中英對照

中國經典名句

引言大全

陳善偉 編

Chan Sin-wai

A DICTIONARY OF
CHINESE POPULAR
SAYINGS
AND
FAMOUS QUOTES

商務印書館

中英對照中國經典名句引言大全
A Dictionary of Chinese Popular Sayings and Famous Quotes

作者：陳善偉
Author：Chan Sin-wai
責任編輯：黃家麗
Executive Editor：Betty Wong
封面設計：涂　慧
Cover Design：Tina Tu
出版：商務印書館(香港)有限公司
香港筲箕灣耀興道 3 號東滙廣場 8 樓
Published by ：The Commercial Press (H.K.) Limited
8/F, Eastern Central Plaza,
3 Yiu Hing Road, Shau Kei Wan, Hong Kong
http://www.commercialpress.com.hk
發行：香港聯合書刊物流有限公司
香港新界荃灣德士古道220－248號荃灣工業中心16樓
Distributed by：The SUP Publishing Logistics (H.K.) Limited
16/F, Tsuen Wan Industrial Centre, 220－248 Texaco Road,
Tsuen Wan, NT, Hong Kong
印刷：美雅印刷製本有限公司
九龍觀塘榮業街6號海濱工業大廈4樓A室
Printed by：Elegance Printing and Book Binding Co. Ltd.
Block A, 4th Floor, Hoi Bun Building
6 Wing Yip Street, Kwun Tong, Kowloon, Hong Kong
版次：2021 年 5 月第 1 版第 1 次印刷
© 2021 商務印書館（香港）有限公司
Edition：First Edition, First Printing, May 2021
ISBN 978 962 07 0586 1
Printed in Hong Kong

目　錄
Contents

Introduction

Aims of this dictionary

This dictionary aims to bring out, in a most idiomatic, readable, and intelligible way, the richness and beauty in the popular sayings and famous quotes in Chinese literature and culture that are most representative of the mind and spirit of the Chinese people through the ages. It puts together the sources and translations of a large number of popular sayings and quotes for the consumption of the English-reading public in the world.

Sayings and quotes are used by people of all walks of life in China as a common way to express themselves with a kind of flavour. In the long history of Chinese civilization, a huge amount of sayings and quotes has been created by different people in different ages and by different authors in different genres of writings. This is well described by Larry Herzberg in his article that came out in 2016:

> China is the world's oldest continuous civilization, with over 3,000 years of history. It is, therefore, hardly surprising that the Chinese language is particularly a rich source of wisdom. Arguably no other language or culture has such a huge treasure trove of proverbs and popular sayings that comment on every aspect of the human experience. There are as many as 20,000 literary idioms and tens of thousands of popular maxims and sayings, in addition to the pithy and profound quotes to be gleaned from three millennia of Chinese philosophy and literature. (Herzberg 2016: 295)

This being the case, it is not surprising to find that the use of popular sayings and famous quotes has become a common occurrence in conversations and writings of the Chinese people and the translation of sayings and quotes is essential for the understanding of Chinese culture. This dictionary, therefore, serves different people in different ways. For translators and interpreters, they often have to translate lines of poems, sayings from well-known works, or proverbs from different areas and dialects when translating speeches, biographies, stories or indeed any writing from Chinese into English. For Sinologists and learners of the Chinese language and culture, they would find it helpful to understand the Chinese tradition and people through learning the popular sayings and famous quotes. For the Chinese people in general, this dictionary serves as a primer for them to know the famous lines and sayings as they might not have the time to read or study the original works which might be too long or difficult to understand.

Definitions of "popular sayings" and "famous quotes"

It is perhaps necessary, at the outset, to define "popular sayings" and "famous quotes". In this dictionary, "popular sayings" refer to common sayings, proverbs, end-clippers, and slang. It does not include "idioms" (成語 *chengyu*), which usually have four characters and stories behind them, known collectively as "literary idioms" (e.g. 朝三暮四, originates from the chapter "On the Equality of Things" in *Zhuangzi* 《莊子》, meaning "keep changing one's mind"). As Chinese idioms are easily found in general dictionaries, they have not been included in this dictionary. Common sayings (俗語 *suyu*) are sayings passed down through many generations by the "common people" and they have no set length or form (e.g. 說是一回事，做是另一回事 To say is one thing, to practise is another). Proverbs (諺語 *yanyu*) are short pithy sayings that express traditionally held truths or pieces of advice, based on common sense or experience (好頭不如好尾 A good beginning is not as good as a good ending). It can be seen that very often, common sayings are interchangeable with proverbs as their distinctions are sometimes hard to make. End-clippers (歇後語 *xiehouyu*) are Chinese metaphorical folk sayings made up of two parts, with the first part leading to the intended meaning in the second, usually with the play of words or sound (e.g. 貓哭老鼠—假慈悲 The cat cries over a dead mouse – hypocritical). Slang is informal language or words used by a particular group of people or community (e.g. 狗吃屎，狼吃人 Dogs eat turds, wolves eat people).

"Famous quotes", on the other hand, refer to the most frequently quoted phrases, lines, and expressions from well-known works, famous authors, celebrities, or newsmakers, which are generally inspirational in nature (e.g. 萬般皆下品，惟有讀書高 All pursuits are base, book-learning is exalted, originated from 汪洙：〈神童詩〉Wang Zhu: "Poem of a Talented Boy").

Organization of the dictionary

This dictionary is organized by topics and entries. It has 442 topics and 6,441 entries. All topics have been arranged alphabetically and all entries, by the order of Hanyu Pinyin, the most popular Romanization system of the Chinese language. Most topics are of a general nature, such as "ability" and "clothing", but there are topics which have been specially created to suit the Chinese context, such as "gentleman" (*junzi* 君子), which has been much discussed by Confucian philosophers and scholars, and "Way, the" (*dao* 道), a central concept in the Daoist philosophy. To minimize the number of topics, six related topics have been grouped into three, which include "audacity" (covering "audacity and "bravery"), "laughter" (covering "laughter" and "smile"), and "rite" (covering "rite" and "courtesy").

For entries, they have been arranged by the order of Hanyu Pinyin. The Chinese original in traditional character is given first, followed by the translation, the source in Chinese and its English translation. When an entry is both a popular saying and a famous quote from a work, both sources are listed.

Content analysis

As implied by the title of the dictionary, this work has two parts: popular sayings and famous quotes. Though the 6,441 entries is a far cry from the "tens of thousands of popular maxims and sayings" mentioned by Herzberg, the entries do provide useful data for us to do a content analysis to find out the essential features and sources of popular sayings and famous quotes. Authors or compilers of popular sayings tend to make vague remarks on Chinese sayings, it is believed, however, that it might be better to let the data speak. The following, therefore, is a statistical analysis of the topics covered with the number of entries under each topic, the sources cited in popular sayings and famous quotes, and the number of authors cited in the dictionary with the purpose of revealing how the Chinese people live, behave, think, and do things as presented by the entries.

Topics covered

As mentioned before, the number of topics included in this dictionary is 442. Though it might seem too numerous to some, the number has been settled through trial and error. The entries under each topic range from 2, such as "breath", "danger", "fortune-telling", "song", "star", and "temple", to about 100, such as "talking". This shows to a large extent what are central or peripheral to the Chinese people.

The following is a table showing the topics with more than 50 entries, in descending order.

Topic	Number of entries	Topic	Number of entries
Talking	99	Family	54
Gentleman	83	Wealth	54
Learning	75	Good and evil	54
Money	73	Governance	53
Official	69	Life	53
Doing things	68	Love	53
Wine	68	Reputation	53
People	59	Death	51
Heart	57	Effort	51
Knowledge	55	Flower	50

The above reflects the importance of the Chinese people attach to these areas and it also shows that the preferences of the Chinese people may be different from people of other cultures, such as "Gentleman" 君子 being ranked second in the above list. From the table, we understand that how people say things, behave in a gentlemanly way, acquire learning, and make money are of great concern to the Chinese people. Perhaps we could discuss more deeply on these popular issues.

Talking

The Chinese people place great emphasis on the way they talk, what should be talked about, how to avoid offending others in their talking, and how to judge a person by his speech. All these are to a certain extent illustrated by the following quotes.

How to talk

長話不可短說。

A long story cannot be told short.

> 俗語 Common saying

處世戒多言，言多必失。

In conducting yourself in society, do not talk more than is necessary, otherwise there will be slips in what you say.

> 朱用純《朱子家訓》Zhu Yongchun: *Percepts of the Zhu Family*

打開天窗說亮話。

Not to mince one's words.

> 俗語 Common saying

對啥人說啥話。

Say the right thing to the right person.

> 俗語 Common saying

What should be talked about

粗話無害，甘言無益。

Hard words are harmless and fine words are of no benefit.

> 諺語 Proverb

多言數窮，不如守中。

Talking much is exhaustive, and it would be better to keep things to oneself.

> 老子《道德經》Laozi: *Daodejing*

多嘴討人厭。

Loquacity is disgusting.

> 俗語 Common saying

逢人且說三分話，未可全拋一片心。

When you talk to people, you tell them a small part of what you want to say, don't tell them all what is really on your mind.

> 《增廣賢文》*Words that Open up One's Mind and Enhance One's Wisdom*

可與言而不與之言，失人；不可與之言而與之言，失言。

If you don't talk to somebody whom you can talk to, you lose the person; if you talk to somebody whom you cannot talk to, you waste your words.

> 孔子《論語‧衛靈公篇第十五》Confucius: Chapter 15, *The Analects of Confucius*

Avoid offending others in speech

說者無心，聽者有意。

The speaker has no particular intention in saying something, but one who listens reads one's own meaning into it.

> 俗語 Common saying

喜時之言多失信，怒時之言多失體。

One often breaks one's promise when happy, and one often speaks in inappropriate terms when angry.

陳繼儒《安得長者言》Chen Jiru: *How to Get Advice from the Elders*

Judge a person by his speech

不以言舉人，不以言廢人。

Don't recommend a person by his words or reject a person by his words.

孔子《論語·衛靈公篇第十五》Confucius: Chapter 15, *The Analects of Confucius*

Gentleman

"Gentleman" (*junzi* 君子) is a central concept in Confucianism. According to Confucius, Mencius and other Confucian scholars, a gentleman, in stark contrast to a "petty man" (*xiaoren* 小人), is one who is courteous, dignified, prudent, honest, virtuous, fearless, loyal, obedient, learned, forgiving, supportive, well-disciplined, and can live with poverty. Popular quotes related to some of the above characteristics of a "gentleman" are given below.

Courteous

君子敬而無失，與人恭而有禮。

A gentleman maintains reverence without errors, and is courteous and polite to others.

孔子《論語·顏淵篇第十二》Confucius: Chapter 12, *The Analects of Confucius*

Dignified

君子不重則不威。

If a gentleman does not behave with dignity, he will not command any respect.

孔子《論語·學而篇第一》Confucius: Chapter 1, *The Analects of Confucius*

君子矜而不爭，羣而不黨。

A gentleman is dignified and not quarrelsome. He is sociable but not cliquey.

孔子《論語·衛靈公篇第十五》Confucius: Chapter 15, *The Analects of Confucius*

君子泰而不驕，小人驕而不泰。

A gentleman is dignified but not proud whereas a petty man is proud but not dignified.

孔子《論語·子路篇第十三》Confucius: Chapter 13, *The Analects of Confucius*

Fearless

君子不憂不懼。

A gentleman does not worry about or fear anything.

孔子《論語·顏淵篇第十二》Confucius: Chapter 12, *The Analects of Confucius*

Forgiving

君子不念舊惡。

A gentleman forgives the past wrong doings of others.

孔子《論語·公冶長篇第五》Confucius: Chapter 5, *The Analects of Confucius*

Honest

君子不宛言而取富，不屈行而取位。

A gentleman does not get wealth by blandishing words nor get an official position by dishonest acts.

戴德《大戴禮記·曾子制言中》Dai De: "Zengzi about Behaviour, Part 2", *Records of Rites by Dai the Elder*

Learned

君子博學於文，約之以禮。

A gentleman is widely versed in culture and bound by the rites.

孔子《論語・雍也篇第六》Confucius: Chapter 6, *The Analects of Confucius*

君子不羞學，不羞問。

A gentleman is not ashamed to learn from or consult with others.

劉向《說苑・卷十六談叢》Liu Xiang: Chapter 16, "The Thicket of Discussion", *Garden of Persuasion*

君子好學不厭，自強不息。

A gentleman is eager to learn and not tired of learning and makes ceaseless efforts to strengthen himself.

司馬光《司馬文正公集》Sima Guang: *Collected Works of Sima Guang*

Live with poverty

君子安貧，達人知命。

A gentleman can be contented with poverty and a discerning person knows his lot.

王勃〈秋日登洪府滕王閣餞別序〉Wang Bo: "Ascending the Tengwang Pavillion of the Hong Family to Bid Farewell"

君子固窮，小人窮斯濫矣。

A gentleman stands firm in poverty while a petty man will lose his self-control in poverty.

孔子《論語・衛靈公篇第十五》Confucius: Chapter 15, *The Analects of Confucius*

君子憂道不憂貧。

A gentleman is worried about the Way but not poverty.

孔子《論語・衛靈公篇第十五》Confucius: Chapter 15, *The Analects of Confucius*

Prudent

君子食無求飽，居無求安，敏於事而慎於言。

A gentleman does not seek for a full stomach when eating, comfort in living, but he is earnest in doing things and cautious in what he says.

孔子《論語・學而篇第一》Confucius: Chapter 1, *The Analects of Confucius*

君子於其言，無所苟而已矣。

A gentleman is concerned about there being no slips in what he says.

孔子《論語・子路篇第十三》Confucius: Chapter 13, *The Analects of Confucius*

Supportive

君子成人之美，不成人之惡。

A gentleman helps others to achieve their goals and he does not help others to achieve what is bad.

孔子《論語・顏淵篇第十二》Confucius: Chapter 12, *The Analects of Confucius*

君子莫大乎與人為善。

The greatest attribute of a gentleman is his helping people to do good deeds.

孟軻《孟子・公孫丑上》Meng Ke: Chapter 2, Part 1, *Mencius*

君子周急不繼富。

A gentleman helps those in urgent needs but does not add wealth to the rich.

孔子《論語・雍也篇第六》Confucius: Chapter 6, *The Analects of Confucius*

Virtuous

德勝才，謂之君子。

He whose virtue is better than his talent is known as a gentleman.

司馬光《資治通鑑・周紀》Sima Guang: "Annals of the Zhou Dynasty", *Comprehensive Mirror to Aid in Government*

君子懷德，小人懷土。

A gentleman cherishes virtue, whereas a petty person, land.

孔子《論語·里仁篇第四》Confucius: Chapter 4, *The Analects of Confucius*

君子以果行育德。

A gentleman acts resolutely to nourish virtue.

《易經·蒙·象》"Image", Hexagram *Meng*, *The Book of Changes*

We can gather from the above that of all the Confucian concepts related to the "gentleman", which must be numerous, the virtues mentioned above are of the greatest concern to the Chinese people.

Learning

Learning is greatly revered in China. Learning is considered by the Chinese people as one of the most effective ways to cultivate one's personality, climb the ladder of success through the civil service examination, and gain fame and status through one's literary writings. It is generally believed that diligence in learning and devotion to study will help one attain one's goals in life.

This mentality is manifested to a great extent by the following saying, which is:

書中自有黃金屋，書中自有顏如玉。

In books there are houses made of gold and women as beautiful as jade.

趙恆：〈勵學篇〉Zhao Heng: "Encouragement to Learning"

Other popular quotes related to learning are given below.

Breadth in learning

博學而不窮，篤學而不倦。

Learn extensively and never end; practise resolutely and never feel tired.

《禮記·儒行第四十一》Chapter 41, "The Conduct of a Confucian Scholar", *The Book of Rites*

學不必博，要之有用。

Learning does not need to be comprehensive, for what is important is that it is useful.

羅大經《鶴林玉露·學仕》Luo Dajing: "Learning and Officialdom", *Jade Dew of the Crane Forest*

Devotion to learning

凡學，必務盡業，心則無營。

In learning, one must make one's utmost efforts to progress and one's mind should not go astray.

呂不韋《呂氏春秋·勸學》Lu Buwei: "Exhortation to Learning", *Master Lu's Spring and Autumn Annals*

Difference between learning and not learning

苟不學，曷為人。

If you do not learn, how can you behave like a decent person?

王應麟《三字經》Wang Yinglin: *Three-character Classic*

好學者如禾如稻，不學者如蒿如草。

A person who is fond of learning is like a grain or rice, and a person who does not like learning is like wormwood or weed.

《增廣賢文》Words that *Open up One's Mind and Enhance One's Wisdom*

人學始知道，不學亦枉然。

A person who begins to learn knows what is the proper way and a person who does not learn will live a life in vain.

《增廣賢文》*Words that Open up One's Mind and Enhance One's Wisdom*

Diligence in learning

古人學問無遺力，少壯工夫老始成。

The ancient people spared no efforts in learning because the efforts they made when young would begin to materialize when old.

陸游：〈冬夜讀書示子聿〉Lu You: "For My Son When Reading Books on a Night in Winter"

人不學，不如物。

He who does not learn is not as good as an animal.

王應麟《三字經》Wang Yinglin: *Three-character Classic*

學問勤中得。

Learning is acquired through diligence.

汪洙：〈神童詩〉Wang Zhu: "Poem of a Talented Boy"

Goal of learning

大學之道，在明明德，在親民，在止於至善。

The way of great learning lies in displaying enlightened virtue, loving the people, and coming to rest in the utmost goodness.

《禮記‧大學第四十二》Chapter 42, "The Great Learning", *The Book of Rites*

古之學者為己，今之學者為人。

Scholars in ancient times studied for self-improvement whereas scholars today study to serve other people.

孔子《論語‧憲問篇第十四》Confucius: Chapter 14, *The Analects of Confucius*

Process of learning

夫學者猶種樹也，春玩其華，秋登其實。

Learning is like planting trees, allowing us to enjoy their flowers in spring and harvest their fruits in autumn.

顏之推《顏氏家訓‧勉學》Yan Zhitui: "Exhortation to Learning", *Family Instructions of Master Yan*

君子之學也，入乎耳‧著乎心。

The learning of a gentleman is such that it enters through his ears and stored in his mind.

荀況《荀子‧勸學第一》Xun Kuang: Chapter 1, "Exhortation to Learning", *Xunzi*

學而不己，闔棺乃止。

Learning is ceaseless and it ends when one is encased in coffin.

韓嬰《韓詩外傳‧卷八》Han Ying: Chapter 8, *The Outer Commentary to the Book of Songs by Master Han*

Teachers and learning

古之學者必有師。

Those who learned in ancient times must have teachers.

韓愈〈昌黎先生集‧師說〉Han Yu: "On Teaching", *Collected Works of Han Yu*

Money

It is true that Buddhism and Confucianism warn people of the evils of desires, particular desires of wealth, yet from the quotes in this dictionary, it is found that the Chinese people truly know that without money, one cannot get what one wants. Money has always been an important part of their life. Some view money negatively, others, positively.

Attraction of money

青酒紅人面，財帛動人心。

Good wine reddens the face of a person while money excites one's heart.

> 諺語 Proverb
> 西周生 《醒世姻緣傳·第十二回》 Xi Zhousheng: Chapter 12, *Stories of Marriage to Awaken the World*

Contempt on money

財物糞土輕，仁義泰山重。

Money and property are light as refuse whereas benevolence and righteousness, heavy as Mount Tai.

> 西周生 《醒世姻緣傳·第三十四回》 Xi Zhousheng: Chapter 34, *Stories of Marriage to Awaken the World*

多金非為貴，安樂值錢多。

Much money is of little value, peace and contentment are worth great wealth.

> 佚名 《名賢集》 Anonymous: *Collected Sayings of Famous Sages*

銀錢如糞土，臉面值千金。

Money is but dirt but the sense of shame is worth one thousand taels of gold.

> 崔復生 《太行志·第二十四章》 Cui Fusheng: Chapter 24, *Records of Taixing*

Evils of money

金錢為萬惡之源。

Money is the source of all evil things.

> 俗語 Common saying

Greed for money

人心節節高於天，越是有錢越愛錢。

Man is insatiably greedy; the more money one has the more one wants.

> 諺語 Proverb

Happiness with money

有錢萬事足。

One is satisfied with everything when he has money.

> 茅盾 《霜葉紅似二月花·第五章》 Mao Dun: Chapter 5, *The Frosty Leaves Are Red As Flowers in the Second Month of the Year*

有錢像條龍，無錢變條蟲。

When one has money, one is like a dragon. When one does not have money, one is like a worm.

> 諺語 Proverb

Necessity of money

燈裏無油點不亮，手裏無錢難煞人。

A lantern without oil cannot be lit bright. A person without money in his hand is hard pressed.

> 俗語 Common saying

Power of Money

可以使鬼者錢也，可以使人者權也。

It is money that can control the ghost and it is power that can order people about.

> 楊慎 《丹鉛總錄·卷七》 Yang Shen: Chapter 7, *Complete Records of Proofreading*

錢聚如兄，錢散如奔。

When you have money, people treat you as an elder brother; when you don't, people run away from you.

諺語 Proverb
佚名：〈來生債‧第一折〉Anonymous: Scene 1, "The Debt in the Future Life"

天下道理千千萬，沒錢不能把事辦。
There are thousands of hows and whys, but without money you can do nothing.

俗語 Common saying
崔復生《太行志‧第七章》Cui Fusheng: Chapter 7, *Records of Taixing*

瞎子見錢眼也開，和尚見錢經也賣。
Money will open a blind person's eyes and will make a monk sell his prayer book.

諺語 Proverb
曹玉林《甦醒的原野‧第二章》Cao Yulin: Chapter 2, *The Awaken Plain*

有錢道真語，無錢語不真。
What is said by the rich is believed and what is said by the poor is not.

《增廣賢文》*Words that Open up One's Mind and Enhance One's Wisdom*

Spending of money

錢要花在刀刃上。
Money should be used on where it is needed most.

俗語 Common saying

使錢容易賺錢難，莫把銀錢作等閒。
It is easy to spend money but difficult to earn it, so you should not make light of money.

諺語 Proverb

張三有錢不會使，李四會使卻無錢。
Some have money but they do not know how to use it; others have no money, yet they know how to use it.

諺語 Proverb
錢希言《戲瑕‧卷三》Qian Xiyan: Chapter 3, *Jokes about Flaws*

Sources cited

The sourcs of all the entries of the popular sayings and famous quotes are listed and translated in this dictionary. The task of tracing and translating the sources of all the entries is daunting. It needs considerable efforts in researching and re-searching the sources and putting them into the target language.

There are 3,438 entries of popular sayings, and 3,865 entries of famous quotes, which means that around 40 percent of the entries are sayings, and the remaining 60 percent, quotes.

A breakdown of the sources of popular sayings is given below:

Sources of popular sayings	Number of entries
Common sayings	1,976
Proverbs	1,105
End-clippers	349
Slang	8

It can be seen that there are 3,081 entries from common sayings and proverbs, making up 90%, whereas end-clippers and slang take up just 10%. In other words, most of things people in China say are common sayings and proverbs and they seldom use end-clippers and slang to express themselves.

For famous quotes, they come from a large number of sources, involving a large number of authors and a wide range of works in different ages. There are, nevertheless, some works which are more frequently quoted than others, which are given in the following table.

Sources of famous quotes (Works)	Number of entries
《論語》 The Analects of Confucius	219
《增廣賢文》 Words that Open up One's Mind and Enhance One's Wisdom	204
《孟子》 Mencius	139
《紅樓夢》 A Dream of the Red Chamber	121
《道德經》 Daodejing	115
《禮記》 The Book of Rites	115
《史記》 Records of the Grand Historian	94
《莊子》 Zhuangzi	86
《左傳》 Zuo's Commentary on the Spring and Autumn Annals	75
《水滸傳》 Outlaws of the Marshes	66
《西遊記》 Journey to the West	57
《易經》 The Book of Changes	55
《金瓶梅》 The Plum in the Golden Vase	52
《三國演義》 Romance of the Three Kingdoms	48
《荀子》 Xunzi	46
《醒世恒言》 Stories to Awaken the World	44
《淮南子》 Huainanzi	42
《詩經》 The Book of Odes	39
《孫子兵法》 The Art of War	38
《戰國策》 Strategies of the Warring States	35
《尚書》 The Book of History	34
《後漢書》 History of the Later Han	29
《韓非子》 Hanfeizi	28
《警世通言》 Stories to Caution the World	26
《儒林外史》 An Unofficial History of the World of Literati	26
《三國志》 Records of the Three Kingdoms	26

These twenty-six works with over twenty entries in the dictionary show the Confucian concepts shape the thinking and behaviour of the Chinese people in a great way. A brief study of the five top-listed works would allow us to have a better understand of the listing.

The Analects of Confucius

The Analects of Confucius《論語》, which has 219 entries, is the most cited work in this dictionary. It is a collection of sayings and ideas attributed to Confucius and the work was compiled and written by his disciples. Central to Confucianism are concepts of moral cultivation through benevolence (*ren*仁), respect for others, and behave in the way of a gentleman (*junzi*). Some of the popular quotations from *The Analects of Confucius* are given below as examples.

己所不欲，勿施於人。
Do not impose on others what you yourself do not desire.

孔子《論語‧衛靈公篇第十五》Confucius: Chapter 15, *The Analects of Confucius*

志士仁人，無求生以害仁，有殺身以成仁。
People of aspirations and benevolence do not harm benevolence for life, but sacrifice life to accomplish benevolence.

孔子《論語‧衛靈公篇第十五》Confucius: Chapter 15, *The Analects of Confucius*

非禮勿視，非禮勿聽，非禮勿言，非禮勿動。
Do not look if it is not in accordance with the rites; do not listen if it is not in accordance with the rites; do not speak if it is not in accordance with the rites; and do not move if it is not in accordance with the rites.

孔子《論語‧顏淵篇第十二》Confucius: Chapter 12, *The Analects of Confucius*

有朋自遠方來，不亦樂乎。
Isn't it a pleasure to have friends coming afar to visit you?

孔子《論語‧學而篇第一》Confucius: Chapter 1, *The Analects of Confucius*

君子博學於文，約之以禮。
A gentleman is widely versed in culture and bound by the rites.

孔子《論語‧雍也篇第六》Confucius: Chapter 6, *The Analects of Confucius*

君子求諸己，小人求諸人。
A gentleman makes demands of himself whereas a petty person makes demands of others.

孔子《論語‧衛靈公篇第十五》Confucius: Chapter 15, *The Analects of Confucius*

Words that Open up One's Mind and Enhance One's Wisdom

Words that Open up One's Mind and Enhance One's Wisdom《增廣賢文》is second on the list. This work, which was compiled during the Ming period, contains many aphorisms that came from the wisdom of ancient sages. It helps children to develop their personality in the right direction. The following are examples from this work.

兩耳不聞窗外事，一心祇讀聖賢書。
One turns a deaf ear to what is happening in the outside world but concentrates on one's studies of books by the sages.

入門休問榮枯事，觀看容顏便得知。
When you enter into a house, do not ask about that things that thrive or wither, just look at one's facial expressions and you know how the things are.

有意栽花花不開，無心插柳柳成蔭。
To grow flowers purposely, you get no flowers; to plant willows casually, you get shade.

饒人不是痴漢，痴漢不會饒人。
One who forgives other is not a stupid person and a stupid man does not forgive others.

相識滿天下，知心能幾人。

You may have friends all over the world, but only a few of them are intimate ones.

Mencius

There are 139 entries from the *Mencius* 《孟子》, written by Meng Ke, generally known as a second sage who was an exponent of Confucius's concept. He believed in innate goodness of the individual, saying that "human nature is good". He also held the view that people are more important than the ruler and that righteousness should be valued over benefits. Some of his ideas cited in the dictionary are given below.

盡信《書》，不如無《書》。

If you trust *The Book of History* without reserve, it would be better for you not to have it.

孟軻《孟子‧盡心章句下》Meng Ke: Chapter 7, Part 2, *Mencius*

生亦我所欲也，義亦我所欲也，二者不可得兼，捨生而取義者也。

Life is what I want and righteousness is also what I want. If I cannot have both, I would give up my life to accomplish righteousness.

孟軻《孟子‧告子章句上》Meng Ke: Chapter 6, Part 1, *Mencius*

以不忍人之心，行不忍人之政，治天下可運之掌上。

When you use a commiserating heart to run a commiserating administration, then governing the country can be controlled in one's hand.

孟軻《孟子‧公孫丑上》Meng Ke: Chapter 2, Part 1, *Mencius*

惻隱之心，人皆有之；羞惡之心，人皆有之；恭敬之心，人皆有之；是非之心，人皆有之。

Everyone has a heart for compassion; everyone has a heart for the dislike of shame; everyone has a heart for respect; and everyone has a heart for right and wrong.

孟軻《孟子‧告子章句上》Meng Ke: Chapter 6, Part 1, *Mencius*

民為貴，社稷次之，君為輕。

People are most valuable, next are the national altars of the soil and grain, and the ruler is insignificant.

孟軻《孟子‧盡心章句下》Meng Ke: Chapter 7, Part 2, *Mencius*

故天將降大任於斯人也，必先苦其心誌，勞其筋骨，餓其體膚，空乏其身，行拂亂其所為，所以動心忍性，曾益其所不能。

Thus, when Heaven is going to give a great responsibility to someone, it first makes his mind endure suffering, his sinews and bones experience toil, and his body to suffer hunger. It inflicts him with poverty and disrupts everything he tries to build. In this way Heaven stimulates his mind, stabilizes his temper and enhances his weak abilities.

孟軻《孟子‧告子章句下》Meng Ke: Chapter 6, Part 2, *Mencius*

Daodejing

Daodejing 《道德經》 by Laozi, more commonly known by his original name Li Er 李耳, has been extremely popular with the Chinese people. It came as no surprise when the table shows that this Daoist classic is the fourth most-quoted work. This work has around 5,000 characters, divided into 81 chapters. The following quotations serve to illustrate the ideas expressed by Li Er.

天下之至柔，馳騁天下之至堅。

The softest in the world can freely control over the hardest in the world.

老子《道德經》Laozi: *Daodejing*

無為無所不為。
One does nothing and yet everything is done.

老子《道德經・第四十八章》Laozi: Chapter 48, *Daodejing*

上善若水，水善利萬物而不爭。
The highest goodness is like water, which benefits myriad things but does not contend with them.

老子《道德經・第八章》Laozi: Chapter 8, *Daodejing*

治大國若烹小鮮。
Running a large country is like cooking a small fish.

老子《道德經・第六十章》Laozi: Chapter 60, *Daodejing*

無名天地之始，有名萬物之母。
The unnamed is the beginning of heaven and earth and the named is the mother of myriad things.

老子《道德經・第一章》Laozi: Chapter 1, *Daodejing*

天下萬物生於有，有生於無。
All things in the world are born of something and something is born of nothing.

老子《道德經》Laozi: *Daodejing*

It should also be noted that a considerable number of quotes come from the four great classical novels i.e., 《紅樓夢》 *A Dream of the Red Chamber* (121 entries), 《水滸傳》 *Outlaws of the Marshes* (66 entries), 《西遊記》 *Journey to the West* (57 entries), and 《三國演義》 *Romance of the Three Kingdoms* (48 entries). Taken together, these popular novels have 292 entries. A brief discussion of these works and a provision of quotes from these works therefore seem in order.

A Dream of the Red Chamber

A Dream of the Red Chamber 《紅樓夢》was written in vernacular Chinese by Cao Xueqin 曹雪芹 of the Qing Dynasty. Later, Gao E 高鶚 added forty more chapters to the original eighty, so the novel has 120 chapters. It is believed that the work is Cao's semi-autobiography, describing the rise and decline of his family. It is a novel of remarkable achievement in terms of the number of characters and his observation of the life and structures of the eighteenth-century China. Some of the well-known quotes are given below.

爾今死去儂收葬，未卜儂身何日喪。
Now you are dead and I come to bury you, and nobody can tell when I will die.

曹雪芹《紅樓夢》Cao Xueqin: *A Dream of the Red Chamber*

一朝春盡紅顏老，花落人亡兩不知。
One day spring will go and beauty will fade; and without knowing it, flowers will fall and people will die.

曹雪芹《紅樓夢・第二十七回》Cao Xueqin: Chapter 27, *A Dream of the Red Chamber*

世事洞明皆學問，人情練達即文章。
A thorough understanding of the affairs of the world is knowledge, and rich experience in human relationships is literature.

曹雪芹《紅樓夢》Cao Xueqin: *A Dream of the Red Chamber*

滿紙荒唐言，一把辛酸淚。
Pages full of idle words, brushed with bitter tears.

曹雪芹 《紅樓夢》 Cao Xueqin: *A Dream of the Red Chamber*

假作真時真亦假，無為有處有還無。

When false is taken for true, true becomes false; if non-being turns into being, being becomes non-being.

曹雪芹 《紅樓夢》 Cao Xueqin: *A Dream of the Red Chamber*

字字看來皆是血，十年辛苦不尋常。

Every character that you read is laboured by my blood. Ten years of hardship is not all that simple.

曹雪芹 《紅樓夢》 Cao Xueqin: *A Dream of the Red Chamber*

Outlaws of the Marshes

Outlaws of the Marshes 《水滸傳》 was written by Shi Nai'an 施耐庵 (1296-1371), a novelist of the early Ming. It is a story about a group of 108 outlaws who gathe Red at Mount Liang to form an army, which was later granted an amnesty and sent by the government to fight against foreign invaders and suppress rebel forces. Some quotes from the novel are listed below.

有緣千里來相會，無緣對面不相逢。

With fate, people will come to meet from a thousand miles away; without fate, though people face each other, they never meet.

施耐庵 《水滸傳》 Shi Nai'an: *Outlaws of the Marshes*

殺人可恕，天理難容。

If killing people can be forgiven, this is against the law of heaven.

施耐庵 《水滸傳．第十回》 Shi Nai'an: Chapter 10, *Outlaws of the Marshes*

聞名不如見面，見面勝似聞名。

To know someone by his repute is not as good as meeting him face to face.

施耐庵 《水滸傳．第三回》 Shi Nai'an: Chapter 3, *Outlaws of the Marshes*

十八般武藝，樣樣精通。

One is skilled in using each and every one of the eighteen weapons.

施耐庵 《水滸傳．第二回》 Shi Nai'an: Chapter 2, *Outlaws of the Marshes*

世事有成必有敗，為人有興必有衰。

In mundane affairs, there are successes as well as failures. In human life, there are rises and falls.

施耐庵 《水滸傳．第一百一十四回》 Shi Nai'an: Chapter 114, *Outlaws of the Marshes*

酒不醉人人自醉，色不迷人人自迷。

It is not wine that intoxicates people but people intoxicating themselves and it is not women who beguile men but men beguiling themselves.

施耐庵 《水滸傳．第四回》 Shi Nai'an: Chapter 4, *Outlaws of the Marshes*

Journey to the West

Journey to the West 《西遊記》 is a novel written by Wu Cheng'en 吳承恩 (1506-1582) of the Ming Dynasty. It is an account of the pilgrimage of Xuanzang to India to obtain Buddhist sutras and his return to the Chinese empire and the journey was frought with many trials and suffering. In the journey, Xuanzang had Sun Wukong, Zhu Bajie and Sha Wujing as his protectors who helped him as a way to atone for their sins. Quotes from this novel include the following.

既在佛會下，都是有緣人。
All in the Buddhist community are brought together by the same lot.

吳承恩《西遊記‧第三十六回》Wu Cheng'en: Chapter 36, *Journey to the West*

孫悟空跳不出如來佛的掌心。
Be unable to escape from another person's control however clever and capable one may be.

吳承恩《西遊記‧第七回》Wu Cheng'en: Chapter 7, *Journey to the West*

道高一尺，魔高一丈。
When virtue rises one foot, vice rises ten.

吳承恩《西遊記‧第五十回》Wu Cheng'en: Chapter 50, *Journey to the West*

Romance of the Three Kingdoms

Romance of the Three Kingdoms《三國演義》is a historical novel attributed to Luo Guanzhong 羅貫中 (1320-1400). It is a story that takes place in the last days of the Han Dynasty when warlords struggle for supremacy and eventually three kingdoms, Shu, Wei, and Wu, take shape. The three kingdoms contend with each other until the empire is finally reunified. The following are quotes from the novel.

良禽擇木而棲，賢臣擇主而事。
Clever birds choose their trees when they perch and wise ministers choose a king to serve.

羅貫中《三國演義‧第三回》Luo Guanzhong: Chapter 3, *Romance of the Three Kingdoms*

三個臭皮匠，勝過一個諸葛亮。
Three cobblers with their wits combined is better than Zhuge Liang the master mind.

羅貫中《三國演義‧第七十五回》Luo Guanzhong: Chapter 75, *Romance of the Three Kingdoms*

既生瑜，何生亮。
Since heaven has given birth to me, Zhou Yu, why heaven still gave birth to Zhu Geliang?

羅貫中《三國演義》Luo Guanzhong: *Romance of the Three Kingdoms*

賠了夫人又折兵。
Lose a lady and suffer a defeat.

羅貫中《三國演義‧第五十五回》Luo Guanzhong: Chapter 55, *Romance of the Three Kingdoms*

蜀中無大將，廖化作先鋒。
In the kingdom of the blind, the one-eyed is king.

羅貫中《三國演義‧第一百一十三回》Luo Guanzhong: Chapter 113, *Romance of the Three Kingdoms*

說曹操，曹操就到。
Speak of the devil, and he is sure to appear.

羅貫中《三國演義‧第十四回》Luo Guanzhong: Chapter 14, *Romance of the Three Kingdoms*

天下大勢，分久必合，合久必分。
The general trend under heaven is that there is bound to be unification after prolonged division and division after prolonged unification.

羅貫中《三國演義》Luo Guanzhong: *Romance of the Three Kingdoms*

It can be seen that a considerable number of famous quotes have come from the four great classical novels.

Authors quoted

The number of authors quoted in this dictionary is exceedingly large, totalling 685. If the nineteen works of unknown authorship are also included, the total number of authors and non-authors reaches 704. In other words, we have to translate 6,441 entries of works by 704 authors from the ancient times to the present, involving the intralingual translation of classical Chinese into modern Chinese and from modern Chinese to plain English. The work of translation is extremely heavy and difficult.

Based on statistics, it is noted that there are a number of authors whose works are more frequently cited than others, as shown below.

Sources of famous quotes (Authors)	Number of citations	Sources of famous quotes (Authors)	Number of citations
李白 Li Bai	72	王維 Wang Wei	24
蘇軾 Su Shi	64	歐陽修 Ouyang Xiu	23
杜甫 Du Fu	63	屈原 Qu Yuan	22
白居易 Bai Juyi	48	毛澤東 Mao Zedong	20
陶淵明 Tao Yuanming	36	關漢卿 Guan Hanqing	17
韓愈 Han Yu	32	杜牧 Du Mu	14
陸游 Lu You	28	劉禹錫 Liu Yuxi	13

It can be seen that the four most-quoted persons are Li Bai, Su Shi, Du Fu, and Bai Juyi. It would be interesting to look into the reasons for their popularity.

Li Bai

The fact that Li Bai (701–762), a poet of the Tang Dynasty, is top on the popularity list is no mere coincidence. He is probably the best-known poet in China, whose poems on the pleasures of friendship, the depth of nature, solitude, and the joys of drinking wine win the hearts of the Chinese people. Poems that show these traits of Li Bai's poems are given below.

Friendship

桃花潭水深千尺，不及汪倫送我情。
The Peach Blossom Lake is one thousand feet deep, but it is not as deep as the parting sorrow that Wang Lun expressed to me.
　　李白：〈贈汪倫〉Li Bai: "To Wang Lun"

Nature

孤帆遠影碧空盡，惟見長江天際流。
The lonely boat and its shadows in the distance have gone to the end of the blue sky and all I could see was the water of the Changjiang River flowing to the edge of heaven.
　　李白：〈黃鶴樓送孟浩然之廣陵〉Li Bai: "Seeing off Meng Haoran to Guangling at the Yellow Crane Tower"

<u>Solitude</u>

桃花流水宛然去，別有天地非人間。

The peach blossoms flow silently away with the running water, This is a world of its own, unlike the world of man.

李白：〈山中答問〉Li Bai: "Conversations in the Mountain"

<u>Wine</u>

人生得意須盡歡，莫使金樽空對月。

When one has one's way in life, one must enjoy it to the full. The golden wine cup must not face the moon unfilled.

李白：〈將進酒〉Li Bai: "About to Drink Wine"

且樂生前一杯酒，何須身後千載名。

It is better to enjoy a cup of wine while you're still alive, for what is the use of gaining a thousand years of glory when you're dead?

李白：〈行路難〉Li Bai: "Moving forward on the Road is Difficult"

Su Shi

The second most-quoted person is Su Shi (1037-1101), also known by his pen-name Su Dongbo 蘇東坡, who was a writer, poet, painter, calligrapher, and statesman of the Song Dynasty. The poems and *ci*-poems of Su Shi have enjoyed a long history of great popularity and exerted huge influence on the intelligentia in China. Themes of his *ci*-poems are related to the natural phenomenon and his disappointment at officialdom. Some of his well-known lines are given below.

<u>Friendship</u>

千里送鵝毛，物輕情意重。

A goose feather sent from a thousand miles away may be light in weight, but the feelings it conveys are deep.

蘇軾：〈揚州以土物寄少游〉Su Shi: "Sending Local Products from Yangzhou to Qin Guan"

<u>Life</u>

泥上偶然留指爪，鴻飛那復計東西。

On the mud it by chance leaves a footprint. When the goose flies away, how can you reckon the east or west?

蘇軾：〈和子由澠池懷舊〉Su Shi: "Meditating on the Past with Ziyou at Pond Mian"

人有悲歡離合，月有陰晴圓缺。

In human life, there are joy and sorrow, parting and reunion. For the moon, it has darkness and brightness, fullness and wane.

蘇軾：〈水調歌頭〉Su Shi: "To the Tune of Prelude to the Melody of Water"

<u>Things</u>

人似秋鴻來有信，事如春夢了無痕。

People are like wild geese who come faithfully in autumn, and things are like dreams in spring without a trace.

蘇軾：〈正月二十日與潘郭二生出郊尋春，忽記去年是日同至女王城作詩，乃和前韻〉Su Shi: "I Went to Spring Outing with Scholars Pan and Guo on the Twentieth of the First Month and Recalled Suddenly that We Went to the Empress City to Write Poems on the Same Day Last Year, I Therefore Write this Poem to Respond, in the Same Rhyme"

Du Fu

The third most-quoted person is Du Fu (712 – 770), a prominent Tang poet, who, along with Li Bai, has been generally called the greatest of the Chinese poets. His poems have a strong sense of history and moral engagement, and he exhibited excellent skills in poetry writings. Some of his popular lines are given below.

Friendship

花徑不曾緣客掃，蓬門今始為君開。
My flowered path has not been swept for any guests. My thatched gate for the first time opened just for you.

杜甫：〈客至〉Du Fu: "A Visitor Arrived"

正是江南好風景，落花時節又逢君。
This is just the time when the scenery of the south of the Yangzi River is beautiful, and I meet you again at the time when petals fall.

杜甫：〈江南逢李龜年〉Du Fu: "Encountering Li Guinian in the South of the Yangzi River"

Livelihood

安得廣廈千萬間，大庇天下寒士俱歡顏。
If only there were thousands of spacious houses, to shelter all the people in the world, much to the joy of the poor.

杜甫：〈茅屋為秋風所破歌〉Du Fu: "Song of My Thatch House Torn down by Autumn Wind"

Music

此曲祇應天上有，人間能得幾回聞。
This piece of music should only exist in heaven above, how rare can it be heard in the world of men?

杜甫：〈贈花卿〉Du Fu: "To the Goddess of Flowers"

Patriotism

出師未捷身先死，長使英雄淚滿襟。
But Zhuge Liang died before he succeeded, and this made heroes after him shed tears that wetted their sleeves.

杜甫：〈蜀相〉Du Fu: "The Premier of Shu"

Poetry-writing

讀書破萬卷，下筆如有神。
When you have read more than ten thousand books, you can write like being helped by a god.

杜甫：〈奉贈韋左丞丈二十二韻〉Du Fu: "A Twenty-two-line Poem Presented to Minister Wei Ji"

Bai Juyi

Bai Juyi (772–846), the last of the top-four most-quoted person, was a renowned poet of the Tang Dynasty who for a time served as a government official. His poems are mainly on his career and observations made about everyday life. His best-known poems are 〈長恨歌〉("Song of Everlasting Grief") and 〈琵琶行〉("Song of a *Pipa* Player") and most of his best-known lines come from these two poems. Four lines are given below to illustrate this point.

回眸一笑百媚生，六宮粉黛無顏色。

When she turned back and smiled, so much charm was generated, making all the ladies of the Six Palaces lose their lustre.

白居易：〈長恨歌〉Bai Juyi: "Song of Everlasting Grief"

在天願作比翼鳥，在地願為連理枝。

In heaven, we hope we are birds flying with wings entwined; on earth, we hope we are intertwined branches on a tree.

白居易：〈長恨歌〉Bai Juyi: "Song of Everlasting Grief"

同是天涯淪落人，相逢何必曾相識。

As we both are losers in this world, does it matter whether we have met before?

白居易：〈琵琶行，並序〉Bai Juyi: "Song of a *Pipa* Player, with a Foreword"

千呼萬喚始出來，猶抱琵琶半遮面。

We hailed and urged her many times before she would rise and come, still half-concealing her face with the *Pipa* she carried.

白居易：〈琵琶行，並序〉Bai Juyi: "Song of a *Pipa* Player, with a Foreword"

He was also known for his *ci*-poetry, from which some popular lines come.

思悠悠，恨悠悠，恨到歸時方始休，月明人倚樓。

My thoughts are endless, so is my grief. My grief would not cease until my husband comes back. The moon is bright, and I lean on the balcony.

白居易：〈長相思〉Bai Juyi: "To the Tune of Everlasting Longing"

More observations can be made from the table given above. First, three of the four most popular persons were poets, which shows to a great extent that people like lines from poems most. Second, of the fourteen popular persons, nine of them were of the Tang Dynasty, which implies that works of the Tang poets have a great influence on the Chinese people. Third, the popularity of the poems of Tao Yuanming is perhaps a reflection of the proclivity of the Chinese people to withdraw from the hustle and bustle of a city life to seek serenity in the remote rustic areas. Fourth, Mao Zedong stands out as the most-quoted person of the contemporary period, due partly to his political status in China and partly to his excellent skills in poetry writing.

Goals and methods of translation

Goals of translation

As with all types of translations, the goal of translating sayings and quotes is to reproduce as faithfully as possible what the original or author intends to express. What we hope to achieve are translations which are faithful to the original, semantically correct, pragmatically effective, stylistically appropriate, and highly acceptable to the target reader.

Methods of translating sayings and quotes

While the goal and standards of translation could be the same for all types of texts, the methods of translation in general vary with the specific text in question and it is not infrequent to translate the same text differently due to textual or contextual considerations. Several observations could be made on the translation of sayings and quotes.

First, the context of the text. It should be noted that in many cases the translation of sayings and quotes is essentially a full translation of short sentences or a partial translation or fragmented translation of a long text, both with very limited context. The decontextualized texts have to be contextualized by the translator in order to bring out the intended meaning in the original.

Sayings with a limited context

以備不時之需。

Against a rainy day.

俗語 Common saying

Partial translation

好讀書，不求甚解。

He takes delight in reading but does not seek to understand the details.

陶淵明，〈五柳先生傳〉Tao Yuanming: "Biography of the Scholar Wuliu"

恃人不如自恃也；人之為己者，不如己之自為也。

To rely on others is not as good as relying on yourself; to ask others to do something for you is not as good as doing it by yourself.

韓非《韓非子·外儲說右下第三十五》Han Fei: Chapter 35, "Outer Congeries of Sayings, Part 2", *Hanfeizi*

Second, the issue of culture. As many sayings and quotes are deeply rooted in history, an understanding of the Chinese culture is essential in translating them. This is particularly the case with philosophical and religious texts. Two examples are given below.

History

司馬昭之心，路人皆見。

The villain's intent is known to all.

陳壽《三國志·魏書·高貴鄉公傳》Chen Shou: "Biography of Township Duke of Gaogui", "History of the State of Wei", *Records of the Three Kingdoms*

Philosophy

道生一，一生二，二生三，三生萬物。

The Way begets one, one begets two, two begets three, and three begets the myriad things.

老子《道德經·第四十二章》Laozi: Chapter 42, *Daodejing*

Third, the issue of language. Sayings are usually of the informal register and quotes are more formal, as illustrated by the following two examples.

Informal register

貓要捕鼠，必先伏下身子。

A cat stoops before it catches a mouse.

俗語 Common saying

Formal register

居安思危，思則有備，有備無患。

When living in peace, we have to think of danger. If we think, then we will be prepared. If we are prepared, then we will have no worries.

左丘明《左傳·襄公十一年》Zuo Qiuming: "The Eleventh Year of the Reign of Duke Xiang", *Zuo's Commentary on the Spring and Autumn Annals*

The classical Chinese in the text, when putting it into modern English, has to go a stage of intralingual translation before interlingual translation can be done. The following is an example.

乞火不若取燧，寄汲不若鑿井。
It would be better to obtain a fire-maker than beg for fire, better to dig a well ourselves than beg for water from others.

劉安《淮南子‧覽冥訓第六》Liu An: Chapter 6, "Peering into the Obscure", *Huainanzi*

When translating the above sentence in *Huainanzi*, an intralingual translation was done. 乞火不若取燧，寄汲不若鑿井, which is in classical Chinese, was translated into modern Chinese as: 向鄰居借火不如自己取得火的燧和技術，借別人的井汲水不如自己家院裏鑿口井" (Wang 2012: 143), which was translated into English as shown above (Chan 2009: 139).

Fourth, the issue of consistency. It must be noted that a major difference that lies between translating sayings and quotes and other types of writings is that sayings and quotes come from a great variety of sources and a wide range of authors whereas other types of writings are more specific in terms of domain, theme, style, and terminology, and this makes consistency in translation hard to achieve.

In view of the above difficulties, it is not possible to use different methods to translate different texts. The basic strategy of this author is to render the sayings and quotes as literally as possible and as freely as necessary. (Chan 1998: 66-73) In actual practice, the following methods have been used to translate the entries.

First, to adopt existent translations. The following is an example:

和合故能諧。
If there is concord and unity, there is harmony.

管仲《管子‧兵法第十七》Guan Zhong: Chapter 17, "Methods of Warfare", *Guanzi*

This translation was based on the translation by W. Allyn Rickett (1985). One major difficulty of this method involves the search for existent translations of the source text and how to choose the most acceptable translation. Take *The Art of War* by Sun Wu as an example. It is estimated that between 1905 and 2003, there were over forty translations of the work. By now, fifteen years later, the number of translations of this work must have reached sixty. The way to choose a good translation of a certain work is to look at the academic background of the translator and the track records of his/her translations and publications. No method, of course, is totally reliable.

Second, to modify existent translations. In many cases, existent translations may not be totally acceptable. A translator has to make changes to the translations to fit the context. The following is an example.

衙齋臥聽蕭蕭竹，疑是民間疾苦聲。
I laid on the bed in the studio of the magistrate's residence and listened to the rattling of the bamboos, and I suspected it was the bitter voice of suffering from the people.

鄭板橋：〈濰縣署中畫竹呈年伯包大中丞括〉Zheng Banqiao: "Painting Bamboos at the Official Residence of Wei County Presented to Bao Kuo, the Magistrate"

The above is my translation. It was based on the translation of Anthony Cheung and Paul Gurofsky (1987: 39), which is as follows:

In my office study, resting, I listen to bamboos mournful in the wind. Is it the suffering of the oppressed people, I wonder?

Third, to maintain consistency in translation. It is true that sayings and quotes are multifarious and complex, yet consistency must be maintained to facilitate an adequate understanding of the Chinese culture and philosophy. Take the idea of ren 仁 as an example. It can be translated variantly as "benevolence", "humanity", or "human-heartedness". In this dictionary, ren has been translated consistently as "benevolence".

The following are examples of translating ren as "benevolence" in different source texts.

《論語》 *The Analects of Confucius*
克己復禮為仁。一日克己復禮，天下歸仁焉。
Control the self and return to rites is benevolence. When one day the self is controlled and rites are restored, all under heaven will return to benevolence.
孔子《論語 · 顏淵篇第十二》Confucius: Chapter 12, *The Analects of Confucius*

《禮記》 *The Book of Rites*
力行近乎仁。
Performing good deeds gets one closer to benevolence.
《禮記 · 中庸第三十一章》Chapter 31, "Doctrine of the Mean", *The Book of Rites*

《莊子》 *Zhuangzi*
愛人利物之謂仁。
Loving people and benefitting things is known as benevolence.
莊周《莊子 · 外篇天地第十二》Zhuang Zhou: Chapter 12, "Heaven and Earth", "Outer Chapters", *Zhuangzi*

《左傳》 *Zuo's Commentary on the Spring and Autumn Annals*
親仁善鄰，國之寶也。
Be close to benevolent people and kind to neighbouring states, these are the precious qualities of a country.
左丘明《左傳 · 隱公六年》Zuo Qiuming: "The Sixth Year of the Reign of Duke Yin", *Zuo's Commentary on the Spring and Autumn Annals*

《老子》 *Laozi*
天地不仁，以萬物為芻狗。
Heaven and earth are unbenevolent, for they regard myriad things as straw dogs.
老子《道德經 · 第八章》Laozi: Chapter 8, *Daodejing*

The above shows that regardless of which source ren occurs, it has been consistently translated as "benevolence".

Methods of translatng the titles of the works cited

This dictionary contains a large number of titles of literary and philosophical works, far exceeding the works listed in the "Authors and works quoted in the dictionary" as they do not include titles of works other than books. Titles can be divided into several types and translated in different ways.

(1) Short and straightfoward titles, which can be translated literally, such as:
孫中山：〈上李鴻章書〉 Sun Yat-sen: "Letter to Li Hungzhang"
吳南生《革命母親李梨英》 Wu Nansheng: *My Revolutionary Mother Li Liying*

杜甫：〈江村〉Du Fu: "Riverside Village"

(2) Short but complicated titles, which have to be understood before translating, such as:

程趾祥 Cheng Zhixiang《此中人語》 *Sayings of an Insider*
黃鈞宰 Huang Junzai《金壺七墨》 *Seven Essays from the Golden Pot*
李匡義 Li Qiangyi, author of《資暇集》 *Collection of Leisure Time Notes*
魯迅 Lu Xun《而已集》 *And that's that*
羅大經 Luo Dajing《鶴林玉露》 *Jade Dew of the Crane Forest*
馬銀春 Ma Yinchun, author of 《沒有最好只有更好》 *The Best Has Gotten Better*

(3) Long but straightforward titles, which can be translated literally, such as:

蘇軾：〈送安敦秀才失解西歸〉Su Shi: "Seeing off Scholar An Dun Who Failed in the Civil Service Examination and Returned Home Westward"
黃庭堅：〈郭明甫作西齋於潁請予賦詩〉Huang Tingjian: "Poem Written at the Request of Kuo Mingfu Who Built the West Studio at Yingwei"
曹靖華《歎往昔，獨木橋頭徘徊無終期》 *A Sigh on the Past: Hovering at the End of a Single-log Bridge without End*

(4) Long and complicated titles, such as:

唐裴休 Tang Peixiu：《黃蘗山斷際禪師傳心法要》 *Essentials in the Method of the Transmission of Mind by the Chan Master Duanji of the Huang Nie Mountain*
鄭板橋：〈濰縣署中畫什呈年伯包大中丞括〉Zheng Banqiao: "Painting Bamboos at the Official Residence of Wei County Presented to Bao Kuo, the Magistrate"
杜牧：〈題宣州開元寺水閣閣下宛溪夾溪居人〉Du Mu: "Inscribing a Poem on the Water Pavilion of the Kaiyuan Temple in Xuanzhou for Layman Jiaxi Living at the Wan Brook beneath the Pavilion"

(5) Titles containing rare works, such as:

《尚書‧旅獒》 "Hounds of Lu", *The Book of History*
黃晞《聱隅子》Huang Xi: *Aoyuzi*

(6) Titles of popular works with fairly standardized translations, such as:

曹雪芹《紅樓夢》Cao Xueqin, *A Dream of the Red Chamber*
施耐庵《水滸傳》Shi Nai'an: *Outlaws of the Marshes*
陳壽《三國志》Chen Shou: *Records of the Three Kingdoms*
孔子《論語》Confucius: *The Analects of Confucius*
孫武《孫子兵法》Sun Wu: *The Art of War by Sunzi*
孟軻《孟子》Meng Ke: *Mencius*
蘭陵笑笑生《金瓶梅》Lanling Xiaoxiaosheng: *The Plum in the Golden Vase*

(7) Titles of popular works without standardized translations, such as:

吳趼人《二十年目睹之怪現狀》Wu Jianren: *Bizarre Happenings Eyewitnessed over Two Decades*
《增廣賢文》 *Words that Open up One's Mind and Enhance One's Wisdom*

(8) Titles of non-Chinese origin, such as:

《般若波羅蜜多心經》 *Prajna Paramita Heart Sutra*
《大般涅槃經》 *Mahāparinirvāṇa Sūtra*

In title translation, several points need to be noted.

(1) Polysemy

Some words are polysemous. Take the character *shu* 書as an example. *Shu* has several meanings, which have to be translated differently, depending on context.

(a) as "letter"

董卓：〈上何進書〉 Dong Zhuo: "A Letter to He Jin"
司馬遷：〈報任安書〉 Sima Qian: "A Letter in Response to Ren An"

(b) as "history"

范曄《後漢書》 Fan Ye: *History of the Later Han*
李百藥《北齊書》 Li Baiyao *History of the Northern Qi*

(c) as "works"

程顥，程頤《二程全書》 Cheng Hao and Cheng Yi: *Complete Works of Cheng Hao and Cheng Yi*
商鞅《商君書》 Shang Yang: *The Works of Shang Yang*

Another example is *zhuan* 傳, which can be translated variously, depending on context.

(d) as "biography"

葛洪 Ge Hong《神仙傳》 *Biographies of Divine Immortals*

(e) as "account"

劉璋 Liu Zhang《斬鬼傳》 *Account of Ghost-beheading*

(f) as "story"

西周生 Xi Zhousheng《醒世姻緣傳》 *Stories of Marriage to Awaken the World*

(g) untranslated

羅貫中 Luo Guanzhong《平妖傳》 *Taming Devils*
馬烽 Ma Feng《呂梁英雄傳》 *Heroes of the Lu Liang Mountain*

There are other variant expressions relating to *zhuan*, such as

(1) *houzhuan* 後傳

(a) as "sequel"

陳忱 Chen Chen:《水滸後傳》 *A Sequel to the Outlaws of the Marshes*

(2) *quan zhuan* 全傳

(a) as "biography"

高陽 Gao Yang:《胡雪巖全傳》 *A Biography of Hu Xueyan*
無垢道人 Wugou Daoren《八仙全傳》 *Biographies of the Eight Immortals*

(b) as "full biography"

郭小亭 Guo Xiaoting《濟公全傳》 *A Full Biography of Jigong*

(c) as "story"

錢彩 Qian Cai《説岳全傳》 *A Story of Yue Fei*

(d) as "history"

《説呼全傳》 *A History of the Shuo Family*

(e) as "complete history"

吳浚 Wu Jun《飛龍全傳》 *A Complete History of the Flying Dragon*

(f) not translated

陳汝衡 Chen Ruheng《説唐演義全傳》 *Romance of the Tang Dynasty*

(3) *waizhuan* 外傳

(a) as "supplementary commentary"

韓嬰 Han Ying《韓詩外傳》 *Supplementary Commentary on The Book of Songs by Master Han*
王夫之 Wang Fuzhi《周易外傳》 *Supplementary Commentary on The Book of Changes*

(4) *xinzhuan* 新傳

(a) as "new biography"

孔厥，袁靜 Kong Jue and Yuan Jing《新兒女英雄傳》*New Biographies of Heroes and Heroines*

(2) Omission

Some parts in the titles of works may not be translated as they are semantically inessential, such as:

孔子《論語·顏淵篇第十二》Confucius: Chapter 12, *The Analects of Confucius*
Note: 顏淵篇 is not translated because this name, which is placed at the beginning of the first sentence of the chapter, does not carry any specific meaning.
孟軻《孟子·公孫丑上》Meng Ke: Chapter 2, Part 1, *Mencius*
Note: 公孫丑 is not translated because this name, which is placed at the beginning of the first sentence of the chapter, does not carry any specific meaning.

(3) Consistency

When a certain expression has been translated in a certain way, then all identical expressions should be translated in the same way. Take *yanyi* 演義 as an example. Since the famous novel《三國演義》by 羅貫中 Luo Guanzhong has been translated as *Romance of the Three Kingdoms*, "romance" has been a standard term to translate *yanyi*, thus we have the following works translated in the same manner.

許廑父《民國演義》Xu Qinfu: *Romance of the Republic*
許仲琳《封神演義》Xu Zhonglin: *Romance of the Investiture of the Deities*

By the same token, *tongsu yanyi* 通俗演義 is translated as "popular romance", as shown in the following examples.

蔡東藩《民國史通俗演義》Cai Dongfan: *Popular Romance of the Republican Period*
蔡東藩《元史通俗演義》Cai Dongfan: *Popular Romance of the Yuan Dynasty*
蔡東藩《南北史通俗演義》Cai Dongfan: *Popular Romance of the Southern and Northern Dynasties*

(4) Primary and secondary meanings

There are titles with expressions which can be translated either by its primary meaning or its derived meaning. Take *fengyun* 風雲 as an example.

Primary meaning

(a) as "wind and clouds"

羅貫中：〈風雲會〉Luo Guanzhong: "The Meeting of Wind and Clouds"

Derived meaning

(b) as "war"

鮑昌《庚子風雲》Bao Chang: *The War in 1900-1901*

(c) as "changes"

劉江《太行風雲》Liu Jiang *Changes in Taixing*

Concluding remarks

Translating the most popular sayings and famous quotes from the best-known works of the best-known poets and writers throughout the ages is both a great challenge and a source of great enjoyment. It is hoped that all the efforts spent on selecting and translating them are well made and that the translations have done justice to the authors and writers.

It must be added, before closing, that this dictionary is different from other dictionaries in at least one way: dictionaries of other types are usually for reference and consultation, but this dictionary is for enjoyment and enrichment. The young would find it informative and inspirational to know the wit and wisdom of their ancestors, the matured would find the life experience of other people in other times and places a shared treasure, while the senior could find enjoyment to know how other people of their age look at life and even after life.

I sincerely hope that the sayings and quotes in this dictionary serve to enhance our understanding of Chinese culture in a way that has never been done before.

References

Chan, Sin-wai (tr.) (2009) *Famous Chinese Sayings Quoted by Wen Jiabao*, Hong Kong: Chung Hwa Book Co. (H.K.) Ltd.

Chan, Sin-wai (1998) "In defence of literalism: My experience in translating *Stories by Gao Yang*", *The Bumanities Bulletin* 5:66-73.

Cheung, Anthony and Paul Gurofsky (trs.) (1987) *Cheng Pan-ch'iao: Selected Poems, Calligraphy, Paintings and Seal Engravings*, Hong Kong: Joint Publishing Co. (HK) 三聯書店(有限)公司.

Herzberg, Larry (2016) "Chinese Proverbs and Popular Sayings", in Chan Sin-wai (ed.), *Routledge Encyclopedia of the Chinese Language*, London and New York: Routledge, 295-327.

Rickett, Allyn W. (1985) *Guanzi: Political, Economic, and Philosophical Essays from Early China: A Study and Translation*, Princeton: Princeton University Press.

Wang, Chunyong 王春永 (2012) 《溫家寶總理經典引句解說》全新修訂本(*Famous Chinese Sayings quoted by Wen Jiabao*), newly revised edition Hong Kong: Chung Hwa Book Co. (H.K.) Ltd. 中華書局.

Ability

八十老公挑擔子 —— 心有餘而力不足。 An eighty-year-old man carrying a shoulder pole with loads – the spirit is willing, but the flesh is weak. 【歇後語 End-clipper】

八仙過海，各顯神通。 Like the Eight Immortals crossing the sea, each shows their prowess. 【李綠園《歧路燈・第六十八回》Li Luyuan: Chapter 68, *Lamp on a Forked Road*】

抱真才者，人不知不慍。 One who is really talented will not be infuriated when people don't know him. 【王文祿《海沂子・真才論》Wang Wenlu:"On Real Talents", *Haiyizi*】

本地薑不辣。 Local ginger is not pungent enough. 【俗語 Common saying】

本事不是吹的。 Real ability is not shown by boasting. 【石玉昆《三俠五義・第三十一回》Shi Yukun: Chapter 31, *The Three Heroes and Five Gallants*】

不能則學，疑則問。 If you can't do something, learn it; if you have doubts, enquire about it. 【戴德《大戴禮記・曾子制言上》Dai De:"Zengzi about Behaviour, Part 1", *Records of Rites by Dai the Elder*】

不怕無能，就怕無恆。 Inability is not to be feared, but inconsistency is. 【俗語 Common saying】

不勝其任，而處其位，非此位之人也。 A person who is incapable of shouldering the responsibilities his position involves but is placed in that position is not a person for the position. 【墨翟《墨子・親士卷一》Mo Di: Chapter 1, "Staying Close to Scholars", *Mozi*】

才者，德之資也；德者，才之帥也。 Ability supports virtue while virtue commands ability. 【司馬光《資治通鑑・周紀》Sima Guang:"Annals of the Zhou Dynasty", *Comprehensive Mirror to Aid in Government*】

唱戲要嗓子，拉弓要膀子。 To act in an opera, one needs a good voice. To draw a bow, one needs strong arms. 【鈕驃〈蕭長華先生談戲曲訣諺〉Niu Biao:"Mr Xiao Changhua on the Important Things in Chinese Opera"】

大事做不來，小事又不做。 Be incapable of doing great things, yet disdain minor tasks. 【俗語 Common saying】

短綆不可以汲深。 A short rope cannot draw water from a deep well. 【莊周《莊子・外篇・至樂第十八》Zhuang Zhou: Chapter 18, "Ultimate Joy", "Outer Chapters", *Zhuangzi*】【荀況《荀子・榮辱篇第十一》Xun Kuang: Chapter 11, "On Honour and Disgrace"】

多能多幹多勞碌，不得浮生半日閒。 Capable people toil all the

time without resting even half a day in their lifetime. 【施世綸《施公案·第一百零五回》Shi Shilun: Chapter 105, *Cases of Judge Shi*】

高不成，低不就。 One who is unfit for a high position, but unwilling to take a lower one. 【陳師道〈宿柴城〉Chen Shidao: "Lodging at the Cai City"】

高者不說，說者不高。 A person with superb skill does not boast, while a person who boasts does not have real skill. 【佚名《丸經·崇古章·卷上》Anonymous: "Chapter on Worshipping the Ancient", Volume 1, *The Classic of Herbal Pills*】

各盡所能，按勞分配。 From each according to his ability, to each according to his work. 【俗語 Common saying】

狗屎做鞭子 —— 文（聞）又文（聞）不得，武（舞）又武（舞）不得。 A whip made from a dog's droppings is useless–a person who could neither be a scholar nor a soldier. 【歇後語 End-clipper】

紅牛黑牛，能拉犁的都是好牛。 It does not matter whether the ox is red or black in colour, for any ox that can pull the plough is a good ox. 【柳青《創業史·一部十八章》Liu Qing: Chapter 18, Part 1, *History of Creating Business*】

肩不能挑擔，手不能提籃。 One cannot carry a pole on one's shoulder nor a basket in one's hand. 【張南莊《何典·第六卷》Zhang Nanzhuang: Chapter 6, *From Which Classic*】

簡能而任之，擇善而從之。 Select the capable to take office and choose the best to follow. 【魏徵〈諫太宗十思疏〉Wei Zheng: "Memorial Containing Ten Recommendations for Deliberation for Emperor Taizong"】

快馬不用鞭催，響鼓不用重錘。 A fast horse needs no whipping and with a loud drum you do not need a heavy hammer. 【諺語 Proverb】

老鼠吃貓 —— 自不量力。 A mouse wanting to eat a cat-overrating its own abilities. 【歇後語 End-clipper】

六十歲學吹打 —— 心有餘力不足。 Learning how to blow a trumpet and beat a gong at the age of sixty – the spirit is willing, but the flesh is weak. 【歇後語 End-clipper】

沒有打虎藝，不敢上山崗。 Without the ability to catch a tiger, one dare not go to the mountains. 【諺語 Proverb】

能貓不叫，叫貓不能。 A mewing cat is never a good mouser. 【諺語 Proverb】

能人背後有能人。 Behind every capable person there is another more capable person. 【佚名〈隋何賺風魔蒯徹·第三折〉Anonymous: Scene 3, "Sui He, Zhi Zhuan, and Kuai Che, Who Feigned Madness"】

能中有能，強中有強。For every capable person, there is another more capable person. For every strong person, there is another stronger person.【佚名《衣襖車》Anonymous: *Carriages of Yi Ao*】

蚍蜉撼大樹，可笑不自量。A tiny insect trying to shake a tree is ridiculously overrating itself.【韓愈〈調張籍〉Han Yu: "Teasing Zhang Ji"】

巧者多勞拙者閒。The able have a lot to do while the clumsy stay idle.【吳承恩《西遊記·第四十六回》Wu Cheng'en: Chapter 46, *Journey to the West*】

巧者勞而智者憂，無能者無所求。Those with good skills have to work hard, those with great intelligence have to worry a lot, while those who are incapable have nothing to look for.【莊周《莊子·雜篇·列御寇第三十二》Zhuang Zhou: Chapter 32, "Lie Yukou", "Miscellaneous Chapters", *Zhuangzi*】

人各有能有不能。Everyone has something he is capable of doing and something he is incapable of doing.【左丘明《左傳·定公五年》Zuo Qiuming: "The Fifth Year of the Reign of Duke Ding", *Zuo's Commentary on the Spring and Autumn Annals*】

人盡其才，物盡其用。People deploy in full their abilities and resources are put to their best use.【孫中山〈上李鴻章書〉Sun Yat-sen: "Letter to Li Hongzhang"】

人之所不學而能者，其良能也；所不慮而知者，其良知也。An ability that people do not have to learn to own is their intuitive ability and the knowledge that they do not have to learn is their intuitive knowledge.【孟軻《孟子·盡心章句上》Meng Ke: Chapter 7, Part 1, *Mencius*】

山高有個頂，海深有個底，唯獨本領無邊。A high mountain has a top, a deep sea has a bottom, but ability is boundless.【俗語 Common saying】

螳臂擋車，不知自量。Using mantis shanks to stop a carriage, one overrates one's own ability.【莊子《莊子·內篇·人間世第四》Zhuang Zhou: Chapter 4, "Human World", "Inner Chapters", *Zhuangzi*】

天生我材必有用，千金散盡還復來。The abilities that heaven endowed me must have some use. Though I spend a thousand taels of gold, I will in time get them back.【李白〈將進酒〉Li Bai: "About to Drink Wine"】

文不文，武不武。Be neither competent for civil purposes nor military purposes.【韓愈〈瀧吏〉Han Yu: "The Officer at the Rapids"】

無所不會，無所不能。There is nothing one cannot do and nothing one is not able to do.【諺語 Proverb】

眾人之中，必有能人。Among many, there must be people of ability.【俗語 Common saying】

自己無能，埋怨刀鈍。 An incompetent worker quarrels with his tools. 【俗語 Common saying】

Achievement

畢其功於一役。 Accomplish something at one stroke. 【孫中山《民報‧發刊辭》Sun Yat-sen:"Inaugural Statement", *People's Journal*】

成大事者不拘小節。 One who wants to make great achievements does not bother oneself with small matters. 【范曄《後漢書‧陳蕃傳》Fan Ye:"Biography of Chen Fan", *History of the Later Han*】

成大事者不惜小費。 One who wants to make great achievements does not mind spending small sums. 【吳趼人《二十年目睹之怪現狀‧第八十八回》Wu Jianren: Chapter 88, *Bizarre Happenings Eyewitnessed over Two Decades*】

成事不足，敗事有餘。 One is incapable of achieving things, but liable to spoil everything. 【曾樸《續孽海花‧第四十二回》Zeng Pu: Chapter 42, *Sequel to Flower on the Ocean of Sin*】

出乎其類，拔乎其萃。 Be distinguished in one's kind and the best among the selected. 【孟軻《孟子‧公孫丑上》Meng Ke: Chapter 2, Part 1, *Mencius*】

大筆寫大字，大人幹大事。 A large writing brush writes big characters and a large-minded person does great things. 【諺語 Proverb】

功成名遂身退。 Retire when you have achieved success and acquired fame. 【老子《道德經‧第二十五章》Laozi: Chapter 25, *Daodejing*】

究天人之際，通古今之變，成一家之言。 Probe into the junction between heaven and man, comprehend changes that have taken place from the past to the present, and create a philosophy of one's own. 【司馬遷《史記‧太史公自序》Sima Qian:"Author's Preface", *Records of the Grand Historian*】

君子成人之美。 A true man is always ready to help others to attain their aims. 【孔子《論語‧顏淵篇第十二》Confucius: Chapter 12, *The Analects of Confucius*】

牆裏開花牆外香。 One's achievement is usually known outside one's own unit. 【海岩《死於青春》Hai Yan: *Die of Youth*】

三不朽：立德、立功、立言。 There are three long-lasting accomplishments: establishing one's virtue, one's achievements, and one's views. 【左丘明《左傳‧襄公二十四年》Zuo Qiuming:"The Twenty-Fourth Year of the Reign of

Duke Xiang", *Zuo's Commentary on the Spring and Autumn Annals*】

士別三日，當刮目相看。When a scholar has been absent for three days it is necessary to rub one's eyes before recognizing him.【陳壽《三國志‧吳志‧呂傳》Chen Shou: "Biography of Lu", "History of the Wu", *Records of the Three Kingdoms*】

Action

八字還沒有一撇。Nothing is definite yet.【俗語 Common saying】

白玉不雕，美珠不文，質有餘也。White jade does not need carving, beautiful pearls do not need ornamentation, for they have superior qualities.【劉安《淮南子‧説林訓第十七》Liu An: Chapter 17, "Discourse on Woods", *Huainanzi*】

不見魚出水，不下釣魚竿。Until one sees the fish one does not cast the fishing line.【李滿天《水向東流‧第七章》Li Mantian: Chapter 7, *Water Flows to the East*】

不矜細行，終累大德。If one does not attend to small actions seriously, it will affect one's achievement in great matters.【《尚書‧旅獒》"Hounds of Lu", *The Book of History*】

秤砣落在棉花上 —— 沒回音。Weights having fallen on cotton–there is no reply.【歇後語 End-clipper】

穿着雨衣打傘 —— 多此一舉。Using an umbrella while wearing a raincoat–engaging in unnecessary action.【歇後語 End-clipper】

大開方便之門。Do everything to suit somebody's convenience.【馮惟敏〈僧尼共犯‧第四折〉Feng Weimin: Act 4, "Monks and Nuns Committing Crimes Together"】

東一鎯頭西一棒子。Act in a disorderly way.【俗語 Common saying】

動莫若敬，居莫若儉，德莫若讓，事莫若諮。Nothing is better than act with respect, live in frugality, concede in cultivating virtue, and consult others in handling things.【左丘明《國語‧周語下》Zuo Qiuming: "The Language of Zhou, Part 2", *National Languages*】

斷而敢行，鬼神避之。When you are decisive and courageous to act, ghosts will stay away from you.【司馬遷《史記‧李斯列傳》Sima Qian: "Biography of Li Si", *Records of the Grand Historian*】

凡事應量力而行。Everything has to be done according to one's capacities.【俗語 Common saying】

非知之難，行之惟難；非行之難，終之斯難。The difficult thing is not just to know something, but to do something; the difficult thing is not even to do something, but to be persistent in doing something. 【《貞觀政要》Notes on the Political Governance of Zhenguan】

趕十五不如趕初一。 Better do something early on the first than late on the fifteenth of a month. 【吳南生《革命母親李梨英》Wu Nansheng: My Revolutionary Mother Li Liying】

顧前不顧後。 Attend to what is before one and leave the future to take care of it. 【曹雪芹《紅樓夢・第六十八回》Cao Xueqin: Chapter 68, A Dream of the Red Chamber】

光說不算，做出看看。 Fine words do not count. One should do some practical work and show it to others. 【俗語 Common saying】

好話說盡，壞事做盡。 Say the nicest things and do the dirtiest things. 【俗語 Common saying】

橫插一扛子。 Interfere flagrantly. 【俗語 Common saying】

話講當面，事辦當時。 Say to one's face and do there and then. 【諺語 Proverb】

火上澆油，爐中熾炭。 Pour oil on the fire and add fuel to the flames in the furnace. 【施耐庵《水滸傳・第六十三回》Shi Nai'an: Chapter 63, Outlaws of the Marshes】

疾風掃落葉。 Be as powerful and quick in action as the strong wind sweeping away fallen leaves. 【陳壽《三國志・魏書・辛毗傳》Chen Shou: "Biography of Xin Pi", "History of the State of Wei", Records of the Three Kingdoms】

己所不欲，勿施於人。 Do not impose on others what you yourself do not desire. 【孔子《論語・衛靈公篇第十五》Confucius: Chapter 15, The Analects of Confucius】

江邊賣水 —— 多餘。 Selling water by the riverside–superfluous. 【歇後語 End-clipper】

今日事，今日畢。 Never put off till tomorrow what you can do today. 【俗語 Common saying】

井邊賣水 —— 多此一舉。 Selling water by the side of a well–making an unnecessary move. 【歇後語 End-clipper】

靜如處女，動如脫兔。 When still, it's like a maiden. When in action, it is as nimble as an escaping hare. 【孫武《孫子兵法・九地第十一》Sun Wu: Chapter 11, "The Nine Situations", The Art of War by Sunzi】

可一而不可再。 Once is enough. 【俗語 Common saying】【歸有光〈崑山縣倭寇始末書〉Gui Youguang: "A Full Account of the Japanese Pirates in Kunshan County"】

口說無憑，做出便見。 What is said is without evidence while what is done can be seen. 【凌濛初《二刻拍案驚奇・第一卷》Ling Mengchu: Chapter 1, Amazing Tales, Volume Two】

快刀斬亂麻。Cut a tangle of hemp with a sharp knife. 【李百藥《北齊書・文宣帝紀》Li Baiyao: "Basic Annals of Emperor Xuan", *History of the Northern Qi*】

雷聲大，雨點少。The thunder is loud, but raindrops are few. 【釋道原《景德傳燈錄・文益禪師》Shi Daoyuan: "Chan Master Wenyi", *Records of the Transmission of the Lamp in the Jingde Period*】

力行近乎仁。Performing good deeds gets one closer to benevolence. 【《禮記・中庸第三十一章》Chapter 31, "Doctrine of the Mean", *The Book of Rites*】

量力而動，其過鮮矣。Act according to one's capacity, one will seldom make mistakes. 【左丘明《左傳・僖公二十年》Zuo Qiuming: "The Twentieth Year of the Reign of Duke Xi", *Zuo's Commentary on the Spring and Autumn Annals*】

路不行不到，事不做不成。If one does not walk, one cannot reach one's destination. If one does not do things, nothing can be accomplished. 【張作為《原林深處・第三章》Zhang Zuowei: Chapter 3, *Deep in the Forest*】

訥於言而敏於行。Slow of speech but quick in action. 【孔子《論語・里仁篇第四》Confucius: Chapter 4, *The Analects of Confucius*】

能說不如能行。Eloquence is not as good as action. 【俗語 Common saying】

能行之者，未必能言；能言之者，未必能行。Those who can do it may not be able to say it and those who can say it may not be able to do it. 【司馬遷《史記・孫子吳起列傳》Sima Qian: "Biographies of Sun Zi and Wu Qi", *Records of the Grand Historian*】

你做初一，我做十五。Answer blows with blows. 【俗語 Common saying】

騎驢拿拐杖 —— 多此一舉。Riding a donkey and holding a crutch–an unnecessary action. 【歇後語 End-clipper】

三個指頭拾田螺。As simple as picking up a field snail with three fingers. 【俗語 Common saying】

事者，生於慮，成於務，失於傲。Things are born out of planning, completed in practice, but lost in arrogance. 【管仲《管子・乘馬第五》Guan Zhong: Chapter 5, "On Horse-back Riding", *Guanzi*】

說得好不如做得好。Well done is better than well said. 【俗語 Common saying】

說來容易做時難。It's easier said than done. 【凌濛初《二刻拍案驚奇・第十八卷》Ling Mengchu: Chapter 18, *Amazing Tales, Volume Two*】

說是一回事，做是另一回事。To say is one thing, to practise is another. 【俗語 Common saying】

太陽底下點燈 —— 多餘。
Lighting a lamp in the sun is superfluous. 【歇後語 End-clipper】

螳螂捕蟬，豈知黃雀在後。A mantis catches a cicada without knowing that a siskin is at its back waiting to eat it. 【《增廣賢文》Words that Open up One's Mind and Enhance One's Wisdom】

退一步，進二步。A step backward now is to make two steps forward in the future. 【俗語 Common saying】

脫褲子放屁。Strip off one's pants to fart – an unnecessary action. 【俚語 Slang】

瞎子戴眼鏡 —— 多餘。A blind person wearing glasses–all for show. 【歇後語 End-clipper】

下得深水擒蛟龍，留在淺灘捕魚蝦。Those who go deep into the sea catch the dragon whereas those who stay in shoals catch only fish and shrimps. 【俗語 Common saying】

行必先人，言必後人。One must act before others and speak after others. 【戴德《大戴禮記·曾子立事》Dai De: "Zengzi Establishes Things", Records of Rites by Dai the Elder】

行成於思，毀於隨。A deed is accomplished through taking thought and fails through drifting with the stream. 【韓愈〈進學解〉Han Yu: "Explanation of Progress in One's Study"】

行動有三分財氣。In action itself there is certain wealth. 【吳承恩《西遊記·第六十八回》Wu Cheng'en: Chapter 68, Journey to the West】

行事不可任心，說話不可任口。Action must not be discretionary, speech must not be casual. 【申居郎《西巖贅語》Shen Juyun, Remarks by Shen Juyun】

揚揚止沸，不如釜底抽薪。To stop water from boiling, it is better to take away firewood from under the cauldron. 【董卓〈上何進書〉Dong Zhuo: "A Letter to He Jin"】

一動不如一靜。To take no action is better than to take any. 【張端義《貴耳集·卷上》Zhang Duanyi: Volume 1, Collection of Things Heard】

一之謂甚，其可再乎。Once it is too much, how can it be repeated? 【左丘明《左傳·僖公五年》Zuo Qiuming: "The Fifth Year of the Reign of Duke Xi", Zuo's Commentary on the Spring and Autumn Annals】

以其人之道，還治其人之身。Deal with a person as he deals with you. 【朱熹《中庸集註·第十三章》Zhu Xi, Chapter 13, Notes on the Doctrine of the Mean】

佔着毛坑不拉屎。Block the path of others. 【諺語 Proverb】

照葫蘆畫瓢。Draw a dipper with a gourd as a model–to copy without using one's creativity. 【魏泰《東軒筆錄·第一卷》Wei Tai: Volume 1, Remarks Recorded at the East Studio】

祇聽樓梯響，不見人下來。Steps on the stairs are heard, but nobody really gets down. 【司馬文森《風雨桐江》Sima Wensen: *The Tong River in Wind and Rain*】

鐘不敲不響，燈不點不亮。Bells will not ring until struck and lamps will not be bright until lit. 【諺語 Proverb】

Adaptation

到甚麼山上唱甚麼歌。Sing different songs on different mountains. 【毛澤東〈反對黨八股〉Mao Zedong: "Against the Stereotyped Party Writing"】

高田宜黍稷，低田宜稻麥。Highlands are fit for growing millet and broomcorn, while lowlands for rice and wheat. 【羅願《爾雅翼‧卷一》Luo Yuan: Volume 1, *Wings to the Erya*】

看菜吃飯，量體裁衣。Eat according to the dishes cooked and make clothes according to one's figure. 【毛澤東〈反對黨八股〉Mao Zedong: "Against the Stereotyped Party Writing"】

隨機應變，因地制宜。Adjust to changing circumstances and adapt to local conditions. 【趙爾巽《清史稿‧卷四百二十一‧朱嶟傳》Zhao Erxun: Chapter 421, "Biography of Zhu Zun", *Draft History of the Qing Dynasty*】

Adultery

姦近殺，賭近賊。Adultery is close to murder and gambling, to theft. 【凌濛初《初刻拍案驚奇‧第三十六卷》Ling Mengchu: Chapter 36, *Amazing Tales, Volume One*】

姦情連命案，賭博出賊情。Adultery often leads to murder, and gambling to theft. 【馮夢龍《警世通言‧第三十五卷》Feng Menglong: Chapter 35, *Stories to Caution the World*】

母狗不掉尾，公狗不上身。If the bitch does not raise her tail, the male dog cannot copulate. 【蘭陵

笑笑生《金瓶梅‧第七十六回》Lanling Xiaoxiaosheng: Chapter 76, *The Plum in the Golden Vase*】

拿賊拿贓，捉姦捉雙。If you go to arrest thieves, you must find the booty. If you go to discover adultery, you must catch both the adulterer and the adulteress. 【胡太初《晝簾緒論‧治獄》Hu Taichu: "Managing the Prison", *An Introduction to Governing While Resting During the Day*】

撒手不為姦。When a man and a woman are separated, you cannot accuse them of adultery. 【關漢卿〈望江亭‧第一摺〉Guan Hanqing: Scene 1, "River-side Pavilion"】

偷漢婆娘害四鄰。An adulteress does harm to her neighbours. 【諺語 Proverb】

夤夜入人家，非姦即盜。One who enters another's house stealthily at midnight is either an adulterer or a thief. 【喬孟符〈金錢記‧二折〉Qiao Mengfu: Scene 2, "The Golden Coins"】

捉賊見贓，捉姦見雙。Catch a thief and find the loot; catch the adulterers and find the pair. 【李文蔚〈燕青博魚‧第三折〉Li Wenhui: Scene 3, "Yan Qing Gambling on Fish"】

Advancement

八級工拜師父——精益求精。A top-grade worker taking a teacher–keep improving 【歇後語 End-clipper】

百尺竿頭，更進一步。Though one is at the tip of a hundred-foot-long pole, one can still make further progress. 【釋道原《景德傳燈錄‧卷十》Shi Daoyuan: Chapter 10, *Records of the Transmission of the Lamp in the Jingde Period.*】

不怕慢，祇怕站。Going slowly is better than standing still. 【《增廣賢文》*Words that Open up One's Mind and Enhance One's Wisdom*】

踩着別人肩膀往上爬。To advance at the expense of others. 【俗語 Common saying】

長風破浪會有時，直掛雲帆濟滄海。There will be a day when a strong wind comes to skim the waves, and I'll hoist my sails high to cross the vast ocean. 【李白〈行路難〉Li Bai:"Moving Forward on the Road is Difficult"】

沉舟側畔千帆過，病樹前頭萬木春。A thousand sails pass by the shipwreck and ten thousand saplings shoot up beyond the withe Red trees. 【劉禹錫〈酬樂天揚州初逢席上見贈〉Liu Yuxi:"Presented to Bai Juyi When First Meeting Him at a Feast in Yangzhou"】

春筍破土——節節昇。Spring bamboo shoots breaking up through the ground shoot up joint by joint–a continuous rise. 【歇後語 End-clipper】

得尺則尺，得寸則寸。Get a foot and it is a foot gained, get an inch and it is an inch gained. 【劉向《戰國策‧秦策三》Liu Xiang:"Strategies of the State of Qin, Part 3", *Strategies of the Warring States*】

得一步，進一步。A step gained is a step forward. 【吳承恩《西遊記‧

第九十四回》Wu Cheng'en: Chapter 94, *Journey to the West*】

後進趕先進，先進更先進。The less advanced strive to catch up with the more advanced, and the more advanced become the most advanced. 【俗語 Common saying】

進不求名，退不辭罪。Advances are not made to gain fame and retreats are not done to avoid punishment. 【孫武《孫子兵法・虛實第六》Sun Wu: Chapter 6, "The Void and Substance", *The Art of War by Sunzi*】

近水樓台先得月。A person in a favourable position gains special advantage. 【蘇麟〈殘句〉Su Lin: "Fragmented Lines"】【俞文豹《清夜錄》Yu Wenbao: *Records of a Clear Night*】

困龍終有上天時。A trapped dragon will eventually fly back to the sky. 【俗語 Common saying】

鯉魚跳龍門。Endeavour to make a success of oneself. 【陸佃《埤雅・釋魚》Lu Dian: "Explaining fish", *Enlarged Erya*】

其進銳者，其退速。Those who advance quickly will retreat with speed. 【孟軻《孟子・盡心章句下》Meng Ke: Chapter 7, Part 2, *Mencius*】

千叮囑，萬叮囑。Give advice repeatedly. 【俗語 Common saying】

人到事中迷，就怕沒人提。When people are lost in a matter, what they need most is a reminder. 【諺語 Proverb】

人往高處走，水往低處流。People endeavour to rise while water flows downward. 【俗語 Common saying】

人向上走，水向下流。People endeavour to move upward while water flows downward. 【俗語 Common saying】

若登高必自卑，若涉遠必自邇。If you want to climb up, you must begin from a low place. If you want to trek to a distant place, you must start from somewhere close. 【《禮記・中庸第三十一章》Chapter 31, "Doctrine of the Mean", *The Book of Rites*】

一代更比一代強。The new generation is superior to the previous one. 【俗語 Common saying】

一人得道，雞犬升天。When a person is promoted, all who are connected with him or her benefit. 【王充《論衡・道虛第二十四卷》Wang Chong: Chapter 24, "Untruths", *Critical Essays*】

Advantage

肥水不流別人田。Water that can fertilize my land will not go to the fields of other people. 【俚語 Slang】

逢着好處便安身。One settles down with what advantages one comes across. 【張南莊《何典·第七卷》Zhang Nanzhuang: Chapter 7, *From Which Classic*】

火在遠處是明燈，它在近處燒灼人。The fire which lights up at a distance will burn us when near. 【俗語 Common saying】

討便宜處失便宜。One who wants to take advantage of others will get the worst of it. 【馮夢龍《醒世恆言·第十六卷》Feng Menglong: Chapter 16, *Stories to Awaken the World*】

天時不如地利，地利不如人和。Favourable weather is less important than geographical advantages, and geographical advantages are less important than harmony among people. 【孟軻《孟子·公孫丑上》Meng Ke: Chapter 2, Part 1, *Mencius*】

未見其利，先見其害。Suffer a loss before an uncertain gain. 【俗語 Common saying】

向陽花木易逢春。Flowers and trees exposed to the sun sprout and bloom early. 【俞文豹《清夜錄》Yu Wenbao: *Records of a Clear Night*】

一長便形一短。With one advantage, there is bound to be a disadvantage. 【羅懋登《三寶太監西洋記·第九十三回》Luo Maodeng: Chapter 93, *Sanbao Eunuch's Voyage to the Western Ocean*】

有百害而無一利。Have everything to lose and nothing to gain. 【諺語 Proverb】

有百利而無一弊。Have every advantage and no drawback. 【諺語 Proverb】

有利必有弊。/ 有一利必有一弊。Everything has its advantages as well as disadvantages./ An advantage is inevitably accompanied by a disadvantage. 【諺語 Proverb】【吳趼人《二十年目睹之怪現狀·第四十六回》Wu Jianren: Chapter 46, *Bizarre Happenings Eyewitnessed over Two Decades*】

針無兩頭利。There is no needle with both ends pointed. 【諺語 Proverb】

針衹有一頭尖 —— 沒有十全十美。Sugar cane is never sweet at both ends – one cannot have it both ways. 【歇後語 End-clipper】

Advice

不聽老人言，吃虧在眼前。 If one does not listen to the advice of the old people, one will suffer immediate losses. 【俗語 Common saying】

不聽忠言，莫怪無禮。 If you don't listen to good advice, don't blame me for being rude to you 【俗語 Common saying】

東說向東，西說向西。 Inclined to the east when hearing advice from the east and the west when advised from the west. 【吳承恩《西遊記‧第四十六回》Wu Cheng'en: Chapter 46, *Journey to the West*】

好言不聽，禍必臨身。 If one refuses to follow good advice, one will court disaster for oneself. 【馮夢龍《喻世明言‧第二十卷》Feng Menglong: Chapter 20, *Stories to Instruct the World*】

君子贈人以言，庶人贈人以財。 A gentleman gives people advice while the ordinary people give others money. 【荀況《荀子‧大略第二十七》Xun Kuang: Chapter 27, "Great Compendium", *Xunzi*】

老虎推磨 —— 不吃這一套。 Turn a deaf ear to a person's advice. 【歇後語 End-clipper】

老太婆吃黃蓮 —— 苦口婆心。 An old woman eating Chinese goldthread has a bitter taste in her mouth – one is giving well-meant advice. 【歇後語 End-clipper】

良言一句三冬暖，惡語傷人六月寒。 A word of kindness keeps one warm in the coldest time, while vicious slander makes one feel cold even in the hottest time. 【《增廣賢文》Words that Open up One's Mind and Enhance One's Wisdom】

啟進善之門。 Open the door for the fine words. 【柳宗元〈賀赦表〉Liu Zongyuan: "A Memorial Congratulating Amnesty"】

千人之諾諾，不如一士之諤諤。 The acquiescence of a thousand people is not comparable to a piece of honest advice from a single person. 【司馬遷《史記‧商君列傳》Sima Qian: "Biography of Lord Shang", *Records of the Grand Historian*】

人不勸不善，鐘不敲不鳴。 A person would not do good without admonitions and a bell does not chime without being tolled. 【《增廣賢文》Words that Open up One's Mind and Enhance One's Wisdom】

若要好，問三老。 If you want to do a good job, you should ask at least three old persons for advice. 【諺語 Proverb】【康海〈中山狼‧第三折〉Kang Hai: Scene 3, "Zhongshan Wolf"】

他山之石，可以攻玉。 Stones from other hills may serve to polish the jade of this one. 【《詩經‧小雅‧鶴鳴》"The Screaming of the Crane", "Minor Odes of the Kingdom", *The Book of Odes*】

聽人勸，吃飽飯。 Listen to others' advice and you will have enough to eat. 【俗語 Common saying】

聽人勸，得一半。 Listen to others' advice and you will be half way to success. 【俗語 Common saying】

問遍千家成行家。 After asking many experts for advice, one becomes an expert oneself. 【俗語 Common saying】

言能聽，道乃進。 When words can be heard, the Way will move forward. 【《史記》 Records of the Grand Historian】

忠言逆耳利於行。 Honest advice offends the ear but is good for the conduct. 【司馬遷《史記·留侯世家》Sima Qian: "House of Liu Hou", Records of the Grand Historian】

Age

觀音菩薩 —— 年年十八。 The Goddess of Mercy is eighteen years old every year – one is forever young. 【歇後語 End-clipper】

今年花似去年好，去年人到今年老。 The flowers this year are as beautiful as last year, but a person who came here last year becomes older this year. 【岑參〈韋員外家花樹歌〉Cen Shen: "Song of the Flowery Tree in an Official's Home"】

今朝一歲大家添，不是人間偏我老。 Today we all put on another year, but I'm not the only person who gets older in this world. 【陸游〈木蘭花〉Lu You: "Magnolia"】

臘月的白菜 —— 動（凍）了心。 One has come to an age when one's thoughts turn to courtship and sex. 【歇後語 End-clipper】

莫言三十是年少，百歲三分已一分。 Don't say that one is young at thirty, for it is a third of your life if you live up to a hundred years. 【白居易〈花下自勸酒〉Bai Juyi: "Urging Myself to Drink Wine under the Flowers"】

年四十而見惡焉，其終也已。 When a person at forty is still an object of dislike, this will remain so to the end of his life. 【孔子《論語·陽貨篇第十七》Confucius: Chapter 17, The Analects of Confucius】

七八月的南瓜 —— 皮老心不老。 Just like pumpkins in the seventh or eighth month of the lunar year, one's skin is old but one's heart is young. 【歇後語 End-clipper】

七十風前燭，八十瓦上霜。 A person at seventy is like a candle exposed to the wind, and a person at eighty, the hoarfrost on tiles. 【諺語 Proverb】

七十猶種樹，旁人莫笑痴。At seventy, I still plant trees, but you bystanders don't laugh at me. 【袁枚〈栽樹自嘲〉Yuan Mei: "Self-mockery When Planting Trees"】

人到三十花正旺。A person at thirty is like flowers in full bloom. 【諺語 Proverb】

人到中年萬事休。People at their middle age are good for nothing. 【佚名〈陳州糶米〉Anonymous: "Selling Rice at Chenzhou"】

人活六十不遠行。A person who has lived for sixty years must not travel far. 【俗語 Common saying】

三人同行小的苦。The youngest of a trio of partners is always the one who suffers. 【關漢卿〈蝴蝶夢·二折〉Guan Hanqing: Scene 2, "Butterfly Dream"】

三十不榮，四十不富，五十看看尋死路。If a person does not become a nobility at thirty, get rich at forty, then he should be looking for death at fifty. 【馮夢龍《喻世明言·第三十三卷》Feng Menglong: Chapter 33, Stories to Instruct the World】

三十以後，才知天高地厚。Only when one has past the age of thirty can one understand that heaven is high and the earth thick. 【諺語 Proverb】

三歲看大，七歲看老。You can find a man in a three-year-old boy and an old man in a seven-year-old boy. 【俗語 Common one is three】

三歲看到老。You can see how one's old age would be when one is three years old. 【俗語 Common saying】

少年經不得順境，中年經不得閒境，晚年經不得逆境。One cannot have a smooth life in one's youth, an easy life in one's mid-age, and adversity in one's old age. 【曾國藩〈人生三境〉Zeng Guofan: "Three Stages in One's Life"】

十五而笄，二十而嫁。A girl should bind up her hair at fifteen and marry at twenty. 【《禮記·內則第十二》Chapter 12, "Pattern of the Family", The Book of Rites】

十五而有志於學。At fifteen, one makes up one's mind to learn. 【孔子《論語·為政篇第二》Confucius: Chapter 2, The Analects of Confucius】

世間何物催人老，半是雞聲半馬蹄。What are the things that age us? Half is the crow of the cock and half is the horse hoofs. 【王有齡〈題旅店〉Wang Youling: "Inscribing on an Inn"】

熟得早，老得早 Soon matured, soon aged. 【諺語 Proverb】

歲年不饒人。Age shows no mercy to anyone. 【陶淵明〈雜詩〉Tao Yuanming: "Miscellaneous Poems"】

五十不造屋，六十不種樹，七十不製衣。At fifty, one will not build a house; at sixty, one will not plant trees, and at seventy, one will not make new clothes.【曾廷枚《古諺閒譚・種樹諺》Zeng Tingmei: "Proverbs on Planting Trees", *Chats on Ancient Proverbs*】

五十杖於家，六十杖於鄉，七十杖於國，八十杖於朝。At fifty, one is privileged to carry a cane in the house, at sixty in one's village, at seventy in the capital, and at eighty, at the court.【《禮記・王制第五》Chapter 5, "Regulations of a King", *The Book of Rites*】

一年又過一年春，百歲曾無百歲人。One spring after another, few have ever lived a hundred years.【宋之問〈宴城東莊〉Song Zhiwen: "The East Lodge at Yancheng"】

有錢四十稱年老，無錢六十逞英雄。A rich man claims to be too old to work when he is only forty, while a poor man has to play the hero when he is already sixty.【諺語 Proverb】

又況人之壽，幾人能百歲。What is more is about the life of a person and few people can live to a hundred years long.【邵雍〈人生一世吟〉Shao Yong: "Ode on a Life Time"】

汩餘若將不及兮，恐年歲之不吾與。Years pass like running water, and I'm afraid time will not wait for me.【屈原《楚辭・離騷》Qu Yuan: "The Sorrows at Parting", *The Song of Chu*】

月過十五光明少，人過中年萬事休。The moon becomes less bright after the fifteenth of the lunar month and people reaching the middle age lose interest in doing anything.【《增廣賢文》Words that Open up One's Mind and Enhance One's Wisdom】

Anger

挨了棒的狗 —— 氣急敗壞。A dog beaten with a club is flustered and angry.【歇後語 End-clipper】

不遷怒，不貳過。Don't take your anger out on others nor make the same mistake twice.【孔子《論語・雍也篇第六》Confucius: Chapter 6, *The Analects of Confucius*】

吹鬍子瞪眼睛。Snort and stare in anger.【俗語 Common saying】

敢怒不敢言。Angry but not dare to speak out.【褚人獲《隋唐演義・第七十八回》Zhu Renhuo: Chapter 78, *Heroes in Sui and Tang Dynasties*】

惱一惱，老一老；笑一笑，少一少。Anger makes you older, and laughter, younger.【胡文煥《類修要訣》Hu Wenhuan: *Essential Classified Instructions on Self-Cultivation*】

息卻雷霆之怒，罷卻虎狼之威。Stop your thunderbolt-like anger and your tiger- or wolf-like intimidating behaviour. 【《增廣賢文》 *Words that Open up One's Mind and Enhance One's Wisdom*】

眾怒難犯，專欲難成。 It is dangerous to go against the anger of the masses and it is difficult to secure the exclusive authority to oneself. 【左丘明《左傳·襄公十年》Zuo Qiuming: "The Tenth Year of the Reign of Duke Xiang", *Zuo's Commentary on the Spring and Autumn Annals*】

Ant

螞蟻搬泰山。 Ants can move Mount Tai. 【諺語 Proverb】

螞蟻啃骨頭。 Ants gnawing at a bone. 【諺語 Proverb】

螞蟻雖然小，大山啃得掉。 Small as the ants are, they are capable of gnawing away a high mountain. 【諺語 Proverb】

寧做螞蟻腿，不做麻雀嘴。 Better to be the leg of an ant than the beak of a sparrow. (Meaning: Hard work is better than empty talk.) 【俗語 Common saying】

熱鍋上的螞蟻。 Like an ant in a hot pot. 【諸人獲《隋唐演義·第十九回》Zhu Renhuo: Chapter 19, *Heroes in Sui and Tang Dynasties*】【吳敬梓《儒林外史·第六回》Wu Jingzi: Chapter 6, *An Unofficial History of the World of Literati*】

Appearance

疤癩眼兒照鏡子——自找難看。 One with a scarred eyelid looking into a mirror–exposing one's own defects. 【歇後語 End-clipper】

凡人不可貌相，海水不可斗量。 Never judge a person by his appearance and the waters of the sea by bushels. 【馮夢龍《醒世恆言·賣油郎獨佔花魁》Feng Menglong: "The Oil Vendor and His Pretty Bride", *Stories to Awaken the World*】

凡外重者內拙。 All who give weight to outward appearance are inwardly clumsy. 【莊周《莊子·達生》 "Dasheng", *Zhuangzi*】

凡重外者撰內。 All who give weight to something outside are inwardly clumsy. 【列御寇《列子·黃帝第二》Lie Yukou: Chapter 2, "The Yellow Emperor", *Liezi*】

肥而不胖，瘦而不癟。 Plump but not fat, slender but not shrivelled. 【俗語 Common saying】

風采不減當年。 As good-looking as ever.【諺語 Proverb】

何其相似乃爾。 What a striking similarity.【諺語 Proverb】

花木瓜，空好看。 A papaya that looks good is empty inside.【施耐庵《水滸傳‧第二十四回》Shi Nai'an: Chapter 24, *Outlaws of the Marshes*】

金玉其外，敗絮其中。 Fair without but foul within.【劉基〈賣柑者言〉Liu Ji: "Words from an Orange Vendor"】

扒了皮的癩蛤蟆 —— 活着討厭，死了還嚇人。 A skinned toad– disgusting while alive, dreadful when dead.【歇後語 End-clipper】

人貌相似，人心不同。 People may be similar in appearance but different in heart.【馮夢龍《醒世恆言‧第十卷》Feng Menglong: Chapter 10, *Stories to Awaken the World*】

人有同貌人，物有同形物。 There are people who have the same appearance as there are things which have the same shape.【施世綸《施公案‧第一百四十四回》Shi Shilun: Chapter 144, *Cases of Judge Shi*】

人有相似，物有相同。 There are people who look alike and there are things which resemble each other.【俗語 Common saying】

色即是空，空即是色。 Forms are empty, and emptiness is form.【《般若波羅蜜多心經》*Prajna Paramita Heart Sutra*】

撒泡尿自己照照。 Piss on the ground and look at your face in the puddle.【吳敬梓《儒林外史‧第三回》Wu Jingzi: Chapter 3, *An Unofficial History of the World of Literati*】

外表老實，骨子奸詐。 One who looks honest but is actually full of machinations and deceit.【俗語 Common saying】

外貌雖變，骨子依舊。 One's appearance might have changed, but one is still the same as before.【俗語 Common saying】

外甥多像舅。 Nephews are often like their maternal uncle.【俗語 Common saying】

繡花枕頭，虛有其表。 An embroidered pillow is beautiful without, but empty within.【俗語 Common saying】

以貌取人，失之子羽。 A fair face may be a foul bargain.【司馬遷《史記‧仲尼弟子列傳》Sima Qian: "Biographies of the Disciples of Confucius", *Records of the Grand Historian*】

銀樣蠟槍頭。 Fine in appearance but of no use in reality.【吳晗〈神仙會和百家爭鳴〉Wu Han: "The Meeting of Fairies and the Contest of a Hundred Schools of Thought"】

貞婦愛色，納之以禮。 A chaste woman who loves good looks will get it through proper decorum.【《增廣賢文》*Words that Open up One's Mind and Enhance One's Wisdom*】

質勝文則野，文勝質則史。 When one's simplicity is in excess of his elegance, he looks uncultivated; when one's elegance is in excess of his simplicity, he looks superficial. 【孔子《論語‧雍也篇第六》Confucius: Chapter 6, *The Analects of Confucius*】

Army

兵敗如山倒。 A rout is like a landslide. 【俗語 Common saying】

兵不在多，而在於精。 An army does not rely on its number, but on quality. 【羅貫中《三國演義》Luo Guanzhong: *Romance of the Three Kingdoms*】

兵貴乎勇不貴乎多。 An army is valued for its courage, not in numbers. 【俗語 Common saying】

兵隨將令草隨風。 Soldiers follow orders as grass follows wind. 【馮志《敵後武工隊‧第四章》Feng Zhi: Chapter 4, *Armed Working Team Behind Enemy Lines*】

兵無將而不動，蛇無頭而不行。 Soldiers without a commander cannot act as a snake without a head cannot crawl. 【俗語 Common saying】

車轔轔，馬蕭蕭，行人弓箭各在腰。 Chariots rumble, horses neigh, and the soldiers each bears bow and arrows by their waist. 【杜甫〈兵車行〉Du Fu: "Song of the War Chariots"】

風聲鶴唳，草木皆兵。 The rattle of the wind, the cry of the cranes, every blade of grass and every tree are like an advancing army. 【房玄齡等《晉書‧謝玄傳》Fang Xuanling *et al*: "Biography of Xie Xuan", *History of the Jin*】

好鐵不打釘，好男不當兵。 Good iron is not used to make nails and good men do not serve as soldiers. 【俗語 Common saying】

救兵如救火。 To save an army is as urgent as fighting a fire. 【夏敬渠《野叟曝言‧第一百回》Xia Jingqu: Chapter 100, *Imprudent Discourse of a Wild Old Man*】

師克在和，不在眾。 An army that is victorious relies on unity, not on the number of soldiers. 【左丘明《左傳‧桓公十一年》Zuo Qiuming: "The Eleventh Year of the Reign of Duke Huan", *Zuo's Commentary on the Spring and Autumn Annals*】

王者之兵，勝而不驕，敗而不怨。 An army of true kingship is not arrogant when victorious, nor whining when defeated. 【商鞅《商君書‧戰法》Shang Yang: "Military Strategy", *The Works of Shang Yang*】

養兵千日，用兵一時。 Maintain an army for a thousand days to use it for a time. 【馬致遠〈漢宮秋‧第一折〉Ma Zhiyuan: Scene 1, "Autumn in the Han Palace"】

遠道行兵，以食為重。Provisions are important for troops in a long march. 【俗語 Common saying】

Arrogance

驕奢淫逸，所自邪也。Arrogance, extravagance, lewdness, and dissipation are what depraved oneself. 【左丘明《左傳‧隱公三年》Zuo Qiuming:"The Third Year of the Reign of Duke Yin", Zuo's Commentary on the Spring and Autumn Annals】

居上位而不驕，在下位而不憂。When occupying a high position, one should not be arrogant; when one is in a low position, one should not be worried. 【《易經‧坤‧文言》"The Record of Wen Yan", Hexagram Kun, The Book of Changes】

老子天下第一。Regard oneself as the best in the world. 【俗語 Common saying】

氣焰囂張，不可一世。Swaggering like conquering heroes. 【俗語 Common saying】

人生大病，祇是一傲字。A serious illness of a human being is nothing but arrogance. 【王陽明《傳習錄》Wang Yangming: Records of Teaching and Practicing】

夜郎自大，利令智昏。One is blinded by one's presumptuous self-conceit and overweening aspirations. 【俗語 Common saying】

在上不驕，高而不危。When you are in a high position, you must not be arrogant, then even though you are above others, you will not be in peril. 【《孝經‧諸侯章第三》Chapter 3:"The Feudal Princes", The Book of Filial Piety】

自滿者敗，自矜者愚。A conceited person will fail and an arrogant person is stupid. 【《易經‧豐》Hexagram feng, The Book of Changes】

Aspiration

必有天下之大志，而後能立天下之大事。One must have lofty aspirations to influence the entire world if one wants to achieve significant things in the world. 【陳亮《漢論‧高帝朝》Chen Liang:"The Reign of Emperor Gao", On Han Dynasty】

才自清明志自高，生於末世運偏消。You are talented and have lofty aspirations, yet born in a time of twilight, you run out of luck.【曹雪芹《紅樓夢》Cao Xueqin: *A Dream of the Red Chamber*】

處世各有志。 Each has their own aspirations in society.【俗語 Common saying】

多一分享用，少一分志氣。 More comfort, less aspiration.【申涵光《荊園小語》Shen Hanguang: *Remarks from the Jing Garden*】

共在人間說天上，不知天上憶人間。 Together in this world of man, we talk in praise of heaven, yet we don't know that the Goddess of the Moon yearns for life in the world of man.【邊貢〈嫦娥〉Bian Gong: "Chang E, Goddess of the Moon"】

古之所謂得志者，非軒冕之謂也。 In ancient times, those who achieved their aspirations did not refer to getting high-ranking positions.【莊周《莊子‧外篇‧繕性第十六》Zhuang Zhou: Chapter 16, "Mending Nature", "Outer Chapters", *Zhuangzi*】

恨鐵不成鋼。 Regret that one's offsprings do not live up to one's expectations.【曹雪芹《紅樓夢‧第九十六回》Cao Xueqin: Chapter 96, *A Dream of the Red Chamber*】

虎瘦雄心在。 A thin tiger still has great aspirations.【馬致遠〈青衫淚‧第一折〉Ma Zhiyuan: Scene 1, "Tears of the Blue-Gowned"】

君子以致命逐志。 A gentleman sacrifices his life to realize his aspirations.【《易經‧困‧象》"Image", Hexagram *Kun*, *The Book of Changes*】

老驥伏櫪，志在千里。烈士暮年，壯心不已。 I am like an old war-horse lying in the stable, longing to gallop a thousand miles. I'm a patriotic man in the twilight years, yet I still have endless lofty aspirations.【曹操〈龜雖壽〉Cao Cao: "Though the Tortoise Lives Long"】

立大志，展宏圖。 Cherish high aspirations and carry out a great plan.【諺語 Proverb】

立志須是光明正大。 Aspirations should be made in a bright and broad way.【陳淳《北溪字義‧志》Chen Chun: "Gazette", *Meanings of Characters at Northern River*】

耐得心頭氣，方為有志人。 Only one who can bear humiliation can become a person with lofty aspirations.【俗語 Common saying】

男兒無志，鈍鐵無鋼。 A man without aspirations is like dull iron without steel.【諺語 Proverb】

男兒志在四方。 A man who has high aspirations can realize them anywhere in the world.【關漢卿〈裴度還帶‧第三折〉Guan Hanqing: Scene 3, "Pei Du Returned the Belt He Found"】

駑駘之才，無志騰驤。 An inferior horse has no ambition to gallop.【蒲松齡《聊齋誌異‧司文郎‧卷八》Pu Songling: Chapter 8, "Siwen Lang", *Strange Stories from a Chinese Studio*】

盼星星，盼月亮。Long for something or somebody day and night.【俗語 Common saying】

窮且益堅，不墜青雲之志。The worse the situation, the firmer we stand. Our lofty and noble aspirations would not flag.【王勃〈秋日登洪府滕王閣餞別序〉Wang Bo: "Ascending the Tengwang Pavilion of the Hong Family to Bid Farewell on an Autumn Day, with a Preface"】

窮天人之際，通古今之變，成一家之言。Explore in full the relationship between heaven and man, understand thoroughly the changes that have taken place in the past and present, and form one's own theory.【司馬遷〈報任安書〉Sima Qian: "A Letter in Response to Ren An"】

人各有志，不可強求。People have their own aspirations and you cannot force them to follow you.【佚名〈金雀記・第八齣〉Anonymous: Scene 8, "Story of a Golden Bird"】

人貴有志，學貴有恆。What is valued in a person is his will and what is valued in learning is perseverance.【諺語 Proverb】

人憑志氣虎憑威。A person depends on his aspirations as a tiger on its might.【俗語 Common saying】

人窮志不窮。A person may be poor but he has lofty aspirations.【張恨水《夜深沉・第四十回》Zhang Henshui: Chapter 40, The Night is Deep】

人窮志短，馬瘦毛長。When people are poor, their aspirations are meagre. When horses are skinny, their hair looks long.【惟白《建中靖國續燈錄》Wei Bai: Continuation of the Record of the Transmission of the Lamp from the Jianzhong to Jingguo Years】

人若無志，與禽獸同類。People without aspirations are the same species as beasts.【孟軻《孟子》Meng Ke: Mencius】

人往高處走，水往低處流。People endeavour to rise and water flows downwards.【俗語 Common saying】

人望幸福樹望春。People aspire to happiness and trees wait for the advent of spring.【鮑昌《庚子風雲・二部第二十五章》Bao Chang: Chapter 25, Part 2, The War in 1900-1901】

人心高過天，想做皇帝想成仙。People have aspirations higher than the sky for they hope to become emperors and gods.【俗語 Common saying】

三軍可奪帥也，匹夫不可奪志也。The commander of a large army can be taken away, but not the aspirations of an ordinary person.【孔子《論語・子罕篇第九》Confucius: Chapter 9, The Analects of Confucius】

上游無止境。One can always aim higher.【諺語 Proverb】

身不危者，志不廣也。If one has not endured adversities, one's

aspirations would not be great. 【劉晝《劉子‧激通第五十二》Liu Zhou: Chapter 52, "Strike to Penetrate", *Works of Master Liu Zhou*】

身可危也，而志不可奪也。 Though one's person may be in peril, one's aspirations cannot be taken from one.【《禮記‧儒行第四十一》Chapter 41, "The Conduct of a Confucian Scholar", *The Book of Rites*】

樹雄心，立壯志。Aim high and have lofty aspirations.【諺語 Proverb】

為天地立心，為生民立命，為往聖繼絕學，為萬世開太平。To ordain conscience for Heaven and Earth, to secure life and fortune for the people, to continue the lost teachings of past sages, and to establish peace for all future generations. 【張載《張子語錄》Zhang Zai: *The Sayings of Zhang Zai*】

無志山壓頭，有志能搬山。 Without aspirations, one feels as if a mountain is bearing down on him; with aspirations, one can move a mountain.【諺語 Proverb】

心比天高，命比紙薄。One's aspirations are higher than the sky, but one's fate is thinner than paper.【曹雪芹《紅樓夢‧第五回》Cao Xueqin: Chapter 5, *A Dream of the Red Chamber*】

心在天山，身老滄州。My heart is still with the Heavenly

Mountain and my body grows old by the riverside.【陸游〈訴衷情〉Lu You: "Expressing My Innermost Feelings"】

燕雀安知鴻鵠之志哉。How can swallows and sparrows know the aspirations of a swan? 【司馬遷《史記‧陳涉世家》Sima Qian: "House of Chen She", *Records of the Grand Historian*】

一簫一劍平生意，負盡狂名十五年。My life-long aspiration is to roam about with a flute a sword, yet my wild reputation is but a waste in the last fifteen years.【龔自珍〈漫感〉Gong Zizhen: "Random Thoughts"】

亦余心之所善兮，雖九死其猶未悔。To achieve what I hold dear to my heart, I would not regret even though I might have to die nine times.【屈原〈離騷〉Qu Yuan: *The Sorrows at Parting*】

有志不分男女。There is no clear distinction between men and women when it comes to aspirations.【俗語 Common saying】

有志不在年高。A person's will has little to do with how advanced his or her age is.【諺語 Proverb】

有志不在年少，無志空活百歲。With aspirations, one can achieve much even though he is not advanced in age; without aspirations, one can achieve nothing even though he lives a hundred years.【石玉昆《三俠五

義·第八十一回》Shi Yukun: Chapter 81, *The Three Heroes and Five Gallants*】

有志者事竟成。 Success goes to the determined. 【諺語 Proverb】

丈夫四海志，萬里猶比鄰。 A man's aspirations are set on the four seas; to him, ten thousand miles seem but next door. 【曹植〈贈白馬王彪〉Cao Zhi: "Presented to Wang Biao, Prince of Baima"】

丈夫志四海，我願不知老。 A man sets his aspirations on the four seas, and I would prefer not to know the coming of old age. 【陶淵明〈無題〉Tao Yuanming: "Untitled Poem"】

志不可滿，樂不可極。 Aspirations cannot be too much and pleasure cannot be excessive. 【《禮記·曲禮上第一》Chapter 1, "Summary of the Rules of Propriety, Part 1", *The Book of Rites*】

志不可慢，時不可失。 Aspirations cannot be relaxed and time should not be lost. 【程顥，程頤《二程全書》Cheng Hao and Cheng Yi: *Complete Works of Cheng Hao and Cheng Yi*】

志不立，天下無可成之事。 Without making an ambition, nothing can be accomplished in the world. 【王陽明〈教條示龍場諸生〉Wang Yangming: "Instructions for Students at Longchang"】

志不求易，事不避難。 For aspirations, don't go for the easy; for things, don't dodge the difficult. 【范曄《後漢書·虞詡列傳》Fan Ye: "Biographies of Yu Yu", *History of the Later Han*】

志小不可以語大事。 Do not discuss important things with a person who has small ambitions. .【陸九淵《語錄》Lu Jiuyuan: *Records of My Sayings*】

志小難成大事。 It is difficult to achieve great things with small aspirations. 【俗語 Common saying】

Attack

出頭的椽子先爛。 People in the limelight bear the brunt of attack. 【俗語 Common saying】

打半邊鼓 —— 旁敲側擊。 Beating only one side of a drum – a flank attack. 【歇後語 End-clipper】

打擊別人，抬高自己。 Attack others so as to build up oneself. 【俗語 Common saying】

打蛇打七寸。 Hit where it hurts. 【俗語 Common saying】

攻堅不怕堡壘硬。 Attack its strong point without fearing that it's a strong fortress. 【俗語 Common saying】

攻其一點，不及其餘。 Pounce on one point and ignore all others. 【俗語 Common saying】

攻無不克，戰無不勝。Conquer everything in attack and win all the battles. 【劉向《戰國策・秦策一》Liu Xiang: "Strategies of the State of Qin, Part 1", *Strategies of the Warring States*】

含血噴人，先污其口。One who spurts blood on others makes one's own mouth dirty first. 【曉瑩《羅湖野錄・卷二》Xiao Ying: Volume 2, *Record of Anecdotes from Lake Luo*】

明槍易躲，暗箭難防。It is easy to dodge a spear in the open, but hard to guard against an arrow shot in the dark. 【羅貫中《平妖傳・第三回》Luo Guanzhong: Chapter 3, *Taming Devils*】

槍打出頭鳥。The leading bird is to be shot first. 【《增廣賢文》*Words that Open up One's Mind and Enhance One's Wisdom*】

羣起而攻之。All rise and attack. 【孔子《論語・先進篇第十一》Confucius: Chapter 11, *The Analects of Confucius*】

人不犯我，我不犯人。We will not attack unless we are attacked. 【毛澤東〈論政策〉Mao Zedong: "On Policies"】

善攻者，敵不知其所守；善守者，敵不知其所攻。One who is good at attacking makes the enemy fail to know what to be defended; one who is good at defence makes the enemy fail to know what to attack. 【孫武《孫子兵法・虛實第六》Sun Wu: Chapter 6, "The Void and Substance", *The Art of War by Sunzi*】

守則不足，攻則有餘。To defend is inadequate, but to attack is more than enough. 【孫武《孫子兵法・軍形第四》Sun Wu: Chapter 4, "Tactical Dispositions", *The Art of War by Sunzi*】

以我之長，攻敵之短。Utilize my strong points to attack the enemy at his weak points. 【俗語 Common saying】

祇可智取，不可強攻。The only way to conquer the enemy is by strategy, not by strong attack. 【俗語 Common saying】

Attitude

不相菲薄不相師。Do not despise others, nor imitate each other. 【袁枚〈論詩絕句〉Yuan Mei: "On Poetry, a Quatrain"】

風吹浪打不動搖。Even when one is blown by the wind and beaten by the waves, one remains unmoved. 【俗語 Common saying】

該和則和，該嚴則嚴。Be gentle when it is necessary and stern when the occasion warrants. 【俗語 Common saying】

拐子走路 —— 左右搖擺。When a cripple walks, he sways from side to side – just as a person is vacillating.【歇後語 End-clipper】

一腳踏兩隻船。Keep a foot in both camps.【俗語 Common saying】

口服心不服。Agree in words, but oppose at heart.【俗語 Common saying】

口服心也服。Say yes and mean it.【俗語 Common saying】

樂天知命故不憂。Rejoice in heaven and understand its decrees and one will have no worries.《易經・繫辭上》"Appended Remarks, Part 1", *The Book of Changes*】

冷一陣，熱一陣。Cold for a while and hot for another.【俗語 Common saying】

拿得起，放得下。Be able to advance or retreat.【俗語 Common saying】

能進能出，能上能下。Can enter or withdraw, or be moved up or down.【俗語 Common saying】

寧為玉碎，不為瓦全。One would rather die with honour than survive with dishonour.【李百藥《北齊書・元景安傳》Li Baiyao: "Biography of Yuan Jing'an", *History of the Northern Qi*】

寧作太平犬，莫作離亂人。Better be a dog in times of general peace than a man in the midst of civil wars.【施惠《幽閨記・第十九齣：偷兒擋路》Shi Hui: Act 19: Blocked on the road when stealing the child, *Stories from the Secluded Chamber*】

牆上一苑草，風吹兩邊倒。A tuft of gass atop the wall sways right and left in the wind.【諺語 Proverb】

牆上一株草，隨風四面倒。The grass on the top of a wall sways with the wind on every side.【諺語 Proverb】

牆頭草，隨風倒。The grass on the top of a wall sways with the blowing of the wind.【諺語 Proverb】

強人腿下還給人留條路。Even bandits leave a way out for others.【俗語 Common saying】

軟不吃，硬不吃。Be neither persuaded nor coerced.【俗語 Common saying】

水裏的葫蘆 —— 兩邊擺。A calabash shell in water sways from side to side.【歇後語 End-clipper】

銅板切豆腐 —— 兩面光。A bean curd knife is sharp on both sides.【歇後語 End-clipper】

惟敬可以勝怠，惟勤可以補拙，惟儉可以養廉。Reverence can overcome laziness, diligence can make up for weaknesses, and frugality can keep one away from corruption.【張伯行《困學錄集粹》Zhang Boxing: *Collections of Difficult Subjects of Study*】

下士者得賢，下敵者得友，下眾者得譽。 He who is humble to scholars wins the heart of the worthy people; he who is humble to his enemy wins friends; and he who is humble to the people wins their praise. 【尸佼《尸子‧明堂第四》Shi Jiao: Chapter 4, "The Enlightenment Hall", *Shizi*】

袖筒裏入棒槌 —— 直出直入。 Frankly and to the point. 【歇後語 End-clipper】

一人倒，眾人踩。 When a person falls, all tread on him. 【俗語 Common saying】

有餘則不泰，不足則自如。 When you have more than enough, don't be arrogant; when you don't have enough, take it easy. 【黃晞《聱隅子‧大中篇》Huang Xi: Chapter 2, *Aoyuzi*】

中立而不倚。 Stand straight in the middle without leaning to either side. 【《禮記‧中庸第三十一章》Chapter 31, "Doctrine of the mean", *The Book of Rites*】

Audacity

不敢說半個不字。 Not dare to utter the slightest dissent. 【俗語 Common saying】

吃了豹子膽。 Be filled with courage. 【俗語 Common saying】

初生之犢不怕虎。 A newborn calf makes little of tigers. 【羅貫中《三國演義‧第七十四回》Luo Guanzhong: Chapter 74, *Romance of the Three Kingdoms*】

大膽天下去得，小心寸步難行。 A bold person can go anywhere in the world, but a timid person does not dare to move even a small step. 【馮夢龍《警世通言‧第二十一卷》Feng Menglong: Chapter 21, *Stories to Caution the World*】

大勇若怯，大智若愚。 He who has great courage looks timid; he who has great wisdom looks unintelligent. 【蘇軾〈賀歐陽少師致仕啟〉Su Shi: "Congratulating Ouyang Shaoshi on Taking up His Official Appointment"】

膽大心細，事事如意。 If one is bold and careful in doing things, everything will follow one's wishes. 【俗語 Common saying】

刀山火海也敢闖。 Dare to climb a mountain of swords or plunge into a sea of flames. 【俗語 Common saying】

多個人，多個膽。 More people, more courage. 【俗語 Common saying】

粉骨碎身渾不怕，要留清白在人間。 I am not afraid of my body being ground to powder or broken into pieces so that I could leave a clean reputation to the world. 【于謙〈石灰吟〉Yu Qian: "A Song on Lime"】

紅梅傲雪凌霜開。 The plum trees brave snow and frost and blossom defiantly. 【俗語 Common saying】

虎頭抓蒼蠅。 Catch flies on the tiger's head. 【俗語 Common saying】

見義不為，無勇也。 One who hesitates to do what is righteous is without courage. 【孔子《論語‧為政篇第二》Confucius: Chapter 2, *The Analects of Confucius*】

氣壯如牛，膽小如鼠。 As strong as a bull but as timid as a mouse. 【陳壽《三國志‧魏書‧元天賜傳》Chen Shou: "Biography of Yuan Tianci", "History of the State of Wei", *Records of the Three Kingdoms*】

人多膽子壯。 Sheer numbers can pluck up people's courage. 【俗語 Common saying】

人急造反，狗急跳牆。 Despair gives courage to a coward. 【曹雪芹《紅樓夢‧第二十七回》Cao Xueqin: Chapter 27, *A Dream of the Red Chamber*】

捨得一身剮，敢把皇帝拉下馬。 One who is not afraid of being cut into pieces dares to unhorse the emperor. 【曹雪芹《紅樓夢‧第六十八回》Cao Xueqin: Chapter 68, *A Dream of the Red Chamber*】

雖千萬人吾往矣。 Even when there are thousands and thousands of soldiers, I'll still go forward. 【孟軻《孟子‧告子章句上》Meng Ke: Chapter 6, Part 1, *Mencius*】

天不怕，地不怕。 There is nothing one fears, either in heaven or on earth. 【曹雪芹《紅樓夢‧第四十五回》Cao Xueqin: Chapter 45, *A Dream of the Red Chamber*】

一人捨命，萬夫莫敵。 Ten thousand people are no match to a person who is willing to sacrifice his life. 【俗語 Common saying】

一身都是膽。 Be very brave. 【陳壽《三國志‧蜀書‧趙雲傳》Chen Shou: "Biography of Zhao Yun", "History of the State of Wei", *Records of the Three Kingdoms*】

勇於敢則殺，勇於不敢則活。 He who is brave and daring will be killed and he who is brave but not daring will stay alive. 【老子《道德經‧第七十三章》Laozi: Chapter 73, *Daodejing*】

知恥近乎勇。 Knowing what shame is gets one closer to courage. 【《禮記‧中庸第三十一章》Chapter 31, "Doctrine of the Mean", *The Book of Rites*】

Autumn

空山新雨後，天氣晚來秋。After a fresh rain on the deserted mountain, the evening air brings the coldness of autumn. 【王維〈山居秋暝〉Wang Wei:"Autumn Dusk at a Mountain Lodge"】

落霞與孤鶩齊飛，秋水共長天一色。The evening clouds and solitary wild ducks fly in the sky while waters in autumn and the boundless sky merge in a single tint. 【王勃〈秋日登洪府滕王閣餞別序〉Wang Bo:"Ascending the Tengwang Pavilion of the Hong Family to Bid Farewell on an Autumn Day, with a Preface"】

秋至滿山多秀色，春來無處不花香。When autumn comes, the entire mountain has many beautiful scenes. When spring comes, there is no place that is not filled with the fragrance of flowers. 【《增廣賢文》Words that Open up One's Mind and Enhance One's wisdom】

三秋不抵一麥忙。Three autumns together are not as busy as a harvest of wheat. 【俗語 Common saying】

山明水淨夜來霜，數樹深紅出淺黃。The mountain is bright, the water is clear, and the frost comes in at night. Some trees are deep red, emerging from those in light yellow. 【劉禹錫〈秋詞二首〉Liu Yuxi: Qin Guan:"Two Poems on Autumn"】

山抹微雲，天連衰草。The mountain is brushed by a wisp of cloud and the sky is joined with a boundless spread of dead grass. 【秦觀〈滿庭芳〉Qin Guan:"A Garden Full of Blossoms"】

山僧不解數甲子，一葉落知天下秋。Monks in the mountains do not know how to count the years, but they know that the falling of one leaf heralds the autumn. 【唐庚《唐子西語錄》Tang Geng: Sayings of Tang Geng】

十分秋色無人管，半屬蘆花半蓼花。There is no one to appreciate autumn in its full beauty, which is made up in part by the reed catkins and in part by the knotweed. 【黃庚〈江村即事〉Huang Geng:"Impromptu Poem Written by the Riverside"】

梧桐一葉落，天下盡知秋。When the first leaf falls from the Wutong tree, the whole world knows that autumn has come. 【汪灝，張逸少等《廣羣芳譜・木譜六・桐》Wang Hao, Zhang Yishao, et al:"Tong trees", "Trees, Part 6", Extended Notes of the Peiwen Study on All Various Herbs】

一年容易又中秋。Days in the year go by swiftly and it is mid-autumn again. 【諺語 Proverb】

一秋一春，物故者新。From autumn to spring, things that are old become new. 【劉基〈司馬

季主論卜〉Liu Ji:"Sima Jizhu's Talk on Divination"】

一曲高歌一樽酒，一人獨釣一江秋。With a bottle of wine I sing loudly. All by myself, I alone angle a river of autumn. 【王士禎〈題秋江獨釣圖〉Wang Shizhen:"Inscribing on a Painting of Angling in a River of Autumn"】

Bamboo

風動竹梢，如翻麥浪。When the wind blows over the tips of the bamboo trees, it is like wheat billowing. 【沈復《浮生六記·卷二》Shen Fu: Chapter 2, *Six Chapters of a Floating Life*】

寧可食無肉，不可居無竹。無肉令人瘦，無竹令人俗。I would rather eat without meat than live without bamboos. No meat makes one thin, but no bamboos makes one vulgar. 【鄭板橋〈詠竹詩〉Zheng Banqiao:"A Poem on Bamboo"】

細細的葉，疏疏的節；雪壓不倒，風吹不折。Tiny leaves and scattered joints. Snow can't press it down, nor can the blowing of the wind break it. 【鄭板橋〈題墨竹圖〉Zheng Banqiao:"Inscribing on a Painting of Bamboos in Ink"】

竹憐新雨後，山愛夕陽時。Bamboos are affectionate after a fresh rain and mountains are lovable at the time of sunset. 【錢起〈贈闕下裴舍人〉Qian Qi:"Presented to Secretary Pei of the Imperial Palace"】

Beauty

八月的荷花 —— 一時鮮。A lotus flower in the eighth month – fleeting beauty. 【歇後語 End-clipper】

比花花不語，比玉玉無香。She is so beautiful that when she is compared to a flower, the flower is silent and when she is compared to jade, the jade is not fragrant. 【諺語 Proverb】

避色如避仇，避風如避箭。One avoids a beautiful girl as if she was an enemy and avoids a wind as if it was an arrow. 【吳承恩《西遊記·第二十回》Wu Cheng'en: Chapter 20, *Journey to the West*】

閉月羞花之容，沉魚落雁之貌。A woman is so beautiful that it makes the moon hide away, the flowers blush, the fish sink and the wild geese drop from the sky. 【吳敬梓《儒林外史·第十回》Wu Jingzi: Chapter 10, *An Unofficial History of the World of Literati*】

不愛江山愛美人。 A king might give up his throne for a beautiful woman. 【陳于王〈題桃花扇傳奇〉Chen Yuwang: "Inscribing on the *Legend of the Peach Blossom Fan*"】

蛾眉本是嬋娟刀，殺盡風流世上人。 Beautiful women are like beautiful knives, they kill all the lustful men in the world. 【馮夢龍《警世通言‧第三十八卷》Feng Menglong: Chapter 38, *Stories to Caution the World*】

蛾眉不肯讓人。 Beautiful women are not willing to concede to others. 【駱賓王〈為徐敬業討武曌檄〉Luo Binwang: "A Proclamation on Behalf of Xu Jinye Condemning Empress Wu Zhao"】

風采不減當年。 As good-looking as ever. 【俗語 Common saying】

各花入各眼。 Beauty is in the eye of the beholder. 【俗語 Common saying】

漢皇重色思傾國，御宇多年求不得。 The Han emperor was fond of beautiful women and longed to have one, but he could not get one after years of running the empire. 【白居易〈長恨歌〉Bai Juyi: "Song of Everlasting Grief"】

紅顏女子多薄命。 Beautiful women are mostly unfortunate in life. 【《增廣賢文》*Words that Open up One's Mind and Enhance One's Wisdom*】

紅顏未老恩先斷。 Her beauty has not yet gone but the favours of the emperor have ceased. 【白居易〈後宮詞〉Bai Juyi: "The Inner Palace"】

佳人慕高義，求賢良獨難。 A beautiful lady longs for a man with a noble character, yet it is especially hard to find a worthy one. 【曹植〈美女篇〉Cao Zhi: "Beautiful Lady"】

佳人難得，才子難逢。 Beautiful women and talented scholars are few and far between. 【陸人龍《三刻拍案驚奇‧第三卷》Lu Renlong: Chapter 3, *Amazing tales, Volume three*】

佳人自來多命薄。 From of old, beautiful women are mostly unfortunate in life. 【王實甫〈西廂記‧第二本第三折〉Wang Shifu: Act 2, Scene 3, *Romance of the Western Bower*】

絕代有佳人，幽居在空谷。 The most lovely lady of her day is now leading a solitary life in this deserted valley. 【杜甫〈佳人〉Du Fu: "Beautiful Lady"】

老鴰窩裏出鳳凰。 A phoenix grows up in a family of old swans. 【曹雪芹《紅樓夢‧第六十五回》Cao Xueqin: Chapter 65, *A Dream of the Red Chamber*】

梨花一枝春帶雨。 She is like a branch of pear flowers in the spring rain. 【柳永〈傾杯〉Liu Yong: "Drink up the Wine"】

眉似春山，眼如秋水。 Her brows are like hills in spring and her eyes, water in autumn. 【劉鶚《老殘遊記‧第九回》Liu E: Chapter 9, *The Travels of Lao Can*】

美而不自知，吾以美之更甚。 When a beauty does not know her own beauty, I think she is even more beautiful. 【莊周《莊子·外篇·山木第二十》Zhuang Zhou: Chapter 20, "The Mountain Tree", "Outer Chapters", *Zhuangzi*】

美女入室，惡女之仇。 When a beautiful woman enters a house, ugly women in it will be jealous of her. 【司馬遷《史記·外戚世家》Sima Qian: "House of the External Relatives", *Records of the Grand Historian*】

美人不在衣。 A beautiful lady does not rely on clothes. 【俗語 Common saying】

美人如花隔雲端。 My beautiful lady is like a flower beyond the clouds. 【李白〈長相思〉Li Bai: "Lovesickness"】

美人如玉劍如虹。 A lady as beautiful as jade and a sword as iridescent as a rainbow. 【龔自珍〈夜坐〉Gong Zizhen: "Sitting in the Evening"】

美人少子，艷花無實。 A beautiful woman without a son is like beautiful flowers without fruit. 【俗語 Common saying】

嫫母有所美，西施有所醜。 There is beauty in the ugliest woman and ugliness in the greatest beauty. 【劉安《淮南子·説山訓第十六》Liu An: Chapter 16, "Discourse on Mountains", *Huainanzi*】

南國有佳人，容華若桃李。 There is a beautiful woman in the southern state, with looks as pretty as peach and plum blossoms. 【曹植〈雜詩〉Cao Zhi: "Miscellaneous Poems"】

如花美眷，怎敵似水流年。 A lady as beautiful as flowers cannot fight against the years that flow away like water. 【曹雪芹《紅樓夢》Cao Xueqin: *A Dream of the Red Chamber*】

三月三日天氣新，長安水邊多麗人。 The air is refreshing on the third day of the third month and there are many beautiful women by the side of the waters of Chang'an. 【杜甫〈麗人行〉Du Fu: "Song of Beautiful Women"】

色不迷人人自迷，情人眼裏出西施。 Beauty does not ensnare men, it is men who ensnare themselves, and beauty is in the eye of the beholder. 【黃增〈集杭州俗語詩〉Huang Zeng: "Poem Made up of Common Sayings in Hangzhou"】

色授魂與，心愉一側。 The girl casts amorous glances at the man who is enchanted by her and both of them are very happy. 【司馬相如〈上林賦〉Sima Xiangru: "Ode on Shanglin Park"】

十八廿三，抵過牡丹。 Girls aged between eighteen and twenty-three are as beautiful as peony blossoms. 【蔡東藩《民國通俗演義·第一五八回》Cai Dongfan: Chapter 158, *Popular Romance of the Republican Period*】

天地有大美而不言。 Heaven and earth has its great beauty which is beyond description. 【莊周《莊子·外篇·知北遊第二十二》：Zhuang Zhou: Chapter 22, "Knowledge Wanders North", "Outer Chapters", *Zhuangzi*】

天生麗質難自棄，一朝選在君王側。 No one of such natural beauty could for long stay hidden, and one day she was chosen to attend the emperor. 【白居易〈長恨歌〉Bai Juyi: "Song of Everlasting Grief"】

惟草木之零落兮，恐美人之遲暮。 As grass will wither and trees will decay, I'm afraid beauties will grow old. 【屈原《楚辭·離騷》Qu Yuan: "The Sorrows at Parting", *The Song of Chu*】

要美不要命。 One is willing to risk one's life to become more beautiful. 【俗語 Common saying】

一白三分俏。 White skin makes a woman more beautiful. 【俗語 Common saying】

一顧傾人城，再顧傾人國。 When she cast a glance, she could bring down a city; when she cast another glance, she could ruin a country. 【李延年〈佳人歌〉Li Yannian: "Song of a Beauty"】

一俊遮百醜。 A beautiful face covers up many defects and deficiencies. 【俗語 Common saying】

一自西施採蓮後，越中生女盡如花。 Ever since the beauty Xi Si plucked the lotus flowers in Yuejiang, all the girls born there were as pretty as flowers. 【朱彝尊〈越江詞〉Zhu Yizun: "Song of Yuejiang"】

以色事他人，能得幾時好。 If a woman tries to please others with her beauty, how long can she enjoy that? 【李白〈妾薄命〉Li Bai: "Ill-fated Concubine"】

尤物足以移人。 A bewitching woman is powerful enough to enchant a man. 【左丘明《左傳·昭公二十八年》Zuo Qiuming: "The Twenty-Eighth Year of the Reign of Duke Zhao", *Zuo's Commentary on the Spring and Autumn Annals*】

有美一人，宛如清揚。 There is a beautiful girl, who is so sweet with clear and bright eyes. 【《詩經·鄭風·野有蔓草》"There Are Tall Weeds in the Fields", "Odes of the State of Zheng", *The Book of Odes*】

有一美人兮，見之不忘，一日不見兮，思之如狂。 There is a beauty whom I cannot forget after seeing her. If I don't see her for one day, I'll go mad thinking of her. 【司馬相如〈鳳求凰〉Sima Xiangru: "A Phoenix Seeking His Mate"】

自古紅顏多薄命。 From of old, beautiful women are mostly unfortunate in life. 【吳承恩《西遊記·第七十回》Wu Cheng'en: Chapter 70, *Journey to the West*】

自古佳人多命薄。 From of old, beautiful women are mostly

unfortunate in life. 【蘇軾〈薄命佳人〉 Su Shi:"Hapless Beauty"】

The beginning and the end

篳路藍縷，以啟山林。 Drive a cart in ragged clothes to open up the mountains and forests. 【左丘明《左傳·宣公十二年》Zuo Qiuming:"The Twelfth Year of the Reign of Duke Xuan", *Zuo's Commentary on the Spring and Autumn Annals*】

不善始者不善終。 An ill beginning, an ill end. 【諺語 Proverb】

不忘其所始，不求其所終。 Don't forget how it begins, but don't enquire into how it would end. 【莊周《莊子·內篇·大宗師第六》: Zhuang Zhou: Chapter 6, "The Great Ancestral Teacher", "Inner Chapters", *Zhuangzi*】

重打鑼鼓另開戲。 Make a fresh start. 【俗語 Common saying】

歹收場不如好收場。 A good ending is better than a bad one. 【俗語 Common saying】

凡事起頭難。 To begin is difficult. 【俗語 Common saying】

凡事總有開頭。 Everything must have a beginning. 【俗語 Common saying】

好頭不如好尾。 A good beginning is not as good as a good ending. 【諺語 Proverb】

好戲在後頭。 The best fish swims near the bottom. 【俗語 Common saying】

結局好，樣樣好。 All's well that ends well. 【俗語 Common saying】

謹其所始，慮其所終。 Be careful at the beginning in order to provide against the end. 【禮記·緇衣第三十三》Chapter 33, "The Black Robes", *The Book of Rites*】

九層之台，起於壘土。 A nine-layered terrace begins with a pile of earth. 【老子《道德經·第六十四章》Laozi: Chapter 64, *Daodejing*】

開頭好，好一半。 Well begun is half done. 【俗語 Common saying】

開頭好，結果好。 A good beginning leads to a good ending. 【俗語 Common saying】

起頭容易結梢難。 It is easy to start something but difficult to conclude it. 【吳承恩《西遊記·第九十六回》Wu Cheng'en: Chapter 96, *Journey to the West*】

起頭易，到底難。 It is easy to start well but difficult to end well. 【凌濛初《初刻拍案驚奇·第三十四卷》Ling Mengchu: Chapter 34, *Amazing Tales, Volume One*】

千里之行，始於足下。 A journey of a thousand miles begins with the first step. 【老子《道德經・第六十四章》Laozi: Chapter 64, *Daodejing*】

善始者實繁，克終者蓋寡。 Those who make the beginning are really many, but those who make it to the end are few. 【魏徵〈諫太宗十思疏〉Wei Zheng: "Memorandum Containing Ten Recommendations for Deliberation for Emperor Taizong"】

慎終如始，則無敗事。 If you are as prudent at the end as you are at the beginning, you will have no failure. 【老子《道德經・第六十四章》Laozi: Chapter 64, *Daodejing*】

萬事起頭難。 Everything is hard in the beginning. 【諺語 Proverb】

有頭有尾，有始有終。 There is a beginning and an end, from start to finish. 【施耐庵《水滸傳・第十二回》Shi Nai'an: Chapter 12, *Outlaws of the Marshes*】

祇有善始，才能善終。 Only by a good beginning can it end well. 【俗語 Common saying】

Behaviour

八十歲的奶奶搽粉 —— 老俏皮。 An eighty-year-old granny applying powder to her face– inappropriate behaviour. 【歇後語 End-clipper】

板板六十四。 Very rigid. 【范寅《越諺・數目之諺》Fan Yin: "Proverbs of Numbers", *Proverbs of the State of Yue*】

閉塞眼睛捉麻雀。 Behave like blindfolding one's eyes to catch sparrows. 【諺語 Proverb】

標新立異，惹人注目。 Attract attention by doing something unconventional. 【俗語 Common saying】

不立異以為高，不逆情以干譽。 Don't be unconventional and take it as a superb strategy and don't go against common sense to achieve fame. 【歐陽修〈縱囚論〉Ouyang Xiu: "On the Release of Prisoners"】

不能越雷池一步。 Do not dare to go one step beyond the limit. 【房玄齡等《晉書・庾亮傳》Tang Xuanling, *et al*: "Biography of Yu Liang", *History of the Jin*】

不期修古，不法常可。 We don't follow the ancient way, nor abide by the fixed rules. 【韓非《韓非子・五蠹第四十九》Han Fei: Chapter 49, "Five Vermin", *Hanfeizi*】

蒼蠅叮破蛋。 Flies go for cracked eggs. 【俗語 Common saying】

察其言，觀其行。 Examine what one says and then watch what one does. 【孔子《論語・為政篇第

二》Confucius: Chapter 2, *The Analects of Confucius*】

待人寬容如待己。 Treat people with broadmindedness like the way you treat yourself.【俗語 Common saying】

道不行，乘桴浮於海。 If my way does not make any headway, I will take a boat and float out to the sea.【孔子《論語·公冶長篇第五》Confucius: Chapter 5, *The Analects of Confucius*】

得放手時須放手。 Be lenient whenever one can.【關漢卿〈竇娥冤·第二折〉Guan Hanqing: Scene 2, "The Injustice to Dou E"】

丟了肥肉啃骨頭。 Throw away the meat to gnaw on the bone.【俗語 Common saying】

躲了初一，躲不了十五。 One may get off today, but not tomorrow.【諺語 Proverb】

放開肚皮吃飯，立定腳跟做人。 Eat as much as one can and conduct oneself with a firm footing.【王晫《今世説·卷八》Wang Zhuo: Chapter 8, *Modern Tales of the World*】

胳膊往外扭。 One turns one's arm outward. (Meaning: One is biasd in favour of outsiders)【蘭陵笑笑生《金瓶梅·第八十一回》Lanling Xiaoxiaosheng: Chapter 81, *The Plum in the Golden Vase*】

胳膊總是往裏彎。 The arm always turns inward.【俗語 Common saying】

各走各的陽關道。 Each goes their own way.【俗語 Common saying】

功歸人，過歸己。 Give credit to others and take the blame on oneself.【陳希夷《心相篇》Chen Xiyi: *Essay on Mind and Appearance*】

姑娘送出門，不關娘家事。 The behaviour of a married daughter has nothing to do with her parents' home.【俗語 Common saying】

顧前不顧後。 Drive ahead without considering the consequences.【曹雪芹《紅樓夢·第六十八回》Cao Xueqin: Chapter 68, *A Dream of the Red Chamber*】

顧三不顧四。 Do things in a thoughtless way.【曹雪芹《紅樓夢·第六十八回》Cao Xueqin: Chapter 68, *A Dream of the Red Chamber*】

好狗不攔路。 Good dogs don't play the part of a stumbling block.【俗語 Common saying】

好漢不吃眼前虧。 A wise man does not put up a fight when the odds are against him.【俗語 Common saying】

和尚腦袋上塗油——滑頭。 Putting oil on a monk's shaven head, it becomes a slippery head – one is a slippery fellow.【歇後語 End-clipper】

己所不欲，勿施於人。 Do unto others as you would have others do unto you.【孔子《論語·顏淵篇第十二》Confucius: Chapter 12, *The Analects of Confucius*】

夾着尾巴做人。 Behave oneself by tucking one's tail between one's legs. 【俗語 Common saying】

見不得人的勾當。 Deeds that cannot bear the light of day. 【俗語 Common saying】

君子有三戒：少年戒色，中年戒鬥，老年戒得。 There are three things that a gentleman must guard against: against lust in youth, against quarrels in adulthood, and against covetousness in dotage.【孔子《論語·季氏篇第十六》Confucius: Chapter 16, *The Analects of Confucius*】

刻苦自己，厚待別人。 Be strict with oneself but lenient towards others. 【俗語 Common saying】

老者安之，朋友信之，少者懷之。 Give comfort to the aged, trust to friends and care to the young. 【孔子《論語·公冶長篇第五》Confucius: Chapter 5, *The Analects of Confucius*】

明人不做暗事。 An honest person does not do anything underhanded. 【俗語 Common saying】

唸完經趕和尚。 Kick away a person after using him or her. 【俗語 Common saying】

螃蟹不忘橫着爬 —— 專走斜道。 Crabs will not change their way of crawling sideways – they specialize in going the evil ways. 【歇後語 End-clipper】

破鼓亂人捶。 A person who is down gets kicked by all. 【俗語 Common saying】

氣忌盛，心忌滿，才忌露。 Avoid impetuosity in temper, arrogance at heart, and showing off one's talent. 【呂坤《呻吟語·人品》Lu Kun: "Character of a Person", *Groaning Words*】

千日行善，善猶不足；一日行惡，惡自有餘。 If one does good things for a thousand days, it is still not enough. If one does bad things for one day, that will be too much.【吳承恩《西遊記·第二十八回》Wu Cheng'en: Chapter 28, *Journey to the West*】

牆倒眾人推。 Everybody hits a person who is down. 【曹雪芹《紅樓夢·第二十五回》Cao Xueqin: Chapter 25, *A Dream of the Red Chamber*】

舉世皆濁我獨清，眾人皆醉我獨醒。 The entire world is soiled, but I alone am clean. All people are drunk, but I alone am sober. 【屈原《楚辭·漁父》Qu Yuan: "The fisherman", *The Songs of Chu*】

日月經天，江河行地。 Like the sun and moon passing through the sky and lakes and rivers flowing across the land 【范曄《後漢書·馮衍傳》Fan Ye: "Biography of Feng Yan" in *History of the Later Han*】

上樑不正下樑歪。 If the upper beam is not straight, the lower ones will be crooked. 【蘭陵笑笑生《金瓶梅·第二十六回》Lanling

Xiaoxiaosheng: Chapter 26, *The Plum in the Golden Vase*】

身正不怕影子斜。A straight body is not afraid of a crooked shadow.【俗語 Common saying】

生平不作虧心事，夜半敲門也不驚。One who does not do anything against one's conscience will not be frightened by a knock at the door at midnight.【諺語 Proverb】

十目所視，十手所指，其嚴乎！When we are looked at by ten pairs of eyes and pointed at by ten hands, isn't this a daunting situation!《禮記·大學第六》Chapter 6, "The Great Learning", *The Book of Rites*】

士雖有學，而行為本焉。It is not enough to have knowledge, a scholar must behave like one with learning.【墨翟《墨子·修身卷二》Mo Di: Chapter 2, "Cultivating the Person", *Mozi*】

是真名士自風流。A real scholar can afford to be eccentric.【俗語 Common saying】

俗人昭昭，我獨昏昏。Worldly people tend to praise themselves while I alone prefer to keep a low profile.【老子《道德經·第二十章》Laozi: Chapter 20, *Daodejing*】

同類不相殘。A dog does not eat a dog.【俗語 Common saying】

推人落井，落井下石。Push somebody down a well and then drop rocks on him.【俗語 Common saying】

玩人喪德，玩物喪志。Playing pranks on people ruins your virtue; over-indulgence in things ruins your aspirations.【《尚書·旅獒》"Hounds of Lu", *The Book of History*】

吾日三省吾身。I reflect on myself three times a day.【孔子《論語·學而篇第一》Confucius: Chapter 1, *The Analects of Confucius*】

小心天下去得，大意百事吃虧。Being careful, one can go anywhere in the world; being careless, one will suffer in everything.【諺語 Proverb】

雅而不俗，恭而不倨。Elegant without vulgarity, respectable without arrogance.【諺語 Proverb】

一而再，再而三。Again and again.【俞萬春《蕩寇志·第三十九回》Yu Wanchun: Chapter 39, *A Record of the Eradication of Bandits*】

遇風隨風，遇水隨水。When there is a wind, one goes with the wind and when there is a water current, one goes with the current.【俚語 Slang】

正人先正己。To ask others to behave well, one should first behave well himself.【俗語 Common saying】

Belief

不可不信，也不可全信。Don't disbelieve something or totally believe it. 【俗語 Common saying 】

寧可信其有，不可信其無。Rather believe that something exists than not. 【俗語 Common saying】

信則有，不信則無。If you believe it, it exists; if you don't, there is no such thing at all. 【俗語 Common saying】

Benevolence

愛人利物之謂仁。Loving people and benefitting things is known as benevolence. 【莊周《莊子·外篇 天地第十二》Zhuang Zhou: Chapter 12, "Heaven and Earth", "Outer Chapters", *Zhuangzi*】

夫仁，天之尊爵也，人之安宅也。Benevolence is an honourable title conferred by heaven and a comfortable home for people. 【孟軻《孟子·公孫丑上》Meng Ke: Chapter 2, Part 1, *Mencius*】

剛、毅、木、訥近仁。If you are firm, enduring, simple, and modest, you are close to benevolence. 【孔子《論語·子路 篇第十三》Confucius: Chapter 13, *The Analects of Confucius*】

苟有仁人，何必周親。If there are benevolent people around, there is no need to rely on one's closest relatives. 【尸佼《尸子· 綽子第十一》Shi Jiao: Chapter 11, "Generous Fellows", *Shizi*】

克己復禮為仁。一日克己復禮，天下歸仁焉。Control the self and return to rites is benevolence. When one day the self is controlled and rites are restored, all under heaven will return to benevolence. 【孔子《論語·顏淵 篇第十二》Confucius: Chapter 12, *The Analects of Confucius*】

口不貪嘉味，耳不樂逸聲，目不淫於色，身不懷於安。The mouth is not greedy for good tastes, the ears do not enjoy frivolous music, the eyes are not enchanted by sexual attraction, and the body does not embrace comfort. 【左丘明《國語·楚語下》 Zuo Qiuming: "The Language of Chu, Part 2", *National Languages*】

求仁而得仁。Obtaining benevolence when seeking benevolence. 【孔子《論語·述而 篇第七》Confucius: Chapter 7, *The Analects of Confucius*】

仁不輕絕，智不簡功。A benevolent person does not break off relations easily and a wise person does not overlook others' merits. 【諺語 Proverb】

【劉向《戰國策・燕策三》Liu Xiang: "Strategies of the State of Yan, No.3", *Strategies of the Warring States*】

仁不輕絕，智不輕怨。 A benevolent person does not break off relations easily and a wise person does not complain recklessly.【諺語 Proverb】【劉向《戰國策・燕策三》Liu Xiang: "Strategies of the State of Yan, No.3", *Strategies of the Warring States*】

仁，人之安宅也。 Benevolence is a peaceful residence of a person.【孟軻《孟子・盡心章句下》Meng Ke: Chapter 7, Part 2, *Mencius*】

仁，人心也。 Benevolence is the heart of a person.【孟軻《孟子・告子章句上》Meng Ke: Chapter 6, Part 1, *Mencius*】

仁人之所以為事者，必興天下之利，除去天下之害，以此為事者也。 What a benevolent person engages in is to promote with certainty what benefits the world and remove what harms the world, and this is his sole business.【墨翟《墨子・兼愛卷十四至十六》Mo Di: Chapters 14-16: "Universal Love", *Mozi*】

仁言不如仁聲之入人深也。 Words of benevolence do not enter the hearts of people as deeply as a reputation for benevolence.【孟軻《孟子・盡心章句下》Meng Ke: Chapter 7, Part 2, *Mencius*】

仁義長，財義短。 A relationship that is based on benevolence is long and a relationship that is based on money is short.【俗語 Common saying】

仁義值千金。 Benevolence and righteousness are worth a thousand pieces of gold.【增廣賢文》*Words that Open up One's Mind and Enhance One's Wisdom*】

仁遠乎哉？我欲仁，斯仁至矣。 Is benevolence far away? If I want to be benevolent, benevolence would come to me right away.【孔子《論語・述而篇第七》Confucius: Chapter 7, *The Analects of Confucius*】

仁者安仁，知者利仁。 A benevolent person finds peace in benevolence and a wise person finds benevolence advantageous to him.【孔子《論語・里仁篇第四》Confucius: Chapter 4, *The Analects of Confucius*】

仁者必有勇，勇者不必有仁。 A benevolent person undoubtedly has courage, but a courageous person does not necessarily have benevolence.【孔子《論語・憲問篇第十四》Confucius: Chapter 14, *The Analects of Confucius*】

仁者不富，富者不仁。 A benevolent person is not rich and a rich person is not benevolent.【孟軻《孟子・滕文公上》Meng Ke: Chapter 5, Part 1, *Mencius*】

仁者，人也；親親為大。 Benevolence is about people, the most important of which is to love one's relatives.【《禮記・中

仁者無不愛也，急親賢之為務。
A benevolent person does not have anything that he does not love, but what is most important to him is to earnestly honour the worthy.【孟軻《孟子‧盡心章句下》Meng Ke: Chapter 7, Part 2, *Mencius*】

仁人無敵於天下。 A benevolent person is invincible in the world.【孟軻《孟子‧盡心章句下》Meng Ke: Chapter 7, Part 2, *Mencius*】

仁者以其所愛及其所不愛，不仁者以其所不愛及其所愛。 A benevolent person proceeds from what he loves to what he does not love, whereas a person without benevolence proceeds from what he does not love to what he loves.【孟軻《孟子‧盡心章句下》Meng Ke: Chapter 7, Part 2, *Mencius*】

仁者，義之本也，順之體也，得之者尊。 Benevolence is the root of righteousness and the embodiment of deferential consideration, and those who have benevolence are honoured.【《禮記‧禮運第九》Chapter 9, "Conveyance of Rites", *The Book of Rites*】

惟仁者可好也，可惡也，可高也，可下也。 Only a benevolent person can like and dislike, be high or be low.【左丘明《國語‧楚語下》Zuo Qiuming: "The Language of Chu, Part 2", *National Languages*】

唯仁者能好人，能惡人。 Only a benevolent person is capable of liking or disliking others.【孔子《論語‧里仁篇第四》Confucius: Chapter 4, *The Analects of Confucius*】

志士仁人，無求生以害仁，有殺身以成仁。 People of aspirations and benevolence do not harm benevolence for life, but sacrifice life to accomplish benevolence.【孔子《論語‧衛靈公篇第十五》Confucius: Chapter 15, *The Analects of Confucius*】

Birds

愛叫的麻雀不長肉。 Sparrows that like crying do not have much flesh.【俗語 Common saying】

白鳥一雙臨水立，見人驚起入蘆花。 A pair of white egrets stood by the riverside. upon seeing people, they were startled and flew into the reed catkins.【戴復古〈江村晚眺〉Dai Fugu: "An Evening View of a Riverside Village"】

布穀鳴於孟夏，蟋蟀吟於始秋。 Cuckoos call in early summer and crickets chirp in early autumn.【范曄《後漢書‧襄楷列傳》Fan Ye: "Biography of Xiang Kai", *History of the Later Han*】

黃鶴一去不復返，白雲千載空悠悠。 Once the yellow crane has gone it never comes back again, leaving behind the white clouds stretching in vain for a thousand years. 【崔顥〈黃鶴樓〉Cui Hao:"Yellow Crane Tower"】

舊時王謝堂前燕，飛入尋常百姓家。 Swallows that once nested before the halls of Wang Dao and Xian An have now flown into the homes of the ordinary folk. 【劉禹錫〈烏衣巷〉Liu Yuxi:"Black Robe Lane"】

兩箇黃鸝鳴翠柳，一行白鷺上青天。 A pair of orioles sing among the green willows; a flight of egrets soar into the sky. 【杜甫〈絕句〉Du Fu:"A Quatrain"】

籠中之鳥，網中之魚。 A bird in the cage and a fish in the net. 【羅貫中《三國演義・第二十一回》Luo Guanzhong: Chapter 21, *Romance of the Three Kingdoms*】

籠子養鳥，越養越小。 When a bird is raised in a cage, it becomes smaller and smaller. 【俗語 Common saying】

麻雀雖小，五臟俱全。 Small as it may be, the sparrow has all the vital organs. 【俗語 Common saying】

漠漠水田飛白鷺，陰陰夏木囀黃鸝。 A white egret hovers over the mists of watery fields; and a yellow oriole warbles in the dark summer foliage. 【王維〈積雨輞川莊作〉Wang Wei: "Written at My Wang Chuan Lodege after a Long Rain"】

泥上偶然留指爪，鴻飛那復計東西。 On the mud a goose by chance leaves a footprint. When it departs it flies east or west. 【蘇軾〈和子由澠池懷舊〉Su Shi:"Meditating on the Past with Ziyou at Pond Nian"】

鳥飛返故鄉兮，狐死必首丘。 A bird flies back to its native place and a dying fox turns his head to its mound. 【屈原《離騷・九章・哀郢》Qu Yuan:"Lament for Ying", "Nine Pieces", *The Sorrows at Parting*】

鳥貴有翼，人貴有智。 A bird is valued for its wings, a person, his intelligence. 【俗語 Common saying】

鳥急了奔林，人急了投親。 Birds when in danger fly into woods, people, turn to their relatives. 【俗語 Common saying】

鳥倦飛而知返。 Birds, tired of flying, know their way back to their nests. 【陶淵明〈歸去來兮辭〉Tao Yuanming:"Returning Home"】

鳥去鳥來山色裏，人歌人哭水聲中。 In the tints of the mountain, birds come and go. In tune with the sound of streams, people sing and weep. 【杜牧〈題宣州開元寺水閣閣下宛溪夾溪居人〉Du Mu:"Inscribing a Poem on the Water Pavilion of the Kaiyuan Temple in Xuanzhou for Layman Jiaxi Living at the Wan Brook Beneath the Pavilion"】

鳥無翅不飛，蛇無頭不行。 A bird without wings cannot fly and a snake without a head cannot crawl. 【施耐庵《水滸傳・第六十回》

Shi Nai'an: Chapter 60, *Outlaws of the Marsh*】

鳥之將死，其鳴也哀。 When dying, a bird's cry is mournful. 【孔子《論語·泰伯篇第八》Confucius: Chapter 8, *The Analects of Confucius*】

飄飄何所似，天地一沙鷗。 What do I look like in my aimless drifting? A seagull drifting between heaven and earth. 【杜甫〈旅夜書懷〉Du Fu:"Venting My Feeling While Travelling at Night"】

禽有禽言，獸有獸語。 Birds and animals have their own languages. 【吳承恩《西遊記·第一回》Wu Cheng'en: Chapter 1, *Journey to the West*】

雀往旺處飛。 Birds always fly to prosperous places. 【曹雪芹《紅樓夢·第六十五回》Cao Xueqin: Chapter 65, *A Dream of the Red Chamber*】

山鳥月中寒，夢醒梅花下。 A mountain bird feels cold in the chilly moonlight, and when it wakes up, it is actually perching under the peach blossoms. 【魏際瑞〈梅花臥鳥〉Wei Jirui:"Bird Perching under Peach Blossoms"】

山上無樹不落鳥。 Birds will not come and perch in a mountain without trees. 【俗語 Common saying】

天好燕高飛，天變掠地過。 Swallows fly high in good weather, but they fly past the ground when the weather gets worse. 【俗語 Common saying】

天下的鳥總往亮處。 All birds in the world fly to bright places. 【俗語 Common saying 】

一雙百香花梢語，四顧無人忽下來。 A pair of myna chatter at the tip of a flower, and seeing there is no one around, they sudden fly down to the ground. 【楊萬里〈積雨小霽〉Yang Wanli:"A Break in the Clouds after Extended Rain"】

眾鳥高飛盡，孤雲獨去閒。 The birds have all flown high and away, and a solitary cloud has just floated lazily by. 【李白〈獨坐敬亭山〉Li Bai:"Sitting Alone at Mount Jingting"】

自去自來堂上燕，相親相近水中鷗。 The swallows in the hall come in and out by themselves, and the gulls in the waters snuggle against each other as they please. 【杜甫〈江村〉Du Fu:"Riverside Village"】

Blessing

吃虧是福。 One is blessed if one suffers losses. 【鄭板橋：匾額 Zheng Banqiao: Plaque】

吃了是福，穿了是祿。 Able to enjoy food and wear fair clothes is really a blessing. 【俗語 Common saying】

和平就是福。 Peace is a blessing in itself. 【俗語 Common saying】

Blood

血濃於水，疏不間親。 Blood is thicker than water. 【俗語 Common saying】

血債要用血來還。 Blood debts must be paid in blood. 【俗語 Common saying】

一腔熱血勤珍重，灑去猶能化碧濤。 My passionate blood must be cherished and treasured. My blood, when shedded, can still be turned into clear waves. 【秋瑾〈對酒〉Qiu Jin: "Facing the Wine"】

以血還血，以牙還牙。 An eye for an eye and a tooth for a tooth. 【俗語 Common saying】

Boats

船破又遇頂頭風。 Meet unfavourable winds when the boat is broken. 【馮夢龍《醒世恆言》Feng Menglong: *Stories to Awaken the World*】

好船不怕迎風開。 A good boat does not fear sailing against the wind. 【俗語 Common saying】

兩岸猿聲啼不盡，輕舟已過萬重山。 While monkeys on both banks of the river howled without cease, my light boat had already passed ten thousand mountains. 【李白〈早發白帝城〉Li Bai: "Leaving the White Emperor Town at Dawn"】

南人使船，北人使馬。 Southerners are good at sailing boats, northerners, riding horses. 【羅貫中《三國演義·第五十四回》Luo Guanzhong: Chapter 54, *Romance of the Three Kingdoms*】

破船經不起迎頭浪。 A broken boat cannot stand the attack of high billows. 【高雲覽《小城春秋·第一章》Gao Yunlan: Chapter 1, *Spring and Autumn of a Small town*】

艄公多了打爛船。 Too many steersmen will wreck the boat. 【俗語 Common saying】

水淺不是泊船處。 A boat should not be anchored in a shallow stretch of water. 【釋普濟《五燈會元·卷四·趙州從諗禪師》Shi Puji: Chapter 4, "Chan Master Chong Shen of Zhaozhou", *A Compendium of the Five Lamps*】

停舟暫相問，或恐是同鄉。 I stop my boat just to ask you, in case

we might have come from the same hometown. 【崔顥〈長干曲〉Cui Hao:"A Riverside Song"】

中流失船，一壺千金。 When a boat wrecks in midstream, a gourd is worth one thousand taels of gold. 【鶡冠子《鶡冠子‧卷下‧學問》Jie Guanzi:"Learning", Part 2, *Jieguanzi*】

Books

藏書不讀如藏木。 Collecting books without reading them is like collecting wood. 【俗語 Common saying】

盡信《書》，不如無《書》。 If you trust *The Book of Documents* without reserve, it would be better for you not to have it. 【孟軻《孟子‧盡心章句下》Meng Ke: Chapter 7, Part 2, *Mencius*】

舊書不厭百回讀。 One never gets tired of reading an old book a hundred times over. 【蘇軾〈送安敦秀才失解西歸〉Su Shi:"Seeing off Scholar An Dun Who Failed in the Civil Service Examination and Returned Home Westward"】

兩耳不聞窗外事，一心祇讀聖賢書。 One turns a deaf ear to what is happening in the outside world but concentrates on one's study of books by the sages. 【《增廣賢文》*Words that Open up One's Mind and Enhance One's Wisdom*】

買田買地不如買書。 Buying fields and land is not as good as buying books. 【《增廣賢文》*Words that Open up One's Mind and Enhance One's Wisdom*】

人生讀書之日，最是難得。 The days when a person reads books are most precious in the life of a person. 【左宗棠《左文襄公全集‧與子書》Zuo Zongtang:"A Letter to My Son", *Complete Works of Zuo Zongtang*】

書當快意讀易盡，客有可人期不來。 The reading of a book that is interesting easily ends, and the agreeable guest whom I long to see does not come. 【陳師道〈絕句〉Chen Shidao:"A Quatrain"】

書到用時方恨少。 When one needs to solve a problem, one regrets how little reading he has done. 【陸游〈格言聯〉Lu You: Couplet with Idioms】

書讀百遍，其義自見。 When you read a book a hundred times, you will understand its meaning naturally. 【陳壽《三國志‧魏書‧王肅傳》Chen Shou:"Biography of Wang Shu", "History of the State of Wei", *Records of the Three Kingdoms*】

書猶藥也，善讀可以醫愚。 Books are like medicine. A good reading of books may cure one's stupidity. 【劉向《說苑‧卷三建本》

Liu Xiang: Chapter 3, "Building the Foundation", *Garden of Persuasions* 】

書中自有黃金屋，書中自有顏如玉。 In books there are houses made of gold and women as beautiful as jade. 【趙恆〈勵學篇〉Zhao Heng: "Encouragement to Learning"】

萬卷藏書宜子弟，十年種木長風煙。 Ten thousand volumes of books in my collection benefit my children, ten years of planting trees enhances landscape. 【黃庭堅〈郭明甫作西齋於穎尾請予賦詩〉Huang Tingjian: "Poem Written at the Request of Kuo Mingfu Who Built the West Studio at Yingwei"】

新書不厭百回看。 A new book is worth reading a hundred times. 【俗語 Common saying】

要知古今事，須讀五車書。 If one wants to know the past and present, one must read five cartloads of books. 【莊周《莊子・雜篇・天下第三十三》Zhuang Zhou: Chapter 33, "All under Heaven", "Miscellaneous Chapters", *Zhuangzi*】

要知天下事，須讀古人書。 If you want to know affairs in the world, you must read a lot of classics. 【馮夢龍《醒世恆言・三孝廉讓產立高名》Feng Menglong: "Three Devoted Brothers Win Honour by Yielding Family Property to One Another", *Stories to Awaken the World*】

一時勸人以口，百世勸人以書。 For a short time, one admonishes people with speech, but for a hundred generations, one admonishes people with books. 【袁了凡〈了凡四訓〉Yuan Liaofan: "Four Admonitions of Liaofan"】

有書借人為痴，借書送還為痴。 One who lends books to others is stupid and one who returns the books one has borrowed is also stupid. 【俗語 Common saying】

有書堆數仞，不如讀盈寸。 Having books piled up dozens of feet high is not as good as reading one inch of them. 【劉岩〈雜詩〉Liu Yan: "Miscellaneous Poems"】

紙上得來終覺淺，絕知此事要躬行。 What we learn from books is obviously rather superficial. We must know that things have to be put into practice. 【陸游〈冬夜讀書示子聿〉Lu You: "For My Son Ziyu When Reading Books on an Evening in Winter"】

Borrowing

冬不借衣，夏不借扇。 Do not borrow clothes from a person in winter, nor a fan in summer. 【俗語 Common saying】

借而不還，再借就難。If you borrow without paying back the money, it will be difficult to lend you again.【俗語 Common saying】

借而能還，再借不難。If you borrow and pay back the money, it will be easy for you to borrow money next time.【俗語 Common saying】

劉備借荊州，一借不回頭。Liu Bei borrowed Jianzhou City, but he never gave it back.【Common saying】

勤於借者懶於還。He who is diligent in borrowing is lazy in repaying.【俗語 Common saying】

Brains

後腦勺子上長瘡 —— 自己看不見以為別人也看不見。The boil that is on the back of one's head– one cannot see it and believes that other people cannot see it either.【歇後語 End-clipper】

花崗石腦袋。A person whose brain is ossified.【俗語 Common saying】

摸不着頭腦。Be unable to understand what it is all about.

【曹雪芹《紅樓夢・第八十一回》Cao Xueqin: Chapter 81, *A Dream of the Red Chamber*】

錢串子腦袋。A person who puts money above everything else.【俗語 Common saying】

四肢發達，頭腦簡單。The four limbs are well-developed, yet the brain is moronic.【俗語 Common saying】

Breath

八十歲的老頭吹喇叭 —— 上氣不接下氣。An eighty-year-old man blowing a trumpet is always out of breath.【歇後語 End-clipper】

倒抽一口冷氣。Draw a cold breath.【俗語 Common saying】

口不喘氣，臉不泛紅。One is not out of breath nor even faintly flushed.【俗語 Common saying】

氣不喘，臉不紅。One is not out of breath, nor does he even flush.【俗語 Common saying】

上氣不接下氣。One is out of breath.【無垢道人《八仙全傳・第

Bribery

官無大小，要錢一般。Officials high or low all take bribes. 【俗語 Common saying】

賄賂成風，貪官遍地。Bribery is rife and corrupt officials are found all over the country. 【俗語 Common saying】

及弟不必讀書，作官何須事業。One does not need to study to pass the imperial examination or devote to one's work to get promoted. 【彭定求等《全唐詩 · 卷八百七十六》Peng Dingqiu et al: Chapter 876, *Complete Tang Poems*】

要是當官不貪財，良田美屋哪裏來？If officials do not take bribes, where do their land and houses come from? 【俗語 Common saying】

一不貪賄，二不枉法。Neither take bribes nor break the law. 【俗語 Common saying】

一任清知府，十萬雪花銀。Serving one term as the magistrate of a prefecture, one would get a hundred thousand taels of white silver. 【吳敬梓《儒林外史 · 第八回》Wu Jingzi: Chapter 8, *An Unofficial History of the World of Literati*】

Brothers

本是同根生，相煎何太急。We are born from the same roots, why should you treat me so harshly? 【曹植〈七步詩〉Cao Zhi: "A Seven-Step Poem"】

搭伙還是親兄弟。Brothers are in the end the best partners. 【俗語 Common saying】

打虎還得親兄弟，上陣須教父子兵。To beat a tiger, one has to rely on the help of one's brother. To go into a battle, father and sons must rely on each other.

【《增廣賢文》*Words that Open up One's Mind and Enhance One's Wisdom*】

度盡劫波兄弟在，相逢一笑泯恩仇。We remain brothers after all the calamities, let's forgo our old grudges with a smile and meet again. 【魯迅〈題三義塔〉Lu Xun: "Inscription for the Stupa of the Three Fidelities"】

好兄弟，勤算賬。Even between good brothers, you should keep constraints and clear accounting. 【俗語 Common saying】

落地為兄弟，何必骨肉親。
When people are born, they
are brothers. Why must they be
related in kinship? 【陶淵明〈雜詩〉
Tao Yuanming: "Miscellaneous Poems"】

難得者兄弟，易得者田地。It is
difficult to have brothers, but
easy to get land. 【馮夢龍《喻世明
言‧第十卷》Feng Menglong: Chapter
10, *Stories to Instruct the World*】

親兄弟，明算賬。Even brothers
should keep careful accounts.
【諺語 Proverb】

四海皆兄弟，誰為行路人。
Within the four seas, all men
are brothers, who are the
strangers on the way? 【佚名〈別
詩〉Anonymous: "Parting Poem"】

四海之內，皆兄弟也。Within the
four seas, all men are brothers.
【孔子《論語‧顏淵篇第十二》
Confucius: Chapter 12, *The Analects of
Confucius*】

兄弟貧窮一條心。Poor brothers
are of one mind. 【《增廣賢文》
*Words that Open up One's Mind and
Enhance One's Wisdom*】

兄弟如手足，妻子如衣服。
Brothers are like hands and feet
while the wife is like clothes. 【陳
壽《三國志‧蜀書‧二主妃子傳》Chen
Shou: "Biography of Liangzhu Imperial
Concubine", "History of the State of
Wei", *Records of the Three Kingdoms*】

兄弟鬩於牆，外禦其侮。Brothers
quarrel at home, but join hands
when defending against attacks
from without. 【《詩經‧小雅‧常
棣》"Changdi, "Minor Odes of the
Kingdom", *The Book of Odes*】

長兄為父，長嫂為娘。The eldest
brother is like the father, and
his wife, the mother. 【佚名〈殺狗
記‧第六齣〉Anonymous: Scene 6, "An
Account of Dog-Killing"】

Brutality

六月裏日頭，晚娘的拳頭。
The scorching sun in the sixth
month and the fists of the
stepmother are unbearable. 【俗
語 Common saying】

Buddha

初次見佛勝似怕鬼。The first
time you see a Buddha is more
frightening than a devil. 【俗語
Common saying】

多一位菩薩多一爐香。With the
addition of one more Buddha,
there will be incense burning
for one more incense burner. 【趙

樹理《李有才板話》Zhao Shuli: *Rhymes of Li Youcai*】

放下屠刀，立地成佛。 The moment a butcher throws away his knife, he becomes a Buddha on the spot. 【釋普濟《五燈會元·卷五十三》Shi Puji: Chapter 53, *A Compendium of the Five Lamps*】

佛面上塗金 —— 淺薄。 The gilt on the face of a Buddha image is just a thin coating – something is shallow or superficial. 【俗語 Common saying】

和尚念經 —— 老一套。 A monk chanting scriptures is repeating the same old story. 【歇後語 End-clipper】

既在佛會下，都是有緣人。 All in the Buddhist community are brought together by the same lot. 【吳承恩《西遊記·第三十六回》Wu Cheng'en: Chapter 36, *Journey to the West*】

見個菩薩燒炷香。 When we see a Buddha, we burn some incense. 【俗語 Common saying】

泥菩薩過河 —— 自身難保。 The clay Buddhas, when fording a river, cannot even protect themselves. 【馮夢龍《警世通言·第四十卷》Feng Menglong: Chapter 40, *Stories to Caution the World*】

平時不燒香，臨時抱佛腳。 One does not burn incense when all is well, but clasp Buddha's feet only in crisis. 【劉敔《中山詩話》Liu Ban: *Poetry Talks at Zhongshan*】

窮人有個窮菩薩。 The poor have a poor Buddha to protect them. 【俗語 Common saying】

求佛求一尊。 If you seek help, pray to just one Buddha. 【俗語 Common saying】

人有幾等人，佛有幾等佛。 There are different classes of people, so are the Buddhas. 【唐芸洲《七劍十三俠》Tang Yunzhou: *Seven Swords and Thirteen Swordsmen*】

人爭一口氣，佛爭一爐香。 People struggle for their life and Buddha, for incense. 【蘭陵笑笑生《金瓶梅·第七十六回》Lanling Xiaoxiaosheng: Chapter 76, *The Plum in the Golden Vase*】

寺破僧醜，也看佛面。 Even when the temple may be broken and the monks in it may be ugly, you should consider the face of the Buddha. 【馮夢龍《警世通言·第一卷》Feng Menglong: Chapter 1, *Stories to Caution the World*】

送佛送到西天。／送佛送到西。 If you accompany the Buddha, accompany Him to the Western Paradise. 【文康《兒女英雄傳·第九回》Wen Kang: Chapter 9, *Biographies of Young Heroes and Heroines*】

檀木雕的菩薩 —— 靈是不靈，就是穩。 Like a Buddha carved out of sandalwood, it is not effective, but steady. 【歇後語 End-clipper】

小廟供不下大菩薩。 A small temple cannot house a big Buddha. 【俚語 Slang】

心堅即是佛。 A strong mind makes a person a Buddha. 【俗語 Common saying】

一子皈依，九祖升天。 When a child of the family is converted to Buddhism, nine of his ancestors are promoted to heaven. 【俗語 Common saying】

以心傳心，不立文字。 The Buddhist dharma is taught through the mind, not through the written word. 【慧能《六祖壇經》Hui Neng: The Sixth Patriarch's Platform Sutra】

有佛地方妖怪多，有福地方罪惡多。 Where there is a Buddha, there are many monsters; where there is good fortune, there are many evils. 【俗語 Common saying】

真菩薩面前，切莫假燒香。 Before a real Buddha, do not burn false joss sticks. 【俗語 Common saying】

Bullying

八哥兒啄柿子 —— 挑軟的欺。 A myna pecks only at soft persimmons–one only bullies the weak. 【歇後語 End-clipper】

大蟲吃小蟲。 The big worm eats the small one. 【李伯元《文明小史・第二十二回》Li Boyuan: Chapter 22, A Short History of Civilization】【茅盾《子夜》Maodun：Ziye】

大魚吃小魚，小魚吃蝦米。 Big fish eat small fish, and small fish eat small shrimps. 【劉向《説苑・卷十五指武》Liu Xiang: Chapter 15, "Pointing at War", Garden of Persuasions】

瓜兒祇揀軟處捏。 One chooses only the soft part of a melon to pinch. 【蘭陵笑笑生《金瓶梅・第五十九回》Lanling Xiaoxiaosheng: Chapter 59, The Plum in the Golden Vase】

好人受人欺。 A nice person is always bullied by others. 【俗語 Common saying】

老實人到處有人欺。 An honest person is bullied everywhere. 【俗語 Common saying】

老太太吃柿子 —— 揀軟和的捏。 An old lady chooses only soft persimmons to bite–bully the weak. 【歇後語 End-clipper】

雷公打豆腐 —— 專揀軟的欺。 The God of Thunder strikes the bean curd – bullies pick on the soft. 【歇後語 End-clipper】

雷公打小雞，專揀弱的欺。 The God of Thunder strikes the chicks – bullies pick on the weak. 【歇後語 End-clipper】

良善被人欺，慈悲生禍害。 A good man might be bullied and a kind man might have disasters. 【蘭陵笑笑生《金瓶梅・第三十八回》Lanling Xiaoxiaosheng: Chapter 38, The Plum in the Golden Vase】

龍游淺水遭蝦戲，虎落平陽被犬欺。 A dragon stranded in shallow water is teased by prawns and a tiger goes down to a plain is bullied by dogs. 【《增廣賢文》 *Words that Open up One's Mind and Enhance One's Wisdom*】

欺人是禍，饒人是福。 Bullying people invites disasters and forgiving people is a blessing in itself. 【鄭德輝〈老君堂·第一折〉 Zheng Dehui: Scene 1, "Hall of the Venerable Sovereign"】

騎在頭上，拉屎拉尿 Ride on the back of the people and piss and shit on them. 【俗語 Common saying】

騎在頭上，作威作福 Ride roughshod over one's subordinates. 【俗語 Common saying】

乞丐不帶棒，狗也要來欺。 Without a stick in hand, a beggar will be bullied by a dog. 【俗語 Common saying】

強量不如商量。 Coercion is not as good as consultation. 【俗語 Common saying】

人難欺，馬難騎。 People are not easily bullied as horses are difficult to ride. 【諺語 Proverb】

人欺不是辱，人怕不是福。 Being bullied by others is no shame to one and being dreaded by others is no blessing to one. 【《增廣賢文》 *Words that Open up One's Mind and Enhance One's Wisdom*】

人欺天不欺，吃虧是便宜。 One who is bullied by people is not bullied by God, so one who bears an insult gains advantage. 【俗語 Common saying】

人善被人欺，馬善被人騎。 A kind person is often bullied and a willing horse, ridden on. 【俗語 Common saying】

軟的欺，硬的怕。 Bully the weak and be scared of the strong. 【王實甫〈西廂記·第二本楔子〉 Wang Shifu: Act 2, Prologue, *Romance of the Western Bower*】

盛氣凌人，不可一世。 Throw one's weight about and become overbearing. 【俗語 Common saying】

瘦狗莫踢，病馬莫欺。 Do not kick a lean dog and never bully an ill horse. 【俗語 Common saying】

泰山可移，民不可欺。 Mount Tai can be removed, but people cannot be bullied. 【俗語 Common saying】

以大欺小，以富壓貧。 The big bully the small and the rich oppress the poor. 【俗語 Common saying】

遇事沒心計，處處受人欺。 Without calculating everything, one will be bullied everywhere. 【俗語 Common saying】

Business

重打鑼鼓另開張。 Reopen a business to the beating of gongs and drums. 【俗語 Common saying】

創業容易守業難。 It is easy to set up a business but hard to keep it going. 【俗語 Common saying】

公是公，私是私。 Business is business and friends are friends. 【俗語 Common saying】

開店容易守店難。 It is easy to open a shop but difficult to keep it going. 【俗語 Common saying】

人無笑臉莫開店。 A person without a smiling face should not open a shop. 【俗語 Common saying】

生意興隆通四海，財源茂盛達三江。 Prosperity in business reaches the four seas and financial resources come from the three rivers. 【俗語 Common saying】【對聯 Couplet】

Buying and selling

百金買駿馬，千金買美人。 With a hundred taels of gold you buy a fine horse and with a thousand taels of gold you buy a beautiful woman. 【屈復〈偶然作〉Qu Fu:"Impromptu poem"】

不吃不喝，不成買賣。 Transactions will not be made without dining and drinking. 【俗語 Common saying】

買不來有錢在，賣不出有貨在。 If you cannot buy the goods, you have your money, and if you cannot sell the goods, you have your goods. 【俗語 Common saying】

買賣不成仁義在。 The deal is not made, but the goodwill is still there. 【梁斌《紅旗譜・第一卷》Liang Bin: Chapter 1, *Song of the Red Flag*】

買賣人有三分耐性。 A merchant is somehow patient. 【施世綸《施公案・第一百二十八回》Shi Shilun: Chapter 128, *Cases of Judge Shi*】

買西瓜要看皮色。 To buy a water melon, you must first judge its rind. 【俗語 Common saying】

買業不明問中人，娶妻不明問媒人。 When one buys a property and has some doubts, ask the real estate agent. If one wants to marry a woman, ask the matchmaker. 【諺語 Proverb】

買一個，饒一個。 Buy one and get one free. 【吳承恩《西遊記・第二十回》Wu Cheng'en: Chapter 20, *Journey to the West*】

賣菜的吃黃葉，賣鞋的赤腳跑。 The shoemaker's wife often goes

in ragged shoes. 【俗語 Common saying】

賣飯的不怕大肚漢。 One who sells food is not afraid of a glutton. 【吳浚《飛龍全傳‧第十三回》Wu Jun: Chapter 13, *A complete history of the Flying Dragon*】

賣瓜的不說瓜苦。 Melon vendors would never say that their melons are bitter in taste. 【俗語 Common saying】

賣酒不說酒酸。 The wine merchant never says his wine is sour. 【韓非《韓非子‧外儲說右上第三十四》Han Fei: Chapter 34, "Outer congeries of sayings, Part 1", *Hanfeizi*】

寧可賣了悔，休要悔了賣。 Rather regret after selling the goods than sell the goods after regret. 【蘭陵笑笑生《金瓶梅‧第十一回》Lanling Xiaoxiaosheng: Chapter 11, *The plum in the golden vase*】

千賣萬賣，折本不賣。 One can sell one's goods at any time but not when one may lose money. 【王有光《吳下諺聯‧第二卷》Wang Youguang: Chapter 2, *Proverb couplets of the Wu dialect*】

一分行情一分貨。 Nothing for nothing, and very little for a halfpenny. 【俗語 Common saying】

一分錢一分貨。 Give value for value. 【俗語 Common saying】

要的般般有，才是買賣。 You can only do good business when you have everything the customers want. 【蘭陵笑笑生《金瓶梅‧第六十六回》Lanling Xiaoxiaosheng: Chapter 66, *The Plum in the Golden Vase*】

祇有錯買，沒有錯賣。 It is the buyer not the seller that errs. 【俗語 Common saying】

Care

大意失荊州。 Carelessness causes heavy losses. 【羅貫中《三國演義‧第七十五回》Luo Guanzhong: Chapter 75, *Romance of the Three Kingdoms*】

關懷備至，體貼入微。 Be deeply concerned with somebody and give meticulous care to him. 【吳趼人《二十年目睹之怪現狀‧第三十八回》Wu Jianren: Chapter 38, *Bizarre Happenings Eyewitnessed Over Two Decades*】

急人之所急。 Be anxious about what others are anxious about. 【文康《兒女英雄傳‧第三十九回》Wen Kang: Chapter 39, *Biographies of Young Heroes and heroines*】

善游者溺，善騎者墮。 Good swimmers drown and good riders fall. 【劉安《淮南子‧原道訓第一》Liu An: Chapter 1, Searching out the Way, *Huainanzi*】

慎於言者不嘩，慎於行者不伐。 He who is careful of his words

is not pretentious; he who is careful of his deeds does not praise himself. 【韓嬰《韓詩外傳 · 卷三》Han Ying: Chapter 3, *Outer Commentary on the Book of Songs by Master Han*】

疏忽一時，痛苦一世。 A momentary negligence causes a lifelong suffering. 【俗語 Common saying】

言輕則招憂，行輕則招辜，貌輕則招辱，好輕則招淫。 Careless words incur worries; careless actions cause troubles; careless appearance brings humiliation, careless likings cause lust. 【揚雄《法言 · 修身》Yang Xiong: "Cultivating One's Person", *Exemplary Figures*】

戰戰兢兢，如臨深淵，如履薄冰。 One is apprehensive and cautious as if one is on the brink of a deep valley or treading on thin ice. 【《詩經 · 小雅 · 小旻之什》"Decade of Xiao Min", "Minor Odes of the Kingdom", *The Book of Odes*】

住在狼窩邊，小心不為過。 Living near a wolf's den, you can never be cautious enough. 【俗語 Common saying】【張行《武陵山下 · 第五回》Zhang Xing: Chapter 5, *Under Mount Wuling*】

Cat

不管白貓黑貓，能捉老鼠就是好貓。 It does not matter whether a cat is white or black in colour, for any cat that catches mice is a good cat. 【鄧小平《鄧小平文選 · 第一卷 · 怎樣恢復農業生產（1962年7月7日）》Deng Xiaoping: "How to restore agricultural produce? (7 July 1962)", Volume 1, *Selected Works of Deng Xiaoping*】

打死一隻貓，救活千隻鼠。 When a cat is killed, a thousand mice will be saved. 【俗語 Common saying】

好貓不作聲。 A cat that is good at catching mice does not mew. 【俗語 Common saying】

貓兒一跑，耗子就鬧。 When the cat is away, the mice will play. 【俗語 Common saying】

貓哭老鼠 —— 假慈悲。 The cat cries over a dead mouse – hypocritical. 【歇後語 End-clipper】【如蓮居士《說唐全傳 · 第六二回》Layman Ru Lian: Chapter 62, *The Story of Tang Dynasty*】

貓鼠不可同穴。 Cats and mice cannot live in the same cave. 【司馬光《資治通鑒 · 魏明帝景初三年》Sima Guang: "The Third Year of Jingchu in the Reign of Emperor Mingdi of Wei", *Comprehensive Mirror in Aid of Governance*】

貓養的狗不親。 A dog does not love a cat that raises itself up. 【俗語 Common saying】

三斤貓能降千百斤鼠。 A cat weighing three catties can conquer a mouse weighing a thousand catties. 【俗語 Common saying】

養貓捕鼠，蓄犬防家。 Raise a cat to catch mice and raise a dog to look after the house. 【佚名《殺狗記‧第二十五齣》Anonymous: Scene 25, "An Account of Dog-killing"】

Cause

冰凍三尺，非一日之寒。 It takes more than one cold day for the river to freeze three feet deep. 【左丘明《左傳‧襄公三十一年》Zuo Qiuming:"The Thirty-first Year of the Reign of Duke Xiang", *Zuo's Dommentary on the Spring and Autumn Annals*】

凡事均有因。 Everything has a cause. 【諺語 Proverb】

各有因緣莫羨人。 Everyone has his own lot and should not envy others. 【俗語 Common saying】【金纓《格言聯璧》Jin Ying: *Couplets of Maxims*】

話出有因，事出有根。 Every word has its reason and everything has its cause. 【李寶嘉《官場現形記‧第四回》Li Baojia: Chapter 4, *Officialdom Unmasked*】

事有因，話有緣。 Everything has its cause and every word has its reason. 【諺語 Proverb】

是草有根，是話有因。 Every blade of grass has its roots and every word, its reason. 【諺語 Proverb】

視其所以，觀其所由。 See what a person does and observe the cause. 【孔子《論語‧為政第二》Confucius: Chapter 2, *The Analects of Confucius*】

樹荊棘得刺，樹桃李得蔭。 If you plant brambles, you get thorns; if you plant peach and plum trees, you get shade. 【馮夢龍《警世通言‧第十八卷》Feng Menglong: Chapter 18, *Stories to Caution the World*】

水有源頭樹有根，葫蘆有藤話有因。 Waters have their origins, trees their roots, gourds their vines and words their causes. 【諺語 Proverb】

斬草必須除根。 When you weed, you must dig up the roots. 【諺語 Proverb】

斬草不除根，逢春又發青。 If you weed without digging up the roots, next spring the grass will grow again. 【諺語 Proverb】

Cause-effect

不管三七二十一。 Regardless of the consequences. 【劉向《戰國策・齊策一》Liu Xiang: "Strategies of the State of Qi", No. 1, *Strategies of the Warring States*】

不因漁父引，怎得見波濤？ If there is no fisherman leading our way, how can we see the great waves? 【《增廣賢文》*Words that Open up One's Mind and Enhance One's Wisdom*】

不種今年竹，哪得來年笋。 If one does not plant bamboo this year, how can one get bamboo shoots next year? 【諺語 Proverb】

開好花，結好果。 Good blossoms will yield good fruit. 【諺語 Proverb】

惡因生惡果。 Sin yields bitter fruits. 【俗語 Common saying】

風不搖，樹不動。 If there is no wind, the tree will not shake. 【蘭陵笑笑生《金瓶梅・第七十五回》Lanling Xiaoxiaosheng: Chapter 75, *The Plum in the Golden Vase*】

怪樹有怪丫叉。 A strangely shaped tree has strangely shaped branches. 【余邵魚《東周列國志・第六十四回》Yu Shaoyu: Chapter 64, The *Chronicles of the Eastern Zhou Kingdoms*】

關門養虎，虎大傷人。 To rear a tiger at home, one will be hurt by the tiger when it grows up. 【錢彩《說岳全傳・第四十回》Qian Cai: Chapter 40, *A Story of Yue Fei*】

腳上的泡，自己走的。 The blisters on one's feet are caused by one's own walk. 【俗語 Common saying】

末大必折，尾大不掉。 A tree with a large top must break and a tail that is too large cannot wag. 【左丘明《左傳・昭公十一年》Zuo Qiuming: "The Eleventh Year of the Reign of Duke Zhao", *Zuo's Commentary on the Spring and Autumn Annals*】

千里之堤，潰於蟻穴。 Slight negligence may lead to great disaster. 【劉安《淮南子・人間訓第十八》Liu An: Chapter 18, "In the World of Man", *Huainanzi*】

前人開路後人行。 One generation opens the road on which another generation travels. 【諺語 Proverb】

前人栽樹，後人乘涼。 One generation plant the trees under whose shade another generation rests. 【頤瑣《黃繡球》Yi Suo: "Yellow Hydrangea"】

前世不修今世苦。 The lack of self-cultivation in the previous life will result in suffering in present life. 【俗語 Common saying】

甚麼樹結甚麼果。 As the tree, so the fruit. 【俗語 Common saying】

玩火者必自焚。 He who plays with fire will perish by fire. 【左丘明《左傳・隱公四年》Zuo Qiuming: "The Fourth Year of the Reign of Duke Yin", *Zuo's Commentary on the Spring and Autumn Annals*】

玩劍者必死於劍下。 One who plays with the sword will perish with the sword. 【諺語 Proverb】

先開花，後結果。 Flowers first, fruits afterwards. 【俗語 Common saying】

先有耕耘，後有收穫。 Sowing before reaping. 【俗語 Common saying】

一分耕耘，一分收穫。 No pain, no gain. 【俗語 Common saying】

以損人開始，以害己告終。 Sow the wind and reap the whirl wind. 【諺語 Proverb】

因因果果，無因無果。 Cause results in effect. When there is no cause, there is no effect. 【俗語 Common saying】

有白必有黑，有甜就有苦。 Where there is whiteness, there is blackness; where there is sweetness, there is bitterness. 【諺語 Proverb】

有果必有因。 Every why has a wherefore. 【俗語 Common saying】【佛教語 Buddhist saying】

栽甚麼樹結甚麼果，撒甚麼種子開甚麼花。 You get the kind of fruits from the kind of trees you plant and you have the kind of flowers from the kind of seeds you sow. 【李玉和《紅燈記》Li Yuhe: "The Red Lantern"】

種瓜得瓜，種豆得豆。 As a man sows, so shall he reap. 《大般涅槃經》 *Mahāparinirvāṇa Sūtra*】

種牡丹得花，種蒺藜得刺。 He who plants peony gets flowers and he who plants thorny vines gets the pricks. 【魯迅《而已集·答有恆先生》Lu Xun: "A Letter in Reply to Mr. Youheng", *The Collection: And That's That*】

種麻得麻，種豆得豆。 You get hemp when you plant hemps, and you get beans when you plant beans. 【《增廣賢文》*Words that Open up One's Mind and Enhance One's Wisdom*】

種田有穀，養豬有肉。 Plough a field to get grain; raise pigs to get meat. 【諺語 Proverb】

Change

安危相易，禍福相生。 Safety and danger are alternate; misfortune and fortune are mutually dependent. 【莊周《莊子·雜篇·則陽第二十五》Zhuang Zhou: Chapter 25, "Sunny", "Miscellaneous Chapters", *Zhuangzi*】

變古亂常，不死則亡。 Those who change traditional rules and conventions will die or flee.【司馬遷《史記‧袁盎晁錯列傳》Sima Qian:"Biographies of Yuan Ang and Chao Cuo", *Records of the Grand Historian*】

洞中方七日，世上已千年。
One has only stayed in a cave for seven days, yet outside a thousand years have passed.【馮夢龍《醒世恆言‧第三十八卷》Feng Menglong: Chapter 38, *Stories To Awaken the World*】

翻手為雲，覆手為雨。With a turn of one's hand, clouds are produced. With another turn, rain is produced.【杜甫〈貧交行〉Du Fu:"Friendship in Poverty"】

高山為淵，深谷為陵。High mountains become deep pools and deep valleys become hills.【葛洪《抱朴子‧內篇‧黃白第十六》Ge Hong: Chapter 16, "Yellow and White", "Inner Chapters", *Master Who Embraces Simplicity*】

苟日新，日日新，又日新。If you can improve yourself in a day, do so each day, forever building on improvement.【《禮記‧大學第四十二》Chapter 42, The Great Learning, *The Book of Rites*】

官事隨時變。Official affairs change all the time.【諺語 Proverb】【老舍《老張的哲學》Lao She:"The Philosophy of Zhang"】

化腐朽為神奇。Turn something rotten into a beautiful thing.【莊周《莊子‧外篇‧知北遊第二十二》: Zhuang Zhou: Chapter 22, "Knowledge Wanders North", "Outer Chapters", *Zhuangzi*】

換湯不換藥。Old wine in new bottle.【馬南邨《燕山夜話》Ma Nancun:"Night Talk on Mount Yan"】

江河不老，朝代易換。Rivers and mountains do not grow old, but dynasties change quickly.【諺語 Proverb】

今日愛東，明日愛西。Drift east today and west tomorrow.【曹雪芹《紅樓夢‧第九回》Cao Xueqin: Chapter 9, *A Dream of the Red Chamber*】

禮義法度者，應時而變者也。Rites, righteousness, and laws should change according to times.【莊周《莊子‧外篇‧天道第十三》: Zhuang Zhou: Chapter 13, "The Way of Heaven", "Outer Chapters", *Zhuangzi*】

六十年風水輪流轉。There is a change of fortune every sixty years.【俗語 Common saying】

貓兒眼 —— 看時候變。The eyes of a cat change with time.【歇後語 End-clipper】

貓兒眼 —— 時時變。Be as adaptable as a cat's eyes to light.【歇後語 End-clipper】

年年歲歲花相似，歲歲年年人不同。Year after year, the flowers are always alike, but year after year, people are different.【劉希夷《代白頭吟》Liu Xiyi:"Admonition On Behalf of a White-haired Old Man"】

騎驢逛燈 —— 走着瞧。Riding on a donkey to watch a lantern show – just wait and see. 【歇後語 End-clipper】

窮則變，變則通，通則久。Coming to a deadlock leads to changes; changes lead to solutions; solutions lead to sustainability. 【《易經‧繫辭下》 "Appended Remarks", Part 2, *The Book of Changes*】

讓高山低頭，叫河水讓路。Let the high mountains bow their heads and the rivers give their ways. 【俗語 Common saying】

人事有代謝，往來成古今。People and worldly matters must endure ups and downs. As time comes and goes, today becomes history in one day. 【孟浩然〈與諸子登峴山〉Meng Haoran: "Climbing the Xian Mountain with Friends"】

人有悲歡離合，月有陰晴圓缺。Men have sorrow and joy, parting and reunion while the moon has darkness and brightness, does wax and wane. 【蘇軾〈水調歌頭〉Su Shi: "To the Tune of Prelude to the Melody of Water"】

日月經天，江河行地。As permanent as the sun and moon passing through the sky, the rivers flow across the land. 【范曄《後漢書‧桓譚馮衍傳》Fan Ye: "Biographies of Heng Tan and Feng Yan", *History of the Later Han*】

三十年河東，三十年河西。Life is full of ups and downs. 【吳敬梓

《儒林外史‧第四十六回》Wu Jingzi: Chapter 46, *An Unofficial History of the Scholars*】

山難改，性難改。It is difficult to move a mountain as it is hard to change human nature. 【西周生《醒世姻緣傳‧第六十二回》Xi Zhousheng: Chapter 62, *Stories of Marriage to Awaken the World*】

十年河東，十年河西。Life is full of ups and downs. 【諺語 Proverb】

士別三日，刮目相看。One should be given a different look even though there are only three days of separation 【陳壽《三國志‧吳志‧呂蒙傳》Chen Shou: "Biography of Lu Meng", "History of Wu", *The Records of the Three Kingdoms*】

世變人亦變。As the world changes, so do people. 【俗語 Common saying】

罈子裏養王八 —— 越養越抽抽 If you ever experience the wind and rain outside, you will become less and less promising. 【歇後語 End-clipper】

湯武革命，順乎天而應乎人。The revolutionary changes made by Tang and Wu are in accordance with the will of heaven and in response to the wishes of the people. 【《易經‧革‧象》"Image", "Hexagram *Ge*", *The Book of Changes*】

堂屋椅子輪流坐，媳婦也有做婆時。The seats in the great hall all come in rotation – the daughter-in-law will someday be the mother-in-law. 【俗語 Common saying】

天不變，道亦不變。 If the sky does not change, the rules will not change. 【班固《漢書·董仲書傳》Ban Gu: "Biography of Dong Zhongshu", *The Book of Han*】

外甥打燈籠 — 照舅（照舊）。 Remain unchanged. 【歇後語 End-clipper】

萬變不離其宗。 All the myriad changes will not deviate from the original purpose. 【荀況《荀子·儒效第八》Xun Kuang: Chapter 8, "The Achievements of the Confucians", *Xunzi*】

萬事變遷，世事無常。 Everything changes and nothing lasts forever. 【諺語 Proverb】

萬事如棋動局，一世如駒過隙。 Everything is like a chess piece moving on a chessboard and one's lifetime is like a horse galloping over a crack. 【《增廣賢文》*Words that Open up One's Mind and Enhance One's Wisdom*】

閒雲潭影日悠悠，物換星移幾度秋。 The sun, reflecting the idle clouds in the pools, is forever there. But things have changed, stars have moved, and years have come and gone. 【王勃《秋日登洪府滕王閣餞別序》Wang Bo: "Preface to a Farewell Feast Atop the Prince Teng's Pavilion in Autumn"】

朽木不可雕也，糞土之牆不可圬也。 Rotten wood cannot be carved; a wall of dungs cannot be cleaned. 【孔子《論語·公冶長篇第五》Confucius: Chapter 5, *The Analects of Confucius*】

一百八十度大轉變。 An about-face change. 【俗語 Common saying】

一時比不得一時。 Times have changed. 【俗語 Common saying】

以不變應萬變。 To cope with changes by remaining unchanged. 【俗語 Common saying】【道家語 Daoist saying】

魚放三日臭，久住招人嫌。 Fish smells in three days and company will get hate after living together for long. 【俗語 Common saying】

自信者不可以誹譽遷也。 He who is confident of himself cannot be changed by praise or slander. 【劉安《淮南子·詮言訓第十四》Liu An: Chapter 14, "An Explanatory Discourse", *Huainanzi*】

Character

板板六十四。 Being stubborn. 【周遵道《豹隱紀談》Zhou Zundao: *Remarks in Retirement*】

吃軟不吃硬。 One is open to persuasion but not to coercion. 【醉月山人《狐狸緣全傳·第三回》】

Zuiyue Shanren: Chapter 3, *A Full Story of Fox Marriage*】

乖僻自是，悔誤必多。 A person who is eccentric and opinionated errs and regrets a lot.【朱柏廬《治家格言》Zhu Pailu: *Maxims for Managing a Family*】

乾魚不能給貓做枕頭。 A dried fish cannot be used as a cat's pillow.【吳承恩《西遊記・第五十五回》Wu Cheng'en: Chapter 55, *Journey to the West*】

江山易改，本性難移。 It is easy to change mountains and rivers but difficult to change a person's character.【臧懋循《元曲選・佚名〈謝金吾〉三》Zang Maoxun: "Xie Jinwu", Part 3, *Anthology of Yuan Plays*】

茅房的石頭，又臭又硬。 Being stubborn.【俗語 Common saying】

千人千品，萬人萬相。 A thousand people have a thousand characters and ten thousand people, ten thousand appearances.【諺語 Proverb】

日久見人心。 Time reveals a person's true character.【陳元靚《事林廣記・卷九》Chen Yuanliang: Chapter 9, *Comprehensive Records of Affairs*】

三歲孩兒定八十。 The character of a person at age three is already formed and will never change【俗語 Common saying】

三歲看到老 You can predict manhood at age three.【諺語 Proverb】

十個光棍九個倔。 Nine out of the ten single men are stubborn.【柳青《狠透鐵・第十卷》Liu Qing: Chapter 10, *Cruelty that Penetrates Iron*】

鐵公雞 毛不拔。 An iron cock will not give up even a feather.【歇後語 End-clipper】【吳敬梓《儒林外史・第二十八回》Wu Jingzi: Chapter 28, "Outer Chapters", *An Unofficial History of the Scholars*】

頭頂生瘡，腳底流膿 —— 壞透了。 Be rotten from head to foot.【歇後語 End-clipper】

Charm

吃了迷魂湯。 Be possessed by a woman's beauty.【蘭陵笑笑生《金瓶梅・第二十六回》Lanling Xiaoxiaosheng: Chapter 26, *The Plum in the Golden Vase*】

回眸一笑百媚生，六宮粉黛無顏色。 When she turned back and smiled, so much charm was revealed, making all the ladies of the Six Palaces at once saw dull and colourless.【白居易〈長恨歌〉Bai Juyi: "Song of Everlasting Grief"】

妙在不言中。 The charm lies in what is left unsaid.【郭璞《江賦》Guo Pu: "Ode to River"】

明媚嫻雅，端莊瑩靜。Charming, elegant, and reserved.【劉鶚《老殘遊記‧第八回》Liu E: Chapter 8, *The Travels of Lao Can*】

我見青山多嫵媚，料青山見我應如是。It occurs to me that the green mountains are charming, and I would expect the feeling to be mutual.【辛棄疾〈賀新郎〉Xin Qiji:"To the Tune of Congratulating the Bridegroom"】

徐娘半老，風韻猶存。A woman in her middle age is still attractive.【李延壽《南史‧後妃傳下》Li Yanshou:"Biographies of Imperial Wives and Concubines", Part 2, *History of the Southern Dynasties*】

Chastity

餓死事小，失節事大。Starving to death is a small matter, but losing one's chastity is a serious one.【程顥，程頤《二程全書‧遺書‧二十二》Cheng Hao and Cheng Yi:"Posthumous Works", No. 22, *Complete Works of Cheng Hao and Cheng Yi*】

節女不事兩夫。A chaste woman never remarries.【司馬遷《史記‧田單列傳》Sima Qian:"Biography of Tian Dan", *Records of the Grand Historian*】

窮義夫，富節婦。A poor husband has his righteousness and a rich widow has her chastity.【諺語 Proverb】

貞女不更二夫。A chaste woman never remarries.【司馬遷《史記‧田單列傳》Sima Qian:"Biography of Tian Dan", *Records of the Grand Historian*】

Cheating

八哥兒啄柿子 —— 挑軟的。Being used to bullying the weak.【歇後語 End-clipper】

變戲法的瞞不了敲鑼的。People in the know cannot be tricked.【諺語 Proverb】

掛羊頭，賣狗肉。Bait-and-switch【釋惟白《續傳燈錄‧第三十一卷》Shi Weibai: Chapter 31, *A Sequel to the Records of the Transmission of the Lamp*】

老太太吃柿子 —— 揀軟和的捏。Being used to bullying the weak.【歇後語 End-clipper】

瞞上不瞞下。Cheating with the subordinates, not letting the superiror know.【李寶嘉《官場現形記‧第三十六回》Li Baojia: Chapter 36, *Officialdom Unmasked*】

拿着金碗討飯吃 —— 裝窮叫苦。
One begs for food with a gold bowl – make a poor mouth. 【歇後語 End-clipper】

能瞞一人眼，瞞不了千人眼。
You can hide something from one person but can't from a thousand people. 【俗語 Common saying】

騙得了一時，騙不過一世。 You can cheat for once, but you cannot cheat forever. 【俗語 Common saying】

騙人一次，招疑一世。 He who has cheated once will be suspected for the rest of his life. 【俗語 Common saying】

騙殺人，弗償命。 One who cheated somebody to death does not need to pay with his own life. 【王有光《吳下諺聯・第二卷》Wang Youguang: Chapter 2, *Proverb Couplets of the Wu Ddialect*】

上大當，吃大虧。 Be badly fooled and suffer severely. 【俗語 Common saying】

上當祇有一回。 A fox is not taken twice in the same snare. 【俗語 Common saying】

銅銀買病豬 —— 大家偷歡喜。
Each of the two hugs himself on having cheated the other. 【歇後語 End-clipper】

外以欺於人，內以欺於心。
Outwardly, one deceives others and inwardly one deceives oneself. 【韓愈《昌黎先生集・原毀》Han Yu:"Origin of Defamation", *Collected Works of Han Yu*】

我無爾詐，爾無我虞。 I do not cheat you and you do not hoodwink me. 【左丘明《左傳・宣公十五年》Zuo Qiuming:"The Fifteenth Year of the Reign of Duke Xuan", *Zuo's Commentary on the Spring and Autumn Annals*】

下民易虐，上蒼難欺。 It is easy to bully people but difficult to deceive heaven. 【洪邁《容齋隨筆》Hong Mai: *Notes from Rong Studio*】

Chicken

公雞抱窩，母雞叫明。 It is unreasonable for a cock sits on eggs and a hen crows to herald daybreak. 【克非《春潮急・上卷第六回》Ke Fei: Volume 1, Chapter 6, *Spring Tide Comes Rapidly*】

雞出籠早，當天雨到。 If the chickens come out of their coops early, it will rain during the day. 【俗語 Common saying】

雞多不下蛋，人多吃閒飯。 If there are too many hens, they will not lay eggs; if there are too many people, they will be idlers. 【諺語 Proverb】

雞兒不吃無工之食。One cannot accept favours or gifts for no reason.【吳承恩《西遊記・第四十七回》Wu Cheng'en: Chapter 47, *Journey to the West*】

雞寒上樹，鴨寒下水。When a chicken feels cold, it gets on the tree and when a duck feels cold, it goes into water.【諺語 Proverb】

雞毛飛上天。Chicken feathers can fly up to heaven.【俗語 Common saying】

雞窩裏藏不住鳳凰。A chicken coop cannot hold a phoenix.【諺語 Proverb】

雞窩裏飛出鳳凰。Phoenixes soar out of a chicken coop.【俗語 Common saying】

雞知將旦，鶴知夜半。A rooster knows the coming of dawn and a crane, midnight.【劉安《淮南子・說山訓第十六》Liu An: Chapter 16, "Discourse on Mountains", *Huainanzi*】

家雞哪有野鶩好。A hen at home is not as good as a wild duck.【俗語 Common saying】

Children

褓母的孩子 —— 人家的。A nanny's children – belongs to others.【歇後語 End-clipper】

多子女，多勞累。More kids, more toil.【俗語 Common saying】

兒孫自有兒孫福。The children have their own happiness.【周密《癸辛雜識續集・葉李紀夢詩》Zhou Mi: "A Poem to Narrate Dreams by Ye Li of the Song Dynasty", *A Sequel to Notes Taken at the Kuxin Road*】

隔層肚皮隔重山。A belly in between is like a mountain in between - a man's mind is unpredictable.【凌濛初《初刻拍案驚奇・第三十八卷》Ling Mengchu: Chapter 38, *Amazing Tales, Volume One*】

孩兒口裏討實信。One can get the truth from a child's mouth.【俗語 Common saying】

孩子離開娘，瓜兒離開秧。When a child leaves his mother, it is like a melon torn off the vine.【俗語 Common saying】

孩子是娘的肉。A child is a mother's flesh.【俗語 Common saying】

虎門無犬種。You won't find a puppy in a tiger's den.【俗語 Common saying】

嬌兒無孝，嬌妻作亂。A spoiled son is unfilial and a petted wife troublesome.【俗語 Common saying】

嬌子如殺子。To spoil a child is to kill him.【諺語 Proverb】

嬌養不如歷艱。It is better to ask the children to go through difficulties than to pamper them.【俗語 Common saying】

老媽抱孩子 —— 人家的。An amah holding a baby in her arms – belongs to others.【歇後語 End-clipper】

六十無孫，老樹無根。One ages sixty without a grandson is like an old tree without roots.【諺語 Proverb】

沒兒沒女是神仙。A childless couple are as happy as gods.【俗語 Common saying】【茅盾《霜葉紅似二月花》Mao Dun:"Frost Leaves Red like the February Blossoms"】

茄子開黃花 —— 縱（種）壞了。The eggplant blooms in yellow – (pun) the child is spoiled.【歇後語 End-clipper】

人在父母前，永遠是孩子。One is always a child in the eyes of one's parents.【俗語 Common saying】

三歲看大，七歲看老。You can foresee one's manhood at the age of three and agedness at seven.【俗語 Common saying】

三歲行徑知八十。From the behaviours of a child of three, one can foresee what he will be like at the age of eighty.【俗語 Common saying】

十月懷胎，一朝分娩。Children are born after they have been in the womb for ten months.【諺語 Proverb】

始作俑者，其無後乎。For those who invented the earthen figures to be buried with the dead, did they ever think of having no male offspring?【孟軻《孟子・梁惠王上》Meng Ke: Chapter 1, Part 1, Mencius】

是兒女，眼前冤。Sons and daughters are born to get back debts their parents owned them in their previous existence.【俗語 Common saying】【佛家語 Buddhist saying】

五十不見孫，至死不鬆心。Without grandchildren at fifty, one dies with an ever-lasting regret.【俗語 Common saying】

昔別君未婚，兒女忽成行。You were not engaged when we parted, and now, all of a sudden, your sons and daughters stand in a row.【杜甫〈贈衛八處士〉Du Fu:"Presented to Scholar-recluse Wei the Eighth"】

小孩子嘴裏討實話。It is easy to trick children into telling the truth.【俗語 Common saying】

小樹要砍，小孩要管。A child needs discipline as a sapling needs pruning.【諺語 Proverb】

燕子銜泥空費力，乳燕羽豐各自飛。The swallow building her nest is wasting her energy, for when the little swallows' wings

grow strong, they will fly away.
【諺語 Proverb】

一般兒女兩般心。 A girl's mind is unpredictable. 【俗語 Common saying】

一生兒女債，半世老婆奴。 A wife and children are a man's burdens. 【諺語 Proverb】

祇愁不養，不愁不長。 The only worry is that you have no children; if so, you need not worry about their growth. 【俗語 Common saying】

逐令天下父母心，不重生男重生女。 This has made parents everywhere to look upon a son as less important than a daughter. 【白居易〈長恨歌〉Bai Juyi: "Song of Everlasting Grief"】

Choice

二者必居其一。 Either one or another. 【孟軻《孟子・公孫丑下》Meng Ke: Chapter 2, Part 2, Mencius】

慌不擇路，饑不擇食。 When one is frightened, one does not choose roads; when one is hungry, one does not choose food. 【俗語 Common saying】

會選的選兒郎，不會選的選田莊。 He who chooses well chooses a son-in-law; he who chooses badly chooses land. 【俗語 Common saying】

饑不擇食，寒不擇衣。 When one is hungry, one does not choose food. When one feels cold, one does not choose clothes. 【施耐庵《水滸傳・第三回》Shi Nai'an: Chapter 3, Outlaws of the Marshes】

籃子裏挑花，越挑越眼花。 If you choose flowers from a basket, the longer time you choose the worse you get. 【俗語 Common saying】

良禽擇木而棲，賢臣擇主而事。 Clever birds choose their trees when they perch and wise ministers choose a king to serve. 【羅貫中《三國演義・第三回》Luo Guanzhong: Chapter 3, Romance of the Three Kingdoms】

兩害相權取其輕。 Accept the lesser of two evils. 【王圻《續文獻通考・卷三百九十四》Wang Qi: Chapter 394, Sequel to the Comprehensive Study of Literary and Documentary Sources】

蘿蔔青菜，各有所愛。 One man's meat is another man's poison. 【俗語 Common saying】

鳥則擇木，人則擇主。 A bird chooses its tree, while a person, his master. 【左丘明《左傳・哀公十一年》Zuo Qiuming: "The Eleventh year of the Reign of Duke Ai", Zuo's Commentary on the Spring and Autumn Annals】

窮鳥不擇枝。A tired bird will stay on any branch. 【俗語 Common saying】

雙木橋好走，獨木橋難行。A bridge with two logs is easy to walk, whereas a bridge with a single log isn't. 【俗語 Common saying】

退而求其次。Have no alternative but to go for the second best. 【曹靖華《歎往昔：獨木橋頭徘徊無終期》Cao Jinghua:"A Sigh on the Past: Hovering at the End of a Single-log Bridge Without End"】

Cleverness

聰明反被聰明誤。Being too smart of one's own good. 【蘇軾〈洗兒詩〉Su Shi:"On Bathing My Son"】

聰明人不上二次當。A silly fish will be caught twice with the same bait. 【俗語 Common saying】

聰明一世，糊塗一時。Smart as a rule, but this time a fool. 【馮夢龍《警世通言·第三卷》Feng Menglong: Chapter 3, *Stories to Caution the World*】

聰明一世，懵懂一時。Wise for a lifetime but foolish at a critical moment. 【徐元《八義記·第三十二齣》Xu Yuan: Scene 32, *The Story of the Eight Righteous Heroes*】

聰明有種，富貴有根。Cleverness is by birth, wealth is from heritage. 【俗語 Common saying】

聰明子弟少容顏。Clever men are rarely endowed with good looks. 【俗語 Common saying】

個人聰明有限，集體智慧無窮。The wisdom of an individual is limited, but collective wisdom is boundless. 【俗語 Common saying】

光棍不吃眼前虧。A clever person will not suffer injury for the present. 【老舍《柳屯的》Lao She："The Story of Liu Tunde"】

撿了芝麻，丟了西瓜。Aware of trivial matters yet neglecting the important ones. 【黃小配《廿載繁華夢·第三十四回》Huang Xiaopei: Chapter 34, *A Two-decade Dream of Glory*】

旗桿上掛燈籠 —— 高明。A lantern hanging on a flagpole is high and bright – one is clever and skilful. 【歇後語 End-clipper】

人皆養子望聰明，我被聰明誤一生。All people raise children and hope that they will be clever, yet my entire life has been ruined by my cleverness. 【蘇軾〈洗兒詩〉Su Shi:"On Bathing My Son"】

三個臭皮匠，勝過一個諸葛亮。Two heads are better than one. 【羅貫中《三國演義·第七十五回》Luo Guanzhong: Chapter 75, *Romance of the Three Kingdoms*】

三個蠢人當個明人，三個明人當個知縣。 Three slow persons together become clever and three clever persons together become a magistrate.【俗語 Common saying】

無知若是福，聰明反為愚。 If ignorance is bliss, then cleverness is folly.【俗語 Common saying】

小事聰明，大事糊塗。 Penny wise and pound foolish.【俗語 Common saying】

一人不抵二智。 Two heads are better than one.【西周生《醒世姻緣傳‧第八十四回》Xi Zhousheng: Chapter 84, *Stories of Marriage to Awaken the World*】

Clothing

粗衣淡飯就是福。 Simple clothes and food are a blessing in themselves.【俗語 Common saying】【黃庭堅《四休導士詩序》Huang Tingjian: "The Collection of Poems of Four Retired Priests"】

當今世上目頭淺，祇重衣裳不重人。 Nowadays people in the world are all short-sighted, they judge a person by clothes they wear but not their character.【俗語 Common saying】

二八月，亂穿衣。 There is no rule for clothing in early spring and autumn.【俗語 Common saying】

佛要金裝，人要衣裝。 Clothes make the man, dressed to the nines.【馮夢龍《醒世恆言‧第一卷》Feng Menglong: Chapter 1, *Stories to Awaken the World*】

明中妝梳暗撩人。 Some women dress beautifully to attract men.【凌濛初《初刻拍案驚奇‧第三十二卷》Ling Mengchu: Chapter 32, *Amazing Tales, Volume One*】

男要俏，一身皂；女要俏，一身孝。 A man who wants to look handsome should dress in dark and a woman who wants to look beautiful should dress in light.【俗語 Common saying】

人靠衣裳馬靠鞍。 Clothes make a person just as a saddle makes a horse.【俗語 Common saying】

人靠衣裝，佛靠金裝。 Clothes make the man, dressed to the nines.【沈自晉《望湖亭記‧第十齣》Shen Zijin: Scene 10, *Account of Lake-overlooking Pavillion*】

人配衣裳馬配鞍。 Clothes make the man just as a saddle makes a horse.【俗語 Common saying】

人憑衣裝馬憑鞍。 Clothes make a person just as a saddle makes a horse.【俗語 Common saying】

人是衣裳馬是鞍。 A dress to a person is like a saddle is to a horse.【俗語 Common saying】

若要俏，添重孝。 To look charming, you had to better be dressed in white. 【馮夢龍《警世通言・第三十五卷》Feng Menglong: Chapter 35, *Stories to Caution the World*】

生看衣裳熟看人。 At the first meeting with a stranger, people look at clothes. When they are familiar with each other, people look at the personality. 【李英儒《還我山河・第三十三章》Li Yingru: Chapter 33, *Give Me back My Homeland*】

十個麻皮九個俏。 Nine out of ten persons with pockmarked faces are smartly dressed. 【俗語 Common saying】

十個禿子九個富。 Nine out of ten bald-headed men are rich. 【俗語 Common saying】

未食五月糭，寒衣不入櫃。 Don't put one's winter clothes into the camphorwood before Dragon Boat Festival. 【諺語 Proverb】

屋要人襯，人要衣襯。 A good house needs good people to live in it and a good man needs good clothes to decorate him. 【俗語 Common saying】

先敬羅衣後敬人。 Respect the fine clothes before the man. 【俗語 Common saying】

新三年，舊三年，縫縫補補又三年。 My suit has been worn for six years, but I can make it last another three years. 【俗語 Common saying】

要暖粗布衣，要好自小妻。 To warm yourself, wear coarse clothes; to have a good marriage, get your wife whom you've known since childhood. 【俗語 Common saying】

衣食足而後知禮義。 When people are well-fed and well-clad, they know how to be courteous and righteous. 【管仲《管子・牧民第一》Guan Zhong: Volume 1: "Shepherding the People", *Guanzi*】

衹重衣衫不重人。 Respect one's clothes but not his character. 【釋普濟《五燈會元・卷十一・繼昌禪師》Shi Puji: Chapter 11, "Chan Master Jichang", *A Compendium of the Five Lamps*】

Cloud

撥開雲霧見青天。 The wind blows away the clouds to reveal the blue sky. 【羅貫中《三國演義・第六十五回》Luo Guanzhong: Chapter 65, *Romance of the Three Kingdoms*】

不畏浮雲遮望眼，衹緣身在最高層。 We have no fear of the clouds that may block our view, as we are already on the summit. 【王安石〈登飛來峯〉Wang Anshi: "Climbing up Mount Feilai"】

多大的雲下多大的雨。 Act according to one's ability. 【聶海〈靠山堡〉Nie Hai:"Near-mountain Fort"】

黑雲壓城城欲摧。 War bearing down on the city threaten to crush it. 【李賀〈雁門太守行〉Li He:"Yan Men Governor"】

落絮無聲春墮淚，行雲有影月含羞。 The catkins fall noiselessly like tears shed by spring, and a demure moon hides behind shadows of the moving clouds. 【吳文英〈浣溪沙〉Wu Wenying:"To the Tune of Sand of Silk-washing Stream"】

片雲足以蔽日。 A single cloud is enough to blot out the sun. 【諺語 Proverb】

如墮五里霧中。 Like being lost in the clouds. 【范曄《後漢書·張霸傳》Fan Ye:"Biography of Zhang Ba", History of the Later Han】

山中何所有？嶺上多白雲。祇可自怡悅，不堪持贈君。 What is there in the mountain? There are many white clouds over its peak. This can only be appreciated by myself, but I cannot take and give you. 【陶弘景〈詔問山中何所有賦詩以答〉Tao Hongjing:"Poem Written in Reply to the Question Asked by the Emperor in His Edict"】

行到水窮處，坐看雲起時。 When facing adversity and desperation, put aside the gains and losses, there may be a new light. 【王維〈終南別業〉Wang Wei: My Cottage at Mount Zhongnan】

雲厚者雨必猛，弓勁者箭必遠。 When clouds are thick, the rain will be heavy. When the bow is strongly pulled, the shoot will be far. 【葛洪《抱朴子·外篇·喻蔽第四十三》Ge Hong: Chapter 43, "Clarifying Obscurities", "Outer Chapters", Master Who Embraces Simplicity】

雲生從龍，風生從虎。 Clouds are created by dragons, and the wind, by tigers. 【《易經·乾卦·九五》Chapter 95, "Hexagram Qian Guo", The Book of Changes】

雲有雲路，水有水路。 Clouds follow their courses as waters flow theirs. 【俗語 Common saying】

早霞主雨，晚霞主晴。 Rosy morning clouds indicate rainy day, and a rosy sunset means fine weather. 【俗語 Common saying】

Colour

青，取之於藍，而青於藍。 Indigo blue is extracted from the indigo plant, but it is bluer than the plant itself. 【荀況《荀子·勸學第一》Xun Kuang: Chapter 1, "Exhortation to Learning", Xunzi】

深紅淺紫，鴨綠鵝黃 The hues of scarlet, light purple, duck-green and goose-yellow. 【蘇軾〈次荊公韻・其一〉Su Shi: No. 1, "Poem Inspired by Wang Anshi"】

五色令人目盲，五音令人耳聾，五味令人口爽。 Feeding one's eyes with the five colours make people blind, delivering one's ears with five sounds make people deaf, providing one's tongue with the five tastes make people lose their sense of taste. 【老子《道德經・第十二章》Laozi: Chapter 12, *Daodejing*】

Coming and going

八月十五的月餅 —— 一盆子來一盆子去。 The coming and going is like mooncakes at the Mid-Autumn Festival, with one plateful being brought in and one being taken away. 【歇後語 End-clipper】

乘興而來，敗興而歸。 Come in high spirits but return disappointed. 【房玄齡等《晉書・王徽之傳》Fang Xuanling *et al*: "Biography of Wang Huizhi", *The Book of the Jin*】

古往今來，世事如麻。 Throughout the ages, countless complicated events had taken place. 【俗語 Common saying】

合則留，不留則去。 Stay if the condition is agreeable and leave if it's not. 【蘇軾〈范增論〉Su Shi: "On Fan Zeng"】

雞蛋下山 —— 滾蛋。 Eggs rolling down a mountain – go away. 【歇後語 End-clipper】

舊的不去，新的不來。 Out with the old, in with the new. 【俗語 Common saying】

來得明，去得白。 Clear come, clear go. 【俗語 Common saying】

來得容易去得快。 Light come, light go. 【俗語 Common saying】

來得早不如來得巧。 To come early is not as good as to come in time. 【俗語 Common saying】

來如春夢幾多時，去似朝雲無覓處。 It comes like a vernal dream that cannot stay. It goes like morning clouds that vanish traceless. 【白居易〈花非花〉Bai Juyi: "A Flower It Seemed"】

來如風雨，去似微塵。 Thing comes suddenly like the storm, and it leaves vaguely like the dust. 《增廣賢文》*Words that Open up One's Mind and Enhance One's Wisdom*】

來無影，去無蹤。 It comes without a shadow and leaves without a trace. 【吳承恩《西遊記・第八十一回》Wu Cheng'en: Chapter 81, *Journey to the West*】

來也匆匆，去也沖沖。Come in a rush, and go with a flush. 【俗語 Common saying】

前腳剛走，後腳又到。One arrives when the other has just left. 【諺語 Proverb】

悄悄的我走了，正如我悄悄的來，我揮一揮衣袖，不帶走一片雲彩。Quietly, I leave, just as quietly, I came. I flicked my sleeve, without taking away a wisp of cloud with me. 【徐志摩〈再別康橋〉Xu Zhimo: "Farewell to Cambridge"】

輕輕的我走了，正如我輕輕的來。我輕輕的招手，作別西天的雲彩。Softly, I leave, just as softly, I came. I softly waved my hands, bidding farewell to the rosy clouds in the western sky. 【徐志摩〈再別康橋〉Xu Zhimo: "Farewell to Cambridge"】

請神容易送神難。Calling up an evil spirit is easy but sending it away is difficult. 【俗語 Common saying】

去者日以疏，來者日以親。What has gone has become distant day by day, and what is yet to come is becoming close day by day. 【佚名《古詩十九首》Anonymous: *Nineteen Ancient Poems*】

時來則來，時往則往。When it's time for you to come, come; when it's time for you to go, go. 【揚雄《法言‧問明》Yang Xiong: "Consult for Clarification", *Exemplary Figures*】

水裏來，湯裏去。Money comes and goes. 【李寶嘉《文明小史‧第五十三回》Li Baojia: Chapter 53, *A Short History of Civilization*】

他來我去，他去我來。When he comes, I'll go. When he goes, I'll come. 【俗語 Common saying】

小的不去，大的不來。Venture a small fish to catch a great one. 【俗語 Common saying】

招之即來，揮之即去。Come when being summoned and go at the wave of one's hand. 【蘇軾〈王忠儀真贊序〉Su Shi: "Preface to a Portrait of Wang Zhongyi"】

Company

伴君如伴虎。Companying a king is like living with a tiger. 【佚名《說呼全傳‧第四回》Anonymous: Chapter 4, *A History of the Shuo Family*】

跟好人，學好人。If you keep a company of good people, you will learn to become a good person. 【諺語 Proverb】

近朱者赤，近墨者黑。If you lie down with dogs, you get up with fleas. 【傅玄〈太子少傅箴〉Fu Xuan: "Motto of the Prince's Tutor"】

立身成敗，在於所染。The success or failure of one's position hinges on the environment one surrounds with.【魏徵〈十漸不克終疏〉Wei Zheng:"Ten Warnings to Changes Taking Place"】

兩人成伴，三人不歡。Two is company, three is a crowd.【俗語 Common saying】

陪太子讀書 —— 沒戲了。Companying the prince to study–hopeless.【歇後語 End-clipper】

親賢人，遠小人。Be close to worthy men and keep away from petty men.【諸葛亮〈前出師表〉Zhuge Liang:"Former Chu Shi Biao"】

染於蒼則蒼，染於黃則黃。Dyed in dark green, silk becomes dark green; dyed in yellow, silk becomes yellow.【墨翟《墨子‧所染卷三》Mo Di: Chapter 3, "Colored by the Environment," *Mozi*】

人伴賢良志轉高。In the company of virtuous and able men, one becomes intelligent.【俗語 Common saying】

捨命陪君子。Keep somebody company at all costs.【老舍《正紅旗下》Lao She: *Under the Red Banner*】

Comparison

比空不空，比忙不忙。Compared with the idle, I'm not idle; compared with the busy, I'm not busy.【俗語 Common saying】

比山還高，比海還深。Higher than mountains and deeper than seas.【俗語 Common saying】

比上不足，比下有餘。Worse off than the best but better off than the worst.【張華〈鷦鷯賦〉Zhang Hua:"Song of Wood Wren"】

比月還潔，比日還光。Whiter than the moon and brighter than the sun.【俗語 Common saying】

蝙蝠不自見，笑他梁上燕。The bat does not see its own ugliness but laughs at the swallow nesting on the beam.【佚名〈玉泉子〉Anonymous:"Master Jade Sources"】

冰炭不同爐。Ice and charcoal cannot be placed in the same furnace.【韓非《韓非子‧顯學第五十》Han Fei: Chapter 50, "Eminence in Learning", *Hanfeizi*】

不比不知道，一比嚇一跳。If one does not compare, one is in the dark. Once one compares, one gets a start.【俗語 Common saying】

不怕不識貨，就怕貨比貨。Don't worry about goods being not appreciated, they will come out well when compared to other goods.【俗語 Common saying】

不怕低，祇怕比。 Not worry about the low price, but about making comparisons. 【俗語 Common saying】

不可同日而語。 Cannot be mentioned in the same breath. 【劉向《戰國策·趙策二》Liu Xiang:"Strategies of the State of Zhao", No. 2, *Strategies of the Warring States*】

此山不如那山青。 This mountain is not as green as that mountain. 【俗語 Common saying】

東方不亮西方亮，黑了南方有北方。 When it is dark in the east, there is light in the west; when things get dark in the south, there is still light in the north. 【毛澤東〈中國革命戰爭的戰略問題〉Mao Zedong:"Problems of Strategy in China's Revolutionary War"】

好漢手下有好漢，英雄背後有英雄。 In this world, brave men have braver one. Behind heroes, there are people who are more heroic. 【吳浚《飛龍全傳·第四十一回》Wu Jun: Chapter 41, *The Story of the Flying Dragon*】

老鴉罵豬黑。 The pot calls the kettle black. 【克非《春潮急·第四二回》Ke Fei: Chapter 42, *Spring Tide Comes Rapidly*】

沒有最好，祇有更好。 The best has gotten better. 【馬銀春《沒有最好只有更好》Ma Yinchun: *The Best Has Gotten Better*】

莫道君行早，更有早行人。 Do not say that you start early, for there are people earlier than you.thrown away. 【釋道原《景德傳燈錄·卷二十二》Shi Daoyuan: Chapter 22, *The Jingde Record of the Transmission of the Lamp*】

強中更有強中手。 Among the capable people, there could be people who are more capable than others. 【羅貫中《三國演義·第十七回》Luo Guanzhong: Chapter 17, *Romance of the Three Kingdoms*】

人比人得死，貨比貨得扔。 When compared with others, some who are not so good would feel too shamed to live; when compared with other goods, some goods are of poor quality should be thrown away. 【俗語 Common saying】

人比人，氣死人。 Comparison is odious. 【俗語 Common saying】

人前莫說人長短，始信人中更有人。 Do not comment on the strong or weak points of others in public for there are always people who are better. 【俗語 Common saying】

人外有人，天外有天。 There are always people with better abilities as there are heavens beyond heavens. 【諺語 Proverb】

山外青山樓外樓，更有能人在後頭。 There are mountains beyond mountains, towers beyond towers, and capable persons behind capable persons. 【諺語 Proverb】

山外青山天外天，更有能人在後邊。 There are mountains

beyond mountains, heavens beyond heavens, and capable persons behind capable persons. 【諺語 Proverb】

山外有山，天外有天。 There are mountains beyond mountains, and heavens beyond heavens. 【諺語 Proverb】

鐵罐莫說鍋粘灰，鯽魚莫說鯉駝背。 A pot must not call a kettle black. 【諺語 Proverb】

萬事不怕比，一比心裏明。 Everything can be compared for it is through comparison that one can get a better understanding. 【俗語 Common saying】

五十步笑百步。 The pot calls the kettle black. 【孟軻《孟子·梁惠王上》Meng Ke: Chapter 1, Part 1, *Mencius*】

相比之下，方見其長。 Gain by contrast. 【俗語 Common saying】

小巫見大巫。 Pale in comparison. 【陳琳〈答張紘書〉Chen Lin: "A Letter in Reply to Zhang Xuan"】

一代不如一代。 Each generation is worse than the preceding one. 【王君玉《國老談苑·第二卷》Wang Junyu: Chapter 2, *Chitchat of Retired Minister*】

一年不如一年。 Each year is worse than the preceding one. 【俗語 Common saying】

一蟹不如一蟹。 Each one is worse than the preceding one. 【蘇軾〈艾子雜說〉Su Shi: "Remarks by Ai Zi"】

Competition

百花齊放，百家爭鳴。 Let a hundred flowers blossom and a hundred schools of thought contend. 【毛澤東〈關於正確處理人民內部矛盾的問題〉Mao Zedong: "On the Correct Handling on Contradictions among the People"】

不能望其項背。 One falls far behind that cannot see the neck and back of the one in front. 【汪琬〈與周處士書〉Wang Wan: "A Letter to Zhou Hongrang"】

不在人前，不落人後。 One is neither ahead of others nor lag behind them. 【俗語 Common saying】

不爭一日之短長。 Not seeking for a temporary superiority. 【俗語 Common saying】

鬥勇不如鬥智。 Competing with force is not as good as competing with wisdom. 【俗語 Common saying】

多一個香爐，多一位神道。 The more the competitors, the

keener the competition. 【俗語 Common saying】

二虎不同山。Two tigers can't stay in the same mountain. 【俗語 Common saying】

夫唯不爭，故無尤。He who does not compete with others is free from blunder. 【老子《道德經・第八章》Laozi: Chapter 8, *Daodejing*】

弗與人爭，要與天爭。Do not contend with human beings, but with heaven. 【俗語 Common saying】

既生瑜，何生亮。Since heaven has given birth to me, Zhou Yu, why heaven still gave birth to Zhu Geliang? 【羅貫中《三國演義・第五十七回》Luo Guanzhong: Chapter 57, *Romance of the Three Kingdoms*】

以其不爭，故天下莫能與之爭。He who does not compete with others will have no one in the world to compete with him. 【老子《道德經・第六十六章》Laozi: Chapter 66, *Daodejing*】

友誼第一，比賽第二。Friendship comes first, and competition second. 【俗語 Common saying】

走錯一粒子，輸了一盤棋。One wrong move may lose the game. 【俗語 Common saying】

Complaint

發瓮肚子氣。Pour out one's grievances. 【俗語 Common saying】

非所怨而怨。Don't complain about what you shouldn't. 【左丘明《左傳・襄公二十六年》Zuo Qiuming: "The Twenty-sixth Year of the Reign of Duke Xiang", *Zuo's Commentary on the Spring and Autumn Annals*】

怪人不知禮，知禮不怪人。One who complains about others does not know rites, and one who knows rites does not complain about others. 【諺語 Proverb】

怪人須在腹，相見又何妨。Complain about others in one's heart and it's no harm to get along with them. 【羅貫中《粉妝樓・第六十回》Luo Guanzhong: Chapter 60, *The Chamber of Powder and Rouge*】

怪張三，怨李四。Go around blaming everybody. 【彭養鷗《黑籍冤魂・第一六回》Peng Yang'ou: Chapter 16, *The Curse of Opium*】

和大怨，必有餘怨。When great resentment is settled, there will surely be lingering resentment. 【老子《道德經・第七十九章》Laozi: Chapter 79, *Daodejing*】

拉不出屎來怨茅房。One complains about the toilet when he failed to empty his bowels. 【老舍〈龍鬚溝・一幕〉Lao She: Scene 1, "The Dragon-beard Ditch"】

臉醜怪不着鏡子。One who has an ugly face should not complain about the mirror.【袁靜、孔厥《新兒女英雄傳·第七回》Yuan Ting and Kong Jue: Chapter 7, *New Biography of Heroes and Heroines*】

明哲保身，但求無過。Be worldly wise and play safe and avoid blame.【毛澤東〈反對自由主義〉Mao Zedong: "Against Liberalism"】

人平不語，水平不流。A peaceful person does not complain and still water does not flow.【釋普濟《五燈會元·卷十八》Shi Puji: Chapter 18, *A Compendium of the Five Lamps*】

上不怨天，下不尤人。Neither complain against heaven nor blame the people.【《禮記·中庸·第三十一章》Chapter 31, "Doctrine of the Mean", *The Book of Rites*】

我不怨別人，別人誰怨我。If you do not complain about others, who will complain about you?【俗語 Common saying】

有冤伸冤，有苦訴苦。Redress the wrong when you are wronged, and speak out your suffering when you are made to suffer.【俗語 Common saying】【周立波《暴風驟雨·第一部·十二》Zhou Libo: Volume 1, Chapter 12, *The Hurricane*】

怨人者窮，怨天者無志。He who complains against others is at the end of his tether; he who complains against heaven has no aspirations.【荀況《荀子·榮辱第四》Xun Kuang: Chapter 4, "Honour and Disgrace", *Xunzi*】

怨在不捨小過，患在不預定謀。Complaints arise when small faults are not forgiven; troubles arise when a consistent strategy is not prepared in advance.【黃石公《素書·安禮》Huang Shigong: "Securing Rites", *Book of Plain Truths*】

怨之所聚，亂之本也。The accumulation of resentment is the cause of disorder.【左丘明《左傳·成公十六年》Zuo Qiuming: "The Sixteenth year of the Reign of Duke Cheng", *Zuo's Commentary on the Spring and Autumn Annals*】

在邦無怨，在家無怨。Have no grumbles against you in the country and have no grumbles against you in the family.【孔子《論語·顏淵篇第十二》Confucius: Chapter 12, *The Analects of Confucius*】

張三怪李四，李四怪張三。Blame each other.【俗語 Common saying】

自知者不怨人，知命者不怨天。Those who know themselves do not blame others and those who know their fate do not blame heaven.【荀況《荀子·榮辱第四》Xun Kuang: Chapter 4, "Honour and Disgrace", *Xunzi*】

Composure

横不是，竖不是。 Feel out of place. 【曹雪芹《紅樓夢‧第四十四回》Cao Xueqin: Chapter 44, *A Dream of the Red Chamber*】

任憑風浪起，穩坐釣魚船。 Sit tight in the fishing boat despite the rising wind and waves. 【毛澤東〈在中國共產黨第八屆中央委員會第二次全體會議上的講話四〉Mao Zedong:"Fourth Address at the Second Plenum of the Eighth Chinese Communist Party Central Committee"】

身居虎穴，從容鎮定。 Remain composed even when one is in the enemy's lair. 【俗語 Common saying】

Concubine

情願做空中一隻鳥，勿願做房中一個小。 Rather be a bird in the sky than a concubine in the house. 【諺語 Proverb】

若要家不和，娶位小老婆。 If one wants to spoil the harmony at home, the best way is to take a concubine. 【俗語 Common saying】

挑柴賣草，不給人家做小。 Working hard is better than being a concubine. 【諺語 Proverb】

錫鐵當不了銀，小老婆算不了人。 Tin cannot be regarded as silver and a concubine is not regarded as a human being. 【諺語 Proverb】

一女獲寵，全家富貴。 If a girl became a favourite concubine, her family naturally rose in status and enjoyed great wealth and luxury. 【俗語 Common saying】

有錢切莫娶後婚，一個牀上兩條心。 Do not take a second wife even though you are rich, otherwise your partner will be heartbroken. 【諺語 Proverb】

Connection

一環扣一環。 Things are closely linked. 【諺語 Proverb】

一環折，全鏈斷。 When one link is broken, the whole chain is broken. 【諺語 Proverb】

Contempt

不放在眼裏。Look down on somebody.【曹雪芹《紅樓夢‧第六十九回》Cao Xueqin: Chapter 69, *A Dream of the Red Chamber*】

狗眼看人低。To look down on a person.【俗語 Common saying】

人必自輕而後人輕之，人必自重而後人重之。Respect yourself and others will respect you.【諺語 Proverb】

眼睛生在額角上。To look down on a person.【俗語 Common saying】

眼睛生在頭頂上 —— 目中無人。With one's eyes at the top of his head – treat others with contempt.【歇後語 End-clipper】

眼珠裏沒人。Being a snob.【俗語 Common saying】

在上位，不陵下。When you are in a high position, do not treat your inferiors with contempt.【《禮記‧中庸第十四章》Chapter 14, "Doctrine of the Mean", *The Book of Rites*】

祇要自家上進，那怕人家看輕。As long as you desire to do better, you need not worry that others look down on you.【諺語 Proverb】

Contentment

大廈千間，不過身眠七尺。There might be thousands of buildings, yet what one needs is no more than a space of seven feet to sleep in.【石玉崑《三俠五義‧第七回》Shi : Chapter 7, *The Three Heroes and Five Gallants*】

禍莫大於不知足。There is no greater disaster than discontent.【老子《道德經‧第四十六章》Laozi: Chapter 46, *Daodejing*】

人心不知足，有得五穀想六穀。Man is never content. When he has five kinds of grain, he wants to have six.【諺語 Proverb】

人心不足，得隴望蜀。Man never feels satisfied and desires for more.【范曄《後漢書‧岑彭傳》Fan Ye:"Biography of Cen Peng", *History of the Later Han*】

人心不足蛇吞象。A person whose heart is not content is like a snake trying to swallow an elephant.【佚名《山海經‧海內南經》Anonymous: "Classic of Regions Within the Seas: South", *The Classic of Mountains and Seas*】

知足不辱，知止不殆。He who knows he is contented will not be humiliated; he who knows when to stop will not be in danger.【老子《道德經‧第四十四章》Laozi: Chapter 44, *Daodejing*】

知足常足，終身不辱。If one knows what is enough, he is always contented, and will not be disgraced in his whole life. 【《增廣賢文》Words that Open up One's Mind and Enhance One's Wisdom】

知足心常樂，能忍身自安。A person who is contented is always happy and a person who is tolerant is always calm. 【俗語 Common saying】

知足者不可以勢利誘也。He who is contented with what he has cannot be lured by power or benefits. 【劉安《淮南子・詮言訓第十四》Liu An: Chapter 16, "An Explanatory Discourse", Huainanzi】

知足者，不以利自累也。He who is contented with what he has does not hurt himself for benefits. 【莊周《莊子・雜篇・讓王第二十八》Zhuang Zhou: Chapter 28, "Abdicating Kingship", "Miscellaneous Chapters", Zhuangzi】

知足者常樂。A person who is contented is always happy. 【老子《道德經・第四十六章》Laozi: Chapter 46, Daodejing】

知足者富，強行者有志。One who is contented with what one has is with wealth, and one who works hard has one's aspirations. 【老子《道德經・第三十三章》Laozi: Chapter 33, Daodejing】

知足之足，常足矣。The contentment of feeling contented is an eternal contentment. 【老子《道德經・第四十六章》Laozi: Chapter 46, Daodejing】

Control

不怕官，祇怕管。One is not afraid of officials but one's immediate superior. 【施耐庵《水滸傳・第二十八回》Shi Nai'an: Chapter 28, Outlaws of the Marshes】

大缸擲骰子 —— 沒跑兒。Dice casts in a vat – cannot get out of trouble. 【歇後語 End-clipper】

端他碗，服他管。If one depends on somebody for livelihood, one has to listen to him. 【俗語 Common saying】

斧頭吃鑿子，鑿子吃木頭。There is always one thing to conquer another. 【俗語 Common saying】

官無三日緊。The government exercises a strict control but it never lasts long. 【羅貫中《平妖傳・第十四回》Luo Guanzhong: Chapter 14, Taming Devils】

呼之則來，揮之則去。Have somebody at one's beck and call. 【蘇軾〈王仲儀真贊序〉Su Shi: "Preface to a Poem Praising Wang Zhongyi"】

既在矮檐下，不得不低頭。Being under low eaves, one has to lower one's head.【吳承恩《西遊記・第二十八回》Wu Cheng'en: Chapter 28, *Journey to the West*】

沒籠頭的馬。A horse without a halter is in freedom.【曹雪芹《紅樓夢・第八回》Cao Xueqin: Chapter 8, *A Dream of the Red Chamber*】

木偶跳舞 —— 幕後操縱。When puppets dance, strings are pulled by others behind the scenes.【歇後語 End-clipper】

人欲役人，必先役己。People who want to control others should first control themselves.【諺語 Proverb】

孫悟空跳不出如來佛的掌心。Even the clever and capable one is unable to escape from another person's control even.【吳承恩《西遊記・第七回》Wu Cheng'en: Chapter 7, *Journey to the West*】

天下之至柔，馳騁天下之至堅。The softest in the world can freely control over the hardest in the world.【老子《道德經・第四十三章》Laozi: Chapter 43, *Daodejing*】

天要下雨，娘要嫁人。There is no way to stop heaven from raining or one's mother from remarrying.【俗語 Common saying】

先發制人，後發制於人。He who takes the action first controls others; he who takes the action later is being controlled by others.【班固《漢書・項籍傳》Ban Gu:"Biography of Xiang Ji", *The Book of Han*】

一手遮天，一手蓋地。Cover up all the truth and take control of everything like covering the sky with one hand and the earth with another.【孔厥，袁靜《新兒女英雄傳・第十回》Kong Jue and Yuan Jing: Chapter 10, *New Biographies of Heroes and Heroines*】

隻手不能遮天。One hand cannot cover the sky.【俗語 Common saying】

Cost

羊毛出在羊身上。Whatever is given is paid for.【俗語 Common saying】

Country

苟利國家生死以，豈因禍福避趨之。If it benefits my country, I would sacrifice my life, and I would not dodge it due to fortune or misfortune. 【林則徐〈赴戍登程口占示家人〉Lin Zexu: "To My Family Members before Boarding at Chengkuo to Shu"】

國必自伐，然後人伐之。 If you do not treasure your own country and destroy it, others will destroy your country after you. 【孟軻《孟子・離婁上》Meng Ke: Chapter 4, Part 1, *Mencius*】

國不務大，而務得民心。 A country does not have to be large, but it has to win the heart of the people. 【戴德《大戴禮記・保傅》Dai De: "Preceptors and Masters", *Records of Rites by Dai the Elder*】

國富民安，國強民歡。 When a country is rich, people enjoy peace. When a country is strong, people are happy. 【俗語 Common saying】

國家將興，必有禎祥。國家將亡，必有妖孽。 When a country is about to rise, there must be propitious signs; when a country is about to fall, there must be abnormalities. 【《禮記・中庸第三十一章》Chapter 31, "Doctrine of the Mean", *The Book of Rites*】

國家興亡，匹夫有責。 Everybody is responsible for the rise and fall of their country. 【顧炎武《日知錄・卷十三》Gu Yanwu: Chapter 13, *Records of Daily Knowledge*】

國將不國，何以為家。 When a country will no longer be a country, what should people rely on to have their homes? 【俗語 Common saying】

國將興，聽於民；國將亡，聽於神。 When a country is about to rise, people's cheers will be heard. When a country is about to fall, it depends on gods. 【左丘明《左傳・莊公三十二年》Zuo Qiuming: "The Thirty-second Year of the Reign of Duke Zhuang", *Zuo's Commentary on the Spring and Autumn Annals*】

國無怨民曰強國。 A country without dissatisfied people is a strong country. 【商鞅《商君書・去強》Shang Yang: "Removing the Strong", *The Book of Lord Shang*】

國一日不可無君，家一日不可無主。 A country cannot do without a leader even for a day and a family cannot do without a head even for a day. 【施耐庵《水滸傳・第六十回》Shi Nai'an: Chapter 60, *Outlaws of the Marshes*】

國以民為本，民以食為天。 A country takes the people as its base and people take food as their heaven. 【司馬遷《史記・酈生陸賈列傳》Sima Qian: "Biographies of Li Yiji and Lu Gu", *Records of the Grand Historian*】

國以民為基，貴以賤為本。 A country takes the people as its foundation and the noble take the humble as their base. 【王符《潛夫論・救邊》Wang Fu: "Rescuing the Frontiers", *Critical Essays of Qianfu*】

南北一家，兄弟一堂。 People all over the country are of the same family and together like brothers under the same roof. 【俗語 Common saying】

溥天之下，莫非王土。 All the land under heaven is without exception the king's land. 【《詩經‧小雅‧北山》 "The Northern Hills", "Minor Odes of the Kingdom", *The Book of Odes*】

親仁善鄰，國之寶也。 Be close to benevolent people and kind to neighbouring states, these are the precious qualities of a country. 【左丘明《左傳‧隱公六年》 Zuo Qiuming: "The Sixth Year of the Reign of Duke Yin", *Zuo's Commentary on the Spring and Autumn Annals*】

全國一盤棋。 Coordinate all the activities of the country as in a game of chess. 【鄧小平〈前十年為後十年做好準備〉 Deng Xiaoping: "The Last Ten Years is a Good Preparation for the Coming Ten Years"】

山圍故國周遭在，潮打空城寂寞回。 The old country surrounded by hills are still here, and the waves that lash at the empty city recede with loneliness. 【劉禹錫〈石頭城〉 Liu Yuxi: "Stony Town"】

商女不知亡國恨，隔江猶唱後庭花。 The singsong girls did not know the sadness of losing the country, and still sang the Backyard Flowers on the other side of the river. 【杜牧〈泊秦淮〉 Du Mu: "Mooring at Qinhuai River"】

身貴自由，國貴自主。 The individual values freedom and the state values autonomy. 【嚴復《原強》 Yan Fu: *On Strength*】

四十年來家國，三千里地山河。 A reign of forty years with a land of over three thousand miles. 【李煜〈破陣子〉 Li Yu: "To the Tune of Breaking the Ranks"】

四萬萬人齊下淚，天涯何處是神州。 All the four hundred million people shed their tears because the country is broken and it no longer exists in the world. 【譚嗣同〈有感一章〉 Tan Sitong: "A Poem to Express My Feelings"】

天下之本在國，國之本在家，家之本在身。 The basis of the world is the state, the state, the family, the family, the individuals. 【孟軻《孟子‧離婁上》 Meng Ke: Chapter 4, Part 1, *Mencius*】

危邦不入，亂邦不居。 One neither enters a state which is in critical situation, nor dwell in a state which is in disorder. 【孔子《論語‧泰伯篇第八》 Confucius: Chapter 8, *The Analects of Confucius*】

小樓昨夜又東風，故國不堪回首月明中。 Last night, the east wind blew past my little tower and beneath the bright moon, I can't bear to think back on my old kingdom. 【李煜〈虞美人〉 Li Yu: "To the Tune of the Beauty of Yu"】

一心中國夢，萬古下泉詩。 We have longed to see a reunified

China, as this is reflected in the ancient ode Xiaquan. 【鄭思肖〈德祐二年歲旦二首〉Zheng Sixiao:"Two Poems Written on the First Day of the Second Year of the Reign of Deyou"】

憂勞可以興國，逸豫可以亡身，自然之理也。 Worries and toil can lead to the rise of a country, whereas ease and complacency may lead to one's doom. These are natural principles. 【歐陽修〈五代史‧伶官傳序〉Ouyang Xiu:"Preface to the Biographies of Musicians and Performers", *History of the Five Dynasties*】

周雖舊邦，其命維新。 Although Zhou was an ancient state, it had a reform mission. 【《詩經‧小雅‧文王》"King of Wen", "Minor Odes of the Kingdom", *The Book of Odes*】

Covering-up

狐狸尾巴 —— 藏不住。 A fox cannot hide its tail. 【歇後語 End-clipper】【楊炫之《洛陽伽藍記》Yang Xuanzhi: *The Story of Arāma in Luoyang*】

麻有袋裏藏不住錐子。 A gunny sack cannot hide a pointed pricker. 【諺語 Proverb】

麻臉姑娘愛擦粉，癩痢娘娘好戴花。 A girl with a pockmarked face like powering her face and a woman with favus on her head likes wearing flowers. 【俗語 Common saying】

窮瞞不住，富遮不住。 Poverty cannot be concealed and wealth cannot be covered up. 【諺語 Proverb】

窮遮不得，醜瞞不得。 Poverty cannot be concealed and an ugly face cannot be covered up. 【諺語 Proverb】

Criticism

挨罵的不低，罵人的不高。 The abused is not degraded, the abuser, not upgraded. 【諺語 Proverb】

打擊別人，抬高自己。 Attack others to build up oneself. 【俗語 Common saying】

對着和尚罵禿賊。 Curse baldheads before a monk. 【魯迅《彷徨‧肥皂》Lu Xun:"Soap", *Wandering*】

非我而當者，吾師也；是我而當者，吾友也；諂諛我者，吾賊也。 He who criticizes me correctly is my teacher, he who praises me correctly is my friend, but he who insidiously flatters me is my foe. 【荀況《荀

子・修身第二》Xun Kuang: Chapter 2, "Cultivating the Person", *Xunzi*】

橫眉冷對千夫指，俯首甘為孺子牛。I never succumb to the enemy, but I am willing to serve my people like an ox bowing its head.【魯迅〈自嘲〉Lu Xun: "Self-mockery"】

冷一句，熱一句。Make cold and biting remarks.【俗語 Common saying】

美服人指，美珠人估。Fine clothes are much criticized and beautiful pearls are much commented on.【張居正《張太岳文集》Zhang Juzheng: *Collected Works of Zhang Juzheng*】

批判從嚴，處理從寬。Be strict in criticism and lenient in punishment.【俗語 Common saying】

批評必須當前，閒談莫論人非。When you criticize a person, do it in his face, and when you chat, don't speak ill of others behind their backs.【金纓〈格言聯璧〉Jin Ying: "Couplets of Maxims"】

人之生，不幸不聞過，大不幸無恥。In one's lifetime, what is unfortunate is not to hear criticisms, and what is most unfortunate is not to have shame.【周敦頤《通書・幸》Zhou Dunyi: "Fortune", *Comprehending The Book of Changes*】

問誰毀之，小人譽之。If you asked who discredits you? It is those petty people who flatter and compliment you.【孔子《論語・衛靈公篇第十五》Confucius: Chapter 15, *The Analects of Confucius*】

小罵大幫忙。Criticize in a small way but help in a big way.【俗語 Common saying】

Cunningness

吃人不吐骨。Bloodsucking.【端木蕻良《曹雪芹・第二十七章》Duanmu Hongliang: Chapter 27, *Cao Xueqin*】

大奸似忠，大詐似信。A man who is very cunning looks faithful, and a man who is very crafty looks honest.【《明史・卷一六四・黃澤傳》Chapter 164, *The History of Ming*】

呆裏奸，直裏彎。A person may seem to be foolish, but is actually crafty. He may seem to be honest, but is actually wicked.【佚名〈漁樵記・二折〉Anonymous: Scene 2, "Records of a Fisherman and Woodcutter"】

機關算盡太聰明，反誤了卿卿性命。All your clever calculations and intrigues have brought you nothing but your doom.【曹雪芹《紅樓夢・第五回》Cao Xueqin: Chapter 5, *A Dream of the Red Chamber*】

巧言令色，鮮矣仁。 It is rare that a person with cunning words and ingratiating countenance to be benevolent.【孔子《論語·學而篇第一》Confucius: Chapter 1, *The Analects of Confucius*】

巧詐不如拙誠。 To be cunning and deceitful is not as good as to be clumsy but honest.【韓非《韓非子·說林上第二十二》Han Fei: Chapter 22, "On Forests", Part 1, *Hanfeizi*】

越奸越狡越貧窮，奸狡原來天不容。 The more cunning and crafty you are, the poorer you will be; for cunningness and craftiness will never be sanctioned by heaven.【佚名《名賢集》Anonymous: *Collected Sayings of Famous Sages*】

Custom

百里不同風，千里不同俗。 There are different manners and different customs in different places.【應劭《風俗通義序》Ying Shao: *Comprehensive Meaning of Customs and Mores*】

各處各鄉俗，一處一規矩。 Every place and village have their own customs. Each unit has its own rules.【諺語 Proverb】

離家三里遠，別是一鄉風。 Go three miles from home and you find different habits and customs.【吳承恩《西遊記·第十五回》Wu Cheng'en: Chapter 15, *Journey to the West*】

入國問禁，入鄉問俗。 When you enter a country, enquire for the taboos; when you cross a boundary, ask about the customs.【《禮記·曲禮上第一》Chapter 1, "Summary of the Rules of Propriety", Part 1, *The Book of Rites*】

入鄉隨谷，出水隨灣。 Do in Rome as the Romans do.【諺語 Proverb】

十里不同風，百里不同俗。 There are different manners within ten miles and different customs within a hundred miles.【俗語 Common saying】

十里不同俗。 Ten miles apart, but the customs are rather different.【諺語 Proverb】

鄉下獅子鄉下舞。 Lion dance in the country should be performed only in the country.【俗語 Common saying】

一鄉一俗，一灣一曲。 Each village has its own customs and each river has its own bends.【諺語 Proverb】

Danger

前門拒虎，後門進狼。 Drive the tiger way from the front door and let a wolf in at the back. 【李贄《史綱評要・周紀》Li Zhi: "Chronicle of the Zhou Dynasty", *Highlights of History with Critical Comments*】

前門拒狼，後門防虎。 Guard against the tiger at the back door while repelling the wolf at the front gate. 【諺語 Proverb】

前門拒狼，後門進虎。 Let the tiger in through the back door while repelling the wolf through the front gate. 【諺語 Proverb】

前門驅狼，後門防虎。 Rebuff the tiger at the back door while repelling the wolf at the front gate. 【諺語 Proverb】

前門驅狼，後門拒虎。 Drive the wolf out of the front gate and prevent the tiger from entering through the back door. 【諺語 Proverb】

前門走狼，後門進虎。 The wolf has left by the front door, but the tiger has entered through the back door. 【諺語 Proverb】

螳螂捕蟬，黃雀在後。 The mantis stalks the cicada but it is unaware of the oriole behind. 【莊周《莊子・外篇・山木第二十》Zhuang Zhou: Chapter 20, "The Mountain Tree", "Outer Chapters", *Zhuangzi*】

剃頭刀擦屁股 —— 懸得乎。Clean the buttocks with a barber's knife – dangerous enough. 【歇後語 End-clipper】

烏龜吃巴豆 —— 不知死活。 A tortoise eating croton oil seeds – unaware of the death ahead. 【歇後語 End-clipper】

一縷之任繫千鈞之量。 A hair bearing the weight of one thousand catties. 【班固《漢書・枚乘傳》Ban Gu: "Biography of Mei Cheng", *History of the Han*】

一鳥知險，合羣得驚。 When a bird detects danger, the entire flock gets the warning. 【俗語 Common saying】

Daughter

嫁出去的女兒，潑出去的水。 A married daughter is like poured-out water. 【俗語 Common saying】

女兒是娘的掛心鈎。 A daughter is always on her mother's mind. 【俗語 Common saying】

生個女兒賠賤貨。 The birth of a daughter means the loss of money. 【俗語 Common saying】

生女猶得嫁比鄰，生男埋沒隨百草。 If you bear a girl, she can still marry to a neighbour. If you bear a boy, he will lie unburied in the battlefield among the weeds. 【杜甫〈兵車行〉Du Fu: "Song of War Chariots"】

瘦女兒，胖媳婦。A slim daughter becomes a plump wife after marriage. 【陸人龍《三刻拍案驚奇·第四卷》Lu Renlong: Chapter 4, *Amazing Tales, Volume Three*】

無兒女也貴。Without a son, a daughter is valued as well. 【俗語 Common saying】

養女不教如養豬，養兒不教如養驢。To raise a daughter up without disciplining her is like raising a pig; to raise a son up without disciplining him is like raising a donkey. 【《增廣賢文》Words that Open up One's Mind and Enhance One's Wisdom】

Day and night

長夜茫茫無盡期。The night drags on without end. 【諺語 Proverb】

從此無心愛良夜，任他明月下西樓。From then on, I will not care for a good night, and let the bright moon fall behind the West Tower. 【李益〈寫情〉Li Yi: "A Sketch of My Feelings"】

過一天，算一天。Muddle through days with no thoughts of tomorrow. 【俗語 Common saying】

哄了一日是兩晌。Cheat to muddle through days. 【蘭陵笑笑生《金瓶梅·第三十一回》Lanling Xiaoxiaosheng: Chapter 31, *The Plum in the Golden Vase*】

今日不為，明日亡貨。昔之日已往而不來矣。If you don't work hard today, you will run out of money tomorrow. Time passed, gone are gone. 【管仲《管子·乘馬第五》Guan Zhong: Chapter 5, "On Military Taxes", *Guanzi*】

明日復明日，明日何其多。One today is worth two tomorrows. 【錢鶴灘〈明日歌〉Qian Hetan: "Song of Tomorrow"】

日有短長，月有死生。There are short and long days while there are full and curved moons. 【孫武《孫子兵法·虛實第六》Sun Wu: Chapter 6, "The Void and Substance", *The Art of War by Sunzi*】

世人苦被明日累，春去秋來老將至。People are bitterly misled by tomorrow; spring gone, autumn come, and old age is around. 【錢鶴灘〈明日歌〉Qian Hetan: "Song of Tomorrow"】

我生待明日，萬事成蹉跎。If I wait for tomorrow all my life, all things will be delayed. 【錢鶴灘〈明日歌〉Qian Hetan: "Song of Tomorrow"】

棄我去者，昨日之日不可留。
亂我心者，今日之日多煩憂。
Things in the past did not stay,
I was deserted and left alone by
time passing, yet today gives me
so much trouble and anxiety.
【李白〈宣州謝朓樓餞別校書叔雲〉
Li Bai:"Farewell to Uncle Yun, The Imperical Librarian, at Xie Tiao's Tower in Xuanzhou"】

夜長人自起，星月滿空江。The
night is long, and as I wake
up, the stars and moon fill the
vacant river.【李益〈水宿聞雁〉Li
Yi:"Lodging on a River and Hearing the
Wild Geese"】

Death

不生不死，不死不生。No birth,
no death; no death, no birth.
【莊周《莊子・內篇・大宗師第六》：
Zhuang Zhou: Chapter 6, "The Great
Ancestral Teacher", "Inner Chapters",
Zhuangzi】

不是你死，便是我活。Either of
us dies.【俗語 Common saying】

不是魚死，就是網破。Either the
fish dies or the net is broken.【諺
語 Proverb】

春蠶到死絲方盡，蠟炬成灰淚始
乾。The silkworm spins silk
until it dies and a candle dries
its tears until it turns to ashes.
【李商隱〈無題〉Li Shangyin:"Untitled
Poem"】

冬天的大葱 —— 葉黃根枯心不
死。One is reconciled and died
without closing one's eyes.【歇後
語 End-clipper】

爾今死去儂收葬，未卜儂身何日
喪。Now you are dead and I
come to bury you, and nobody
can tell when I will die.【曹雪芹
《紅樓夢・第二十七回》Cao Xueqin:
Chapter 27, *A Dream of the Red Chamber*】

粉身碎骨，在所不惜。One
does not flinch even if one is
threatened with destruction.【俗
語 Common saying】

飛蛾撲火 —— 自取滅亡。A moth
flying into the flame is seeking
for its own death.【歇後語 End-
clipper】【姚思廉《梁書・到漑傳》Yao
Silian:"Biography of Dao Gai", The *Book
of Liang*】

服毒又上吊 —— 死定了。Taking
poison and hanging oneself–
sure to die.【歇後語 End-clipper】

古來雖有死，好在不先知。
Though death has been with us
from of old, what is good is that
we don't know it in advance.【袁
枚〈栽樹自嘲〉Yuan Mei:"Self-Mockery
When Planting Trees"】

棺材店裏咬牙 —— 恨人不死。
One grits one's teeth in a coffin
shop, cursing on all who are not
dying.【歇後語 End-clipper】

棺材裏的生意 —— 賺死人的錢。
Doing business in a coffin is
making money out of the dead –
trying to make money by all
possible means. 【歇後語 End-
clipper】

棺材裏伸手 —— 死要錢。
Stretching out one's hand from a
coffin is greedy for money even
after death. 【歇後語 End-clipper】

棺材裏伸頭 —— 死不要臉。
Poking out one's head out of a
coffin is dead to all feelings of
shame. 【歇後語 End-clipper】

棺材上畫老虎 —— 嚇死人。
Painting a tiger on a coffin to
frighten the dead – to frighten
the dead only. 【歇後語 End-clipper】

棺材頭上放砲 —— 嚇死人。
Exploding firecrackers on a
coffin to frighten the dead –
nobody will be frightened. 【歇後
語 End-clipper】

好死不如賴活着。 A living dog is
better than a death lion. 【俗語
Common saying】

耗子舔貓鼻子 —— 找死。 A
mouse licking a cat's nose is
courting its own death. 【歇後語
End-clipper】

黃泉路上無老少。 Death regards
no ages. 【俗語 Common saying】

可憐無定河邊骨，猶是春閨夢裏
人。 Pity the scattered bones
along the River Wuding, for
these dead soldiers are still in
the dreams of their wives far
away. 【陳陶〈隴西行〉Chen Tao: :
"Song of Longxi"】

老肥豬上屠場 —— 挨刀的貨。
An old pig entering a
slaughterhouse – ready to die.
【歇後語 End-clipper】

兩眼朝了天。 Kick the bucket. 【俗
語 Common saying】

馬上摔死英雄漢，河中淹死會水
人。 Heroes who are good at
riding often die by falling off the
horse; good swimmers are often
drowned. 【諺語 Proverb】

貓舔虎鼻梁 —— 找死。 A cat
licking a tiger's nose is to seek
for death. 【歇後語 End-clipper】

哪裏黃土不埋人。 It is
unnecessary to be over-clingged
to your hometown, it does not
matter where your death will
be. 【俗語 Common saying】

寧可站着死，決不跪着生。 Would
rather die than surrender. 【俗語
Common saying】

儂今葬花人笑痴，他年葬儂知是
誰？ Now I bury flowers and
people laugh at my folly, but
who knows who will bury me
in the future? 【曹雪芹《紅樓夢・第
二十七回》Cao Xueqin: Chapter 27, *A
Dream of the Red Chamber*】

千夫所指，無疾而死。 When a
thousand people point their
accusing fingers at a person,
he will die even though he is
not ill. 【班固《漢書・王嘉傳》Ban

Gu:"Biography of Wang Jia", *History of the Han*】

強梁者不得其死。 Those who are violent will be in a bad death. 【老子《道德經・第四十二章》Laozi: Chapter 42, *Daodejing*】

秋後的螞蚱 —— 蹦躂不了幾天 Like a locust in late autumn, they live short. 【歇後語 End-clipper】

求生不得，求死不能。 One can neither live nor die. 【李伯元《文明小史・第三十七回》Li Boyuan: Chapter 37, *A Short History of Civilization*】

人不知死，車不知翻。 A person does not know death till it comes as a car does not know what it is up to until it overturns. 【俗語 Common saying】

人固有一死，死有重於泰山，或輕於鴻毛。 All people die, but their death varies depending on their values. 【司馬遷〈報任安書〉Sima Qian:"A Letter in Reply to Ren An"】

人叫人死人不死，天叫人死人才死。 A person will not die if somebody orders him to die, but a person will die if Heaven orders him to die. 【西周生《醒世姻緣傳・第七十五回》Xi Zhousheng: Chapter 75, *Stories of Marriage to Awaken the World*】

人生百年，終歸一死。 Everyone will eventually die. 【沈復《浮生六記・卷三》Shen Fu: Chapter 3, *Six Chapters of a Floating Life*】

人生自古誰無死，留取丹心照汗青。 Ever since time immemorial, men die eventually. Let me leave a loyal heart to shine in the pages of history. 【文天祥〈過零丁洋〉Wen Tianxiang:"Crossing the Lingding Ocean"】

人死不記仇。 When a person dies, others' wrongs are forgotten. 【俗語 Common saying】

人死不能復生。 The dead cannot be brought to life again. 【俗語 Common saying】

人死如燈滅。 Death is like a lamp being put out. 【俗語 Common saying】

人死萬事休。 Death ends everything. 【俗語 Common saying】

人要人死天不肯，天要人死有何難。 If a person wants another person to die, Heaven can disagree. If Heaven wants a person to die, it has no difficulties. 【郭小亭《濟公全傳・上卷》Guo Xiaoting: Part 1, *A Full Biography of Jigong*】

人之將死，其言也善。 When a person is about to die, his words are kind. 【孔子《論語・泰伯篇第八》Confucius: Chapter 8, *The Analects of Confucius*】

人之所惡莫甚於死。 What is most disliked by people is death. 【孟軻《孟子・告子章句上》Meng Ke: Chapter 6, Part 1, *Mencius*】

三寸氣在千般用，一旦無常萬事休。 There are many matters to look forward when one is alive, but once one is dead, all things are finished. 【諺語 Proverb】

善泅者死於水，善戰者死於兵。 Good swimmers eventually are drowned and good fighters are killed at battles. 【劉安《淮南子‧原道訓第一》Liu An: Chapter 1, "Searching Out the Way", *Huainanzi*】

捨死不怕禍。 A person who does not fear death will not be afraid of disasters. 【俗語 Common saying】

視死若生者，烈士之勇也。 To regard death as life is the courage of a martyr. 【莊周《莊子‧外篇‧秋水第十七》：Zhuang Zhou: Chapter 17, "Autumn Floods", "Outer Chapters", *Zhuangzi*】

壽星老兒上吊 —— 活膩了。 A long-living old chap hanging himself – asking for trouble. 【歇後語 End-clipper】

順之者昌，逆之者亡。 Those who submit to me will flourish, and those who are against me will perish. 【司馬遷《史記‧太史公自序》Sima Qian: "Author's Preface", *Records of the Grand Historian*】

死不死，活不活。 One can neither live nor die. 【曹雪芹《紅樓夢‧第六十八回》Cao Xueqin: Chapter 68, *A Dream of the Red Chamber*】

死而不義，非勇也。 One whose death is not with morality is not bravery. 【左丘明《左傳‧文公二年》Zuo Qiuming: "The Second year of the Reign of Duke Wen", *Zuo's Commentary on the Spring and Autumn Annals*】

死而後已，不亦遠乎。 Only with death does the road come to an end. Isn't that long? 【孔子《論語‧泰伯篇第八》Confucius: Chapter 8, *The Analects of Confucius*】

死生有命，富貴由天。 Life is fated and fortunes destined. 【孔子《論語‧顏淵篇第十二》Confucius: Chapter 12, *The Analects of Confucius*】

死生有命，禍福在天。 Life is fated, misfortunes destined. 【俗語 Common saying】

死無葬身之地。 Die without a place to be buried. 【王世貞《鳴鳳記‧寫本》Wang Shizhen: "Hand-written Copy", *Records of a Phoenix's Cry*】

死有重於泰山，有輕於鴻毛。 The meaning of death varies depending on one's own values. 【司馬遷〈報任安書〉Sima Qian: "A Letter in Response to Ren An"】

兔死狐悲，物傷其類。 The fox mourns over the death of the hare; like mourns over the death of fellows. 【羅貫中《三國演義‧第八十九回》Luo Guanzhong: Chapter 89, *Romance of the Three Kingdoms*】

為國而死，雖死猶榮。 Dying for one's country is a glorious death. 【俗語 Common saying】

我自橫刀向天笑，去留肝膽兩崑崙。 I smiled towards the sky in the execution ground, though it comes to death, the spirit will stay like Mount Kunlun.【譚嗣同〈絕命詩〉Tan Sitong:"Poem before Death"】

烏龜吃巴豆 —— 不知死活。A tortoise eating croton–getting into trouble.【歇後語 End-clipper】

武大郎服毒 —— 吃也死，不吃也死。Wu Dalang's dose of poison – sure to die without retreatment.【歇後語 End-clipper】

昔人已乘黃鶴去，此地空餘黃鶴樓。The immortal has flown away on a yellow crane, and only Yellow Crane Tower remained.【崔顥〈黃鶴樓〉Cui Hao:"Yellow Crane Tower"】

昔日戲言身後意，今朝都到眼前來。Once in the past we joked about what it would be after we die, but now it has all come true to me.【元稹〈遣悲懷〉Yuen Zhen:"Giving Vent to Sorrow"】

閻王下帖子 —— 真要命。Like the King of Hell dispatching invitation cards – be really terrible.【歇後語 End-clipper】

閻王爺叫你三更死，誰留人到五更。The King of Hell decide the death without any dealays.【諺語 Proverb】【曹雪芹《紅樓夢‧第十六回》Cao Xueqin: Chapter 16, A Dream of the Red Chamber】

一朝春盡紅顏老，花落人亡兩不知。One day spring will go and beauty will fade; flowers will fall and people will die without knowing it.【曹雪芹《紅樓夢‧第二十七回》Cao Xueqin: Chapter 27, A Dream of the Red Chamber】

一人拼命，萬夫莫當。Nobody can stop a person who works desperately.【羅貫中《粉妝樓‧第二十二回》Luo Guanzhong: Chapter 22, The Chamber of Powder and Rouge】

一日無常萬事休。Death ends everything.【諺語 Proverb】《大般涅槃經‧卷一》"Volume 1", Mahāparinirvāṇa Sūtra】

一雙空手見閻王。Everyone goes and sees the King of Hell with their hands empty.【張南莊《何典‧第三卷》Zhang Nanzhuang: Chapter 3, From Which Classic】

一死以謝天下。To kill oneself to alleviate the anger of the people.【俗語 Common saying】

與其忍辱生，不如光榮死。Better dying in glory than living in shame.【諺語 Proverb】

死無大事。Nothing is dreadful to a person who is willing to die.【諺語 Proverb】

Debt

不怕該債的精窮，祇怕討債的英雄。No matter how poor the debtor is, only the great creditor who is hard to handle matters.

【諺語 Proverb】【吳敬梓《儒林外史·第五十二回》Wu Jingzi: Chapter 52, *An Unofficial History of the Scholars*】

負債容易清債難。 Owing a debt is easy, but clearing it is difficult. 【俗語 Common saying】

好賬不如無。 Debts under no pressure of repayment are not as good as having no debts. 【俗語 Common saying】

好借好還，再借不難。 If one returns what one has borrowed on time, it will not be difficult for one to borrow again. 【吳承恩《西遊記·第十六回》Wu Cheng'en: Chapter 16, *Journey to the West*】

好借債，窮得快。 One who likes borrowing money becomes poor soon. 【俗語 Common saying】

還錢常記借錢時。 When you pay your debts, always think of how kind the creditor is. 【佚名《名賢集》Anonymous: *Collected Sayings of Famous Sages*】

還債一身輕。 When the debts are paid, one feels relaxed. 【俗語 Common saying】

借債還債，窟窿還在。 To incur debt in order to repay another debt, it never comes to an end. 【諺語 Proverb】【李綠園《歧路燈·第三十回》Li Yuyuan: Chapter 30, *Lamp on a Forked Road*】

借債還債，一時寬泰。 To pay debts with borrowed money, you feel relieved for but a short time. 【諺語 Proverb】【范寅《越諺·卷上》Fan Yin: Part 1, *Proverbs of the State of Yue*】

借債要忍，還債要狠。 Try not to borrow money, but be resolved to pay your debts. 【諺語 Proverb】【李綠園《歧路燈·第三十回》Li Yuyuan: Chapter 30, *Lamp on a Forked Road*】

冷怕起風，窮怕欠債。 When feeling cold, one is afraid of winds and when one is poor, he is afraid of debts. 【諺語 Proverb】

沒有不用還的債。 There is no such debt that one need not to pay. 【俗語 Common saying】

寧少閻王債，莫欠小鬼錢。 Better not deal with troublesome people. 【諺語 Proverb】

前欠未清，免開尊口。 Do not ask to borrow money again before you pay off your old debts. 【諺語 Proverb】

前賬未清，後賬又來。 While the old debts are still outstanding, new debts have incurred. 【諺語 Proverb】

欠錢怨財主。 Debtor blames the creditor. 【俗語 Common saying】

欠債要清，許願要還。 A debt needs to be cleared, and a promise has to be kept. 【諺語 Proverb】

人窮窮在債，天冷冷在風。 Poverty lies with debts and feeling cold lies with wind. 【諺語 Proverb】

人窮思舊債。 When a person is poor, he remembers the old debts others owed him. 【俗語 Common saying】【李涵秋《近十年目睹之怪現狀·第一回》Li Hanqiu: Chapter 1, *Bizarre Happenings Eyewitnessed Over the Last Ten Years*】

人死萬債休。 Death pays all debts. 【俗語 Common saying】

人死債爛。 Death pays all debts. 【俗語 Common saying】

人死賬不死。 A person dies, but his debts do not die. 【諺語 Proverb】

忍嘴不欠債。 Try your best to avoid debts. 【諺語 Proverb】

虱多不癢，債多不愁。 When lice are all over one, one does not feel itchy. When one has lots of debts, one stops worrying. 【諺語 Proverb】

無債一身輕。 One feels relieved when one is out of debt. 【俗語 Common saying】

血債要用血來還。 An eye for an eye. 【諺語 Proverb】

與其欠錢，不如賣田。 One would rather sell his land than owing a debt. 【譚嗣同〈報貝元微書〉Tan Sitong: "A Letter in Reply to Friend Bei"】

債多了不愁。 When there are too many debts, one stops worrying. 【蔡東藩《民國通俗演義·第十一回》Cai Dongfan and Xu Qinfu: Chapter 11, *Popular Romance of the Republican Period*】

Decision

打錯了算盤。 Make a wrong decision. 【俗語 Common saying】

當斷不斷，終受其亂。 One who is indecisive will suffer from one's indecision in the end. 【司馬遷《史記·春申君列傳》Sima Qian: "Biographies of Lord Chunshen", *Records of the Grand Historian*】

弈者舉棋不定，不勝其耦。 If a chess player is unsure where to place the game pieces, he will not prevail over his rival. 【左丘明《左傳·襄公二十五年》Zuo Qiuming: "The Twenty-fifth Year of the Reign of Duke Xiang", *Zuo's Commentary on the Spring and Autumn Annals*】

謀事在人，成事在天。 Man proposes, heaven disposes. 【羅貫中《三國演義·第一百零三回》Luo Guanzhong: Chapter 103, *Romance of the Three Kingdoms*】

丫鬟帶鑰匙 —— 當家不作主。 Manage with no power. 【歇後語 End-clipper】

魚，我所欲也。熊掌，亦我所欲也。二者不可得兼，捨魚而取熊掌者也。 I like fish and the bear's paw. But if I cannot have both of them, I will forgo fish and take the bear's paw. 【孟軻《孟子‧告子章句上》Meng Ke: Chapter 6, Part 1, *Mencius*】

Degree

比山還高，比海還深。 Higher than mountains and deeper than seas. 【俗語 Common saying】

有過之而無不及。 It is higher rather than lower than standard. 【孔子《論語‧先進篇第十一》Confucius: Chapter 11, *The Analects of Confucius*】

Desire

見素抱樸，少私寡慾。 Stay simple and unadorned, curb selfishness and desires. 【老子《道德經‧第十九章》Laozi: Chapter 19, *Daodejing*】

騎着驢騾思駿馬。 When riding on a donkey or a mule, one feels unsatisfied and thinks of a steed. 【吳承恩《西遊記‧第一回》Wu Cheng'en: Chapter 1, *Journey to the West*】

千金難買心頭好。 Money cannot buy what one loves. 【俗語 Common saying】

人心難滿，欲壑難填。 It is difficult to satisfy the heart of a person as it is difficult to fill up the gully of desires. 【諺語 Proverb】

人欲可斷，天理可循。 Men's desires can be curbed as the rules of the nature can be followed. 【佚名《名賢集》Anonymous: *Collected Sayings of Famous Sages*】

生亦我所欲也，義亦我所欲也，二者不可得兼，捨生而取義者也。 Life is what I want; righteousness is also what I want. If I cannot have both, I would give up my life to accomplish righteousness. 【孟軻《孟子‧告子章句上》Meng Ke: Chapter 6, Part 1, *Mencius*】

養心莫善於寡欲。 In nourishing one's mind, there is nothing better than having few desires. 【孟軻《孟子‧盡心章句上》Meng Ke: Chapter 7, Part 1, *Mencius*】

一人難稱百人意。 You cannot please everyone. 【諺語 Proverb】

一人難如千人意。 You cannot please everyone. 【俗語 Common saying】

一鞋難合千雙腳。 You cannot please everyone. 【俗語 Common saying】

欲致魚者先通水，欲致鳥者先樹木。 If you want to have fish, you need to lead water in first; if you want to have birds, you need to plant trees first.【劉安《淮南子・說林訓第十六》Liu An: Chapter 16, "Discourse on Mountains", *Huainanzi*】

Destiny

不是一家人，不進一家門。 A married woman always has the same character as her husband's family.【諺語 Proverb】

不是冤家不聚頭。 Enemies are destined to meet each other.【鄭廷玉《楚昭公・第二折》Zheng Yanyu: Scene 2, "Duke Zhao of Chu"】

打入十八層地獄。 Shut somebody in the eighteenth hell.【俗語 Common saying】

但是詩人多薄命，就中淪落不過君。 Most poets had a sorry fate, but none of them fell as down-and-out as you.【白居易〈李白墓〉Bai Juyi: "Tomb of Li Bai"】

好醜命生成。 Fortunes and misfortunes are destined.【俗語 Common saying】

盡人事，聽天命。 Do one's best and leave all else to destiny.【李汝珍《鏡花緣・第六回》Li Ruzhen: Chapter 6, *Flowers in the Mirror*】

郎中醫病，不能醫命。 A medical doctor can cure your disease but not your fate.【俗語 Common saying】

命該井裏死，河裏淹不煞。 One who is destined to die in the well cannot be drowned in a river.【劉江《太行風雲・第四十二回》Liu Jiang: Chapter 42, *Changes in Taixing*】

命裏八尺，難得一丈。 If one is destined to have only eight feet, one cannot get ten.【姜樹茂《漁港之春・第四章》Jiang Shumao: Chapter 4, *Spring in a Fishing Port*】

命裏有時終須有，命裏無時求也無。 What is meant for you never passes; what is not destined for you never stays.【蘭陵笑笑生《金瓶梅・第十四回》Lanling Xiaoxiaosheng: Chapter 14, *The Plum in the Golden Vase*】

莫非命也，順受其正。 As everything is destined, we should submissively take destiny in a positive way.【孟軻《孟子・盡心章句上》Meng Ke: Chapter 7, Part 1, *Mencius*】

人各有緣份。 Fortune is pre-destined.【俗語 Common saying】

生有時，死有時。 Birth and death are predetermined.【俗語 Common saying】

同船過渡，皆是有緣。 Passengers on the same boat to cross a river

are linked by fate. 【諺語 Proverb】
【石玉崑《小五義·第二十四回》Shi
Yukun: Chapter 24, *The Five Younger
Gallants*】

同呼吸，共命運。 Share the same
breath and the same fate. 【俗語
Common saying】

同人不同命，同傘不同柄。
Different people have different
fates as different umbrellas have
different handles. 【諺語 Proverb】
【歐陽山《三家巷·第一回》Ouyang
Shan: Chapter 1, *Three-family Lane*】

萬般皆是命，半點不由人。
Everything is destined and
nothing can be changed. 【俗語
Common saying】【馮夢龍《警世通言·
第十七卷》Feng Menglong: Chapter 17,
Stories to Caution the World】

萬事不由人作主，一心難與命爭
衡。 People cannot decide on
anything for it is difficult to rival
with destiny which arranges
everything for them. 【羅貫中
《三國演義·第一百零三回》Luo
Guanzhong: Chapter 103, *Romance of the
Three Kingdoms*】

萬事分已定，浮生空自忙。 All
things are determined by fate,
so what people strive for in their
lives is simply useless. 【《增廣賢
文》*Words that Open up One's Mind and
Enhance One's Wisdom*】

無奇不成書，無緣不相逢。 A
book cannot be written without
strange happenings; a meeting
will not take place without

predestination. 【俗語 Common
saying】

無緣錯過，有緣遇上。 Without
a predestined relationship,
people miss each other at an
arm's length; with a predestined
relationship, people meet
unexpectedly. 【俗語 Common
saying】

相好命好，命好相好。 With a
good appearance, one is sure
to have a good fate; with a good
fate, one is sure to have a good
appearance. 【俗語 Common saying】
【董說《西遊補·第十三回》Dong
Shuo: Chapter 13, *A Supplement to
Journey to the West*】

一命二運三風水，四積陰德五
讀書。 Fate first, luck second,
geomancy third, virtue fourth,
and education fifth. 【俗語
Common saying】

一條船上的人。 People in the
same boat. 【俗語 Common saying】

一飲一啄，莫非前定。 Every life
is pre-destined. 【俗語 Common
saying】

有緣千里來相會，無緣對面不
相逢。 With fate, people will
come to meet from a thousand
miles away; without fate, though
people face each other, they
never meet. 【施耐庵《水滸傳·第
三十五回》Shi Nai'an: Chapter 35,
Outlaws of the Marshes】

知命者不怨天，知己者不怨人。
He who knows his fate does not
resent heaven; he who knows

himself does not resent others. 【劉安《淮南子・繆稱訓第十》Liu An: Chapter 10, On Erroneous Designations, *Huainanzi*】

自古書生多薄命。 From of old, scholars have shared a sorry fate. 【俗語 Common saying】

Destruction

一個臭螺螄，搞壞一鍋湯。 One rotten apple soils the barrel. 【俗語 Common saying】

Determination

不到黃河心不死。 One will never give up until everything is over. 【李寶嘉《官場現形記・第十七回》Li Baojia: Chapter 17, *Officialdom Unmasked*】

不怕路難，就怕志短。 A tough life is not to be feared, but a weak mind is. 【諺語 Proverb】

赴湯蹈火，在所不辭。 Come hell or high water. 【諺語 Proverb】

橫下一條心。 Be determined to do something. 【俗語 Common saying】

君子貞而不諒。 A gentleman is determined for righteousness but not stubborn. 【孔子《論語・衞靈公篇第十五》Confucius: Chapter 15, *The Analects of Confucius*】

明知山有虎，偏向虎山行。 One knows perfectly well that there are tigers in the mountain, and yet one is all the more determined to go deep into the mountain. 【諺語 Proverb】【紀昀《閱微草堂筆記》Ji Yun: *Jottings from the Thatched Hut for Reading the Subtleties*】

大變不足畏，祖宗不足法，人言不足恤。 The changes in waether need not to be feared, the ancestors' rules need not to follow, and people's comment need not to be worried about. 【脫脫等《宋史・王安石傳》Toktoghan, et al:"Biography of Wang Anshi", *History of the Song*】

天下無難事，只怕有心人。 Nothing is impossible to a willing mind. 【王驥德〈韓夫人題紅記〉Wang Jide:"A Poem Inscribed by Mrs Han on a Red Leaf"】

心堅石也穿。 With determination, you can succeed in anything. 【諺語 Proverb】【封特卿《離別難》Feng Teqing:"Parting Is Hard"】

一人倒下，萬人起來。 When one falls, thousands more will rise. 【俗語 Common saying】

有志者，事竟成。 A person with determination will succeed in everything. 【范曄《後漢書·耿弇傳》Fan Ye:"Biography of Di He", *History of the Later Han*】

Difference

不分青紅皂白。 Unable to tell the difference between black and white. 【《詩經·大雅·桑柔》"Soft Leaves of the Mulberry Tree", "Greater Odes of the Kingdom", *The Book of Odes*】

不可以道里計。 The differences are beyond measure. 【章炳麟〈東京留學生歡迎會演説辭〉Zhang Binglin:"Speech at the Welcoming Party for Chinese Students Studying in Tokyo"】

道不同，不相為謀。 Birds of different feathers do not flock together. 【孔子《論語·衛靈公篇第十五》Confucius: Chapter 15, *The Analects of Confucius*】

風馬牛不相及。 As different as chalk and cheese. 【左丘明《左傳·僖公四年》Zuo Qiuming:"The Fourth Year of the Reign of Duke Xi", *Zuo's Commentary on the Spring and Autumn Annals*】

木沒一樣木，人沒一樣人。 No trees are identical, so are people. 【俗語 Common saying】

求大同，存小異。 Seeking for the common ground on the major issues while accepting differences on the minor ones. 【諺語 Proverb】

失之毫釐，差之千里。 A little error leads to a large discrepancy. 【戴德《大戴禮記·保傅》Dai De:"Preceptors and Masters", *Records of Rites by Dai the Elder*】

一個在天上，一個在地下。 As different as chalk and cheese. 【俗語 Common saying】【周而復《上海的早晨·第三部·第二十一章》Zhou Erfu: Chapter 21, Volume 3, *Morning in Shanghai*】

一龍九種，種種各別。 A dragon has nine varieties of offspring, each variety is different from the other. 【俗語 Common saying】【曹雪芹《紅樓夢·第九回》Cao Xueqin: Chapter 9, *A Dream of the Red Chamber*】

指頭伸出有長短。 Everyone has his own strengths and weaknesses. 【俗語 Common saying】

Difficulty

處處碰釘子。 One meets with difficulties whatever one does. 【俗語 Common saying】

大有大的難處。 The great have difficulties of their own. 【曹雪芹《紅樓夢·第六回》Cao Xueqin: Chapter 6, *A Dream of the Red Chamber*】

大有大難，小有小難。 The great have their great difficulties, and the small, their small difficulties. 【諺語 Proverb】

刀快不怕脖子粗。 With good qualities and power, one can get over any challenges. 【俗語 Common saying】【劉江《太行風雲·第二十一回》Liu Jiang: Chapter 21, *Changes in Taixing*】

凍豆腐 —— 難辦（拌）。 Frozen bean curd is hard to be mixed with anything else – hard to deal with matters. 【歇後語 End-clipper】

趕鴨子上樹 —— 難上難。 Driving a duck up a tree – extremely difficult. 【歇後語 End-clipper】

鋼鐵怕火煉，困難怕志堅。 Iron fears the fire; difficulties fear a strong will. 【諺語 Proverb】

見困難就上，見榮譽就讓。 One should take the difficult matters for oneself and leave glory and honour to others. 【諺語 Proverb】

見難不救，枉為人也。 A person who does not save others in danger is not much of a human. 【諺語 Proverb】

看事容易做事難。 A matter may look easy but difficult to do. 【諺語 Proverb】

困難留給自己，方便讓給別人。 Difficulties for oneself but conveniences for others. 【諺語 Proverb】

難者不會，會者不難。 Things are difficult for those who don't know how to handle, but easy for those who know. 【王濬卿《冷眼觀·第十二回》Wang Junqing: Chapter 12, *Casting a Cold Eye*】

窮當益堅，老當益壯。 When in a difficult situation, one should stand firmly. When one gets old, he should be even stronger in aspiration. 【范曄《後漢書·馬援傳》Fan Ye: "Biography of Ma Huan", *History of the Later Han*】

三尖瓦絆倒人。 A small piece of tile can make a person stumble. 【諺語 Proverb】【李綠園《歧路燈·第五十八回》Li Luyuan: Chapter 58, *Lamp on a Forked Road*】

天下無難事，祇怕有心人。 Nothing is impossible to a strong mind. 【俗語 Common saying】【曹雪芹《紅樓夢·第四十九回》Cao Xueqin: Chapter 49, *A Dream of the Red Chamber*】

圖難於其易，為大於其細。 To overcome hardship, one should begin with the easy one; to accomplish what is lofty, one should begin with the small.

【老子《道德經‧第六十三章》Laozi: Chapter 63, *Daodejing*】

雄關漫道真如鐵，而今邁步從頭越。 Mount Luo is as strong as iron and roads are long, we the soldiers are walking across them with big steps. 【毛澤東〈憶秦娥‧婁山關〉Mao Zedong: "Passing Mount Luo", *Recalling Qin Maiden*】

一方困難，八方支援。 When one place is in trouble, assistance comes from all sides. 【《中國青年報‧又一曲共產主義的凱歌》(1960 年 2 月 28 日) "Another Song of Triumph for Communist", *China Youth Daily* (28 February 1960)】

知困然後能自強。 Only when one feels puzzled about certain knowledges, he will encourage himself to go further. 【《禮記‧學記第十八》Chapter 18, "Records on the Subject of Education", *The Book of Rites*】

Diligence

勤而不儉，枉費其勤。 If a man is industrious but not frugal, being industrious is meaningless. 【諺語 Proverb】

勤奮為成功之母。 Diligence is the mother of success. 【諺語 Proverb】

勤勞出碩果。 Diligence brings about fruitful results. 【俗語 Common saying】

勤力可以不貧，謹身可以避禍。 Diligence can save one from poverty and prudence can dodge disasters. 【賈思勰《齊民要術》Jia Sixie: *Important Ways to Unite the People*】

勤能補拙，儉以養廉。 Diligence makes up for one's dullness; frugality nourishes honesty. 【邵雍〈弄筆吟〉Shao Yong: "Playing with the Writing Brush"】

勤勤懇懇，埋頭苦幹。 Diligent and hardworking. 【諺語 Proverb】

勤勤懇懇，一絲不苟。 Work diligently and conscientiously and with the greatest care. 【諺語 Proverb】【司馬遷〈報任少卿書〉Sima Qian: "A Letter in Reply to Ren Shaoqing"】

勤是搖錢樹，儉是聚寶盆。 Diligence is fortune's right hand, and frugality her left. 【諺語 Proverb】

勤有功，嬉無益。 Diligence does one good while indolence brings no good. 【王應麟《三字經》Wang Yinglin: *Three-character Classic*】

人勤地不懶。 If the tiller is diligent, the farmland will become fertile. 【諺語 Proverb】

人勤地生寶，人懶地生草。 If people are diligent, the land produces treasures; if people are lazy, the land produces weeds. 【諺語 Proverb】

書山有路勤為徑，學海無邊苦作舟。 There is no royal road to learning. 【韓愈《古今賢文・勸學篇》 Han Yu:"Exhortation to Study", *Good Writings of the Past and Present*】

惟天地之無窮兮，哀人生之長勤。 Thinking of the vastness of heaven and earth, bemoaning the long travail in one's life. 【屈原《離騷・遠遊》Qu Yuan:"Travelling Far", *The Sorrows at Parting*】

要人知重勤學，怕人知事莫做。 If you want to be famous, you must study hard; if you do not want to be known for bad behaviour, do not do it. 【馮夢龍《警世通言・第三十三卷》Feng Menglong: Chapter 33, *Stories to Caution the World*】

一生之計在於勤。 The most decisive thing for life is diligence. 【《增廣賢文》*Words that Open up One's Mind and Enhance One's Wisdom*】

Diplomacy

凡交，近則必相靡以信，遠則必忠之以言。 Intercourse among close friends should be with trust and keep our promise with distant friends. 【莊周《莊子・內篇・人間世第四》Zhuang Zhou: Chapter 4, "Human World", "Inner Chapters", *Zhuangzi*】

兩國相爭，不斬來使。 Messengers should not be killed when two countries are at war.

【羅貫中《三國演義・第四十五回》Luo Guanzhong: Chapter 45, *Romance of the Three Kingdoms*】

召遠在修近，閉禍在除怨。 To win distant friends relies on keeping a good relationship with your neighbours; to avoid disasters relies on getting rid of animosity. 【管仲《管子・版法第七》Guan Zhong: Chapter 7, "Tablets Inscribed with Standards", *Guanzi*】

Disaster

禍不入慎家之門。 A prudent person avoids all disasters. 【諺語 Proverb】

禍從天降，災向地生。 Misfortune happens all of a sudden. 【施耐庵《水滸傳・第四十五回》Shi Nai'an: Chapter 45, *Outlaws of the Marshes*】

禍到臨頭才念佛。 One starts praying only when disaster is imminent. 【俗語 Common saying】 【老舍《大地龍蛇・第一幕》Lao She: Act 1, *Dragons and Snakes of the Great Earth*】

禍到臨頭後悔遲。 When disaster is imminent, it is too late to repent. 【李開先《林沖寶劍記．第五十齣》Li Kaixian: Scene 50, "The Story of Lin Chong's Sword"】

禍來如山倒，禍去如抽絲。 Mischiefs come by the pound and go away by the ounce. 【諺語 Proverb】

禍由自取，非命非系。 Misfortune is something man brings upon himeself and is not necessarily determined by fate. 【諺語 Proverb】

去民之患，如除腹心之疾。 To remove the calamities of the people is like taking away an illness of the heart. 【蘇轍〈上神宗皇帝書〉Su Che: "A Memorial to Emperor Shengzong"】

天大旱，人大乾。 Fight the big drought with redoubled energy. 【俗語 Common saying】

圖一時之苟安，貽百年之大患。 A moment's easiness can bring a century of calamities. 【俗語 Common saying】

災來如山倒，災去如抽絲。 Disasters come quickly and go away slowly. 【俗語 Common saying】【曹雪芹《紅樓夢．第五十二回》Cao Xueqin: Chapter 52, *A Dream of the Red Chamber*】

Distance

不積跬步，無以至千里。 Without the accumulation of short steps, it is impossible to travel a thousand miles. 【荀況《荀子．勸學第一》Xun Kuang: Chapter 1, Exhortation to Learning, *Xunzi*】

近若咫尺，遠若山河。 We are close by a distance of one foot, yet we seem to be separated far apart like hills and rivers. 【俗語 Common saying】【劉義慶《世說新語．傷逝》Liu I-ching: Chapter 17, "Grieving for the Departed", *A New Account of the Tales of the World*】

十萬八千里。 Poles apart. 【釋道原《景德傳燈錄．卷十三》Shi Daoyuan: Chapter 13, *Records of the Transmission of the Lamp in the Jingde Period*】

Doctor

急驚風偏遇慢郎中。 When one has something urgent to do, one meets with a person of slow action. 【凌濛初《二刻拍案驚奇．第三十三卷》Ling Mengchu: Chapter 33, *Amazing Tales, Volume Two*】

久病成良醫。 Prolonged illness makes a patient a good doctor. 【俗語 Common saying】

良醫不自醫。 Good doctors do not treat themselves. 【俗語 Common

saying】【李夢陽〈梅山先生墓志銘〉Li Mengyang:"The Epitaph of Mei Shan"】

三折肱，為良醫。 He who has broken his arm three times makes a good surgeon. 【左丘明《左傳・定公十三年》Zuo Qiuming:"The Thirteenth Year of the Reign of Duke Ding", *Zuo's Commentary on the Spring and Autumn Annals*】

少年木匠老郎中。 Carpenters should be young and doctors old. 【諺語 Proverb】【胡祖德《滬諺・卷上》Hu Zhude: Part 1, *Shanghainese Proverbs*】

醫病要找病根兒，打魚要看浪花兒。 To cure a patient, you must find out the cause of his illness; to catch fish, you must pay attention to the condition of the waves. 【俗語 Common saying】

醫不叩門，有請才行。 A doctor does not visit patients; he comes only upon invitation. 【俗語 Common saying】

醫得病，醫不得命。 A person's disease can be cured, but not his mentality. 【諺語 Proverb】【李漁《蜃中樓・第二十二回》Li Yu: Chapter 22, *The Building in Mirage*】

醫得身，醫不得心。 The body can be cured, but mentality cannot be cured. 【諺語 Proverb】

醫者父母心。 Doctors have kind hearts towards their patients like parents towards their children. 【諺語 Proverb】

庸醫殺人不用刀。 A charlatan doctor can kill a person without using a scalpel. 【諺語 Proverb】

自做郎中無藥醫。 A doctor cannot cure his own diseases. 【諺語 Proverb】

Dog

狗不嫌家貧。 Dogs show no aversion to poor families. 【諺語 Proverb】【《增廣賢文》Words that Open up One's Mind and Enhance One's Wisdom】

狗不以善吠為良，人不以善言為賢。 We don't regard dogs good in barking as good dogs and people who are eloquent as virtuous people. 【莊周《莊子・雜篇・徐無鬼第二十四》Zhuang Zhou: Chapter 24, "Ghostless Xu", "Miscellaneous Chapters", *Zhuangzi*】

狗吃屎，狼吃人。 Dogs eat turds, wolves eat people. 【俚語 Slang】

狗急也要跳牆。 A dog in desperation will leap on to the wall. 【王重民，王慶菽，向達，周一良，啟功，曾毅公編《敦煌變文集・燕子賦》Wang Zhongmin, Wang Qingshu, Xiang Da, Zhou Yiliang, Qi Gong, Zeng Yigong, etc.:"Ode to Sparrows", *A Collection of Proses at Dunhuang*】

狗瘦主人羞。 A lean dog puts its master to shame. 【俗語 Common saying】

狗嘴裏吐不出象牙。 What do you expect from a pig but a grunt? 【臧懋循《元曲選・遇上皇・第一折》Zang Maoxun: Act 1, "Meeting the Emperor", *Anthology of Yuan Plays*】

好狗不擋道。 Great barkers are no biters. 【諺語 Proverb】

好狗抵不了狼多。 Even a brave dog cannot resist many wolves. 【俗語 Common saying】

癩狗扶不上牆。 An unpromising person cannot be made useful. 【俗語 Common saying】【曹雪芹《紅樓夢・第六十八回》Cao Xueqin: Chapter 68, *A Dream of the Red Chamber*】

猛犬不吠，吠犬不猛。 A ferocious dog does not bark, and a barking dog is not ferocious. 【俗語 Common saying】

Doing things

愛叫的鳥兒 —— 不做窩。 A bird that loves to sing does not make a nest – all talk and no action. 【歇後語 End-clipper】

不幹則已，一幹到底。 Once one starts doing something, one carries it through. 【俗語 Common saying】

不為不可成，不求不可得。 Don't do something which cannot be completed; don't seek for something which cannot be obtained. 【管仲《管子・牧民第一》 Guan Zhong: Volume 1, "Shepherding the People", *Guanzi*】

吃糧不管事。 Taking benefits without doing anything. 【俗語 Common saying】【曹雪芹《紅樓夢・第九十三回》Cao Xueqin: Chapter 93, *A Dream of the Red Chamber*】

除了死法有活法。 Besides traditional ways, there are flexible ways of doing things. 【俗語 Common saying】【張南莊《何典・第一卷》Zhang Nanzhuang: Chapter 1, *From Which Classic*】

從容幹好事，性急生岔子。 Without haste, you can do things in a nice way; if you are impetuous, you make mistakes easily. 【俗語 Common saying】

打油的錢不買醋。 One cannot spend the money exclusive for cooking oil on vinegar at the same time. 【諺語 Proverb】

耳聽千遍，不如手過一遍。 Hearing about doing something for a thousand times is not as good as doing it in person. 【諺語 Proverb】

凡事不可造次，凡人不可輕視。 Everything cannot be done rashly and everybody cannot be taken lightly. 【諺語 Proverb】

反其道而行之。 Act in a diametrically opposite way. 【司馬遷《史記・淮陰侯列傳》Sima Qian: "Biography of the Marquis of Huaiyin", *Records of the Grand Historian*】

各吹各的號，各唱各的調。 Each blows his own bugle and sings his own tune without interfering with each other. 【俗語 Common saying】

各打鑼鼓各唱戲。 Each beats their own drums and gongs and sings their own songs without interfering with each other. 【諺語 Proverb】

狗咬刺猬 —— 無處下口。 A dog tries to bite a hedgehog but does not know where to start. 【歇後語 End-clipper】

光鼓槌子 —— 打不響。 A drumstick can't make much noise without a drum. 【歇後語 End-clipper】

過猶不及，有餘猶不足也。 Going beyond the limit is as bad as falling short. 【賈誼《新書・容經》Jia Yi: "Chapter on *Rongjng*", *New Writings*】

合理可作，小利莫爭。 You can do reasonable things, but do not fight for negligible profits. 【《增廣賢文》*Words that Open up One's Mind and Enhance One's Wisdom*】

會家不忙，忙家不會。 An expert does not work in haste while a layman does. 【吳承恩《西遊記・第七十六回》Wu Cheng'en: Chapter 76, *Journey to the West*】

會者不難，難者不會。 It is not difficult for one who knows how to do something, and one who finds it difficult does not know how. 【王濬卿《冷眼觀・第十二回》Wang Junqing: Chapter 12, *Casting a Cold Eye*】

今日事，今日畢。 Never put off till tomorrow what can be done today. 【俗語 Common saying】

老鼠咬烏龜 —— 沒法下手。 A mouse tries to bite a tortoise but does not know where to start. 【歇後語 End-clipper】

兩條腿走路。 Do something in two ways. 【俗語 Common saying】【中共中央委員會，國務院〈關於教育工作的指示〉（一九五八年九月）Central Committee of the Communist Party of China, State Council: "The Instructions on Educational Work" (September 1958)】

臨淵羨魚，不如退而結網。 Rather than standing by the pond and longing for fish, one should go back and make a net. 【班固《漢書・董仲書傳》Ban Gu: "Biography of Dong Zhongshu", *History of the Han Dynasty*】

貓嘴裏挖泥鰍 —— 辦不到。 It is impossible to take a loach out of a cat's mouth. 【歇後語 End-clipper】

敏於事而慎於言。 Be diligent in work and cautious in speech. 【孔子《論語・學而篇第一》Confucius: Chapter 1, *The Analects of Confucius*】

明修棧道，暗渡陳倉。 Pretend to prepare to advance along one

path while secretly going along another. 【司馬遷《史記·高祖本紀》 Sima Qian:"Annals of Gaozu", *Records of the Grand Historian*】

摸着石頭過河。 Cross a river by feeling the stones in the water. 【俗語 Common saying】

拿衣提領，張網抓綱。 Bringing out the essential points. 【俗語 Common saying】

拿魚先拿頭，刨樹要刨根。 To catch a fish, you must grasp its head; to dig up a tree, you must dig out its roots. 【諺語 Proverb】【郭澄清《大刀記·第十章》Guo Chengqing: Chapter 10, *Story of a Big Sword*】

平生不作虧心事，半夜敲門心不驚。 A good conscience is a soft pillow 【蘭陵笑笑生《金瓶梅·第四十七回》Lanling Xiaoxiaosheng: Chapter 47, *The Plum in the Golden Vase*】

遷延因循，一事無成。 If one procrastinates, nothing will be accomplished. 【俗語 Common saying】

勸了身子，動不了心。 You can advise somebody not to do something, but you can't stop him from thinking about it. 【俗語 Common saying】

瘸子擔水 —— 一步步來。 Like a cripple carrying water – step by step. 【歇後語 End-clipper】

人多好辦事。 Many hands make light work. 【俗語 Common saying】

人有不為也，而後可以有為。 A person has to decide what to forgo so he can make accomplishments. 【孟軻《孟子·離婁上》Meng Ke: Chapter 4, Part 1, *Mencius*】

若要人不知，除非己莫為。 If you don't want anyone to find out, don't do it. 【枚乘〈上書諫吳王〉 Mei Cheng:"Submitting a Memorial to Admonish King Wu"】

少說空話，多幹實事。 Less empty talk and more practical work. 【俗語 Common saying】

生米煮成熟飯。 What is done cannot be undone. 【沈受先《三元記·遣妾》Shen Shouxian:"Sending Away My Concubine", *Winning the First Place in Three Examinations*】

事寬則完，急難成效。 If you do something calmly, you will finish it. If you do something in a hurry, you will not achieve any results. 【施耐庵《水滸傳·第六十七回》Shi Nai'an: Chapter 67, *Outlaws of the Marshes*】

事無不可對人言。 Nothing one has done cannot be told to others. 【諺語 Proverb】【脫脫等《宋史·司馬光傳》Toktoghan, *et al*:"Biography of Sima Guang", *History of the Song*】

事無大小，關心者亂。 No matter how urgent or less important the matter is, a person paying too much attention on it will mess it up. 【俗語 Common saying】

事無三不成。 Nothing can be done without countless efforts. 【俗語 Common saying】

事之難易，不在小大，務在知時。 Whether something is easy or difficult does not depend on its size, but on knowing the right time to do it. 【呂不韋《呂氏春秋·首時》Lu Buwei: "Beginning of Time", *Master Lu's Spring and Autumn Annals*】

說到那裏，做到哪裏。 Do what one says. 【俗語 Common saying】

說來容易做時難。 Easier said than done. 【俗語 Common saying】

天下之患，莫大於不知其然而然。不知其然而然者，是拱手而待亂也。 The greatest trouble of the country is no clue for the roots of disorder. 【蘇軾〈策略·第一〉Su Shi: Chapter 1, *Strategies*】

天下大事，必作於細。 Great things in the world must have small beginnings. 【老子《道德經·第六十三章》Laozi: Chapter 63, *Daodejing*】

萬事起頭難。 Everything is difficult at the beginning. 【諺語 Proverb】

為事逆之則敗，順之則成。 You fail at doing something if you oppose it; you succeed if you conform to it. 【莊周《莊子·雜篇·漁父第三十一》Zhuang Zhou: Chapter 31, "The Old Fisherman", "Miscellaneous Chapters", *Zhuangzi*】

為者常成，行者常至。 With determination, you will

succeed in doing anything. 【晏嬰《晏子春秋·內篇·雜下》Yan Ying: "Miscellaneous", Part 2, "Inner Chapters", *Master Yan's Spring and Autumn Annals*】

無為其所不為，無欲其所不欲。 Don't do what you should not do, and don't crave for what does not belong to you. 【孟軻《孟子·盡心章句上》Meng Ke: Chapter 7, Part 1, *Mencius*】

無為無所不為。 Following the laws of nature can accomplish anything. 【老子《道德經·第四十八章》Laozi: Chapter 48, *Daodejing*】

先抓西瓜，再抓芝麻。 Pick up the watermelons first and then the sesame seeds. 【俗語 Common saying】

消停作好事。 Calm and unhurried, you will make accomplishments. 【俗語 Common saying】

羞刀難入鞘。 Once it is started, go through with it. 【俗語 Common saying】

言之易，行之難。 To know is easy, but to do is difficult. 【呂不韋《呂氏春秋·不苟論》Lu Buwei: "Nothing Indecorous", *Mater Lu's Spring and Autumn Annals*】

要想人不知，除非己莫為。 If one does not want others to find out, don't do it. 【俗語 Common saying】

一不做，二不休。 Once it is started, go through with it. 【趙

元一《奉天錄·卷四》Zhao Yuanyi: Chapter 4, *Records of Fengtian*】

一步一個腳印。 One step leaves one footprint – do things in a down-to-earth manner. 【俗語 Common saying】

一人做事一人當。 One is responsible for what one has done. 【俗語 Common saying】【許仲琳《封神演義·第十二回》Xu Zhonglin: Chapter 12, *Romance of the Investiture of the Deities*】

一生依樣畫葫蘆。 All one's life, one is copying mechanically. 【陶谷〈題翰林院壁詩〉Tao Gu: "Inscribing a Poem on a Wall in the Imperial Academy"】

以其人之道，還治其人之身。 Deal with a person as he deals with one. 【朱熹《中庸集注·第十三章》Zhu Xi: Chapter 13, *Collected Annotations of the Golden Mean*】

有事覺天短，無事覺天長。 When there are things to do, one feels the day is short; when there is nothing to do, one feels the day is long. 【俗語 Common saying】

有所不為而後可以有所為。 Refrain from doing something in order to be able to achieve something else. 【孟軻《孟子·離婁下》Meng Ke: Chapter 4, Part 2, *Mencius*】

欲速則不達。 More haste, less speed. 【孔子《論語·子路篇第十七》Confucius: Chapter 13, *The Analects of Confucius*】

欲投鼠而忌器。 Throw something at a rat, but afraid to break the vase – being indecisive. 【班固《漢書·賈誼傳》Ban Gu: "Biography of Jia Yi", *History of the Han*】

早知今日，何必當初。 If I'd known then what was going to happen, I wouldn't have done it in the beginning. 【俗語 Common saying】

早知今日，悔不當初。 If I'd known better what was going to happen, I wouldn't have done it in the beginning. 【俗語 Common saying】

知其不可為而為之。 Do something even though one knows that it is impossible to succeed. 【孔子《論語·憲問篇第十四》Confucius: Chapter 14, *The Analects of Confucius*】

鐘在寺裏，聲在外邊。 The bell is in the temple but its sound is heard outside – your reputation represents your behaviours. 【俗語 Common saying】【席浪仙《石點頭·卷八》Xi Lang-xian: Chapter 8, *Nodding of Stone*】

豬往前拱，雞往後扒 —— 各有各的活路。 Everybody has his own ways of doing things. 走一步是一步。 Deal with things one step at a time. 【俗語 Common saying】

走走看看，不如親手幹幹。 Better do it yourself than standing by and watching it done. 【諺語 Proverb】

做着不避，避着不做。If you do something, don't hide it; if you want to hide it, do not do it.【諺語 Proverb】

Dragon

龍多不治水。Too many dragons won't control the flood–too many people involving in a matter will mess it up.【俗語 Common saying】

龍多旱，人多亂。Many dragons lead to a drought and many people create confusion.【諺語 Proverb】

龍生龍，鳳生鳳。Like begets like.【俗語 Common saying】

龍生龍子，虎生虎兒。A dragon bears dragon cubs and a tiger, tiger cubs–like begets like.【《增廣賢文》Words that Open up One's Mind and Enhance One's Wisdom】

寧養一條龍，不養十個熊。Would rather have one dragon than a dozen bears–one rare talents is better than dozens of mediocre people.【俗語 Common saying】

死水不藏龍。A dragon does not stay in stagnant water–talented genius do not want to be neglected.【釋普濟《五燈會元·卷十四》Shi Puji: Chapter 14, A Compendium of the Five Lamps】

一龍九種，種種各別。A dragon begets nine off-springs and each one is different.【曹雪芹《紅樓夢·第九回》Cao Xueqin: Chapter 9, A Dream of the Red Chamber】

一龍生九子，九子九個樣。A dragon begets nine off-springs and all of them are different in appearance.【俗語 Common saying】

Dream

白天做夢 —— 胡思亂想。Dreaming in the daytime–going off into wild flights of fancy.【歇後語 End-clipper】

春夢了無痕。A vernal dream vanishes without a trace.【蘇軾〈正月二十日與潘郭二生出郊尋春，忽記去年是日同至女王城作詩，乃和前韻〉Su Shi: "A Poem Written on the Twentieth Day of the First Month When I Had a Spring Outing with the Two Gentlemen Pan and Guo and Suddenly Recalling that on the Same Day Last Year, We also Arrived at the Nuwang Town and Wrote Poems, with the Same Rhymes"】

方其夢也，不知其夢也。When you are dreaming, you do not realize that you are dreaming.【莊周《莊子·內篇·齊物論第二》】

Zhuang Zhou: Chapter 2, "On the Equality of Things", "Inner Chapters", *Zhuangzi*】

飛機上做夢 —— 空想。 Dreaming on an airplane – building castles in the air. 【歇後語 End-clipper】

古今如夢，何曾夢覺，但有舊歡新怨。 The past and present are like dreams, from which nobody has ever waken, and what are left are old joys and new sorrows. 【蘇軾〈永遇樂〉Su Shi:"To the Tune of the Joy of Eternal Union"】

開了眼睛說夢話 —— 白日做夢。 Talking in one's sleep with one's eyes open – day-dreaming. 【歇後語 End-clipper】

夢福得禍，夢笑得哭。 If you get fortune in your dream, you will have misfortune. If there are laughters in your dream, you will have crying. 【凌濛初《二刻拍案驚奇‧第十九卷》Ling Mengchu: Chapter 19, *Amazing Tales, Volume Two*】

夢魂慣得無拘檢，又踏楊花過謝橋。 My soul in dreams is carefree; I tread the willow catkins to her abode. 【晏幾道《鷓鴣天》Yan Jidao:"To the Tune of Partridge in the Sky"】

夢火焚者主發財。 If one dreams of fire burning, it forecasts one's wealth. 【俗語 Common saying】【許仲元《三異筆談‧卷三》Xu Zhongyuan: Chapter 3, *Sketches of Three Strangenesses*】

夢是心頭想。 A dream is what one has in mind. 【關漢卿〈雙赴

夢‧第二折〉Guan Hanqing: Scene 2, "Both Visiting a Dream"】

南人不夢駝，北人不夢象。 Southerners do not dream of camels and northerners, elephants – you cannot imagine without getting experience from real-life. 【諺語 Proverb】

蜻蜓搖石柱 —— 妄想。 A dragonfly hoping to shake down a stone pillar is sheer fantasy. 【歇後語 End-clipper】【吳承恩《西遊記‧第四十二回》Wu Cheng'en: Chapter 42, *Journey to the West*】

日有所思，夜有所夢。 What you think in the day will be in your dream. 【俗語 Common saying】

人似秋鴻來有信，事如春夢了無痕。 People can keep a promise like wild geese that come faithfully in every autumn, and things in the past are like dreams in spring without a trace. 【蘇軾〈正月二十日與潘郭二生出郊尋春，忽記去年是日同至女王城作詩，乃和前韻〉Su Shi:"A Poem Written on the Twentieth Day of the First Month When I Had a Spring Outing with the Two Gentlemen Pan and Guo and Suddenly Recalling that on the Same Day Last Year, We also Arrived at the Nuwang Town and Wrote Poems, with the Same Rhymes"】

昔日莊周夢為蝴蝶，栩栩然蝴蝶也。 I once dreamed that I was a butterfly, a beautiful one. 【莊周《莊子‧內篇‧齊物論第二》Zhuang Zhou: Chapter 2, "On the Equality of Things", "Inner Chapters", *Zhuangzi*】

自己的夢自己圓。 Chase your dream by yourself. 【俗語 Common saying】

Duck

笨鴨子上不了架。 A clumsy duck cannot get onto a perch – one without talent cannot achieve something big. 【俗語 Common saying】【孔厥，袁靜《新兒女英雄傳·第二回》 Kong Jue and Yuan Jing: Chapter 2, *New Biographies of Heroes and Heroines*】

打鴨子上架。 Drive a duck onto a perch – forcing someone to do something beyond his capability. 【諺語 Proverb】

三斤鴨子二斤嘴 —— 多嘴多舌。 A duck of two catties has a beak of two cattie – too talkative. 【歇後語 End-clipper】

竹外桃花三兩枝，春江水暖鴨先知。 Several twigs of peach blossoms outside the bamboo fence, and the duck is the first to know when the water turns warm in early spring. 【蘇軾〈惠崇春江晚景〉 Su Shi: "Huichong's Painting of the Evening Scene of a River in Spring"】

Dwarf

矮人面前莫論侏儒。 One does not talk about midgets in front of dwarfs. 【俗語 Common saying】

矮子矮，一肚怪。 A dwarf has a bellyful of tricks. 【俗語 Common saying】

矮子多心事。 A dwarf schemes much. 【俗語 Common saying】

矮子肚裏疙瘩多。 A short person has lots of cunning ideas. 【俗語 Common saying】【沈璟〈義俠記·第十六齣〉 Shen Jing: Scene 16, "Stories of the Righteous and Gallant"】

矮子裏拔將軍 —— 矮中挑長。 Choose the tallest among the dwarfs – choosing the best among the ordinary. 【歇後語 End-clipper】【石玉崑《小五義·第五十三回》 Shi Yukun: Chapter 53, *The Five Younger Gallants*】

矮子騎高馬 —— 上下兩難。 A dwarf riding a tall horse, both suffer. 【歇後語 End-clipper】

矮子上樓梯 —— 步步登高。 A dwarf going upstairs – one has a rise in position. 【歇後語 End-clipper】

矮子坐高櫈 —— 夠不着。A dwarf trying to sit on a tall bench – one can't reach something. 【歇後語 End-clipper】

矮子坐末排看戲 —— 隨人家喝彩 A dwarf watching a play from a last-row seat applauds along with the others – one follows others' suit. 【歇後語 End-clipper】

打倒長人，矮子露臉。When a tall person is struck down, a short person will show his face – when the talented are gone, the ordinary are shown. 【茅盾《色盲》 Mao Dun:"Colour Blindness"】

當着矮子，莫說短話。Don't say the word short before a short person. 【俗語 Common saying】

Ear

百聞不如一見。To see is to believe. 【班固《漢書‧趙充國傳》 Ban Gu:"Biography of Zhao Chongguo", *History of the Han Dynasty*】

聰以知遠，明以察微。His ears were keen to perceive what is far; his eyes were sharp to observe in details. 【司馬遷《史記‧五帝本紀》Sima Qian:"Annals of the Five Emperors", *Records of the Grand Historian*】

東風吹馬耳。Like the east wind blowing at the ears of a horse - not to bat an eye. 【李白〈答王十二寒夜獨酌有懷〉Li Bai:"A Poem in Reply to Wang Shi'e – My Feelings When Angling Alone in a Cold Night"】

耳不聽，心不煩。If one refuses to hear anything, one's mind will not be disturbed. 【俗語 Common saying】【郭小亭《濟公全傳‧第六十五回》Guo Xiao-ting: Chapter 65, *The Story of Master Ji Gong*】

耳聽八方，眼觀六面。With keen ears and sharp eyes. 【孔厥，袁靜《新兒女英雄傳‧第六回》Kong Jue and Yuan Jing: Chapter 6, *New Biographies of Heroes and Heroines*】

耳聽是虛，眼見為實。Seeing is believing. 【劉向《說苑‧卷七政理》 Liu Xiang: Chapter 7, "The Principles of Government", *Garden of Persuasion*】

耳聞不如目見。Seeing is believing. 【劉向《說苑‧卷七政理》 Liu Xiang: Chapter 7, "The Principles of Government", *Garden of Persuasion*】

隔牆須有耳，窗外豈無人。There are ears between walls and people outside the windows – secret talk may get leaked. 【孟德耀〈舉案齊眉‧第二折〉Meng Deyao: Scene 2, "Husband and Wife Treating Each Other with Courtesy"】

隔牆有耳，草中有人。Secret talk may get leaked. 【諺語 Proverb】

過耳之言，不可聽信。Words overheard are not to be trusted. 【諺語 Proverb】【吳承恩《西遊記‧第九回》Wu Cheng'en: Chapter 9, *Journey to the West*】

雞毛堵着耳朵 —— 裝聾作啞。
Have chicken feathers blocking one's ears – pretend to be ignorant. 【歇後語 End-clipper】

兼聽則明，偏聽則暗。 Listen to different sides and you will be enlightened; heed only one side and you will be benighted. 【司馬光《資治通鑒・貞觀二年》Sima Guang: "The Second Year in the Reign of Zhenguan", *Comprehensive Mirror to Aid in Government*】

兩耳不聽心不亂。 If one refuses to hear anything, one's mind will not be disturbed. 【諺語 Proverb】

聾子的耳朵 —— 擺設。 A deaf person's ears are there for ornamentation. 【歇後語 End-clipper】

瓶兒罐兒也有兩個耳朵。 Jars and jugs have two ears, yet people with ears, cannot get updates from others. 【施耐庵《水滸傳・第七十八回》Shi Nai'an: Chapter 78, *Outlaws of the Marshes*】

牆有縫，壁有耳。 Secret talk may get leaked. 【蘭陵笑笑生《金瓶梅・第八十六回》Lanling Xiaoxiaosheng: Chapter 86, *The Plum in the Golden Vase*】

勸了耳朵，勸不了心。 You can advise somebody listen to you and does not do something, but you cannot stop him from thinking about it. 【俗語 Common saying】

三更酒醒殘燈在，臥聽瀟瀟雨打篷。 I woke up from my drunkenness in the third watch of the night and the candle light was still on, and laid on the boat to listen to the rain that pattered on its canvas, bemoaning the misfortune in life. 【陸游〈東關〉Lu You: "East Gate"】

聽話聽音兒，鑼鼓聽聲兒。 Listen for the meaning behind somebody's words like listening for the sound of gongs and drums. 【俗語 Common saying】

聽話聽音，刨樹刨根。 Listen for the meaning behind somebody's words like digging out a tree for the roots. 【俗語 Common saying】【劉流《烈火金鋼・第二十回》Liu Liu: Chapter 20, *Steel Meets Fire*】

聽其言，觀其行。 Listen to what a person says and see how he behaves. 【孔子《論語・公冶長篇第五》Confucius: Chapter 5, *The Analects of Confucius*】

無聽之以耳，而聽之以心。 Don't listen with your ears, think with your heart. 【莊周《莊子・內篇・人間世第四》Zhuang Zhou: Chapter 4, "Human World", "Inner Chapters", *Zhuangzi*】

小孩子耳朵快。 Children have sharp ears. 【俗語 Common saying】

一隻耳朵進，一隻耳朵出。 In at one ear and out at the other. 【俗語 Common saying】

欲人勿聞，莫若勿言。 If you don't want to be heard, you had better keep silent. 【班固《漢書・枚乘傳》Ban Gu: "Biography of Mei Cheng", *History of the Han*】

左耳入，右耳出。 In at one ear
and out at the other. 【俗語
Common saying】

Eating

不乾不淨，吃了沒病。 Eating
food with a little dirt won't kill
you. 【俗語 Common saying】

不能一口吃成胖子。 It is
impossible to achieve something
beyond your capability. 【俗語
Common saying】

吃不飽，穿不暖。 Inadequate
food to eat and clothing to keep
oneself warm. 【俗語 Common
saying】

吃得快，做得快。 Quick at meal,
quick at work. 【俗語 Common
saying】

吃飯防噎，走路防跌。 be careful
not to choke while eating; be
careful not to stumble while
walking. 【俗語 Common saying】【陳
忱《水滸後傳‧第十回》Chen Chen:
Chapter 10, *A Sequel to the Outlaws of the
Marshes*】

吃果嚐味，說話聽音。 When
eating fruit, we enjoy the taste.
When hearing, we listen to the
intended meaning. 【俗語 Common
saying】

吃人的獅子不露齒。 A man-
eating lion never shows its
fangs. 【俗語 Common saying】【梁斌
《紅旗譜‧第十回》Liang Bin: Chapter
10, *Music of Red Flag*】

吃魚吃肉，穿紅着綠。 Eat fish
and meat and wear fine clothes.
【諺語 Proverb】

大嚼大噎，大走多跌。 One
chokes if eating too much and
stumbles if walking too fast –
work with detail-minded
instead of getting things done
in a hurry. 【呂德勝《小兒語》Lu
Desheng: *Words for Young Boys*】

大口吃飯，小口飲酒。 Eat at
pleasure, drink with measure.
【俗語 Common saying】

斗大的饅頭 —— 吃不下嘴。 A big
steamed bun – hard to be taken
a bite. 【歇後語 End-clipper】

毒人的東西莫吃，犯法的事莫做。
Neither eat anything poisonous
nor do anything which violates
the law. 【俗語 Common saying】

多吃無滋味，話多不值錢。 If you
eat too much, the food becomes
tasteless. If you talk too much,
what you say is worthless. 【諺語
Proverb】

多吃飯，少開口。 Eat more,
speak less. 【俗語 Common saying】

過屠門而大嚼。 One chews
when passing through a
butcher's – comfort oneself in

an unrealistic way when one cannot get what one wants. 【桓譚《新論》Huan Tan: *New Disquisitions*】

節飲食以養胃，多讀書以養膽。 Regulate one's diet to nourish the appetite and read more books to foster courage. 【莊周《莊子·雜篇·讓王第二十八》 Zhuang Zhou: Chapter 28, "Abdicating Kingship", "Miscellaneous Chapters", *Zhuangzi*】

口大喉嚨小。 Crave for what beyond your limit. 【俗語 Common saying】

能吃不能幹。 Eat a lot but do nothing. 【俗語 Common saying】

寧吃過頭飯，莫說過頭話。 Eating too much is better than talking too much. 【俗語 Common saying】

寧食開眉粥，莫食愁眉飯。 It is better to stay happy in poor living quality than bemoaning in luxury lives 【俗語 Common saying】

寧可食無肉，不可居無竹。 Living without meat is better than losing my personality. 【蘇軾〈於潛僧綠筠軒〉Su Shi:"With Monk Yuqian in Green Veranda"】

牆上畫餅 —— 中看不中吃。 A cake drawn on the wall can only feed the eye but not the stomach. 【歇後語 End-clipper】

少吃多餐，病好自安。 Eat a little several times a day, your disease will be cured automatically. 【俗語 Common saying】

少吃多滋味，多吃活受罪。 If you eat a little, you will enjoy the taste, but if you eat too much, you will suffer. 【諺語 Proverb】

食不厭精，膾不厭細。 Rice for the worship of ancestors should be full and complete to show your piety; beef for the worship of ancestors should be cut thin and even. 【孔子《論語·鄉黨篇第十》Confucius: Chapter 10, *The Analects of Confucius*】

食不語，寢不言。 Do not converse with others while eating; do not talk in bed. 【孔子《論語·鄉黨篇第十》Confucius: Chapter 10, *The Analects of Confucius*】

食多無滋味。 Overeating kills a person's appetite. 【俗語 Common saying】

食宜樂，飲宜節。 Eat at pleasure and drink with measure. 【俗語 Common saying】

食在口頭，錢在手頭。 Food in the mouth is like money at hand. 【俗語 Common saying】【馮夢龍《警世通言·第三十一卷》Feng Menglong: Chapter 31, *Stories to Caution the World*】

貪多嚼不爛。 Pursuing for quantity instead of quality at work is like biting off more than one can chew. 【凌濛初《二刻拍案驚奇·第五卷》Ling Mengchu: Chapter 5, *Amazing Tales, Volume Two*】

為生而食，不為食而生。 One eats to live, but not lives to eat. 【俗語 Common saying】

惜飯有飯吃，惜衣有衣穿。 Waste not, want not.【俗語 Common saying】

先到竈頭先得食。 Those who are first at the fire will get their dinner first.【俗語 Common saying】

夜飯少吃口，活到九十九。 If you eat less, you can live long.【俗語 Common saying】【郎瑛《七修類稿・卷二十一》Lang Ying: Chapter 21, *Draft Arranged in Seven Categories*】

一口吃不成胖子。 No one grows fat on just one mouthful–it is impossible to achieve something beyond your capability.【俗語 Common saying】

又要馬兒好，又要馬兒不吃草。 You can't expect a horse to run without feeding it.【霽園主人《夜譚隨錄・卷十一・鐵公雞》Jiyuan Zhuren: Chapter 11, "Iron Cock", *Random Notes of Evening Chats*】

早吃好，中吃飽，晚吃少。 Have a good breakfast in the morning, have a full lunch at noon, and have a simple dinner in the evening.【諺語 Proverb】

紙上畫的餅，看得吃不得。 A cake drawn on paper can be seen but not eaten.【俗語 Common saying】

Education

不撒好種，哪得好苗。 Without spreading good seeds, how can we get good seedlings?【俗語 Common saying】

大學不在於有大樓。 It is not buildings that make a university.【梅貽琦〈任清華大學校長就職演講〉Mei Yiqi:"Inagurual Address as President of Tsinghua University"】

得天下英才而教育之。 Get the most talented individuals from the whole kingdom, and teach and nourish them.【孟軻《孟子・盡心章句上》Meng Ke: Chapter 7, Part 1, *Mencius*】

黃金不打難成器。 Gold without being struck cannot turn into useful things.【俗語 Common saying】

教育孩子在母親，教育學生在先生。 The education of a child rests with the mother and the education of a student, the teacher.【俗語 Common saying】

門第雖好，家教第一。 Birth is much, but family education is most important.【諺語 Proverb】

十年樹木，百年樹人。 It takes ten years to grow trees, but a hundred years to rear people.【管仲《管子・權修第三》Guan Zhong: Chapter 3, "Cultivation of Political Power", *Guanzi*】

學校，王政之本也。 Schools are the foundation of ideal government.【歐陽修〈吉州學記〉Ouyang Xiu:"Records of Schools in Jizhou"】

養不教，父之過。教不嚴，師之惰。 Raising a child without teaching him is the fault of a father. Teaching a child without strict guidance is the teacher's laziness.【王應麟《三字經》Wang Yinglin: *Three-character Classic*】

逸居而無教，則近於禽獸。 If one leads an idle life without education, one is close to an animal.【孟軻《孟子·滕文公上》Meng Ke: Chapter 5, Part 1, *Mencius*】

有爺娘生沒爺娘教。 Children have parents but they have no parental guidance.【俗語 Common saying】

玉不琢，不成器。 An uncut gem cannot sparkle.【《禮記·學記第十八》Chapter 18, "Records on the Subject of Education", *The Book of Rites*】

育才造士，為國之本。 Fostering talents and training scholars is the basis of a country.【權德輿《進士策問五道·第五問》Quan Deyu:"Answer for the Fifth Question", *Answers to the Five Questions on Strategies in the Palace Examination*】

子不教，父之過。 It is the father's fault if his son is not educated.【王應麟《三字經》Wang Yinglin: *Three-character Classic*】

Effort

百折不撓，再接再勵。 Never lose heart in spite of repeated failures but continue to make persistent efforts.【諺語 Proverb】

飽食終日，無所用心。 Spend one's day on eating and do nothing.【孔子《論語·陽貨篇第十七》Confucius: Chapter 17, *The Analects of Confucius*】

背着石頭上山。 Carry a rock on one's back to climb a mountain – work hard to gain nothing.【俗語 Common saying】【李光庭《鄉諺解頤·地部》Li Guangting:"Ground", *Country Sayings to Smile at*】

不費吹灰之力。 On a silver platter.【劉鶚《老殘遊記·第十七回》Liu E: Chapter 17, *Travelogue of Lao Can*】

不費一兵一卒。 Without a single effort.【俗語 Common saying】

不入虎穴，焉得虎子。 Nothing venture, nothing gain.【范曄《後漢書·班超列傳》Fan Ye:"Biography of Ban Chao", *History of the Later Han*】

不下大海，難得明珠。 No pain, no gain.【諺語 Proverb】

不作無補之功，不為無益之事。 Don't make any futile effort and

don't do things with no benefits.
【管仲《管子‧禁藏第五十三》Guan
Zhong: Chapter 53, "On Maintaining
Restraint", *Guanzi*】

吃奶的勁都拿出來了。 One has
done one's utmost.【俗語 Common
saying】

乞火不若取燧，寄汲不若鑿井。
It is better to obtain a fire-
maker than begging for fire; it is
better to dig a well oneself than
begging for water from others –
better to solve problems from
the roots.【劉安《淮南子‧覽冥訓第
六》Liu An: Chapter 6, "Peering Into the
Obscure", *Huainanzi*】

出力不討好。 Do a thankless job.
【俗語 Common saying】

大炮打蚊子。 To overkill.【俗語
Common saying】

費九牛二虎之力。 Involve a great
amount of effort.【鄭德輝《孤本
元明雜劇〈三戰呂布‧楔子〉》Cheng
Dehui:"Prologue", "Three Heroes
Fighting Against Lu Bu", *Unique Copies
of Zaju in Yuan and Ming*】

費力不討好。 Efforts made are not
appreciated.【俗語 Common saying】
【老舍〈今年的希望〉Lao She:"Hope of
the Year"】

給死人醫病 —— 白費功夫。
Giving medical treatment to the
dead – a vain effort.【歇後語 End-
clipper】

趕鴨子上架 —— 吃力不討好。
Driving a duck onto a perch –
expending one's efforts to no

good result; force a donkey to
dance.【歇後語 End-clipper】

功到自然成。 Constant effort
yields sure success.【文康《兒
女英雄傳‧第二十三回》Wen Kang:
Chapter 23, *Biographies of Young Heroes
and Heroines*】

海底撈月 —— 一場空。 It's in vain
to fish out the moon from the
bottom of the sea.【歇後語 End-
clipper】

河裏撈月亮 —— 白費勁。 Fishing
for the moon in the river – a vain
effort.【歇後語 End-clipper】

猴子撈月亮 —— 空忙一場 A
monkey trying to fish the moon
out of the water is simply a vain
attempt.【歇後語 End-clipper】

積力之所舉，則無不勝也；
眾智之所為，則無不成也。
Everything made by concerted
efforts is invincible; everthing
done by people's wisdom will be
accomplished.【劉安《淮南子‧主
術訓第九》Liu An: Chapter 9, "Craft of
the Ruler", *Huainanzi*】

家懶外頭勤。 One is a loafer at
home and a hustler outside.【俗
語 Common saying】

將相本無種，男兒當自強。
Generals and ministers are not
born to be so, every young man
should strengthen himself to
achieve their goals.【汪洙《神童
詩》Wang Zhu:"Poem of a Talented
Boy"】

苦恨年年壓金線，為他人作嫁衣裳。 What I deeply regret about is that year after year I sew golden threads to make marriage clothes for others.【秦韜玉《貧女》Qin Taoyu: "A Poor Girl"】

累死沒人買棺材。 Even if you work yourself to death, nobody will buy you a coffin.【俗語 Common saying】

冷水要人挑，熱水要人燒。 Cold water has to be carried home and hot water has to be boiled by somebody.【陳登科《赤龍與丹鳳・第一部・第六章》Chen Dengke: Part 1, Chapter 6, *Red Dragon and Red Phoenix*】

路是人開的，樹是人栽的。 Roads are built by people and trees are planted by people – where there's a will, there's a way.【諺語 Proverb】

路要一步一步地走，飯要一口一口地吃。 One must walk step by step and eat mouthful by mouthful.【諺語 Proverb】

莫問收穫，但問耕耘。 No worry about the harvest, keep on ploughing.【曾國藩《曾國藩日記》Zeng Guofan: *The Diary of Zeng Guofan*】

前人栽樹，後人乘涼。 To sew the seeds of our future success.【諺語 Proverb】

人一能之，己百之；人十能之，己千之。 If others succeed by one ounce of effort, I will make a hundred times as much effort; if others succeed by ten ounces of effort, I will make a thousand times as much effort.【《禮記・中庸第三十一章》Chapter 31, "Doctrine of the Mean", *The Book of Rites*】

日久功夫深，鐵尺磨成繡花針。 Preservance spells success.【諺語 Proverb】

沙裏求油，冰裏求火。 Seek for oil from sand and fire from ice.【俗語 Common saying】

少壯不努力，老大徒傷悲。 A young idler, an old beggar.【佚名〈長歌行〉Anonymous: "Long Poem"】

繩鋸木斷，水滴石穿。 Constant dropping wears the stone.【羅大經《鶴林玉露・乙編・卷四》Luo Dajing: Part 2, Chapter 4, *Jade Dew of the Crane Forest*】

世上無難事，只要肯登攀。 Nothing is hard under the sky, if we dare to climb up high.【毛澤東〈水調歌頭・重上井崗山〉Mao Zedong: "Reascending Jinggang Mountain: To the Tune of Prelude to the Melody of Water"】

死馬當作活馬醫。 Try to save the dead horse as if it is still alive.【俗語 Common saying】【集成《宏智禪師廣錄・卷一》Ji Cheng: Chapter 1, *Extended Records of Chan Master Hong Zhi*】

台上一分鐘，台下十年功。 A minute on stage requires ten years of efforts off stage.【俗語 Common saying】

天時人事兩相扶。 The will of heaven and human efforts

supplement each other.【王濬卿《冷眼觀·第二十五回》Wang Junqing: Chapter 25, *Casting a Cold Eye*】

天行健，君子以自強不息。As Heaven's movement is ever vigorous, a gentleman must ceaselessly strive along.【《易經·乾·象》"Image", "Hexagram *Qian*", *The Book of Changes*】

枉費功勞白費心。Rack one's effort and mind for nothing.【俗語 Common saying】

為山九仞，功虧一簣。Come up short with a lack of final effort.【《尚書·旅獒》"Hounds of Lu", *The Book of History*】

為者常成，行者常至。He who keeps working always accomplishes his task and he who keeps walking arrives at his destination.【晏嬰《晏子春秋·內篇·雜下》Yan Ying: "Miscellaneous", Part 2, "Inner Chapters", *Master Yan's Spring and Autumn Annals*】

無魚撒網空費力。To cast the net where there is no fish is a waste of efforts.【俗語 Common saying】

瞎子點燈 —— 白費蠟。It is as useless as lighting a lamp for a blindman.【歇後語 End-clipper】

先有耕耘，後有收穫。One must first sow before one can reap.【俗語 Common saying】

一把屎一把尿。Blood, sweat, and tears.【俗語 Common saying】

一場歡喜一場空。Draw water with a sieve.【俗語 Common saying】

一粒米，七擔水。A grain of rice needs seven buckets of water to grow.【諺語 Proverb】

一鍬挖不出一口井。A tree will not fall at one blow.【俗語 Common saying】【周立波《暴風驟雨·第一部·第十章》Zhou Libo: Chapter 10, Volume 1, *The Hurricane*】

一人開井，千人食水。A person digs the well and a thousand people benefit and drink from it.【諺語 Proverb】

易如探囊取物。As easy as taking a thing out of one's pocket.【歐陽修〈新五代史·南唐世家〉"Ouyang Xiu", "House of Southern Tang", *A New History of the Five Dynasties*】

因風吹火，用力不多。As the wind blows the fire, we do not have to use much of our efforts to do so.【蘭陵笑笑生《金瓶梅·第八十回》Lanling Xiaoxiaosheng: Chapter 80, *The Plum in the Golden Vase*】

用功不求太猛，但求有恆。Efforts do not have to be too stringent; what we should seek for after is consistency.【曾國藩《曾國藩家書》Zeng Guofan: *Family Letters of Zeng Guofan*】

有錢出錢，有力出力。The rich can donate and the strong, labour.【俗語 Common saying】

有一份熱，發一份光。Contrubute as much as one can.【魯迅《隨感錄·第四十一章·熱風》Lu Xun: Chapter 41, "Hot Wind", *Records of My Random Thoughts*】

有意栽花花不發，無心插柳柳成陰。To grow flowers purposely, you get no flowers; to plant willows casually, you get shade.【羅貫中《平妖傳・第十九回》Luo Guanzhong: Chapter 19, *Taming Devils*】

欲求生快活，須下死功夫。To lead a happy life, you must make painstaking efforts.【俗語 Common saying】【施耐庵《水滸傳・第二十五回》Shi Nai'an: Chapter 25, *Outlaws of the Marshes*】

祇問耕耘，不問收穫。What you sow is more important than what you reap.【俗語 Common saying】

祇要功夫深，鐵柱磨成針。If one works hard enough, one can grind an iron rod into a needle.【諺語 Proverb】【祝穆《方輿勝覽・眉州・磨針溪》Zhu Mu: "Needle-grinding River", "Meizhou", *A Geographic Guide*】

祇要人手多，牌樓搬過河。Many hands make light work.【諺語 Proverb】【俞萬春《蕩寇志・第八十回》Yu Wanchun: Chapter 80, *A Record of the Eradication of Bandits*】

眾擎易舉，獨力難成。By teamwork, things can be done easily; by working alone, one can achieve little.【張岱《募修岳鄂王祠姆疏》Zhang Dai: "A Memorial to Raise Funds to Repair the Temple for Yue Fei"】

竹籃子打水 —— 一場空。One gets nothing by drawing water with a sieve.【歇後語 End-clipper】

Employment

此處不留人，自有留人處。If there is no place for me, there will be other places for me.【陳叔寶〈戲贈陳應〉Chen Shubao: "Present to Chen Ying for Fun"】

此山望着那山高。The grass is always greener on the other side of the fence.【俗語 Common saying】【李光庭《鄉言解頤》Li Guang-ting: *Recalling the Folk Songs of Hometown*】

當差不自在，自在不當差。If one works as an official, one feels uneasy. If one wants to feel free, one should not work as an official.【俗語 Common saying】

東不成，西不就。A person has no success in a certain place but refuses to accept an offer from another.【洪楩《清平山堂話本・刎頸鴛鴦會》Hong Pian: "Cutting Their Throats in a Lover's Meeting", *Qingping Shantang Scripts*】

任賢勿貳，去邪勿疑。Employ the worthy without indecision and remove the bad without doubt.【《尚書・大禹謨》"Counsels of Yu the Great", *The Book of History*】

人得其位，位得其人。The right person for the right position and the right position for the right person. 【俗語 Common saying】

善用人者為之下。One who is good at employing people humbles subordinates. 【老子《道德經·第六十八章》Laozi: Chapter 68, *Daodejing*】

疑人勿使，使人勿疑。If you suspect a person, don't employ him; if you employ a person, don't suspect him. 【脫脫《金史·卷四·本紀第四·熙宗》Toktoghan: Chapter 4, "Annals of the Emperors", "No.4", "Emperor Xizong", *History of the Jin*】

疑則勿任，任則勿疑。Don't employ a person if you suspect him and don't suspect him if you employ him. 【司馬光《資治通鑒·晉安帝義熙十三年》Sima Guang: "The Thirteenth Year of the Reign of Yixi of Emperor Andi of Jin", *Comprehensive Mirror To Aid In Government*】

疑則勿用，用則勿疏。When you suspect someone, don't employ him; but once you employ him, don't estrange him. 【白居易〈策林三·君不行臣事〉Bai Juyi: Chapter 3, "A King Does Not Do Matters Done By Ministers", *A Forest of Strategies*】

用人不疑，疑人不用。If you employ a person, don't suspect him; if you suapect a person, don't use him. 【陳亮〈論開誠之道〉Chen Liang: "On Open-heartedness"】

這山望來那山高，到了那山沒柴燒。Looking from this hill, you think the opposite hill is higher; but after climbing up there, you can't find wood to make a fire. 【俗語 Common saying】

Enemy

不是冤家不聚頭。Enemies are destined to meet. 【俗語 Common saying】【曹雪芹《紅樓夢·二十九回》Cao Xueqin: Chapter 29, *A Dream of the Red Chamber*】

仇人見面，份外眼紅。When enemies meet, their eyes blaze with hate. 【俗語 Common saying】【羅懋登《三寶太監西洋記》Luo Mao-deng: *The Western Voyage of the Eunuch of Three Treasures*】

狗臉親家驢臉皮。Enemies one moment and friends the next. 【俗語 Common saying】

眼中釘，肉中刺。Somebody is like a pest in one's eyes and a thorn in one's flesh. 【李寶嘉《官場現形記·第二十二回》Li Baojia: Chapter 22, *Officialdom Unmasked*】

一斗米養個恩人，一石米養個仇人。A peck of rice wins you a friend; a bushel wins you an enemy. 【俗語 Common saying】【吳

敬梓《儒林外史・第二十二回》Wu Jingzi: Chapter 22, *An Unofficial History of the Scholars*】

一日縱敵，數世之患。 Once you let go of your enemy, it will lead to disaster for several generations. 【左丘明《左傳・僖公三十三年》Zuo Qiuming: "The Thirty-third Year of the Reign of Duke Xi", *Zuo's Commentary on the Spring and Autumn Annals*】

冤家少結，方便多行。 Make less enemies and do more good to others. 【俗語 Common saying】【葉

憲祖《碧蓮繡符・六折》Ye Xianzhu: Scene 6, "Bilian's Embroidered Charm"】

冤家宜解不宜結。 Compromising is always better than deepening the contradictions. 【俗語 Common saying】【錢彩《說岳全傳・第二回》Qian Cai: Chapter 2, *A Story of Yue Fei*】

冤有頭，債有主。 Every wrong has its cause and every debt has its debtor, others should not be involved. 【諺語 Proverb】【釋普濟《五燈會元・卷十六》Shi Puji: Chapter 16, *A Compendium of the Five Lamps*】

Excellence

趕鴨子過河 —— 呱呱叫。 Driving ducks across the river, they quack-quack – one is brilliant. 【歇後語 End-clipper】

龍王爺搬家 —— 厲害（離海）。 The Dragon King moving house is to leave the sea – it's excellent. 【歇後語 End-clipper】

帽子破了邊 —— 頂好。 It couldn't be better. 【歇後語 End-clipper】

Experience

不嚐黃蓮苦，怎知蜜糖甜。 He who has not tasted the bitterness of goldthread would not realize the sweetness of honey. 【諺語 Proverb】

不經一事，不長一智。 A fall in the pit, a gain in the wit. 【曹雪芹《紅樓夢・第六十回》Cao Xueqin: Chapter 60, *A Dream of the Red Chamber*】

不挑擔子不知重，不走長路不知遠。 If one does not carry a load, one does not know what heaviness is. If one does not travel a long road, one does not know what distance is. 【俗語 Common saying】

吃一次虧，學一次乖。 A fall in a pit, a gain in your wit. 【諺語 Proverb】

吃一塹，長一智。A fall in a pit, a gain in your wit.【左丘明《左傳·昭公二十九年》Zuo Qiuming:"The Twenty-ninth Year of the Reign of Duke Zhao", *Zuo's Commentary on the Spring and Autumn Annals*】

齒痛方知齒痛人。Only when one has a toothache will one know that toothache hurts.【俗語 Common saying】

黃毛鴨子下水 —— 不知道深淺。A duckling entering the water does not know how deep it is – one is inexperienced.【歇後語 End-clipper】

見人挑擔不吃力。One does not understand how heavy things are by watching another person carrying things on a pole.【諺語 Proverb】【張南莊《何典·第五卷》Zhang Nanzhuang: Chapter 5, *From Which Classic*】

見識見識，不見不識。Experience is gained only through experience.【諺語 Proverb】

薑還是老的辣。The older, the wiser.【俗語 Common saying】

經風雨，見世面。Been through obstacles.【俗語 Common saying】【毛澤東〈組織起來〉Mao Zedong:"Together"】

經驗大似學問。Experience is more valuable than learning.【俗語 Common saying】【李準《黃河東流去》Li zhun:"Yellow River Flow to East"】

經驗乃智慧之母。Experience is the mother of wisdom.【諺語 Proverb】

經一事，長一智。A fall into a pit is a gain in your wit.【俗語 Common saying】【《新編五代史平話·漢史》"The History of Han", *The War Across Five Dynasties*】

口說不如身逢。Seeing is believing.【司馬光《資治通鑑·唐紀》Sima Guang:"Annals of the Tang Dynasty", *Comprehensive Mirror to Aid in Government*】

沒見過大世面。One who has not seen much of the world.【俗語 Common saying】

碰鼻子轉彎。Draw a lesson from one's failure.【俗語 Common saying】

前車之覆，後車之鑒。The overturned cart ahead is a warning to the carts behind.【劉向《說苑·卷七政理》Liu Xiang: Chapter 7, "The Principles of Government", *Garden of Persuasion*】

前事之不忘，後事之師。Not forgetting the experience one learned from the past will serve as a guide for the future.【劉向《戰國策·趙策一》Liu Xiang:"Strategies of the State of Zhao, No. 1", *Strategies of the Warring States*】

前有車，後有轍。The wheels of the cart leave their tracks behind – learn from mistakes.【俗語 Common saying】

親身下河知深淺，親口嚐梨知酸甜。By going down into the

river, you will know its depth; by taking a bite of a pear, you will know the sweetness. 【張九齡〈文苑英華・謝賜大麥麵狀〉Zhang Jiuling: "A Memorial to Thank the Granting of Wheat Noodles", *Finest Blossoms in the Garden of Literature*】

去年的皇曆 —— 看不得。 Past experience is not applicable now. 【歇後語 End-clipper】

三折肱成良醫。 A person who has broken his arm three times makes a good surgeon – to do something unless one has experienced it oneself. 【俗語 Common saying】【左丘明《左傳・定公十三年》Zuo Qiuming: "The Thirteenth Year of the Reign of Duke Ding", *Zuo's Commentary on the Spring and Autumn Annals*】

上一回當，學一回乖。 If you have been taken in before, you will be wary next time. 【俗語 Common saying】

生薑老的辣，奸人老的滑。 Old foxes want no tutors. 【俗語 Common saying】

事非經過不知難。 Getting to know the reality with experience. 【陸游〈格言聯〉Lu You: "Idiom Couplet"】

水滴集多成大海，經歷集多成學問。 Water-drops gathe Red together forming sea; experience gathe Red together becoming knowledge. 【諺語 Proverb】

要知河深淺，須問過河人。 To know how deep the river is, one must ask the person who has waded through it. 【俗語 Common saying】【吳承恩《西遊記・第二十一回》Wu Cheng'en: Chapter 21, *Journey to the West*】

要知前方路，須問過來人。 If you want to know the road ahead, ask those who have travelled it. 【俗語 Common saying】

要知水深淺，須問過來人。 He who has waded through water knows the depth the best. 【俗語 Common saying】

要知下山路，須問過來人。 If you want to know the road to the bottom of the hill, you should ask those who have travelled it. 【俗語 Common saying】【吳承恩《西遊記・第二十一回》Wu Cheng'en: Chapter 21, *Journey to the West*】

一塹之虧，一智之長。 A fall into the pit, a gain in your wit. 【諺語 Proverb】

欲知河淺深，須問過來人。 To know how deep the river is, one must ask the person who has waded through it. 【俗語 Common saying】

鑿壞而遁，洗耳不聽。 Wash one's ear and refuse to listen. 【劉安《淮南子・齊俗訓第二十六》Liu An: Chapter 26, "Placing Customs On A Par", *Huainanzi*】

Explanation

跳到黃河也洗不清。The misunderstanding is beyond repair.【俗語 Common saying】【文 康《兒女英雄傳・第二十二回》Wen Kang: Chapter 22, *Biographies of Young Heroes and Heroines*】

Eye

出洞的老鼠 —— 東張西望。A rat coming out of its hole peers around.【歇後語 End-clipper】

大眼瞪小眼。Look at each other in silence.【俗語 Common saying】

大中見小，小中見大。We see small details in great things, we see great things in small matters.【沈復《浮生六記・卷二》Shen Fu: Chapter 2, *Six Chapters of A Floating Life*】

但將冷眼看螃蟹，看你橫行到幾時。I watch the crabs with indifference and see how long it can move – persisting in evil brings self-destruction.【《增廣賢文》*Words that Open up One's Mind and Enhance One's Wisdom*】

獨眼龍看書 —— 一目瞭然。A one-eyed person reading a book takes everything at a glance.【歇後語 End-clipper】

獨眼龍相親 —— 一目瞭然。A one-eyed person sizing up his prospective wife takes everything at a glance.【歇後語 End-clipper】

非禮勿視，非禮勿聽，非禮勿言，非禮勿動。Do not look if it is not in accordance with the rites; do not listen if it is not in accordance with the rites; do not speak if it is not in accordance with the rites; and do not move if it is not in accordance with the rites.【孔子《論語・顏淵篇第十二》Confucius: Chapter 12, *The Analects of Confucius*】

隔山不聽娃娃哭。Out of sight, out of mind.【俗語 Common saying】

好戲不厭百回看。A good performance is worth seeing a hundred times.【俗語 Common saying】

見所未見，聞所未聞。Such rare things have never been seen or heard before.【揚雄《法言・淵騫》Yang Xiong: "Yuan and Qian", *Exemplary Sayings*】

見小曰明，守柔曰強。To be able to look into detail is called clear in mind; to be able to hold on to the weak is called strength.【老子《道德經・第五十二章》Laozi: Chapter 52, *Daodejing*】

看在眼裏，記在心裏。What one sees with one's eyes sinks into one's mind.【俗語 Common saying】

可望而不可及。 Can be seen but not reached.【宋之問〈明河篇〉Song Zhi-wen: "River Ming"】

可遠觀而不可褻玩。 Can be seen from a distance yet not to be touched.【周敦頤〈愛蓮說〉Zhou Dunyi: "On My Love of the Lotus"】

拉縴的瞧活兒 —— 往後看。 A boat puller examining his work looks backwards.【歇後語 End-clipper】

老天爺有眼睛。 Heaven is not blind.【俗語 Common saying】

盲人騎瞎馬，夜半臨深池。 A blind person riding a blind horse reaches a deep pool at midnight – act blindly puts you in danger.【劉義慶《世說新語·排調第二十五》Liu Yiqing: Chapter 25, "Taunting and Teasing", *A New Account of the Tales of the World*】

盲人牽瞎馬，一同落深池。 A blind person leads a blind horse and they will both fall into the ditch.【俗語 Common saying】

目不斜視，耳不旁聽。 One is deaf and blind to everything going on around as one is concentrating on something totally – focusing on something solely.【曹雪芹《紅樓夢·第四十八回》Cao Xueqin: Chapter 48, *A Dream of the Red Chamber*】

肉眼不識賢人。 To fail to recognize great man.【程允升《幼學瓊林·卷二夫婦》Cheng Yunsheng: Chapter 2, "Husband and Wife", *Treasury of Knowledge for Young Students*】

視而不見，聽而不聞。 Look without seeing and hear without listening.【《禮記·大學第四十二》Chapter 42, "The Great Learning", *The Book of Rites*】

吾不欲觀之矣。 That is something I don't want to see.【孔子《論語·八佾篇第三》Confucius: Chapter 3, *The Analects of Confucius*】

昔時橫波目，今作流淚泉。 In the past, my eyes doted with love. Today, they become springs of tears.【白居易〈長相思〉Bai Juyi: "To the Tune of Everlasting Longing"】

瞎子吃蒼蠅 —— 眼不見為淨。 The blind eat many flies – what is not seen is regarded as clean.【歇後語 End-clipper】

眼不見為淨。 What is not seen is regarded as clean.【俗語 Common saying】

眼不見，心不煩。 If one refuses to look into anything, one's mind will not be disturbed.【曹雪芹《紅樓夢·第二十九回》Cao Xueqin: Chapter 29, *A Dream of the Red Chamber*】

眼不見，心不念。 Out of sight, out of mind.【諺語 Proverb】

眼大肚子小。 The eye is bigger than the belly.【俗語 Common saying】

眼觀六路，耳聽八方。 Have sharp eyes and keen ears.【許仲琳《封神演義·第五十三回》Xu Zhonglin: Chapter 53, *Romance of the Investiture of the Deities*】

眼若秋水，目如寒星。One's eyes are like water in autumn and stars in a cold night. 【俗語 Common saying】

一人為私，六眼為公。What one person sees may be false but what three persons see may be true. 【俗語 Common saying】

一雙冷眼看世人，滿腔熱血酬知己。I sit on the sidelines towards the world but reward my friends with a bosom of passion. 【袁枚《隨園詩話》Yuan Mei: *Talks on Poetry from the Sui Garden*】

一葉障目，不見泰山。A leaf before the eye shuts out Mount Tai – being shortsighted. 【佚名《鶡冠子・天則第四》Anonymous: Chapter 4, "Principles of Heaven", *Eguanzi*】

有鼻子有眼。Sound convincing. 【俗語 Common saying】

睜一眼，閉一眼。Turning a blind eye to something. 【俗語 Common saying】【老舍〈上任〉Lao She: "Taking up an Appointment"】

祇見其一，不見其二。See only one side of the matter and overlook the other. 【諺語 Proverb】【莊周《莊子・外篇・天論地第十二》Zhuang Zhou: Chapter 12, "Heavens and Earth", "Outer Chapters", *Zhuangzi*】

祇見樹木，不見森林。Unable to see the forest for the trees. 【俗語 Common saying】【毛澤東〈矛盾論〉Mao Zhedong: "On Contradiction"】

中看不中吃。Pleasant to the eye but of no use. 【凌濛初《二刻拍案驚奇・第三十四卷》Ling Mengchu: Chapter 34, *Amazing Tales, Volume Two*】

中看不中用。Pleasant to the eye but of no use. 【俗語 Common saying】

眾人眼裏有桿秤。People have their own views. 【諺語 Proverb】

左眼跳財，右眼跳禍。The twitching of the left eyelid predicts gain and the right eyelid, disaster. 【俗語 Common saying】

Face

暴露真面目。Show one's true colours. 【俗語 Common saying】

不看僧面看佛面。Even if one does not give face to a monk, one has to give face to the Buddha – be lenient to show respect to a third person. 【馮夢龍《醒世恆言・第三十九卷》Feng Menglong: Chapter 39, *Stories to Awaken the World*】

搽粉入棺材 —— 死要面子。Powdering one's face before being put into a coffin – being stubborn pride. 【歇後語 End-clipper】

出門看天色，進門觀臉色。 Look at the weather when you step out; observe the host's face when you step into his house. 【諺語 Proverb】

打狗看主人面。 When beating a dog, find out who's its master – think of the consequences before action. 【蘭陵笑笑生《金瓶梅·第七十九回》Lanling Xiaoxiaosheng: Chapter 79, *The Plum in the Golden Vase*】

打腫臉充胖子。 Slap one's face until it is swollen to make one look like a plump person – try to satisfy one's vanity when one cannot really afford to do so. 【俗語 Common saying】

給臉不要臉。 Give one face, but one does not want it. 【俗語 Common saying】

嬌若春花，媚如秋月。 Her face is as lovely as flowers in spring and as enchanting as the moon in autumn. 【曹雪芹《紅樓夢·第五回》Cao Xueqin: Chapter 5, *A Dream of the Red Chamber*】

老了面皮，飽了肚皮。 One who asks for food loses one's face but fills one's belly. 【俗語 Common saying】【胡祖德《滬諺·卷上》Hu Zhude: Part 1, *Shanghainese Proverbs*】

臉醜怪不着鏡子。 You can't blame the mirror for your ugliness. 【俗語 Common saying】【孔厥，袁靜《新兒女英雄傳·第七回》Kong Jue and Yuan Jing: Chapter 7, *New Biographies of Heroes and Heroines*】

臉面值千金。 The face worths a thousand taels of gold. 【崔復生《太行志·第二十四章》Cui Fusheng: Chapter 24, *Records of Taixing*】

臉上不願心裏願。 One shows unwillingness on one's face, but inwardly one is willing. 【俗語 Common saying】

臉上無肉，必是壞物。 One who has a thin and wretched face is surely a bad person. 【俗語 Common saying】

臉一陣紅，一陣白。 One feels embarrassed that his face turns white and red alternately. 【李伯元《文明小史·第四回》Li Boyuan: Chapter 4, *A Short History of Civilization*】

臉一陣青，一陣黃。 One's face turns green and yellow alternately. 【俗語 Common saying】

面目可憎，語言無味。 One's face and eyes become unappealing and one's conversations are boring. 【韓愈《昌黎先生集·送窮文》Han Yu: "An Essay to Send Away Poverty", *Collected Works of Han Yu*】

面如桃花，眉如新月。 She has a face that resembles peach-blossoms and brows that shaped like a crescent moon. 【俗語 Common saying】

面若桃花，心如蛇蝎。 She has a fair face, but a foul heart. 【俗語 Common saying】

千人一面，萬人一腔。 One thousand people have the same faces and ten thousand people have the same voice – stereotype without new changes. 【曹雪芹《紅樓夢・第一回》Cao Xueqin: Chapter 1, *A Dream of the Red Chamber*】

去年今日此門中，人面桃花相映紅。 Last year on this day in this house, your pink face was set off by the pinkness of the peach blossoms. 【崔護〈題都城南莊〉Cui Hu:"A Poem about a Mansion in the South of the City"】

人臉識高低。 From the face of a person we can judge whether he is good or bad. 【俗語 Common saying】

人面不知何處去，桃花依舊笑春風。 Your face is nowhere to be seen, yet the peach blossoms still welcome in the spring breeze. 【崔護〈題都城南莊〉Cui Hu:"A Poem about a Mansion in the South of the City"】

人面咫尺，人心千里。 The faces of the people may have a distance of a few feet, but their hearts can be a thousand miles apart. 【蘭陵笑笑生《金瓶梅・第八十一回》Lanling Xiaoxiaosheng: Chapter 81, *The Plum in the Golden Vase*】

人人有臉，樹樹有皮。 A person has the face and a tree, the bark – man should have the sense of shame. 【俗語 Common saying】【蘭陵笑笑生《金瓶梅・第七十六回》Lanling Xiaoxiaosheng: Chapter 76, *The Plum in the Golden Vase*】

人無笑面休開店。 A person without a smiling face should not run a business. 【諺語 Proverb】

人要臉，樹要皮。 A person needs face just like a tree needs bark. 【俗語 Common saying】

入門休問榮枯事，觀看容顏便得知。 When you enter into a house, do not ask about that things that thrive or wither, just look at the host's facial expressions and you know how the things are. 【《增廣賢文》*Words that Open up One's Mind and Enhance One's Wisdom*】

容光煥發，神采奕奕。 One is brim with health and in excellent spirits. 【俗語 Common saying】

伸手不打笑臉人。 No one will strike a smiling face. 【俗語 Common saying】

死要面子活受罪。 More nice than wise. 【俗語 Common saying】

往臉上貼金。 Stick gold on somebody's face to beautify him. 【俗語 Common saying】

喜不喜，面上看。 Whether a man is happy can be seen on his face. 【俗語 Common saying】

喜怒不形於色。 Do not show one's anger or happiness on the face. 【陳壽《三國志・蜀書・先主傳》Chen Shou:"Biography of Liu Bei", "History of the State of Wei", *Records of the Three Kingdoms*】

張飛擺屠案 ── 兇神惡煞。 One pulls a long face. 【歇後語 End-clipper】

Fact

擺事實，講道理。 Present the facts and reason things out. 【俗語 Common saying】

丁是丁，卯是卯。 Being conscientious and meticulos 【曹雪芹《紅樓夢・第四十三回》Cao Xueqin: Chapter 43, *A Dream of the Red Chamber*】

該一是一，該二是二。 One is one and two is two – being honest and unambiguous. 【俗語 Common saying】

橋是橋，路是路。 Black and white cannot be confused. 【周 立波《暴風驟雨・第一部・第七章》 Zhou Libo: Chapter 7, Volume 1, *Violent Storms and Heavy Showers*】

事實勝於雄辯。 Facts speak louder than words. 【俗語 Common saying】【魯迅〈熱風〉Lu Xun: "Hot Wind"】

一是一，二是二。 To describe or recount something honestly, unambiguously, and without embellishment. 【俞萬春《蕩寇志・第八十回》Yu Wanchun: Chapter 80, *A Record of the Eradication of Bandits*】

Failure

敗莫大於不自知。 The most important cause for failure is a lack of self-knowledge. 【呂不韋《呂氏春秋・自知》Lu Buwei: "Self-knowledge", *Master Lu's Spring and Autumn Annals*】

半夜叫城門 ── 碰釘子。 To knock on the city gate at midnight – asking for embarrassment. 【歇後語 End-clipper】

兵敗如山倒。 Falling apart like a house of cards – army being defeated thoroughly. 【俗語 Common saying】

鍋膛裏吹火 ── 碰一鼻子灰。 Blowing at the fire in a stove, one has one's nose smudged with ashes – get snubbed or rejected. 【歇後語 End-clipper】

滿必溢，驕必敗。 When a container is too full, it overflows; when a person is too conceited, he fails. 【俗語 Common saying】

棋錯一着滿盤輸。Make a wrong move and you will lose the game.【諺語 Proverb】

失敗乃常情，成功是僥倖。One fails as a rule; one succeeds by luck.【俗語 Common saying】

失敗是成功之母。Failure is the mother of success.【諺語 Proverb】

為山九仞，功虧一簣。A failure is still a failure no matter how close it is to success.【《尚書·旅獒》"Hounds of Lu", The Book of History】

一事無成兩鬢斑，長使英雄痛灑淚。Nothing is achieved when temples have turned grey, this makes a man sad and tearful.【俗語 Common saying】

有小負必有大勝。Small failures will bring a great victory.【俗語 Common saying】【《施公案·第三百三十六回》Chapter 363, Cases of Judge Shi】

Faithfulness

波瀾誓不起，妾心古井水。I swear that no ripples will rise inside me, for my heart is like the dead water of an old well.【孟郊〈烈女操〉Meng Jiao: "The Chastity of a Faithful Widow"】

蕩子行不歸，空床難獨守。The wanderer travels about and never comes home. It is difficult for me to sleep all by oneself in an empty bed.【佚名《古詩十九首》Anonymous: "Nineteen Ancient Poems"】

老天不負有心人。Heaven rewards the faithful.【諺語 Proverb】

Family

婢美妾嬌，非閨房之福。To have good-looking maids and charming concubines is not a blessing to one's family life.【朱用純《朱子家訓》Zhu Yongchun: Precepts of the Zhu Family】

不當家不知柴米貴。One who has not run a family does not know the high cost of fuel and rice.【梁斌《烽煙圖·第八章》Liang Bin: Chapter 8, A Scence of Beacon Fires】

成家容易養家難。To set up a family is easy, but to keep it is difficult.【諺語 Proverb】

當家才知柴米貴，處世方識世情難。Only when one runs a family will one know that rice and firewood are expensive. Only when one conducts oneself in the society will one understand how difficult it is to handle human relationship.【諺語 Proverb】

當家才知柴米價，養子方曉父娘恩。 Only when one runs a family will one know the prices of rice and firewood. Only when one raises one's children will one appreciate parental love. 【諺語 Proverb】【吳承恩《西遊記‧第二十八回》Wu Cheng'en: Chapter 28, *Journey to the West*】

當家三日狗也嫌。 When one is in charge of the affairs of a family for three days, even one's dog dislikes one. 【蘭陵笑笑生《金瓶梅‧第七十五回》Lanling Xiaoxiaosheng: Chapter 75, *The Plum in the Golden Vase*】

好家當，怕三份分。 What is to be worried is that a good family fortune is being divided into three portions. 【諺語 Proverb】【柳青《創業史》Liu Qing: *A Story of Pioneering*】

皇帝也有草鞋親。 Everyone has straw-sandaled relatives. 【諺語 Proverb】【李漁〈連城璧〉Li Yu: "The Baileys in the Cities"】

積不善之家，必有餘殃。 A family that has bad deeds accumulated will surely have more than abundant misery to suffer. 【《易經‧坤‧文言》"The Record of Wen Yan", "Hexagram *Kun*", *The Book of Changes*】

積善之家，必有餘慶。 A family that has good deeds accumulated will surely have more than enough blessings.

【《易經‧坤‧文言》"The Record of Wen Yan", "Hexagram *Kun*", *The Book of Changes*】

家必自毀，而後人毀之。 A family must have destroyed itself before others can destroy it. 【孟軻《孟子‧離婁上》Meng Ke: Chapter 4, Part 1, *Mencius*】

家不和，被人欺。 A family at discord will be bullied by others. 【諺語 Proverb】【鄭國軒《白蛇傳》Zheng Guo-xuan: *The Legend of the White Snake*】

家不和，招禍災。 A family at discord will get disasters. 【諺語 Proverb】

家醜不可外揚。 Domestic shame should not be made public. 【釋普濟《五燈會元‧卷十五》Shi Puji: Chapter 15, *A Compendium of the Five Lamps*】

家大業大，人多事多。 When a family is large, its business is large. When there are many people, there are many problems. 【俗語 Common saying】

家和百事順。 A harmonious family succeeds in everything. 【俗語 Common saying】

家和人和萬事和。 A family living in harmony will bring about a peaceful life to all its members and succeed in everything. 【俗語 Common saying】

家家有本難念的經。 Every family has a skeleton in the cupboard. 【俗語 Common saying】

家教雖嚴，醜事難免。 Even in the best regulated families, bad things are bound to happen. 【俗語 Common saying】

家裏不和外人欺。 Others will get good on a family at discord. 【諺語 Proverb】

家裏事，家裏了。 What happens in the family should be settled in the house. 【俗語 Common saying】

家貧則思良妻，國亂則思良相。 When a family is poor, one cherishes the hope of having a capable wife; when a country is chaotic, one cherishes the hope of having a capable minister. 【司馬遷《史記‧魏世家》Sima Qian: "House of Wei", *Records of the Grand Historian*】

家有患難，鄰里相助。 When a family is in trouble, its neighbours will help. 【俗語 Common saying】【蘭陵笑笑生《金瓶梅‧第十四回》Lanling Xiaoxiaosheng: Chapter 14, *The Plum in the Golden Vase*】

家有家規，國有國法。 A family has family rules to follow, and a country has its laws to regulate. 【諺語 Proverb】

家有千口，主事一人。 A family may have many members but only one master. 【諺語 Proverb】【趙樹理《李家莊的變遷》Zhao Shuli: *Changes of the Li Family*】

家有主，國有王。 A country has a king as a family, a master. 【陳忱《水滸後傳‧第三十四回》Chen Chen: Chapter 34, *A Sequel to the Outlaws of the Marshes*】

家中不和鄰里欺。 A family in discord is insulted by its neighbours. 【諺語 Proverb】【《增廣賢文》*Words that Open up One's Mind and Enhance One's Wisdom*】

將門必有將，相門必有相。 A general's family will have born generals and a minister's family, born ministers. 【司馬遷《史記‧孟嘗君列傳》Sima Qian: "Biography of Lord Mengchang", *Records of the Grand Historian*】

將門出虎子。 A general's family will have brave sons. 【諺語 Proverb】

將相出寒門。 The talented often come from poor families. 【王實甫《西廂記‧第五本第三折》Wang Shifu: Act 5, Scene 3, "Romance of the Western Bower"】

刻薄成家，理無久享。 A family that builds on meanness does not, according to reason, last long. 【朱用純《朱子家訓》Zhu Yongchun: *Precepts of the Zhu Family*】

鳥愛其巢，人愛其家。 Every bird likes its own nest, every person, his family. 【諺語 Proverb】

便宜不過當家。 Perks should be kept inside the family. 【俗語 Common saying】【曹雪芹《紅樓夢‧第六十五回》Cao Xueqin: Chapter 65, *A Dream of the Red Chamber*】

千朵桃花一樹生。 Siblings are of the same mother. 【蘭陵笑笑

生《金瓶梅·第七十八回》Lanling Xiaoxiaosheng: Chapter 78, *The Plum in the Golden Vase*】

清官難斷家務事。 Even a righteous official can't judge family disputes. 【馮夢龍《喻世明言·第十卷》Feng Menglong: Chapter 10, *Stories to Instruct the World*】

窮家難離，熱土難捨。 No one likes to leave one's home and their land. 【孔厥，袁靜《新兒女英雄傳·第六回》Kong Jue and Yuan Jing: Chapter 6, *New Biographies of Heroes and Heroines*】

人家天作，不在人為。 The fortune of a family is decided by heaven, not by what is done by family members. 【凌濛初《二刻拍案驚奇·第二十二卷》Ling Mengchu: Chapter 22, *Amazing Tales, Volume Two*】

三教原來是一家。 The three religions of Confucianism, Buddhism, and Daoism are of the same family. 【俗語 Common saying】

上有老，下有小。 There are parents and children in need of support in a family. 【俗語 Common saying】

同室不操戈。 Members of the same family should not draw swords on each other. 【諺語 Proverb】【曾樸《孽海花·第二十九回》Zheng Pu: Chapter 29, *A Flower in a Sinful Sea*】

屯不露好屯，家不露是好家。 A concealed village is a good village and a concealed family is a good family. 【周立波《暴風驟雨·第二部·第一章》Zhou Libo: Chapter 1, Volume 2, *Violent Storms and Heavy Showers*】

外人難管家務事。 Outsiders cannot interfere with the affairs of one's family. 【俗語 Common saying】

萬兩黃金未為貴，一家安樂值錢多。 Ten thousand taels of gold is not as valuable as peace and happiness in the family. 【鄭之文《旗亭記·第三十八齣》Zheng Zhiwen: Scene 38, "Story of the Flag Pavilion"】

無家一身輕，有錢萬事足。 Without a family, one feels carefree; with money, one feels content with everything. 【歐陽元源《負曝閒談·第十八回》Ouyang Yuanyuan: Chapter 18, *Chats When Basking in the Winter Sun*】

五百年前是一家。 Five hundred years ago, our ancestors might be of the same family. 【俗語 Common saying】【吳敬梓《儒林外史·第二十二回》Wu Jingzi: Chapter 22, *An Unofficial History of the Scholars*】

興家猶如針挑土，敗家好似水推舟。 Money comes like earth scooped up with a needle; it goes like sand washed away by water. 【俗語 Common saying】

一家飽暖千家怨。 A wealthy family is envied by a thousand families. 【俗語 Common saying】

一家不夠，百家相湊。 When one family is in need, a hundred

families come up to help. 【諺語 Proverb】

一家不知一家事。 One family does not know how another family lives. 【俗語 Common saying】

一家打牆，兩家好看。 When one family breaks down a wall, two families will be happy – one man does everything and others gain as well. 【《增廣賢文》 Words that Open up One's Mind and Enhance One's Wisdom】

一家富難顧三家貧。 One rich family cannot take care of three poor families. 【諺語 Proverb】

一家有事，四鄰不安。 When one family gets into trouble, the neighbours cannot be in peace as well. 【諺語 Proverb】

一家有一主。 There is a head in each family. 【施世綸《施公案・第四百四十四回》 Shi Shilun: Chapter 444, *Cases of Judge Shi*】

有國才有家。 The family exists only when the country exists. 【俗語 Common saying】

欲成家，置兩犁；欲破家，置兩妻。 To make your family rich, buy two ploughs; to break up your family, marry two wives. 【宋纁《古今藥石・卷下》 Song Xun: Part 2, *Medical Herbs Past and Present*】

正家而天下定矣。 When all families are in order, the whole world will be in peace. 【《易經・家人・彖》 "Tuan", "Hexagram *Jia Ren*", *The Book of Changes*】

Father and son

白頭父子燈前語，忘卻江湖久別離。 The white-headed father and son chatted before the lamplight, forgetting about the long separation by rivers and lakes. 【楊萬里〈次公秩滿來歸遇上巳寒食同日父子小酌〉 Yang Wanli: "Father and Son Dining on the Eve of the Qingming Festival"】

不痴不聾，不作家翁。 If you are not generous, you can't be a grandfather. 【劉熙《釋名・釋首飾》 Liu Xi: "Explanation of Making-up the Face", *Explanation of Terms*】

慈父之愛子，非為報也。 A kind father loves his son not for a return. 【劉安《淮南子・繆稱訓第十》 Liu An: Chapter 10, On Erroneous Designations, *Huainanzi*】

父不父，子不子。 Fathers neglect their responsibilities as fathers and sons neglect their responsibilities as sons. 【孔子《論語・先進篇第十一》 Confucius: Chapter 11, *The Analects of Confucius*】

父不憂心因子孝，家無煩惱因妻賢。 A father is free from anxiety because his children are filial. A husband is free from worry because his wife is virtuous. 【郭小亭《濟公全傳・第七十二回》Guo Xiaoting: Chapter 72, *Biography of Jigong*】

父若英雄，子必好漢。 If the father is a heroic person, his son will sure be a brave man. 【諺語 Proverb】

父望子成龍。 A father hopes that his son will be a successful person. 【俗語 Common saying】【李白《李太白文集・第三十六回》Li Bai: Chapter 36, *Collected Work of Li Bai*】

父債子償，父業子得。 Debts owned by the father should be repaid by his sons, and the properties of the father should be inherited by his sons. 【俗語 Common saying】

父子不同舟。 Father and son should not take the same boat to avoid accidents happen and the family will lose all the breadwinners. 【俗語 Common saying】

虎父無犬兒。 The apple doesn't fall far from the tree. 【羅貫中《三國演義・第八十三回》Luo Guanzhong: Chapter 83, *Romance of the Three Kingdoms*】

虎狼知父子。 Even animals have the love between father and son, man should have more love between father and son. 【俗語 Common saying】【馮夢龍《喻世明言・第二十一卷》Feng Menglong: Chapter 21, *Stories to Instruct the World*】

老子偷瓜盜果，兒子殺人放火。 The apple doesn't fall far from the tree. 【呂德勝《小兒語》Lu Desheng: *Words for Young Boys*】

老子英雄兒好漢。 A heroic father will have brave sons. 【俗語 Common saying】

嚴父出驥子，慈母出懦子。 A strict father produces a well-bred son, a kind mother, a cowardly son. 【俗語 Common saying】【《增廣賢文》*Words that Open up One's Mind and Enhance One's Wisdom*】

嚴父出孝子，慈母出巧女。 A strict father produces a filial son, a kind mother, a clever daughter. 【俗語 Common saying】

有其父必有其子。 Like father, like son. 【俗語 Common saying】

知子莫若父。 No one knows a man better than his own father. 【羅貫中《三國演義・第二十八回》Luo Guanzhong: Chapter 28, *Romance of the Three Kingdoms*】

子不言父過。 The son should not talk about his father's faults. 【俗語 Common saying】

子用父錢心不痛。 The son never feels sorry to spend his father's money. 【諺語 Proverb】

Fault-finding

肥肉裏挑骨頭 —— 找岔子。
Looking for bones in fat – nit-picking.【歇後語 End-clipper】

橫挑鼻子豎挑眼。Find faults in a petty manner.【老舍〈龍鬚溝·第三幕〉Lao She: Scene 3, "Dragon-beard Ditch"】

哪壺不開提哪壺。Talking about something inappropriate in a wrong time.【俗語 Common saying】

Fear

怕得要死，恨得要命。Beside oneself with fright and hatred.【俗語 Common saying】

吃豆腐也怕扎牙根 —— 小心過份。Be afraid of breaking one's teeth when eating bean curd – be too careful.【楊朔《三千里江山》Yang Shuo: *Three Thousand Miles of Rivers and Mountains*】

重足而立，側目而視。Stand with one foot on another and look sideways at something–beside oneself with fright and hatred.【司馬遷《史記·汲鄭列傳》Sima Qian:"Biographies of Ji and Zheng", *Records of the Grand Historian*】

耗子見到貓。As terrifying as a mouse confronting a cat.【俗語 Common saying】

惶惶不可終日。Be on pins and needles day and night.【諺語 Proverb】

見怪不怪，其怪自敗。Face the fearful without fears and its fearfulness disappears.【曹雪芹《紅樓夢·第九十四回》Cao Xueqin: Chapter 94, *A Dream of the Red Chamber*】

見過鬼怕黑。Once bitten, twice shy.【俗語 Common saying】

來者不懼，懼者不來。Those who come have no fears and those who have fears will not come.【諺語 Proverb】【馮夢龍《醒世恆言·第三十四卷》Feng Menglong: Chapter 34, *Stories to Awaken the World*】

臉不變色，心不跳。Not to show the slightest fear.【俗語 Common saying】

兩腳站得牢，不怕大風搖。Being upright and selfless fears no slander.【諺語 Proverb】

毛骨悚然，通體寒慄。Make one's flesh creep and one shudders all over.【沈復《浮生六記·卷三》Shen Fu: Chapter 3, *Six Chapters of a Floating Life*】

捏一把冷汗。Break into a cold sweat.【宋濂等《元史·趙璧傳》Song Lian, et al.:"Biography of Zhao Bi", *The History of the Yuan Dynasty*】

怕鬼才被鬼嚇着。Only a person who is afraid of a ghost can be scared by it.【俗語 Common saying】

前怕狼，後怕虎。Fear wolves ahead and tigers behind – needless fears. 【西周生《醒世姻緣傳・第三十二回》Xi Zhousheng: Chapter 32, *Stories of Marriage to Awaken the World*】

前怕龍，後怕虎。Fear dragons ahead and tigers behind – needless fears. 【馮惟敏《朝天子・感述》Feng Weimin: "To the Tune of Stating My Feelings: Paying Homage to the Son of Heaven"】

窮怕親，富怕賊。The poor fear kinsmen, the rich fear thieves. 【俗語 Common saying】

三魂丟了七魄。Be frightened out of one's wits. 【俗語 Common saying】

無私故能無畏。When one is selfless, one can be fearless. 【俗語 Common saying】

小恐惴惴，大恐縵縵。Small fears make one restless and great fears, apprehensive. 【莊周《莊子・內篇・齊物論第二》Zhuang Zhou: Chapter 2, "On the Equality of Things", "Inner Chapters", *Zhuangzi*】

Feast

辦酒容易請客難。Preparing a feast is easier than inviting guests to come. 【諺語 Proverb】《客座贅語・卷一》Chapter 1, *The Postscript of Guests*】

富家一席酒，貧漢一年糧。A banquet prepared by a rich family worths a whole year's food for a poor family. 【諺語 Proverb】【呂德勝《小兒語》Lu Desheng: *Words for Young Boys*】

千里搭長棚 —— 沒有不散的筵席。Even the longest feast must break up at last – people have to separate from each other as good time is not constant. 【歇後語 End-clipper】【蘭陵笑笑生《金瓶梅・第八十回》Lanling Xiaoxiaosheng: Chapter 80, *The Plum in the Golden Vase*】

筵前無樂，不成歡笑。Without music at the banquet, people cannot enjoy themselves to the full. 【俗語 Common saying】【喬夢符《揚州夢》Qiao Mengfu: "Yangzhou Dream"】

Feeling

便縱有千種風情，更與何人說。Though I have myriad feelings, to whom should I tell? 【柳永〈雨霖鈴〉Liu Yong: "To the Tune of Bells Ringing in the Rain"】

出戶獨彷徨，秋思當告誰？I go outside and walk back and forth by myself, wondering to whom should I tell my autumn yearnings? 【柳永〈雨霖鈴〉Liu Yong:"To the Tune of Bells Ringing in the Rain"】

此情可待成追憶，只是當時已惘然。These feelings could have become memories to be cherished, but at that time we were bewildered and lost. 【李商隱〈錦瑟〉Li Shangyin:"An Ornamented Zither"】

此情無計可消除，纔下眉頭，卻上心頭。There is no way to dispel the lovesick and sorrow as soon as it just gets off my eyebrows, it goes to my mind. 【李清照〈一剪梅〉Li Qingzhao:"To the Tune of a Twig of Plum Blossoms"】

動天地而泣鬼神。Shocked like moving the heaven and earth and touched like the gods and ghosts weeping. 【汪琬〈烈婦周氏墓表〉Wang Wan:"Tomb Tablet for the Heroic Woman Surnamed Zhou"】

對月傷懷，挑燈自歎。Bewail one's fate to the moon and sigh before the lamp. 【曹雪芹《紅樓夢·第八十回》Cao Xueqin: Chapter 80, A Dream of the Red Chamber】

多情只有春庭月，猶為離人照落花。Only the moon that shone on the courtyard in spring was full of passion, still shedding its light on the fallen petals for the departed lover. 【張泌〈寄人〉Zhang Bi:"Sent to Someone"】

多情自古空餘恨，好夢由來最易醒。From of old, the romantic have many regrets as fond dreams are the easiest to wake up from. 【史清溪〈佚題〉Shi Qingxi:"Without a Title"】

放情者危，節慾者安。Those who are undisciplined in lust will get in danger and those who control their desires are safe. 【桓范《政要論·節慾》Huan Fan:"Controlling Desires", Discussions on Politics】

起雞皮疙瘩。Get goosebumps. 【俗語 Common saying】

千金縱買相如賦，脈脈此情誰訴。A thousand taels of gold might buy a prose as expressive as that by Sima Xiangru, but to whom should I pour out my feelings. 【辛棄疾〈摸魚兒〉Xin Qiji:"To the Tune of Groping for Fish"】

千人萬人之情，一人之情也。The feeling of thousands of people is the same as that of a single person. 【荀況《荀子·不苟第三》Xun Kuang: Chapter 3, "Nothing Indecorous", Xunzi】

親者痛，仇者快。Sadden one's own people and gladden the enemy. 【俗語 Common saying】【朱浮〈為幽州牧與彭寵書〉Zhu Fou:"A Letter to Peng Chong for the Magistrate of Youzhou"】

情欲信，辭欲巧。The feelings should be sincere and the expression should be adept. 【《禮記·表記第三十二》Chapter 32,

"Records of Examples", *The Book of Rites*】

人到情多情轉薄，而今真箇不多情。 When a person is very affectionate, his passion may turn thin, and now he regrets being affectionate.【納蘭性德〈攤破浣溪沙〉Nalan Xingde:"To the Tune of Sand of Silk-washing Stream" (lengthened)】

人非草木，孰能無情。 People are not grass or trees, how is it possible that they have no feelings?【余邵魚《東周列國志·第八十八回》Yu Shaoyu: Chapter 88, *Chronicles of the Eastern Zhou Kingdoms*】

人情薄如紙。 People's sympathy is as thin as paper.【俗語 Common saying】

人若無情，不如草木。 A person without emotion is inferior to grass and wood.【俗語 Common saying】

人若無情，孰能謂人。 If a person has no emotions, how can he be called a man?【余邵魚《東周列國志·第八十八回》Yu Shaoyu: Chapter 88, *Chronicles of the Eastern Zhou Kingdoms*】

人生有情淚沾臆。 Life is emotive and often chests are soaked with tears. Whoever has human feelings will have tears soaking his chest.【杜甫〈哀江頭〉Du Fu:"Grieving by the River"】

人同此心，心同此理。 All people share the same feelings and principles.【俗語 Common saying】

人心是肉長的。 All people are born sympathetic.【俗語 Common saying】

人在人情在，人死一筆勾。 While a person is alive, his favours are remembered; when a person is dead, his favours are totally forgotten.【俗語 Common saying】

十五個吊桶打水，七上八下。 One's restless heart is like fifteen buckets drawing water from a well, with seven buckets drawn up and eight dropped down.【文康《兒女英雄傳·第四十回》Wen Kang: Chapter 40, *Biographies of Young Heroes and Heroines*】

衰蘭送客咸陽道，天若有情天亦老。 Withe Red orchids saw off my guests at the Xianyang way. Heaven would grow old if it had feelings.【李賀〈金銅仙人辭漢歌並序〉Li He:"A Bronze Immortal Takes His Leave to the Han"】

鐵皮釘鋼釘 —— 硬到家。 Be as hard as nails – one does not consider another person's feelings.【歇後語 End-clipper】

言語傳情不如手。 Expression of your feelings with words is sometimes not as good as music and paintings.【諺語 Proverb】【劉商《胡笳十八拍·第六拍》Liu Shang:"The Sixth Song", *Eighteen Songs on a Nomad Flute*】

一片芳心千萬緒，人間沒個安排處。 Full of sorrow in my mind, yet there is no place to leave it.

【李煜〈蝶戀花〉Li Yu: "To the Tune of Butterflies Kissing Flowers"】

語已多，情未了，回首猶重道：記得綠羅裙，處處憐芳草。 Much has been said, yet we have not come to the end of our feelings. Looking back, he said again: If you remember my green silken skirt, have tender regard for the sweet grass wherever you go to miss me. 【牛希濟〈生查子〉Niu Xiji: "To the Tune of the Ripe Quince"】

祇可意會，不能言傳。 That which can only be felt but not spoken. 【莊周《莊子・外篇・天道第十三》: Zhuang Zhou: Chapter 13, "The Way of Heaven", "Outer Chapters", *Zhuangzi*】

Festival

八月十五大過年。 The Mid-Autumn Festival is more important than the Spring Festival. 【俗語 Common saying】

爆竹聲中一歲除，春風送暖入屠蘇。千門萬戶曈曈日，總把新桃換舊符。 A year ends amidst the sound of firecrackers. The spring breeze brings warmth to the wine. All households bask in the rising sun, and people replace the old peachwood charms with new ones. 【王安石〈元日〉Wang Anshi: "Lunar New Year's Day"】

立春雨淋淋，陰陰濕濕到清明。 Drizzling starts on the Beginning of Spring Day, and the rainy period will last until the Qingming Day. 【諺語 Proverb】

清明時節雨紛紛，路上行人欲斷魂。 It drizzles thick on the Qingming days. The traveller on his way is dismayed. 【杜牧〈清明〉Du Mu: "Qingming Festival"】

生前不給父母吃，何必清明去掃墓。 If you do not provide your parents with food when they are still alive, what is the point of sweeping their tombs on the Qingming days? 【俗語 Common saying】

迎新年，除舊歲。 Play the New Year in and lay the old year out. 【俗語 Common saying】

Fighting

城隍廟裏內訌 —— 鬼打鬼。 An internal strife within the temple of the City God is the devils beating the devils – having internal conflicts among the insiders. 【歇後語 End-clipper】

凡鬥者自以為是，而以人為非也。 All fighters firmly believe that

they are on the right side and others are on the wrong side. 【荀況《荀子・榮辱第四》Xun Kuang: Chapter 4, "Honour and Disgrace", *Xunzi*】

凡戰者，以正合，以奇勝。 In general, fighting is about using the normal strategies to meet the enemy, but exceptional tactics to secure victory. 【孫武《孫子兵法・兵勢第五》Sun Wu: Chapter 5, "Strategic Military Power", *The Art of War by Sunzi*】

古之所謂善戰者，勝於易勝者也。 What the ancients called a good fighter is one who won over the enemies who were easy to be defeated. 【孫武《孫子兵法・軍形第四》Sun Wu: Chapter 4, "Tactical Dispositions", *The Art of War by Sunzi*】

拉一派打一派。 Draw in one faction and hit out at another. 【俗語 Common saying】

兩狗爭一骨，相持難下。 Two dogs fighting for a bone will not yield to each other. 【俗語 Common saying】

兩虎相鬥必有一傷。 When two tigers fight, one is sure to get hurt. 【劉向《戰國策・秦策二》Liu Xiang: Part 2, "Strategies of the State of Qin", *Strategies of the Warring States*】

兩軍相遇勇者勝。 When two armies fight, the braver wins. 【諺語 Proverb】【司馬遷《史記・廉頗藺相如列傳》Sima Qian: "Biography of Lian Po and Lin Xianggru", *Records of the Grand Historian*】

兩雄相遇，其鬥必烈。 When two great persons meet, there must be a fierce fight. 【諺語 Proverb】

龍虎相鬥，必有一傷。 When a dragon and a tiger fight, one of them is sure to be injured. 【俗語 Common saying】

鷸蚌相爭，漁翁得利。 If a snipe and a clam are locked in fight, the fisherman will benefit – a quarrel benefits only the third party. 【劉向《戰國策・燕策二》Liu Xiang: "Strategies of the State of Yan, Part 2", *Strategies of the Warring States*】

善戰者不怒，善勝者不懼。 A good fighter does not shower his anger and a good winner is brave. 【老子《道德經・第六十八章》Laozi: Chapter 68, *Daodejing*】

善戰者，立於不敗之地，而不失敵之敗也。 A skilful fighter puts himself in an invincible position and does not miss the opportunity of defeating the enemy. 【孫武《孫子兵法・軍形第四》Sun Wu: Chapter 4, "Pattern of Military", *The Art of War by Sunzi*】

天下雖興，好戰必亡，天下雖安，忘戰必危。 Though the country is now prosperous, if it is fond of fighting, it will surely ruin; though the country is now peaceful, if it neglects military affairs, it will surely be in danger. 【白居易〈白居易集・議兵策〉Bai Juyi: "Discussion on Military Strategies", *Collected Works of Bai Juyi*】

知己知彼，百戰不殆。 Know the enemy and know yourself, and in a hundred battles you will never be in peril. 【孫武《孫子兵法‧謀攻第三》Sun Wu: Chapter 3, "Attack by Stratagem", *The Art of War by Sunzi*】

坐山觀虎鬥。 Shepherds quarrel, the wolf has a winning game. 【司馬遷《史記‧張儀列傳》Sima Qian: "Biography of Zhang Yi", *Records of the Grand Historian*】

Filial piety

百行孝為先。 Of all moral conducts, filial piety comes first. 【孔子《論語‧學而篇》Confucius: Chapter 1, *The Analects of Confucius*】

棒頭上出孝子。 Spare the rod and spoil the son. 【俗語 Common saying】

不孝有三，無後為大。 There are three things which are unfilial and to have no posterity is the gravest of them. 【孟軻《孟子‧離婁上》Meng Ke: Chapter 4, Part 1, *Mencius*】

財主門前孝子多。 There are many filial children in front of the door of a rich man – one does not care about his dignity and shame before fame and wealth. 【俗語 Common saying】

長病無孝子，慈母多敗兒。 Parents with chronic illness have no filial son as they have long been annoyed and a kind mother often spoils prodigal sons. 【俗語 Common saying】

兒忤逆是爹不是。 It is the father's fault if his son is unfilial. 【俗語 Common saying】

夫孝，德之本也，教之所由生也。 Filial piety is the root of virtue and from which education is born. 【《孝經‧開宗明義章第一》Chapter 1, "Opening Explanation", *Book of Filial Piety*】

夫孝，始於事親，中於事君，終於立身。 Filial piety begins with serving one's parents, proceeds to serving one's ruler, and ends at the way one conducts oneself in the society. 【《孝經‧開宗明義章第一》Chapter 1, "Opening Explanation", *Book of Filial Piety*】

父母唯其疾之憂。 Parents always worry about their children's health. 【孔子《論語‧為政篇第二》Confucius: Chapter 2, *The Analects of Confucius*】

教民親愛，莫善於孝。 To teach people to be affectionate and loving, there is nothing better than filial piety. 【《孝經‧廣要道章第十二》Chapter 12, "Broad and Crucial Doctrine", *Book of Filial Piety*】

樂其心，不違其志。 Delight your parents' hearts and do not oppose their wills. 【《禮記‧內則

第十二》Chapter 12, "The Pattern of the Family", *The Book of Rites*】

立身行道，揚名於後世，以顯父母，孝之終也。 When we have established ourselves, we should practice the Way and make our name for posterity to win honours for our parents, this is the accomplishment of filial piety.【《孝經・開宗明義章第一》Chapter 1, "Opening Explanation", *Book of Filial Piety*】

人之行，莫大於孝。 Of all the things people do, nothing is more important than filial piety.【《孝經・聖治章第九》Chapter 9, "Rule by Sagehood," *Book of Filial Piety*】

三年無改於父之道，可謂孝矣。 If the son behave well like he is still under the control of father for three years, he can be called filial.【孔子《論語・學而篇第一》Confucius: Chapter 1, *The Analects of Confucius*】

身體髮膚，受之父母，不敢毀傷，孝之始也。 Our body, hair, and skin are received from our parents, so we dare not injure or wound them, and this is the beginning of filial piety.【《孝經・開宗明義章第一》Chapter 1, "Opening Explanation", *Book of Filial Piety*】

世上難得事，子孝與妻賢。 Filial sons and virtuous wives are hard to find in this world.【俗語 Common saying】【馮夢龍〈萬事足・第十三折〉Feng Menglong: Scene 13, "Everything Is Satisfactory"】

樹欲靜而風不止，子欲養而親不待。 The tree wants to stay still yet the wind will not subside. The son wants to serve his parents, but they are no longer with him.【韓嬰《韓詩外傳・卷九》Han Ying: Chapter 9, *Supplementary Commentary on the Book of Songs by Master Han*】

誰言寸草心，報得三春暉。 Who can say the filial piety of children that is like inch-long grass will ever repay their mothers' love that are the sunlight of full spring?【孟郊〈遊子吟〉Meng Jiao: "Song of a Roamer"】

惟孝順父母，可以解憂。 It is only through filial piety that our stress is relieved.【孟軻《孟子・萬章上》Meng Ke: Chapter 10, Part 1, *Mencius*】

為人子當孝。 As a son, one must fulfil his filial duties.【俗語 Common saying】

孝當竭力，忠則盡忠。 One should do his utmost in doing his filial duties and should not hesitate to sacrifice his life for serving the country with loyalty.【俗語 Common saying】《千字文》 *Thousand Character Classic*】

孝順定生孝順子，忤逆還生忤逆兒。 If one is filial, one will have filial sons; if one is unfilial, one will have unfilial sons.【《增廣賢文》 *Words that Open up One's Mind and Enhance One's Wisdom*】

羊有跪乳之恩，鴉有反哺之義。 A small sheep expresses its gratitude to its mother by while kneeling to take milk from its mother, and a crow feeds its mother to express its affection to its mother.【《增廣賢文》*Words that Open up One's Mind and Enhance One's Wisdom*】

要求順子，先孝爹娘。 If you want to have filial sons, you should first be filial to your own parents.【俗語 Common saying】【呂德勝《小兒語》Lu Desheng: *Words for Young Boys*】

有錢難買子孫賢。 Money cannot buy virtuous offsprings.【俗語 Common saying】

遠燒香不如敬爺娘。 Burning incense to worship god is not as good as doing your filial duties to your parents.【諺語 Proverb】

祇覺當初歡侍日，千金一刻總蹉跎。 I regret that when I recalled the days of serving my parents joyfully at the beginning, I always wasted these valuable chances.【袁枚〈傷心〉Yuan Mei:"Heartbreaking"】

子孝父心寬。 A filial son will put his father's mind at ease.【《增廣賢文》*Words that Open up One's Mind and Enhance One's Wisdom*】

Fire

無火不生煙，無風不起浪。 There is no smoke without fire.【諺語 Proverb】

星星之火，可以燎原。 A single spark can start a great fire.【《尚書・盤庚上》Pan Geng, Part 1, *The Book of History*】

Fish

老魚不上鈎。 An old fish would not be hooked – The experienced will not be tricked.【俗語 Common saying】

鯉魚找鯉魚，鯽魚找鯽魚 —— 物以類聚。 Carps find carps, and crucian carps crucian carps – like attracts like.【歇後語 End-clipper】

荃者所以在魚，得魚而忘荃。 A fish-trap is for catching fish, when fish is caught, the fish-trap is forgotten.【莊周《莊子・雜篇・外物第二十六》Zhuang Zhou: Chapter 26, "External Things", "Miscellaneous Chapters", *Zhuangzi*】

深水有大魚。 There are big fish in the deep water.【俗語 Common saying】

水淺魚不住。 Fish will not stay in shallow water – Talents cannot be nurtured without great resources. 【俗語 Common saying】【李綠園《歧路燈·第八十回》Li Yuyuan: Chapter 80, *Lamp on a Forked Road*】

水淺養不住大魚。 Shallow water cannot breed big fish. 【諺語 Proverb】【李綠園《歧路燈·第八十回》Li Yuyuan: Chapter 80, *Lamp on a Forked Road*】

水清不養魚。 Fish does not come when water is too clean – things cannot go too far. 【俗語 Common saying】

水太清則無魚，人太急則無智。 When the water is too clear, there will be no fish in it. If a person is too impatient, he will have no wisdom. 【增廣賢文》*Words that Open up One's Mind and Enhance One's Wisdom*】

一夜海潮河水滿，鱸魚清曉入池塘。 A night of sea waves fills up the river, and bass go into the pond at dawn. 【宋禧〈即事〉Song Xi:"Impromptu"】

魚失水則死，水失魚猶為水也。 Fish will die when water is lost, but water with the loss of fish is still water – without the Emperor. Ordinary folks stay same; losing the support of ordinary folks, the Emperor is not the Emperor anymore. 【尸佼《尸子·君治第十五》Shi Jiao: Chapter 15, "The Governance of a Ruler", *Shizi*】

魚找魚，蝦找蝦。 Fish looks for fish and shrimps look for shrimps. 【俗語 Common saying】

子非魚，安知魚之樂？ Since you are not a fish, how do you come to know its happiness? 【莊周《莊子·外篇·秋水第十七》：Zhuang Zhou: Chapter 17, "Autumn Floods", "Outer Chapters", *Zhuangzi*】

Flattery

阿諛人人喜，直言人人嫌。 Everyone likes to be flattered and is annoyed by frank words. 【馮夢龍《警世通言·第十七卷》Feng Menglong: Chapter 17, *Stories to Caution the World*】

阿諛有福，直言有禍。 Flattery brings fortune, frank words, disaster. 【蔡東藩《後漢通俗演義·第四十七回》Cai Dongfan: Chapter 47, *Popular Romance of the Later Han*】

吹吹拍拍，拉拉扯扯。 Resort to boasting, flattery, and touting. 【俗語 Common saying】

見大得得拜，見小踢一腳。 Worship the superior and kick the inferior. 【俗語 Common saying】

君子上交不諂，下交不瀆。 A gentleman neither curry favour with his superiors nor look down on his inferiors. 《易經·繫

辭下》"Appended Remarks", Part 2, *The Book of Changes*】

臨下驕者事上必諂。 One who is arrogant to his subordinates is no doubt servile to his superiors. 【諺語 Proverb】

馬兒屁拍到馬腿上。 Lick someone's boots the wrong way. 【俗語 Common saying】【吳趼人《二十年目睹之怪現狀・第六十七回》Wu Jianren: Chapter 67, *Bizarre Happenings Eyewitnessed Over Two Decades*】

你稱我心，我合你意。 You scratch my back and I'll scratch yours. 【俗語 Common saying】

天下省連省，馬屁不穿棚。 The world is made up people in different provinces, yet all of them are not averse to flattery. 【俗語 Common saying】

言不取苟合，行不取苟容。 One neither say something to conform to others nor do something to please others. 【司馬遷《史記・范睢蔡澤列傳》Sima Qian:"Biographies of Fan Sui and Cai Ze", *Records of the Grand Historian*】

在下位，不援上。 When you are in a low position, do not court the flavours of your superiors. 【《禮記・中庸第三十一章》Chapter 31, "Doctrine of the Mean", *The Book of Rites*】

Flower

哀眾芳之蕪穢。 I am sadden by the withering of flowers amid weeds. 【屈原〈離騷〉Qu Yuan: *The Sorrows at Parting*】

白花冷淡無人愛。 Nobody likes the white flowers as they are too pale and simple. 【白居易〈白牡丹〉Bai Juyi:"White Peony"】

百花盛開，萬紫千紅。 Hundreds of flowers are in full bloom, in a riot of colours. 【俗語 Common saying】【朱熹《春日》Zhu Xi:"Spring Day"】

不是花中偏愛菊，此花開盡更無花。 Not that of all the flowers I favour the chrysanthemum, for no flowers will blossom after this flower withers away. 【元稹〈菊花〉Yuan Zhen:"Chrysanthemum"】

不信死花勝活人，請郎今夜伴花眠。 I do not believe that a dead flower is better than a living beauty. You might as well sleep with the flowers tonight. 【唐寅〈題拈花微笑圖〉Tang Yin:"Writing a Poem on the Painting with a Monk Picking a Flower in a Smile"】

春風桃花，十里飄香。 The fragrance of peach blossoms in the spring breeze wafts to ten miles away. 【俗語 Common saying】

春賞梅花，秋聞桂香。 Spring is the time to enjoy the plum blossoms, and autumn, the fragrance of sweet Osmanthus flowers.【俗語 Common saying】

春賞梅花夏賞荷。 Spring is the time to enjoy the plum blossoms, and summer, the lotus flowers.【俗語 Common saying】

地上一枝花，天上千滴露。 A flower on earth needs a thousand drops of dew from heaven.【俗語 Common saying】

各花入各眼。 A flower is beautiful in the eye that appreciates it.【俗語 Common saying】

好花不在多，一朵香滿園。 Good flowers do not win by number as the fragrance of a flower fills an entire garden.【俗語 Common saying】

好花開在一樹。 Good blossoms bloom on the same tree.【俗語 Common saying】

好花易謝，好景難長。 Good flowers are easy to wither and a good fortune does not last long.【俗語 Common saying】

忽如一夜春風來，千樹萬樹梨花開。 Suddenly in a night, the spring breeze comes, and peach bloom on thousands of trees.【岑參〈白雪歌送武判官歸〉Cen Shen:"Song of White Snow to Bid Farewell to Secretary Wu on His Return to the Capital"】

花開堪折直須折，莫待無花空折枝。 When flowers are fit for plucking, you must pluck them. Don't wait until the flowers are gone and you can only pluck the bare twigs.【杜秋娘〈金縷衣〉Du Qiunang:"The Gold-threaded Dress"】

花謝花飛花滿天，紅消香斷有誰憐。 Flowers wither Red, flowers are blown to fly up, and flowers fill the sky. When the redness of the flowers fades and when the fragrance of the flowers is gone, who has pity on them?【曹雪芹《紅樓夢·第二十七章》Cao Xueqin: Chapter 27, *A Dream of the Red Chamber*】

今年花落顏色改，明年花開復誰在。 Petals that fall this year change their colour, but who will still be here when flowers blossom next year.【劉希夷〈代悲白頭翁〉Liu Xiyi:"Sadness on Behalf of a White-haired Old Man"】

今年花勝去年紅，可惜明年花更好，知與誰同。 Flowers this year are redder than last. Perhaps the flowers next year will be finer, but I don't know who will share them with me?【歐陽修〈浪淘沙〉Ouyang Xiu:"To the Tune of Waves Washing over Sand"】

菊，花之隱逸者也。 Chrysanthemum is a flower that is withdrawn and carefree.【周敦頤〈愛蓮說〉Zhou Dunyi:"On My Love of the Lotus"】

看花容易栽花難。 Flowers are pleasant to look at but hard to grow.【俗語 Common saying】

蓮，花之君子者也。 Lotus is a flower like a gentleman. 【周敦頤〈愛蓮說〉Zhou Dunyi: "On My Love of the Lotus"】

林花謝了春紅，太匆匆。 The flowers in the forest have lost their spring hues, all too soon. 【李煜〈相見歡〉Li Yu: "To the Tune of the Joy of Meeting"】

柳絮迎風舞，桃花隨溪流。 The willow catkins dance with the wind and the peach blossoms float with the flowing waters of the river. 【杜甫〈漫興九首‧第一首〉Du Fu: "Nine Quatrain Poems: First Poem"】

落紅不是無情物，化作春泥猶護花。 The fallen red petals are not without feelings, for they turn into mud to fertilize the flowers in spring. 【龔自珍〈己亥雜詩〉Gong Zizhen: "Miscellaneous Poems of the Jihai Years"】

落花無言，人淡如菊。 The falling flowers do not say a word, and a person is calm like chrysanthemums. 【司空圖《二十四詩品‧典雅》Sikong Tu: "Elegance", *Twenty-four Modes of Poetry*】

玫瑰花兒可愛，刺大扎手。 The rose is lovely but prickly. 【諺語 Proverb】【曹雪芹《紅樓夢‧第六十五回》Cao Xueqin: Chapter 65, *A Dream of the Red Chamber*】

梅花優於香，桃花優於色。 Plum blossoms are good for their fragrance, and peach blossoms for their colour. 【俗語 Common saying】

梅須遜雪三分白，雪卻輸梅一段香。 The snow beats the plums with its whiter colour, but the plums make the snow concede by their nicer scent. 【盧梅坡〈雪梅〉Lu Meipo: "Snow Plum"】

梅佔百花魁。 Among flowers the plum ranks first. 【俗語 Common saying】

牡丹花好空入目，棗花雖小結實成。 The peony flowers are good for the eyes but they are fruitless. The jujube flowers, though small, bear fruits. 【《增廣賢文》*Words that Open up One's Mind and Enhance One's Wisdom*】

牡丹，花之富貴者也。 Peony is a flower representing wealth and honours. 【周敦頤〈愛蓮說〉Zhou Dunyi: "On My Love of the Lotus"】

年年歲歲花相似，歲歲年年人不同。 Every year, year after year, the flowers blossom as always. Year after year, every year, people are not the same. 【劉希夷〈代悲白頭翁〉Liu Xiyi: "Sadness on Behalf of a White-haired Old Man"】

弄花一年，看花十日。 It takes a year to raise flowers, but just ten days to watch the blossoming of flowers. 【陸游〈天彭牡丹譜‧風俗記第三〉Lu You: Chapter 3, "Records of Customs", *Treatise on Tianpeng Peonies*】

片片紅梅落，纖纖綠草生。 Petals of plum blossom fall, and the

fine grass grow. 【陸游〈春雨〉Lu You:"Spring Rain"】

平生行樂慣，病起即看花。 I am used to enjoy life and I watch the flowers as soon as I recover from illness. 【麗江木知府〈病起〉House Mu Zhi:"Recovery"】

清水出芙蓉，天然去雕飾。 The lotus that emerges from the clear water is natural without any embellishment. 【李白〈經亂離後天恩流夜郎憶舊游書懷贈江夏韋太守良宰〉Li Bai:"Presented to Wei Liangzai, Chief of Jiangxia Prefecture, to Express My Feelings When Staying At Yelang after Chaos"】

山茶紅似火。 The camellia is red like fire. 【俗語 Common saying】

十里荷花，三秋桂子。 Ten miles of lotus and late-autumn osmanthus seeds. 【柳永〈望海潮〉Liu Yong:"Watching Waves"】

時到花就開。 Flower blossoms when the time comes. 【俗語 Common saying】

桃花流水宛然去，別有天地非人間。 The peach blossoms flow silently away with the running water, this is a world of its own, unlike the world of man. 【李白〈山中答問〉Li Bai:"Conversations in the Mountain"】

桃花一簇開無主，可愛深紅愛淺紅？ No one but Nature owns the burst of peach blossoms, which shall I love best, the pink one or the crimson? 【杜甫〈江畔獨步尋芳〉Du Fu:"Walking Along the Riverside Looking for the Beautiful"】

萬綠叢中一點紅。 A single red flower in the midst of thick foliage. 【王安石〈石榴〉Wang Anshi:"Pomegranate"】

唯有牡丹真國色，花開時節動京城。 Only the peony is the true beauty; when its flowers blossom, it causes a great stir in the capital. 【劉禹錫〈賞牡丹〉Liu Yuxi:"Enjoying Peony"】

無可奈何花落去，似曾相識燕歸來。 Flowers fall, about which nothing much can be done, and the swallows, seemingly familiar, return again. 【晏殊〈浣溪沙〉Yan Shu:"To the Tune of Sand of Silk-washing Stream"】

惜花花結果，愛柳柳成蔭。 Care for flowers and you will have fruit; cherish willows, and you will have shade. 【諺語 Proverb】

小桃無主自開花，煙草茫茫帶晚鴉。 The small peach trees by themselves blossomed, and amidst the misty smokes and grass came the crows returning to the trees in the evening. 【戴復古〈淮村兵後〉Dai Fugu:"The Hui Village after the Battle"】

小小閒花分外紅，野人籬落自春風。 The little idle flowers are particularly red, and the bamboo fences of the rural people have the spring breeze. 【周霆震〈籬間小花〉Zhou

Tingzhen:"Little Flowers amidst the Fences"】

小雨輕風落楝花，細紅如雪點平沙。 The drizzle and breeze blew off the chinaberry flowers, and the small and red petals, like snowflakes, fell flatly on the beach. 【王安石〈鍾山晚步〉 Wang Anshi:"Strolling in the Evening at Mount Zhong"】

尋常一樣窗前月，才有梅花便不同。 Though in front of the window the moon shines as usual, the presence of the plums makes the moon look different. 【杜耒〈寒夜〉Du Lai:"Chilly Night"】

一叢深色花，十戶中人賦。 A bunch of red peonies worth the taxes paid by ten peasant households. 【白居易〈買花〉Bai Juyi:"Buying Flowers"】

一晝一夜，華開者謝。 Within the span of one day and one night, flowers blossom and wither. 【劉基〈司馬季主論卜〉Liu Ji:"Sima Jizhu's Talk on Divination"】

Food

吃得好壞看滋味，手藝高低看技術。 The condition of food depends on the taste and whether the craftsmanship is good or not depends on one's skill. 【俗語 Common saying】

粗茶淡飯吃得飽，粗衣棉衣穿到老。 Simple meals keep your stomach full and simple clothes keep you warm till old age. 【諺語 Proverb】

好飯不怕晚，趣話不嫌慢。 The best food takes time to prepare and the best stories are told slowly. 【諺語 Proverb】

家無隔宿之糧。 Not to know where the next meal comes from. 【諺語 Proverb】

美食不如美器。 Good food is not as important as good tableware. 【俗語 Common saying】

民以食為天。 Food is the first necessity of the people. 【司馬遷《史記‧酈生陸賈列傳》Sima Qian:"Biographies of Li Sheng and Lu Jia", Records of the Grand Historian】

人莫不飲食也，鮮能知味也。 Man eats every day, yet few can appreciate the original taste of food. 【《禮記‧中庸第三十一章》Chapter 31, "Doctrine of the Mean", The Book of Rites】

人無根本，飲食為命。 Men do not have roots, food is most important to men. 【蘭陵笑笑生《金瓶梅‧第七十九回》Lanling Xiaoxiaosheng: Chapter 79, The Plum in the Golden Vase】

食不果腹，衣不蔽體。 Do not have enough food and clothes. 【馮夢龍《警世通言‧第三十一卷》Feng Menglong: Chapter 31, Stories to Caution the World】

食之無味，棄之可惜。It's tasteless when consumed but it's a pity to throw it away – white elephant. 【陳壽《三國志・魏書・武帝紀》Chen Shou: "Annals of Emperor Wu", "History of the state of Wei", *Records of the Three Kingdoms*】

惜飯有飯吃，惜衣有衣穿。Treasure food and you will get rice; treasure clothes and you will get dress. 【諺語 Proverb】

小碗吃飯 —— 靠天（添）。Eating a meal with a small rice bowl – man depends upon Heaven for food. 【歇後語 End-clipper】

一朝無糧，父子不親。If food runs short, the father and sons are estranged. 【諺語 Proverb】

一粥一飯，當思來之不易。One should bear in mind that the production of the congee or rice is not easy to come by. 【朱用純《朱子家訓》Zhu Yongchun: *Precepts of the Zhu Family*】

飲食男女，人之大欲存焉。Food and sex are the great desires of the people. 【《禮記・禮運第九》Chapter 9, "Conveyance of Rites", *The Book of Rites*】

飲食約而精，園蔬勝珍饈。What you eat and drink should be simple and selected. Vegetables in a garden are better than rare delicacies. 【朱用純《朱子家訓》Zhu Yongchun: *Precepts of the Zhu Family*】

飲食之人，則人賤之矣。People who pursue the best only in food are regarded as low by other people. 【孟軻《孟子・告子章句上》Meng Ke: Chapter 6, Part 1, *Mencius*】

有米不愁沒飯吃。When there is rice, you do not need to worry about food. 【諺語 Proverb】

早飯吃得早，中飯吃得飽，夜飯吃得少。Have early breakfast, full lunch, and light supper. 【俗語 Common saying】

煮飯要有米，說話要有理。To make food, you must have rice; to speak, you must be in the right. 【諺語 Proverb】

Foolishness

笨人有笨福。A fool has his own fortune. 【諺語 Proverb】

才德兼亡，謂之愚人。He who has neither talent nor virtue is known as a fool. 【司馬光《資治通鑑・周紀》Sima Guang: "Annals of the Zhou Dynasty", *Comprehensive Mirror to Aid in Government*】

痴人自有痴人福。A fool has his own blessings. 【馮夢龍《古今譚概・卷二十九》Feng Menglong: Chapter 29, *Stories Old and New*】

蠢人饒舌，智者思慮。A stupid person is talkative, a wise person, meditative. 【諺語 Proverb】

刀鈍石來磨，人蠢沒奈何。 A blunt knife can be sharpened on a stone, but nothing can be done if a person is fool.【諺語 Proverb】

戇人自有戇人福。 A fool has his own fortune.【諺語 Proverb】

為戲子落淚，替古人擔憂。 Shedding tears for dramatic characters and worrying for the ancients are unnecessary.【蘭陵笑笑生《金瓶梅‧第二十回》Lanling Xiaoxiaosheng: Chapter 20, *The Plum in the Golden Vase*】

獻醜不如藏拙。 It is wiser to conceal one's stupidity than it is to show oneself up.【諺語 Proverb】

愚人不見現實，賢者洞察未來。 The stupid are blind to the reality while the wise see clearly what lies ahead in the future.【俗語 Common saying】

愚人偏說人愚。 Stupid people often call others stupid.【俗語 Common saying】

愚人之口，毀身之由。 The mouth of a stupid person is the cause of his destruction.【俗語 Common saying】

愚者暗於成事，智者見於未萌。 A stupid person cannot understand the reason to get success while a wise person foresees the success before it takes place.【劉向《戰國策‧趙策二》Liu Xiang: "Strategies of the State of Zhao, No. 2", *Strategies of the Warring States*】

愚者千慮，必有一得。 Among a thousand ideas of a foolish person, there will certainly be one which is correct.【司馬遷《史記‧淮陰侯列傳》Sima Qian: "Biography of the Marquis of Huaiyin", *Records of the Grand Historian*】

Foot

搬起石頭打自己的腳。 Shoot oneself in the foot.【毛澤東〈關於國際新形勢對新華日報記者的談話〉Mao Zedong: "Interview with a *New China Daily* Correspondent on the New International Situation"】

不敢越雷池一步。 Dare not go one step beyond the limit.【庾亮〈報溫嶠書〉Yu Liang: "A Letter in Reply to Wen Qiao"】

出水才看兩腿泥。 Only the end can tell–speak with reason and basis.【《增廣賢文》*Words that Open up One's Mind and Enhance One's Wisdom*】

懶婆娘的裹腳，又長又臭。 Foot-bindings of a slattern are long and smelly–words being too lengthy and pointless.【俗語 Common saying】

企者不立，跨者不行。 He who is on tiptoe cannot stand firm and

he who walks in great strides cannot walk far – pursuing for the impossibilities can never success; pursuing for things to be done quickly will never succeed. 【老子《道德經‧第二十四章》Laozi: Chapter 24, *Daodejing*】

棄之如敝屣。 Cast aside like throwing away an old shoe. 【孟軻《孟子‧盡心章句上》Meng Ke: Chapter 7, Part 1, *Mencius*】

三步並兩步。 With hurried steps. 【諺語 Proverb】【馮夢龍《醒世恒言‧第三十五卷》Feng Menglong: Chapter 35, *Stories to Awaken the World*】

一步趕不上，步步趕不上。 Miss one step and you'll fall behind every step. 【俗語 Common saying】【王希堅〈雨過天晴〉Wang Xijian: "Sunshine after Rain"】

一步未穩，休跨二步。 If one is not sure of the first step, do not take the second one. 【俗語 Common saying】

一步一腳印。 Each step leaves its footmark. 【俗語 Common saying】

有多大的腳，穿多大的鞋。 Get a shoe that fits – do what you can do. 【諺語 Proverb】

足寒傷心，民怨傷國。 Cold feet do harm to the heart and people's enmity does harm to the country. 【黃石公《素書‧安禮》Huang Shigong: "Securing Rites", *Book of Plain Truths*】

Forgiveness

得饒人處且饒人。 Forgive others wherever you can. 【曹雪芹《紅樓夢‧第五十九回》Cao Xueqin: Chapter 59, *A Dream of the Red Chamber*】

虧人是禍，饒人是福。 Treating others unfairly is a disaster and forgiving people is a blessing. 【《增廣賢文》*Words that Open up One's Mind and Enhance One's Wisdom*】

饒人不是痴，過後得便宜。 It is not stupid to forgive others for you will benefit from it in the future. 【諺語 Proverb】

饒人不是痴漢，痴漢不會饒人。 One who forgives others is not stupid and a stupid man does not forgive others. 【《增廣賢文》*Words that Open up One's Mind and Enhance One's Wisdom*】

責人之心責己，恕己之心恕人。 Blame yourself in the way you blam others and forgive others in the way you forgive your own faults. 【《增廣賢文》*Words that Open up One's Mind and Enhance One's Wisdom*】

饒人三分不為痴。 He who forgives others is not an idiot. 【諺語 Proverb】

饒人是福，欺人是禍。 To forgive people is a blessing to oneself, while to bully others is a disaster.【鄭德輝《老君堂・第一折》Zheng Dehui: Scene 1, "Hall of the Venerable Sovereign"】

饒一着，退一步。To forgive others, to give in others. 【《增廣賢文》Words that Open up One's Mind and Enhance One's Wisdom】

Fortune and misfortune

白璧不可為，容容多後福。To do nothing like a purely white jade; harmony with other people will bring you fortune in the future. 【范曄《後漢書・左雄傳》Fan Ye: "Biography of Zuo Xiong", History of the Later Han】

閉門家中坐，禍從天上來。Even if you stay at home, misfortune might befall you. 【馮夢龍《醒世恆言・第二十卷》Feng Menglong: Chapter 20, Stories to Awaken the World】

不經災難不知福。Misfortunes tell us what fortune is. 【俗語 Common saying】

不幸中之大幸。A fortune out of misfortune. 【俗語 Common saying】

才脫虎穴，又入龍潭。Jump out of a dragon's pond into a tiger's den – one misfortune comes on the neck of another. 【俗語 Common saying】

大難不死，必有後福。One who has survived a great disaster will certainly have good fortune in the future. 【俗語 Common saying】

躲過了風暴又遇了雨。One has escaped a storm but has to be caught in a heavy rain–one misfortune comes on the neck of another. 【俗語 Common saying】【曹雪芹《紅樓夢・第一百一回》Cao Xueqin: Chapter 101, A Dream of the Red Chamber】

躲了點鋼槍，撞見喪門劍。Having dodged the spear, there comes the sword. 【俗語 Common saying】【佚名〈關雲長千里獨行・第二折〉Anonymous: Scene 2, "Walking alone for a Thousand Miles"】

躲了雷公，遇見霹靂 —— 禍不單行。Having escaped from the Thunder God, then comes the Lightening God. 【歇後語 End-clipper】【馮夢龍《警世通言・第十八卷》Feng Menglong: Chapter 18, Stories to Caution the World】

方離狼窩，又逢虎口。Out of the wolf's den into the tiger's mouth–one misfortune comes on the neck of another. 【羅貫中《三國演義・第十三回》Luo Guanzhong: Chapter 13, Romance of the Three Kingdoms】

逢凶化吉，遇難呈祥。If anything untoward happens, one's bad luck will turn into good. 【俗語 Common saying】

福從禍中來。Good fortune comes out of bad. 【俗語 Common saying】

福大量大造化大。 Good fortune and great natural capacity make a remarkable workings of fate.【俗語 Common saying】

福生有根，禍生有胎。 Fortune and disaster have their causes.【班固《漢書‧枚乘傳》Ban Gu:"Biography of Mei Cheng", *History of the Han*】

福是禍中來。 Good fortune comes out of bad.【俗語 Common saying】

福無重受日，禍有并來時。 Fortune never repeats itself, whereas trouble comes in pairs.【關漢卿〈蝴蝶夢‧第一折〉Guan Hanqing: Scene 1, "Butterfly Dream"】

福無雙全，禍不單行。 Good fortune does not come in pairs, and disasters do not come alone.【施耐庵《水滸傳‧第三十七回》Shi Nai'an: Chapter 37, *Outlaws of the Marshes*】

福由己發，禍由己生。 Fortune begins from the self and misfortunate is generated by the self.【劉安《淮南子‧繆稱訓第十》Liu An: Chapter 10, "On Erroneous Designations", *Huainanzi*】

福在積善，禍在積惡。 Fortune is about accumulating merits and disaster is about accumulating evils.【黃石公《素書‧安禮》Huang Shigong:"Securing Rites", *Book of Plain Truths*】

福中伏禍，禍中寓福。 In fortune lurks calamity, and in calamity lies fortune.【俗語 Common saying】

福中有禍，禍中有福。 In fortune, there may be misfortune, and in misfortune, fortune.【俗語 Common saying】

甫出龍潭，又入虎穴。 Just out of the dragon's pond, then enters a tiger's den—one misfortune comes on the neck of another.【俗語 Common saying】

黃鼠狼單病鴨子 —— 倒楣越加倒楣。 The weak get victimized most.【歇後語 End-clipper】

禍福同門，利害為鄰。 Fortune and misfortune come from the same source and advantages and disadvantages are closely linked.【劉安《淮南子‧人間訓第十八》Liu An: Chapter 18, "In the World of Man", *Huainanzi*】

禍福無門，唯人所招。 There is no door for misfortune or fortune to come in. It is people themselves who ask for it.【左丘明《左傳‧襄公二十三年》Zuo Qiuming:"The Twenty-third Year of the Reign of Duke Xiang", *Zuo's Commentary on the Spring and Autumn Annals*】

禍莫於不知足。 No disaster is greater than not to be contented with what one has.【老子《道德經‧第四十六章》Laozi: Chapter 46, *Daodejing*】

禍兮福之所倚，福兮禍之所伏。 Disaster is what fortune leans on and fortune is what disaster hides in.【老子《道德經‧第五十八章》Laozi: Chapter 58, *Daodejing*】

禍因惡積，福緣善慶。 Disasters result from evil doings accumulated from the past and blessings from good deeds. 【諺語 Proverb】

禍由惡做，福自德生。 Disasters result from evil doings while blessings come from virtue. 【諺語 Proverb】

禍與福相鄰。 Fortune and misfortune are closely linked. 【荀況《荀子‧大略第二十七》Xun Kuang: Chapter 27, "Great Compendium", *Xunzi*】

禍中寓福，福中伏禍。 There is calamity in good fortune and good fortune in calamity. 【諺語 Proverb】

老天不扶苦命人。 Even Heaven does not help the unlucky. 【諺語 Proverb】

人生禍福總由天。 The fortune and misfortune in the life of a person are always decided by heaven. 【諺語 Proverb】

人有旦夕禍福，天有晝夜陰晴。 People cannot foresee their fortune and misfortune like there are days and nights, rain and sunshine. 【佚名《名賢集》Anonymous: *Collected Sayings of Famous Sages*】

人有禍患，不可生喜幸心。 Do not rejoice over the misfortunes of others. 【朱用純《朱子家訓》Zhu Yongchun: *Precepts of the Zhu Family*】

塞翁失馬，安知非福。 Misfortune may be a blessing in disguise. 【李汝珍《鏡花緣‧第七回》Li Ruzhen: Chapter 7, *Flowers In the Mirror*】

三不幸：幼年喪父，中年喪妻，老年喪子。 There are three misfortunes: death of one's father in youth, widowerhood in middle age, and death of one's son in old age. 【俗語 Common saying】

時來誰不來，時不來誰來。 When fortune comes, all people come; when fortune leaves, all people leave. 【俗語 Common saying】

時來易覓金千兩，運去難賒酒一壺。 When fortune comes, it is easy for me to find ten thousand taels of gold; when fortune leaves, it is difficult for one to buy a pot of wine on credit. 【褚人獲《隋唐演義‧第十四回》Zhu Renhuo: Chapter 14, *Heroes in Sui and Tang Dynasties*】

世有無望之福，又有無望之禍。 In this world, there are unexpected fortunes and misfortunes. 【司馬遷《史記‧春申君列傳》Sima Qian: "Biography of Lord Chunshen", *Records of the Grand Historian*】

是福不是禍，是禍躲不過。 Fortune will not turn into misfortune and misfortune cannot be dodged. 【諺語 Proverb】

瓦片也有翻身日。 Every dog has its day. 【諺語 Proverb】【蔡東藩《元史通俗演義‧第三回》Cai Dongfan: Chapter 3, *Popular Romance of the Yuan*】

屋漏更遭連夜雨。 It never rains but pours. 【高則誠〈琵琶記・第二十三齣〉Gao Zecheng: Scene 23, "A Record on Pipa"】

無功之賞，不義之富，禍之媒也。 Rewards received for no credit and wealth amassed by dishonest means lead to misfortune. 【晏嬰《晏子春秋・內篇・雜下》Yan Ying: "Miscellaneous", "Inner Chapters", Part 2, *Master Yan's Spring and Autumn Annals*】

無妄之災在所難免。 Misfortunes are hard to be avoided. 【俗語 Common saying】

行善獲福，行惡得殃。 Do good and you get fortune; do evil and you get disasters. 【諺語 Proverb】【王重民，王慶菽，向達，周一良，啟功，曾毅公編《敦煌變文集・卷六》Wang Zhongmin, Wang Qingshu, Xiang Da, Zhou Yiliang, Qi Gong, Zeng Yigong, etc.: Chapter 6, *A Collection of Proses at Dunhuang*】

一福壓百禍。 One good fortune neutralizes a hundred misfortunes. 【佛家語 Buddhist saying】

有福同享，有難同當。 Share good and bad times. 【諺語 Proverb】【李寶嘉《官場現形記・第五回》Li Baojia: Chapter 5, *Officialdom Unmasked*】

Fortune-telling

鑼在本山敲不響，隔山敲打響噹噹 A fortune-teller is not honoured in his own country. 【俗語 Common saying】

賣卜賣卦，轉回說話。 Fortune-tellers and diviners are slick and sly in what they say. 【俗語 Common saying】【施耐庵《水滸傳・第六十一回》Shi Nai'an: Chapter 61, *Outlaws of the Marshes*】

賣卦口，沒量斗。 A fortune-teller is slick and sly. 【馮夢龍《警世通言・第十三卷》Feng Menglong: Chapter 13, *Stories to Caution the World*】

Fox

狐狸看雞 —— 越看越稀。 When one asked a fox who looks after one's chicken, their number will dwindle – appointing the wrong person cause big trouble. 【歇後語 End-clipper】

狐狸必首丘。 When a fox dies, its head is sure to lie in the direction of the mountain where it was born – never forget the foundation. 【劉安《淮南子・說林訓第十七》Liu An: Chapter 17, "Discourse on Mountains", *Huainanzi*】

一窩狐狸不嫌騷。 Foxes in the same burrow do not mind each other's foul smells. 【諺語 Proverb】

【趙樹理《賣煙葉》Zhao Shuli: *Selling Tobacco Leaves*】

Friend

不打不成相識。 It takes a fight for people to know each other. 【施耐庵《水滸傳·第三十八回》Shi Nai'an: Chapter 38, *Outlaws of the Marshes*】

不觀其人，但觀其友。 A man is known by the company he keeps. 【俗語 Common saying】

不知其人觀其友。 A man is known by the company he keeps. 【俗語 Common saying】

財盡不交，色盡不妻。 A person who has lost his wealth gets no friends;a woman who has lost her beauty cannot get married. 【吳中情奴〈相思譜·第九折〉Wuzhong Qingnu: Scene 9, "Melody of Mutual Love"】

陳酒味醇，老友情深。 Friendship is like wine, the older the better. 【諺語 Proverb】

大凡君子與君子，以同道為朋；小人與小人，以同利為朋。 In general, the friendship between a gentleman and another is based on sharing the same ideals, whereas the friendship between a petty person and another is based on mutual benefits. 【歐陽修〈朋黨論〉Ouyang Xiu:"On Cliques"】

得一知己，死可無恨。 When one has a bosom friend, one can die without regret. 【俗語 Common saying】

多一個朋友多一條路。 One more friend gives you one more way to go. 【俗語 Common saying】

風物依然，故人已亡。 The scenery is still the same, but my friend is dead. 【諺語 Proverb】

富貴交友易，患難顯真情。 Wealth makes friends, and adversity tests true friendship. 【諺語 Proverb】

甘蔗老的甜，友情老的深。 Old sugarcanes are sweet and long friendships, deep. 【諺語 Proverb】

官情短，私情長。 Friendship between officials lasts short, but that between ordinary people is long. 【俗語 Common saying】

官情如紙薄。 Friendship between officials is as thin as paper. 【諺語 Proverb】【馮夢龍《醒世恆言·第二十七卷》Feng Menglong: Chapter 27, *Stories to Awaken the World*】

觀其友，知其人。 A person is known by the company he keeps. 【諺語 Proverb】

海內存知己，天涯若比鄰。 If you have friends that know you well, you and your friends are closely linked no matter how far you are apart from each other.【王勃〈送杜少府之任蜀州〉Wang Bo:"Seeing off Magistrate Du Who Is Leaving for Shuzhou to Take up His Appointment"】

患難見至交，烈火現真金。 In adversity, true friends are seen as in a blazing fire genuine gold is revealed.【俗語 Common saying】

交惡友不如獨處。 It is better to be alone than in bad company.【俗語 Common saying】

交情歸交情，公事歸公事。 Friendship is friendship, while business is business.【俗語 Common saying】

交友遍天下，知心有幾人。 Even you have friends all over the world, you could only have a few bosom ones.【俗語 Common saying】

結交須勝己，似我不如無。 You make friends with those who are better than you, and you would rathr have no friends than making friends with those who are similar to you.【增廣賢文》Words that Open up One's Mind and Enhance One's Wisdom】

結有德之朋，絕無義之交。 Make virtuous friends but spurn wicked acquaintants.【佚名《名賢集》Anonymous: Collected Sayings of Famous Sages】

今夕復何夕，共此燈燭光。 What lucky night is tonight? We are together in this candlelight.【杜甫〈贈衞八處士〉Du Fu:"Presented to Scholar-recluse Wei the Eighth"】

近人不說遠話。 With close friends, one need not talk in a roundabout way.【俗語 Common saying】

久旱逢甘雨，他鄉遇故知。 It is a pleasure to have a welcome rain after a long drought or run into an old friend in a distant land.【佚名〈四喜詩〉Du Fu:"Poem on Four Delightful Things"】

酒肉弟兄千個有，落難之中無一人。 You may have a thousand wine-and-meat friends, but when you meet with misfortune, you can find none.【俗語 Common saying】【馮夢龍《喻世明言‧第八卷》Feng Menglong: Chapter 8, Stories to instruct the world】

酒肉朋友，柴米夫妻。 Friends come together to have wine and meat and husband and wife are together for firewood and rice – treat different people in different manners.【諺語 Proverb】

居必擇鄰，交必良友。 If one wants to settle down, one must choose your neighbours. If you want to make friends, you must choose the good ones.【佚名《名賢集》Anonymous: Collected Sayings of Famous Sages】

君乘車，我戴笠，他日相逢下車揖。 You sit on a carriage,

while I wear a straw hat. When we meet in the future, hope you will come down from your carriage to greet me. 【《越謠歌》 Folksongs of Yue】

君子過人以為友，不及人以為師。 When a gentleman is better than others, he takes them as friends; when a gentleman is not as good as others, he takes them as his teachers. 【晏嬰《晏子春秋·外篇下》Yan Ying: "Outer Chapters", Part 2, *Master Yan's Spring and Autumn Annals*】

君子絕交不出惡語。 A gentleman terminates a friendship without using any bad language. 【司馬遷《史記·樂毅列傳》Sima Qian: "Biography of Le Yi", *Records of the Grand Historian*】

君子絕交不計仇。 A gentleman severs ties with a friend without rancour. 【俗語 Common saying】

君子以朋友講習。 A gentleman talks and practices with friends. 【《易經·兌·象》"Image", "Hexagram Dui", *The Book of Changes*】

君子以文會友，以友輔仁。 A gentleman makes and meets friends by knowledge and literacy talents, and enhance their own righteousness through the practice among friends. 【孔子《論語·顏淵篇第十二》Confucius: Chapter 12, *The Analects of Confucius*】

君子之交淡如水，小人之交甘若醴。 The friendship of a gentleman is insipid as water while that of a petty man is sweet as wine. 【莊周《莊子·外篇·山木第二十》Zhuang Zhou: Chapter 20, "The Mountain Tree", "Outer Chapters", *Zhuangzi*】

兩好合一好。 The friendship between two people comes from their kindness to each other. 【諺語 Proverb】

麻面無鬚不可交。 Do not make friends with a man whose face is pockmarked and beardless as those have high chance of smallpox infection in the past. 【俗語 Common saying】

莫逆於心，遂相與友。 When there is complete mutual understanding, then there is a making of friendship. 【莊周《莊子·內篇·大宗師第六》：Zhuang Zhou: Chapter 6, "The Great Ancestral Teacher", "Inner Chapters", *Zhuangzi*】

朋友遍天下，同志最知心。 We have friends all over the world and comrades are closest to our hearts. 【諺語 Proverb】

朋友千個少，仇人一個多。 Better to make more friends and less enemies. 【諺語 Proverb】

朋友相衛而不相攻。 Friends protect and do not attack each other. 【俗語 Common saying】

朋友有信。 There is trust between friends. 【孟軻《孟子·滕文公上》Meng Ke: Chapter 5, Part 1, *Mencius*】

貧賤之知不可忘。 Do not forget friends that you made when you

were poor and low-positioned.
【范曄《後漢書・宋弘傳》Fan Ye:"Biography of Song Hong", *History of the Later Han*】

拼將一死酬知己。 One risks death for friendship's sake.【羅貫中《三國演義・第五十回》Luo Guanzhong: Chapter 50, *Romance of the Three Kingdoms*】

千金易得，知心難覓。 One can get a thousand pieces of gold easily and but finding a true friend with an understanding heart is difficult.【諺語 Proverb】

勸君更盡一杯酒，西出陽關無故人。 I sincerely advise you to have another cup of wine, as you'll find none of your old friends west of the Yang Pass.【王維〈送元二使安西〉Wang Wei:"Seeing off Yuan the Second on a Mission to Anxi"】

人生樂在相知心。 A pleasure in life is to have a friend who knows your heart.【王安石〈明妃曲之二〉Wang Anshi:"Song on the Ming Imperial Concubine: No. 2"】

人生交契無老少，論心何必先同調。 In life, friendship is built not on age; it is about heart and there is no need to be of the same voice first.【杜甫〈徒步歸行〉Du Fu:"Returning Home on Foot"】

人以自好而擇友。 One chooses one's friends according to one's preferences.【俗語 Common saying】

少交友，少結怨。 Fewer friends, fewer enemies.【俗語 Common saying】

生死關頭見真情。 At the critical point between life and death, true friendship is seen.【俗語 Common saying】

士為知己者死，女為悅己者容。 A man dies for the one who knows him, and a girl does make up for one who loves her.【劉向《戰國策・趙策一》Liu Xiang:"Strategies of the State of Zhao, No. 1", *Strategies of the Warring States*】

水至清則無魚，人至察則無徒。 When the water is too clear, there will be no fish; when a person is too exacting, he has no friends.【班固《漢書・東方朔傳》Ban Gu:"Biography of Dong Fangsu", *History of the Han*】

歲寒知松柏，患難見交情。 The character of the pine and cypress is shown in frigid winter; the sincerity of one's friend is shown in adverse circumstances.【孔子《論語・子罕篇第九》Confucius: Chapter 9, *The Analects of Confucius*】

萬兩黃金容易得，知心一個也難求。 It is easy to get ten thousand taels of gold but difficult to have a bosom friend.【曹雪芹《紅樓夢・第五十七回》Cao Xueqin: Chapter 57, *A Dream of the Red Chamber*】

往來無白丁。 There is no people with limited knowledge among one's friends.【劉禹錫〈陋室銘〉

Liu Yuxi: "Inscription on My Humble Dwelling"】

未觀其人，先觀其友。 You can judge a person by the friends he keeps. 【諺語 Proverb】

無友不如己者。 Do not makes friends with those who are worse than you. 【孔子《論語·學而篇第一》Confucius: Chapter 1, *The Analects of Confucius*】

物莫如新，友莫如故。 Everything is good when new, but friendship is good when old. 【諺語 Proverb】

相識滿天下，知心能幾人。 You may have friends all over the world, but only a few of them are intimate ones. 【《增廣賢文》 *Words that Open up One's Mind and Enhance One's Wisdom*】

相視而笑，莫逆於心。 Friends look and smile at each other and have complete mutual understanding. 【莊周《莊子·內篇·大宗師第六》: Zhuang Zhou: Chapter 6, "The Great Ancestral Teacher", "Inner Chapters", *Zhuangzi*】

相知無遠近，萬里尚為鄰。 Distance cannot separate true friends who feel so close even when they are thousands of miles apart. 【張九齡〈送韋城李少府〉Zhang Jiuling: "Seeing off Vice-prefect Li of Weicheng"】

詳交者不失人，泛結者多後悔。 He who is prudent in making friends will not lose them; he who makes friends indiscriminately often regret. 【葛洪《抱朴子·外篇·交際第十六》Ge Hong: Chapter 16, "Keeping Company", "Outer Chapters", *The Master Who Embraces Simplicity*】

要作好人，須尋好友。 To be a good person, you must make good friends. 【呂德勝《小兒語》Lu Desheng: *Words for Young Boys*】

一貴一賤，交情乃見。 Friendship is tested when a noble man becomes humble. 【司馬遷《史記·汲鄭列傳》Sima Qian: "Biography of Ji Zheng", *Records of the Grand Historian*】

一回生，二回熟。 Strangers the first time, friends the second. 【諺語 Proverb】

一朝認識，千日朋友。 Once acquainted, people become friends for long. 【俗語 Common saying】

衣不如新，人不如故。 For clothes, the newest are best; for friends, the oldest are best. 【佚名〈古艷歌〉Anonymous: "Love Songs in the Old Days"】

衣服新的好，朋友舊的好。 For clothes, the newest are best; for friends, the oldest are best. 【俗語 Common saying】

衣莫若新，人莫若故。 For clothes, the newest is best; for friends, the oldest are best. 【晏嬰《晏子春秋·內篇雜上第五》Yan Ying: Chapter 5, "Miscellaneous", "Inner Chapters", *Master Yan's Spring and Autumn Annals*】

以利相交，利盡而疏。A friendship built on money will grow thin when money runs low.【俗語 Common saying】

友情濃於酒。Friendship is thicker than wine.【諺語 Proverb】

友誼第一，比賽第二。Friendship first, competition second.【俗語 Common saying】

友者，所以相有也；道不同，何以相有也。Friends are made on what they have in common. If they differ in their principles, how can they have anything in common?【荀況《荀子·大略第二十七卷》Xun Kuang: Chapter 27, "Great Compendium", *Xunzi*】

有朋自遠方來，不亦樂乎。Isn't it a pleasure to have friends coming from afar to visit you?【孔子《論語·學而篇第一》Confucius: Chapter 1, *The Analects of Confucius*】

有錢有酒，必有朋友。A full purse never lacks friends.【俗語 Common saying】

有錢有酒，何愁缺友。A full purse never lacks friends.【俗語 Common saying】

在家靠父母，出門靠朋友。At home, we rely on our parents; away from home, we rely on our friends.【諺語 Proverb】

知己到來言不盡。When bosom friends come, they have endless things to talk about.【諺語 Proverb】【許仲琳《封神演義·第十一回》Xu Zhonglin: Chapter 11, *Romance of the Investiture of the Deities*】

志道者少友，逐俗者多儔。He who is committed to the Way has few friends; he who drifts along with the tide has many partners.【王符《潛夫論·實貢》Wang Fu: "On Recommendations of Substance", *Remarks by a Recluse*】

最難風雨故人來。Treasure the old friend who comes over in a storm.【孫星衍〈楹聯〉Sun Xingyan: "Hall Couplet"】

Frugality

大儉以後，必生奢男。Very frugal parents are sure to have children who live an extravagant life.【俗語 Common saying】【蔡東藩《南北史通俗演義·第九十六回》Cai Dongfan: Chapter 96, *Popular Romance of the Southern and Northern Dynasties*】

儉，德之共也；奢，惡之大也。Frugality is common in all virtues; extravagance is the worst of all vices.【左丘明《左傳·莊公二十四年》Zuo Qiuming: "The Twenty-fourth Year of the Reign of Duke Zhuang", *Zuo's Commentary on the Spring and Autumn Annals*】

儉是致富之本。Frugality is the foundation of wealth.【諺語 Proverb】

勒緊褲腰帶。 Tighten one's belt.
【俗語 Common saying】

省吃省用省求人。If you are frugal in eating and spending, you save the trouble of seeking for help from others. 【諺語 Proverb】

由儉入奢易，由奢返儉難。 It is easy to go from frugality to extravagance, but it is difficult to go from extravagance to frugality. 【張伯行《困學錄集粹》Zhang Boxing: *Collections of Difficult Subjects of Study*】

Fruit

當令果子趁鮮賣。 Sell the fruit when it is still fresh. 【俗語 Common saying】

到處楊梅一樣花 Same trees at all places bear the same fruit. 【俗語 Common saying】

日啖荔枝三百顆，不妨長作嶺南人。 If I can eat three hundred pieces of lichee every day, I wish to be a Lingnan person. 【蘇軾〈食荔枝〉Su Shi:"Eating Lichees"】

一年好景君須記，最是橙黃橘綠時。 The best time and scene of the year you have to remember, it is the time when tangerines are green and oranges golden. 【蘇軾〈贈劉景文〉Su Shi:"To Liu Jingwen"】

一騎紅塵妃子笑，無人知是荔枝來。 The cloud of brown dust behind the horse made the palace concubines smile, and no one knew that it was the delivery of lichees. 【杜牧〈過清華宮〉Du Mu:"Passing the Summer Palace"】

Future

承前啟後，繼往開來。 Carry forward the career pioneered by the predecessors and forge ahead into the future and inherit the past and usher in the future. 【朱國禎《湧幢小品‧曾有菴贈文》Zhu Guozhen:"A Passage Presented to me by Zeng Youyan", *Works at Yongchuang*】

道路曲折，前途光明。 The road ahead will be tortuous, but the future is bright. 【俗語 Common saying】

明日隔山岳，世事相茫茫。 Tomorrow the hills and valleys will separate us again, and neither of us will know what the future holds. 【杜甫〈贈衛八處士〉Du Fu:"Presented to Scholar-recluse Wei the Eighth"】

若要有前程，莫做沒前程。 If you want to have a bright future, don't do anything that harms your future. 【吳承恩《西遊記‧第八回》Wu Cheng'en: Chapter 8, *Journey to the West*】

Gain and loss

賠了夫人又折兵。 Lose one's wife as well as one's soldiers – to suffer a double loss after being tricked. 【羅貫中《三國演義‧第五十五回》Luo Guanzhong: Chapter 55, *Romance of the Three Kingdoms*】

賠上功夫又貼本。 Waste time and money doing something. 【俗語 Common saying】

扁擔沒紮，兩頭打塌。 If we run after two hares, we will catch neither. 【臧懋循《元曲選‧佚名‧合同文字‧第三折》Anonymous: Scene 3, "The Story of a Bond", Zang Maoxun: *Anthology of Yuan Plays*】

捕得老鼠，打破油瓶。 A mouse was caught but an oil bottle broken – loss outweighs the gain. 【釋普濟《五燈會元‧卷十八》Shi Puji: Chapter 18, *A Compendium of the Five Lamps*】

吃小虧佔大便宜。 Suffer small losses for the sake of making great gains. 【俗語 Common saying】

打老鼠傷了玉瓶兒。 Smash a jade vase to catch a rat - loss outweighs the gain. 【曹雪芹《紅樓夢‧第六十一回》Cao Xueqin: Chapter 61, *A Dream of the Red Chamber*】

大失必有小得。 There will be small gains when you have a big loss. 【俗語 Common saying】

當取不取，過後莫悔。 If you did not take what you could take, you cannot regret afterwards. 【施耐庵《水滸傳‧第十五回》Shi Nai'an: Chapter 15, *Outlaws of the Marshes*】

得尺則尺，得寸則寸。 When one gets a foot, it is a foot gained. When one gets an inch, it is an inch gained. 【劉向《戰國策‧秦策三》Liu Xiang: "Strategies of the State of Qin, Part 2", *Strategies of the Warring States*】

得而不喜，失而不憂。 One is neither overjoyed while gaining something nor worried while losing something. 【莊周《莊子‧外篇‧秋水第十七》: Zhuang Zhou: Chapter 17, "Autumn Floods", "Outer Chapters", *Zhuangzi*】

得來容易失去快。 Easy get, easy lose. 【俗語 Common saying】

得失一朝，榮辱千載。 Gains and losses matter only one day, but honours and disgrace last a thousand years. 【劉知幾《史通‧曲筆》Liu Zhiji: "Indirect Misrepresentation", *Generality of Historiography*】

得之易，失之易。得之難，失之難。Easy come, easy go. What is difficult to get is difficult to lose.【施耐庵《水滸傳・第一百一十六回》Shi Nai'an: Chapter 116, *Outlaws of the Marshes*】

趕上城裏的，耽誤了鄉裏的。What one gains in the city is lost in the country.【俗語 Common saying】

混水裏好拿魚。It is easy to catch fish in troubled water.【俗語 Common saying】

今日之失，未必不為後日之得。What is lost today may not be something to be gained in the future.【王陽明〈與薛尚謙書〉Wang Yangming: "A Letter to Xie Shangqian"】

利在一身勿謀也，利在天下必謀之。I will not seek for personal gains, but if the gains benefit the world, I will certainly seek for them.【張仲超《錢氏家訓》Zhang Zhongchao: *Family Instructions of Master Qian*】

麻痺大意，全功盡棄。If you slacken in your vigilance, you might lose all you've gained.【劉向《戰國策・西周策二》Liu Xiang: "Strategies of the Western Zhou, No. 2", *Strategies of the Warring States*】

莫貪意外之財，莫飲過量之酒。Neither crave for ill-gotten gains nor drink excessively.【朱用純《朱子家訓》Zhu Yongchun: *Precepts of the Zhu Family*】

寧捨十畝地，不受啞巴虧。Rather give up ten pieces of land than suffer losses in the dark.【諺語 Proverb】

賠本生意無人做。No one will be interested in doing a losing business.【俗語 Common saying】

人不見害，魚見食而不見鈎。People see the gains but not the danger, and a fish sees the bait but not the hook.【俗語 Common saying】【李汝珍《鏡花緣・第九十二回》Li Ruzhen: Chapter 92, *Flowers in the Mirror*】

塞翁失馬，焉知非福。When the old man on the frontier lost his mare, who could have guessed it was a blessing in disguise?【劉安《淮南子・人間訓第十八》Liu An: Chapter 18, "The World of Man, *Huainanzi*"】

失之東隅，收之桑榆。What is lost in one place can be gained in another place.【范曄《後漢書・馮異傳》Fan Ye: "Biography of Feng Yi", *History of the Later Han*】

輸得自己，贏得他人。Only when you dare to lose can you win others.【諺語 Proverb】【馮夢龍〈雙雄記・第二十五折〉Feng Menglong: Act 25, "A Tale of Two Heroes"】

貪小便宜吃大虧。One who covets a little advantage will lose a lot.【俗語 Common saying】

偷雞不着蝕把米。Try to steal a chicken only to end up losing the rice.【錢彩《說岳全傳・第二十五回》Qian Cai: Chapter 25, *A Story of Yue Fei*】

無功不受祿。 No gains without pains. 【劉向《説苑・卷四立節》 Liu Xiang: Chapter 4, "Upholding Integrity", *Garden of Persuasions*】

無所求則無所獲。 Seek for nothing, nothing will be found. 【俗語 Common saying】

想下水又怕濕腳。 One wants to get into water but would not like to wet one's feet. 【諺語 Proverb】

一手得來，一手失去。 Lose on the swings what one makes on the roundabout. 【俗語 Common saying】

一手難抓兩頭鰻。 If you run after two hares, you will catch neither. 【俗語 Common saying】

一損皆損，一榮皆榮。 When one loses all lose; when one gains, all gain. 【曹雪芹《紅樓夢・第四回》 Cao Xueqin: Chapter 4, *A Dream of the Red Chamber*】

佔小便宜吃大虧。 One who hankers after petty advantages will suffer great losses. 【俗語 Common saying】

Gambling

盜賊出於貧窮。 Robbers and thieves come from the poor. 【《增廣賢文》 *Words that Open up One's Mind and Enhance One's Wisdom*】

賭博出賊情。 Gambling is often involved in robbery. 【諺語 Proverb】

賭近盜，姦近殺。 Gambling is close to robbery, and adultery to murder. 【俗語 Common saying】【馮夢龍《警世通言・第三十五卷》 Feng Menglong: Chapter 35, *Stories to Caution the World*】

賭錢場裏無君子。 There is no gentleman at gambling. 【俗語 Common saying】

賭錢場上無父子。 The relationship of father and son does not exist at gambling. 【諺語 Proverb】【施耐庵《水滸傳・第三十八回》 Shi Nai'an: Chapter 38, *Outlaws of the Marshes*】

喝酒喝厚了，耍錢耍薄了。 Drinking wine together makes friends closer and gambling together estrange friends. 【俗語 Common saying】【老舍《鼓書藝人・第十四章》 Lao She: Chapter 14, *The Drum Singers*】

禍從浮浪起，辱因賭博招。 Dissoluteness starts disaster and gambling brings disgrace. 【施耐庵《水滸傳・第一百零二回》 Shi Nai'an: Chapter 102, *Outlaws of the Marshes*】

久賭神仙輸。 Even gods and immortals will lose if they gamble for a long time. 【諺語 Proverb】

久賭無贏家。Gambling for a long time ends with no winners.【諺語 Proverb】

孔夫子搬家 —— 淨輸（書）。Confucius moving to a new location – all loss.【歇後語 End-clipper】

孔夫子的手巾 —— 包輸（書）。Confucius' handkerchief is for wrapping books – sure to lose.【歇後語 End-clipper】

俏大姐的油頭 —— 輸（梳）得光光的。The sleek hair of a cutie is combed glossy and shiny – one has lost everything through gambling.【歇後語 End-clipper】

情場失意，賭場得意。A loser in love affairs but a winner in gambling.【俗語 Common saying】

窮人忌賭，越賭越窮。A poor person should avoid gambling, for the more he gambles, the poorer he becomes.【俗語 Common saying】

是賭必輸錢。All gamblers lose money.【俗語 Common saying】

輸錢祇為贏錢起。Money lost at gambling is caused by money gained.【俗語 Common saying】

General

矮子裏拔將軍。Choose a general among the dwarfs as for choosing the best among the ordinary.【俗語 Common saying】【石玉崑《小五義·第五十三回》Shi Yukun: Chapter 53, *The Five Younger Gallants*】

敗軍之將，不足言勇。The general of a defeated army is in no position to say that he is brave.【司馬遷《史記·淮陰侯列傳》Sima Qian: "Biography of the Marquis of Huaiyin", *Records of the Grand Historian*】

但使龍城飛將在，不教胡馬度陰山。If General Li Guang of the Dragon City was still alive, no tartar horses would be able to pass Mount Yin.【王昌齡〈出塞二首〉Wang Changling: "Beyond the Frontier, Two Poems"】

過五關，斬六將。Pass through five gates and kill six generals.【羅貫中《三國演義·第二十七回》Luo Guanzhong: Chapter 27, *Romance of the Three Kingdoms*】

將軍百戰死，壯士十年歸。A general dies after fighting a hundred battles, and soldiers return home after ten years.【佚名〈木蘭詞〉Anonymous: "Poem of Mulan"】

將軍不下馬，各自奔前程。Generals, not dismounting from their horses, gallop off to their destinations.【吳承恩《西遊記·第

五十四回》Wu Cheng'en: Chapter 54, *Journey to the West*】

將軍一去，大樹飄零。 Once the general is gone, the leaves are fallen from trees. 【庾信〈哀江南賦〉Yu Xin:"Lament for the South"】

將軍之事，靜以幽，正以治。 The work of a general is to think calmly so that he is unpredictable and upright in managing affairs. 【孫武《孫子兵法‧九地第十一》Sun Wu: Chapter 11, "The Nine Situations", *The Art of War by Sunzi*】

將帥無能，累死三軍。 If the commanders and generals are incompetent, the armies will be fatigued to death. 【左丘明《左傳‧桓公八年》Zuo Qiuming:"The Eighth Year of the Reign of Duke Huan", *Zuo's Commentary on the Spring and Autumn Annals*】

將相本無種，男兒當自強。 Generals and ministers are not born, they achieve their positions through their own efforts. 【汪洙〈神童詩〉Wang Zhu:"Poem of a Talented Boy"】

苗子不造反，將軍不值錢。 Without rebellion, generals are worthless. 【俗語 Common saying】

千金易得，一將難求。 It is easy to get a thousand taels of gold but difficult to get a good general. 【馬致遠〈漢宮秋‧第一折〉Ma Zhiyuan: Scene 1, "Autumn in the Han Palace"】

千軍易得，一將難求。 It is easy to get a thousand soldiers but hard to get a good general. 【馬致遠〈漢宮秋‧第一折〉Ma Zhiyuan: Scene 1, "Autumn in the Han Palace"】

遣將不如激將。 To a general a challenge is better than persuasion. 【吳承恩《西遊記‧第三十一回》Wu Cheng'en: Chapter 31, *Journey to the West*】

強將手下無弱兵。 There are no weak troops under a strong general. 【俗語 Common saying】

強將無弱兵，強祖無弱孫。 There are no weak soldiers under a strong general, and there are no weak grandchildren from a strong grandfather. 【俗語 Common saying】

請將不如激將。 To a general a challenge is more effective than an invitation. 【吳承恩《西遊記‧第三十一回》Wu Cheng'en: Chapter 31, *Journey to the West*】

勸將不如激將。 To a general a challenge is better than persuasion. 【俗語 Common saying】

人不寐，將軍白髮征夫淚。 Nobody could sleep, the general and soldiers' hair turned white, wept. 【范仲淹〈漁家傲‧秋思〉Fan Zhongyan:"Thoughts in Autumn: To the Tune of Fisherman's Pride"】

散將容易聚將難。 It is easy to send generals away, but difficult to gather them. 【俗語 Common saying】

蜀中無大將，廖化作先鋒。
Without young blood, the old
and experienced man has to
deal with challenges in the
first place.【羅貫中《三國演義·
第一百一十三回》Luo Guanzhong:
Chapter 113, *Romance of the Three
Kingdoms*】

太平本是將軍定，不許將軍見太
平。Peace is won by generals,
but they are not allowed to see
peace.【諺語 Proverb】【佚名〈隨何賺
風魔蒯通·第一折〉Anonymous: Scene
1, "Sui He Tricks the Mad Kuai Tong"】

太平不用舊將軍。When peace
prevails, veteran generals are no
longer used.【關漢卿〈哭存孝·第
二折〉Guan Hanqing: Scene 2, "Tears
and Filial Piety"】

鐵將軍把門。A locked door.【俗語
Common saying】【褚人獲《隋唐演義·
第五十八回》Zhu Renhuo: Chapter 58,
Heroes in Sui and Tang Dynasties】

瓦罐不離井上破，將軍難免陣前
亡。A jar used to take water
from a well will be broken in
the well and a general will die
in a battle.【高陽《胡雪巖全傳·平
步青雲》Gao Yang: "A Meteoric Rise", *A
Biography of Hu Xueyan*】

為將之道，當先治心。To be
a good general, he must first
nurture a calm mind.【蘇洵《權
書·心術》Su Xun: "Intention", *Book of
Power Strategy*】

一個將軍一個令 —— 不知聽誰
的。A new general, a new law –
Don't know whom should one
obey.【歇後語 End-clipper】

一將功成萬骨枯。One general
achieves renown over the dead
bodies of ten thousand soldiers.
【曹松〈己亥歲感事〉Cao Song: "The
War Year"】

一身轉戰三千里，一劍曾擋百萬
師。I fought from place to place
for a thousand miles, and my
sword once held up an army of
a million people.【王維〈老將行〉
Wang Wei: "Old General"】

智將不如福將。A wise general is
not as good as a lucky general.
【俗語 Common saying】【曾慥〈類說〉
Zheng Zao: "Theory of Class"】

Gentleman

德勝才，謂之君子。He whose
virtue is better than his talent
is known as a gentleman.【司
馬光《資治通鑒·周紀》Sima
Guang: "Annals of the Zhou Dynasty",
*Comprehensive Mirror to Aid in
Government*】

古之君子，其責己也重以周，其
待人也輕以約。A gentleman in
the old days set a strict and all-
round standard for himself, but
they treated others in a generous
and modest manner.【韓愈《昌
黎先生集·原毀》Han Yu: "Origin of

Defamation," *Collected Works of Han Yu*】

觀棋不語真君子。 A true gentleman watches a game of chess in silence. 【諺語 Proverb】【馮夢龍《醒世恆言・第九卷》Feng Menglong: Chapter 9, *Stories to Awaken the World*】

君子安貧，達人知命。 A gentleman can be contended with poverty and a discerning person knows his lot. 【《增廣賢文》*Words that Open up One's Mind and Enhance One's Wisdom*】

君子博學於文，約之以禮。 A gentleman is widely versed in culture and bound by the rites. 【孔子《論語・雍也篇第六》Confucius: Chapter 6, *The Analects of Confucius*】

君子不奪人之好。 A gentleman does not covet what others prize. 【馬致遠〈馬丹陽三度任風子・第四折〉Ma Zhiyuan: Scene 4, "Ma Danyang Thrice Converts the Butcher Ren"】

君子不鏡於水而鏡於人。 A gentleman does not mirror himself by water but by people to see the misfortune and fortune. 【墨翟《墨子・非攻卷十七至十九》Mo Di: Chapters 17-19, "Condemning Offensive Warfare", *Mozi*】

君子不掠人之美。 A gentleman does not claim credit due to others. 【諺語 Proverb】

君子不念舊惡。 A gentleman forgives the past wrong doings of others. 【孔子《論語・公冶長篇第五》Confucius: Chapter 5, *The Analects of Confucius*】

君子不欺暗室。 A gentleman is honest even when he is alone. 【駱賓王〈螢火賦〉Luo Binwang: "Ode to Glow-worms"】

君子不宛言而取富，不屈行而取位。 A gentleman does not get wealth by blandishing words nor get an official position by dishonest acts. 【戴德《大戴禮記・曾子制言中》Dai De: "Zengzi about Behaviour", Part 2, *Records of Rites by Dai the Elder*】

君子不羞學，不羞問。 A gentleman is not ashamed to learn from or consult with others. 【劉向《說苑・卷十六談叢》Liu Xiang: Chapter 16, "The Thicket of Discussion", *Garden of Persuasions*】

君子不以其所能者病人，不以人之所不能者愧人。 A gentleman neither criticizes others for being unable to do what he can do, nor does he embarrass others for what they cannot do. 【《禮記・表記第三十二》Chapter 32, "Records of Examples", *The Book of Rites*】

君子不以言舉人，不以人廢言。 A gentleman does not recommend a person based on what the person says, and he does not reject what is said because of the person. 【孔子《論語・衛靈公篇第十五》Confucius: Chapter 15, *The Analects of Confucius*】

君子不憂不懼。A gentleman does not worry about or fear anything. 【孔子《論語・顏淵篇第十二》Confucius: Chapter 12, *The Analects of Confucius*】

君子不怨天，不尤人。One neither grumble about Heaven nor blame others. 【孔子《論語・憲問篇第十四》Confucius: Chapter 14, *The Analects of Confucius*】

君子不重則不威。If a gentleman does not behave with dignity, he will not command any respect. 【孔子《論語・學而篇第一》Confucius: Chapter 1, *The Analects of Confucius*】

君子藏器於身，待時而動。A gentleman keeps his weapon about his person and waits for the proper time to move – to keep on learning to prepare for the right time. 【《易經・繫辭下》 "Appended Remarks", Part 2, *The Book of Changes*】

君子成人之美，不成人之惡。A gentleman helps others to achieve their goals and he does not help others to do bad things. 【孔子《論語・顏淵篇第十二》Confucius: Chapter 12, *The Analects of Confucius*】

君子辭貴不辭賤，辭富不辭貧。A gentleman abandons high ranks and does not mind to be in a low position; he abandons wealth and does not mind to be in poverty. 【《禮記・坊記第三十》Chapter 30, "Records of the Dykes", *The Book of Rites*】

君子恥其言而過其行。A gentleman is ashamed of letting his words outstrip his deeds. 【孔子《論語・憲問篇第十四》Confucius: Chapter 14, *The Analects of Confucius*】

君子動口不動手。A gentleman reasons and does not strike others with his fist in a quarrel. 【俗語 Common saying】

君子固窮，小人窮斯濫矣。A gentleman stands firm in poverty while a petty man will lose his self-control in poverty. 【孔子《論語・衛靈公篇第十五》Confucius: Chapter 15, *The Analects of Confucius*】

君子好學不厭，自強不息。A gentleman is eager to learn and not tired of learning and makes ceaseless efforts to strengthen himself. 【司馬光《司馬文正公集》Sima Guang: *Collected Works of Sima Guang*】

君子和而不同，小人同而不和。A gentleman gets along with others but have their own viewpoints. A petty man gets along with others and blindly agrees with them. 【孔子《論語・子路篇第十三》Confucius: Chapter 13, *The Analects of Confucius*】

君子懷德，小人懷土。A gentleman cherishes virtue, whereas a petty person, wealth. 【孔子《論語・里仁篇第四》Confucius: Chapter 4, *The Analects of Confucius*】

君子禍至不懼，福至不喜。A gentleman is fearless when

disaster befalls him and is not overjoyed when blessings come to him.【司馬遷《史記・孔子世家》Sima Qian:"House of Confucius", *Records of the Grand Historian*】

君子矜而不爭，羣而不黨。A gentleman is dignified and not quarrelsome. He is sociable but not cliquey.【孔子《論語・衞靈公篇第十五》Confucius: Chapter 15, *The Analects of Confucius*】

君子進德修業。A gentleman must work hard to cultivate his moral character and enrich his knowledge.【《易經・乾・文言》"The Record of Wen Yan", "Hexagram *Qian*", *The Book of Changes*】

君子敬而無失，與人恭而有禮。A gentleman maintains reverence without errors and is courteous and polite to others.【孔子《論語・顏淵篇第十二》Confucius: Chapter 12, *The Analects of Confucius*】

君子敬以直內，義以方外。A gentleman maintains inward correctness through reverence, and outward correctness through righteousness.【《易經・坤・文言》"The Record of Wen Yan", "Hexagram *Kun*", *The Book of Changes*】

君子居其室，出其言善，則千里之外應之，況其邇者乎！居其室，出其言不善，則千里之外違之，況其邇者乎！When a gentleman living in his house says something good, people of a thousand miles away will echo to it. How much more so for those who are near to him? When he says something bad while living in his house, people of a thousand miles away will contradict him. How much more so for those who are near to him?【《易經・繫辭・上》"Appended Remarks", Part 1, *The Book of Changes*】

君子樂得做君子，小人枉自做小人。A gentleman is happy to be a gentleman, but a petty man is a petty man unintentionally.【《增廣賢文》*Words that Open up One's Mind and Enhance One's Wisdom*】

君子名之必可言也，言之必可行也。When a gentleman names it, it must be spoken of, and when it can be spoken of, it must be practicable.【孔子《論語・子路篇第十三》Confucius: Chapter 13, *The Analects of Confucius*】

君子莫大乎與人為善。The greatest attribute of a gentleman is his helping people to do good deeds.【孟軻《孟子・公孫丑上》Meng Ke: Chapter 2, Part 1, *Mencius*】

君子求諸己，小人求諸人。A gentleman reflects on himself whereas a petty person blames others when he has problems.【孔子《論語・衞靈公篇第十五》Confucius: Chapter 15, *The Analects of Confucius*】

君子上達，小人下達。A gentleman strives for virtues while a petty person strives for money.【孔子《論語・憲問篇第十四》Confucius: Chapter 14, *The Analects of Confucius*】

君子食無求飽，居無求安，敏於事而慎於言。 A gentleman does not seek for a full stomach when eating, comfort in living, but he is earnest in doing things and cautious in what he says. 【孔子《論語‧學而篇第一》Confucius: Chapter 1, *The Analects of Confucius*】

君子思不出其位。 A gentleman does not think beyond his authority. 【孔子《論語‧憲問篇第十四》Confucius: Chapter 14, *The Analects of Confucius*】

君子死義，不可以富貴留也。 A gentleman dies for righteousness and would not stay alive for wealth and rank. 【宋鈃《文子‧九守第三》Song Jin: Chapter 3, "The Nine Observances", *Wenzi*】

君子泰而不驕，小人驕而不泰。 A gentleman is calm and not proud whereas a petty man is proud but not calm. 【孔子《論語‧子路篇第十三》Confucius: Chapter 13, *The Analects of Confucius*】

君子坦蕩蕩，小人長戚戚。 A gentleman is broad-minded while a petty man is always full of anxiety. 【孔子《論語‧述而篇第七》Confucius: Chapter 7, *The Analects of Confucius*】

君子務本，本立而道生。 A gentleman works on the fundamentals. When the fundamentals are established, then virtues come into being. 【孔子《論語‧學而篇第一》Confucius: Chapter 1, *The Analects of Confucius*】

君子惡居下流，天下之惡皆歸焉。 A gentleman hates to be tainted whereas all the evils of the world will go to him. 【孔子《論語‧子張篇第十九》Confucius: Chapter 19, *The Analects of Confucius*】

君子學以聚之，問以辨之，寬以居之，仁以行之。 A gentleman learns to accumulate knowledge and virtues, asks question to clarify everything, treats others with kindness, and acts with benevolence. 【《易經‧乾‧文言》"The Record of Wen Yan", "Hexagram Qiao", *The Book of Changes*】

君子以道充貴，身安為富。 A gentleman regards filling up with the Way as noble and the ease of the self as rich. 【周敦頤《通書‧富貴》Zhou Dunyi: "Wealth and Nobility", *Comprehending The Book of Changes*】

君子以反身修德。 A gentleman reflects on himself to cultivate his virtue. 【《易經‧寒‧象》"Image", "Hexagram *Jian*", *The Book of Changes*】

君子以果行育德。 A gentleman acts resolutely to nourish virtue. 【《易經‧蒙‧象》"Image", "Hexagram *Meng*", *The Book of Changes*】

君子以見善則遷，有過則改。 A gentleman follows when seeing good deeds and corrects himself when committing mistakes. 【《易經‧益‧象》"Image", "Hexagram *Yi*," *The Book of Changes*】

君子以言有物而行有恆。A gentleman speaks in a rational way and his actions are consistent.【《易經・家人・象》“Image”, “Hexagram *Jia Ren*,” *The Book of Changes*】

君子隱而顯，不矜而莊，不厲而威，不言而信。A gentleman is obscure but known to people, not arrogant but dignified, not harsh but to be respected, not talking but trustworthy.【《易經・益・象》“Image”, “Hexagram *Yi*”, *The Book of Changes*】

君子憂道不憂貧。A gentleman is worried about the Way but not poverty.【孔子《論語・衛靈公篇第十五》Confucius: Chapter 15, *The Analects of Confucius*】

君子有三變：望之儼然，即之也溫，聽其言也厲。A gentleman undergoes three changes: when you look at him, he appears to be stern; when you approach him, he is tender; when we hear what he says, his language is firm.【孔子《論語・子張篇第十九》Confucius: Chapter 19, *The Analects of Confucius*】

君子有三畏：畏天命，畏大人，畏聖人之言。A gentleman has three fears: he fears the ordinances of heaven, he fears great men, and he fears the words of sages.【孔子《論語・季氏篇第十六》Confucius: Chapter 16, *The Analects of Confucius*】

君子有勇而無義為亂，小人有勇而無義為盜。When a gentleman has courage but without righteousness, it will be chaos; when a petty man has courage but without righteousness, it will be robbery.【孔子《論語・陽貨篇第十七》Confucius: Chapter 17, *The Analects of Confucius*】

君子有終身之憂，無一朝之患也。A gentleman has life-long worries, but he does not have momentary vexations.【孟軻《孟子・離婁下》Meng Ke: Chapter 4, Part 2, *Mencius*】

君子於其言，無所苟而已矣。A gentleman is serious about his words.【孔子《論語・子張篇第十九》Confucius: Chapter 19, *The Analects of Confucius*】

君子欲訥於言而敏於行。A gentleman is deliberate in speech and swift in action.【孔子《論語・里仁篇第四》Confucius: Chapter 4, *The Analects of Confucius*】

君子喻於義，小人喻於利。A gentleman comprehends what is righteousness, a petty man, self-interest.【孔子《論語・里仁篇第四》Confucius: Chapter 4, *The Analects of Confucius*】

君子在德不在衣。It is virtue but not clothes that makes a gentleman.【諺語 Proverb】

君子貞而不諒。A gentleman is firm, but not stubborn.【孔子《論語・衛靈公篇第十五》Confucius: Chapter 15, *The Analects of Confucius*】

君子之守，修其身而天下平。The principle that a gentleman

holds is to cultivate the person and keep the world in peace. 【孟軻《孟子‧盡心章句上》Meng Ke: Chapter 7, Part 1, *Mencius*】

君子之所為，眾人固不識也。
What is done by a gentleman may not be understandable by people. 【孟軻《孟子‧告子章句下》Meng Ke: Chapter 6, Part 2, *Mencius*】

君子之言，信而有徵，故怨遠於其身。 What a gentleman says is trustworthy and evidenced, blames therefore are way away from him. 【左丘明《左傳‧昭公八年》Zuo Qiuming: "The Eighth Year of the Reign of Duke Zhao", *Zuo's Commentary on the Spring and Autumn Annals*】

君子之言寡而實，小人之言多而虛。 What a gentleman says is little but true; what a petty man says is much but empty. 【劉向《説苑‧卷十六談叢》Liu Xiang: Chapter 16, "The Thicket of Discussion", *Garden of Persuasions*】

君子之於天下也，無適也，無莫也，義之與比。 A gentleman, when dealing with people in the world, should not have the fixed rules, but with righteousness. 【孔子《論語‧里仁篇第四》Confucius: Chapter 4, *The Analects of Confucius*】

君子周而不比，小人比而不周。 A gentleman treats people in fair way without favouritism whereas a petty man gangs up for personal interests. 【孔子《論語‧為政篇第二》Confucius: Chapter 2, *The Analects of Confucius*】

君子周急不繼富。 A gentleman helps those in urgent needs but does not add wealth to the rich. 【孔子《論語‧雍也篇第六》Confucius: Chapter 6, *The Analects of Confucius*】

君子尊賢而容眾，嘉善而矜不能。 A gentleman respects the virtuous and accommodates the common people, praises the capable people and sympathizes with the incompetent. 【孔子《論語‧子張篇第十九》Confucius: Chapter 19, *The Analects of Confucius*】

量小非君子，無毒不丈夫。 A person with a small mind is not a gentleman and a true man is ruthless. 【俗語 Common saying】

路急無君子。 No one is gentleman in a critical moment. 【俗語 Common saying】

門內有君子，門外君子至。 If there are gentlemen at home, gentlemen from other places will come. 【馮夢龍《警世通言‧第一卷》Feng Menglong: Chapter 1, *Stories to Caution the World*】

莫見乎隱，莫顯乎微，故君子慎其獨也。 Nothing is more manifest than the minute; nothing is more manifest than the hidden. A gentleman therefore must be watchful of his behaviour when he is alone. 【《禮記‧中庸第一章》Chapter 1, "Doctrine of the Mean", *The Book of Rrites*】

趨吉避凶者為君子。 A gentleman is one who knows how to seek for fortune and avoid

misfortune.【俗語 Common saying】
【曹雪芹《紅樓夢‧第四回》Cao Xueqin: Chapter 4, *A Dream of the Red Chamber*】

人不知而不愠，不亦君子乎？Isn't he a gentleman when he does not feel offended when people fail to know about him?【孔子《論語‧學而第一》Confucius: Chapter 1, *The Analects of Confucius*】

山中石廣真玉少，世上人多君子稀。There is a lot of stones in the mountains, but jade is scarce; there are many people in the world, but gentlemen are few and far between.【俗語 Common saying】

捨命陪君子。Would rather give up one's life in order to be in the company of a gentleman.【俗語 Common saying】

文質彬彬，然後君子。When one has refinement and good quality, then one is known as gentleman.【孔子《論語‧雍也篇第六》Confucius: Chapter 6, *The Analects of Confucius*】

言念君子，溫其如玉。I think of my husband, who is gentle as a piece of jade.【《詩經‧國風‧秦風‧小戎》"Small Arsenal", "Odes of the States", "Odes of the State of Qin", *The Book of Odes*】

以小人之心，度君子之腹。Gauge the heart of a gentleman by the yardstick of a petty person.【俗語 Common saying】【左丘明《左傳‧昭公二十八年》Zuo Qiuming: "The Twenty-eighth Year of the Reign of Duke Zhao," *Zuo's Commentary on the Spring and Autumn Annals*】

倚強凌弱非君子。One who takes advantage over the weak by being strong is not a gentleman.【高文秀〈澠池會‧第二折〉Gao Wenxiu: Scene 2, "Meeting at Mianchi"】

義動君子，利動小人。A gentleman is moved by righteousness and a petty person, by gains.【諺語 Proverb】【王充《論衡‧答佞第三十三卷》Wang Chong: Chapter 33, "On the Cunning and Artful", *Critical Essays*】

自稱盜賊無須防，自稱君子必須防。It is unnecessary to guard against one who claims to be a thief, but we should watch out for one who claims that he is a gentleman.【俗語 Common saying】

Ghost

白天見鬼——心病。Seeing ghosts in the daytime – anxiety.【歇後語 End-clipper】

不問蒼生問鬼神。The emperor did not ask Jia Yi about the affairs of the people, but about deities and ghosts.【李商隱〈賈生〉 Li Shangyin: "Jia Yi"】

鬼不招不來。 Ghosts will not come unless they are invited.【俗語 Common saying】

鬼怕惡人蛇怕棒。 Ghosts are afraid of evil persons as snakes of sticks.【俗語 Common saying】

鬼也不上門來。 Even a ghost does not come.【吳敬梓《儒林外史・第五十三回》Wu Jingzi: Chapter 53, An Unofficial History of the Scholars】

敬鬼神而遠之，可謂知矣。 Respect the gods and spirits of the dead but keep them at a distance can be called wisdom.【孔子《論語・雍也篇第六》Confucius: Chapter 6, The Analects of Confucius】

人不怕鬼鬼自消。 When people do not fear ghosts, the ghosts will leave.【俗語 Common saying】

招鬼容易驅鬼難。 It is easy to summon a ghost but difficult to drive him away.【俗語 Common saying】

Gift

瓜子不飽實人心。 The melon seeds cannot fill your stomach, but they convey profound feeling.【俗語 Common saying】

瓜子敬客 —— 一點兒心意。 Entertaining one's guests with melon seeds is small hospitality–a small but thoughtful gift.【歇後語 End-clipper】

禮輕情意重。 The gift is trifling but the feeling is profound.【李致遠〈還牢末〉Li Zhiyuan: "A Story of Returning to the Prison"】

千里送鵝毛，物輕情意重。 A goose feather sent from a thousand miles away may be light in weight, but the affection it conveys are deep.【蘇軾〈揚州以土物寄少游〉Su Shi: "Sending Local Products from Yangzhou to Qin Guan"】

區區薄禮，不成敬意。 This small gift is a token of my appreciation.【俗語 Common saying】

人情重似債。 Owing one's favour is as heavy as a debt.【俗語 Common saying】

秀才人情紙一張。 Scholars do not earn much and is able to buy others a paper as a gift–gift is not worthy.【俗語 Common saying】

贈人玫瑰，手有餘香。 The roses in her hand, the flavour in mine.【諺語 Proverb】

Giving and taking

將欲取之，必先與之。 Give in order to take. 【老子《道德經・第三十六章》Laozi: Chapter 36, *Daodejing*】

明中施捨，暗裏填還。 Give alms openly and you will be rewarded in secret. 【佚名《名賢集》Anonymous: *Collected Sayings of Famous Sages*】

卻之不恭，受之有愧。 To decline one's offer would be disrespectful but to accept it is embarrassing. 【孟軻《孟子・萬章下》Meng Ke: Chapter 10, Part 2, *Mencius*】

天下皆知取之為取，莫知與之為取。 People in the world all know they take and gain but they do not realize the way they give is a gain as well. 【范曄《後漢書・桓譚列傳》Fan Ye: "Biography of Heng Tan", *History of the Later Han*】

投我以桃，報之以李。 You give me a peach and I return a plum to you. 【《詩經・大雅・抑》"Pressing, Greater Odes of the Kingdom", *The Book of Odes*】

Glory

一人功成，人人光榮。 The achievement of one person glories all. 【俗語 Common saying】

Goal

不達目的，誓不罷休。 We pledge not to give up until our goal is reached. 【俗語 Common saying】

祇問目的，不問手段。 The end justifies the means. 【俗語 Common saying】

God

神不居功，聖不居德。 God never prides himself on his merits and a sage never prides himself on his virtue. 【諺語 Proverb】

神鬼怕惡人。 Gods and ghosts are afraid of vicious people. 【蘇軾〈艾子雜説〉Su Shi: "Random Remarks by Aizi"】

神鬼怕愣人。 Gods and ghosts are afraid of courageous people – Doing without the thought of consequences is terrifying. 【俗語 Common saying】

神仙相爭，凡人禍殃。 When gods are in discord with each other, people on earth suffer. 【俗語 Common saying】

識破人情便是仙。 One who can see through the ways of the world is god. 【俗語 Common saying】【王濬卿《冷眼觀·第十一回》Wang Junqing: Chapter 11, *Casting a Cold Eye*】

世人都曉神仙好，只有功名忘不了。 People all know that fairies are having a good time, yet they still can't forget fame and honours. 【曹雪芹《紅樓夢·好了歌》Cao Xueqin: "Song of 'Good and Yet'", *A Dream of the Red Chamber*】

天老爺不昧苦心人。 God will not treat badly those who make painstaking efforts. 【俗語 Common saying】【周立波《暴風驟雨·第一部·六》Zhou Libo: Volume 1, Chapter 6, *The Hurricane*】

萬事勸人休瞞昧，舉頭三尺有神明。 A person is urged not to hide from truth or betray one's conscience in all the things involved, for there are gods three feet above one's head. 【《增廣賢文》*Words that Open up One's Mind and Enhance One's Wisdom*】

信神有神在，不信是泥塊。 If you believe in gods, they exist; if you do not believe in them, they are but clay figures. 【俗語 Common saying】

Gold

黃金散盡為收書。 Gold is all spent for the purpose of collecting good books – letting go all wealth to achieve a goal. 【《增廣賢文》*Words that Open up One's Mind and Enhance One's Wisdom*】

黃金無假，阿魏無真。 Gold cannot be faked, but the rare medicinal plant *awei* can. 【《增廣賢文》*Words that Open up One's Mind and Enhance One's Wisdom*】

金子終得金子換。 True gold will find its price. 【俗語 Common saying】【曹雪芹《紅樓夢·第四十六回》Cao Xueqin: Chapter 46, *A Dream of the Red Chamber*】

金子做生鐵賣。 It's selling gold at the price of iron. 【施耐庵《水滸傳·第六回》Shi Nai'an: Chapter 6, *Outlaws of the Marshes*】

烈火見真金。 Pure gold proves its worth in a blazing fire. 【諺語 Proverb】

男兒膝下有黃金。 A man has his dignity like there is gold under his knees. 【諺語 Proverb】

人間祇道黃金貴，不問天公買少年。 In the mundane world, people only say that gold is precious, and they don't ask the King of Heaven how much would it be to buy youth. 【元好問〈無題〉Yuan Haowen:"Untitled Poem"】

生來不讀半行書，祇把黃金買身貴。 The young people do not read half a line in a book and they only want to flaunt their wealth with the gold they have. 【李賀〈嘲少年〉Li He:"Teasing the Young"】

真金不怕洪爐火，石獅不怕雨滂沱。 A person of integrity can stand severe tests. 【諺語 Proverb】

真金不怕火煉。 True gold fears no fire. 【諺語 Proverb】

Good and evil

鋤一惡，長十善。 Getting rid of one evil thing is tantamount to having ten good things. 【脫脫、阿魯圖《宋史・畢士安傳》Toqto'a and Alutu:"Biography of Bi Shi'an", History of the Song】

從來好事必多磨。 From of old, good things have always been strewn with setbacks. 【凌濛初《二刻拍案驚奇・第九卷》Ling Mengchu: Chapter 9, Amazing Tales, Volume Two】

從容幹好事，性急出差子。 With composure, you will succeed; with impatience, accidents always happen. 【諺語 Proverb】

從善如登，從惡如崩。 Learning to be a good man takes time like climbing up a mountain, get a bad influence on somebody is easy like falling down to the ground. 【左丘明《國語・周語》Zuo Qiuming:"The Language of Zhou", Part 2, National Languages】

但行好事，莫問前程。 One does good deeds without thinking of what it will bring in the future. 【《增廣賢文》Words that Open up One's Mind and Enhance One's Wisdom】

多行不義必自斃。 One who often does evil deeds will ruin oneself. 【左丘明《左傳・隱公元年》Zuo Qiuming:"The First year of the Reign of Duke Yin", Zuo's Commentary on the Spring and Autumn Annals】

惡恐人知，便是大惡。 Evil that dreads to be known is a really great evil. 【朱用純《朱子家訓》Zhu Yongchun: Precepts of the Zhu Family】

惡人惡心肝。 An evil person has an evil heart. 【俗語 Common saying】

惡人難做善事。 It is difficult for an evil person to do good things. 【俗語 Common saying】

惡人祇有惡人降。 An evil person can only be subdued by his like. 【俗語 Common saying】

惡人自有惡人磨。 An evil person will be tormented by another evil person.【《增廣賢文》Words that Open up One's Mind and Enhance One's Wisdom】

惡人自有惡相。 Evil-doers have ferocious countenances.【馮夢龍《警世通言・第四卷》Feng Menglong: Chapter 4, Stories to Caution the World】

好事不出門，惡事傳千里。 Good deeds are never heard outside while evil deeds are circulated to a thousand miles away.【諺語 Proverb】【吳承恩《西遊記・第七十三回》Wu Cheng'en: Chapter 73, Journey to the West】

花香風來吹，好事有人傳。 The fragrance of flowers is spread by wind, and good deeds by people.【諺語 Proverb】

積錢積穀不如積德。 Accumulating money or grain is not as good as accumulating merits.【《增廣賢文》Words that Open up One's Mind and Enhance One's Wisdom】

吉人自有天相。 Heaven rewards the good.【諺語 Proverb】【馮夢龍《醒世恆言・第二十五卷》Feng Menglong: Chapter 25, Stories to Awaken the World】

君子見善則遷，有過則改。 A gentleman, upon seeing good deeds done by others, follows suit and when he commits a mistake, he will correct it.【《易經・益・象》"Image", "Hexagram Yi", The Book of Changes】

強邪不壓正。 Evil, no matter how powerful it is, cannot prevail over good.【俗語 Common saying】

取其精華，棄其糟粕。 Keep the good, discard the rest.【魯迅〈拿來主義〉Lu Xun: "Gabism"】

讓了甜桃，去尋酸李。 One gives up sweet pears but seeks for sour plums.【蘭陵笑笑生《金瓶梅・第三十八回》Lanling Xiaoxiaosheng: Chapter 38, The Plum in the Golden Vase】

人不勸不善，鐘不敲不鳴。 People would not do good deeds without persuasion and bells would not make sounds if they are not struck.【《增廣賢文》Words that Open up One's Mind and Enhance One's Wisdom】

人惡人怕天不怕，人善人欺天不欺。 An evil person is feared by others but not Heaven; a kind person is bullied by others but not Heaven.【《增廣賢文》Words that Open up One's Mind and Enhance One's Wisdom】

泥沙俱下，魚龍混雜。 When the waters are mudded, the bad are mixed with the good.【袁枚《隨園詩話・卷一》Yuan Mei: Chapter 1, Talks on Poetry from the Sui Garden】

善不積，不足以成名。惡不積，不足以滅身。 Without accumulating good deeds, it is inadequate to achieve fame; without accumulating evil doings, one will not bring destruction to the self.【《易經・

繫辭下》"Appended Remarks", Part 2, *The Book of Changes*】

善不可失,惡不可長。 Good should not be allowed to perish, nor evil to grow. 【左丘明《左傳·隱公六年》Zuo Qiuming:"The Sixth year of the Reign of Duke Yin", *Zuo's Commentary on the Spring and Autumn Annals*】

善不可外來兮,名可不可以虛作。 Goodness cannot be done by others and fame cannot be made up. 【屈原《楚辭·離騷·九章·抽思》Qu Yuan: Chapter 9, "Stray Thoughts", "The Sorrows At Parting", *The Songs of Chu*】

善惡不同徐,冰炭不同爐。 Good and evil do not go on the same road as ice and burning coal are not in the same furnace. 【韓非《韓非子·顯學第五十》Han Fei: Chapter 50, "Eminence in Learning", *Hanfeizi*】

善惡隨人作,福禍自己招。 A person decides to do good or evil and blessings or disasters are of one's own making. 【《增廣賢文》Words that Open up One's Mind and Enhance One's Wisdom】

善惡昭彰,如影隨形。 Rewards follow good or bad deeds as the shadow follows the figure. 【李汝珍《鏡花緣·第七十一回》Li Ruzhen: Chapter 71, *Flowers in the Mirror*】

善門難開,惡門難閉。 It is difficult to start good deeds or stop evil doings. 【李寶嘉《官場現形記·第三十四回》Li Baojia: Chapter 34, *Officialdom Unmasked*】

善乃福之基。 Good deeds are the foundation of fortune. 【俗語 Common saying】

善若施於人,禍不侵於己。 If you do good to others, no calamity will come upon you. 【佚名《名賢集》Anonymous: *Collected Sayings of Famous Sages*】

善事可作,惡事莫為。 You can do good things, but don't do bad things. 【《增廣賢文》*Words that Open up One's Mind and Enhance One's Wisdom*】

善欲人見,不是真善。 Goodness which is meant to be seen by others is not true goodness. 【朱用純《朱子家訓》Zhu Yongchun: *Precepts of the Zhu Family*】

善則稱人,過則稱己。 When good things are done, give credits to others; when mistakes are made, admit them as your mistakes. 【《禮記·坊記第三十》Chapter 30, "Records of the Dykes", *The Book of Rites*】

善者福,惡者禍。 The good are blessed for fortune and the evil are doomed for misfortune. 【俗語 Common saying】【許仲琳《封神演義·第二十九回》Xu Zhonglin: Chapter 29, *Romance of the Investiture of the Deities*】

上善若水,水善利萬物而不爭。 The highest goodness is like water, which benefits myriad things but does not contend with them. 【老子《道德經・第八章》Laozi: Chapter 8, *Daodejing*】

天下烏鴉一樣黑。In every country dogs bite.【俗語 Common saying】

萬惡為禍水之源。All evils are origins of disasters.【俗語 Common saying】

為善不欲人知。One should not let others know when he is doing good.【俗語 Common saying】

為善則流芳百世。To do good one will leave a name that lasts a hundred generations.【程允升《幼學瓊林・卷三人事》Cheng Yunsheng: Chapter 3, "Human Matters", *Treasury of Knowledge for Young Students*】

為善最樂，為惡難逃。To do good deeds is most enjoyable but it will be difficult to escape from guilt when you do evil deeds. 【《增廣賢文》*Words that Open up One's Mind and Enhance One's Wisdom*】

毋以惡小而為之，毋以善小而不為。Don't do evil things because the vice is insignificant; don't neglect to do good deeds because the goodness is small. 【陳壽《三國志・蜀書・先主傳》Chen Shou: "Biographies of the Ancient Emperors", "History of the State of Wei", *Records of the Three Kingdoms*】

邪不能勝正，假不能勝真。The evil cannot prevail over the good and the false cannot prevail over the true.【俗語 Common saying】

行善得善，行惡得惡。Do good and you will get fortune; do evil and you will get misfortune.【俗語 Common saying】

學壞容易學好難。That which is evil is soon learned. 【俗語 Common saying】

一好百好，一醜百醜。When there is goodness, all will be good. When there is evil, all will be evil.【俗語 Common saying】

一好遮百醜。A single good deed makes up for a hundred ill deeds.【俗語 Common saying】

一善掩百惡。For one good deed a hundred ill deeds should be overlooked.【李漁《十二樓・歸正樓》Li Yu: "Return-to-right Tower", *Twelve Towers*】

一善足以消百惡。One good deed can conquer a hundred ill deeds successively.【諺語 Proverb】【周楫《西湖二集・第十卷》Zhou Ji: Chapter 10, *The West Lake, Second Volume*】

隱惡揚善，執其兩端。To hide one's bad deeds and make known one's good deeds, these two aspects should be held when dealing with people.【《增廣賢文》*Words that Open up One's Mind and Enhance One's Wisdom*】

願無伐善，無施勞。I neither brag about my strengths, nor the services I gave to others.【孔子《論語・公冶長篇第五》Confucius: Chapter 5, *The Analects of Confucius*】

在家不行善，出門大風灌。 If one does not do good at home, he will go against strong winds when he travels. 【諺語 Proverb】

自作孽不可活。 The evils we bring on ourselves are the hardest to bear. 【孟軻《孟子‧離婁上》Meng Ke: Chapter 4, Part 1, *Mencius*】

作善天降百祥，作惡天降百殃。 Doing good, one is blessed by god; doing evil, one will have disaster as punishment given by god. 【《尚書‧伊訓》"Instructions of Yi", *The Book of History*】

Goods

貨要賣當時。 Goods are sold well when in season. 【俗語 Common saying】

貨無大小，缺者便貴。 The price depends on the need. 【馮夢龍《醒世恆言‧第三十五卷》Feng Menglong: Chapter 35, *Stories to Awaken the World*】

便宜沒好貨，好貨不便宜。 Goods that are cheap in price are of poor quality, and goods of good quality are not cheap. 【俗語 Common saying】

一分錢一分貨。 You get what you pay for. 【俗語 Common saying】

一手交錢，一手交貨。 Give me the cash and I'll give you the goods. 【俗語 Common saying】

Gossip

大風吹倒梧桐樹，自有旁人說短長。 When a strong wind blows down a *Wutong* tree, then there will be gossips by the bystanders – injustice comes with complaints and criticism. 【袁枚《隨園詩話》Yuan Mei: *Talks on Poetry from the Sui Garden*】

當面不說，背後亂說。 Say nothing to one's face but gossip behind one's back. 【俗語 Common saying】【毛澤東〈反對自由主義〉Mao Zhedong: "Against Liberalism"】

寡婦門前是非多。 There are many gossips laying in front of a widow's door. 【諺語 Proverb】

來是是非人，去是是非者。 The one who comes as a gossiper is still a gossiper when he goes – whoever causes the incident take responsibility to deal with it. 【蘭陵笑笑生《金瓶梅‧第八十六回》Lanling Xiaoxiaosheng: Chapter 86, *The Plum in the Golden Vase*】

來說是非者，便是是非人。 One who comes to gossip is

a gossiper himself – whoever causes the incident takes responsibility to deal with it. 【俗語 Common saying】《增廣賢文》 *Words that Open up One's Mind and Enhance One's Wisdom*】

流言蜚語滿天飛。 Wild rumours are in the air. 【俗語 Common saying】

明人不說暗話。 An upright person does not gossip about others behind their backs. 【諺語 Proverb】【許晏駢《胡雪巖全傳》Xu Yanpian: *Biographies of Hu Xueyan*】

莫將閒話當閒話，往往事從閒話生。 Don't take gossips for just gossips, for they often cause trouble. 【諺語 Proverb】【金埴《不下帶編·卷六》Jin Zhi: Chapter 6, *Historical Notes of Qing Dynasty*】

人串門子惹是非，狗串門子挨棒錘。 People who gossip around stir up troubles; dogs that wander about are apt to be beaten. 【諺語 Proverb】

人多是非多。 More people, more gossips. 【諺語 Proverb】

人言不可信。 Gossips are not to be believed. 【諺語 Proverb】

人嘴快如風。 Gossips can be spread as fast as wind. 【諺語 Proverb】【李綠園《歧路燈·第六十五回》Li Yuyuan: Chapter 65, *Lamp on A Forked Road*】

識人多處是非多。 If you know many people, there will be much gossips about you. 【諺語 Proverb】

是非祇因多開口，煩惱皆因強出頭。 Gossips are caused by talking too much, and troubles are all caused by coming forward to help others beyond one's ability. 【《增廣賢文》*Words that Open up One's Mind and Enhance One's Wisdom*】

是非終日有，不聽自然無。 There are gossips every day, but if you don't listen to them, they are gone. 【《增廣賢文》*Words that Open up One's Mind and Enhance One's Wisdom*】

誰個背後不說人。 Everyone in the world comments on others behind their backs. 【諺語 Proverb】

誰人背後無人說，哪個人前不說人。 Everyone will be commented by others behind his back, and there is no one who does not comment on others in front of others. 【《增廣賢文》*Words that Open up One's Mind and Enhance One's Wisdom*】

閒口論閒話。 Idle people gossip. 【諺語 Proverb】

眼見方為是，傳言未必真。 What you see with your own eyes is true, but what is gossiped may be false. 【馮夢龍《醒世恆言·第七卷》Feng Menglong: Chapter 7, *Stories to Awaken the World*】

一身不入是非門。 I would not enter those places where gossips are rampant. 【諺語 Proverb】【茅盾《子夜》Mao Dun: Chapter 10, *Midnight*】

張家長，李家短。Gossip about this or that family. 【俗語 Common saying】【施耐庵《水滸傳・第二十一回》Shi Nai'an: Chapter 21, *Outlaws of the Marshes*】

止謗莫於自修。The best way to stop gossips is to mend one's own ways. 【諺語 Proverb】

Governance

愛國治民，能無知乎。When one loves one's country and governs the people, can one achieve them without knowledge? 【老子《道德經・第十章》Laozi: Chapter 10, *Daodejing*】

安定國家，必大焉先。To stabilize a country, top priority must be given to the most important matters. 【左丘明《左傳・襄公三十年》Zuo Qiuming: "The Thirtieth Year of the Reign of Duke Xuan", *Zuo's Commentary on the Spring and Autumn Annals*】

安而不忘危，存而不忘亡，治而不忘亂。When in peace, do not forget the danger may come; when in existence, do not forget the ruin may come; when in order, do not forget the disorder may come. 【《易經・繫辭下》"Appended Remarks, Part 2", *The Book of Changes*】

罷無能，廢無用，損不急之官，塞私門之請。Dismiss the incapable, exterminate the useless, cut down unnecessary officials, and stop backdoorism. 【劉向《戰國策・秦策》Liu Xiang: "Strategies of the State of Qin", *Strategies of the Warring States*】

半部論語治天下。Reading half of the *Analects of Confucius* enables one to rule the empire. 【俗語 Common saying】

得賢者昌，得愚者亡。If a country has virtuous people assisting in governance, it prospers. If it has stupid people assisting in governance, it perishes. 【諺語 Proverb】【《全相平話・卷六》Chapter 6, *Comprehensive Talk*】

德惟善政，政在養民。The virtue of the ruler is seen in his good government, which is in the nourishing of the people. 【《尚書・大禹謨》"Counsels of Yu the Great", *The Book of History*】

凡治天下，必因人情。All who govern the world must accord with the inclinations of the people. 【韓非《韓非子・八經第四十八》Han Fei: Chapter 48, "Eight Canons", *Hanfeizi*】

甘其食，美其服，安其居，樂其俗。(Governance is about) making people's food sweet, their clothes beautiful, their dwellings comfortable, and their customs enjoyable. 【老子

《道德經・第八十章》Laozi: Chapter 80, *Daodejing*】

君仁，莫不仁；君義，莫不義；君正，莫不正。 If a ruler is benevolent, all others will be benevolent; if a ruler is righteous, all others will be righteous; if a ruler is upright, all others will be upright. 【孟軻《孟子・離婁上》Meng Ke: Chapter 4, Part 1, *Mencius*】

君王發狂，百姓遭殃。 When an emperor goes crazy, people suffer. 【諺語 Proverb】

苛政猛於虎也。 Harsh governance is more fearful than a tiger. 【《禮記・檀弓下第四》Chapter 4, "Tangong", Part 2, *The Book of Rites*】

勞心者治人，勞力者治於人。 Those who work with diligence rule, while those who work with their physical strength are being ruled. 【孟軻《孟子・滕文公上》Meng Ke: Chapter 5, Part 1, *Mencius*】

禮世不必一其道，便國不必法古。 Governing a country does not have to always adopt the same way and benefitting a country does not have to always follow the ancient. 【劉向《戰國策・趙策一》Liu Xiang: "Strategies of the State of Zhao, No. 1", *Strategies of the Warring States*】

民之難治，以其智多。 People are difficult to be governed because they are so clever. 【老子《道德經・第六十五章》Laozi: Chapter 65, *Daodejing*】

民之所好好之，民之所惡惡之，此之謂民之父母。 Promote what the people are in favour of; ban what the people hate. This is how the official, known as the parent of the people, should do. 【《禮記・大學第四十二》Chapter 42, "The Great Learning", *The Book of Rites*】

其政悶悶，其民淳淳；其政察察，其民缺缺。 When the government is magnanimous, the people become simple; when the government is harsh, the people become cunning. 【老子《道德經・第五十八章》Laozi: Chapter 58, *Daodejing*】

千年江山八百主。 A country of a thousand years old may have eight hundred rulers. 【俗語 Common saying】【《醒醉石・第十五回》Chapter 15, *Awakened and Drunk Stone*】

清政不怕民反。 A government free from corruption is not afraid of rebellion. 【俗語 Common saying】

取之於民，用之於民。 What is taken from the people is spent on the people. 【諺語 Proverb】

善政不如善教之得民也。 Good governance does not win the hearts of the people as much as good education. 【孟軻《孟子・盡心章句上》Meng Ke: Chapter 7, Part 1, *Mencius*】

天下兼相愛則治，相惡則亂。 The world will be in order when there is universal love, and chaotic when there is universal hatred. 【墨翟《墨子·兼愛卷四》Mo Di: Volume 4, "Universal Love", *Mozi*】

天下之生久矣，一治一亂。 It has been a long time since people in the world came into being and it has been an alternation of a period of good order and a period of disorder. 【孟軻《孟子·滕文公下》Meng Ke: Chapter 5, Part 2, *Mencius*】

徒善不足以為政，徒法不能以自行。 Mind of good deeds alone are not enough for the governing of a country; laws alone cannot be enforced by themselves without implementation. 【孟軻《孟子·離婁上》Meng Ke: Chapter 4, Part 1, *Mencius*】

為國者，必先知民之所苦，禍之所起，然後設之以禁。 Those who govern a country must first know what causes the suffering of the people and the emergence of disasters so that they could take measures to prevent them. 【王符《潛夫論·述赦》Wang Fu: "On Amnesties", *Remarks by a Recluse*】

為善不同，同歸於治；為惡不同，同歸於亂。 Good deeds are done differently, yet what is the same is that they all contribute to good order; evil deeds are done differently, yet what is the same is that they all result in disorder. 【《尚書·蔡仲之命》 "Charge to Cai Zhong", *The Book of History*】

為無為，則無不治。 Act by means of natural rules, then nothing will be in disorder. 【老子《道德經·第三章》Laozi: Chapter 3, *Daodejing*】

為政不及私怨。 Governance has nothing to do with personal grudges. 【諺語 Proverb】

為政不難，不得罪於巨室。 To manage a government is not difficult. It lies on not offending the great families. 【孟軻《孟子·離婁上》Meng Ke: Chapter 4, Part 1, *Mencius*】

為政不在多言。 Those who govern must not talk much of blank words. 【司馬遷《史記·儒林列傳》Sima Qian: "Biographies of Confucian Scholars", *Records of the Grand Historian*】

為政以德，譬如北辰，居其所，而眾星拱之。 He who governs with virtue is like the Pole Star, which remains in its place with a myriad of stars surrounding it. 【孔子《論語·為政篇第二》Confucius: Chapter 2, *The Analects of Confucius*】

為政者不賞私勞，不罰私怨。 He who governs neither award those who contribute to his personal interest nor punish those who have personal grudges against him. 【左丘明《左傳·昭公五年》Zuo Qiuming: "The Fifth Year of the Reign of Duke Zhao", *Zuo's Commentary on the Spring and Autumn Annals*】

為政者，每人而悅之，日亦不足矣。 If a person who governs

tries to please everybody, then he will find that he does not have the days to do his work. 【孟軻《孟子‧離婁下》Meng Ke: Chapter 4, Part 2, *Mencius*】

為政之道，須在寬猛相濟。 Governance is about striking a balance between leniency and strictness. 【左丘明《左傳‧昭公二十年》Zuo Qiuming: "The Twentieth Year of the Reign of Duke Zhao", *Zuo's Commentary on the Spring and Autumn Annals*】

修身齊家治國平天下。 Cultivate the person, regulate the family, rule the country, and give peace to the world. 【《禮記‧大學第四十二》Chapter 42, "The Great Learning", *The Book of Rites*】

以不忍人之心，行不忍人之政，治天下可運之掌上。 When you use a sympathetic heart to implement a sympathetic governance, then governing the country can be easily under the control. 【孟軻《孟子‧公孫丑上》Meng Ke: Chapter 2, Part 1, *Mencius*】

以亂攻治者亡，以邪攻正者亡，以逆攻順者亡。 A chaotic army that attacks a stable one will perish, an evil country that attacks a just one will perish, and a perverse country that attacks a proper one will perish. 【孔子《論語‧憲問篇第十四》Confucius: Chapter 14, *The Analects of Confucius*】

以正治國，以奇用兵。 Govern a country with justice, fight a war with exceptional strategies. 【老子《道德經‧第五十七章》Laozi: Chapter 57, *Daodejing*】

以智治國，國之賊；不以智治國，國之福。 To govern a country by cunning is a disaster to the country; not to govern a country by intelligence is a blessing to the country. 【老子《道德經‧第六十五章》Laozi: Chapter 65, *Daodejing*】

養生喪死無憾，王道之始也。 When people have no regrets about nourishing their living and burying the dead, this is the beginning of royal government. 【孟軻《孟子‧梁惠王上》Meng Ke: Chapter 1, Part 1, *Mencius*】

義人在上，天下必治。 When the righteous people are in authority, the world will certainly be well governed. 【墨翟《墨子‧非命卷三十五至三十七》Mo Di: Chapters 35-37, "Against Fate", *Mozi*】

在知人，在安民。 Those who govern have to understand the subordinates and make people feel secure. 【《尚書‧皋陶謨》"Counsels of Gao Yao", *The Book of History*】

政不可不慎也。務三而己：一曰擇人，二曰因民，三曰從時。 Governance must be very cautious. There are but three tasks involved: first, appoint the right people; second, adhere to the will of the people; and third, time one's actions. 【左丘明《左傳‧

昭公七年》Zuo Qiuming: "The Seventh Year of the Reign of Duke Zhao", *Zuo's Commentary on the Spring and Autumn Annals*】

政通人和，百廢俱興。 The administration is effective and people are united, and all things that fell into disrepair are activated. 【范仲淹〈岳陽樓記〉Fan Zhongyan: "Song of the Yueyang Tower"】

政有毫髮之善，下必知也。 When there is any slightest good thing done by the government, people surely know it. 【白居易〈策林四·采詩〉Bai Juyi: Chapter 4, "Collecting Poems", *A Forest of Strategies*】

政之所興，在順民心。政之所廢，在逆民心。 The reason for the popularity of a government lies with following what is on the mind of the people. The cause for the failure of a government lies with going against what is on the mind of the people. 【管仲《管子·牧民第一》Guan Zhong: Volume 1, "Shepherding the People", *Guanzi*】

知屋漏者在宇下，知政失者在草野。 He who knows the leakage of a house lives under its roof, and he who knows the mismanagement of a state stays on its land. 【王充《論衡·書解第八十二卷》Wang Chong: Chapter 82, "On Literary Works", *Critical Essays*】

治大國若烹小鮮。 Running a large country is like cooking a tasty dish which is just to the right point. 【老子《道德經·第六十章》Laozi: Chapter 60, *Daodejing*】

治國不諱亂。 In the government of a country, do not preclude all possibilities of anarchy. 【蔡東藩《清史通俗演義·第八十回》Cai Dongfan: Chapter 80, *Popular Romance of the Qing Dynasty*】

治國不以禮，猶無耜而耕也。 To govern a country without rites is like tilling a field without a plough. 【《禮記·禮運第九》Chapter 9, "Conveyance of Rites", *The Book of Rites*】

治國去之，亂國就之。 Leave a country which is well governed and go to a country which is in disorder. 【莊周《莊子·內篇·人間世第四》Zhuang Zhou: Chapter 4, "The Human World", "Inner Chapters", *Zhuangzi*】

治國之道，愛民而已。 The way to govern a country is nothing other than loving the people. 【劉向《説苑·卷七政理》Liu Xiang: Chapter 7, "The Principles of Government", *Garden of Persuasion*】

治久必亂，合久必分。 After a prolonged order in a country, there is bound to be disorder; after a prolonged unification, there is bound to be division. 【羅貫中《三國演義·第一回》Luo Guanzhong: Chapter 1, *Romance of the Three Kingdoms*】

治生乎君子。 Order springs from the gentleman. 【荀況《荀子·

王制第九》Xun Kuang: Chapter 9, "Sovereign's Regulations", *Xunzi*】

治天下者，當用天下之心為心。
He who governs a country should regard the heart of the people as his own heart.【班固《漢書·鮑宣傳》Ban Gu:"Biography of Bao Xuan", *History of the Han*】

Grass

草不去根，終當復生。 If the roots of the grass are not removed, the grass will eventually grow again.【司馬光《資治通鑒·卷二百零八》Sima Guang: Chapter 208, *Comprehensive Mirror to Aid In Government*】

芳草鮮美，落英繽紛。 The flowers and grass are fresh and the fallen leaves are dense.【陶淵明〈桃花源記〉Tao Yuanming:"Record of Peach Blossom Spring"】

離離原上草，一歲一枯榮。 Luxuriant is the grass on the plain; once a year, it thrives and wanes.【白居易〈古原草〉Bai Juyi:"Grass on an Ancient Plain"】

年年陌上生秋草，日日樓中到夕陽。 Year after year, the autumn grass grows on the bank. Day after day, the evening glow reaches the tower.【晏幾道〈鷓鴣天〉Yan Jidao:"To the Tune of Partridge in the Sky"】

青青河邊草，鬱鬱園中柳。 Green is the grass on the river banks, the willows are flushy in the garden.【佚名〈古詩十九首〉Anonymous:"Nineteen Ancient Poems"】

十步之間，必有茂草；十室之邑，必有俊士。 Within the space of ten paces, there must be luxuriant grass; within a town of ten households, there must be an outstanding man.【王符《潛夫論·實貢》Wang Fu:"On Recommendations of Substance", *Remarks by a Recluse*】

十步之澤，必有香草；十室之邑，必有忠士。 Within a marsh of ten paces, there must be fragrant grass; within a town of ten households, there must be a loyal man.【劉向《說苑·卷十六談叢》Liu Xiang: Chapter 16, "The Thicket of Discussion", *Garden of Persuasions*】

天涯何處無芳草。 Is there a place in the world where there is no fragrant flower?【蘇軾〈蝶戀花〉Su Shi:"To the Tune of Butterflies Lingering over Flowers"】

野火燒不盡，春風吹又生。 A fire on the plain cannot burn out the grass, for it will grow again when the spring breeze blows.【白居易〈賦得古原草送別〉Bai Juyi:"Grass on an Ancient Plain"】

一番桃李花開盡，惟有青青草色齊。 When the peach and plum

blossoms are over, what is left is the green green grass. 【曾鞏〈城南〉Zeng Gong:"South of the City"】

枝上柳綿吹又少,天涯何處無芳草。 Catkins on the branches have been blown away and got fewer and fewer. The fragrant grass will grow everywhere on earth. 【蘇軾〈蝶戀花〉Su Shi:"To the Tune of Butterflies Lingering over Flowers"】

種豆南山下,草盛豆苗稀。 I grow beans at the foot of the southern hill, weeds run riot but the shoots are few. 【陶淵明〈歸園田居〉Tao Yuanming:"Returning to My Rural Home"】

Gratitude and ingratitude

吃飯不忘種田人。 When you have rice at meal, don't forget those who till the fields. 【俗語 Common saying】

吃了果子忘記樹。 One forgets the tree after eating its fruit. 【俗語 Common saying】

狗咬呂洞賓,不識好人心。 Like the dog that bit Lu Dongbin – you bite the hand that feeds you. 【俗語 Common saying】【曹雪芹《紅樓夢・第二十五回》Cao Xueqin: Chapter 25, *A Dream of the Red Chamber*】

過河打渡子 —— 忘恩負義。 Beating the ferryman after crossing the river is ungrateful. 【歇後語 End-clipper】

過了河就拆橋。 Remove the bridge just after crossing the river. 【宋濂《元史・徹里帖木兒傳》Song Lian:"Biography of Cheli Timur", *History of the Yuan*】

好心當作驢肝肺。 One bites the hand that feeds one. 【俗語 Common saying】【曹雪芹《紅樓夢・第二十八回》Cao Xueqin: Chapter 28, *A Dream of the Red Chamber*】

好心沒善報。 Recompense good with evil. 【俗語 Common saying】

喝水不忘掘井人。 When one drinks water, one does not forget the well-digger. 【俗語 Common saying】【周立波《暴風驟雨・第一部・十八》Zhou Libo: Volume 1, Chapter 18, *The Hurricane*】

記人之恩,忘人之過。 Remember the good deeds done by others and forget the faults committed by others. 【陳壽《三國志・蜀書・秦宓傳》Chen Shou:"Biography of Qin Mi", "History of the State of Shu", *Records of the Three Kingdoms*】

狡兔死,走狗烹。 When the cunning hare is killed, the hound becomes useless and boiled. 【司馬遷《史記・越王勾踐世家》Sima Qian:"House of King Goujian of Yue", *Records of the Grand Historian*】

救了落水狗,反咬你一口。 If you save a drowning dog, it'll bite

you after getting back on shore.
【諺語 Proverb】

君子記恩不記仇。 A gentleman
remembers others' kindness but
not the wrongs he has suffered.
【諺語 Proverb】

寧叫我負天下人，休叫天下人負
我。 Rather let me be ungrateful
to the world than the world to
me.【羅貫中《三國演義・第四回》
Luo Guanzhong: Chapter 4, *Romance of
the Three Kingdoms*】

寧可人負我，不可我負人。
I would rather let others be
ungrateful to me than let me be
ungrateful to others.【羅貫中《三
國演義・第四回》Luo Guanzhong:
Chapter 4, *Romance of the Three
Kingdoms*】

起死人，肉白骨。 Save the dead
to grow the flesh – giving the
greatest kindness.【左丘明《國語・
吳語》Zuo Qiuming: "The Language of
Wu", *National Languages*】

人之有德於我也，不可忘也；
吾有德於人也，不可不忘也。
When people do a favour for us,
we must not forget. When we
do a favour for others, we must
forget it.【劉向《戰國策・魏策四》
Liu Xiang: "Strategies of the State of Wei,
No.4, " *Strategies of the Warring States*】

施恩不望報，望報莫施恩。 He
who offers a favour should not
expect its return, and he who
expects its return should not
confer a favour.【俗語 Common

saying】《八仙全傳・第一回》Chapter
1, *The Story of Eight Deities*】

施惠不記心，受德莫忘恩。 Don't
remember the good things you
did to others, but don't forget
the good things you received
from others.【俗語 Common saying】

施惠勿念，受恩莫忘。 You should
not bear in mind the favour you
give to others, but you should
not forget the favour you receive
from others.【朱用純《朱子家
訓》Zhu Yongchun: *Precepts of the Zhu
Family*】

受人點水之恩，當要湧泉相報。
Being given a bit of favour, one
should do a lot to pay the debt
of gratitude.【《增廣賢文》*Words that
Open up One's Mind and Enhance One's
Wisdom*】

忘恩負義，禽獸之徒。 An
ungrateful person is like birds
or beasts that do not behave in a
human way.【《增廣賢文》*Words that
Open up One's Mind and Enhance One's
Wisdom*】

物有不可忘，或有不可不忘。
There are things that you cannot
forget and there are things that
you cannot but need to forget.
【司馬遷《史記・魏公子列傳》Sima
Qian: "Biography of the Prince of Wei",
Records of the Grand Historian】

飲水不忘挖井人。 When you
drink water, do not forget those
who dig the well.【俗語 Common
saying】

飲水當思挖井人。When you drink water, you should think of those who dig the well. 【俗語 Common saying】

有恩報恩，有仇報仇。Return kindness with kindness and hatred with hatred. 【俗語 Common saying】

有恩不報非君子。He who does not pay for others' kindness is not a gentleman. 【吳承恩《西遊記・第二十七回》Wu Cheng'en: Chapter 27, *Journey to the West*】

Greed

別貪不義財，別喝過量酒。Don't be greedy for ill-gotten gains nor drink excessively. 【俗語 Common saying】

吃一看二眼觀三。Hope for another after gaining one. 【俗語 Common saying】

吃着碗裏，瞧着鍋裏。While eating one dish, one keeps watching for next. 【曹雪芹《紅樓夢・第十六回》Cao Xueqin: Chapter 16, *A Dream of the Red Chamber*】

得一望十，得十望百。When one gets one, he wants ten. When one gets ten, he wants a hundred. 【馮夢龍《醒世恆言・第十七卷》Feng Menglong: Chapter 17, *Stories to Awaken the World*】

人心不足蛇吞象。A greedy person is like a snake trying to swallow an elephant. 【俗語 Common saying】【佚名《山海經・海內南經》Anonymous: "Classic of Regions within the Seas", "South", *Classic of Mountains and Seas*】

人心難滿，溪壑易填。Avarice knows no bounds. 【洪應明《菜根譚・第三百四十四章》Hong Yingming: Chapter 344, *Vegetable Root Discourse*】

貪心不足，反罹其害。One falls victim to one's greed. 【俗語 Common saying】

Grief

長太息以掩涕兮，哀民生之多艱。I sighed for a long time and wiped my tears, saddened by my difficult life. 【屈原〈離騷〉Qu Yuan: "The Sorrows at Parting"】

愁人莫向愁人說，說與愁人轉轉愁。A distressed person should not tell their distress to another distressed person, or the distress will be doubled. 【董説《西遊補・第五回》Dong Shuo: Chapter 5, *A Supplement to the Journey to the West*】

幾時重，自是人生長恨水長東。When will all these happen

again? Is it destined that life is always full of regrets like waters always flow to the east?【李煜〈烏夜啼〉Li Yu:"To the Tune of Crows Crying at Night"】

人怨語聲高。A person with grievances speaks loud.【湯顯祖《牡丹亭‧第四十九齣》Tang Xianzu: Scene 49, "Peony Pavilion"】

人之生也，與憂俱生。When a person is born, his griefs are born with him.【莊周《莊子‧外篇‧至樂第十八》Zhuang Zhou: Chapter 18, "Ultimate Joy", "Outer Chapters", "Zhuangzi"】

思悠悠，恨悠悠，恨到歸時方始休，月明人倚樓。My thoughts are endless, so is my grief. My grief would not cease until my husband comes back. The moon is bright, and I lean on the balcony.【白居易〈長相思〉Bai Juyi:"To the Tune of Everlasting Longing"】

我心傷悲，莫知我哀。My heart is filled with sorrow and sadness, but who knows my misery.【《詩經‧小雅‧采薇》"Gathering Vetch", "Minor Odes of the Kingdom", *The Book of Odes*】

閒坐悲君亦自悲，百年多是幾多時。Sitting alone at home, I grieve for both you and me. In hundred years' lifespan our bliss lasted but a short time.【元稹〈遣悲懷〉Yuen Zhen:"Giving Vent to Sorrow"】

衙齋臥聽蕭蕭竹，疑是民間疾苦聲。Lying in bed in my den, I heard the rustling of bamboos outside, and it just sounded like the moaning of the needy.【鄭板橋〈濰縣署中畫竹呈年伯包大中丞括〉Zheng Banqiao:"In the Magistrate's Office at Weixian I Paint a Bamboo to Present to My Senior, Governor Bao Kuo"】

自是人生常恨水常東。From of old, life is always full of grief and waters always flow to the east.【李煜〈相見歡〉Li Yu:"To the Tune of the Joy of Meeting"】

Growth

百尺高樓從地起。A tower of a hundred feet starts from the ground.【諺語 Proverb】

從無到有，從小到大。Grow from nothing to something and from small to large.【諺語 Proverb】

海不辭水，故能成其大；山不辭土石，故能成其高。The sea does not reject water, so it is able to become great; the mountain does not reject stones, so it is able to become tall.【管仲《管子‧形勢解第六十四》Guan Zhong: Chapter 64, "Explanation of the Conditions and Circumstances", *Guanzi*】

合抱之樹，生於毫末。 A huge tree grows from a tiny seedling. 【老子《道德經‧第六十四章》Laozi: Chapter 64, *Daodejing*】

平地起樓台。 Construct a building or terrace from a level ground. 【徐珂《清稗類鈔‧第二卷》Xu Ke: Chapter 2, *Collection of Old Rules in Qing*】

萬尺高樓起於累土。 A building of ten thousand feet high is built from piling up earth.【老子《道德經‧第六十四章》Laozi: Chapter 64, *Daodejing*】

萬丈高樓平地起。 A tall building of ten-thousand feet rises from a level ground. 【諺語 Proverb】

小時了了，大未必佳。 A precocious child may not be remarkable when grown up. 【劉義慶《世說新語‧言語第二》Liu Yiqing: Chapter 2, "Speech and Conversation", *A New Account of the Tales of the World* 】

由小到大，由少到多。 From small to large, from few to many. 【俗語 Common saying】

Guest

過門都是客。 All those who pass through one's door are one's guests. 【諺語 Proverb】

好客主人多。 One who likes entertaining guests are welcomed by many hosts. 【諺語 Proverb】【黃世仲《廿載繁華夢‧第十四回》Huang Shizhong: Chapter 14, *A Rich Dream that Lasted Two Decades* 】

花徑不曾緣客掃，篷門今始為君開。 My flowered path has not been swept for any guests and now I swept for you. My thatch gate for the first time opened just for you. 【杜甫〈客至〉Du Fu: "A Visitor Arrived"】

客來主不顧，應恐是痴人。 If the host leaves a guest unattended, I am afraid the host must be an idiot.《增廣賢文》*Words that Open up One's Mind and Enhance One's Wisdom*】

客散主人寬。 When the guests are gone the host can relax. 【諺語 Proverb】

羅漢請觀音 —— 客少主人多。 When Buddhist arhats invite the goddess Guanyin, there are more hosts than guests. 【歇後語 End-clipper】

美酒釀成緣好客。 Good wine is brewed for entertaining guests. 【《增廣賢文》*Words that Open up One's Mind and Enhance One's Wisdom*】

強賓不壓主。 Even a powerful guest should not overwhelm the host. 【羅貫中《三國演義‧第十三回》Luo Guanzhong: Chapter 13, *Romance of the Three Kingdoms*】

行客拜坐客。 Guests should first call on the host.【諺語 Proverb】【文康《兒女英雄傳‧第十二回》Wen Kang: Chapter 12, *Biographies of Young Heroes and Heroines*】

一客不煩二主。 One guest should not bother two hosts.【俗語 Common saying】【李綠園《歧路燈‧第二十七回》Li Yuyuan: Chapter 27, *Lamp on a Forked Road*】

在家不會迎賓客，出門方知少主人。 If a person does not treat guest with kindness at home, he will meet few people who treat him with kindness outside.【《增廣賢文》 Words that Open up One's Mind and Enhance One's Wisdom】

主賢客來勤。 A courteous host will have frequent visitors.【諺語 Proverb】【曹雪芹《紅樓夢‧第三十二回》Cao Xueqin: Chapter 32, *A Dream of the Red Chamber*】

座上客常滿，杯中酒不空。 There are always guests taking up all the seats in the house and wine in the cups is never unfilled.【《增廣賢文》 Words that Open up One's Mind and Enhance One's Wisdom】

Habit

少成若天性，習慣如自然。 When young, form good habits as if they are your nature, then habits come naturally to you.【諺語 Proverb】【班固《漢書‧賈誼傳》Ban Gu: "Biography of Jia Yi", *History of the Han*】

習慣成自然。 Habit is a second nature.【諺語 Proverb】【班固《漢書‧賈誼傳》Ban Gu: "Biography of Jia Yi", *History of the Han*】

性相近，習相遠也。 Human nature is alike, but habits make them differ.【孔子《論語‧陽貨篇第十七》Confucius: Chapter 17, *The Analects of Confucius*】

Hair

拔根汗毛，比別人腰粗。 A hair from one's body is thicker than somebody's waist – one is very rich.【曹雪芹《紅樓夢‧第六回》Cao Xueqin: Chapter 6, *A Dream of the Red Chamber*】

白髮悲花落，青雲羨鳥飛。 When my hair turns white, I lament the falling of flowers, and when the sky is blue, I envy the flight of birds.【岑參〈寄左省杜拾遺〉Cen Shen: "To Censor Du Fu"】

白髮未除豪氣在。 White hair has not wiped out my ambition.【陸游〈度浮橋至南臺〉Lu You: "Crossing a Boat-bridge to the South Terrace"】

白髮無情侵老境，青燈有味似兒時。 My white hair has without mercy entered into my old age, while reading under the blue lamplight has rekindled the joy of my boyhood. 【陸游〈度浮橋至南臺〉Lu You:"Crossing a Boat-bridge to the South Terrace"】

公道世間唯白髮，貴人頭上不曾饒。 The fairest thing in the world is white hair, which has no mercy on even a noble head. 【杜牧〈送隱者一絕〉Du Mu:"To a Recluse"】

少年莫笑白頭老，轉眼少年也白頭。 Youth should not laugh at the old with white hair for in the twinkling of an eye, youth's hair will turn white too. 【諺語 Proverb】

少壯能幾時，鬢髮各已蒼。 How long can one stay young and sound? Hair on my temples and my head have turned grey. 【杜甫〈贈衛八處士〉Du Fu:"Presented to Scholar-recluse Wei the Eighth"】

Hand

挨一頓拳頭。 Get a punch. 【俗語 Common saying】

打人沒好手，罵人沒好口。 When one beats something, one will not use a light hand. To scold somebody, one will not use good words. 【俗語 Common saying】

打人莫打膝，道人莫道實。 To beat a person, don't beat his vital part. To talk about a person, don't mention his privacy. 【諺語 Proverb】【袁采《袁氏世範·第二卷》Yuan Cai: Chapter 2, *Models for the World by Master Yuan*】

打人休打臉，罵人休揭短。 When you strike a person with your fist, don't strike their face. When you scold a person, don't mention their faults. 【諺語 Proverb】【蘭陵笑笑生《金瓶梅·第八十六回》Lanling Xiaoxiaosheng. Chapter 86, *The Plum in the Golden Vase*】

打人一拳，防人一腳。 When you strike somebody with your fist, be prepared for his kicking you with his foot. 【石玉昆《三俠五義·第一百零三回》Shi Yukun: Chapter 103, *The Three Heroes and Five Gallants*】

滾油鍋裏撿金子 —— 難下手。 Picking gold out from a pot of boiling oil – difficult to put one's hand into it. 【歇後語 End-clipper】

伸手不見五指。 So dark that you can't see all your fingers in front of you. 【凌濛初《初刻拍案驚奇·第二十四卷》Ling Mengchu: Chapter 24, *Amazing Tales, Volume One*】

手背手心都是肉。 The back and palm of one's hand are both one's flesh. 【俗語 Common saying】

手長衫袖短，人窮顏色低。When the arm is long the sleeve seems short; if a man is poor, he cannot hold up his head. 【俗語 Common saying】

手提一管筆，到處不求人。With a writing brush in hand, one does not need to ask for help. 【俗語 Common saying】【汪洙《神童詩》Wang Zhu: "Poem of a Talented Boy"】

手閒長指甲，心閒長頭髮。When one's hands are idle, one's nails grow long; when one's mind is at leisure, one's hair grows long. 【俗語 Common saying】

手中沒把米，叫雞雞不來。Without a handful of rice in one's hand, one cannot call chickens to come. 【諺語 Proverb】【陸地〈瀑布〉Lu Di: "Waterfall"】

Happiness

百歲開懷能幾日，一生知己不多人。How many happy days you have if you live to a hundred years, and in one's lifetime, you only have a few bosom friends. 【何蘭庭〈斷句〉He Lanting: "Broken Lines"】

得快活，且快活。Enjoy life while you can. 【俗語 Common saying】

獨樂樂不如眾樂樂。Enjoying happiness alone is not as happy as sharing it with others. 【孟軻《孟子·梁惠王上》Meng Ke: Chapter 1, Part 1, Mencius】

福中勤中得。Happiness comes from diligence. 【俗語 Common saying】

黃金未為貴，安樂值錢多。Gold is not value, for peace and happiness are worth a lot of money. 【《增廣賢文》Words that Open up One's Mind and Enhance One's Wisdom】

黃連樹下彈琴 —— 苦中作樂。Try to enjoy oneself despite one's suffering. 【歇後語 End-clipper】

叫化子唱山歌 —— 窮開心。A beggar singing a mountain song – he is poor but happy. 【歇後語 End-clipper】

君子有終身之樂，無一日之憂。A gentleman lives in happiness all his life and does not have worries for a single day. 【荀況《荀子·子論第二十九》Xun Kuang: Chapter 29, "The Way to Be a Son", Xunzi】

樂而不淫，哀而不傷。Joyful but not out of control, sorrowful but not too sad. 【孔子《論語·八佾篇第三》Confucius: Chapter 3, The Analects of Confucius】

寧窮而開心，不富而憂慮。Would rather be poor but happy than rich but anxious. 【諺語 Proverb】

窮亦樂，通亦樂。 Be happy when you are in adversity; be happy when you are in clear mind. 【莊周《莊子・雜篇・讓王第二十八》Zhuang Zhou: Chapter 28, "Abdicating Kingship", "Miscellaneous Chapters", *Zhuangzi*】

仁者樂山，智者樂水。 A benevolent person loves mountains, a wise person, rivers. 【孔子《論語・雍也篇第六》Confucius: Chapter 6, *The Analects of Confucius*】

人生盡是樂，獨苦不知足。 Life is full of happiness, and the only bitterness is people's insatiable wants. 【諺語 Proverb】

身在福中不知福。 One fails to appreciate the happiness one enjoys. 【俗語 Common saying】

時人不識余心樂，將謂偷閒學少年。 My peers don't know what my heart takes delight, and they would say that I idle away and pattern after the young people. 【程顥〈春日偶成〉Cheng Hao: "An Occasional Poem Completed on a Day in Spring"】

一時之樂，終身之苦。 A moment of happiness brings suffering all one's life. 【俗語 Common saying】

一則以喜，一則以悲。 It is a matter for both happiness and sadness. 【諺語 Proverb】

一則以喜，一則以懼。 It is a matter for both rejoice and anxiety. 【孔子《論語・里仁篇第四》Confucius: Chapter 4, *The Analects of Confucius*】

有福不可享盡。 If you have happiness, do not enjoy it to excess. 【曾國藩《曾國藩家書・致澄弟》Zeng Guofan: "A Letter to My Younger Brother Chenghou", *Family Letters of Zeng Guofan*】

有福同享，有難同當。 Share joy and sorrows. 【李寶嘉《官場現形記・第五回》Li Baojia: Chapter 5, *Officialdom Unmasked*】

有福的人不在忙。 A person with a happy lot does not need to be busy. 【王實甫《破窯記・第一折》Wang Shifu: Scene 1, "The Dilapidated Kiln"】

有福的人人服侍，無福之人服侍人。 A person with a happy lot is served while a person of a bad lot serves. 【俗語 Common saying】

至樂無樂，至譽無譽。 Ultimate happiness is free of happiness and the highest fame is free of fame. 【莊周《莊子・外篇・至樂第十八》Zhuang Zhou: Chapter 18, "Ultimate Joy", "Outer Chapters," *Zhuangzi*】

Hardship

不吃苦中苦，難為人上人。
Without being tempered in
great hardships, one cannot
be a person above others. 【諺
語 Proverb】【馮夢龍《警世通言・第
二十四卷》Feng Menglong: Chapter 24,
Stories to Caution the World】

不是一番寒徹骨，哪得梅花放清
香。 Without the coldness that
is chilling to the bone, how can
we have the fragrance of the
plum blossoms? 【裴休〈宛陵錄〉
Pei Xiu: "The Wanling Record of the
Chan Master Huangbo Duanji"】

吃得苦中苦，方為人上人。 Only
those who could endure the
hardest hardships could become
outstanding persons. 【馮夢龍《警
世通言・第二十四卷》Feng Menglong:
Chapter 24, *Stories to Caution the World*】

吃青果 —— 先苦後甜。 Eating
Chinese olives is first bitter, then
sweet – just like first hardship,
then happiness. 【歇後語 End-
clipper】

工夫不負有心人。 Hard work will
certainly be rewarded. 【諺語
Proverb】

沒有功勞，也有苦勞。 One has
done hard work even if he has
not performed meritorious
deeds. 【俗語 Common saying】

人不磨，不成道。 People have
to be tempered in hardships
before they become useful. 【諺語
Proverb】

一不怕苦，二不怕死。 One
neither fear hardship nor death.
【俗語 Common saying】

以苦為樂，以苦為榮。 Feel it a joy
and an honour to work under
hard conditions. 【俗語 Common
saying】

Harm

害人反害己。 If one harms others,
it might come back to one and
harm oneself. 【俗語 Common
saying】

害人害自己。 When one harms
others, one harms oneself. 【俗
語 Common saying】【郭小亭《濟公全
傳・第一百三十七回》Guo Xiaoting:
Chapter 137, *Biography of Jigong*】

害人如害己。 One harms oneself
when harming others. 【俗語
Common saying】

害人之心不可有，防人之心不可
無。 One should not have the
thought of harming others,
but one should be prepared to
prevent others from harming
one. 【俗語 Common saying】

會叫的狗不咬人。 Barking dogs seldom bite. 【俗語 Common saying】

趨利而避害。 Seek for advantages and avoid harm. 【霍諝〈奏記大將軍梁商〉Fo Xu: "Petition to General-in-chief Liang Shang"】

人不害人身不貴，火不燒山地不肥。 A person who does not harm others cannot become a nobility and a mountain without being burnt cannot have a fertile land. 【諺語 Proverb】

Harmony

和合故能諧。 If there is concord and unity, there is harmony. 【管仲《管子·兵法第十七》Guan Zhong: Chapter 17, "Methods of Warfare", Guanzi】

虎鹿不同行。 Tigers and deer do not walk together. 【諺語 Proverb】

家中不和鄰里欺，鄰里不和說是非。 When there is no harmony inside a family, the family will be bullied by its neighbours, when there is no harmony among neighbours, there will be gossips. 【《增廣賢文》Words that Open up One's Mind and Enhance One's Wisdom】

萬物並育而不相害，道並行而不相悖。 All living creatures grow together without harming one another; ways run parallel without interfering with one another. 【《禮記·中庸第三十章》Chapter 30, "Doctrine of the Mean", The Book of Rites】

以和為貴，和而不同。 Harmony is most valuable, but it allows diversity. 【孔子《論語·學而篇第一》Confucius: Chapter 1, The Analects of Confucius】

願人之相美，不樂人之相傷。 I wish people would live in harmony and don't want to see them harming each other. 【范曄《後漢書·孔融傳》Fan Ye: "Biography of Kong Rong", History of the Later Han】

Hatred

但見淚痕濕，不知心恨誰。 The wet stains of her tears has been seen, but no one knows whom she hates in her mind. 【李白〈怨情〉Li Bai: "Grief"】

恨極出毒言。 Poisonous words are used when people hate each other very much. 【俗語 Common saying】

恨生不恨死。 Hate a person when he is alive but not when he is dead. 【俗語 Common saying】

往日無冤，今日無仇。 I bore no grudges against you in the past and I have no enmity with you today. 【施耐庵《水滸傳·第八回》Shi Nai'an: Chapter 8, *Outlaws of the Marshes*】

Head

矮簷之下，怎不低頭。 When one is under the eaves of a low house, one has to bend one's head. 【俗語 Common saying】【施耐庵《水滸傳·第二十八回》Shi Nai'an: Chapter 28, *Outlaws of the Marshes*】

白頭搔更短，渾欲不勝簪。 The white hair on my head becomes shorter from scratching, and it can hardly hold my hairpins. 【杜甫〈春望〉Du Fu: "Spring Sight"】

白頭縱作花園主，醉折花枝是別人。 Even if you become the master of a garden house when the hair of your head is white, it will be others who break the flower twigs in drunkenness. 【雍陶〈勸樂行〉Yong Tao: "Exhortation to Enjoyment"】

背着孩子找孩子 —— 頭腦昏了。 Looking for a child while carrying the child on one's back. 【歇後語 End-clipper】

居人屋簷下，豈敢不低頭。 When one lives under the eaves of another person, one has to bend one's head. 【俗語 Common saying】【施耐庵《水滸傳·第二十八回》Shi Nai'an: Chapter 28, *Outlaws of the Marshes*】

牛皮燈籠 —— 點不透。 One is thick-headed. 【歇後語 End-clipper】

身在屋簷下，怎敢不低頭。 Being under the eaves, dare one not lower one's head. 【俗語 Common saying】【施耐庵《水滸傳·第二十八回》Shi Nai'an: Chapter 28, *Outlaws of the Marshes*】

十步九回頭。 Look back nine times every ten steps. 【俗語 Common saying】【高明〈琵琶記〉Kao Ming: "The Story of *Pipa*"】

頭要冷，心要熱。 Be cool-headed and warm-hearted. 【諺語 Proverb】

一步一回頭。 Look back at every step. 【俗語 Common saying】

Health

不知筋力衰多少，但覺新來懶
上樓。 I do not know how
much my physical power has
weakened down, for I feel lately
that I am too lazy to mount the
tower. 【辛棄疾〈鷓鴣天〉Xin Qiji: "To
the Tune of Partridge in the Sky"】

家有萬貫財，不如一身健。
Health is better than wealth. 【俗
語 Proverb】

健康勝於財富。 Health is better
than wealth. 【俗語 Proverb】

老太太過年 —— 一年不如一年。
Just like an old woman's health,
declining more and more as the
years go by. 【歇後語 End-clipper】

沒病沒痛是神仙。 One who has
no disease is as lucky as a god.
【俗語 Common saying】

若要健，隔夜練。 To be healthy,
you must do exercises at
alternate nights. 【諺語 Proverb】

Heart

哀莫大於心死，而人死亦次
之。 There is nothing more
lamentable than the death of
the heart, even the death of the
body comes second. 【莊周《莊子·
外篇·田子方第二十一》Zhuang Zhou:
Chapter 21, "Esquire Square Field",
"Outer Chapters", *Zhuangzi*】

百人百條心。 A hundred people
have a hundred minds. 【諺語
Proverb】

百人百心，百人百性。 A hundred
people have a hundred minds
and a hundred people have a
hundred kinds of character. 【俗
語 Common saying】

蠶豆開花 —— 黑心 The broad
bean in bloom is black inside –
one is black-hearted. 【歇後語 End-
clipper】

惻隱之心，人皆有之；羞惡之
心，人皆有之；恭敬之心，人
皆有之；是非之心；人皆有
之。 Everyone has a heart for
compassion; everyone has a
heart for the dislike of shame;
everyone has a heart for respect;
and everyone has a heart for
right and wrong. 【孟軻《孟子·告
子章句上》Meng Ke: Chapter 6, Part 1,
Mencius】

膽怯難獲美人心。 A faint heart
never won a fair lady. 【俗語
Common saying】

冬天吃冰棍 —— 心都涼了。 One's
heart sinks. 【歇後語 End-clipper】

豆腐心腸刀子嘴。 One's heart is
as soft as bean curd but one's
mouth is as sharp as a knife. 【俗
語 Common saying】

寡婦的心 —— 三心二意。A widow's heart – of two minds. 【歇後語 End-clipper】

海枯終見底，人死不知心。The bottom of the sea can be seen finally when it dries up, but a person's heart cannot be known even when he dies. 【諺語 Proverb】【杜荀鶴〈感寓〉Du Xunhe:"Inspired Allegories"】

海水可量，人心難測。The sea water is measurable, but a person's heart is unfathomed. 【司馬遷《史記·淮陰侯列傳》Sima Qian:"Biography of the Marquis of Huaiyin", *Records of the Grand Historian*】

好歹人心久後知。Whether a person's heart is good or evil will be revealed in time. 【吳中情奴《相思譜·第二折》Wuzhong Qingnu: Scene 2, "Melody of Mutual Love"】

好心不得好報。A kind heart is often rewarded with evil. 【釋道原《景德傳燈錄·卷十七》Shi Daoyuan: Chapter 17, *Records of the Transmission of the Lamp in the Jingde Period*】

好心當作驢肝肺。Take one's goodwill for ill intent. 【俗語 Common saying】【蘭陵笑笑生《金瓶梅·第二十八回》Lanling Xiaoxiaosheng: Chapter 28, *The Plum in the Golden Vase*】

畫虎畫皮難畫骨，知人知面不知心。In painting a tiger, you can paint its skin but difficult to paint its bones. In knowing a person, you know a person's face but not his heart. 【臧懋循《元曲選·孟漢卿〈魔合羅〉一》Meng Hanxing: Act 1, "Mascot *Moheluo*", Zang Maoxun (ed.) *Anthology of Yuan Plays*】【〈增廣賢文〉Words that Open up One's Mind and Enhance One's Wisdom】

患難之中見人心。Calamity is man's true touchstone. 【俗語 Common saying】

黃河有底，人心沒底。The Yellow River has a bottom, but the human heart doesn't. 【俗語 Common saying】

黃金有價心無價。Gold has a price, but a human heart hasn't. 【俗語 Common saying】

看人看心，聽話聽音。To judge a person, you should know his heart. To understand one's words, you should find the implications. 【諺語 Proverb】

涼了半截兒。One's heart sinks. 【俗語 Common saying】

路遙知馬力，日久見人心。It takes a long journey to test the stamina of a horse and a long time to see the heart of a person. 【陳元靚《事林廣記·警世格言》Chen Yuanliang:"Maxims to Warn the World", *Comprehensive Records of Affairs*】

男子心，海樣深；婦人心，一枚針。A man's heart is as deep as the sea and a woman's heart is as scrupulous as a needle is thin. 【俗語 Common saying】

洛陽親友如相問，一片冰心在玉壺。If relatives at Luoyang ask you about me, just tell them that my heart is still as pure as an ice crystal in a jade vase no matter there are much fame and fortune.【王昌齡〈芙蓉樓送辛漸〉Wang Changling:"Bidding Farewell to Xin Jian at the Lotus Tower"】

懦夫難獲美人心。A faint heart never won a fair lady.【諺語 Proverb】

千金難買 —— 心中願。A thousand taels of gold cannot buy a willing heart.【歇後語 End-clipper】

秋天的雲，少女的心。A young woman's heart is like clouds in autumn.【俗語 Common saying】

人到難處才見心。A person's heart is known when he has difficulties.【俗語 Common saying】

人各有心，心各有見。Each person has his own mind, and every mind has its own opinions.【《增廣賢文》Words that Open up One's Mind and Enhance One's Wisdom】

人居兩地，情發一心。People may be physically separated, but their spirits meet.【曹雪芹《紅樓夢·第二十九回》Cao Xueqin: Chapter 29, A Dream of the Red Chamber】

人靠好心，樹靠好根。A person depends on his kind heart and a tree, on its good roots.【諺語 Proverb】

人心不如其面。The mind of a person is not as easily read as his face.【俗語 Common saying】

人心不同，各如其面。People's hearts differ as their faces do.【左丘明《左傳·襄公三十一年》Zuo Qiuming:"The Thirty-first Year of the Reign of Duke Xiang", Zuo's Commentary on the Spring and Autumn Annals】

人心不似水長流。The heart of a person is unlike the ever-flowing water.【諺語 Proverb】【關漢卿〈竇娥冤〉Quan Hanqing:"The Injustice to Dou E"】

人心參不透。A person's heart cannot be fathomed.【俗語 Common saying】【佚名〈四賢記·第十七齣〉Anonymous: Scene 17, "A Story of Four Sages"】

人心都是肉長的。The heart of a person is flesh.【俗語 Common saying】

人心隔肚皮。The heart of a person is separated by the belly.【錢彩《說岳全傳·第二回》Qian Cai: Chapter 2, A Story of Yue Fei】

人心各異，猶如其面。People's hearts differ as their faces do.【左丘明《左傳·襄公三十一年》Zuo Qiuming:"The Thirty-first Year of the Reign of Duke Xiang", Zuo's Commentary on the Spring and Autumn Annals】

人心換人心。To gain another person's heart, one must give his own.【俗語 Common saying】

人心難測，海水難量。The heart of a person is difficult to fathom as sea water is difficult to measure.【凌濛初《二刻拍案驚奇·

《第二十卷》Ling Mengchu: Chapter 20, *Amazing Tales, Volume Two*】

人心齊，羣山移。 When people are of one heart, they can move the mountains. 【俗語 Common saying】

人心齊，泰山移。 When people are of one heart, they can move Mount Tai. 【俗語 Common saying】

日久見人心。 Time reveals a person's heart. 【陳元靚《事林廣記·警世格言》Chen Yuanliang: "Maxims to Warn the World", *Comprehensive Records of Affairs*】

上下同心者勝。 The side that has superiors and subordinates united in heart will take the victory. 【孫武《孫子兵法·謀攻第三》Sun Wu: Chapter 3, "Attack by Stratagem", *The Art of War by Sunzi*】

上有天，下有地，中間有良心。 Above is heaven, below is earth, and a true heart is in the middle. 【孔厥，袁靜《新兒女英雄傳·第十八回》Kong Jue and Yuan Jing: Chapter 18, *New Biographies of Heroes and Heroines*】

身無綵鳳雙飛翼，心有靈犀一點通。 We do not have the colourful wings of the phoenix to fly side by side, but our hearts, like the magic horns, are linked to each other. 【李商隱〈無題〉Li Shangyin: "Untitled Poem"】

事變知人心。 In an unforeseen event, the true heart of a person is known. 【丁玲《太陽照在桑乾河上·第三十七章》Ding Ling: Chapter 37, *The Sun Shines On the Sanggan River*】

水深易測，人心難量。 The depth of water can be fathomed, but a person's heart cannot. 【諺語 Proverb】

鎖得住人，鎖不住心。 One can physically lock up a person, but one cannot mentally lock up his heart. 【張愛玲《金鎖記》Zhang Ailing: *The Golden Cangue*】

所謂人皆有不忍人之心者：今人乍見孺子將入於井，皆有怵惕惻隱之心。 My reasons for saying that no man is devoid of a heart sensitive to the suffering of others is: suppose a man were, all of a sudden, to see a young child on the verge of falling into a well, he would certainly be moved to compassion. 【孟軻《孟子·公孫丑上》Meng Ke: Chapter 2, Part 1, *Mencius*】

天可度，地可量，惟有人心最難防。 The sky and earth can be measured, but people's hearts cannot. 【白居易〈天可度〉Bai Juyi: *Heaven Can Be Guessed at*】

外貌容易認，內心最難猜。 One's appearance is easy to recognize; one's mind is difficult to fathom. 【諺語 Proverb】

我心如明月，寒潭清皎潔。 My heart is like the bright moon; it is white, pure, and clean. 【寒山〈吾心詩〉Han Shan: "Poem on My Heart"】

無情最是黃金物，變盡天下兒女心。 Gold is the most merciless thing, which changes the hearts of all sons and daughters in the world. 【張恨水《啼笑姻緣‧第一回》Zhang Henshui: Chapter 1, *Cry and Laugh Marriage*】

繫我一生心，負你千行淚。 All my life, my heart is tied to you, yet this is not compensated for the thousand streams of tears you shed. 【柳永〈憶帝京〉Liu Yong:"To the Tune of Recalling the Imperial Capital"】

心安身自安，身安室自寬。 When there is peace of mind, the person is naturally calm, and when the person is calm, the room will be spacious. 【邵雍〈心安吟〉Shao Yong:"Peace of Mind"】

心病還得心藥醫。 The illness of the heart has to be cured by a heart medicine. 【諺語 Proverb】

心裏七上八下。 One feels very perturbed. 【俗語 Common saying】【曹雪芹《紅樓夢‧第二十六回》Cao Xueqin: Chapter 26, *A Dream of the Red Chamber*】

心靜自然涼。 When one's heart is at peace, one naturally feels cool. 【俗語 Common saying】

心去人難留。 When one's heart is gone, it is difficult to keep his body. 【王僧孺〈為姬人自傷〉Wang Zengru:"For a Concubine Hurt by Me"】

心如刀割，淚如雨下。 One's heart is like being cut by a knife and one's tears fall like rain. 【俗語 Common saying】

心如金石堅。 The heart is as constant as metals and stones. 【枚乘〈七發〉Mei Cheng:"Seven Stimuli"】

心如明鏡，物來則照。 The heart is like a shiny mirror, it reflects when things appear. 【王陽明《傳習錄》Wang Yangming: *Records of Teaching and Practicing*】

心正不怕邪。 If the heart is upright, one does not fear any apprehension of depravity. 【俗語 Common saying】

心之所至，百事度外。 When you put your heart into doing something, you will not be concerned with all other things. 【俗語 Common saying】

弦斷可續，心碎難補。 Broken strings can be tied but broken hearts are difficult to be mended. 【俗語 Common saying】

一心不能二用。 No person can do two things at once. 【俗語 Common saying】

易漲易退山溪水，易反易覆小人心。 The water in a mountain stream rises and falls easily, and the mind of a petty person keeps changing. 【《增廣賢文》*Words that Open up One's Mind and Enhance One's Wisdom*】

只願君心似我心，定不負相思意。 I only hope that your heart is like mine, then my love for you will not be in vain. 【李之儀〈卜算子〉Li Zhiyi:"To the Tune of Divination"】

知人知面不知心。One might know the appearance and face of a person, but not his heart. 【《增廣賢文》Words that Open up One's Mind and Enhance One's Wisdom】

最毒婦人心。Nothing is more venomous than a woman's heart. 【許仲琳《封神演義·第十八回》Xu Zhonglin: Chapter 18, *Romance of the Investiture of the Deities*】

Heaven and earth

夫天地者，萬物之逆旅。Heaven and earth is an inn for myriad things. 【李白〈春夜宴桃李園序〉Li Bai: "Preface to a Banquet on a Night in Spring in the Peach and Plum Garden"】

老天爺有眼。Heaven is not blind. 【俗語 Common saying】

上天有好生之德。Heaven has the virtue of making life happy for people. 【《尚書·大禹謨》"Counsels of Yu the Great", *The Book of History*】

上有天，下有地。There is the heaven above and the earth beneath. 【俗語 Common saying】

順天者存，逆天者亡。Those who obey the mandate of heaven will survive, while those who defy it will perish. 【孟軻《孟子·離婁上》Meng Ke: Chapter 4, Part 1, *Mencius*】

天不變，道亦不變。Heaven does not change, so does the Way. 【董仲舒〈舉賢良對策·三〉Dong Zhongshu:, "Recommending the Virtue and Talented Strategy, No.3"】

天不怕，地不怕。Fear neither heaven or earth. 【曹雪芹《紅樓夢·第四十五回》Cao Xueqin: Chapter 45, *A Dream of the Red Chamber*】

天聰明，自我民聰明。Heaven hears and sees, which comes from what the people hear and see. 【《尚書·皋陶謨》"Counsels of Gao Yao", *The Book of History*】

天道無親，常與善人。The Way of heaven does not favour relatives but always helps those who are good. 【老子《道德經·第七十九章》Laozi: Chapter 79, *Daodejing*】

天地不仁，以萬物為芻狗。Heaven and earth are unbenevolent, for they regard myriad things as straw dogs. 【老子《道德經·第五章》Laozi: Chapter 5, *Daodejing*】

天地革而四時成。Heaven and earth undergo changes and the four seasons are formed. 【《易經·革·象》"Image", "Hexagram *Ge*", *The Book of Changes*】

天地尚不能久，而況於人乎。When even heaven and earth cannot be so ruthless and cruel for a long time, how much more so is the case with human beings. 【老子《道德經·第二十三章》Laozi: Chapter 23, *Daodejing*】

天地與我並生，萬物與我為一。 Heaven, earth, and I are born at the same time and the myriad things and I are one. 【莊周《莊子・內篇・齊物論第二》Zhuang Zhou: Chapter 2, "On the Equality of Things", "Inner Chapters", *Zhuangzi*】

天將與之，必先苦之；天將毀之，必先累之。 When heaven wants to give him something, it will make him suffer first; when heaven wants to destroy one, it will exhaust him first. 【劉向《說苑・卷十六談叢》Liu Xiang: Chapter 16, "The Thicket of Discussion", *Garden of Persuasions*】

天上少有，地下全無。 Be seldom seen in heaven and never seen on earth. 【李綠園《歧路燈・第八回》Li Yuyuan: Chapter 8, *Lamp on a Forked Road*】

天上有，地下無。 Exist only in Heaven but not on earth. 【俗語 Common saying】【羅懋登《三寶太監西洋記・第二回》Luo Maodeng: Chapter 2, *The Western Voyage of the Eunuch of Three Treasures*】

天生時而地生財。 Heaven produces the seasons and earth produces wealth. 【《禮記・禮運第九》Chapter 9, "Conveyance of Rites", *The Book of Rites*】

天視自我民視，天聽自我民聽。 What heaven sees comes from what our people see and what heaven hears comes from what our people hear. 【《尚書・泰誓中》"The Great Speech", Part 2, *The Book of History*】

天無絕人之路。 Heaven does not close all doors. 【佚名〈貨郎擔・第四折〉Anonymous: Scene 4, "Travelling Salesman"】

天行有常，不為堯存，不為桀亡。 Heaven has its regular way of running. It neither exists for the sake of the good ruler Yao nor perishes because of the bad ruler Jie. 【荀況《荀子・天論第十七》Xun Kuang: Chapter 17, "Discourse on Heaven", *Xunzi*】

天之道，利而不害。 The way of heaven is to benefit, not to harm. 【老子《道德經・第八十一章》Laozi: Chapter 81, *Daodejing*】

天之所助者，順也；人之所助者，信也。 Heaven helps those who follow the course of nature; people help those who are trustworthy. 【《易經・繫辭上》"Appended Remarks", Part 1, *The Book of Changes*】

天作孽，猶可違；自作孽，不可逭。 When heaven creates disasters, people can still escape from them. But when people create disasters by themselves, they cannot ward them off. 【《尚書・太甲中》"The Great Oath", Part 2, *The Book of History*】

一在天上，一在地下。 One is up in the heaven, the other, on the ground. 【俗語 Common saying】

一在天之涯，一在地之角。 One is at the end of heaven, the other, at a corner of the earth. 【韓愈〈祭

十二郎文〉Han Yu:"Elegy to My Twelfth Nephew"】

有物混成，先天地生。 There is something formed in chaos existing before the birth of heaven and earth. 【老子《道德經·第二十五章》Laozi: Chapter 25, *Daodejing*】

與天地兮同壽，與日月兮同光。 Live as long as heaven and earth and shed light like the sun and moon. 【屈原《離騷·九歌·涉江》Qu Yuan:"Crossing the River", "The Nine Songs", *The Sorrows at Parting*】

Help

幫人幫到底。 When one helps others, help them to the end. 【諺語 Proverb】

呆子幫忙 —— 越幫越忙。 A fool helping out someone – the more he helps, the busier one becomes. 【歇後語 End-clipper】

當其同舟而濟，遇風，其救也如左右手。 Crossing the river in the same boat in the gale, one would go to each other's aid like the right hand helping the left. 【孫武《孫子兵法·九地第十一》Sun Wu: Chapter 11, "The Nine Situations", *The Art of War by Sunzi*】

得道者多助，失道者寡助。 Those who have the Way have many people to help them; those who do not have few people to help. 【孟軻《孟子·公孫丑下》Meng Ke: Chapter 2, Part 2, *Mencius*】

好花也得綠葉扶。 Even good flowers need green leaves to bring out their beauty. 【俗語 Common saying】

皇天不負苦心人。 Heaven helps those who help themselves. 【諺語 Proverb】

己先則援之，彼先則推之。 When you are ahead of others, help them; when others are ahead of you, give them a push. 【戴德《大戴禮記·曾子制言上》Dai De:"Zengzi about Behaviour", Part 1, *Records of rites by Dai the Elder*】

己欲立而立人。 Being able to establish oneself, one should help others to do so. 【孔子《論語·雍也篇第六》Confucius: Chapter 6, *The Analects of Confucius*】

吉兇相救，患難相扶。 The victims of misfortune help each other and those in trouble support each other. 【俗語 Common saying】

濟人須濟急時無。 When you help a person, help him when he is in need. 【諺語 Proverb】【《增廣賢文》Words that Open up One's Mind and Enhance One's Wisdom】

叫天天不應，叫地地不靈。 Cry to the Heaven, it does not reply; cry to the Earth, it does not respond. 【諺語 Proverb】

君子救急不濟富。 A gentleman helps those in need but not the rich. 【孔子《論語‧雍也篇第六》 Confucius: Chapter 6, *The Analects of Confucius*】

爛泥扶不上牆。 A good-for-nothing cannot be made useful by any help. 【俗語 Common saying】

臨危望救，遇難思親。 In danger, one hopes to be saved; in distress, one thinks of one's dear ones. 【諺語 Proverb】【劉流《烈火金鋼‧第六回》Liu Liu: Chapter 6, *Steel Meets Fire*】

路見不平，拔刀相助。 When on one's way one sees anything unfair, one draws one's sword to help the victim. 【釋道原《景德傳燈錄‧卷二十二》Shi Daoyuan: Chapter 22, *Records of the Transmission of the Lamp in the Jingde Period*】

寧給饑人一口，不送富人一斗。 Rather give a mouthful of rice to a hungry person than a bushel of rice to a rich person. 【諺語 Proverb】【石玉昆《三俠五義‧第一百回》Shi Yukun: Chapter 100, *The Three Heroes and Five Gallants*】

窮幫窮，富幫富。 The poor help the poor and the rich, the rich. 【諺語 Proverb】

求爹爹，拜奶奶。 Plead high and low. 【諺語 Proverb】【蘭陵笑笑生《金瓶梅‧第十四回》Lanling Xiaoxiaosheng: Chapter 14, *The Plum in the Golden Vase*】

求人不如求己。 Seeking for help from oneself is better than seeking help from others. 【孔子《論語‧衛靈公篇第十五》Confucius: Chapter 15, *The Analects of Confucius*】

求人須求大丈夫，濟人須濟急時無。 When one seeks for help, seek for help from a true man; if one wants to help a person, you must help him when he urgently needs help. 【《增廣賢文》*Words that Open up One's Mind and Enhance One's Wisdom*】

人到難處才求人。 People ask for help only when they are in difficulties. 【俗語 Common saying】

人靠人幫，花靠葉護。 A person needs the help of others as a flower needs the protection of leaves. 【俗語 Common saying】

人情人情，在人情願。 When it comes to help, it hinges on the willingness of the helper. 【施耐庵《水滸傳‧第三十八回》Shi Nai'an: Chapter 38, *Outlaws of the Marshes*】

同病相憐，同憂相救。 Those who have the same illness sympathize with each other and those who have the same misfortune help each other. 【趙曄《吳越春秋‧闔閭內傳》Zhao Ye: "The Inner Biography of King Helü", *A History of the States of Wu and Yue*】

一方有難，八方支援。 When trouble occurs at one spot, help

comes from all quarters. 【俗語 Common saying】

一人倒，眾人扶。 When a person falls, all lend their support. 【俗語 Common saying】

一人困難，人人相助。 If someone gets into difficulty, everybody is ready to help. 【俗語 Common saying】

一人有難大家幫，一家有事百家幫。 When a person gets into difficulty, everyone comes to help him; when something happens to a family, a hundred families offer them help. 【諺語 Proverb】

魚幫水，水幫魚。 Help one another. 【俗語 Common saying】

與人方便，自己方便。 To help others is to help yourself. 【俗語 Common saying】

遠水不解近渴。 Distant water cannot quench present thirst. 【韓非《韓非子・説林上第二十二》Han Fei: Chapter 22, "On Forests", Part 1, *Hanfeizi*】

遠水不救近火。 Distant water won't put out a fire close at hand. 【韓非《韓非子・説林上第二十二》Han Fei: Chapter 22, "On Forests", Part 1, *Hanfeizi*】

助人為快樂之本。 Helping others is a source of happiness. 【俗語 Common saying】

Hero

不到長城非好漢。 A man who fails to get to the Great Wall is not a hero. 【毛澤東〈清平樂・六盤山〉Mao Zedong: "Mount Liupan: To the Tune of Serene Music"】

不以成敗論英雄。 One does not judge a hero by his success or failure. 【俗語 Common saying】

出師未捷身先死，長使英雄淚滿襟。 Zhuge Liang died before he succeeded, and this made heroes after him shed tears that wetted their sleeves. 【杜甫〈蜀相〉Du Fu: "The Premier of Shu"】

從古英雄成大器，須知半向苦中來。 It must be known that from of old, heroes have all been tempered in hardship. 【俗語 Common saying】

大江東去，浪淘盡，千古風流人物。 The great river flows east, and its waves wash away heroes of a thousand ages. 【蘇軾〈念奴嬌・赤壁懷古〉Su Shi: "Recalling the Past at the Red Cliff: To the Tune of Missing the Charm of a Young Maid"】

風浪裏試舵手，困難中識英雄。 A helmsman is tested in a storm and a hero is recognized in a predicament. 【諺語 Proverb】

風蕭蕭兮易水寒，壯士一去兮不復還。 The wind blew strongly and the waters in Yi River was cold. The hero went out and never returned. 【劉向《戰國策‧荊軻刺秦王‧易水歌》Liu Xiang: "Song of Yi River", "Jing Ke Assassinated Emperor Qin", *Strategies of the Warring States*】

好漢惜好漢。 Heroes are attracted by heroes. 【余邵魚《東周列國志‧第六十二回》Yu Shaoyu: Chapter 62, *Chronicles of the Eastern Zhou Kingdoms*】

慧眼識英雄。 Discerning eyes can tell who the hero is. 【俗語 Common saying】

滾滾長江東逝水，浪花淘盡英雄。 On and on the roaring waters in the Changjiang River flow to the east, its waves scoured like all heroes faded. 【楊慎〈臨江仙‧說秦漢〉Yang Shen: "Chatting about Qin and Han Dynasties: To the Tune of an Immortal by the River"】

江山如此多嬌，引無數英雄競折腰。 China is such a beautiful country, leading countless heroes to concede their homages. 【毛澤東〈沁園春‧雪〉Mao Zedong: "Snow: To the Tune of Spring in the Garden of Qin"】

江山如畫，一時多少豪傑。 The majestic country is like a painting, how many heroes have once gathe Red here. 【蘇軾〈念奴嬌‧赤壁懷古〉Su Shi: "Recalling the Past at the Red Cliff: To the Tune of Missing the Charm of a Young Maid"】

兩雄不并立。 Two heroes cannot stay together in peace. 【羅貫中《三國演義‧第十三回》Luo Guanzhong: Chapter 13, *Romance of the Three Kingdoms*】

兩雄相遇，其鬥必烈。 When Greek meets Greek, then comes the tug of war. 【俗語 Common saying】

亂世出英雄。 Turbulent days bring forth heroes. 【諺語 Proverb】

山僧不識英雄主，何必哓哓問姓名？ The monk in the mountain did not know I'm a hero and an emperor, what is the point of ceaselessly asking my name? 【朱元璋〈題寺壁詩〉Zhu Yuanzhang: "Writing a Poem on a Temple Wall"】

設想英雄垂暮日，溫柔不住住何鄉。 Imagine a hero in his declining years: where can he stay but in the land of addiction of lust. 【龔自珍〈己亥雜詩〉Gong Zizhen: "Poems Written in the Year of Jihai"】

生當作人傑，死亦為鬼雄。 One is an outstanding person when alive and remains a hero when becoming a ghost after death. 【李清照〈夏日絕句〉Li Qingzhao: "A Quatrain on a Summer Day"】

生而為英，死而為靈。 A hero in life will become a god after death. 【歐陽修〈祭石曼卿文〉Ouyang Xiu: "Funeral Oration for Shi Manqing"】

生是英雄，死是英雄。 One is a hero when he is alive and remains to be a hero when he is dead. 【俗語 Common saying】

生為英雄，死作鬼雄。 One is a hero when alive and remains a hero when becoming a ghost after death. 【李清照〈夏日絕句〉Li Qingzhao: "A Quatrain on a Summer Day"】

時勢造英雄。 A hero is nothing but a product of his time. 【俗語 Common saying】

數風流人物，還看今朝。 The real heroes are the past form, you should look foward to the present. 【毛澤東〈沁園春‧雪〉Mao Zedong: "Snow: To the Tune of Spring in the Garden of Qin"】

天下英雄，使君與操，餘子誰堪共酒杯。 You and me are heroes in this world and others are not good enough to drink wine with us. 【劉克莊〈沁園春‧夢方孚若〉Liu Kezhuang: "Dreamt Fang Furuo: To the Tune of the Spring in the Garden"】

天下英雄誰敵手？曹劉。生子當如孫仲謀。 Among the equals in this world, who were the true heroes? Cao Cao and Liu Bei. And even Cao Cao would like to have a son like Sun Zhongmou. 【辛棄疾〈南鄉子〉Xin Qiji: "To the Tune of a Southern Village"】

英雄保明主，俊鳥登高枝。 A hero serves the wise king as a beautiful bird perches on a high branch. 【諺語 Proverb】【石印紅，

章程《護國皇娘傳‧第四十一回》Shi Yinghong and Zhang Cheng: Chapter 41, *A Biography of the Protect-the-country Imperial Concubine*】

英雄不論出身低。 It does not matter that a hero is from a humble family. 【俗語 Common saying】

英雄不失路，何以成功名。 If a hero has not suffered frustrations, how can he achieve success and fame? 【屈大鈞〈贈朱士稚〉Qu Dajun: "Presented to Zhu Shizhi"】

英雄出少年。 Heroes grow out of the young and able. 【俗語 Common saying】

英雄多困於酒色。 Heroes are usually entangled in wine and women. 【俗語 Common saying】

英雄流血不流淚。 Heroes would rather shed blood than tears. 【諺語 Proverb】

英雄莫問出處。 Not every great person was born with a silver spoon in his mouth. 【諺語 Proverb】

英雄難過美人關。 Heroes find it hard to overcome the attraction of beautiful women. 【高陽《胡雪巖全傳‧平步青雲》Gao Yang: "A Meteoric Rise", *A Biography of Hu Xueyan*】

英雄氣短，兒女情長。 The ambition of a hero may be of a short duration, the affection of lovers, however, last long. 【許自

昌〈水滸記・第十八齣〉Xu Zichang: Scene 18, "A Record of the Outlaws of the Marshes"】

英雄識英雄。 Like knows like. 【俗語 Common saying】

英雄所見略同。 Great minds think alike. 【俗語 Common saying】

英雄無用武之地。 A hero without the opportunity to display his abilities. 【陳壽《三國志・蜀書・諸葛亮傳》Chen Shou: "Biography of Zhuge Liang, History of the State of Shu", *Records of the Three Kingdoms*】

英雄行險道，富貴似花枝。 A hero is walking on dangerous roads and wealth and nobility are like flowers on twigs. 【《增廣賢文》*Words that Open up One's Mind and Enhance One's Wisdom*】

英雄造時勢，時勢造英雄。 Heroes create time and circumstances and time and circumstances create heroes. 【俗語 Common saying】【梁啟超〈李鴻章傳〉Liang Qichao: "Biography of Li Hongzhang"】

英雄祇怕病來磨。 A hero is afraid of nothing but a lasting disease. 【俗語 Common saying】

戰爭出英雄。 Heroes emerge from wars. 【俗語 Common saying】

自古英雄出少年。 From of old, heros stood out in their boyhood. 【吳敬梓《儒林外史・第七回》Wu Jingzi: Chapter 7, *An Unofficial History of the Scholars*】

自古英雄都是夢。 From of old, heroes are but a dream. 【韓世忠〈南鄉子〉Han Shizhong: "To the Tune of a Southern Village"】

自古英雄多磨難。 From of old, heroes have experienced more suffering than others. 【孟軻《孟子・告子章句下》Meng Ke: Chapter 6, Part 2, *Mencius*】

History

褒貶無一詞，豈得為良史？ If you do not make any derogatory or appreciative comments, how can you be a good historian? 【王禹偁〈對雪〉Wang Yucheng: "Ode to the Snow"】

行事見於當時，是非公於後世。 What one did at the time will be judged by history. History is created and written by the people. 【朱元璋〈明太祖寶訓〉Zhu Yuanzhang: *Valuable Instructions from the First Emperor of Ming*】

知我罪我，其惟春秋。 People may understand me or criticize me, I will keep doing it and leave it to history for judgment. 【孟軻《孟子・滕文公下》Meng Ke: Chapter 5, Part 2, *Mencius*】

Home

白日放歌須縱酒，青春作伴好還鄉。On this bright day, we sang and drank to our heart's content, and the green spring kept us company on our way home.【杜甫〈聞官軍收河南河北〉Du Fu:"On Hearing the Recapture of the Regions north and South of the Yellow River"】

出外一里，不如屋裏。Going out to travel a mile is not as good as staying at home.【施耐庵《水滸傳·第六十一回》Shi Nai'an: Chapter 61, Outlaws of the Marshes】

大門不出，二門不邁。Stays indoors all the time.【俗語 Common saying】

東搬西搬，虧了一半。A rolling stone gathers no moss.【俗語 Common saying】

金窩銀窩不如自家草窩。Home is home, however humble it may be.【諺語 Proverb】

滿天打油飛。Fly all over the place as one is homeless.【老舍《駱駝祥子·第七章》Lao She: Chapter 7, Rickshaw Boy】

年年躍馬長安市，客舍似家家似寄。You gallop in the capital city of Chang'an year after year. You appear to be in guesthouse more than at home.【劉克莊〈玉樓春〉Liu Kezhuang:"To the Tune of Spring in the Jade Tower"】

娘家住不老。A girl cannot live at her mother's home all her life.

【劉江《太行風雲·第十六回》Liu Jiang: Chapter 16, Changes in Taixing】

鳥愛自己巢，人愛自己家。Birds love their own nests and people love their own home.【俗語 Common saying】

破家值萬貫。Even a tumbledown home is worth a fortune.【諺語 Proverb】

人言落日是天涯，望極天涯不見家。People say that the place where the sun sets is the edge of the earth, yet when I look to the end of the earth, my home cannot be seen.【李覯〈鄉思〉Li Gou:"Thinking of Home"】

樹高千丈，落葉歸根。No matter whether it is east or west, home is the best.【諺語 Proverb】【李寶嘉《官場現形記·第二十二回》Li Baojia: Chapter 22, Officialdom Unmasked】

天下處處不如家。Nowhere in the world is better than home.【諺語 Proverb】

一為遷客去長沙，西望長安不見家。When Jia Yi was banished to Changsha, he looked westward to Chang'an and could not see home.【李白〈與史郎中欽聽黃鶴樓上吹笛〉Li Bai:"Hearing Flute with Scholar Shi on the Yellow Crane Tower"】

在家貧亦好。Home is the best place even if it is poor.【戎昱〈長

安秋夕〉Rong Yu:"Autumn Evening at Chang'an"】

在家千般好，出門事事難。 At home, everything is good; outside, everything is difficult. 【俗語 Common saying】

在家千日好，出門一時難。 It is good to stay at home for a thousand days and it is hard to go out for an hour. 【諺語 Proverb】【褚人獲《隋唐演義‧第十回》Zhu Renhuo: Chapter 10, *Heroes in Sui and Tang Dynasties*】

在家人貴，出家人賤。 At home, one is valued; outside, one is looked down on. 【俗語 Common saying】

眾鳥欣有託，吾亦愛吾廬。 Birds, safe from danger, enjoy their refuge. I love the home I have settled in as well. 【陶淵明〈讀山海經〉Tao Yuanming:"*Reading the Classics of Mountains and Seas*"】

走遍天下，不如家下。 After travelling all over the world, one finds that there is no place like home. 【俗語 Common saying】

Homecoming

大兮起風雲飛揚，威加海內歸故鄉。 A strong wind rises, the clouds fly, and I return to my homeland with the world under my sway. 【劉邦〈大風歌〉Liu Bang:"Strong Wind"】

兒童相見不相識，笑問客從何處來？ The children saw me but did not recognize me and they asked me with a smile, "Stranger, where are you from?" 【賀知章〈回鄉偶書〉He Zhizhang:"Returning to My Hometown"】

何處是歸程，長亭又短亭。 Where is my homeward journey? I can only see the large pavilions after small pavilions. 【李白〈菩薩蠻〉Li Bai:"To the tune of Buddhist Dancers"】

少貪夢裏還家樂，早起前山路正長。 I dream of the pleasure of returning home, but when I wake up in the morning, the road ahead of the mountain is still long. 【歐陽修〈奉使道中作〉Ouyang Xiu:"Written When I Was on My Way to Serve as an Envoy"】

少小離家老大回，鄉音無改鬢毛衰。 I was young when I left home, and was old when I returned. My local accent remained the same, but the hair on my temples was thinner. 【賀知章〈回鄉偶書〉He Zhizhang:"On Homecoming"】

Homesickness

半世無歸似轉蓬，今年作夢到巴東。 Half a lifetime I have not returned home, like a tumbleweed, and this year, in my dream, I get to my hometown Badong. 【陸游〈晚泊〉Lu You: "Mooring a Boat at Night"】

不知何處吹蘆管，一夜征人盡望鄉。 From somewhere blows a tune of reed, evoking homesickness in soldiers all night long. 【李益〈夜上受降城聞笛〉Li Yi: "Listening to a Flute at Night on the Watch Tower of Shouxiang"】

大江流日夜，客心悲未央。 Day and night, the Yangzi River flows on and on, yet the sadness of a wanderer never ends. 【謝朓〈暫使下都夜發新林至京邑贈西府同僚〉Xie Tiao: "To My Colleagues at Xi Fu"】

忽聞歌古調，歸思欲霑巾。 Suddenly I heard you sang the song in the old style, tears of homesickness drenched my handkerchief. 【杜審言〈和晉陵陸丞早春遊望〉Du Shenyan: "Thought in Spring Out"】

今夕為何夕，他鄉說故鄉。 What year is this year? I always talk about hometown in another town. 【袁凱〈客中除夕〉Yuan Kai: "Staying in a Strange Land on New Year's Eve"】

舉頭望明月，低頭思故鄉。 I raised my head to gaze at the bright moon. Lowering my head, I thought of my hometown. 【李白〈靜夜思〉Li Bai: "Thoughts on a Silent Night"】

十年踪跡渾無定，莫更逢人問故鄉。 I have been wandering without a fixed abode for the last ten years, I would not ask about my hometown whenever I run into a person. 【金誠〈江行〉Jin Cheng: "Sailing on a River"】

鄉淚客中盡，孤帆天際看。 I have exhausted my homesick tears in my eyes, and watched a lone sail fading to the skies. 【孟浩然〈早寒有懷〉Meng Haoran: "Thoughts on a Day When Cold Winds Come Early"】

鄉心新歲切，天畔獨潸然。 My homesickness is strong with the approach of the New Year. Before the horizon, I weep alone. 【劉長卿〈新年作〉Liu Changqing: "Written at the Beginning of the New Year"】

一驛復一驛，思親頭易白。 One stage after another, thinking of the dear ones turns my hair grey easily. 【彭汝礪〈武岡路中〉Peng Ruli: "Wugang Road"】

一叫一回腸一斷，三春三月憶三巴。 A chirp of the cuckoo is a break of the heart; I recall Sichuan in the third month of spring. 【李白〈宣城見杜鵑花〉Li Bai: "Seeing Azalea at Xuan City"】

一年將盡夜，萬里未歸人。 The year is about to end tonight, but I'm still ten thousand miles

away without returning home.
【戴叔倫〈除夕夜宿石頭驛〉Dai Shulun:"Lodging at the Stone Inn on New Year's Eve"】

悠悠天宇曠，切切故鄉情。
Longlasting is the spacious heaven, deep are my home feelings.【張九齡〈西江夜行〉Zhang Jiuling:"Night Walk In Xijiang"】

月色不可掃，客愁不可道。The moonbeams cannot be swept away, and the sadness of a wanderer cannot be told.【李白〈擬古·其八〉Li Bai "Poems Imitating the Ancients, No. 8"】

Hometown

君自故鄉來，應知故鄉事。You come from my native village, you should know the village affairs.【王維〈雜詩三首·其二〉Wang Wei: "Three Poems, No.2"】

離鄉背井，流離失所。Leave one's hometown and wander about.【俗語 Common saying】【王實甫《西廂記·二本第四折》Wang Shifu: Act 4, Scene 2, "Romance of the Western Bower"】

美不美，鄉中水，親不親，故鄉人。Sweet or not, it is water from hometown; close or not, they are people from the same hometown.【《增廣賢文》*Words that Open up One's Mind and Enhance One's Wisdom*】

犬臥花陰雞唱午，依稀風景是吾鄉。The dogs are lying under the shade of the flowers and the cocks are crowing at noon; such a scenery is somewhat like what my native home is like.【李翔〈東阿即事〉Li Xiang:"Dong'e, a Poem Written out of Inspiration"】

日暮鄉關何處是，煙波江上使人愁。The sun sets, and where is my hometown? The mist and ripples on the river make me sad.【崔顥〈登黃鶴樓〉Cui Hao:"Climbing up the Yellow Crane Tower"】

人不離鄉，鳥不離枝。People are unwilling to leave their hometown as birds, their woodlands.【諺語 Proverb】【李英儒〈戰鬥在滹沱河上〉Li Yingru:"*Fight by River Hutuo*"】

樹高千丈，落葉歸根。A tree may grow to a height of one thousand feet, yet its leaves fall down to the roots.【諺語 Proverb】【李寶嘉《官場現形記·第二十二回》Li Baojia: Chapter 22, *Officialdom Unmasked*】

兔子沿山跑，還來歸舊窩。A rabbit runs about in the mountains, but it returns to its old burrow.【俗語 Common saying】【蘭陵笑笑生《金瓶梅·第八十七回》Lanling Xiaoxiaosheng: Chapter 87, *The Plum in the Golden Vase*】

未老莫還鄉，還鄉須斷腸。 When you are not yet old, don't return to your hometown. Once you return, it would break your heart. 【韋莊〈菩薩蠻〉Wei Zhuang: "To the Tune of Buddhist Dancers"】

Honesty

誠實是上策。 Honesty is the best policy. 【諺語 Proverb】

誠實重於珠寶。 Honesty is more valuable than jewels and treasures. 【諺語 Proverb】

當着真人，不說假話。 In front of an honest person, don't say things which are not true. 【諺語 Proverb】【吳敬梓《儒林外史·五十回》Wu Jingzi: Chapter 50, *An Unofficial History of the Scholars*】

道不拾遺，夜不閉戶。 People do not take any articles left by the roadside and doors need not be bolted at night. 【韓非《韓非子·外儲說左上第三十二》Han Fei: Chapter 32, "Outer Congeries of Sayings", Part 1, *Hanfeizi*】

凡事從實，積福自厚。 When one practices honesty in doing everything, one's happiness is sure to build up enormously. 【佚名《名賢集》Anonymous: *Collected Sayings of Famous Sages*】

反身而誠，樂莫大焉。 Nothing is more pleasant than you find yourself an honest person on reflection. 【孟軻《孟子·盡心章句上》Meng Ke: Chapter 7, Part 1, *Mencius*】

鑑明，則塵垢不止。 When a mirror is clean, there will be no dust or dirt on it. 【莊周《莊子·內篇·德充符第五》Zhuang Zhou: Chapter 5, "Symbols of Virtue Fulfilled", "Inner Chapters", *Zhuangzi*】

老老實實，勤勤懇懇。 Be honest and hardworking. 【俗語 Common saying】

老實常在，說空常敗。 An honest person is always safe and a prattler is always a loser. 【佚名《名賢集》Anonymous: *Collected Sayings of Famous Sages*】

明人不做暗事。 An honest person does not deal underhand. 【諺語 Proverb】【吳昌齡〈張天師〉Wu Changling: "Master Zhang"】

莫信直中直，須防仁不仁。 Do not believe all are honest who appear honest, but beware lest the semblance of goodness turn out to be the reverse. 【《增廣賢文》*Words that Open up One's Mind and Enhance One's Wisdom*】

養正邪自退。 If one is honest, evil influence will leave him by itself. 【俗語 Common saying】【李綠園《歧路燈·第三十六回》Li Yuyuan: Chapter 36, *Lamp on a Forked Road*】

夜不閉戶，道不拾遺。 People do not bolt their doors at night nor take anything left by the roadside. 【韓非《韓非子‧外儲說左上第三十二》Han Fei: Chapter 32, "Outer Congeries of Sayings", Part 1, *Hanfeizi*】

忠厚人常在。 An honest and tolerant person extends his good fortune to his off-springs. 【諺語 Proverb】

做老實人，說老實話，辦老實事。 Be an honest person, honest in word and honest in deed. 【俗語 Common saying 】

Honour

一榮俱榮，一損俱損。 We are bound together for good or ill. 【曹雪芹《紅樓夢‧第四回》Cao Xueqin: Chapter 4, *A Dream of the Red Chamber*】

Hope

抱一線希望。 Hope against hope. 【俗語 Common saying】

老太太哭大妞兒 —— 沒盼兒。 The grandma weeping for her dead daughter – it's hopeless. 【歇後語 End-clipper】

留得五湖明月在，不愁無處下金鈎。 As long as the five lakes and the bright moon are there, you don't have to worry about having no place to cast down the golden hook. 【《增廣賢文》*Words that Open up One's Mind and Enhance One's Wisdom*】

山重水複疑無路，柳暗花明又一村。 It seems that there is no road beyond the layered ridges and winding rivers, yet amidst the shady willows and bright flowers is another village. 【陸游〈遊山西村〉Lu You: "Touring Shanxi Village"】

上天無路，入地無門。 All hopes and dreams were dashed. 【釋悟明《聯燈會要‧卷二十八》Shi Wuming: Chapter 28, *Essential Materials from the Chan School's Successive Lamp Records*】

Horse

車如流水馬如龍。 Carriages flew like water and horses, a dragon. 【李煜〈望江南〉Li Yu: "To the Tune of Watching the South"】

道遠知驥，世偽知賢。 We know a horse by the long distance it runs; and we distinguish a virtuous person from other hypocritical people. 【曹植〈矯志〉 Cao Zhi:"Where There is a Will"】

得十良馬，不若得一伯樂。 Having ten good horses is not as good as having a horse expert Bo Le. 【呂不韋《呂氏春秋・贊能》Lu Buwei:"Praising the Capable", *Master Lu's Spring and Autumn Annals*】

公眾馬，公眾騎。 Public horses are for the public to ride. 【俗語 Common saying】

好馬不吃回頭草。 A good horse will not turn back to graze in the same place. 【李漁《憐香伴・議遷》 Li Yu:"Discussion on Transfer", *Female Relationships*】

馬不吃夜草不肥。 Without eating hay during the night, a horse will not grow fat. 【俗語 Common saying】【增廣賢文》*Words that Open up One's Mind and Enhance One's Wisdom*】

世有伯樂，然後有千里馬。千里馬常有，而伯樂不常有。 Only when there is a horse connoisseur Bo Le can there be a horse that can run a thousand miles. Horses that can run a thousand miles are commonplace, but horse connoisseurs like Bo Le are rare. 【韓愈《雜說四・馬說》Han Yu: No.4, "On Horses", *Random Remarks*】

一馬不配兩鞍。 One cannot put two saddles on one horse. 【俗語 Common saying】

Human being

人是肉長的。 All people are born sympathetic. 【俗語 Common saying】

人是鐵，飯是鋼。 A human being is iron but food is steel – only when you are full, you get energy. 【俗語 Common saying】

人是無價寶。 A human being is a priceless treasure. 【俗語 Common saying】

人為萬物之靈。 Of all the beings, man is most intelligent. 【《尚書・泰誓上》"The Great Speech", Part 1, *The Book of History*】

人之所以異於禽獸者幾希。 What differs a human being from an animal is virtues. 【孟軻《孟子・離婁下》Meng Ke: Chapter 4, Part 2, *Mencius*】

萬物人為貴。 Of all things in this world, human beings are the most valuable. 【劉向《說苑・卷十七雜言》Liu Xiang: Chapter 17, "Miscellaneous Words", *Garden of Persuasions*】

仙人亦是凡人做。 Immortals were originally human beings. 【俗語 Common saying】

Humiliation

長子住在矮檐下。 Like a tall man living under low eaves. 【俗語 Common saying】【施耐庵《水滸傳 · 第二十八回》Shi Nai'an: Chapter 28, *Outlaws of the Marshes*】

人必自侮，然後人侮之。 A person must insult himself before he is insulted by others. 【孟軻《孟子 · 離婁上》Meng Ke: Chapter 4, Part 1, *Mencius*】

忍辱至三公。 If you endure humiliation, you will get a high position as prime minister. 【諺語 Proverb】

士可殺，不可辱。 A scholar can be killed, but not humiliated. 【《禮記 · 儒行第四十一》Chapter 41, "The Conduct of a Confucian scholar", *The Book of Rites*】

侮人還自侮，說人還自說。 Humiliating others is equal to humiliating oneself and speaking ill of others is equal to speaking ill of oneself. 【馮夢龍《警世通言 · 第九卷》Feng Menglong: Chapter 9, *Stories to Caution the World*】

知止常止，終身不恥。 If a person knows the limits and always knows when to stop doing something, he will not be humiliated in his whole life. 【《增廣賢文》*Words that Open up One's Mind and Enhance One's Wisdom*】

Hunger

飽漢不知餓漢饑。 A well-fed person does not know what hunger is like to the starving. 【李寶嘉《官場現形記 · 第四十五回》Li Baojia: Chapter 45, *Officialdom Unmasked*】

飽人不知餓人饑，富人不知窮人苦。 The well-fed do not know the hunger of the ill-fed and the rich do not know the suffering of the poor. 【俗語 Common saying】

吃了上頓沒有下頓。 Be half starved. 【俗語 Common saying】

廚中有剩飯，路上有饑人。 There is left-over rice in the kitchen, but there are starving travellers on the way. 【佚名《名賢集》Anonymous: *Collected Sayings of Famous Sages*】

肚皮貼在脊梁上 —— 餓得要命。 With one's belly sticking to the back of one's body – one is starving to death. 【歇後語 End-clipper】

餓得死懶漢，餓不死窮漢。 A lazy man can starve to death, a poor man won't. 【俗語 Common saying】【草明《今日》Cao Ming: *Today*】

餓漢肚飽思美食。 A hungry person, after satisfying his

hunger, will look for good food. 【俗語 Common saying】

餓雞不怕打，餓人不顧臉。 A hungry chicken is not afraid of beating and a hungry person is thick-skinned. 【諺語 Proverb】

餓了甜如蜜，飽了蜜不甜。 Hunger is the best sauce. 【諺語 Proverb】

餓殺不如為盜。 One would rather be a robber than die in hunger. 【俗語 Common saying】【孫犁《風云初記·第二十一回》Sun Li: Chapter 21, *The First Story*】

餓眼見瓜皮。 Hungry eyes see and are appealed to the skin of a water melon. 【俗語 Common saying】【蘭陵笑笑生《金瓶梅·第五十五回》Lanling Xiaoxiaosheng: Chapter 55, *The Plum in the Golden Vase*】

湖廣熟，天下足。 When Hunan and Hubei have a bumper harvest, the whole country will be free from hunger. 【諺語 Proverb】【杜文瀾《古謠諺》Du Wenlan:"Ancient Proverbs"】

饑時飯，渴時漿。 Food for the hungry and soup for the thirsty. 【馮夢龍《喻世明言·第十卷》Feng Menglong: Chapter 10, *Stories to Instruct the World*】

饑一頓，飽一頓。 One is hungry at one moment but full at another. 【俗語 Common saying】

饑者易食，寒者易衣。 It is easy to feed a hungry person and clothe a cold person. 【尸佼《尸子·神明第十三》Shi Jiao: Chapter 13, "Spiritual Enlightenment", *Shizi*】

饑者易為食，渴者易為飲。 The hungry are readily satisfied with any food and the thirsty with any drink. 【孟軻《孟子·公孫丑上》Meng Ke: Chapter 2, Part 1, *Mencius*】

老天爺餓不死瞎眼家雀兒。 Heaven will not let even a blind sparrow starve. 【俗語 Common saying】

民饑而無食，寒而無衣。 People suffer hunger without food and cold without clothing. 【管仲《管子·輕重篇第七十二》Guan Zhong: Chapter 72, "Weighing and Balancing Economic Factors", *Guanzi*】

民可百年無貨，不可一朝有饑。 People can do without treasures for a hundred years, but they must not go hungry for a single day. 【賈思勰《齊民要術》Jia Sixie: *Important Ways to Unite the People*】

農夫不努力，餓死帝王君。 If farmers do not work hard, the kings and lords will starve to death. 【俗語 Common saying】

萬事好當，一饑難忍。 Everything is bearable except hunger. 【俗語 Common saying】【《八賢傳》The Story of Eight Talents】

以食愈饑，以學愈愚。 Food cures hunger and study cures ignorance. 【劉向《説苑·卷三建本》Liu Xiang: Chapter 3, "Building the Foundation", *Garden of Persuasions*】

Husband and wife

柴米夫妻，酒肉朋友。 Firewood and rice bind husband and wife and wine and meat pull friends together.【諺語 Proverb】

秤不離砣，公不離婆。 A steelyard does not part with the weight and a husband, his wife.【孫錦標《通俗常言疏證‧什物》Sun Jinbiao: "Miscellaneous Items", *Mistakes and Corrections in Nantong Dialects and Proverbs*】

得意夫妻欣永守，負心朋友怕重逢。 A happy couple enjoys being together to the end of their lives. An ungrateful friend dreads reunion.【諺語 Proverb】【李綠園《歧路燈‧第一百零七回》Li Yuyuan: Chapter 107, *Lamp on a Forked Road*】

恩愛夫妻不到頭。 Husband and wife who love each other cannot live together to the end of their lives.【李漁《十二樓‧鶴歸樓》Li Yu: "Crane-returning Tower", *Twelve Towers*】

夫婦和而家道成。 When the husband and wife are in harmony, the welfare of the family will be secured.【程允升《幼學瓊林‧卷二夫婦》Cheng Yunsheng: Chapter 2, "Husband and Wife", *Treasury of Knowledge for Young Students*】

夫婦死同穴，父子貧賤離。 Husband and wife share the same grave when they die, and father and son will be separated in poverty or adversity.【陳師道〈別三子〉Chen Shidao: "Parting with My Three Sons"】

夫婦之道，有義則合，無義則離。 The way of husband and wife is that when they have affection, they stay together, and when they do not have affection, they go separate ways.【班固《漢書‧孔光傳》Ban Gu: "Biography of Kong Guang", *History of the Han*】

夫妻本是同林鳥，大限到來各自飛。 Husband and wife are originally like birds in the same forest, each will fly away when death comes.【馮夢龍《警世通言》Feng Menglong: *Stories to Caution the World*】

夫妻且說三分話，未可全拋一片心。 When husband and wife talk, they should tell each other a small part of what they want to tell, not all on their minds.【汪廷訥《種玉記‧第二十八齣》Wang Tingna: Scene 28, "Planting Jade"】

夫妻同牀，心隔千里。 Husband and wife sleep on the same bed, yet their minds are a thousand miles apart.【郭小亭《濟公全傳‧第一百一十四回》Guo Xiaoting: Chapter 114, *Biography of Jigong*】

夫妻無隔夜之仇。 Husband and wife never hate each other over the next day.【俗語 Common saying】

夫妻者，非有骨肉之恩也。愛則親，不愛則疏。 Husband and

wife have no kinship between them; they are intimate when mutually in love and distant when not in love. 【韓非《韓非子‧備內第十七》Han Fei: Chapter 17, "Guarding against the Interior", *Hanfeizi*】

夫仁則妻賢。 A good husband makes a good wife. 【諺語 Proverb】

雞公不啼雞婆啼。 The cock does not crow, but the hen does. 【俗語 Common saying】

幾家夫婦同羅帳，幾家飄散在他州？ How many husbands and wives can live together under the thin silk curtains and how many of them are scattered in different places? 【佚名〈吳歌〉 Anonymous:"Song of Wu"】

結髮為夫妻，恩愛兩不疑。 We have become husband and wife, and the love between us is beyond doubt. 【蘇武〈留別妻〉Su Wu:"Message I Left to My Wife before Parting with Her"】

捆綁不成夫妻。 To tie a man and a woman together would not make them husband and wife. 【諺語 Proverb】【毛澤東〈在中國共產黨第八屆中央委員會第二次全體會議上的講話〉Mao Zedong:"A Talk Given at the Second Plenum of the Eighth Chinese Communist Party Central Committee"】

滿堂兒女，當不得半席夫妻。 Many daughters and sons cannot compare with one's husband or wife. 【西周生《醒世姻緣傳‧第六十四回》Xi Zhousheng: Chapter 64, *Stories of Marriage to Awaken the World*】

美女累其夫。 A beautiful woman gets her husband into trouble. 【臧懋循《元曲選‧遇上皇‧第二折》Zang Maoxun: Act 2, "Meeting the Emperor", *Anthology of Yuan Plays*】

妻以夫為榮，母以子為貴。 A wife enjoys the honour because of her husband and a mother becomes noble because of her son. 【諺語 Proverb】

女大兩，黃金長；女大三，黃金山。 When the wife is two years older than her husband, gold at home will increase; when the wife is three years older than her husband, gold at home will be accumulated like a mountain. 【蘭陵笑笑生《金瓶梅‧第七回》Lanling Xiaoxiaosheng: Chapter 7, *The Plum in the Golden Vase*】

少年夫妻老來伴。 A young couple becomes companions to each other when old. 【諺語 Proverb】

少年夫妻甜如蜜。 Life to young couples is as sweet as honey. 【諺語 Proverb】

使君自有婦，羅敷自有夫。 You have your wife and I have my husband. 【佚名〈陌上桑〉 Anonymous:"Mulberry Lane"】

小夫妻吵架，越吵越親熱。 When a young couple quarrel, they get more intimate when the quarrel gets heated. 【俗語 Common saying】

休嫌官不要，夫妻直到老。 Don't choose your husband by his position, for what is important is that your husband and you will live to old age. 【羅貫中《平妖傳・第三十五回》Luo Guanzhong: Chapter 35, *Taming Devils*】

一日夫妻百年恩。 We are husband and wife in a day and our love will last for a hundred years.【蘭陵笑笑生《金瓶梅・第七十三回》Lanling Xiaoxiaosheng: Chapter 73, *The Plum in the Golden Vase*】

哲夫成城，哲婦傾城。 A wise husband founds a city but a wise wife overthrows it.【《詩經・大雅・瞻卬》"Looking Up", "Greater Odes of the Kingdom", *The Book of Odes*】

Illness

病從口入，禍從口出。 Illness enters the body from the mouth and misfortune comes from the mouth.【傅玄《傅子》Fu Xuan: *The Works of Fuzi*】

病急亂投醫。 When a person is critically ill, he will turn in desperation to any doctor.【王濬卿《冷眼觀・第二十五回》Wang Junqing: Chapter 25, *Casting a Cold Eye*】

病來如山倒，病去如抽絲。 Illness comes quickly like a landslide and goes slowly like cocoons reeling off raw silk.【俗語 Common saying】【曹雪芹《紅樓夢・第五十二回》Cao Xueqin: Chapter 52, *A Dream of the Red Chamber*】

病人多長命。 A person with illness usually enjoys longevity.【俗語 Common saying】

病無良藥，自解自樂。 There is no good medicine for illness. One has to liberate from it and feel happy about it.【諺語 Proverb】

【徐野君《春波影・第三齣》Xu Yejun: Scene 3, "Shadows of Spring Waves"】

不醉多愁醉多病，幾回愛酒又停杯。 I'm not concerned about my troubles but about my illness; for a number of times I want to drink wine but put down my cup without drinking it.【李覯〈索酒〉Li Gou: "Asking for Wine"】

毒病毒藥醫。 A poisonous disease should be cured with poisonous medicine.【俗語 Common saying】

多病方知健是仙。 Only when you often fall ill will you know that staying healthy is a blessing in itself.【諺語 Proverb】

久病成良醫。 Prolonged illness makes a good doctor of a patient.【左丘明《左傳・定公十三年》Zuo Qiuming: "The Thirteenth Year of the Reign of Duke Ding", *Zuo's Commentary on the Spring and Autumn Annals*】

久病牀前無孝子。 There is no filial son by the bedside of a patient who has prolonged illness. 【俗語 Common saying】

良藥苦口利於病，忠言逆耳利於行。 Good medicine is bitter in the mouth but good for the disease; honest advice offends the ear but is good for the conduct. 【司馬遷《史記‧留侯世家》Sima Qian: "House of Liu Hou", *Records of the Grand Historian*】

人吃五穀生百病。 It is normal that people eat all kinds of grains and suffer all kinds of diseases. 【俗語 Common saying】

無病不知有病苦。 Those who do not have illness do not know the suffering of those who have. 【俗語 Common saying】

無病當思有病時。 Think of illness when you do not have it. 【俗語 Common saying】

無病即神仙。 One who has no disease is god. 【俗語 Common saying】

無病一身輕，有子萬事足。 Without disease, one feels happy and carefree; with a son, one is content with everything. 【凌濛初《初刻拍案驚奇‧第二十卷》Ling Mengchu: Chapter 20, *Amazing Tales, Volume One*】

小兒無詐病。 A child does not feign illness. 【俗語 Common saying】

心病從來無藥醫。 There is no medicine for the disease of the heart. 【佚名《碧桃花‧二折》Anonymous: Scene 2, "Verdure Peach Blossom"】

心病還須心藥醫。 The diseases of the heart can be cured by medicine for the heart. 【曹雪芹《紅樓夢‧第九十回》Cao Xueqin: Chapter 90, *A Dream of the Red Chamber*】

心裏痛快百病消。 Having ease of mind, one will get rid of all diseases. 【諺語 Proverb】

心裏有病自己知。 One knows clearly what trouble he himself has at heart. 【俗語 Common saying】

治病不如防病。 Prevention is better than cure. 【俗語 Common saying】

治病要趁早，除害要除了。 A disease should be treated early; an evil must be rooted out. 【俗語 Common saying】

自己有病自家知。 One is aware of his own illness. 【俗語 Common saying】【王有光《吳下諺聯》Wang Youguang: *Collection of Proverbs*】

Influence

百足之蟲，死而不僵。 A centipede does not topple over even when dead – Although people and things decay and fall, the illusion of prosperity can still be maintained. 【蕭統《昭明文選‧曹冏〈六代論〉》Cao Jiong:"On the Six Dynasties in Xiao Tong (ed.)", *Zhaoming's Selection of Literary Writings*】

虎死不落架。 A tiger is dead but its skeleton does not fall down. 【王少堂《武松‧第一回》Wang Shaotang: Chapter 1, *Wu Song*】

牽一髮而動全身。 The pull of a hair may move the whole body. 【龔自珍〈自春徂秋偶有所感觸〉Gong Zizhen:"From Spring to Autumn: Occasional Thoughts"】

一石激起千重浪。 A stone tossed into a pond raises a thousand ripples. 【諺語 Proverb】

一隻爛，隻隻爛。 A rotten thing causes all other things to rot. 【俗語 Common saying】

Integrity

安能摧眉折腰事權貴，使我不得開心顏。 How can I serve the rich and the powerful subserviently, and make myself unhappy?【李白〈夢遊天姥吟留別〉Li Bai:"Ascended Mount Tian in a Dream – A Farewell Song"】

不為五斗米折腰。 Not to lose one's integrity for the salary of five bushels of rice. 【房玄齡等《晉書‧陶潛傳》Tang Xuanling, *et al*:"Biography of Tao Yuanming", *History of the Jin*】

不要人誇好顏色，祇留正氣滿乾坤。 I do not want others to praise the beauty of the painting, I just want to leave a spirit of righteousness to fill heaven and earth. 【王冕〈題墨梅〉Wang Mian:"Inscribing on a Painting of Peach blossoms in Ink"】

根深不怕風搖動，樹正何愁月影斜。 A tree with deep roots is not afraid of the wind that shakes it and a tree that is upright does not worry about its shadow in the moon is being slanted. 【《增廣賢文》*Words that Open up One's Mind and Enhance One's Wisdom*】

古之至人，先存諸己而後存諸人。 The best people in ancient times cultivated their integrity first and then helped others to do so. 【莊周《莊子‧內篇‧人間世第四》Zhuang Zhou: Chapter 4, "Human World", "Inner Chapters", *Zhuangzi*】

疾風知勁草。 The integrity of a person is tested in a crisis. 【范曄《後漢書・銚期王霸邳遵列傳》Fan Ye: "Biography of Wang Ba", *History of the Later Han*】

寧可正而不足，不可邪而有餘。 I would rather be upright and do not have enough to go by than being evil and having more. 【《增廣賢文》*Words that Open up One's Mind and Enhance One's Wisdom*】

千磨萬擊還堅勁，任爾東西南北風。 Bamboo stays firm and strong against endless beatings, regardless of the wind from north or south, or east or west. 【鄭板橋〈題竹石〉Zheng Banqiao: "On Bamboo and Rock"】

時窮節乃見，── 垂丹青。 A person's true integrity is revealed in times of stress, and this is what the painters portray in their works. 【文天祥〈正氣歌〉Wen Tianxiang: "Song of Righteousness"】

體面自己立。 One's dignity is established all by himself. 【俗語 Common saying】

天地有正氣，雜然賦流形。 There is a spirit of righteousness in heaven and earth and this spirit gives rise to different and varied forms. 【文天祥〈正氣歌〉Wen Tianxiang: "Song of Righteousness"】

威武不屈，富貴不淫。 One is neither intimidated by authority or force nor subdued by wealth or rank. 【孟軻《孟子・滕文公下》Meng Ke: Chapter 5, Part 2, *Mencius*】

吾愛孟夫子，風流天下聞。 I adore Master Meng, whose literary talent is known to the entire world. 【李白〈贈孟浩然〉Li Bai: "Presented to Meng Haoran"】

仰不愧於天，俯不怍於人。 Looking up, one is not abashed before heaven; looking down, one is not ashamed before others. 【孟軻《孟子・盡心章句上》Meng Ke: Chapter 7, Part 1, *Mencius*】

予獨愛蓮之出於淤泥而不染，濯清漣而不妖。 My special love of the lotus flower is because it grows in mud but remains unsullied, baths in clear water but is not coquettish. 【周敦頤〈愛蓮說〉Zhou Dunyi: "On My Love of the Lotus"】

真金不怕火煉。 True gold fears no fire. 【俗語 Common saying】

Intelligence

卑賤者最聰明，高貴者最愚蠢。 The lowly are most intelligent; the noble are most ignorant. 【毛澤東〈新觀察・卑賤者最聰明，高貴者最愚蠢〉（一九五八年五月十八日、二十日）Mao Zedong: "The Lowly Are Most Intelligent; the Noble Are Most Ignorant", *New Observer* (18-20 May 1958)】

盜雖小人，智過君子。Thieves are people of little significance, yet they are more intelligent than a gentleman.【諺語 Proverb】【費袞《梁溪漫志》Fei Gun: *Stories of Liangxi*】

鼓樓的燈籠 —— 高明。A lantern on a drum tower is high and bright–high intelligence.【歇後語 End-clipper】

明者舉大略細，不忮不求。An intelligent person focuses on what is important and ignores what is trivial, and he is not jealous or overcritical of others.【葛洪《抱朴子·外篇·接疏第二十九》Ge Hong: Chapter 29, "Meeting Visitors", "Outer Chapters", *The Master Who Embraces Simplicity*】

明者遠見於未萌，而知者避危於無形。An intelligent person has foresight to see things before happening and a wise person avoids danger without any trace.【司馬遷《史記·司馬相如列傳》Sima Qian:"Biographies of Sima Xiangru", *Records of the Grand Historian*】

人有隔宿之智。People might be more intelligent after a night's sleep.【諺語 Proverb】

雖有至知，萬人謀之。Though you might be the most intelligent, you still need ten thousand people to work things out for you.【莊周《莊子·外篇·外物第二十六》Zhuang Zhou: Chapter 26, "External Things", "Miscellaneous Chapters", *Zhuangzi*】

頭大冇腦, 腦大長草。A stupid person is without intelligence.【俗語 Common saying】

知也者，爭之器也。Intelligence is a weapon of contention.【莊周《莊子·內篇·人間世第四》Zhuang Zhou: Chapter 4, "Human World", "Inner Chapters", *Zhuangzi*】

智養千口，力養一人。With intelligence, one can support a thousand people; with physical strength, one can only support one.【諺語 Proverb】

Intention

鱷魚上岸 —— 來者不善。A crocodile climbing up on the bank comes with ill intent.【歇後語 End-clipper】

黃鼠狼給雞拜年 —— 沒安好心。The weasel pays a New-year visit to a chick–without good intentions.【歇後語 End-clipper】

來者不善，善者不來。Those who come have ill intent and those who have good intent do not come.【諺語 Proverb】

流水下灘非有意，白雲出岫本無心。Water flowing to the beach is without intention, and white clouds arising from the hill is without design. 【《增廣賢文》 *Words that Open up One's Mind and Enhance One's Wisdom*】

墨魚肚腸河豚肝 —— 又黑又毒。 The intestine of an ink fish and the liver of a globefish – black and venomous. 【歇後語 End-clipper】

圖窮匕首見。 The real intention is revealed in the end. 【劉向《戰國策・燕策三》 Liu Xiang: "Strategies of the State of Yan, No.3", *Strategies of the Warring States*】

項莊舞劍，意在沛公。 Act with an ulterior motive. 【司馬遷《史記・項羽本紀》 Sima Qian: "Annals of Xiang Yu", *Records of the Grand Historian*】

言者所以在意，得意而忘言。 Words are for the expression of meaning, so once the meaning is obtained the words can be forgotten. 【莊周《莊子・外篇・外物第二十六》 Zhuang Zhou: Chapter 26, "External Things", "Miscellaneous Chapters", *Zhuangzi*】

歪嘴和尚唸歪經。 A monk with a crooked mouth chants a sutra in a crooked way. 【俗語 Common saying】

咬人的狗兒不露齒。 Dogs that bite do not bare their teeth. 【張國賓《羅李郎・第三折》 Zhang Guobing: Scene 3, "Master Luo Li"】

一片好心，反成惡意。 One's good will is being turned about as bad intentions. 【施耐庵《水滸傳・第二十二回》 Shi Nai'an: Chapter 22, *Outlaws of the Marshes*】

Intimidation

扯着老虎尾巴 —— 抖威風。 Wield a tiger's tail to intimidate others. 【歇後語 End-clipper】

打的丫環，嚇的小姐。 Beat the maid to intimidate the young lady. 【王少堂《武松・第三回》 Wang Shaotang: Chapter 3, *Wu Song*】

打了騾子馬受驚。 If you whip a mule, the horse will be scared. 【諺語 Proverb】【曲波《林海雪原・第四章》 Qu Bo: Chapter 4, *Tracks in the Snowy Forest*】

打死閻王，嚇死小鬼。 Kill the King of Hell and the goblins will be scared to death. 【俗語 Common saying】

拉大旗作虎皮。 Drape oneself in a tiger skin to intimidate people. 【俗語 Common saying】【魯迅《且介亭雜文末編・答徐懋庸並關於抗日統一戰線問題》 Lu Xun: "Last Compilation, in Reply to Xu Maoyong and Questions about the Anti-Japanese United Front"】

殺雞給猴看 —— 懲一儆百。 Kill the chicken to frighten the monkey. 【歇後語 End-clipper】

Jealousy

堆土於岸，水必湍之。 When sand piles up on the shore, it will be lashed by water. 【李康〈運命論〉Li Kang: "On Fate"】

婦人不嫉便是德。 A woman who is not jealous is virtuous. 【俗語 Common saying】

爵高者人妒之。 People envy those high in rank. 【列禦寇《列子‧說符第八》Lie Yukou: Chapter 8, "Explaining Conjunctions", Liezi】

女無美惡，入宮見妒；士無賢不肖，入朝見疑。 A woman, regardless of her looks, will be a target of jealousy once she is called to enter an imperial palace. A scholar, regardless of his virtue, will be a target of suspicion once he is called to enter the court. 【司馬遷《史記‧扁鵲倉公列傳》Sima Qian: "Biographies of Bian Que and the Duke of Cang", Records of the Grand Historian】

人高招忌，樹大招風。 A high-ranking person is apt to cause jealousy as a tall tree catches the wind. 【諺語 Proverb】

人含智，則嫉之。 People with wisdom are envied. 【劉晝《劉子‧言苑第五十四章》Liu Zhou: Chapter 54, "Garden of Speech", Works of Master Liu Zhou】

人有喜慶，不可生妒忌心。 Don't be jealous when people have things to celebrate. 【朱用純《朱子家訓》Zhu Yongchun: Precepts of the Zhu Family】

十個女人九個妒。 Nine out of ten women are jealous. 【俗語 Common saying】

無錢吃酒，妒人面赤。 Without money to drink wine, one is jealous of a man with a red face. 【諺語 Proverb】

Judgement

裁縫的尺子 —— 量人不量己。 A tailor's ruler is to measure others, but not himself. 【俗語 Common saying】

從果看樹，從事看人。 Judge a tree by its fruit and a person, what he does. 【俗語 Common saying】

當局者迷，旁觀者清。 Outsiders see things clearer than those involved. 【劉鶚《老殘遊記‧第十三回》Liu E: Chapter 13, The Travels of Lao Can】

隔着門縫瞧人，把人看偏了。 If we peer at a person through a crack, he looks flat. 【俗語 Common saying】

觀其行而知其人。A person is judged by his deeds. 【俗語 Common saying】

觀人必於其微。To observe a person, one must examine the small things he does. 【俗語 Common saying】【李寶嘉《官場現形記・第五十六回》Li Baojia: Chapter 56, *Officialdom Unmasked*】

觀人如觀玉，拙眼喜譏評。Judging a person is like judging jade, the uninformed like to criticize. 【陸游〈雜興十首〉Lu You: "Ten Miscellaneous Poems"】

看樹看果實，看人看作為。Judge a tree by its fruit and judge a person by his deeds. 【俗語 Common saying】

寧可不識字，不可不識人。Not knowing how to read books is better than not knowing how to judge people. 【曾國藩〈冰鑒〉Zeng Guofan: "Ice Judge"】

牆裏開花牆外香。Local talents are not as valued as foreign ones. 【諺語 Proverb】

權，然後知輕重；度，然後知長短。By weighing, we know which is light and which is heavy; by measuring, we know which is long and which is short. 【孟軻《孟子・梁惠王上》Meng Ke: Chapter 1, Part 1, *Mencius*】

勿以己度人。Don't judge others by yourself. 【韓嬰《韓詩外傳・卷三》Han Ying: Chapter 3, *Supplementary Commentary on the Book of Songs by Master Han*】

勿以言取人，勿以貌取人。Neither judge people solely by their words nor by their appearance. 【司馬遷《史記・仲尼弟子列傳》Sima Qian: "Biographies of the Disciples of Confucius", *Records of the Grand Historian*】

相馬以輿，相士以居。To judge a horse, you should watch it pulling a cart; to judge a person you should examine his conduct in everyday life. 【司馬遷《史記・仲尼弟子列傳》Sima Qian: "Biographies of the Disciples of Confucius", *Records of the Grand Historian*】

要客觀看人，別感情用事。Judge a person objectively, and don't give yourself over to blind emotions. 【俗語 Common saying】

直尺量不準曲線。A straight ruler cannot measure curves correctly. 【諺語 Proverb】

Justice

公道自在人心。Justice lies naturally on the hearts of the people. 【俗語 Common saying】

理正不怕官。With justice on one's side, one is not afraid of an official. 【諺語 Proverb】

理直則氣壯，理虧則詞窮。With justice on one's side, one is bold and assured; without it, one will be speechless.【俗語 Common saying】【曹雪芹《紅樓夢‧第一百一十八回》Cao Xueqin: Chapter 118, *A Dream of the Red Chamber*】

人情歸人情，公道歸公道。Human relations are human relations and justice is justice.【俗語 Common saying】【黎汝清《萬山紅遍‧第九章》Li Ruqing: Chapter 9, *Red Over Country*】

人同此心，心同此理。The sense of justice and rationality is the same with everybody.【俗語 Common saying】【文康《兒女英雄傳‧第九回》Wen Kang: Chapter 9, *Biographies of Young Heroes and Heroines*】

人爭正氣，魚爭上水。People struggle for justice while fish fight for water.【俗語 Common saying】

天網恢恢，疏而不漏。The net of Heaven is large and has large meshes, but it lets nothing bad through.【老子《道德經‧第七十三章》Laozi: Chapter 73, *Daodejing*】

物不平則鳴。Injustice will cry out.【韓愈〈送孟東野序〉Han Yu: "Preface to a Poem on Bidding Farewell to Meng Dongye"】

有理不在聲高。A loud voice does not signify that justice is on the speaker's side.【釋普濟《五燈會元‧卷二十》Shi Puji: Chapter 20, *A Compendium of the Five Lamps*】

有理走遍天下，無理寸步難行。With justice on your side, you can go anywhere in the world; without justice, it is difficult for you to move a single step.【俗語 Common saying】

Killing

案板上的肉 —— 任人宰割。Meat on a chopping block can be butchered by others at will.【歇後語 End-clipper】

打死人要抵命，哄死人不抵命。If you beat somebody to death, you have to pay with your life, but if you coax somebody to death, you need not pay for that.【諺語 Proverb】

風高放火，月黑殺人。When the wind blows hard, it is time to set fire. When the night is dark, it is an opportunity to murder.【鞭然子《拊掌錄》Chan Ranzi: *Clapping-hand Stories*】

來一殺一，來兩殺雙。When one person comes, I will kill one person. When two persons come, I will kill a pair.【俗語 Common saying】

殺不辜者，得不祥焉。He who kills the innocent will have misfortunes.【墨翟《墨子‧法儀卷

四》Mo Di: Chapter 4, "On Standards and Rules", *Mozi*】

殺得人，救得人。 One can kill people and also save people.【施耐庵《水滸傳‧第九回》Shi Nai'an: Chapter 9, *Outlaws of the Marshes*】

殺敵要用槍，還得本領強。 To kill an enemy, you have to use a gun, but it depends on how well your skill is.【俗語 Common saying】

殺人不過頭點地。 To kill a person just means to put his head on the ground.【俗語 Common saying】【文康《兒女英雄傳‧第十六回》Wen Kang: Chapter 16, *Biographies of young heroes and heroines*】

殺人不見血。 Killing a person without spilling blood.【馮夢龍《醒世恆言‧第三十五卷》Feng Menglong: Chapter 35, *Stories to Awaken the World*】

殺人不眨眼。 Killing a person without batting an eyelid.【釋普濟《五燈會元‧卷二十二‧緣德禪師》Shi Puji: Chapter 22, "Chan Master Yuande", *A compendium of the five lamps*】

殺人抵命，借債還錢。 A murderer must pay with his life and a debtor must pay his debt.

【諺語 Proverb】【凌濛初《初刻拍案驚奇‧第三十三卷》Ling Mengchu: Chapter 33, *Amazing Tales, Volume One*】

殺人可恕，天理難容。 If killing people can be forgiven, this is against the law of heaven.【施耐庵《水滸傳‧第十回》Shi Nai'an: Chapter 10, *Outlaws of the Marshes*】

殺人須見血。 Blood must be seen if one kills a person.【施耐庵《水滸傳‧第九回》Shi Nai'an: Chapter 9, *Outlaws of the Marshes*】

殺人一萬，自損三千。 To kill ten thousand people, you lose three thousand people of your own.【《增廣賢文》*Words that Open up One's Mind and Enhance One's Wisdom*】

殺身成仁，捨生取義。 Kill oneself to achieve benevolence and sacrifice oneself to accomplish righteousness.【孟軻《孟子‧告子章句上》Meng Ke: Chapter 6, Part 1, *Mencius*】

同類不相殘。 One will not kill his own kind.【俗語 Common saying】

紙筆殺人不用刀。 Paper and writing brush can be used to kill people without using a knife.【俗語 Common saying】

Kindness

慈不掌兵，義不主財。 A kind person cannot command an army, a righteous person cannot be in charge of finance.【諺語 Proverb】

你敬我一尺，我還你一丈。 Kindness is always returned tenfold.【諺語 Proverb】

善人者，不善人之師；不善人者，善人之資。 One who is kind to others is a teacher for those who are unkind to others; One who is unkind to others is a lesson for those who are kind to others. 【老子《道德經‧第二十七章》Laozi: Chapter 27, *Daodejing*】

以德報德，則民有所勸；以怨報怨，則民有所懲。 When kindness is returned by kindness, people are persuaded to be kind. When enmity is returned by enmity, people will be warned not to have enmity. 【《禮記‧表記第三十二》Chapter 32, "Records of examples", *The Book of Rites*】

Knife

白刀子入，紅刀子出。 In goes a white knife and out comes a red knife. 【曹雪芹《紅樓夢‧第七回》Cao Xueqin: Chapter 7, *A Dream of the Red Chamber*】

刀把兒遞外人。 Give other people the handle against oneself. 【陳壽《三國志‧魏書‧王衛二劉傅傳》Chen Shou: "Biographies of Wang Wei'er and Liu Fu", "History of the Wei", *Records of the Three Kingdoms*】

利刀割體瘡易合，惡語傷人恨不消。 The wound caused by a sharp knife cutting one's body can be healed easily, but the hatred resulting from being hurt by vicious language cannot be removed easily. 【《增廣賢文》*Words that Open up One's Mind and Enhance One's Wisdom*】

Knowledge

斑鳩吃螢火蟲 —— 肚裏明。 A turtledove eating up a firefly is bright in the belly–have a clear understanding of things. 【歇後語 End-clipper】

扁擔挑燈籠 —— 兩頭兒明。 When hanging lanterns at both ends of a carrying pole, both ends are bright–both sides understand. 【歇後語 End-clipper】

不出戶知天下事。 Without going out, you still can know the affairs of the world. 【老子《道德經‧第四十七章》Laozi: Chapter 47, *Daodejing*】

不憤不啟，不悱不發。 I do not open up the truth to one who is not eager to get knowledge, nor help out anyone who is not anxious to explain himself. 【孔

子《論語・述而篇第七》Confucius: Chapter 7, *The Analects of Confucius*】

不患人之不己知，患不知人也。 You should not be troubled by the failure of others not appreciating your abilities, but rather your failure to appreciate theirs.【孔子《論語・學而篇第一》 Confucius: Chapter 1, *The Analects of Confucius*】

不認識東南西北。 Don't have any sense of direction.【俗語 Common saying】

不知而言不智，知而不言不忠。 To say something one does not know is unwise and not to say something one knows is disloyal.【韓非《韓非子・初見秦第一》Han Fei: Chapter 1, "The First Meeting with the King of Qin", *Hanfeizi*】

不知而自以為知，百禍之宗也。 If one does not know but thinks that he knows, this is the source of hundreds of disasters.【呂不韋《呂氏春秋・謹聽》Lu Buwei: "Be Cautious in Listening", *Master Lu's Spring and Autumn Annals*】

不知者不罪。 Those who are ignorant are not to be blamed. 【錢彩《說岳全傳・第六十三回》Qian Cai: Chapter 63, *A Story of Yue Fei*】

從一椿知百椿。 From one thing, one knows a hundred things of the same kind.【俗語 Common saying】

但知其一，不知其二。 Know one aspect of something without knowing another aspect.【余邵

魚《東周列國志・第五回》Yu Shaoyu: Chapter 5, The *Chronicles of the Eastern Zhou Kingdoms*】

到處留心皆學問。 Knowledge is gained through observation of things around you.【諺語 Proverb】

多做長知識，久病成良醫。 Repeated practice helps one accumulate knowledge and prolonged illness makes a doctor of a patient.【諺語 Proverb】 【左丘明《左傳・定公十三年》Zuo Qiuming: "The Thirteenth year of the Reign of Duke Ding", *Zuo's Commentary on the Spring and Autumn Annals*】

觀音生子 ── 天知道。 The Goddess of Mercy giving birth to a baby – Heaven knows.【歇後語 End-clipper】

攃面杖吹火 ── 一竅不通。 Try to blow up a fire through a rolling-pin – not to know anything about something.【歇後語 End-clipper】

井蛙不可以語於海者，拘於虛也；夏蟲不可以語於冰者，篤於時也。 You can't discuss the ocean with a well frog as it is limited by the space it lives in and you can't discuss ice with a summer insect for it is bound to a single season.【莊周《莊子・外篇・秋水第十七》: Zhuang Zhou: Chapter 17, "Autumn Floods", "Outer Chapters", *Zhuangzi*】

近水知魚性，近山識鳥音。 If you live close to water, you know the behaviour of fish; if you live close to a mountain, you know the chirping of birds. 【《增廣賢文》 *Words that Open up One's Mind and Enhance One's Wisdom*】

馬不知臉長。 Men are blind in their own cause. 【諺語 Proverb】

賣金須向識金家。 Sell gold to those who know how to judge it. 【陳汝衡《說唐演義全傳·第五回》Chen Ruheng: Chapter 5, *Romance of the Tang Dynasty*】

沒吃過豬肉也見過豬跑。 Have some knowledge of a certain subject. 【曹雪芹《紅樓夢·第十六回》Cao Xueqin: Chapter 16, *A Dream of the Red Chamber*】

明於知己，暗於知彼。 Good at knowing oneself but poor at knowing others. 【諺語 Proverb】

能知而不能行者，非真知也。真知則無不能行矣。 Knowledge that can be learned but cannot be practiced is not real knowledge. Real knowledge can surely be put into practice. 【譚嗣同《仁學》Tan Sitong: *An Exposition of Benevolence*】

牛不知角彎，馬不知臉長。 An ox does not know that its horns are bent and a horse does not know that its face is long. 【諺語 Proverb】

千金難買早知道。 A word before is worth two behind. 【諺語 Proverb】

強不知以為知。 Pretend to know what one does not know. 【凌濛初《二刻拍案驚奇·第一卷》Ling Mengchu: Chapter 1, *Amazing Tales, Volume Two*】

秋天賣涼粉 —— 不識時務。 Selling bean jelly in autumn shows no understanding of the times. 【歇後語 End-clipper】

人不知，鬼不覺。 Not known by anybody. 【佚名〈爭報恩·第一折〉Anonymous: Scene 1, "Fighting to Return the Favours"】

人非生而知之者，孰能无惑。 No one is born wise or learned, how can we be free of doubts? 【韓愈《昌黎先生集·師說》Han Yu: "On Teaching", *Collected Works of Han Yu*】

人固未易知，知人亦未易也。 People are not easy to know and knowing people is not easy. 【司馬遷《史記·范睢蔡澤列傳》Sima Qian: "Biographies of Fan Sui and Cai Ze", *Records of the Grand Historian*】

人貴有自知之明。 What is to be valued is that one knows one's own limitations. 【老子《道德經·第三十三章》Laozi: Chapter 33, *Daodejing*】

人看起小，馬看蹄走。 One knows a person from how he grows up from young age and a horse from how it runs with its hooves. 人未知，神先知。 What a person does not know, God knows first. 【黃世仲《廿載繁華夢·第十三回》Huang Shizhong: Chapter 13, *A Rich Dream that Lasted Two Decades*】

人無自知煩惱多。 People who lack self-knowledge will have many troubles. 【俗語 Common saying】

人有知學，則有力矣。People with knowledge and learning are powerful.【王充《論衡・效力第三十七卷》Wang Chong: Chapter 37, "The Display of Energy", *Critical Essays*】

人知之，亦囂囂；人不知，亦囂囂。If people know it, I would be happy; if people don't, I would also be happy.【孟軻《孟子・盡心章句上》Meng Ke: Chapter 7, Part 1, *Mencius*】

如人飲水，冷暖自知。When drinking the water, only the drinker knows whether it is hot or cold.【唐裴休〈黃蘗山斷際禪師傳心法要〉Tang Peixiu: "Essentials in the Method of the Transmission of Mind by the Chan Master Duanji of the Huang Nie Mountain"】

三人知，天下曉。When three people know it, all know it.【俗語 Common saying】

上知天文，下知地理。One who knows astronomy in heaven above and geography on earth.【《易經・上經》Book 1, *The Book of Changes*】

神不知，鬼不覺。Without being known either by god or by ghost – without anybody knowing it.【凌濛初〈初刻拍案驚奇・第二卷〉Ling Mengchu: Chapter 2, *Amazing Tales, Volume One*】

生我者父母，知我者足下也。I was born by my parents, but you are the one who knows me well.【司馬遷《史記・管晏列傳》Sima Qian: "Biographies of Guan (Zhong) and Yan (Ying)", *Records of the Grand Historian*】

世事洞明皆學問，人情練達即文章。A thorough understanding of the affairs of the world is knowledge, and rich experience in human relationships is literature.【曹雪芹《紅樓夢・第五回》Cao Xueqin: Chapter 5, *A Dream of the Red Chamber*】

天知地知，你知我知。This is something known only to heaven and earth, and you and I.【佚名〈女姑姑・第二折〉Anonymous: Scene 2, "Aunt"】

聞一知二，舉一反三。Having learnt one, one knows two, and infers the whole from a single instance.【孔子《論語・公冶長篇第五》Confucius: Chapter 5, *The Analects of Confucius*】

屋漏在上，知之在下。The leakage is on the roof and it is the one who lives under it knows it.【王充《論衡・答佞第三十三卷》Wang Chong: Chapter 33, "On the Cunning and Artful", *Critical Essays*】

吾生也有涯，而知也無涯。Life is finite while knowledge is infinite.【莊周《莊子・內篇・養生主第三》Zhuang Zhou: Chapter 3, "Essentials for Nourishing Life", "Inner Chapters", *Zhuangzi*】

秀才不出門，便知天下事。Without stepping outside the house, a scholar knows all the affairs in the world.【老子《道德

經‧第四十七章》Laozi: Chapter 47, *Daodejing*】

啞巴吃餃子 —— 心裏有數。 **One knows what to do.** 【歇後語 End-clipper】

樣樣皆通，樣樣稀鬆。 **Know everything but not specialize in any.** 【諺語 Proverb】

一門不到一門黑。 **Without knowledge of a branch of learning, you will be in the dark about that field.** 【王濬卿《冷眼觀‧第十二回》Wang Junqing: Chapter 12, *Casting a Cold Eye*】

一竅通，百竅通。 **By knowing one method you will know all.** 【吳承恩《西遊記‧第二回》Wu Cheng'en: Chapter 2, *Journey to the West*】

一問三不知。 **Not to know anything.** 【左丘明《左傳‧哀公二十七年》Zuo Qiuming: "The twenty-seventh Year of the Reign of Duke Ai", *Zuo's Commentary on the Spring and Autumn Annals*】

一在明裏，一在暗裏。 **One is in the know, the other, in the dark.** 【俗語 Common saying】

以其所知推其所未知。 **Based on what is known to predict what is not yet known.** 【梁啟超《梁啟超文集‧慧觀》Liang Qichao: "Wise Views", *Collected Works of Liang Qichao*】

易則易知，簡則易從。 **If it is easy, it is easy to know; if it is simple, it is easy to follow.** 【《易經‧繫辭上》"Appended Remarks", Part 1, *The Book of Changes*】

有不知則有知，無不知則無知。 **If one knows that there are things that he does not know, he has knowledge. If he thinks that there is nothing he does not know, he does not have knowledge.** 【王夫之《張子正蒙注‧卷四》Wang Fuzhi: Chapter 4, *Annotations on Correct Discipline for Beginners by Zhang Zai*】

有道之士，貴以近知遠，以今知古，以所見知所不見。 **A person who knows the Way is valued for knowing the far by the near, understanding the ancient by the present, and perceiving the invisible by the visible.** 【呂不韋《呂氏春秋‧察今》Lu Buwei: "Perceive the Present", *Master Lu's Spring and Autumn Annals*】

有眼不識泰山。 **One fails to recognize an important person.** 【施耐庵《水滸傳‧第二回》Shi Nai'an: Chapter 2, *Outlaws of the Marshes*】

欲人勿知，莫若勿為。 **If you don't want your action to be known, do not do it.** 【班固《漢書‧枚乘傳》Ban Gu: "Biography of Mei Cheng", *History of the Han*】

欲知人，必須自知。 **If you want to know others, you must know yourself first.** 【王詡《鬼谷子‧反應第二》Wang Xu: Chapter 2, "Reciprocal Reaction", *Master of the Ghost Valley*】

知不知，尚矣。不知知，病矣。 **He who knows there are**

something he does not know is intelligent; he who does not know but thinks that he knows is sick. 【老子《道德經‧第七十一章》Laozi: Chapter 71, *Daodejing*】

知己知彼，將心比心。 Know yourself and you know others, and compare your feelings with those of others. 【《增廣賢文》*Words that Open up One's Mind and Enhance One's Wisdom*】

知其然，不知其所以然。 Know the hows but not the whys. 【李節〈錢潭州疏言禪師詣太原求藏經詩序〉Li Jie: "Preface to a Poem Bidding Farewell to Buddist Master Shu Yan of Tanzhou who Goes to Taiyuan to Seek the Tripitaka Sutra"】

知其一，不知其二。 One knows only a thing about something, but not other things about it. 【《詩經‧小雅‧小旻之什》"Decade of Xiao Min", "Minor Odes of the Kingdom", *The Book of Odes*】

知人者智，自知者明。 He who knows others is wise and he who knows himself has insight. 【老子《道德經‧第三十三章》Laozi: Chapter 33, *Daodejing*】

知識就是力量。 Knowledge is power. 【諺語 Proverb】

知是行之始，行是知之成。 Knowledge is the beginning of practice, and practice is the accomplishment of knowledge. 【王陽明《傳習錄》Wang Yangming: *Records of Teaching and Practicing*】

知者不言，言者不知。 Those who know do not speak and those who speak do not know. 【老子《道德經‧第五十六章》Laozi: Chapter 56, *Daodejing*】

知之為知之，不知為不知，是為知也。 To say you know when you know and you don't when you don't, this is knowledge. 【孔子《論語‧為政篇第二》Confucius: Chapter 2, *The Analects of Confucius*】

知之必好之，好之必求之，求之必得之。 When you know it, you will like it; when you like it, you will seek for it; when you seek for it, you will get it. 【程顥，程頤《河南程氏粹言‧論學篇》Cheng Hao and Cheng Yi: "On Learning", *Sayings of Cheng Hao and Cheng Yi of Henan*】

知之者不如好之者，好之者不如樂之者。 Those who know it are not as good as those who are fond of it and those who are fond of it are not as good as those who find joy in it. 【孔子《論語‧雍也篇第六》Confucius: Chapter 6, *The Analects of Confucius*】

Laughter / smile

別人笑我忒瘋癲，我笑別人看不穿。 People laugh at me for being too crazy, but I laugh at people for being too worldly. 【唐

寅〈桃花庵歌〉Tang Yin:"Song of Peach Blossom Nunnery"】

不見採蓮人，但聞花中語。 I did not see the lotus-seed pickers, but I heard laughters amongst the lotus flowers. 【瞿時行〈採蓮曲〉Qu Shixing:"Lotus Picking Song"】

打情罵俏，惹人譏笑。 A coquette is laughed at by others. 【俗語 Common saying】

滑天下之大稽。 The most ridiculous thing in the world. 【魯迅《花邊文學‧小品文的生機》Lu Xun:"The Lease of Life for Essays", *Fringed Literature*】

皮笑肉不笑。 Put on a false smile. 【俗語 Common saying】【柳青《創業史》Liu Qing: *A Story of Pioneering*】

千金難買一笑。 A thousand taels of gold cannot buy a smile. 【俗語 Common saying】【司馬遷《史記‧周本紀》Sima Qian:"Annals of Zhou", *Records of the Grand Historian*】

巧笑倩兮，美目盼兮。 Her sweet smile is charming and her pretty eyes, clear and bright. 【《詩經‧衛風‧碩人》"The Shuo People", "Odes of Wei", *The Book of Odes*】

笑口常開，青春常在。 Keep a smiling face, and you will always feel young. 【俗語 Common saying】

笑一笑，十年少；愁一愁，白了頭。 Smile and you are ten years younger; worry and your head turns gray. 【諺語 Proverb】

一笑解千愁。 A smile can erase a thousand worries. 【俗語 Common saying】

一笑勝百美。 Her smile outshines all the beautiful women around her. 【俗語 Common saying】

一笑值千金。 A smile is worth a thousand taels of gold. 【俗語 Common saying】

Law

包公審案 —— 鐵面無私。 Magistrate Bao trying a case – a face as impartial as cast iron. 【歇後語 End-clipper】

當堂不讓父，舉手不留情。 At court, one does not concede to one's father. In fighting, one strikes without leniency. 【俗語 Common saying】【施世綸《施公案‧第一百七十六回》Shi Shilun: Chapter 176, *Cases of Judge Shi*】

惡法等於無法。 A bad law is worse than no law. 【俗語 Common saying】

惡人先告狀。 The rowdy person brings lawsuit against his victims before he himself is prosecuted. 【諺語 Proverb】【魯迅《兩地書》Lu Xun: *Letters between Two Places*】

法不阿貴，人人平等。The law does not fawn on the noble for everyone is equal before the law.【韓非《韓非子・有度第六》Han Fei: Chapter 6, "Having Regulations", *Hanfeizi*】

法不仁，不可以為法。A law that is not benevolent cannot be a law.【墨翟《墨子・法儀卷一》Mo Di: Volume 1, "Principles of Law", *Mozi*】

法令滋彰，盜賊多有。The more laws and regulations, the more thieves and robbers.【老子《道德經・第五十七章》Laozi: Chapter 57, *Daodejing*】

法律面前，人人平等。Everyone is equal before the law.【俗語 Common saying】

法律治光棍，惡狗治橫人。The law punishes scoundrels and a fierce dog punishes the rude.【俗語 Common saying】

法能為買賣，官可做人情。The law can be traded and government posts can be given as gifts.【羅貫中《粉妝樓・第五十八回》Luo Guanzhong: Chapter 58, *The Chamber of Powder and Rouge*】

法無三日嚴，草是年年長。If the law is not strictly followed for less than three days, illegal activities will occur like grass which grows year after year.【文康《兒女英雄傳・第四回》Wen Kang: Chapter 4, *Biographies of Young Heroes and Heroines*】

法之不行，自上犯之。The law cannot be enforced as the upper class does not follow it.【司馬遷《史記・商君列傳》Sima Qian:"Biography of Lord Shang", *Records of the Grand Historian*】

鋼刀雖快，不斬無罪之人。A sword is sharp, but it does not kill an innocent person.【李雨堂《五虎征西・第四十六回》Li Yutang: Chapter 46, *Five Tigers Conquering the West*】

告人一狀三世冤。To accuse a person at law makes three generations of foes.【俗語 Common saying】

官法不容情。The law does not spare anyone's sensibilities.【諺語 Proverb】

官無悔筆，罪不重科。Court decisions cannot be changed and a criminal cannot be sentenced twice for the same crime.【俗語 Common saying】【馮夢龍《古今譚概・卷二十九》Feng Menglong: Chapter 29, *Stories Old and New*】

國有國法，家有家規。A country has its laws, just as a family has its rules.【俗語 Common saying】

國有王法，廟有清規。A country has its laws and a temple has monastic rules.【郭小亭《濟公全傳・第三回》Guo Xiaoting: Chapter 3, *Biography of Jigong*】

和尚打傘 —— 無法（髮）無天。A bonze under an open umbrella has no hair and can't see the sky – lawless and godless.【歇後語 End-clipper】

家有家規，軍有軍法。 A family has family rules and an army has army rules. 【諺語 Proverb】

君子懷刑，小人懷惠。 A gentleman has the sanctions of law on his mind, whereas the petty person is concerned about the generous treatment they may receive. 【孔子《論語‧里仁篇第四》Confucius: Chapter 4, *The Analects of Confucius*】

君子行法，以俟命而已矣。 A gentleman acts according to law is leaving the results to destiny. 【孟軻《孟子‧盡心章句下》Meng Ke: Chapter 7, Part 2, *Mencius*】

禮禁未然之前，法施已然之後。 Rites serve to stop in advance what has not taken place, while laws act on what is has happened. 【司馬遷《史記‧太史公自序》Sima Qian: "Author's Preface", *Records of the Grand Historian*】

立法不可不嚴，行法不可不恕。 In enacting laws, severity is essential; in executing laws, leniency should be tempered with justice. 【諺語 Proverb】【金纓《格言聯璧‧從政》Jin Ying: "Governance", *Couplets of Maxims*】

律設大法，禮順人情。 Laws are created to maintain the national system and rites are used to keep the harmonious relations of people. 【范曄《後漢書‧卓茂傳》Fan Ye: "Biography of Zhuo Mao", *History of the Later Han*】

偶然犯事叫作過，立志犯法叫作惡。 Occasional mistakes are but faults, intended violations of law are crimes. 【俗語 Common saying】

懼法朝朝樂，欺公日日憂。 If you are afraid of the laws, you will be happy every day. If you cheat the public, you will be worried every day. 【《增廣賢文》*Words that Open up One's Mind and Enhance One's Wisdom*】

人情大於王法。 Human feelings are more important than imperial laws. 【諺語 Proverb】

人隨王法草隨風。 A person abides by the law just as the grass sways before the wind. 【俗語 Common saying】

人心似鐵，官法如爐。 The heart of a person is like iron and the laws of the government are like a furnace. 【《增廣賢文》*Words that Open up One's Mind and Enhance One's Wisdom*】

十場官司九場和。 Nine out of ten lawsuits will have no winner nor loser. 【俗語 Common saying】

世不患無法，而患無必行之法也。 In this world, having no laws is not what worries us, what is worrying is that there is no law which must be executed. 【桓寬《鹽鐵論‧申韓》Huan Kuan: "Shen Buhai and Han Feizi", *Discussions on Salt and Iron*】

世易時移，變法宜矣。 With the change of generations and the

passage of time, it is right to reform the laws. 【呂不韋《呂氏春秋‧察今》 Lu Buwei:"Perceive the Present", *Master Lu's Spring and Autumn Annals*】

事急無法律，路急無君子。 Necessity knows no law. 【俗語 Common saying】

王者犯法，與庶民同罪。 If a prince violates the law, he must be punished like an ordinary person. 【司馬遷《史記‧商君列傳》 Sima Qian:"Biography of Lord Shang", *Records of the Grand Historian*】

一法立，一弊生。 For every law there springs a drawback. 【俗語 Common saying】

一日官司十日打。 Fight a lawsuit for one day and it will go on for ten. 【俗語 Common saying】

有治人，無治法。 There are people who rule, but no laws that rule. 【荀況《荀子‧君道第十二》 Xun Kuang: Chapter 12, "The Way to be a Lord", *Xunzi*】

緣法而治，按功而賞。 Follow the laws in governing, and give rewards according to merits. 【商鞅《商君書‧君臣》 Shang Yang:"The Ruler and Ministers", *The Works of Shang Yang*】

知情不舉，罪加一等。 One who conceals what he knows of a case is doubly guilty. 【石玉昆《三俠五義‧第八十一回》 Shi Yukun: Chapter 81, *The Three Heroes and Five Gallants*】

Laziness

不怕晚，祗怕懶。 Better late than never. 【俗語 Common saying】

大懶使小懶 —— 懶對懶。 The laziest order about the less lazy. 【歇後語 End-clipper】

東不管，西不管，吃飯選大碗。 A person who does not concern himself with anything but chooses to eat with a large bowl. 【俗語 Common saying】

凍的是懶人，餓的是閒人。 A lazy person freezes and an idle person starves. 【諺語 Proverb】

惰而侈則貧，力而儉則富。 One who is lazy and extravagant will be poor. One who is diligent and frugal will be rich. 【管仲《管子‧形勢解第六十四》 Guan Zhong: Chapter 64, "Explanation of the Conditions and Circumstances", *Guanzi*】

逢讒必懶，逢懶必讒。 One who is greedy for good food is sure to be lazy and one who is lazy is sure to be greedy for good food. 【俗語 Common saying】

橫針不拈，竪針不動。 Be too lazy to thread a needle. 【諺語 Proverb】

【曹雪芹《紅樓夢‧第六十二回》Cao Xueqin: Chapter 62, *A Dream of the Red Chamber*】

家懶外頭勤。 A loafer at home and a hustler outside. 【俗語 Common saying】

懶惰無善行。 A lazy person cannot do good deeds. 【俗語 Common saying】

懶驢上磨屎尿多。 Idle folks lack no excuses. 【俗語 Common saying】

懶驢無輕馱，懶人無輕活。 A lazy sheep thinks its wool heavy. 【俗語 Common saying】

莫生懶惰意，休起怠荒心。 Neither loaf on the job nor seek for an easy life. 【吳承恩《西遊記‧第八十二回》Wu Cheng'en: Chapter 82, *Journey to the West*】

木頭人 —— 推一推，動一動。 A wooden person never moves without a push on it. 【歇後語 End-clipper】

四體不勤，五穀不分。 One who neither toils with his four limbs nor tells the five cereals apart. 【孔子《論語‧微子篇第十八》Confucius: Chapter 18, *The Analects of Confucius*】

討飯三年懶做官。 One gets used to living in idleness. 【俗語 Common saying】

踢倒油瓶也不扶。 One will not put up the oil bottle that one has kicked down. 【俗語 Common saying】

頹惰自甘，家道難成。 If one is lazy and self-indulgent, it is difficult to keep the house going. 【朱用純《朱子家訓》Zhu Yongchun: *Precepts of the Zhu Family*】

Leader

大匠無棄材。 To a great master, no materials are disposable. 【曹植〈當欲游南山行〉Cao Zhi:"Wanting to Roam about in the Southern Mountains"】

大國為臣不如小國為君。 Would rather be a leader than a follower. 【管仲《管子‧匡君小匡第二十》Guan Zhong: Chapter 20, "Rectification of the Lord", "Third Register", *Guanzi*】

給牽着鼻子走。 Be led by the nose. 【俗語 Common saying】【劉白羽《第二個太陽‧第九章》Liu Baiyu: Chapter 9, *The Second Sun*】

海上無魚蝦自大。 A dwarf in Lilliput would be thought a superbeing. 【俗語 Common saying】

火車跑得快，全靠車頭帶。 A train runs fast because of the pull of the locomotive. 【俗語 Common saying】

鳥中之鳳，魚中之龍。 Like the phoenix among birds and a dragon among fish, one stands out from one's fellows.【諺語 Proverb】

寧為雞口，莫為牛後。 Better be the head of a dog than the tail of a lion.【劉向《戰國策・韓策一》Liu Xiang:"Strategies of the State of Han, No. 1", *Strategies of the Warring States*】

寧做雞頭不做牛尾。 Better be the head of a dog than the tail of a lion.【劉向《戰國策・韓策一》Liu Xiang:" Strategies of the State of Han, No. 1", *Strategies of the Warring States*】

擒賊先擒王。 To catch rebels first catch their chief.【杜甫〈前出塞九首・其六〉Du Fu: "Nine Poems out of the Border, No. 6"】

人無頭不行，鳥無翅不騰。 People will not act without a leader and birds cannot fly without wings. 【石玉崑《小五義・第八十二回》Shi Yukun: Chapter 82, *The Five Younger Gallants*】

人有頭，家有主。 People have leaders as families, heads.【俗語 Common saying】

山中無老虎，猴子稱大王。 When there is no tiger in a mountain, monkeys call themselves king. 【吳敬梓《儒林外史・第三回》Wu Jingzi: Chapter 3, *An Unofficial History of the Scholars*】

蛇無頭不行。 A snake without a head cannot crawl.【諺語 Proverb】 【施耐庵《水滸傳・第六十回》Shi Nai'an: Chapter 60, *Outlaws of the Marshes*】

蜀中無大將，廖化當先鋒。 In the country of the blind, the one-eyed man is king.【羅貫中《三國演義・第一百一十三回》Luo Guanzhong: Chapter 113, *Romance of the Three Kingdoms*】

天無二日，國無二主。 Heaven does not have two suns, and a country, two rulers.【孟軻《孟子・萬章上》Meng Ke: Chapter 10, Part 1, *Mencius*】

一馬當先，萬馬奔騰。 One horse takes the lead and ten thousand horses gallop after it.【俗語 Common saying】

一山難容二虎。 It is difficult to have two tigers in a mountain. 【俗語 Common saying】【歐陽山《三家巷・第十五章》Ouyang Shan: Chapter 15, *Three Alleys*】

Leaf

見一葉落而知歲之將暮。 On seeing the fall of a single leaf, we know that the year is coming to an end.【劉安《淮南子・說山訓第十六》Liu An: Chapter 16, "Discourse on Mountains", *Huainanzi*】

落葉滿空山，何處尋行跡。
The fallen leaves covered the deserted mountain, where could I find your way?【韋應物〈寄全椒山中道士〉Wei Yingwu:"To the Mountain Hermit at Quanjiao"】

秋色在葉，秋聲在竹。The colour of autumn is on the leaves, and the sound of autumn, on the bamboo.【諺語 Proverb】

停車坐愛楓林晚，霜葉紅於二月花。I stop my carriage, sit and enjoy the maple forest in the evening. The frosted maple leaves are redder than flowers in the second month of the year.【杜牧〈山行〉Du Mu: "Driving by the Mountain"】

無邊落木蕭蕭下，不盡長江滾滾來。Boundless leaves rustle down in the whistling wind, and the waters in the Changjiang River flow without cease.【杜甫〈登高〉Du Fu:"Ascending the Height"】

一葉葉，一聲聲，空階滴到明。A leaf follows by a leaf, a sound follows by another sound, they drop to the empty steps till morning.【溫庭筠〈更漏子〉Wen Tingyun:"Water Clock"】

Learning

八十歲學吹打 —— 上氣不接下氣。Learn to play trumpet and drum at the age of eighty – being out of breath.【歇後語 End-clipper】

八十歲學繡花 —— 老來奮發。An old dog will learn no new tricks.【歇後語 End-clipper】

博學而不窮，篤學而不倦。Learn extensively and never end; practise resolutely and never feel tired.【《禮記・儒行第四十一》Chapter 41, "The Conduct of a Confucian Scholar", The Book of Rites】

博學而篤志，切問而近思。Learn widely and be resolute in your aspirations, enquire earnestly and reflect on what is at hand.【孔子《論語・子張篇第十九》Confucius: Chapter 19, The Analects of Confucius】

博學之，審問之，慎思之，明辯之，篤行之。Learn extensively, enquire carefully, think deeply, analyse intelligently, and practise diligently.【《禮記・中庸第三十一章》Chapter 31, "Doctrine of the Mean", The Book of Rites】

不能則學，不知則問。If you can't do it, learn it; if you don't know, ask about it.【荀況《荀子・非十二子第六》Xun Kuang: Chapter 6, "Against the Twelve Masters", Xunzi】

不怕不知，祇怕不學。Lack of knowledge is not as terrible as refusing to learn.【諺語 Proverb】

不學不成，不問不知。If you don't learn, you have no achievement; if you don't ask, you have no knowledge.【王充《論衡・實知第七十八卷》Wang Chong: Chapter 78,

"The Knowledge of Truth", *Critical Essays*】

不知理義，生於不學。 Ignorance of principles and righteousness is due to a lack of learning. 【呂不韋《呂氏春秋‧勸學》Lu Buwei:"Exhortation to Learning", *Master Lu's Spring and Autumn Annals*】

大凡為學，先須立志。 In general, those who intend to learn must first establish their determination. 【張履祥《初學備忘》Zhang Luxiang: *Memorandum for Beginners of Learning*】

大學之道，在明明德，在親民，在止於至善。 The way of great learning lies in displaying enlightened virtue, loving the people, and coming to rest in the utmost goodness. 【《禮記‧大學第四十二》Chapter 42, "The Great Learning", *The Book of Rites*】

獨學而無友，則孤陋而寡聞。 Learning all by oneself without discussing with friends, one becomes ignorant and ill-informed. 【《禮記‧學記第十八》Chapter 18, "Records on the Subject of Education", *The Book of Rites*】

凡學，必務盡業，心則無營。 In learning, one must make one's utmost efforts to progress and one's mind should not go astray. 【呂不韋《呂氏春秋‧勸學》Lu Buwei:"Exhortation to Learning", *Master Lu's Spring and Autumn Annals*】

凡學之道，嚴師為難。 In general, the way of learning is most beset by the difficulty of finding a strict teacher. 【《禮記‧學記第十八》Chapter 18, "Records on the Subject of Education", *The Book of Rites*】

夫學者猶種樹也，春玩其華，秋登其實。 Learning is like planting trees, allowing us to enjoy their flowers in spring and harvest their fruits in autumn. 【顏之推《顏氏家訓‧勉學》Yan Zhitui:"Exhortation to Learning", *Family Instructions of Master Yan*】

苟不學，曷為人。 If you do not learn, how can you behave like a decent person? 【王應麟《三字經》Wang Yinglin: *Three-Character Classic*】

古人學問無遺力，少壯工夫老始成。 The ancient people spared no efforts in learning because the efforts they made when young would begin to materialize when old. 【陸游〈冬夜讀書示子聿〉Lu You:"For My Son When Reading Books on a Night in Winter"】

古之學者必有師。 Those who learned in ancient times must have teachers. 【韓愈《昌黎先生集‧師說》Han Yu:"On Teaching", *Collected Works of Han Yu*】

古之學者為己，今之學者為人。 Scholars in ancient times studied for self-improvement whereas scholars today study to serve other people. 【孔子《論語‧憲問篇第十四》Confucius: Chapter 14, *The Analects of Confucius*】

好學近乎知。Fond of learning gets one closer to wisdom. 【《禮記‧中庸第三十一章》Chapter 31, "Doctrine of the Mean", *The Book of Rites*】

好學者如禾如稻，不學者如蒿如草。A person who is fond of learning is like a grain or rice, and a person who does not like learning is like wormwood or weed. 【《增廣賢文》*Words that Open up One's Mind and Enhance One's Wisdom*】

活到老，學到老。One is never too old to learn. 【俗語 Common saying】

見者易，學者難。Seeing something done is easy, but learning how to do it is difficult. 【《增廣賢文》*Words that Open up One's Mind and Enhance One's Wisdom*】

君子取人貴恕，及論學術，則不得不嚴。A gentleman values forgiveness in treating people, but when it comes to scholarship, he has to be very strict. 【方東樹《昭昧詹言》Fang Dongshu: *Casual Words by Zhaomei*】

君子之學貴慎始。A gentleman is cautious when he starts learning something. 【劉蓉《養晦堂詩文集‧習慣說》Liu Rong: "On Habit", *Collected Essays from the Hall of Seclusion*】

君子之學也，入乎耳，著乎心。The learning of a gentleman is such that it enters through his ears and stored in his mind. 【荀況《荀子‧勸學第一》Xun Kuang: Chapter 1, "Exhortation to Learning", *Xunzi*】

沒學爬就學走。Learn to run before learning to walk. 【俗語 Common saying】

前頭烏龜爬上路，後背烏龜趁路爬。When the tortoise in front climbs up the path, the tortoise behind follows. 【俗語 Common saying】

人不學，不如物。He who does not learn is not as good as an animal. 【王應麟《三字經》Wang Yinglin: *Three-Character Classic*】

人不學，不知義。A person who does not learn does not know what is righteousness. 【《禮記‧學記第十八》Chapter 18, "Records on the Subject of Education", *The Book of Rites*】

人而不學，雖無憂，如禽何？A person who does not learn, though free of worries, is not different from an animal. 【揚雄《法言‧學行》Yang Xiong: "Learning and Behaviour", *Exemplary Sayings*】

人生識字憂患始。Miseries in life begin with literacy. 【蘇軾〈石蒼舒醉墨堂〉Su Shi: "Shi Cangshu's Hall of Inebriant Ink"】

人學始知道，不學亦枉然。A person who begins to learn knows what is the proper way and a person who does not learn will live a life in vain. 【《增廣賢文》*Words that Open up One's Mind and Enhance One's Wisdom*】

人之學，如渴而飲河海，大飲則大盈，小飲則小盈。 To people, learning is like drinking from the river or the sea when they are thirsty. If they drink much, they gain much. If they drink little, they gain little. 【馬總《意林・物理論》Ma Zong: "On Principles Relating to Things", *Forest of Opinions*】

人之於學，避其所難而姑為其易者，斯自棄也矣。 In learning, if people elude what is difficult and just go for what is easy, this is self-renunciation. 【程顥，程頤《河南程氏粹言・論學篇》Cheng Hao and Cheng Yi: "On Learning", *Sayings of Masters Cheng of Henan*】

善學者，借人之長以補其短。 A good learner is one who borrows what others are good at to make up what one lacks. 【呂不韋《呂氏春秋・用眾》Lu Buwei: "Fulfill the Number", *Master Lu's Spring and Autumn Annals*】

數不盡的星星，渡不完的學海。 Stars are countless and the sea of learning is limitless. 【諺語 Proverb】

天下學問無邊。 Learning under heaven is boundless. 【俗語 Common saying】

為學日益，為道日損。 When pursuing learning, knowledge is increased daily; when pursuing the Way, actions are reduced daily. 【老子《道德經・第四十八章》Laozi: Chapter 48, *Daodejing*】

為學如堆木，後來者居上。 Learning is like piling up logs of wood, the later ones are on top of others. 【司馬遷《史記・汲鄭列傳》Sima Qian: "Biography of Ji Zheng", *Records of the Grand Historian*】

溫故而知新，可以為師矣。 If you review what you have learned and know new things, you can become a teacher. 【孔子《論語・為政篇第二》Confucius: Chapter 2, *The Analects of Confucius*】

務正學以言，無曲學以阿世。 Strive to base your words on correct learning and don't twist your learning around to flatter the age. 【司馬遷《史記・儒林列傳》Sima Qian: "Biographies of Confucian Scholars", *Records of the Grand Historian*】

習善則善，習惡則惡。 Learn what is good and you will be good; learn what is evil and you will be evil. 【俗語 Common saying】

修學好古，實事求是。 Pursue learning and love the ancient classics, and seek truth from facts. 【班固《漢書・河間獻王傳》Ban Gu: "Biography of King Xian of Hejian", *History of the Han*】

學百藝而無一精。 Jack of all trades and master of none. 【諺語 Proverb】

學不必博，要之有用。 Learning does not need to be comprehensive, for what is important is that it is useful. 【羅大經《鶴林玉露・學仕》Luo

Dajing:"Learning and Officialdom", *Jade Dew of the Crane Forest*】

學不可以已。 Learning cannot be ceased.【荀況《荀子‧勸學第一》Xun Kuang: Chapter 1, "Exhortation to Learning", *Xunzi*】

學不厭，智也。 Learning tirelessly, you will gain wisdom.【孟軻《孟子‧公孫丑上》Meng Ke: Chapter 2, Part 1, *Mencius*】

活到老，學到老。 One lives and learns to one's old age.【諺語 Proverb】

學道如愚，才能稱賢。 In learning, you must learn as if you were stupid and then you can become a sage.【諺語 Proverb】

學而必習，習而必行。 After learning, one must review. After review, one must practise.【顏元《習齋言行錄》Yan Yuan: *Records of Speech and Acts in the Studio of Practice*】

學而不能行謂之病。 We call it sickness when what is learned cannot be put into practice.【莊周《莊子‧雜篇‧讓王第二十八》Zhuang Zhou: Chapter 28, "Abdicating Kingship", "Miscellaneous Chapters", *Zhuangzi*】

學而不思則惘，思而不學則殆。 He who learns but does not think is lost; he who thinks but does not learn remains puzzled.【孔子《論語‧為政篇第二》Confucius: Chapter 2, *The Analects of Confucius*】

學而不厭，誨人不倦。 Be insatiable in learning and tireless in teaching.【孔子《論語‧述而篇第七》Confucius: Chapter 7, *The Analects of Confucius*】

學而不己，闔棺乃止。 Learning is ceaseless and it ends when one is encased in coffin.【韓嬰《韓詩外傳‧卷八》Han Ying: Chapter 8, *Supplementary Commentary on the Book of Songs by Master Han*】

學而時習之，不亦悅乎。 Isn't it a pleasure to try out constantly what one has learned?【孔子《論語‧學而篇第一》Confucius: Chapter 1, *The Analects of Confucius*】

學好，千日不足；學壞，一日有餘。 A thousand days is not enough to learn to be good, but one day is more than enough to learn to be bad.【羅懋登《三寶太監西洋記‧第九十八回》Luo Maodeng: Chapter 98, *Sanbao Eunuch's Voyage to the Western Ocean*】

學好三年不得，學壞三日便成。 One cannot learn to be good in three years but one can learn to be bad in just three days.【俗語 Common saying】

學貴心悟，守舊無功。 What is to be valued in learning is to understand with one's own heart and one cannot achieve anything by sticking to the old conventions.【張載《經學理窟‧義理》Zhang Zai:"Righteousness and Principles", *The Profundities of the Classics*】

學壞容易學好難。 It is easy to learn what is bad but difficult to

learn what is good. 【俗語 Common saying】

學進於振而廢於窮。 Learning progresses with efforts and retreats when neglected. 【王符《潛夫論・贊學》Wang Fu:"In Praise of Learning", *Remarks by a Recluse*】

學然後知不足。 It is only through learning that you know your inadequacies. 【《禮記・學記第十八》Chapter 18, "Records on the Subject of Education", *The Book of Rites*】

學如不及，猶恐失之。 If I lag behind others in learning, I am still worried that I might forget what I learn. 【孔子《論語・泰伯篇第八》Confucius: Chapter 8, *The Analects of Confucius*】

學如逆水行舟，不進則退。 Learning is like sailing against the current; if it does not advance, it drops back. 【《增廣賢文》*Words that Open up One's Mind and Enhance One's Wisdom*】

學如牛毛，成如麟角。 Those who learn are as many as hairs on an ox, but those who succeed are as rare as phoenix feathers. 【蔣濟〈萬機論〉Jiang Ji:"On State Affairs"】

學識如何觀點書。 To know the learning of a person, you should examine how he punctuates classics. 【李匡義《資暇集・卷上》Li Qiangyi: Part 1, *Collection of Leisure Time Notes*】

學問就是路。 Learning is a road in itself. 【俗語 Common saying】

學問學問，不懂就問。 Learning is about asking questions whenever you do not understand. 【俗語 Common saying】

學問勤中得。 Learning is acquired through diligence. 【汪洙〈神童詩〉Wang Zhu:"Poem of a Talented Boy"】

學問之道，其得之不難者，失之必易。 The way of learning is such that what is not difficult to be acquired will be lost easily. 【魏源《魏源集・默觚》Wei Yuan:"Mogu", *Works of Wei Yuan*】

學問之道無他，求其放心而已矣。 The way of learning is nothing other than putting one's mind at rest. 【孟軻《孟子・告子章句上》Meng Ke: Chapter 6, Part 1, *Mencius*】

學者非必為仕，而仕者必如學。 One who learns may not be learning with the sole purpose of taking office; one who has taken office must learn. 【荀況《荀子・大略第二十七》Xun Kuang: Chapter 27, "Great Compendium", *Xunzi*】

學者貴於行之，而不貴於知之。 What is valued in learning is practice, not mere knowledge. 【司馬光〈答孔文仲司戶書〉Sima Guang:"A Letter in Reply to Kong Wenzhong"】

學者如登山焉，愈而益高。 The pursuit of learning is like climbing a mountain: the more you move, the higher you climb. 【徐幹《中論・治學》Xu Gan:"How to Learn", *Balanced Discourses*】

有匪君子，如切如磋，如琢如磨。A fine gentleman, when engaged in learning, is like cutting, grinding, carving, and polishing jade. 【《詩經‧衛風‧淇奧》"Banks of the Qi River", "Odes of Wei", *The Book of Odes*】

幼而學，壯而行。Learn while young and practise it when grown up. 【王應麟《三字經》Wang Yinglin: *Three-Character Classic*】

至博而約於精，深思而敏於行。Learn extensively but condense what you learn to the essentials; think deeply and be diligent in practice. 【方孝孺〈書籤〉Fang Xiaoru: "Bookmark"】

鐘不敲不自鳴，人不學心不靈。A bell without being struck does not toll and a person without learning cannot become clever. 【諺語 Proverb】

Leisure

不用閉門防俗客，愛閒能有幾人來？There is no need to close the door to prevent vulgar guests from coming, as I love leisure, there will be few visitors. 【呂夷簡〈天華寺〉Lu Yijian: "Tianhua Temple"】

此中有真意，欲辯已忘言。There is a profound truth in these things, but the moment I intend to explain it, the words slip me. 【陶淵明〈飲酒〉Tao Yuanming: "Drinking Wine"】

忙裏偷閒，苦中作樂。Snatch a little leisure from the rush of business and be happy amidst adverse circumstances. 【陳造〈同陳宰黃簿遊靈山八首〉Chen Zao: "Visiting Mount Ling with Chen Zai, Huang Bu, Eight Poems"】

清閒錢難買。Leisure is not something that money can easily buy. 【俗語 Common saying】

求閒不得閒。One who seeks leisure deliberately will not have leisure. 【司空圖〈漫書五首〉Sikong Tu: "Random Writings, Five Poems"】

日長睡起無情思，閒看兒童捉柳花。On a long day, I wake up from my nap with a mind empty of thoughts. I leisurely watch the children chasing willow catkins. 【楊萬里〈初夏睡起〉Yang Wanli: "Waking up in Early Summer"】

若問閒情都幾許？一川煙草，滿城風絮，梅子黃時雨。How much leisurely feelings do I have? As much as a river full of hazy grass, a town full of wind-borne catkins, and a sky full of plum-ripening seasonal rain. 【賀鑄〈青玉案〉He Zhu: "To the Tune of Green Jade Table"】

山寺日高僧未起，算來名利不如閒。The monks of the temple do not get up until the sun is high in the sky; so one who aspires to fame and fortune has not as much enjoyment as the other one who does nothing. 【高明〈琵琶記·第十六·丹陛陳情〉Gao Ming: Chapter 16, "Dan Bi Making His Case", "Tale of the *Pipa*"】

天津橋上無人識，獨倚欄杆看落暉。 I was on the Tianjin Bridge. Nobody knew me and I leaned against the balustrades all by myself to watch the setting sun. 【黃巢〈自題畫像〉Huang Chao: "Inscribing Self-Portrait"】

天意憐幽草，人間重晚晴。 The will of Heaven pities the solitary grass, and the world of man treasures the beautiful evening.

【李商隱〈晚晴〉Li Shangyin: "Fine Evening"】

因過竹院逢僧話，又得浮生半日閒。 As I passed by the bamboo court, I met a monk and conversed with him. Thus I had half a day's leisure in this floating life. 【李涉〈登山〉Li She: "Climbing up a Mountain"】

終年無客常關閉，終日無心常自閒。 Since no one visits me the whole year round, my hut is always closed. Since every day my mind is not occupied, I always enjoy my leisure. 【王維〈答張五弟〉Wang Wei: "A Reply to Brother Zhang"】

Letter

尺紙從頭徹尾空，憶人全在不言中。 The letter you sent me is totally blank; you miss me without any words. 【郭暉遠之妻〈寄夫〉Wife of Guo Huiyuan: "Sent to My Husband"】

烽火連三月，家書抵萬金。 The flames of war have been burning for three months and letters from home are worth ten thousand pieces of gold. 【杜甫〈春望〉Du Fu: "Spring Sight"】

紅紙一封書後信，綠芽十片火前春。 A letter on red paper follows a letter; ten fire-roasted-spring tea leaves green-budded. 【白居易〈謝李六郎中寄新蜀茶〉Bai Juyi: "Thanking Li Xuan for Sending

Me Newly Plucked Tea Leaves from Sichuan"】

江水三千里，家書十五行，行行無別語，祇道早還鄉。 Waters in the river run for three thousand miles and I received a family letter of fifteen lines. There is nothing said in each line, just repeating the same words: "Come back to the hometown as early as you can". 【袁凱〈京師得家書〉Yuan Kai: "Receiving a Family Letter at the Capital"】

山盟雖在，錦書難托。 Our oath is still in our hearts, but it's hard to convey our feelings through brocade letters.【陸游〈釵頭鳳〉Lu You:"The Phoenix Hairpin"】

天外魚書絕，征人豈念家？ In the distant land, it is not possible to communicate by letters; do the soldiers miss their families? 【宋凌雲〈偶成〉Song Lingyun:"Impromptu Poem"】

一行書信千行淚，寒到君邊衣到無。 A thousand streams of tears stained every line of my letter: has the robe arrived upon the coming of the cold weather? 【陳玉蘭〈寄夫〉Chen Yulan:"To My Husband"】

Life

曖曖遠人村，依依墟里煙。 The distant villages are dim, and the smoke from the neighbouring chimneys is gentle. 【陶淵明〈歸園田居〉Tao Yuanming:"Returning to My Rural Home"】

飽食終日，無所用心。 Loaf around all day long and do nothing. 【孔子《論語・陽貨篇第十七》Confucius: Chapter 17, The Analects of Confucius】

晨興理荒穢，帶月荷鋤歸。 Early in the morning, I rise to remove the weeds; under the moonlight I return home carrying my shovel on my shoulder. 【陶淵明〈歸園田居〉Tao Yuanming:"Returning to My Rural Home"】

燈紅酒綠，紙醉金迷。 Lead a life of debauchery. 【李涵秋《近十年目睹之怪現狀・第三回》Li Hanqiu: Chapter 3, Bizarre Happenings Eyewitnessed over the Last Ten Years】

燈火不夜，笙歌長春。 The lights of the lanterns turn the night into day. The flutes and singing make an eternal spring. 【俗語 Common saying】

對酒當歌，人生幾何。 We should sing in front of the wine. How long does our life last? 【曹操〈短歌行〉Cao Cao:"A Short Poem"】

飯來張口，衣來伸手。 Open one's mouth to be fed and hold out one's hands to be dressed. 【文康《兒女英雄傳・第三十一回》Wen Kang: Chapter 31, Biographies of Young Heroes and Heroines】

浮生若夢，不可強求。 Our floating life is like a dream, there is no point trying to get everything. 【俗語 Common saying】

浮生若夢，為歡幾何？ Our floating life is like a dream, but how much pleasure can we indulge in? 【李白〈春夜宴桃李園序〉Li Bai:"Preface to a Banquet on a Night in Spring in the Peach and Plum Garden"】

久在樊籠裏，復得返自然。 Long confined in a cage, I am again at one with nature. 【陶淵明〈歸田園

居〉Tao Yuanming:"Returning to My Rural Home"】

糧收萬石，也要粗茶淡飯。 Even when one has ten thousand bushels of grain, one still needs to have simple food and plain tea.【俗語 Common saying】

沒有十全十美的人生。 There is no rose without a thorn.【諺語 Proverb】

千金難買一口氣。 Even a thousand taels of gold cannot buy you one breath of life.【孔厥，袁靜《新兒女英雄傳·第二十四回》Kong Jue and Yuan Jing: Chapter 24, *New Biographies of Heroes and Heroines*】

前世不修今世苦。 The lack of self-cultivation in morals in one's previous existence is responsible for one's sufferings in the present life.【俗語 Common saying】

且喜胸中無一事，一生常在平易中。 I am glad that there is nothing on my mind, so my life has always been in ease and comfort.【徐積〈送晦叔〉Xu Ji:"To Uncle Hui"】

人生百年如過客。 One may live a hundred years, yet one is but a transient guest of this world.【康海〈王蘭卿·第四折〉Kang Hai: Scene 4, "Wang Lanqing"】

人生到處知何似？應似飛鴻踏雪泥。 Do you know what it is like moving from one place to another throughout one's life? It is, I should say, like a swan's traces on mud or snow.【蘇軾〈和子由澠池懷舊〉Su Shi:"Meditating on the Past with Ziyou at Pond Min"】

人生得意須盡歡，莫使金樽空對月。 When one has one's way in life, one must enjoy it to the full. The golden wine cup must not face the moon unfilled.【李白〈將進酒〉Li Bai:"About to Drink Wine"】

人生短暫，日近墓穴。 Life is short. Each day one is getting closer to the grave.【俗語 Common saying】

人生苦短，及時行樂。 Life is regrettably short and one should enjoy oneself while there is still time.【俗語 Common saying】

人生寄一世，奄忽若飆塵。 The life of a person lasts but one generation; it is like dust swirling by wind.【佚名《古詩十九首·今日良宴會》Anonymous:"Today We Hold a Splendid Banquet", *Nineteen Ancient Poems*】

人生看得幾清明。 How many times in one's life can one see such snowy and lovely plum blossoms?【蘇軾〈東欄梨花〉Su Shi:"Plum Blossoms at the East Gate"】

人生如白駒過隙。 The life of a person is like a white horse passing by a crevice.【莊周《莊子·外篇·知北遊第二十二》：Zhuang Zhou: Chapter 22, "Knowledge Wanders North", "Outer Chapters", *Zhuangzi*】

人生如航海。 Life is like a voyage.【俗語 Common saying】

人生如寄。 Life is like boarding in this world. 【曹丕〈善哉行〉Cao Pi: "Do Good Work"】

人生如夢，一樽還酹江月。 Life is like a dream, so allow me to librate a cup of wine to the river. 【蘇軾〈念奴嬌·赤壁懷古〉Su Shi:"Meditating on the Past at Red Cliff: To the Tune of Missing the Charm of a Young Maid"】

人生如朝露。 Life is like the morning dew. 【班固《漢書·蘇武傳》Ban Gu:"Biography of Su Wu", *History of the Han*】

人生如盞走馬燈。 Life is like a running horse lantern. 【俗語 Common saying】

人生若塵露，天道邈悠悠。 Life is like dust and dew, but the way of heaven is everlasting. 【秦嘉〈贈婦詩〉Qin Jia:"To a Woman"】

人生失意無南北。 Disappointment in life makes no difference between south and north. 【王安石〈明妃曲〉Wang Anshi:"Song of the Ming Imperial Concubine"】

人生天地間，忽如遠行客。 Man lives between heaven and earth, as sudden as a guest travelling from afar. 【佚名《古詩十九首·青青陵上柏》Anonymous:"Green, Green Cypress on the Mound", *Nineteen Ancient Poems*】

人生天地之間，若白駒過隙，忽然而已。 A person's life in heaven and earth is like a white horse galloping past a crevice. It is all but in a sudden. 【莊周《莊子·外篇·知北遊第二十二》：Zhuang Zhou: Chapter 22, "Knowledge Wanders North", "Outer Chapters", *Zhuangzi*】

人生無根蒂，飄如陌上塵。 Without a root and a base, a person's life drifts like dust on the path. 【陶淵明〈雜詩〉Tao Yuanming:"A Random Poem"】

人生無坦途。 Life is not a plain sail. 【俗語 Common saying】

人生似幻化，終當歸空無。 Life is just like an illusion; it eventually will return to emptiness. 【陶淵明〈歸園田居〉Tao Yuanming:"Returning to Country and Farming"】

人生一盤棋。 Life is but a game of chess. 【俗語 Common saying】

人生在世不稱意，明朝散髮弄扁舟。 As things in the world do not go the way I want, I shall let loose my hair and take to a small boat tomorrow morning. 【李白〈宣州謝朓樓餞別校書叔雲〉Li Bai:"Farewell to Uncle Yun, the Imperial Librarian, at Xie Tiao's Tower in Xuanzhou"】

人生值艱難，不如路旁草。 When one's life is in difficulty, it is not worth the grass by the roadside. 【方回〈路旁草〉Fang Hui:"Grass by the Roadside"】

人生祇似風前絮，歡也零星，悲也零星，都作連江點點萍。 Life is just like catkins before the wind, with bits of joy and bits of sorrow; all of them are bits of floating weeds in a river. 【王國維

〈採桑子〉Wang Guowei: "To the Tune of Picking Mulberries"】

人生總有盡頭日。 The life of a person will eventually come to an end.【俗語 Common saying】

人世幾登高，寂寞黃花酒。 How many times in our life will we pass the Qingming Festival? I silently drink the chrysanthemum wine alone.【汪時元〈九日舟中〉Wang Shiyuan: "In a Boat on the Qingming Festival"】

人世幾回傷心事，山形依舊枕寒流。 How many times, in this human world, do we have sad events, yet the mountains, as ever, pillow the cold water.【劉禹錫〈西塞山懷古〉Liu Yuxi: "Meditating on the Past at West Fort Mountain"】

人是水中泡。 A person is but a bubble in water.【俗語 Common saying】

人生在世一場戲。 Life is but a drama on stage.【俗語 Common saying】

生活生活，非生而活。 Life is not about living to be alive.【俗語 Common saying】

生，亦我所欲也；義，亦我所欲也。二者不可兼得，捨生而取義者也。 I like life and I also like righteousness. But if I have to choose between them, I will forsake life and take righteousness.【孟軻《孟子·告子章句上》Meng Ke: Chapter 6, Part 1, Mencius】

生於憂患，死於安樂。 We thrive in adversity and perish in ease and comfort.【孟軻《孟子·告子章句下》Meng Ke: Chapter 6, Part 2, Mencius】

盛年不重來，一日難再晨。 The prime of our lives does not come again, and a day can never dawn twice.【陶淵明〈雜詩〉Tao Yuanming: "Miscellaneous Poems"】

世路如今已慣，此心到處悠然。 I am now used to life high and low, and my heart is at ease wherever I go.【張孝祥〈西江月〉Zhang Xiaoxiang: "To the Tune of the Moon over the West River"】

世事一場大夢，人生幾度秋涼。 Things in this world are a huge dream, for how many times we have the cool autumn in our life.【蘇軾〈西江月·黃州中秋〉Su Shi: "Mid-Autumn at Huangzhou: To the Tune of the Moon over the West River"】

世事雲千變，浮生夢一場。 Things in this world have myriad changes like clouds, and the floating life is but a dream.【王庭筠〈書西齋〉Wang Tingyun: "Shuxi Studio"】

誰道人生無再少，門前流水尚能西。 Who says that people can never regain their youth again? Even the running water before the gate can flow westward.【蘇軾〈浣溪沙〉Su Shi: "To the Tune of Sand of Silk-Washing Stream"】

舞台小人生，人生大舞台。 The stage is a miniature of life and

life is a large stage. 【俗語 Common saying】

誤落塵網中，一去三十年。For thirty years, I have, by accident, been enmeshed in the web of worldly affairs. 【陶淵明〈歸田園居〉Tao Yuanming:"Returning to My Rural Home"】

賢人多薄命。Able and virtuous people are mostly unfortunate in life. 【諺語 Proverb】

小舟從此逝，江海寄餘生。I might go in a small boat to spend the rest of my life on rivers and seas. 【蘇軾〈臨江仙·夜歸臨皋〉Su Shi:"Returning to Lingao by Night: To the Tune of an Immortal by the River"】

行樂須及時。Enjoy life before it is too late. 【李白〈月下獨酌〉Li Bai:"Drinking Alone under the Moon"】

休道黃金貴，安樂最值錢。Don't say that gold is valuable, as living in peace and content is worth more. 【關漢卿〈裴度還帶·第二折〉Guan Hanqing: Scene 2, "Pei Du Returned the Belt He Found"】

尋尋覓覓，冷冷清清，淒淒慘慘戚戚。All my life, I have been searching for something I missed. I feel cold and lonely, dreadfully hurtful and sorrowful. 【李清照〈聲聲慢〉Li Qingzhao:"To the Tune of Adagio"】

中年歲月苦風飄。The months and years at middle age are bitter, like floating with the wind. 【黃遵憲〈海上雜感〉Huang Zunxian:"Random Thoughts at Sea"】

Life and death

哀莫哀兮生別離，樂莫樂兮心相惜。Nothing is more sorrowful than the separation of the living and the dead, and nothing is happier than loving each other. 【屈原《離騷·九歌·少司令》Qu Yuan:"The Little Lords of Life", "The Nine Songs", *The Sorrows at Parting*】

不求同年同日生，但求同年同日死。We would not ask to have been born on the same day of the same year, but we want to die on the same day of the

same year. 【關漢卿《單刀會》Guan Hanqing:"Single-sword Meeting"】

不生亦不滅，不常亦不斷，不一亦不異，不來亦不去。Neither born nor destroyed; neither permanent nor ceased; neither identical nor different; neither comes nor goes. 【龍樹《中論·皈敬偈》Nagarjuna:"Dedicatory Verses", *Treatise on the Middle Path Doctrine*】

不是你死，就是我亡。Either you or I have to die. 【俗語 Common saying】

方生方死，方死方生。 Things are now life and death; now death and life. 【莊周《莊子・內篇・齊物論第二》Zhuang Zhou: Chapter 2, "On the Equality of Things", "Inner Chapters", *Zhuangzi*】

螻蟻尚且貪生，為人何不惜命。 Even mole crickets and ants care for life, let alone human beings. 【諺語 Proverb】【馬致遠〈薦福碑・第三折〉Ma Zhiyuan: Scene 3, "Fortune-recommending Tablet"】

寧可站着死，不願跪着生。 One would rather die on one's feet than live on one's knees. 【俗語 Common saying】

寧鳴而死，不默而生。 I would rather die for speaking out than to live and be silent. 【范仲淹〈靈烏賦〉: Fan Zhong Yan: "Ode to the Owl"】

拼死吃河豚 —— 不要命了。 Eating a globefish–risking one's life. 【歇後語 End-clipper】

求生不得，求死不能。 Can neither live or die. 【俗語 Common saying】

人居一世間，忽若風吹塵。 People live for a lifetime, as sudden as the wind blowing away the dust. 【曹植〈薤露行〉Cao Zhi: "Song on the Dew on Oniongrass"】

人生百年，終歸一死。 Even if one lives to one hundred years old, one eventually will die. 【沈復《浮生六記・卷三》Shen Fu: Chapter 3, *Six Chapters of a Floating Life*】

人生不過百，常懷千歲憂。 One's life is no more than a hundred years, yet one worries about things in a thousand years. 【佚名《古詩十九首》Anonymous: *Nineteen Ancient Poems*】

人生但講前三十。 The life of a person is all about what has been achieved in the first thirty years. 【俗語 Common saying】

人生非金石，豈能長壽考？ The life of a human being is not gold or stone, how can we live to old age? 【佚名《古詩十九首》Anonymous: *Nineteen Ancient Poems*】

人生天地之間，若白駒之過卻，忽然而已。 The existence of a human being in the space between heaven and earth is as swift as a white colt galloping past a chink. 【莊周《莊子・外篇・知北遊第二十二》: Zhuang Zhou: Chapter 22, "Knowledge Wanders North", "Outer Chapters", *Zhuangzi*】

人生一世，草生一秋。 A person lives only one lifetime and grass lasts only an autumn. 【《增廣賢文》Words that Open up One's Mind and Enhance One's Wisdom】

人生自有命，但恨生日稀。 The life of a person is destined, what is regrettable is that our living days are short. 【孔融〈雜詩〉Kong Rong: "Miscellaneous Poems"】

人死不能復生。 A dead person cannot be restored to life. 【俗語 Common saying】

人為刀俎，我為魚肉。 One is like a piece of meat placed on one's chopping block – one's life is at the mercy of those in power. 【司馬遷《史記‧項羽本紀》Sima Qian: "Annals of Xiang Yu", *Records of the Grand Historian*】

人有生死，物有毀壞。 For human beings, there are life and death; for things, there is wear-and-tear or destruction. 【俗語 Common saying】

日方中方睨，物方生方死。 The sun at noon is the sun beginning to set and a being born is a being beginning to die. 【莊周《莊子‧雜篇‧天下第三十三》Zhuang Zhou: Chapter 33, "All under Heaven", "Miscellaneous Chapters", *Zhuangzi*】

善生者必善死。 He who lives his life well will surely die in a good way. 【莊元臣《叔苴子》Zhuang Yuanchen: *Shujuzi*】

生不帶來，死不帶去。 At birth, one does not bring anything; at death, one does not take away anything. 【俗語 Common saying】

生的偉大，死的光榮。 A great life and a glorious death. 【俗語 Common saying】

生而辱，不如死而榮。 Living in disgrace is not as good as dying in honour. 【司馬遷《史記‧范睢蔡澤列傳》Sima Qian: "Biographies of Fan Sui and Cai Ze", *Records of the Grand Historian*】

生命短促，藝術流長。 Life is short but art is long. 【俗語 Common saying】

生乃死之始，死即生之歸。 Birth is the beginning of death and death is the end of life. 【俗語 Common saying】

生死中年兩不堪，生非容易死非甘。 At midage, life and death are both painful things, for life is not easy and death is not voluntary. 【郁達夫〈病中作〉Yu Dafu: "Written during Illness"】

生以救時，死以明道。 When alive, one saves the society from danger; when dead, one seeks to illustrate the Way. 【王通《中說‧周公》Wang Tong: "Lord Zhou", *Analects of Wenzhongzi*】

生有益於人，死不害於人。 When alive, one benefits people; when dead, one does not leave a legacy of trouble. 【《禮記‧檀弓上第三》Chapter 3, "Tangong, Part 1", *The Book of Rites*】

生於憂患而死於安樂也。 We survive in adversity and perish in ease and comfort. 【孟軻《孟子‧告子章句下》Meng Ke: Chapter 6, Part 2, *Mencius*】

生在蘇州，食在廣州，穿在杭州，死在柳州。 It would be perfect for one to be born in Suzhou, fed in Guangzhou, clad in Hangzhou, and buried in Liuzhou. 【俗語 Common saying】

事死如事生，事亡如事存。 One serves the dead as if they

were still alive and serves the departed as if they were still around. 【《禮記・中庸第三十一章》 Chapter 31, "Doctrine of the Mean", *The Book of Rites*】

天地無終極，人命若朝霞。 Heaven and earth have no end, but the life of a person is like morning dew. 【曹植〈送應氏二首〉 Cao Zhi: "Two Poems Presented to the Person Surnamed Ying"】

天地之大德曰生。 Life is the greatest virtue of heaven and earth. 【《易經・繫辭上》 "Appended Remarks, Part 1", *The Book of Changes*】

同生死，共患難。 Together we share life and death, weal and woe. 【魏徵《隋書・鄭譯傳》 Wei Zheng: "Biography of Zheng Yi", *History of the Sui*】

有其生必有其死。 What has life will have death. 【俗語 Common saying】

Livelihood

長太息以掩涕兮，哀民生之多艱。 I sigh and wipe away my tears, lamenting the difficult livelihood of the people. 【屈原 《楚辭・離騷・九章・抽思》 Qu Yuan: Chapter 9, "Stray Thoughts", "The Sorrows at Parting", *The Songs of Chu*】

此處無緣，他鄉再化。 If one cannot find alms here, one will beg in other places. 【諺語 Proverb】

飯有三餐不餓，衣有三件不破。 One would not be hungry when one has three meals a day. One is satisfied when one has three clothes which are intact. 【諺語 Proverb】

管山的吃山，管水的吃水。 Those who manage mountains rely on mountains for their livelihood, and those who tend rivers rely on the rivers for their livelihood. 【吳敬梓《儒林外史・第四十一回》 Wu Jingzi: Chapter 41, *An Unofficial History of the World of Literati*】

過一天算一天。 Live one day at a time. 【俗語 Common saying】

開門七件事：柴米油鹽醬醋茶。 There are seven daily needs: fuel, rice, oil, salt, soya sauce, vinegar, and tea. 【諺語 Proverb】

兩腳忙忙走，祇為身和口。 The two feet keep themselves busy for the body and mouth's sake. 【俗語 Common saying】

寧可自食其力，不可坐吃山空。 Rather earn one's living than use up all one's fortune by sitting idle and eating. 【諺語 Proverb】

日求三餐，夜求一宿。 Seek to have three meals a day and sleep at night. 【諺語 Proverb】

一方水土養一方人。 Each place has its own way of supporting its inhabitants. 【俗語 Common saying】

欲求溫飽，勤儉為要。 To get enough to eat and wear, you must first be hardworking and frugal. 【諺語 Proverb】

Living

吃飯不管事。 Lead an idle life. 【俗語 Common saying】

吃賣命飯的。 Earn a living by risking one's neck. 【俗語 Common saying】【曹禺〈日出・第一幕〉Cao Yu: Scene 1, "Sunrise"】

久居別家招人嫌。 To stay in others' home too long incurs odium. 【俗語 Common saying】

久住令人賤。 One who lives in others' home for a long time will be looked down on. 【《增廣賢文》Words that Open up One's Mind and Enhance One's Wisdom】

久住令人厭，勤來親也疏。 One who stays long at others' home will be detested. Frequent visits will make a relative distant. 【《增廣賢文》Words that Open up One's Mind and Enhance One's Wisdom】

鄰國相望，雞犬之聲相聞。民至老死，不相往來。 This is a place where the neighbouring kingdoms are in sight of one another and the cries of the roosters and the barking of dogs can be heard, and people never visit one another until they are old or about to die. 【老子《道德經・第八十章》Laozi: Chapter 80, Daodejing】

日食三餐，夜眠一榻。 One needs three meals a day and a bed to rest at night. 【吳承恩《西遊記・第五回》Wu Cheng'en: Chapter 5, Journey to the West】

獅虎不羣居。 Lions and tigers live by themselves. 【諺語 Proverb】

相見好，同住難。 It's nice to see each other from time to time, but to live together is difficult. 【諺語 Proverb】

相見易得好，久住難為人。 It is easy to have a good impression of each other when two persons meet each, but it will be difficult to live together for a long time. 【《增廣賢文》Words that Open up One's Mind and Enhance One's Wisdom】

小屋平頭墟落里，炊煙起處是人家。 Rows of small houses are built in villages; where there is smoke floating, there is a family living there. 【趙秉文〈北都望雪〉Zhao Bingwen: "Watching Snow from the Northern Capital"】

心安茅屋穩。 With ease of mind, one feels content living in a hut. 【范立本《明心寶鑑》Fan Liben: The Precious Mirror that Enlightens the Heart】

Longevity

飯後百步走，能活九十九。 Walk a mile after your meal, and you will have longevity of life. 【俗語 Common saying】

福如東海，壽比南山。 May your fortune be as boundless as the East Sea and your life as longlasting as the South Mountain. 【朱權〈荊釵記・第三齣〉Zhu Quan: Act 3, "The Bramble Hairpin"】

古人誰不死，何必較壽折。 The ancients without exception all died, and there is no point to compare longevity. 【蘇軾〈屈原塔〉Su Shi: "Qu Yuan Pagoda"】

皇帝有錢，難買萬萬歲。 However rich an emperor is, he cannot buy longevity. 【俗語 Common saying】

人活百歲不嫌多。 No one is tired of longevity even when one lives to a hundred years old. 【俗語 Common saying】

人間五福，惟壽為先。 Of the five kinds of happiness on earth, longevity comes first. 【諺語 Proverb】【沈泰《盛明雜劇・同甲會》Shen Tai: "The Meeting of People of the Same Age", Variety Plays from the High Ming】

人有可延之壽，亦有可折之壽。 The life of a person can be either lengthened or shortened. 【馮夢龍《喻世明言・第三十一卷》Feng Menglong: Chapter 31, Stories to Instruct the World】

善能壽老，惡能早亡。 To do good works, one can expect to live a long life; to do evil deeds, one will die young. 【《增廣賢文》Words that Open up One's Mind and Enhance One's Wisdom】

壽不利貧祇利富。 Longevity is only for the rich, not the poor. 【呂南公〈勿願壽〉Lu Nangong: "Don't Long for Longevity"】

與天地兮同壽，與日月兮齊光。 Be as long-living as heaven and earth and as bright as the sun and moon. 【屈原〈離騷〉Qu Yuan: The Sorrows at Parting】

要做長命人，莫做短命事。 If you want to live a long life, do not do evil deeds that injure your chances of longevity. 【俗語 Common saying】

Love

愛不貴濃而貴長。 Love is not valued for its thickness, but for its length. 【俗語 Common saying】

愛而知其惡，憎而知其善。 Like a person and yet you know what is not right in him; dislike a person and yet you know what is good in him. 【《禮記‧曲禮上第一》Chapter 1, "Summary of the Rules of Propriety, Part 1", *The Book of Rites*】

愛情不分貧富。 Love makes no distinction between the rich and the poor. 【俗語 Common saying】

愛情誠可貴，千萬莫求拜。 It is true that love is to be treasured, but it must be stressed that you should not beg for it. 【俗語 Common saying】

愛人者，人恆愛之。 One who loves others is loved by them. 【孟軻《孟子‧離婁下》Meng Ke: Chapter 4, Part 2, *Mencius*】

愛之欲其生，惡之欲其死。 If you love a person, you want him to live; if you hate a person, you want him to die. 【孔子《論語‧顏淵篇第十二》Confucius: Chapter 12, *The Analects of Confucius*】

不見也相思苦，便見也相思苦。 When we are separated, I am sick with love. When we meet, I am sick with love. 【鄭板橋〈踏莎行‧無題〉: Zheng Banqiao: "To the Tune of Walking on Grass: Without a Title"】

不堪盈手贈，還寢夢佳期。 As I cannot give you a handful of moonlight, I shall go back to sleep and dream of the good times we share together. 【張九齡〈望月懷遠〉Zhang Jiuling: "Gazing at the Moon and Thinking of My Loved One Far away"】

不能自愛，焉能愛人。 One who does not love oneself cannot love others. 【俗語 Common saying】

不寫情詞不寫詩，一方素帕寄心知。 I don't write love songs or love poems, a silk handkerchief says all my heart wants to say. 【佚名〈民歌〉Anonymous: "Folk Song"】

曾經滄海難為水，除卻巫山不是雲。 One who has experienced the waters of Canghai would not regard other waters as waters, and one who has seen the clouds of Mount Wu would not regard other clouds as clouds. 【元稹〈離思〉Yuan Zhen: "Thoughts of the Departed"】

痴心女子負心漢。 An infatuated girl being deserted by a heartless man. 【王實甫〈西廂記‧第三本第四折〉Wang Shifu: Act 3, Scene 4, "Romance of the Western Bower"】

臭豬頭有爛鼻子來聞。 A lover has no judge of beauty. 【俗語 Common saying】

但見新人笑，那聞舊人哭。 People only saw the new bride smiling, but would not hear the weeping of the ex-wife. 【杜甫〈佳人〉Du Fu: "A Beautiful Lady"】

但教心似金鈿堅，天上人間會相見。 I hope that our hearts would stay as true as gold, and we would meet in heaven above or in the world of men below. 【白居易〈長恨歌〉Bai Juyi: "Song of Everlasting Grief"】

多情爭似無情。 True love conceals. 【柳永〈清平樂・越調〉Liu Yong: "Chinese Opera from the Henan Province: To the Tune of Purity and Peace"】

泛愛眾而親仁。 Love one's fellow people and stay close to benevolence. 【孔子《論語・學而篇第一》Confucius: Chapter 1, *The Analects of Confucius*】

芳心既許，永矢不變。 A girl who loves a man will remain faithful to him forever. 【俗語 Common saying】

枋榔樹一條心。 Love somebody heart and soul. 【俗語 Common saying】

過盡千帆皆不是，斜暉脈脈水悠悠。 Many sails have passed me by, but not the one I have been waiting for. 【溫庭筠〈夢江南〉Wen Tingyun: "To the Tune of Dreaming of the South"】

海枯石爛心不變。 Seas may run dry and rocks may crumble, yet our hearts remain loyal to each other. 【俗語 Common saying】

海枯石爛，永不變心。 Seas may run dry and rocks may crumble, yet my loyalty to you will never change. 【俗語 Common saying】

海誓山盟，永不變心。 Lovers make solemn vows and pledges, promising each other that their hearts will never change. 【俗語 Common saying】

後宮佳麗三千人，三千寵愛在一身。 In the Inner Palace there were three thousand beauties, yet all the favours for them were now bestowed on her only. 【白居易〈長恨歌〉Bai Juyi: "Song of Everlasting Grief"】

花自飄零水自流，一種相思，兩處閒愁。 Blossoms fall by themselves and water flows by itself; we have the same lovesickness, yet it is sorrow at two places. 【李清照〈一剪梅〉Li Qingzhao: "To the Tune of a Twig of Plum Blossoms"】

換我心，為你心，始知相憶深。 By exchanging my heart with yours, you would know how deeply I love you. 【顧夐〈訴衷情〉Gu Xiong: "To the Tune of Revealing the Inner Feelings"】

慧劍斬情絲。 Sever the thread of love with a sword of wisdom. 【俗語 Common saying】

今年元夜時，月與燈依舊，不見去年人，淚濕春衫袖。 This year on the night of the Lantern Festival, the moon and the lanterns are as before. My love from last year is nowhere to be seen, tears drench the sleeves of my spring dress. 【歐陽修〈生查子〉Ouyang Xiu: "To the Tune of Ripe Quince"】

兩情若是久長時，又豈在朝朝暮暮？ If our love will endure long, it makes no difference that we do not live together day and night. 【秦觀〈鵲橋仙〉Qin Guan: "To the Tune of an Immortal at the Magpie Bridge"】

落花有意，流水無情。 The fallen flowers pine for love, yet the flowing water does not have any feelings. 【釋惟白《續傳燈錄‧第二十九卷》Shi Weibai: Chapter 29, *A Sequel to the Records of the Transmission of the Lamp*】

男子痴，一時迷；女子痴，沒藥醫。 A man who is infatuated with a woman clings to her for only a short period of time, whereas a woman who is infatuated with a man cannot be cured by any medicine. 【諺語 Proverb】【徐復祚〈投梭記‧第二十齣〉Xu Fuzuo: Scene 20, "Picking Shuttles"】

平生不會相思，才會相思，便害相思。 I do not know until now what lovesickness is, then I know and I have since been addicted to it. 【徐再思〈折桂令‧春情〉Xu Zaisi: "Lovesickness"】

千年長交頸，歡愛不相忘。 We will not be separated for a thousand years and our joy and love will never be forgotten. 【佚名〈古絕句〉Anonymous: "An Ancient Quatrain"】

人人要結後生緣，儂祇今生結目前。 Everyone wants to tie knots in their future life, I only want to do so presently. 【黃遵憲〈山歌〉Huang Zunxian: "Mountain Song"】

人生自是有情癡，此恨不關風與月。 In our life, we cannot get away from love. My present grief has nothing to do with the moon and breezes. 【歐陽修〈玉樓春〉Ouyang Xiu: "To the Tune of Spring in the Jade Tower"】

仁者以其所愛及其所不愛。 A benevolent person extends his kindness from the ones he loves to the ones he doesn't love. 【孟軻《孟子‧盡心章句下》Meng Ke: Chapter 7, Part 2, *Mencius*】

日久不見，感情易變。 If lovers don't see each other for a long time, their love is apt to change. 【俗語 Common saying】

入我相思門，知我相思苦。長相思兮長相憶，短相思兮無窮極。 If you enter the gates of my longing, you will understand the depth of my pain. Long longings have lasting memories, while short longings never end. 【李白〈秋風詞〉Li Bai: "Autumn Breeze"】

若有變心，天雷擊頂。 If I cease to be faithful to you, thunder will strike me dead. 【俗語 Common saying】

三百六十病，唯有相思苦。 Of the three hundred and sixty sicknesses, lovesickness is the hardest to endure. 【馮夢龍《醒世恆言‧第二十八卷》Feng Menglong: Chapter 28, *Stories to Awaken the World*】

山盟雖在，錦書難托。 My pledge of love is still there, but it is hard to convey it through letters. 【陸游〈釵頭鳳〉Lu You: "To the Tune of Phoenix Hairpin"】

身無彩鳳雙飛翼，心有靈犀一點通。 Though we don't have on our body a pair of wings of the colourful phoenix, our hearts are linked and beat in unison. 【李商隱〈無題〉Li Shangyin:"Untitled Poem"】

他生莫作有情痴，人天無地着相思。 In my future life I will not be a person obsessed with love, for in this mundane world there is no place for me to place my lovesickness. 【況周頤〈浣溪沙〉Kuang Zhouyi:"One Thousand Years Old"】

天不老，情難絕，心似雙絲網，中有千千結。 Heaven does not grow old and love can never be severed. The heart is like two overlapping spider webs, with thousands of knots. 【張先〈千秋歲〉Zhang Xian:"One Thousand Years Old"】

天長地久，此心不變。 Heaven and earth are longlasting and my heart remains unchanged. 【俗語 Common saying】

天各一方，愛情不改。 Though separated in two different places under the sky, the love between lovers remains unchanged. 【俗語 Common saying】

天下多少有情事，世間滿眼無奈人。 Under heaven, there are many affairs of love; in the world of man, our eyes are filled with hopeless people. 【曹雪芹《紅樓夢》Cao Xueqin: A Dream of the Red Chamber】

天涯地角有窮時，祇有相思無盡處。 Even the sky has its limits and the earth has its bounds, however, my lovesickness does not end anywhere. 【晏殊〈木蘭花〉Yan Shu:"Magnolia Lyrics"】

投我以木瓜，報之以瓊琚。匪報也，永以為好也。 You give me a quince, and I give you in return a green jade. The jade is not for returning your favour, but to show my love to you forever. 【《詩經・衞風・木瓜》"Quince", "Odes of Wei", The Book of Odes】

問世間，情為何物？ I ask people in this world, what sort of a thing love is? 【元好問〈摸魚兒〉Yuan Haowen:"To the Tune of Groping for Fish"】

我泥中有你，你泥中有我。 In my mud, there is you and in your mud, there is me. 【管道升〈我儂詞〉Guan Daosheng:"You and I"】

相思病，無藥醫。 There is no medicine to cure lovesickness. 【俗語 Common saying】

襄王有夢，神女無心。 King of Chu, Xiang, dreamt of the beautiful girl in his dream, but the girl was not interested in him. 【宋玉〈高唐賦〉Song Yu:"Rhapsopy on the Gaotang Shrine"】

心相連，永不變。 Our hearts are linked: this will never change. 【俗語 Common saying】

心心復心心，結愛務在深。 Your heart and my heart, our hearts

are closely linked.【孟郊〈結愛〉Meng Jiao:"Entwined Love"】

心中事，眼中淚，意中人。Things in my heart, tears in my eyes, and the person on my mind.【張先〈行香子〉Zhang Xian:"Song of Incense"】

一把慧劍斬情絲。A sword of wisdom severs threads of love.【俗語 Common saying】

一朝情義淡，樣樣不順眼。Faults are thick where love is thin.【諺語 Proverb】

一朝人落泊，愛情生翼飛。When poverty comes in at the door, love flies out of the window.【俗語 Common saying】

一絲柳，一寸柔情。Each catkin of willow is an inch of tender passion.【吳文英〈風入松〉Wu Wenying:"To the Tune of Wine in the Pines"】

一枝穠艷露凝香，雲山巫雨枉斷腸。Dew on a twig of the red peony emits fragrance and our intimate contacts wring the hearts.【李白〈清平調〉Li Bai:"To the Tune of Purity and Peace"】

以前喜歡一個人，現在喜歡一個人。In the past, I loved a person. Now I like being all by myself.【俗語 Common saying】

易求無價寶，難得有情郎。It is easy to get priceless treasures but difficult to have a man who loves you.【魚玄機〈贈鄰女〉Yu Xuanji:"To the Girl Next Door"】

有情喝水飽。/ 有情飲水飽。People in love could satisfy their hunger only by drinking water.【俗語 Common saying】

欲人之愛己也，必先愛人；欲人之從己也，必先從人。If you want to be loved, you must love others first; if you want to be obeyed, you must obey others first.【左丘明《國語‧晉語四》Zuo Qiuming:"The Language of Jin, Part 4", *National Languages*】

願得一心人，白首不相離。I hope to have a person endearing to my heart and we will not be separated from each other even when we are white-haired.【卓文君〈白頭吟〉Zhuo Wenjun:"Song of White Hair"】

在天願作比翼鳥，在地願為連理枝。In heaven, we hope we are birds flying with wings entwined; on earth, we hope we are intertwined branches on a tree.【白居易〈長恨歌〉Bai Juyi:"Song of Everlasting Grief"】

知之愈深，愛之彌堅。The more you know it, the firmer you love it.【俗語 Common saying】

坐結行亦結，結盡百歲月。Sitting or walking, our hearts are closely linked; linked together, for as long as a hundred years.【孟郊〈結愛〉Meng Jiao:"Entwined Love"】

Loyalty

不怕虎生三個口，祇怕人有兩樣心。／不怕虎生三張嘴，只怕人有兩樣心。One is not afraid of a tiger with three mouths but is afraid of a person with a divided loyalty.【諺語 Proverb】

好馬不備二鞍，好女不嫁二夫。A good horse does not have two saddles and a good woman does not marry twice.【佚名《名賢集》Anonymous: *Collected Sayings of Famous Sages*】

火要空心，人要忠心。Fire must have a hollow inside and a human heart must be loyal.【王少堂《武松‧第八回》Wang Shaotang: Chapter 8, *Wu Song*】

家貧知孝子，國亂顯忠臣。A family in poverty tries the filial piety of a son and a country in trouble tests the loyalty of a minister.【佚名《名賢集》Anonymous: *Collected Sayings of Famous Sages*】

盡忠不能盡孝。One who is loyal to the country cannot stay at home to do his filial duties.【俗語 Common saying】【施世綸《施公案‧第六十二回》Shi Shilun: Chapter 62, *Cases of Judge Shi*】

身在曹營心在漢。One is in the Cao camp but one's mind is with the Han camp.【羅貫中《三國演義‧第二十五回》Luo Guanzhong: Chapter 25, *Romance of the Three Kingdoms*】

十室之邑，必有忠信。Even in a small place with ten families, there must be loyal and trustworthy people.【孔子《論語‧公冶長篇第五》Confucius: Chapter 5, *The Analects of Confucius*】

一臣不事二主。A person does not serve two masters.【褚人獲《隋唐演義‧第四十九回》Zhu Renhuo: Chapter 49, *Heroes in Sui and Tang Dynasties*】

忠臣不事二主。A loyal minister never serves two kings.【褚人獲《隋唐演義‧第四十九回》Zhu Renhuo: Chapter 49, *Heroes in Sui and Tang Dynasties*】

忠孝難兩全。／忠孝兩難全。Loyalty and filial piety are difficult to attain at the same time.【俗語 Common saying】

忠孝為立身之本。Loyalty and filial piety are the foundations for building up a person's good character.【俗語 Common saying】

Luck

倒他八輩子的楣。Have bad luck through and through.【俗語 Common saying】

凡人皆有得意時。Every dog has his day.【俗語 Common saying】

黃河尚有澄清日，豈可人無得運時。 There is still a chance for the Yellow River to have days when its waters become clear, how can it be that people don't have the time when luck is with them?【《增廣賢文》Words that Open up One's Mind and Enhance One's Wisdom】

爛眼睛招蒼蠅 —— 倒楣透了。 A festering eye attracts flies – bad luck.【歇後語 End-clipper】

無巧不成書。 By sheer luck.【俗語 Common saying】【馮夢龍《醒世恆言‧賣油郎獨佔花魁》Feng Menglong: "The Oil Vendor and His Pretty Bride", Stories to Awaken the World】

瞎貓逮死耗子 —— 碰運氣。 A blind cat caught a dead mouse– sheerluck.【歇後語 End-clipper】

運去金成鐵，時來鐵似金。 When with luck, gold turns into iron in value. When out of luck, iron is like gold in value.【《增廣賢文》Words that Open up One's Mind and Enhance One's Wisdom】

運窮君子拙，家富小兒嬌。 When out of luck, a gentleman becomes clumsy; when rich, one's children are spoiled.【俗語 Common saying】【趙琦美《古今雜劇‧元‧秦簡夫‧東堂老‧第一折》Zhao Qimei: Qin Jianfu: Scene 1, "The Elder of the Eastern Hall", Dramas of Ancient and Recent Times】

Lying

扯謊不打草稿。 One lies without having to draft it.【俗語 Common saying】

撒謊不臉紅。 One tell lies without one's face turning red and one's heart feeling ashamed.【俗語 Common saying】

狗不吃屎 —— 騙人。 A dog that does not eat shit–playing false.【歇後語 End-clipper】

鬼門關出告示 —— 鬼話連篇。 A notice put up at the Gate of Hell is full of devilish words – a pack of lies.【歇後語 End-clipper】

謊言的腿短，走不遠。 Lies have short legs, they won't travel long.【諺語 Proverb】

謊言腿不長。 Lies are always lame. 謊言掩蓋不了事實。 Lies cannot cover up the facts.【諺語 Proverb】

開大口，說大話。 Open one's mouth wide and talk big.【吳承恩《西遊記‧第八十一回》Wu Cheng'en: Chapter 81, Journey to the West】

說瞎話嘴長疔。 A blister will rise on the tongue that tells a lie.【俗語 Common saying】

天不着風兒晴不得，人不着謊兒成不得。 The sky cannot clear

up without winds and people cannot succeed without telling lies. 【蘭陵笑笑生《金瓶梅·第七十二回》Lanling Xiaoxiaosheng: Chapter 72, *The Plum in the Golden Vase*】

無謊不成媒。 Without telling lies, one cannot be a matchmaker. 【馮夢龍《醒世恆言·第七卷》Feng Menglong: Chapter 7, *Stories to Awaken the World*】

一步八個謊。 Tell eight lies every step. 【佚名〈氣英布·第二折〉Anonymous: Scene 2, "Teasing Ying Bu"】

真人面前不說假。 Before a really honest person, one will not tell lies. 【吳敬梓《儒林外史·第五十回》Wu Jingzi: Chapter 50, *An Unofficial History of the World of Literati*】

睜着眼睛說瞎話。Lie brazenly. 【諺語 Proverb】

Machination

機關算盡，一朝覆亡。 There is too much scheming, causing its doom eventually. 【俗語 Common saying】

千算萬算，不及天算。 No matter how much you scheme, you can't match the decision of Heaven. 【諺語 Proverb】

司馬昭之心，路人皆見。 The villain's intent is known to all. 【陳壽《三國志·蜀書·諸葛亮傳》

Chen Shou: "Biography of Zhuge Liang", "History of the State of Shu", *Records of the Three Kingdoms*】

用心計較般般錯，退步思量事事寬。 If you are deliberately fussy and calculating, everything is wrong. If you step back and think, everything is fine and you will feel relaxed. 【《增廣賢文》*Words that Open up One's Mind and Enhance One's Wisdom*】

Magnanimity

海納百川，有容乃大。 The sea takes in hundreds of rivers and hold them as it is big. 【林則徐：家中對聯 Lin Zexu: Home Couplet】

海水不可斗量。 The sea cannot be measured by bushels. 【吳承恩《西遊記·第六十二回》Wu Cheng'en: Chapter 62, *Journey to the West*】

河海不擇細流。 Rivers and seas do not refuse small streams. 【司馬遷《史記·李斯列傳》Sima Qian: "Biography of Li Si", *Records of the Grand Historian*】

量大福也大，機深禍亦深。 Broad-minded, one will enjoy great fortune; crafty, one will have great disasters. 【諺語 Proverb】【施耐庵《水滸傳・第十九回》Shi Nai'an: Chapter 19, *Outlaws of the Marshes*】

量小福也小。 Narrow-minded, one will enjoy but little fortune. 【諺語 Proverb】【西周生《醒世姻緣傳・第九十一回》Xi Zhousheng: Chapter 91, *Stories of Marriage to Awaken the World*】

心寬不在屋寬。 Broad-mindedness has nothing to do with the breadth of the room onc lives in. 【瞿灝《通俗編・居處》Di Hao: "Residence", *Common Things*】

心寬出少年。 Broad-mindedness makes one young. 【諺語 Proverb】【王濬卿《冷眼觀・第二十五回》Wang Junqing: Chapter 25, *Casting a Cold Eye*】

心寬增壽，愁能催老。 Broad-mindedness can make one live long and worry can make one become old quickly. 【諺語 Proverb】

蚊子放屁 —— 小氣。 A mosquito breaking wind is a small wind – one is stingy. 【歇後語 End-clipper】

屋寬不如心寬。 A broad house is not as good as a broad mind. 【諺語 Proverb】

有容，德乃大。 If one has forbearance, one's virtue will be great. 《尚書・君陳》"Lord Chen", *The Book of History*】

宰相肚裏可撐船。 The heart of a prime minister should be large enough to sail a boat. 【俗語 Common saying】

祇要心寬，弗用屋寬。 Broad-mindedness is better than a spacious house. 【俗語 Common saying】

Makeshift

把黃牛當馬騎。 Take an ox as a horse and ride on its back. 【俗語 Common saying】【李六如《六十年的變遷・第六章》Li Liuru: Chapter 6, *The Changes in the Last Sixty Years*】

拆東牆，補西牆。 Tear down the east wall to mend the west wall. 【俗語 Common saying】

無牛捉了馬耕田 —— 退而求其次。 Get a horse to do the ploughing when one does not have an ox. 【歇後語 End-clipper】

移東籬，補西障。 Remove the east fence to mend the west fence. 【釋普濟《五燈會元・卷十八》Shi Puji: Chapter 18, *A Compendium of the Five Lamps*】

Make-up

奴僕勿用俊美，妻妾切忌艷妝。Do not employ maids or servants who are beautiful or handsome, and your wife and concubine must avoid putting on too much make-up. 【朱用純《朱子家訓》Zhu Yongchun: *Percepts of the Zhu Family*】

三分人材，七分打扮。The natural figure is thirty percent while the make-up is seventy. 【俗語 Common saying】

三分顏色七分妝。One's look is thirty percent while one's make-up is seventy. 【俗語 Common saying】

長得俏來總是俏，打扮俏來惹人笑。A beautiful woman is born so and an ugly woman is laughed at if she dresses herself up. 【諺語 Proverb】

妝罷低聲問夫婿，畫眉深淺入時無。When I have finished my make-up, I asked my husband in a low voice, "Have I painted my eyebrows with a thickness that is right in fashion?" 【朱慶餘〈近試上張水部〉Zhu Qingyu: "To Waterworks Minister Zhang Ji on the Eve of the Palace Examination"】

Man

大人不華，君子務實。An honourable man is not ostentatious and a gentleman is pragmatic. 【王符《潛夫論‧敘錄》Wang Fu: "Summary", *Remarks by a Recluse*】

大人者，不失其赤子之心者也。A broad-minded man is one who does not lose his newborn-baby heart. 【孟軻《孟子‧離婁上》Meng Ke: Chapter 4, Part 1, *Mencius*】

好漢不吃眼前虧。A true man does not put up a fight when the odds are against him. 【諺語 Proverb】

好漢不打妻，好狗不咬雞。A brave man does not beat his wife and a good dog does not bite a chicken. 【諺語 Proverb】

好漢不當兵，好鐵不打釘。A good man does not join the army and good iron is not used to make nails. 【諺語 Proverb】

好漢不誇當年勇。A true man does not boast of his past bravery. 【諺語 Proverb】

好漢流血不流淚。A brave man would rather shed blood than tears. 【諺語 Proverb】

好男不事二君。A good man does not serve two rulers. 【諺語 Proverb】

茫茫四海人無數，哪個男兒是丈夫。There are countless people in this boundless world, which men are the true men? 《增廣賢文》Words that Open up One's Mind and Enhance One's Wisdom】

男兒志在四方。A man is ready to realize his aspirations anywhere in the world. 【左丘明《左傳‧僖公二十三年》Zuo Qiuming: "The Twenty-Third Year of the Reign of Duke Xi", Zuo's Commentary on the Spring and Autumn Annals】

男人靠得住，母豬會上樹。If a man could be trusted, a female pig could climb up a tree. 【俗語 Common saying】

男人能作主，是貓能逮鼠。A man backs up his wife as naturally as a cat catches a mouse. 【俗語 Common saying】

男子無醜相。No man is ugly in appearance. 【俗語 Common saying】

強漢不離時。A great man should conform to the trend of the time. 【俗語 Common saying】

世間不少奇男子，誰肯沙場萬里行。There are many capable men in this world, yet who is willing to go to the battle fields and expeditions of thousands of miles. 【明思宗〈贈秦良玉〉Emperor Sizong of Ming: "To Qin Liangyu"】

無毒不丈夫。One who is not ruthless is not a truly great man. 【俗語 Common saying】【馬致遠〈漢宮秋‧第一折〉Ma Zhiyuan: Scene 1, "Autumn in the Han Palace"】

Man and woman

痴男勝過巧女。A stupid man is better than a crafty woman. 【俗語 Common saying】

好狗不和雞鬥，好男不和女鬥。A good dog will not fight with a chicken and a good man will not fight with a woman. 【俗語 Common saying】【張恨水《丹鳳街‧第十六章》Zhang Henshui: Chapter 16, Crimson Phoenix Street】

好男不吃分家飯，好女不穿嫁時衣。A decent man does not live on his inheritance and a good woman does not wear clothes from her own home after she marries. 【蘭陵笑笑生《金瓶梅》Lanling Xiaoxiaosheng: The Plum in the Golden Vase】

郎騎竹馬來，繞牀弄青梅。同居長干里，兩小無嫌猜。You came around on a bobby horse, encircled the railings of the well and we played when plums are green. We both lived in Chang'gan Lane, and both of us were children, innocent and carefree. 【李白〈長干行〉Li Bai:"Song of Chang'gan Lane"】

每一個成功的男人後面有一個偉大的女人。 There is a great woman behind every successful man. 【諺語 Proverb】

男不男，女不女。 Neither fish, flesh, nor fowl. 【俗語 Common saying】

男當家，女插花。 The husband runs the family while the wife decorates the house. 【俗語 Common saying】

男女授受不親。 Man and woman should not allow hands to touch in giving or receiving something. 【《禮記・坊記第三十》Chapter 30, "Records of the Dykes", *The Book of Rites*】

男無妻，家無主；女無夫，身無主。 A man without a wife lacks someone to manage his household affairs. A woman without a husband lacks

someone to depend on. 【俗語 Common saying】【佚名〈鴛鴦被・第一折〉Anonymous: Scene 1, "Mandarin Duck Quilt"】

男以強為貴，女以弱為美。 A man is valued by his power, and the beauty of a woman lies in her weakness. 【俗語 Common saying】

男要勤，女要勤，三時茶飯不求人。 A man has to be diligent and so does a woman, so that they will not ask for help for their meals. 【諺語 Proverb】【蘇復之〈金印記・第十六齣〉Su Fuzhi: Scene 16, "The Gold Seal"】

男主外，女主內。 A man is engaged in affairs outside the home and a woman takes charge of affairs at home. 【諺語 Proverb】

自古嫦娥愛少年。 From of old, young ladies love young men. 【曹雪芹《紅樓夢・第四十六回》Cao Xueqin: Chapter 46, *A Dream of the Red Chamber*】

Management

半路上殺出個程咬金。 Have an unexpected interferer poking his nose into the matter. 【褚人獲《隋唐演義・第四回》Zhu Renhuo: Chapter 4, *Heroes in Sui and Tang Dynasties*】

兵來將擋，水來土掩。 When soldiers come, we stop them with our generals, and when

water flows in, we keep it back with earth. 【趙琦美《古今雜劇・雲台門聚二十八將》Zhao Qimei:"Gathering of Twenty-Eight Generals at Yuntai Gate", *Dramas of Ancient and Recent times*】

大王外出，小鬼跳梁。 When the King of Hell is away, ghosts will play. 【諺語 Proverb】

得放手時須放手。When one can free oneself from something, one must do so.【關漢卿〈竇娥冤‧第二折〉Guan Hanqing: Scene 2, "The Injustice to Dou E"】

凡事當留餘地，得意不宜再往。One must leave some leeway for everything and it is not appropriate to go further when you get what you want.【朱用純《朱子家訓》Zhu Yongchun: *Percepts of the Zhu Family*】

凡事留人情，回頭好相見。In doing everything, one must be empathic and allow for others' needs, so that one can get along with them in the future.【俗語 Common saying】

各立門戶，各自為政。Each sets up its own unit and acts on its own will.【俗語 Common saying】

國政易，家政難。It is easy to manage affairs of a country, but difficult to deal with affairs of a family.【諺語 Proverb】

老貓不在家，耗子鬧翻天。When the old cat is away from home, the mice will play.【俗語 Common saying】

貓不在家，耗子造反。When the cat is away from home, mice rebel.【諺語 Proverb】【張恨水《金粉世家‧第二十四回》Zhang Henshui: Chapter 24, *A Golden Family*】

貓兒不在，鼠兒自在。When the cat is away, the mice will play.【諺語 Proverb】

人存政舉，人亡政息。With the person in charge, the policies and regulations of an organization is upheld; without the person in charge, they are in vain.【《禮記‧中庸第三十一章》Chapter 31, "Doctrine of the Mean", *The Book of Rites*】

人盡其位，位得其人。Put the right person in the right position.【諺語 Proverb】

世上人管世上事。People of this world manage affairs of this world.【俗語 Common saying】

閻王不在，小鬼翻天。When the King of Hell is away, goblins will rebel.【俗語 Common saying】

一朝天子一朝臣。When there is a change of sovereignty, there will be a change of all the ministers.【湯顯祖〈牡丹亭‧第十五齣〉Tang Xianzu: Scene 15, "Peony Pavilion"】

用人容易識人難。It is easy to use a person but difficult to understand him or her.【蔡東藩《後漢通俗演義‧第十四回》Cai Dongfan: Chapter 14, *Popular Romance of the Later Han*】

用人者，取人之長，避人之短。In deploying people one takes their strong points and avoid their shortcomings.【魏源《魏源集‧默觚》Wei Yuan: "Mogu", *Works of Wei Yuan*】

執一而應萬，握要而治詳。Grasp one key point to handle ten thousand things; master the essentials to manage the trivialities. 【劉安《淮南子‧人間訓 第十八》Liu An: Chapter 18, "In the World of Man", *Huainanzi*】

Manhood

大丈夫不可無志。A true man should not be without aspirations. 【俗語 Common saying】

大丈夫敢做敢當。A true man dares to act and dares to take the responsibility. 【俗語 Common saying】

大丈夫見義勇為。A true man is ready to take up the cudgels for a just cause. 【郭沫若〈南冠草‧第 三幕〉Guo Moruo: Scene 3, "Nanguan Grass"】

大丈夫流血不流淚。A true man is ready to bleed without shedding any tears. 【俗語 Common saying】

大丈夫能屈能伸。A true man knows when to yield and when not. 【俗語 Common saying】

大丈夫言出如山。A true man keeps his promise as firm as a mountain. 【俗語 Common saying】

Marriage

出嫁的姑娘 —— 滿面春風。A girl who is going to get married– beaming with satisfaction. 【歇後 語 End-clipper】

初嫁從親，再嫁由身。A woman follows her parents' wish in her first marriage, but she follows her own wish in her second marriage. 【施耐庵《水滸傳‧第 二十五回》Shi Nai'an: Chapter 25, *Outlaws of the Marshes*】

鳳凰不配烏鴉。A phoenix must not marry to a crow. 【俗語 Common saying】

夫病而娶婦，則有勿藥之喜。A sick man who gets married will not need medicine. 【吳德旋《初 月樓聞見錄‧續錄‧第四卷》Wu Dexuan: Chapter 4, *A Sequel to What I hear and See from the Crescent Moon Tower*】

夫婚姻，禍福之階也。Marriage is a ladder to happiness or misery. 【左丘明《國語‧周語》Zuo Qiuming:"The Language of Zhou", *National Languages*】

父母之命，媒妁之言。A marriage that follows the order of the parents and the words of a matchmaker. 【孟軻《孟子‧滕 文公下》Meng Ke: Chapter 5, Part 2, *Mencius*】

歸妹，天地之大義也。 The marrying away of young women is the most important thing in heaven and earth.【《易經·歸妹》"The Marrying away of the Young Sister", *The Book of Changes*】

好姻緣棒打不散。 Good marriage cannot be broken by force.【曹雪芹《紅樓夢·第九十回》Cao Xueqin: Chapter 90, *A Dream of the Red Chamber*】

還君明珠雙淚垂，恨不相逢未嫁時。 With tears streaming down, I return the bright pearls to you. Why didn't we meet before I was married?【張籍〈節婦吟〉Zhang Ji: "Song of a Faithful Widow"】

皇帝的女兒不愁嫁。 The emperor's daughter does not worry about her marriage.【諺語 Proverb】

婚前不睜眼，婚後傻了眼。 Marry in haste, repent at leisure.【俗語 Common saying】

婚前明，婚後瞎。 Keep one's eyes open before marriage, but half shut after marriage.【俗語 Common saying】

嫁出的女，潑出的水。 A married daughter is like poured-out water.【曾樸《孽海花·第二十二回》Zeng Pu: Chapter 22, *Flower on an Ocean of Sin*】

嫁出去的女，賣出去的地。 A married daughter is like sold land.【西周生《醒世姻緣傳·第四十八回》Xi Zhousheng: Chapter 48, *Stories of Marriage to Awaken the World*】

嫁雞隨雞，嫁狗隨狗。 When a woman marries a chicken, stick with a chicken, a dog, stick with a dog.【歐陽修〈歐陽文忠集·代鳩婦言〉Ouyang Xiu: "Speaking in Defence of Women", *Collected Works of Ouyang Xiu*】

嫁女擇佳婿，毋索重聘。 When you marry off your daughter, select a good son-in-law and don't demand too much bethrothal money from him.【朱用純《朱子家訓》Zhu Yongchun: *Percepts of the Zhu Family*】

媒婆口，沒量斗。 The mouth of a matchmaker is like a bushel without standard measurement.【天然癡叟《石點頭·第十二卷》Tianran Chisou: Chapter 12, *Stone Nodding*】

門前冷落車馬稀，老大嫁作商人婦。 The door of my house was quiet and seldom any horses or carriages came. I grew older and was married to a merchant.【白居易〈琵琶行，並序〉Bai Juyi: "Song of a *Papa* Player, with a Foreword"】

窈窕淑女，君子好逑。 A fair lady would be a spouse whom a gentleman would love to have.【《詩經·周南·關雎》"Cooing Turtledoves", "The Odes of Zhou and the South", *The Book of Odes*】

男大當婚，女大當嫁。 A man, when grown up, should take a wife, and a woman, a husband.【俗語 Common saying】

男女居室，人之大倫也。A man living with a woman is the greatest relationship for human beings.【孟軻《孟子・萬章上》Meng Ke: Chapter 10, Part 1, *Mencius*】

寧嫁窮漢子，莫嫁孩蛋子。A girl would rather marry a poor guy than an ignorant guy.【俗語 Common saying】

寧娶大家奴，勿要小家女。Rather marry a maid servant in a rich and influential family than a daughter of a small family.【俗語 Common saying】

女怕嫁錯郎。A woman is afraid of marrying a wrong man.【俗語 Common saying】

配了千個，不如先個。Having remarried a thousand times, a woman finds the first is the best.【俗語 Common saying】

破人婚，九世貧。One who breaks another's marriage will be poor for nine generations.【俗語 Common saying】

千里姻緣一線牽。People a thousand miles apart may be linked, like a thread, by marriage.【李復言《續玄怪錄・訂婚店》Li Fuyan:"Inn of Betrothal", *Sequel to the Records of the Mysterious and Strange*】

強扭的瓜兒不甜，強撮的婚姻不美。A melon forcibly picked off is not sweet and a forced marriage will not be happy.【俗語 Common saying】

是姻緣棒打不回。Predestined marriage cannot be broken even by beating with a club.【曹雪芹《紅樓夢・第九十回》Cao Xueqin: Chapter 90, *A Dream of the Red Chamber*】

桃之夭夭，灼灼其華。之子於歸，宜其室家。The peach tree is young and elegant and its flowers, dazzling. A young lady is getting married, and she will put her home and family in good order.【《詩經・周南・桃夭》"The Peach Tree is Young and Elegant", "The Odes of Zhou and the South", *The Book of Odes*】

天成一對，地配一雙。Heaven makes them a pair, Earth matches them a couple.【俗語 Common saying】

天上無雲不下雨，地下無媒不成親。Without clouds in the sky, there would be no rain; without match-makers on earth, there would be no marriage.【諺語 Proverb】

同姓不攀親。A man and a woman with the same family name should not marry.【俗語 Common saying】

鮮花插在牛糞上。It is like sticking a lovely flower in a cow dung.【諺語 Proverb】

小姑居處本無郎。The abode of a maiden is without a man.【李商隱〈無題〉Li Shangyin:"Untitled Poems"】

一家有女百家求。When there is a girl in the family, a hundred

families will come to seek a marriage alliance. 【《增廣賢文》 *Words that Open up One's Mind and Enhance One's Wisdom*】

一樹梨花壓海棠。 One is married to a woman many years younger than oneself. 【蘇軾〈戲張先〉Su Shi:"Teasing Zhang Xian"】

姻緣本是前生定，不是姻緣莫強求。 Marriage is predestined, which should not be forcibly sought. 【馮夢龍《喻世明言·第五卷》Feng Menglong: Chapter 5, *Stories to Instruct the World*】

姻緣五百年前定。 Husband and wife are predestined five hundred years ago. 【邱心如《筆生花·第三十一回》Qiu Xinru: Chapter 31, *The Flowering Writing Brush*】

姻緣姻緣，事非偶然。 Marriage is by no means a coincidence. 【佚名〈隔江鬥智·第一折〉Anonymous: Scene 1, "Fight a Battle of Wit across the River"】

有情人終成眷屬。 Lovers finally become husband and wife. 【王實甫〈西廂記·第五本第四折〉Wang Shifu: Act 5, Scene 4, "Romance of the Western Bower"】

姊姊不嫁，耽擱了妹妹。 If the elder sister is not married, the younger sister's marriage will be delayed. 【俗語 Common saying】

執子之手，與子偕老。 Holding your hand in mine, I will grow old with you. 【《詩經·邶風·擊鼓》 "Beating the Drum", "The Odes of Bei", *The Book of Odes*】

之子于歸，言秣其君。 When that woman marries me, I must first feed the horses before taking her home. 【《詩經·國風》"Odes of the States", *The Book of Odes*】

竹門對竹門，木門對木門。 Choose a husband or wife with a similar family background. 【諺語 Proverb】

Martial art

十八般武藝，樣樣精通。 One is skilled in using each and every one of the eighteen weapons. 【施耐庵《水滸傳·第二回》Shi Nai'an: Chapter 2, *Outlaws of the Marshes*】

Matching

城隍廟的鼓錘 —— 一對。 Be as alike as a pair of drumsticks at the city temple. 【歇後語 End-clipper】

刀對刀，槍對槍。 Sword against sword and spear against spear. 【俗語 Common saying】

惡虎難鬥肚裏蛇。 Even a ferocious tiger is no match for the snake hidden inside its own belly.【諺語 Proverb】【吳承恩《西遊記‧第四十五回》Wu Cheng'en: Chapter 45, *Journey to the West*】

惡人自有惡人磨。 A wicked person will be harassed by others of their ilk.【馮夢龍《喻世明言‧第八卷》Feng Menglong: Chapter 8, *Stories to Instruct the World*】

斧頭吃鑿子，鑿子吃木頭。 The axe strikes the chisel, and the chisel strikes the wood – there is always one thing to conquer another.【諺語 Proverb】

胳膊扭不過大腿。 The arm cannot resist a leg.【諺語 Proverb】

寡不敵眾，弱難勝強。 A few cannot resist many and it is difficult for the weak to defeat the strong.【俗語 Common saying】

花對花，柳對柳，破畚箕配斷掃帚。 Flowers match with flowers, willows with willows and broken dustbins with broken brooms.【俗語 Common saying】

雞蛋碰不過石頭。 An egg cannot match a rock when they strike each other.【諺語 Proverb】

精明鬼碰上精明鬼。 The shrewd meet the shrewd.【俗語 Common saying】

龍配龍，鳳配鳳。 Let beggars match with beggars.【俗語 Common saying】

驢唇不對馬嘴。 A donkey's lips do not match a horse's jaws.【俗語 Common saying】

你有半斤，我有八兩。 Six of one and half a dozen of the other.【俗語 Common saying】

你有乾坤，我有日月。 Both are evenly matched.【俗語 Common saying】

牛頭不對馬嘴。 The head of an ox does not match with the mouth of a horse.【李寶嘉《官場現形記‧第十六回》Li Baojia: Chapter 16, *Officialdom Unmarked*】

棋逢對手，將遇良才。 A chess-player meeting his match and a general coming up against a worthy foe.【施耐庵《水滸傳‧第三十四回》Shi Nai'an: Chapter 34, *Outlaws of the Marshes*】

棋逢敵手難藏行。 One cannot hide one's trick when one meets one's match in a chess game.【俗語 Common saying】

強龍難壓地頭蛇。 The mighty dragon cannot subdue a snake in its old haunts.【俗語 Common saying】

強中自有強中手。 However strong one is, one often meets a stronger match.【羅貫中《三國演義‧第十七回》Luo Guanzhong: Chapter 17, *Romance of the Three Kingdoms*】

拳來拳打，刀來刀擋。 Fist for fist and sword for sword.【俗語 Common saying】

三拳不敵四手。 Three fists are no match for four hands.【馬烽《呂梁英雄傳‧第二十九回》Ma Feng: Chapter 29, *Heroes of the Lu Liang Mountain*】

石板上甩烏龜——硬碰硬。 A tortoise pounding a slabstone – a case of the tough confronting the tough.【歇後語 End-clipper】

雙拳難敵四手。 Two fists cannot ward off the attack of four hands.【褚人獲《隋唐演義‧第二十二回》Zhu Renhuo: Chapter 23, *Heroes in Sui and Tang Dynasties*】

銅盆碰上鐵刷子——一個比一個硬。 A copper pan against an iron brush – diamond cut diamond.【歇後語 End-clipper】

萬夫不當之勇。 Ten thousand people are no match for him.【施惠〈幽閨記‧第四齣：罔害璠良〉Shi Hui: Act 4: Harming Pan Liang, *Tale of the Secluded Chambers*】

文來文對，武來武對。 Civility meets civility, violence meets violence.【俗語 Common saying】

小不能敵大。 The small cannot resist the big.【俗語 Common saying】

小草擋不住大浪。 Small grass cannot stop big waves.【俗語 Common saying】

小鬼鬥不過閻王。 Small devils cannot contend with the King of Hell.【諺語 Proverb】

惺惺惜惺惺。 The clever people like the clever people.【俗語 Common saying】

一報還一報。／以牙還牙 Tit for tat.【俗語 Common saying】

一拳來，一腳去。 A Roland for an Oliver.【俗語 Common saying】

一人拼命，萬夫莫當。 Ten thousand people are no match for one who is desperate.【羅貫中《粉妝樓‧第五十八回》Luo Guanzhong: Chapter 58, *Cosmetical Building*】

一手不敵雙拳，雙拳不敵四手。 A hand is no match for two and two hands are no match for four.【馮夢龍《醒世恆言‧第二十九卷》Feng Menglong: Chapter 29, *Stories to Awaken the World*】

一套配一套，歪鍋配扁灶。 A crooked pot is matched by a crooked stove.【俗語 Common saying】

一物降一物。 There is always one thing to conquer another.【俗語 Common saying】

以打對打，以拉對拉。 Stick for stick and carrot for carrot.【俗語 Common saying】

針尖對麥芒。 Diamond cut diamond.【俗語 Common saying】

Matter

按下葫蘆浮起瓢。Too busy to attend to all matters. 【諺語 Proverb】

半斤對五兩 —— 一回事。Half a catty against five taels –the same thing. 【歇後語 End-clipper】

大路朝天 —— 各走一邊。As the main road leads to the end of the world, each one can take one's own way. 【歇後語 End-clipper】

爹死娘嫁人 —— 各人願各人。When one's father is dead and one's mother is remarried, each one has to look after oneself. 【歇後語 End-clipper】

對事不對人。What is discussed is on the matter, not on any particular person. 【俗語 Common saying】

凡事到頭終有救。In the end things will mend. 【俗語 Common saying】

公而忘私，國而忘家。Public matters come before private ones and the state comes before the family. 【吳敬梓《儒林外史·第六回》Wu Jingzi: Chapter 6, *An Unofficial History of the World of Literati*】

狗拿耗子，多管閒事。A dog trying to catch mice is to poke its nose into other people's business. 【文康《兒女英雄傳·第三十四回》Wen Kang: Chapter 34, *Biographies of Young Heroes and Heroines*】

護國寺買駱駝 —— 沒那事。Buying camels in Huguo Temple–no such thing. 【歇後語 End-clipper】

論事不論人。Discuss matters without discussing any particular person. 【俗語 Common saying】

眉毛鬍子一把抓。Try to grasp the eyebrows and the beard all at once. 【俗語 Common saying】

你走你的陽關道，我走我的獨木橋。You walk along your broad road and I, my single-log bridge. 【俗語 Common saying】

區區小事，何足掛齒。Such small things are not worth mentioning. 【俗語 Common saying】

世上無難事，祗怕有心人。Nothing in this world is difficult for one who gives one's mind to it. 【俗語 Common saying】

事不關己，己不勞心。If a thing has nothing to do with one, onedoes not need to worry about it. 【俗語 Common saying】

事不關己莫多問。If a thing has nothing to do with you, don't ask anything about it. 【俗語 Common saying】

事不關心，關心則亂。If one is not concerned about a matter, one's concern will disturb the matter. 【俗語 Common saying】

事要多知，酒要少吃。 Know more things but drink less wine. 【佚名《名賢集》Anonymous: *Collected Sayings of Famous Sages*】

事有兩面，有利有弊。 Everything has two sides: the advantages and the disadvantages. 【諺語 Proverb】

天下大事，必作於細。 Great things under heaven all have small beginnings. 【老子《道德經・第六十三章》Laozi: Chapter 63, *Daodejing*】

無事不登三寶殿。 One never goes to the temple without any business. 【馮夢龍《警世通言・第二十八卷》Feng Menglong: Chapter 28, *Stories to Caution the World*】

閒事不管，問事不知。 Don't bother yourself with others' business and say you don't know when asked. 【俗語 Common saying】

閒事休管，飯吃三碗。 Don't bother yourself with other's business and you will have

three bowls of rice a meal. 【俗語 Common saying】

小事糊塗，大事不糊塗。 Be confused about trivial matters, but wise about important matters. 【脫脫等《宋史・呂端傳》Toktoghan, *et al*: "Biography of Lu Duan", *History of the Song*】

小事精明，大事糊塗。 Wise about trifles but muddle-headed about important things. 【俗語 Common saying】

小事注意，大事自成。 Take care of the pence and the pounds will take care of themselves. 【俗語 Common saying】

一二三五八 —— 沒事（四）。 One, two, three, five, and six – nothing goes amiss. 【歇後語 End-clipper】

一事不煩二主。 Do not bother two persons with one matter. 【釋惟白《續傳燈錄・堂遠禪師》Shi Weibai: "Chan Master Tang Yuan", *A Sequel to the Records of the Transmission of the Lamp*】

Medicine

拔出膿來，才是好膏藥。 A good poultice is one that draws out the pus. 【諺語 Proverb】【孔厥，袁靜《新兒女英雄傳・第七回》Kong Jue and Yuan Jing: Chapter 7, *New Biographies of Heroes and Heroines*】

毒藥苦口利於病。 Good medicine, though bitter to the mouth,

is effective in curing illness. 【司馬遷《史記・留侯世家》Sima Qian: "House of Liu Hou", *Records of the Grand Historian*】

服藥千朝，火如獨寢一宵。 Taking tonic for a thousand days is not as good as sleeping alone for one night. 【諺語 Proverb】

服藥求神仙，多為藥所誤。Those who hope to become immortals by taking elixir are often harmed by the medicine.【佚名《古詩十九首》Anonymous: *Nineteen Ancient Poems*】

葫蘆裏賣甚麼藥。What's at the back.【凌濛初《二刻拍案驚奇·第十四卷》Ling Mengchu: Chapter 14, *Amazing Tales, Volume Two*】

換湯不換藥。The water is changed, but not the medicine.【張南莊《何典·第三卷》Zhang Nanzhuang: Chapter 3, *From Which Classic*】

療未患之疾，通不和之氣。Cure an illness that is not yet contracted and dredge the discordant vital energy.【葛洪《抱朴子·內篇·登涉第十七》Ge Hong: Chapter 17, "Climbing Mountains and Crossing Rivers", "Inner Chapters", *The Master Who Embraces Simplicity*】

靈丹妙藥，治不好該死的病。No panacea in the world can cure fatal diseases.【俗語 Common saying】

賣狗皮膏藥。Sell quack medicine.【俗語 Common saying】

猛藥起沉疴。Desperate diseases must have desperate cures.【俗語 Common saying】

偏方治大病。Folk prescriptions often cure serious diseases.【俗語 Common saying】

三分吃藥，七分靠養。/ 三分治療七分養。Resting is a better cure than taking medicine./ Treatment of an illness is thirty percent while resting is seventy.【俗語 Common saying】

施藥不如施方。To give out medicine is not as good as to give prescriptions.【俗語 Common saying】

說真方，賣假藥。The prescription is true, but the medicine isn't.【佚名〈廣成子·第二折〉Anonymous: Scene 2, "Master of Vast Accomplishment"】

說嘴郎中無好藥。A physician who boasts cannot have good medicine.【張南莊《何典·第三卷》Zhang Nanzhuang: Chapter 3, *From Which Classic*】

雖有神藥，不如少年。Miracle-working medicine is not as good as youth.【任昉《述異記·卷下》Ren Fang: *Accounts of Strange Things*, Part 2】

瞎子害眼睛 ── 沒治了。A blind person hurts his eyes–incurable.【歇後語 End-clipper】

藥補不如食補。Diet cures more than doctors.【李時珍《本草綱目·第八卷》Li Shizhen: Chapter 8, *Chinese Herbal Manual*】

藥不執方，病不定症。Medicine has no fixed prescriptions for diseases have no fixed symptoms.【俗語 Common saying】

藥不執方，合宜而用。Medicine has no fixed prescriptions, so it can be used as long as it cures properly.【諺語 Proverb】【吳承恩

《西遊記・第六十九回》Wu Cheng'en: Chapter 69, *Journey to the West*】

藥苦治病，甜言誤人。 Bitter medicine cures people, but sweet words mislead them. 【諺語 Proverb】

藥能醫假病，酒不解真愁。 Medicine can cure a fake illness and wine cannot remove real worries. 【《增廣賢文》*Words that Open up One's Mind and Enhance One's Wisdom*】

藥醫不死病，佛度有緣人。 Medicine can only cure diseases that are not fatal and Buddha releases souls that are fated. 【俗語 Common saying】【馮夢龍《醒世恆言・第十卷》Feng Menglong: Chapter 10, *Stories to Awaken the World*】

藥醫不死病，死病無藥醫。 Medicine can only cure diseases that are not fatal, but there is no medicine against death. 【俗語 Common saying】【張南莊《何典・第三卷》Zhang Nanzhuang: Chapter 3, *From Which Classic*】

治標不治本。 Cure the symptoms, not the disease. 【俗語 Common saying】

Meeting

不知來歲牡丹時，再相逢何處。 Who knows when the peony blossoms next year, who knows where we shall meet again. 【葉清臣〈賀聖朝〉Ye Qingcheng: "Congratulations to the Holy Court"】

從別後，憶相逢，幾回魂夢與君同。 Since we parted, I still remember our meeting, and for several times, I dreamed that we were together. 【晏幾道〈鷓鴣天〉Yan Jidao: "To the Tune of Partridge in the Sky"】

春草明年綠，王孫歸不歸。 Next year when the grass in spring turns green, will you, my travelling friend, come here again? 【王維〈送別〉Wang Wei: "Seeing Somebody Off"】

此時一別何時見，邊撫兒身舔兒面。 How will we meet again after this parting? I hugged my son and kissed his face. 【謝榛〈賣子歎〉Xie Qin: "Sighs When Selling My Son"】

此生何處不相逢。 In this lifetime, we might meet anywhere in this world. 【杜牧〈送人〉Du Mu: "Seeing a Person off"】

但聞其名，未見其人。 I have heard of his name but have not met him in person. 【施世綸《施公案・第二百三十七回》Shi Shilun: Chapter 237, *Cases of Judge Shi*】

分明一見怕魂消，卻愁不到魂消處。 Though I know only too well that my soul will be crippled when I see you, yet my fear is that I cannot get this opportunity. 【鄭板橋〈踏莎行〉Zheng Banqiao: "To the Tune of Hiking through the Suo Grass"】

浮萍尚有相逢日，人豈全無見面時。 When even floating weeds may come together some day, how could it be that people have no chance to meet each other? 【俗語 Common saying】【曹雪芹《紅樓夢·第七十二回》Cao Xueqin: Chapter 68, *A Dream of the Red Chamber*】

何當共剪西窗燭，卻話巴山夜雨時。 When shall we trim the wicks of the candles together by the west window again, and chat on the evening rain that fell on Mount Ba? 【李商隱〈夜雨寄北〉Li Shangyin: "Written on a Rainy Night to My Wife in the North"】

記得那年花下，深夜，初識謝娘時。 I recall that year, under the cover of flowers and late at night, I met you for the first time. 【韋莊〈荷葉盃〉Wei Zhuang: "To the Tune of Lotus-Leaf Cup"】

今日重逢深院裏，一種溫存猶昔。 Today we meet gain in this secluded courtyard, there is a kind of tenderness as of old. 【鄭板橋〈金縷曲〉Zheng Banqiao: "The Golden Thread"】

今夕何夕，見此邂逅。 What night is tonight? We are here meeting each other. 【《詩經·國風》"Odes of the States", *The Book of Odes*】

今宵賸把銀釭照，猶恐相逢是夢中。 Tonight I keep lighting up the silver lamp, for fear that our meeting is but a dream. 【晏幾道〈鷓鴣天〉Yan Jidao: "To the Tune of Partridge in the Sky"】

今夜故人來不來，教人立盡梧桐影。 Are you, my dear friend, coming or not this evening? I have been standing here waiting for you till the shadow of the *wutong* tree is almost gone. 【呂岩〈梧桐影〉Lu Yan: "Written on a Rainy Night to My Wife in the North"】

馬逢伯樂而嘶，人遇知己而死。 A horse neighs when meeting its admirer and one will die for one's confidant. 【羅貫中《三國演義·第六十回》Luo Guanzhong: Chapter 60, *Romance of the Three Kingdoms*】

人生不相見，動如參與商。 People often do not meet up with each other in life, as they move like the morning and evening stars. 【杜甫〈贈衛八處士〉Du Fu: "Presented to Scholar-recluse Wei the Eighth"】

人生何處不相逢。 People, though separated, will meet somewhere in life sooner or later. 【晏殊〈金柅園〉Yan Shu: "Gold Pear Garden"】

人有見面之情。 People have feelings after a face-to-face meeting. 【俗語 Common saying】

人在對面，人隔千里。 People facing each other may have their hearts separated by a thousand miles. 【俗語 Common saying】

如今俱是異鄉人，相見更無因。
Now we all become strangers living in different places far away from home, there is no cause for us to meet again. 【韋莊〈荷葉杯〉Wei Zhuang:"To the Tune of Lotus Leaf Cup"】

如聞其聲，如見其人。 Seem to hear his voice and see him in person. 【韓愈《昌黎先生集·獨孤申叔哀辭》Han Yu:"Elegy for Dugu Shenzhu", *Collected Works of Han Yu*】

三日不相見，莫作舊時看。
Without seeing each other for three days, one should not look at the other the way one used to. 【陳壽《三國志·吳書·呂蒙傳》Chen Shou:"Biography of Lu Meng", "History of the Wu", *Records of the Three Kingdoms*】

十年別淚知多少，不道相逢淚更多。 I don't know how many tears I shed during the ten-year separation, and I was surprised that I shed even more tears when we met. 【徐熥〈酒店逢李大〉Xu Teng:"Meeting Li Da at an Inn"】

數面成親舊。 After several meetings people become acquaintances. 【陶淵明〈答龐參軍詩序〉Tao Yuanming:"A Poem in Response to Adjutant Pang, with Preface"】

抬頭不見低頭見。 Meet regularly or frequently. 【俗語 Common saying】

天涯流落思無窮，既相逢，卻匆匆。 I have been wandering around the world with endless thoughts of you. No sooner than we met, then you departed in a hurry. 【蘇軾〈江城子·別徐州〉Su Shi:"On leaving Xuzhou: To the Tune of a Riverside Town"】

天涯原咫尺，此地又逢君。
The world is just a tiny place, and here we meet again. 【俗語 Common saying】

同是天涯淪落人，相逢何必曾相識。 As we both are losers in this world, it doesn't really matter whether we have met before or not. 【白居易〈琵琶行，並序〉Bai Juyi:"Song of a *Pipa* Player, with a Foreword"】

聞名不如見面，見面勝似聞名。
To know someone by his repute is not as good as meeting him face to face. 【施耐庵《水滸傳·第三回》Shi Nai'an: Chapter 3, *Outlaws of the Marshes*】

相見時難別亦難，東風無力百花殘。 Meeting with each other is difficult and parting with each other is also difficult. When the east wind is feeble, all flowers wither. 【李商隱〈無題〉Li Shangyin:"Untitled Poem"】

一日不見，如三秋兮。 Not meeting one a day is like a separation of three autumns. 【《詩經·王風·采葛》"Plucking Cloth-Creeper", "Odes around the Capital", *The Book of Odes*】

月上柳梢頭，人約黃昏後。 The moon rose to the tip of the

willows, my love and I kept our tryst after dusk. 【歐陽修〈生查子〉Ouyang Xiu: "To the Tune of Ripe Quince"】

乍見翻疑夢，相悲各問年。 When I ran into you, I suspected it was a dream, and we asked our age in sadness. 【司空曙〈雲陽館與韓紳宿別〉Sikong Shu: "Staying Overnight at the Yunyang Inn to Bid Farewell to Han Shen"】

正是江南好風景，落花時節又逢君。 This is just the time when the scenery of the south of the Yangzi River is beautiful, and I meet you again at the time when petals fall. 【杜甫〈江南逢李龜年〉Du Fu: "Encountering Li Guinian in the South of the Yangzi River"】

昨夜星辰昨夜風，畫樓西畔桂堂東。 Last night the stars were glittering, the wind blowing. We met at the western side of the painted tower and eastern side of the cassia hall. 【李商隱〈無題〉Li Shangyin: "Untitled Poem"】

Memory

白髮宮女在，閒坐說玄宗。 The white-haired palace maids are still alive, sitting idly to chat about anecdotes of Emperor Xuanzong. 【元稹〈行宮〉Yuan Zhen: "Summer Palace"】

跛者不忘屨，眇者不忘視。 A lame person does not forget the shoes he used to wear when he was not lame and a blind person does not forget what he used to see when he was not blind. 【諺語 Proverb】【蒲松齡《聊齋誌異・巧娘・卷二》Pu Songling: Chapter 2, "Qiao Niang", Strange Stories from a Chinese Studio】

貴人多忘事。 Great people are apt to have short memories. 【王定保《唐摭言・卷二》Wang Dingbao: Chapter 2, Garnered Words from the Tang Dynasty】

記得快，忘得快。 Soon learned, soon forgotten. 【俗語 Common saying】

擱在脖子後頭。 Let slip from one's mind. 【曹雪芹《紅樓夢・第一百二十回》Cao Xueqin: Chapter 120, A Dream of the Red Chamber】

拋到九霄雲外。 Put entirely out of mind. 【劉禹錫〈同樂天登棲靈寺塔〉Liu Yuxi: "Climbing the Pagoda at Spirit Lodge Monastery, with Le Tian"】

強記不如善悟。 A retentive memory is not as good as a comprehensive mind. 【諺語 Proverb】

人不忘其所忘，而忘其所不忘，是謂誠忘。 People do not forget what they should forget and forget what they should not forget, and this is known as true forgetfulness. 【莊周《莊子・內篇・

德充符第五》：Zhuang Zhou: Chapter 5, "Symbols of Virtue Fulfilled", "Inner Chapters", *Zhuangzi*】

心記不如筆記。 What is memorized is not as good as what is written. 【俗語 Common saying】

一目十行，過目不忘。 Memorize something with one reading. 【俗語 Common saying】

一日不死，一日不忘。 It will stay in my memory as long as I live. 【俗語 Common saying】

Message

都云作者癡，誰解其中味。 Everyone says that the author is obsessed, who knows the messages he delivers. 【曹雪芹《紅樓夢》Cao Xueqin: *A Dream of the Red Chamber*】

馬上相逢無紙筆，憑君傳語報平安。 We met while riding on the horseback without paper or a writing brush, so I relied on you to convey my words: tell them I am safe and well. 【岑參〈逢入京使〉Cen Shen: "Meeting a Messenger Going to the Capital"】

言有盡而意無窮。 There is an end to the words, but not to their message. 【嚴羽《滄浪詩話・詩辨》Yan Yu: "Poetic Differentiate", *Canglang Poetry Talks*】

雲中誰寄錦書來，雁字回時，月滿西樓。 Who sent me a brocade letter through the clouds? When the wild geese return, in formation, the West Tower will be full of moonbeams. 【李清照〈一剪梅〉Li Qingzhao: "To the Tune of a Twig of Plum Blossoms"】

Method

定法不是法。 A fixed and rigid method is not a good one. 【文康《兒女英雄傳・第三十三回》Wen Kang: Chapter 33, *Biographies of Young Heroes and Heroines*】

跟和尚借梳子——找錯了人。 Asking a monk to lend you a comb–you have gone to the wrong person. 【歇後語 End-clipper】

和尚廟裏借梳子——走錯門了。 Asking a monk in a temple for a comb is getting into the wrong way. 【歇後語 End-clipper】

一法通，百法通。 Once you grasp a key method, you understand a hundred related methods. 【羅貫中《平妖傳・第十三回》Luo Guanzhong: Chapter 13, *Taming Devils*】

一竅通，百竅通。 Once you grasp a key method, you understand a hundred related methods. 【吳承恩《西遊記・第二回》Wu Cheng'en: Chapter 2, *Journey to the West*】

Mind

二人同心，其利斷金。 If two persons are of the same mind, it has a sharpness that is capable of breaking gold./If two persons are of the same mind, earth can become gold. 【《易經・繫辭上》 "Appended Remarks, Part 1", *The Book of Changes*】【周楫《西湖二集・胡少保平倭戰功》Zhou Ji: "Military Merits of the Imperial Tutor Hu Who Conquered the Japanese", *The West Lake, Second Volume*】

黑心當被雷擊。 One who is evil-minded will be struck by lightning. 【俗語 Common saying】

黑心人倒有馬兒騎。 An evil-minded person has a horse to ride. 【俗語 Common saying】

葷油蒙了心。 Be befuddled. 【俗語 Common saying】

將心比，同一理。 Judge other people's minds by one's own. 【俗語 Common saying】

君子勞心，小人勞力。 A gentleman works with his mind while a petty man toils with his labour. 【左丘明《左傳・襄公九年》Zuo Qiuming: "The Ninth Year of the Reign of Duke Xiang", *Zuo's Commentary on the Spring and Autumn Annals*】

可意會不可言傳。 Can be grasped by the mind but cannot be expressed in words. 【莊周《莊子・外篇・天道第十三》: Zhuang Zhou: Chapter 13, "The Way of Heaven", "Outer Chapters", *Zhuangzi*】

明以照暗室，理以照人心。 A lamp is to light up a dark room and truth is to enlighten people's minds. 【諺語 Proverb】

難得糊塗，吃虧是福。 Pretending to be foolish is not easy and suffering a loss is a blessing. 【鄭板橋〈對聯〉Zheng Banqiao: A Couplet】

千金難買兩同心。 A thousand taels of gold is not as good as two people of one mind. 【馮夢龍《醒世恆言・第九卷》Feng Menglong: Chapter 9, *Stories to Awaken the World*】

人多心難齊。 Many people, many minds. 【諺語 Proverb】

人各有心，心各有愛。 Every person has his own mind and every mind its own liking. 【《增廣賢文》*Words that Open up One's Mind and Enhance One's Wisdom*】

人在心不在。 One is here, but one's mind isn't. 【俗語 Common saying】

外貌容易認，內心最難猜。One's appearance is easy to recognize, but one's mind is difficult to fathom.【諺語 Proverb】

為人總有懵懂時。 One has a fool in one's sleeve.【俗語 Common saying】

心靈的財富才是唯一真正的財富。The wealth of the mind is the only true wealth.【諺語 Proverb】

修身在正其心。The cultivation of the person depends on the rectification of the mind.【《禮記‧大學第四十二》Chapter 42:"The Great Learning", *The Book of Rites*】

啞巴吃餃子——心裏有數。When a dumb man eats dumplings, he knows what's what.【歇後語 End-clipper】

一家同心，糞土成金。When all members of a family are of the same mind, even useless things become gold.【俗語 Common saying】

一娘生九子，連娘十條心。Many people, many minds.【諺語 Proverb】

一日個猴兒一百條心。A hundred monkeys have a hundred minds.【俗語 Common saying】

一心不可二用。You cannot concentrate your mind on two things at the same time.【俗語 Common saying】

英雄所見略同。Great minds think alike.【陳壽《三國志‧蜀書‧龐統傳》Chen Shou:"Biography of Pang Tong", "History of the State of Shu", *Records of the Three Kingdoms*】

Minister

臣為君死，妻為夫亡。A minister dies for his emperor, a wife, her husband.【俗語 Common saying】【劉一清《錢塘遺事‧第八卷》Liu Yiqing: Chapter 8, *Anecdotes of Qiantang*】

勁松彰於歲寒，貞臣見於國危。The toughness of the pine is exhibited in the year-end coldness and the loyalty of ministers is manifested when a country is in a crisis.【潘嶽〈西征賦〉Pan Yue:"Ode to the Western Expedition"】

親賢臣，遠小人。Keep close to the good ministers and keep away from petty people.【諸葛亮〈前出師表〉Zhuge Liang:"First Memorial on Dispatching the Troops"】

求忠臣必於孝子之門。Loyal ministers must be sought from families with filial sons.【范曄《後漢書‧韋彪傳》Fan Ye:"Biography of Wei Biao", *History of the Later Han*】

為臣當忠，交友當義。A minister should be loyal to his king and friends should be righteous.【諺語 Proverb】【褚人獲《隋唐演義‧第

五十五回》Zhu Renhuo: Chapter 58, *Heroes in Sui and Tang Dynasties*】

為臣當忠，為子要孝。 A minister should be loyal to his king and a son should be filial to his parents.【諺語 Proverb】【褚人獲《隋唐演義・第五十五回》Zhu Renhuo: Chapter 55, *Heroes in Sui and Tang Dynasties*】

賢臣擇主而侍。 A worthy minister chooses his king to serve.【羅貫中《三國演義・第三回》Luo Guanzhong: Chapter 3, *Romance of the Three Kingdoms*】

相門必有相，將門必有將。 In the family of a minister, there will be ministers to be born in the future and in the family of a general, there will be generals born in the future.【司馬遷《史記・孟嘗君列傳》Sima Qian: "Biography of Lord Mengchang", *Records of the Grand Historian*】

忠臣不怕死，怕死不忠臣。 A loyal minister is not afraid of death and one who is afraid of death is not a loyal minister.【諺語 Proverb】

忠臣不事二主。 A loyal minister will not serve two kings.【褚人獲《隋唐演義・第四十九回》Zhu Renhuo: Chapter 49, *Heroes in Sui and Tang Dynasties*】

忠臣不易主，志士不言私。 A loyal minister will not change to serve a different king and a person with lofty aspirations seeks no personal gains.【俗語 Common saying】

佐不務多，而務得賢臣。 A ruler does not have to have many advisors, but he has to have virtuous ministers.【戴德《大戴禮記・保傅》Dai De: "Perceptors and Masters", *Records of Rites by Dai the Elder*】

Missing somebody

北寒妾已知，南心君不見。 I as your wife know the coldness in the north, but you cannot see my yearnings for you in the south.【鮑令暉〈古意贈今人〉Bao Linghui: "Old Sentiments Presented to a Man of Today"】

不曾遠別離，安知慕儔侶？ If you and your lover have not been separated far away, how can you know the feelings of missing your lover?【張華〈情詩〉Zhang Hua: "Love Poem"】

出有日，還無期，結巾帶，長相思。 You have the date of departure, but not a date for return. I knit a scarf for you to express my everlasting longing.【蘇伯玉妻《盤中詩》Wife of Su Boyu: "Poem on a Tray"】

春心莫共花爭發，一寸相思一寸灰。 Do not let the amorous

heart vie with the flowers in blossom, for every inch of longing is an inch of candle ash. 【李商隱〈無題四首〉Li Shangyin: "Four Untitled Poems"】

獨在異鄉為異客，每逢佳節倍思親。 I am a lonely stranger in a strange land; every time a festive occasion comes around, I miss all the more my dear ones. 【王維〈九月九日憶山東兄弟〉Wang Wei: "Thinking of My Brothers in Shandong on the Ninth Day of the Ninth Month"】

故人入我夢，明我長相憶。 My old friend came into my dream, knowing that I have been missing him. 【杜甫〈夢李白二首〉Du Fu: "Dreaming of Li Bai: Two Poems"】

紅豆生南國，春來發幾枝。願君多採擷，此物最相思。 Red beans grow in the south, and they appear on branches when spring comes. I hope you would gather as many as you can, for these beans are the best forget-me-nots. 【王維〈相思〉Wang Wei: "Longings"】

見鞍思馬，睹物思人。 Seeing the saddle, one thinks of one's horse; seeing the thing, one thinks of one's owner. 【俗語 Common saying】

君住長江頭，妾住長江尾，日日思君不見君，共飲長江水。 I live at the head of the Changjiang River, and I live at the end of the river. Every day I miss you but cannot see you, and we both drink the water of the river. 【李之儀〈卜算子〉Li Zhiyi: "To the Tune of Fortune Telling"】

人逢佳節倍思親。 Every time a fest comes around, people miss all the more their loved ones. 【王維〈九月九日憶山東兄弟〉Wang Wei: "Thinking of My Brothers in Shandong on the Ninth Day of the Ninth Month"】

人想人，苦煞人。 Missing each other makes one suffer. 【俗語 Common saying】

人想人，沒法治。 What is most incurable is to miss each other. 【俗語 Common saying】

生當復來歸，死當長相思。 I will return to see you if I'm alive and I will miss you forever if I die. 【蘇武〈留別妻〉Su Wu: "Message I Left to My Wife Before Parting With Her"】

十年生死兩茫茫，不思量，自難忘。 For ten years the living and the dead have been separated. Though not thinking of you, naturally I cannot forget. 【蘇軾〈江城子〉Su Shi: "To the Tune of a Riverside Town"】

思君令人老，歲月忽已晚。 Missing you ages me, and all of a sudden, I'm in my twilight days and years. 【佚名《古詩十九首》Anonymous: *Nineteen Ancient Poems*】

所謂伊人，在水一方。 The person I miss is on the other side of the river. 【《詩經·秦風·蒹

葭》"Reeds", "Odes of the State of Qin", *The Book of Odes*】

一日不見，如隔三秋。A day absent from you is like three seasons.【《詩經‧王風‧采葛》 "Plucking Cloth-Creeper", "Odes around the Capital", *The Book of Odes*】

一日不見，如三月兮。【《詩經‧鄭風‧子衿》"Blue-Collared Lad", "Odes of the State of Zheng", *The Book of Odes*】

祇願君心似妾心，定不負相思意。I only wish that your heart is like my heart, then my love for you will not be unrequited.【李之儀〈卜算子〉Li Zhiyi: "To the Tune of Fortune Telling"】

仲可懷也，人之多言，亦可畏也。I miss you, Zhongzi, but I am afraid of the gossips of the people.【《詩經‧鄭風‧將仲子》"To Zhongzi", "Odes of the State of Zheng", *The Book of Odes*】

Mistake

不怕有過，祇怕不改。Making mistakes is not to be feared, but leaving them uncorrected is.【俗語 Common saying】

不求有功，但求無過。One is not interested in making contributions, but making no mistakes.【俗語 Common saying】

不做不錯，多做多錯。Those who do nothing make no mistakes; those who do a lot make a lot of mistakes.【俗語 Common saying】

差之毫釐，謬以千里。A little mistake can lead to a great disaster.【《增廣賢文》*Words that Open up One's Mind and Enhance One's Wisdom*】

成功少碰壁多。Keep making mistakes.【俗語 Common saying】

懲前毖後，治病救人。Learn from past mistakes to avoid future ones and cure the illness

to save the patient.【俗語 Common saying】

錯一遍，精一遍。A mistake one makes is a gain in one's wit.【諺語 Proverb】

錯走道回得來，錯行事回不來。If one takes a wrong road, one can return, but if one does something wrong, one cannot undo it.【俗語 Common saying】

大人不記小人過。A broad-minded man rarely remembers mistakes committed by people below him.【石玉昆《三俠五義‧第三十三回》Shi Yukun: Chapter 33, *The Three Heroes and Five Gallants*】

非其罪，雖累辱而不愧也。If the mistakes are not made by one, one should not feel ashamed even though one is repeatedly wronged by others.【司馬遷《史記‧日者列傳》Sima Qian: "Biographies of Soothsayers", *Records of the Grand Historian*】

改過不嫌遲。It is never too late to repent.【俗語 Common saying】

過而不改，是為過矣。Errors not corrected are errors.【孔子《論語‧衞靈公篇第十五》Confucius: Chapter 15, *The Analects of Confucius*】

過日聞而德日新。Learn about your mistakes every day and renew your virtue every day.【白居易〈策林四‧納諫〉Bai Juyi: Chapter 4, "Accepting Admonitions", *A Forest of Strategies*】

過則勿憚改。When you make mistakes, you should not be afraid of correcting them.【孔子《論語‧子罕篇第九》Confucius: Chapter 9, *The Analects of Confucius*】

靜坐當思己過，閒談莫論人非。When sitting alone, think about your own faults. When chatting, don't talk about others' errors.【金纓《格言聯璧》Jin Ying: *Couplets of Maxims*】

君子之過也，如日月之食焉；過也，人皆見之，更也，人皆仰之。The mistakes of a gentleman is like the eclipses of the sun and moon. When he makes a mistake, all people see it; when he corrects a mistake, all people respect him.【孔子《論語‧子張篇第十九》Confucius: Chapter 19, *The Analects of Confucius*】

君子有過則謝以質，小人有過則謝以文。When a gentleman makes a mistake, he apologizes with sincerity; when a petty person makes a mistake, he apologizes by glossing over it.【司馬遷《史記‧孔子世家》Sima Qian:"House of Confucius", *Records of the Grand Historian*】

孔子也有三分錯。Even Confucius made mistakes.【俗語 Common saying】

老手也有失算時。Even an old hand sometimes makes mistakes.【俗語 Common saying】

棋無一着錯。Do not make any false move in a chess game.【諺語 Proverb】【蔡東藩《明史通俗演義‧第二十一回》Cai Dongfan: Chapter 21, *Popular Romance of the Ming Dynasty*】

千里長堤，潰於蟻穴。An ant-hole may cause the collapse of a thousand-mile dyke.【韓非《韓非子‧喻老第二十一》Han Fei: Chapter 21, "Illustrating Laozi's Teaching", *Hanfeizi*】

人不錯成仙，馬不錯成龍。Everybody makes mistakes or he becomes a Daoist immortal. Every horse makes mistakes or it becomes a dragon.【諺語 Proverb】

人不知己過，牛不知力大。A person who does not know the mistakes he made is just like an ox which does not know the great power it has.【諺語 Proverb】

人非聖賢，孰能無過。People are not saints and sages, how can they be free from making mistakes?【左丘明《左傳‧宣公二

年》Zuo Qiuming: "The Second Year of the Reign of Duke Xuan", *Zuo's Commentary on the Spring and Autumn Annals*】

人皆有過，改之為貴。 Everyone makes mistakes and what is to be valued is the correction of mistakes.【徐元〈八義記‧第六齣〉Xu Yuan: Scene 6, "The Story of the Eight Righteous Heroes"】

人誰無過？過而能改，善莫大焉。 Who doesn't make mistakes? Nothing is better than correcting one's mistakes when one has committed them.【左丘明《左傳‧宣公二年》Zuo Qiuming: "The Second Year of the Reign of Duke Xuan", *Zuo's Commentary on the Spring and Autumn Annals*】

人有錯手，馬有失蹄。 A person makes mistakes as a horse trips.【俗語 Common saying】

慎勿談人之過，切勿矜己之長。 Be careful not to gossip about others' weaknesses, and don't be eager to display your own strengths.【朱用純《朱子家訓》Zhu Yongchun: *Percepts of the Zhu Family*】

聖人也有三分錯。 Even a sage makes some mistakes.【俗語 Common saying】

是人孰能無過。 How can any human being be free from mistakes?【左丘明《左傳‧宣公二年》Zuo Qiuming: "The Second Year of the Reign of Duke Xuan", *Zuo's Commentary on the Spring and Autumn Annals*】

萬事皆從急中錯。 Countless mistakes are the result of impetuosity.【諺語 Proverb】

瞎子打架 —— 抓住不放。 Two blind persons fighting with each other – each grasps tightly to the other.【歇後語 End-clipper】

先正自己，再正他人。 Correct yourself before you correct others.【俗語 Common saying】

小錯不改，大錯即來。 If we leave small mistakes uncorrected, big ones will follow.【俗語 Common saying】

小患不治成大災。 A small mistake uncorrected will bring great disaster.【諺語 Proverb】

小人之過也必文。 A petty man is sure to gloss over his faults.【孔子《論語‧子張篇第十九》Confucius: Chapter 19, *The Analects of Confucius*】

行年五十當知四十九年之非。 At the age of fifty we should know the errors of forty-nine years.【劉安《淮南子‧原道訓第一》Liu An: Chapter 1, "Searching out the Way", *Huainanzi*】

一步錯，步步錯。 Take a false step and you will make mistakes in every step.【諺語 Proverb】

一錯，豈可再錯。 Having made one mistake, how can you make yet another?【俗語 Common saying】

一失足成千古恨，再回頭已百年身。 A false step might cause a life-long regret and when you turn around again, you are already a hundred years old. 【魏子安〈花月痕〉Wei Zi'an: "Traces of Flowers and the Moon"】

一時之錯，終身之恨。 The mistake of a moment causes a lifetime of repentance. 【諺語 Proverb】

一誤不能再誤。 Having made one mistake, one is not allowed to make another. 【俗語 Common saying】

有則改之，無則加勉。 If one has made mistakes, correct them. If one has not, then take it as encouragement. 【朱熹《論語集注》Zhu Xi: *Annotations of the Analects of Confucius*】

朝過夕改，君子與之。 If mistakes made in the morning are corrected in the evening, it will be appreciated by a gentleman. 【班固《漢書·翟方進傳》Ban Gu: "Biography of Di Fangjin", *History of the Han*】

知錯改錯不算錯，知錯不改錯中錯。 A mistake that is corrected after being found is no longer a mistake, but a mistake that is not corrected after being found is a mistake of mistakes. 【俗語 Common saying】

知錯容易改錯難。 It is easy to find a mistake but difficult to correct it. 【俗語 Common saying】

知錯必改，便是聖賢。 A person who knows his fault and corrects is a sage. 【俗語 Common saying】

仔細不怕多，粗心出差錯。 You can never be too meticulous; carelessness may cause errors. 【俗語 Common saying】

走錯一步棋。 Make a wrong move. 【諺語 Proverb】

Modelling

不法古，不修今。 Do not follow the ancients nor stick to the present. 【商鞅《商君書·開塞》Shang Yang: "Opening and Plugging", *The Works of Shang Yang*】

法乎其上，僅得其中；法乎其中，則得其下。 If one models after the best, what one merely gets will be mediocre. If one models after the mediocre, then what one gets will be inferior. 【唐太宗《帝範·卷四》Emperor Taizong of Tang: Chapter 4, *Rules for an Emperor*】

舉一反三，觸類旁通。 A single item typifies all the rest. 【俗語 Common saying】

前頭烏龜爬上路，後背烏龜趁路爬。 As the tortoise in front has climbed up the path, the tortoise behind will follow suit –pattern after others. 【俗語 Common saying】

人法地，地法天，天法道，道法自然。 Man models himself after earth, earth models itself after heaven, heaven models itself after the Way, and the Way models itself after nature. 【老子《道德經‧第二十五章》Laozi: Chapter 25, *Daodejing*】

一犬吠影，百犬吠聲。 When one dog barks at a shadow, a hundred dogs barks at the noise. 【王符《潛夫論‧賢難》Wang Fu: "Difficulties of Worthies", *Remarks by a Recluse*】

Modesty

滿招損，謙受益。 Complacency incurs losses whereas modesty brings benefits. 【《尚書‧大禹謨》 "Counsels of Yu the Great", *The Book of History*】

謙，德之柄也。 Modesty is the essence of virtue. 【《易經‧繫辭上》 "Appended Remarks, Part 2", *The Book of Changes*】

謙虛的人常思己過，驕傲的人祇論人非。 A modest person often ponders over his mistakes and a conceited person only gossips about the errors made by other people. 【俗語 Common saying】

Money

財帛動人心。 Money is tempting. 【錢彩《說岳全傳‧第八回》Qian Cai: Chapter 8, *A Story of Yue Fei*】

財散人安樂。 When money is spent, peace of mind is possible. 【俗語 Common saying】

財上分明大丈夫。 A true man is beyond reproach in monetary matters. 【《增廣賢文》 *Words that Open up One's Mind and Enhance One's Wisdom*】

財物糞土輕，仁義泰山重。 Money and property are light as refuse whereas benevolence and righteousness, heavy as Mount Tai. 【西周生《醒世姻緣傳‧第三十四回》Xi Zhousheng: Chapter 34, *Stories of Marriage to Awaken the World*】

得人錢財，替人消災。 When you receive money from others, you must remove disasters for them. 【俗語 Common saying】

燈裏無油點不亮，手裏無錢難煞人。 A lantern without oil cannot be lit bright. A person without money in his hand is hard pressed. 【俗語 Common saying】

多金非為貴，安樂值錢多。 Much money is of little value, peace

and contentment are worth great wealth. 【佚名《名賢集》Anonymous: *Collected Sayings of Famous Sages*】

多求不如省費。Trying to get more money is not as good as trying to economize. 【司馬光〈招軍札子〉Sima Guang: "A Memorial on Army Recruitment"】

棺材裏伸手 —— 死要錢。Be greedy for money. 【歇後語 End-clipper】

花了錢，擋了災。Money is spent to prevent a disaster. 【俗語 Common saying】

歡喜破財，不在心上。Losing money in happiness is not a pity. 【凌濛初《二刻拍案驚奇 · 第十一卷》Ling Mengchu: Chapter 11, *Amazing Tales, Volume Two*】

會尋不如省用。One who knows how to make money is not as good as one who knows how to economize. 【俗語 Common saying】

會賺錢，會使錢。One should know how to make money and how to spend it. 【俗語 Common saying】

金錢為萬惡之源。Money is the source of all evil things. 【俗語 Common saying】

君子愛財，取之有道。A gentleman cherishes money and he gets it through proper means. 【《增廣賢文》*Words that Open up One's Mind and Enhance One's Wisdom*】

可以使鬼者錢也，可以使人者權也。It is money that can control the ghost and it is power that can order people about. 【楊慎《丹鉛總錄 · 卷七》Yang Shen: Chapter 7, *Complete Records of Proofreading*】

老子打洞 —— 兒子受用。The father earns, the son spends. 【歇後語 End-clipper】

臨財勿苟得，臨難勿苟免。Don't be unscrupulous in monetary matters or shrink in face of disasters. 【《禮記 · 曲禮上第一》Chapter 1, "Summary of the Rules of Propriety, Part 1", *The Book of Rites*】

羅鍋兒上山 —— 錢（前）緊。A humpback climbing a mountain–short of money. 【歇後語 End-clipper】

馬蹄刀瓢裏切菜 —— 滴水不漏。As stingy as cutting vegetables with a hoof-paring knife in a wooden spoon. 【歇後語 End-clipper】

買醬油的錢不能買醋。Money for soya bean sauce cannot be spent on buying vinegar. 【俗語 Common saying】

每日省一錢，三年併一千。If you save a dollar a day, you will save a thousand in three years. 【俗語 Common saying】

鬧裏有錢，靜處安身。In a noisy area, there is money to be gained; in a quiet area, people have a comfortable life. 【《增廣賢文》*Words that Open up One's Mind and Enhance One's Wisdom*】

寧可無錢，不可無恥。 One would rather be short of money than have no shame. 【諺語 Proverb】

破財是擋災。 Losing money will prevent disasters that may befall one. 【俗語 Common saying】

千錢難買一個願。 A thousand cash cannot buy the willingness of a person. 【俗語 Common saying】

錢財乃身外之物。 Money is something external to our physical being. 【嫩川主人《世無匹‧第三回》E Chun Zhuren: Chapter 3, *Unrivalled in the World*】

錢盡情義絕。 When money is gone, the relationship stops. 【諺語 Proverb】【西泠野樵《繪芳圖‧第十四回》Xiling Yejiao: Chapter 14, *Paintings of Flowers*】

錢聚如兄，錢散如奔。 When you have money, people treat you as an elder brother; when you don't, people run away from you. 【諺語 Proverb】【佚名〈來生債‧第一折〉Anonymous: Scene 1, "The Debt in the Future Life"】

錢買眾人和。 Money can buy harmony. 【俗語 Common saying】

錢親人不親。 It is money that keeps people close together but not people themselves. 【諺語 Proverb】【鄭廷玉〈忍字記‧楔子〉Zheng Tingyu: Prologue, "The Word 'Forbearance'"】

錢生錢，利生利。 Money begets money, and profits beget profits. 【俗語 Common saying】

錢是人之膽。 Money accounts for people's courage. 【俗語 Common saying】

錢要花在刀刃上。 Money should be used on where it is needed most. 【俗語 Common saying】

錢在前頭，人在後頭。 Money goes first and people follow. 【俗語 Common saying】

錢在手邊，食在嘴邊 —— 難留住。 Money in the hand and food in the mouth are difficult to hold onto. 【歇後語 End-clipper】

親生兒不如傍身錢。 One's own son is not as good as money on hand. 【俗語 Common saying】

青酒紅人面，財帛動人心。 Good wine reddens the face of a person while money excites one's heart. 【諺語 Proverb】【西周生《醒世姻緣傳‧第十二回》Xi Zhousheng: Chapter 12, *Stories of Marriage to Awaken the World*】

人情是人情，數目要算清。 Balance accounts with somebody in spite of intimacy. 【諺語 Proverb】

人為財死，鳥為食亡。 People die for money as birds die for food. 【《增廣賢文》*Words that Open up One's Mind and Enhance One's Wisdom*】

人心節節高於天，越是有錢越愛錢。 Man is insatiably greedy; the more money one has the more one wants. 【諺語 Proverb】

少花錢，多辦事。 Spend less but do more. 【俗語 Common saying】

捨命不捨財。 One would rather give up one's life than one's money. 【石玉崑《續小五義・第五十一回》Shi Yukun: Chapter 82, *A Second Sequel to The Five Younger Gallants*】

生時招不來，死時帶不去。 Money is something that you cannot easily get when you're alive or take away with you when you die. 【袁枚〈錢〉Yuan Mei: "Money"】

使錢容易賺錢難，莫把銀錢作等閒。 It is easy to spend money but difficult to earn it, so you should not make light of money. 【諺語 Proverb】

世上錢多賺不盡，朝裏官多做不盡。 There is so much money in the world that you cannot earn all of it. There are so many positions in the royal court that you cannot hold all of them. 【唐寅〈一世歌〉Tang Yin: "Song of a Life"】

說大話，使小錢。 Talk big but spend little money. 【諺語 Proverb】

他財莫要，他馬莫騎。 Do not try to get money that belongs to others; do not ride another's horse. 【諺語 Proverb】【范受益〈尋親記・第二十一齣〉Fan Shouyi: Scene 21, "Seeking Parents"】

天下道理千千萬，沒錢不能把事辦。 There are thousands of hows and whys, but without money you can do nothing. 【俗語 Common saying】【崔復生《太行志・第七章》Cui Fusheng: Chapter 7, *Records of Taixing*】

銅錢斷親戚，銀子壞朋友。 Money cuts off family ties and friendship. 【俗語 Common saying】

銅錢眼裏翻斤斗。 Turn somersaults in the square hole of a coin. 【諺語 Proverb】【張南莊《何典・第二卷》Zhang Nanzhuang: Chapter 2, *From Which Classic*】

無錢難辦稱心事。 Without money one cannot do things in a satisfactory way. 【俗語 Common saying】

勿貪意外之財，勿飲過量之酒。 Don't covet money that is not expected and don't drink more than you can drink. 【朱用純《朱子家訓》Zhu Yongchun: *Percepts of the Zhu Family*】

瞎子見錢眼也開，和尚見錢經也賣。 Money will open a blind person's eyes and will make a monk sell his prayer book. 【諺語 Proverb】【曹玉林《甦醒的原野・第二章》Cao Yulin: Chapter 2, *The Awakened Plain*】

小錢不去，大錢不來。 If a small amount of money does not go out, a large amount of money will not come in. 【諺語 Proverb】

小錢有大用。 A small amount of money can be of great use. 【俗語 Common saying】

衙門八字開，有理無錢莫進來。 The gate of a government office

is wide open, but those who are in the right yet without money should not come in. 【諺語 Proverb】

腰中有錢腰不軟，手中無錢手難鬆。 With money in one's pocket, one can straighten one's back; without money in hand, one feels embarrassed. 【俗語 Common saying】【李綠園《歧路燈‧第七十四回》Li Luyuan: Chapter 74, *Lamp on a Forked Road*】

一分錢掰兩半用。 Live in a small way. 【俗語 Common saying】

一錢逼死英雄漢。 The lack of money has driven a dauntless man to a dead end. 【李綠園《歧路燈‧第二十三回》Li Luyuan: Chapter 23, *Lamp on a Forked Road*】

一錢不落虛空地。 Not a single cent is to be spent uselessly. 【李寶嘉《官場現形記‧第十二回》Li Baojia: Chapter 12, *Officialdom Unmasked*】

義斷親離祇為錢。 Money is the cause of unrighteousness and the alienation of relatives. 【俗語 Common saying】

銀錢如糞土，臉面值千金。 Money is but dirt but the sense of shame is worth one thousand taels of gold. 【崔復生《太行志‧第二十四章》Cui Fusheng: Chapter 24, *Records of Taixing*】

用錢容易賺錢難。 It is easy to use money but difficult to make it. 【俗語 Common saying】

有道之錢方可取。 Take only the money that is earned in a clean way. 【俗語 Common saying】

有分本事賺分錢。 You make the amount of money that your skill deserves. 【俗語 Common saying】

有錢膽就壯。 With money, one can be bold. 【劉鶚《老殘遊記‧第十九回》Liu E: Chapter 19, *Travelogue of Lao Can*】

有錢道真語，無錢語不真。 What is said by the rich is believed and what is said by the poor is not. 【《增廣賢文》*Words that Open up One's Mind and Enhance One's Wisdom*】

有錢蓋百醜。 Money covers all sins. 【俗語 Common saying】

有錢路路通。 Money can buy every success. 【俗語 Common saying】

有錢難買翻生藥。 Even with money, one cannot buy a medicine that can bring the dead to life. 【俗語 Common saying】

有錢能解語，無錢語不聽。 If you have money, people will understand you; if you have no money, no one will take the trouble to listen to you. 【佚名《名賢集》Anonymous: *Collected Sayings of Famous Sages*】

有錢能使鬼推磨。 Money can control the ghost. 【劉義慶《幽明錄‧新鬼》Liu Yiqing: "New Ghosts", *Records of the Dark and Light*】

有錢能說話，無錢話不靈。With money, you can make decisions; without it, you have no say.【俗語 Common saying】

有錢能通神路。Money can buy your way to heaven.【俗語 Common saying】

有錢萬事足。One is satisfied with everything when he has money.【茅盾《霜葉紅似二月花·第五章》Mao Dun: Chapter 5, *The Frosty Leaves are Red as Flowers in the Second Month of the Year*】

有錢未必有福。Money does not always bring happiness.【俗語 Common saying】

有錢像條龍，無錢變條蟲。When one has money, one is like a dragon. When one does not have money, one is like a worm.【諺語 Proverb】

有錢也難買一身安。Money cannot buy safety.【諺語 Proverb】

有錢諸事辦。With money you can succeed in everything.【俗語 Common saying】

張三有錢不會使，李四會使卻無錢。Some have money but they do not know how to use it; others have no money, yet they know how to use it.【諺語 Proverb】【錢希言《戲瑕·卷三》Qian Xiyan: Chapter 3, *Jokes about Flaws*】

掙得多，花得快。The more money one earns, the faster one spends.【俗語 Common saying】

掙錢容易積錢難。It is easy to earn money but difficult to keep it.【俗語 Common saying】

祇識銀錢不認人。Know only money but not people.【俗語 Common saying】

左手來，右手去。Money comes to the left hand and goes with the right.【俗語 Common saying】

Monk

和尚廟對着尼姑庵 —— 沒事也有事。When a monastery faces a convent, scandals will take place sooner or later.【歇後語 End-clipper】

和尚無兒孝子多。Monks do not have sons, but they have lots of filial people.【諺語 Proverb】【曹雪芹《紅樓夢·第八十五回》Cao Xueqin: Chapter 85, *A Dream of the Red Chamber*】

和尚置梳篦 —— 無用。Monks buy combs – useless.【歇後語 End-clipper】

寺僧吃四方。Monks have food to eat wherever they go.【諺語 Proverb】

新來和尚好撞鐘。A new monk likes tolling the bell.【俗語 Common saying】【李綠園《歧路燈·

第八回》Li Luyuan: Chapter 8, *Lamp on a Forked Road*】

厭惡和尚，恨及袈裟。 Those who dislike monks also hate monkish vestments.【俗語 Common saying】

遠來的和尚會唸經。 A monk from afar knows how to chant scriptures.【俗語 Common saying】

丈二和尚，摸不着頭腦。 One cannot touch the head of a monk who is twelve feet tall.【周楫《西湖二集·第二十八卷》Zhou Ji: Chapter 28, *The West Lake, Second Volume*】

捉住和尚要辮子。 Take hold of a monk and ask for his pigtail.【王濬卿《冷眼觀·第二十一回》Wang Junqing: Chapter 21, *Casting a Cold Eye*】

走了和尚走不了廟。 A monk may run away, but the temple cannot run away with him.【丁玲《太陽照在桑乾河上·第三十二章》Ding Ling: Chapter 32, *The Sun Shines on the Sanggan River*】

做一天和尚，敲一天鐘。 As long as one remains a monk, one rings the bell.【李伯元《文明小史·第四十四回》Li Boyuan: Chapter 44, *A Short History of Civilization*】

Moon

本待將心托明月，誰知明月照溝渠。 I was about to entrust my heart to the bright moon, yet it shines on the gutter.【凌濛初《拍案驚奇》Ling Mengchu: *Amazing Tales*】

此生此夜不長好，明月明年何處看。 My life and tonight cannot be so good forever. Next year, where shall I see the bright moon?【蘇軾〈中秋月〉Su Shi: "To the Tune of Mid-Autumn Moon"】

但願人長久，千里共嬋娟。 I only hope that our relationship will be long-lasting, watching the moon even when we are a thousand miles apart.【蘇軾〈水調歌頭〉Su Shi: "To the Tune of Prelude to the Melody of Water"】

當時明月在，曾照彩雲歸。 At that time the moon was there, it once lit the way home for the colourful clouds.【晏幾道〈臨江仙〉Yan Jidao: "To the Tune of an Immortal by the River"】

獨上江樓思渺然，月光如水水如天。 Alone I climb up the Riverside Tower, the moonlight is like water, and the water like heavens.【趙嘏〈江樓感舊〉Zhao Gu: "Recalling the Past on the Riverside Tower"】

多情最是波心月，一路相隨伴我歸。 The moon on the centre of the river is most passionate, for it follows me and keeps me company on my way home.【龔栩〈歸自莊北〉Gong Xu: "Returning from Zhuangbei"】

二十四橋仍在，波心蕩冷月無聲。The twenty-four bridges are still there, the waves are rolling, and the cold moon is quiet. 【姜夔〈揚州慢〉Jiang Kui:"To the Tune of Yangzhou Adagio"】

共看明月應垂淚，一夜鄉心五處同。Together we gaze at the bright moon and surely shed our tears. Though we are scattered in five different places, we share the same longings for home tonight. 【白居易〈自河南經亂〉Bai Juyi:"After the Disorder in Henan"】

古人今人若流水，共看明月皆如此。The ancient people and people today go away like flowing water, yet they all gaze at the moon in the same manner. 【李白〈把酒問月〉Li Bai:"I asked the Moon with a Wine Cup in Hand"】

海上生明月，天涯共此時。A bright moon rises over the sea; far apart we enjoy the moon at the same time. 【張九齡〈望月懷遠〉Zhang Jiuling:"Gazing at the Moon and Thinking of My Dear One Far away"】

江畔何人初見月，江月何年初照人。Who first saw the moon on this riverbank? What year did this river moon first shine on men? 【張若虛〈春江花月夜〉Zhang Ruoxu:"A Flowery Moonlit Night by the Spring River"】

今人不見古時月，今月曾經照古人。People today do not see the moon in ancient times, but the moon tonight did shine on the ancient people. 【李白〈把酒問月〉Li Bai:"I asked the Moon with a Wine Cup in Hand"】

今夜月明人盡望，不知秋思在誰家。Tonight, the moon is bright and all people watch it, yet I don't know which family has autumn thoughts. 【王建〈十五夜望月〉Wang Jian:"Gazing at the Moon at Night on the Fifteenth of the Lunar Month"】

俱懷逸興壯思飛，欲上青天攬明月。Both you and I have the buoyant mood and elated spirit, wishing to fly to the blue sky to embrace the bright moon. 【李白〈宣州謝朓樓餞別校書叔雲〉Li Bai:"Farewell to Uncle Yun, the Imperial Librarian, at Xie Tiao's Tower in Xuanzhou"】

舉杯邀明月，對影成三人。I raise my cup to invite the bright moon. It throws my shadow and makes us a party of three. 【李白〈月下獨酌〉Li Bai:"Drinking Alone under the Moon"】

露從今夜白，月是故鄉明。From tonight the dew will be white with frost, and the moon that shines on our hometown is bright. 【杜甫〈月夜憶舍弟〉Du Fu:"Thinking of My Brothers on a Moonlit Night"】

明月不常圓，好花容易落。A bright moon does not last long and beautiful flowers wither easily.【蘭陵笑笑生《金瓶梅‧第

明月出天山，蒼茫雲海間。 The bright moon rises from Mount Tian, and it shines amonga vast and misty sea of clouds. 【李白〈關山月〉Li Bai:"Moon over the Mountain Pass"】

明月幾時有，把酒問青天。 How often do we have the bright moon? With a cup of wine in hand, I ask the blue sky?【蘇軾〈水調歌頭〉Su Shi:"To the Tune of Prelude to the Melody of Water"】

明月如霜，好風如水，清景無限。 The bright moon is like frost, the fine breeze, water, and the scene is clear and boundless. 【蘇軾〈永遇樂〉Su Shi:"To the Tune of the Joy of Eternal Union"】

明月松間照，清泉石上流。 The bright moon shines on the pines, and the clear spring flows over the pebbles. 【王維〈山居秋暝〉Wang Wei:"Autumn Dusk at a Mountain Lodge"】

暮從碧山下，山月隨人歸。 Dusk descends from the green mountain, and the moon over the mountain follows me on my way home. 【李白〈下終南山過斛斯山人宿置酒〉Li Bai:"Descending Zhongnan Mountain and Meeting Husi the Hermit"】

人生代代無窮已，江月年年望相似。 Human life is endless from generations to generations, and the moon over the river looks the same year after year. 【張若盧〈春江花月夜〉Zhang Ruoxu:"A Night of Flowers and Moon on a River in Spring"】

人有悲歡離合，月有陰晴圓缺。 People have sorrows and joys, partings and unions, just as the moon may be dim or bright, waxing or waning. 【蘇軾〈水調歌頭〉Su Shi:"To the Tune of Prelude to the Melody of Water"】

山近月遠覺月小，便道此山大於月。 When the mountain is near and the moon is far, then one feels that the moon is small, and says that the mountain is larger than the moon. 【王陽明〈蔽月山房〉Wang Yangming:"Moon-concealing Mountain Lodge"】

山月不知心裏事，水風吹落眼前花。 The moon in the mountain does not know what is on my mind, and the wind on the water blows off the flowers before my eyes. 【温庭筠〈望江南〉Wen Tingyun:"To the Tune of Looking at the South"】

誰共我，醉明月。 Who will join me, in getting drunk under a bright moon?【辛棄疾〈賀新郎〉Xin Qiji:"To the Tune of Congratulating the Bridegroom"】

水中撈月 —— 一場空。 It comes to nothing when trying to scoop up the moon from the water. 【歇後語 End-clipper】

天階月色涼如水，臥看牽牛織女星。 The steps in the open space

and moonlight are cool as water, and I laid down and gazed at the Herdboy and Weaving Maid stars. 【杜牧〈秋夕〉Du Mu: "Evening in Autumn"】

同來望月人何處？風景依稀似去年。 Where are those who came to gaze at the moon with me last year? The scene is very much that of last year. 【趙嘏〈江樓感舊〉Zhao Gu: "Recalling the Past on the Riverside Tower"】

聞道欲來相問訊，西樓望月幾回圓。 How many full moons I have watched from my western tower, ever since I learned that you'll come again. 【韋應物〈寄李儋元錫〉Wei Yingwu: "Sent to Li Dan, Styled Yuanxi"】

溪邊小立苦待月，月知人意偏遲出。 I stand by the stream waiting for the moon to rise, but the moon knows my impatience and takes its time. 【楊萬里〈釣雪舟中霜夜望月〉Yang Wanli: "Gazing at the Moon in a Frosty Evening While Fishing Snow in a Boat"】

小時不識月，呼作白玉盤。 When I was a child, I didn't know what the moon was, so I called it a white jade plate. 【李白〈古朗月行〉Li Bai: "Walking under the Moon"】

小舟輕似一鷗飛，戀月隨風慣不歸。 The small boat was light as a flying seagull. I was attracted by the moon, and so I followed the wind and forgot about returning home. 【許棐〈秋江漁文〉Xu Fei: "Walking under the Moon"】

新月有圓夜，人心無滿時。 There are times when the moon is not full, but people are never satisfied. 【釋普濟《五燈會元・卷十六》Shi Puji: Chapter 16, A Compendium of the Five Lamps】

星多不擋月。 Stars, no matter how numerous, cannot cover the light of the moon. 【俗語 Common saying】

一個是水中月，一個是鏡中花。 One is the moon in water and the other, a flower in a mirror. 【曹雪芹《紅樓夢》Cao Xueqin: A Dream of the Red Chamber】

一輪明月，飛彩凝輝。 Rays of the bright moon are in full splendour. 【曹雪芹《紅樓夢・第一回》Cao Xueqin: Chapter 13, A Dream of the Red Chamber】

一年明月今宵多，人生由命非由他，有酒不飲奈若何。 The moon tonight is the fullest of the year. One's life is destined, not controlled by others. How can we not drink wine? 【韓愈〈八月十五夜贈張功曹〉Han Yu: "Presented to Zhang of the Personnel Assessment Section, on the Evening of the Fifteenth of the Eighth Month"】

月出松際雲，清光滿籬舍。 The moon comes out through pine-trees that reach the clouds, and the moonlight fills up my bamboo cottage. 【沈侗〈松際月〉Shen Zhuo: "Moon among the Pines"】

月到天心處，風來水面時。 It is the time when the moon is on

the centre of the sky and the wind is blowing on the face of the water. 【邵雍〈清夜吟〉Shao Yong: "On a Clear Night"】

月到中秋分外明。 The moon at mid-autumn is exceptionally bright. 【馮夢龍《醒世恆言》Feng Menglong: *Stories to Awaken the World*】

月華皎潔，銀光瀉地。 The moonlight was bright and clear, its silvery beams flooded the ground. 【俗語 Common saying】

月近中秋白，風從半夜清。 The moon becomes bright when it is close to mid-autumn, and the wind becomes cool from the midnight. 【高士談〈不眠〉Gao Shitan: "Sleepless"】

月落烏啼霜滿天，江楓漁火對愁眠。 The moon went down, a raven cried, and frost filled the sky. With sadness in my heart I fell asleep with maple leaves and fishing lights dimly in sight. 【張繼〈楓橋夜泊〉Zhang Ji: "Mooring at Night by the Maple Bridge"】

月滿則虧，水滿則溢。 The moon waxes only to wane and water brims only to overflow. 【曹雪芹《紅樓夢·第十三回》Cao Xueqin: Chapter 13, *A Dream of the Red Chamber*】

月色滿天，霜華遍地。 The sky was flooded with moonlight and hoarfrost covered the ground. 【施耐庵《水滸傳·第二回》Shi Nai'an: Chapter 2, *Outlaws of the Marshes*】

月色朦朧，星辰昏暗。 The moonlight was obscure and the stars were dim. 【施耐庵《水滸傳·第六十八回》Shi Nai'an: Chapter 68, *Outlaws of the Marshes*】

月子彎彎照九州，幾家歡樂幾家愁。 The crescent moon shines all the nine provinces. How many families are happy? How many families are sad? 【佚名〈吳歌〉Anonymous: "Song of Wu"】

中天月色好誰看。 The light of the moon in the middle of the sky is beautiful, but who will appreciate it. 【杜甫〈宿府〉Anonymous: "Staying at a General's Headquarters"】

Morning

東方欲曉，曙光微露。 Dawn is about to break in the east, and the morning light glimmers on the horizon. 【俗語 Common saying】

黎明即起，灑掃庭除，要內外整潔。 One gets up when dawn breaks, sprinkles water onto and sweeps the floor in the courtyard and rooms to ensure that the house is clean and tidy inside and outside. 【朱用純《朱子家訓》Zhu Yongchun: *Percepts of the Zhu Family*】

天明還得黑一陣子。 It's always darkest before dawn. 【俗語 Common saying】

一日之計在於晨。 An hour in the morning is worth two in the evening. 【蕭繹《纂要‧梁元帝》 Xiao Yi: "Emperor Yuandi of Liang", *Essentials*】

早起三朝當一天。 To get up early for three mornings is equal to one day of time. 【諺語 Proverb】

Mother

雞無三隻腿，娘有兩條心。 A chicken does not have three legs, but a mother has two hearts. 【諺語 Proverb】

六月的日頭，晚娘的拳頭。 A step-mother's fist is like the scorching sun in summer. 【諺語 Proverb】【吳敬梓《儒林外史‧第五回》 Wu Jingzi: Chapter 5, *An Unofficial History of the World of Literati*】

親娘絮肩，後娘絮邊。 One's own mother puts more cotton on the shoulders when she makes cotton-padded clothes for the son, but his stepmother puts more cotton on the edges. 【俗語 Common saying】

有奶便是娘。 Where there is milk there is a mother. 【諺語 Proverb】

Mother and children

慈母手中線，遊子身上衣。 The thread in the kind mother's hand is for making clothes worn on a travelling son. 【孟郊〈遊子吟〉 Meng Jiao: "Song of a Travelling Son"】

兒不嫌母醜。 A child never dislikes his ugly mother. 【俗語 Common saying】

母不嫌兒醜。 A mother never dislikes her ugly child. 【俗語 Common saying】

母慈悲，子孝順。 If the mother is kind, her son will be filial. 【賈仲名〈對玉梳‧第一折〉 Jia Zhongming: Scene 1, "Finding a Match for the Jade Comb"】

母親眼裏無醜兒。 In the eyes of the mother, not a single child of hers is ugly. 【俗語 Common saying】

娘想兒，長江水，兒想娘，扁擔長。 The time for a mother to think of her son is as long as the waters of Changjiang, whereas the time for a son to think of his mother is as short as a carrying pole. 【諺語 Proverb】

有其母必有其女。 Like mother, like daughter. 【俗語 Common saying】

Mountain

不上高山，不顯平地。 One who has not ascended a high mountain cannot appreciate the level ground. 【西周生《醒世姻緣傳・第九十六回》Xi Zhousheng: Chapter 96, *Stories of Marriage to Awaken the World*】

不識廬山真面目，祇緣身在此山中。 I don't know the true face of Mount Lu, for it was only by chance that I happened to be in this mountain. 【蘇軾〈題西林壁〉Su Shi:"Inscribing the Wall of a West Forest Temple"】

採菊東籬下，悠然見南山。 I pick chrysanthemums by the eastern hedge and gaze leisurely at the southern hills. 【陶淵明〈飲酒〉Tao Yuanming:"Drinking Wine"】

好山十里都如畫，更與橫排一徑松。 Ten miles of fine mountains is like a painting. It also has a path of pine trees lying sideways in a row. 【楊萬里〈江上松徑〉Yang Wanli:"A Pine Path on the River"】

橫看成嶺側成峯，遠近高低各不同。 When you look at the mountain sideways, the mountain has ranges and peaks. It is different if you look at it from afar, from a close distance, from a height, and from a low point. 【蘇軾〈題西林壁〉Su Shi:"Inscribing the Wall of a West Forest Temple"】

忽聞海上有仙山，山在虛無縹渺間。 By chance, he heard of a mountain of immortals in the seas, and this mountain was in a state of visual voidness. 【白居易〈長恨歌〉Bai Juyi:"Song of Everlasting Grief"】

會當凌絕頂，一覽眾山小。 I hope one day I could climb up to the summit of Mount Tai, where I could take a sweeping gaze, with all other mountains looking so small. 【杜甫〈望嶽〉Du Fu:"Gazing down from Mount Tai"】

空山不見人，但聞人語響。 In the deserted mountain, one cannot see anybody, but can hear the sound of people's voice. 【王維〈鹿柴〉Wang Wei:"Luchai Village"】

名人如高人，豈可久不見。 A famous mountain is like an extraordinary person, how can we leave it unseen for a long while? 【陸游〈夜坐憶剡溪〉Lu You:"Remembering the Yan River While Sitting at Night"】

寧過三山，不過一水。 Rather cross over three mountains than a river. 【諺語 Proverb】

怕走崎嶇路，莫想攀高峯。 One who is afraid of the uneven paths can never reach the summit of a high mountain. 【諺語 Proverb】

平蕪盡處是春山，行人更在春山外。 At the end of the plain lie the mountains in spring, and my rider husband has gone beyond the mountains. 【歐陽修〈踏莎行〉Ouyang Xiu:"To the Tune of Hiking through the Suo Grass"】

恰似遮不住的青山隱隱，流不斷的綠水悠悠。 It is like the dimly visible mountains that cannot be concealed and the long blue water that flows without end. 【曹雪芹《紅樓夢·紅豆詞》Cao Xueqin:"Song of Red Beans", *A Dream of the Red Chamber*】

千重峯巒，萬頃巨浪。 A thousand layers of mountain peaks and ten thousand acres of seething waves. 【俗語 Common saying】

千山鳥飛絕，萬徑人蹤滅。 In a thousand mountains, no birds are flying, and on ten thousand paths, there are no traces of people. 【柳宗元〈江雪〉Liu Zongyuan:"River in Snow"】

千嶂裏，長煙落日孤城閉。 Amidst a thousand mountains, a long streak of smoke and the setting sun shut down a solitary town. 【范仲淹〈漁家傲·江雪〉Fan Zhongyan:"River Snow: To the Tune of the Pride of Fishermen"】

青山不盡一重重，重重如畫中。 Green hills extend on and on, one after one; one after one, just like in a picture. 【劉敏中〈阮郎歸〉Liu Minzhong:"To the Tune of the Return of Master Yuan"】

青山不老，綠水長存。 The green mountains never grow old and the blue waters flow on forever. 【羅貫中《三國演義·第六十回》Luo Guanzhong: Chapter 60, *Romance of the Three Kingdoms*】

青山遮不住，畢竟東流去。 The green mountain cannot stop water from flowing, and the river keeps flowing eastward. 【辛棄疾〈菩薩蠻·書江西造壁〉Xin Qiji:"Written on the Zaokou Cliff in Jiangxi: To the Tune of Buddhist Dancers"】

入眼青山看不厭，傍船白鷗自相親。 I never feel tired of watching the green mountain that is pleasing to the eye, and the white gulls that perch on the side of the boat are kissing each other. 【劉著〈月夜泛舟〉Liu Zhu:"Sailing a Boat in a Moonlit Night"】

山不厭高，海不厭深。 Mountains can't be deemed too high and water, too deep. 【曹操〈短歌行〉Cao Cao:"A Short Poem"】

山不在高，有仙則名。水不在深，有龍則靈。 A hill does

not have to be high; it becomes famous if there is an immortal in it. A river does not have to be deep; it becomes holy if there is a dragon in it. 【劉禹錫〈陋室銘〉Liu Yuxi:"Inscription on My Humble Dwelling"】

山高才顯威嚴，水清才顯好看。Only high mountains look majestic and clear waters look beautiful. 【俗語 Common saying】

山高遮不住太陽。A high mountain cannot shut out the sun. 【曹雪芹《紅樓夢·第二十四回》Cao Xueqin: Chapter 24, *A Dream of the Red Chamber*】

山高能容四面看。A beautiful mountain can be viewed from all sides. 【諺語 Proverb】

山近月遠覺月小，便道此山大於月。When the mountain is close and the moon is far, you feel that the moon is small, and say that the mountain is larger than the moon. 【王陽明〈蔽月山房〉Wang Yangming:"The Mountain Lodge that Conceals the Moon"】

山巒相接，河水相連。Mountain ranges are linked and rivers are merged. 【俗語 Common saying】

山氣日夕佳，飛鳥相與還。The tints of the mountain are fine in the evening, while the flying birds one follows the other return to their nests. 【陶淵明〈飲酒〉Tao Yuanming:"Drinking Wine"】

山深失小寺，湖盡得孤亭。When the mountain is deep, the small temple is out of sight. When the lake is dry, a solitary pagoda is in sight. 【唐庚〈栖禪暮歸書所見〉Tang Geng:"What I Saw When Returning Home in the Evening After Staying in a Buddhist Temple"】

山水之樂，得之心而寓之酒也。The pleasure of the mountain and river is obtained in the heart and lodged in wine. 【歐陽修〈醉翁亭記〉Ouyang Xiu:"The Story of the Old Drunkard Pavillion"】

山隨平野盡，江入大荒流。The mountains end at the open plain, and the river flows into the wilderness. 【李白〈渡荊門送別〉Li Bai:"Sailing through the Thorn Gates to See off a Friend"】

山外青山樓外樓，西湖歌舞幾時休。Beyond the mountain is the green hill, and beyond one mansion is another; when will the dancing and singing at West Lake come to an end? 【林洪〈西湖〉Lin Hong:"The West Lake"】

上了一山又一山，一山更比一山高。When you climb up a mountain, there is yet another mountain to climb, and the mountain is higher than another mountain. 【俗語 Common saying】

上山容易下山難。Going uphill is easy but going downhill is difficult. 【俗語 Common saying】

深山畢竟藏猛虎，大海終須納細流。Remote mountains after all hide fierce tigers and the big sea eventually accept waters from small rivers. 【《增廣賢文》Words that Open up One's Mind and Enhance One's Wisdom】

泰山不卻微塵，積小壘成高大。 Mount Tai does not refuse minute particles of sand and itaccumulates small grains and increases its height. 【佚名《名賢集》Anonymous: *Collected Sayings of Famous Sages*】

泰山不讓壤土。 Mount Tai does not reject small amounts of earth. 【李斯〈諫逐客書〉Li Si:"Admonition against Ordering Guests to Leave"】

五嶽尋仙不辭遠，一生好入名山遊。 I did not mind the distance and went to the Five Mountains to seek fairies. All my life, I like climbing up and roaming about in mountains. 【李白〈廬山謠寄盧侍御盧舟〉Li Bai:"Song of Mount Lu – To Censor Lu Xuzhou"】

下山容易上山難。 Going downhill is easy but going uphill is difficult. 【俗語 Common saying】

有了青山，不愁俊鳥不來。 When there is a green mountain, beautiful birds are sure to come. 【俗語 Common saying】

一登一陟一回顧，我腳高時他更高。 I looked back each time I climbed higher and found that when my feet were high, the mountain is even higher. 【楊萬里〈過上湖嶺望招賢江南北山〉Yang Wanli:"Looking at the Mountain after passing the Lake"】

一丘一壑也風流。 Each hill and vale has a beauty of its own. 【辛棄疾〈鷓鴣天〉Xin Qiji:"To the Tune of Partridge in the Sky"】

一折青山一扇屏，一灣碧水一條琴。 Each bend of green hill is a screen and each bay of water is a zither. 【劉嗣綰〈自錢塘至桐廬舟中雜詩〉Liu Siguan:"Random Thoughts When Sailing in a Boat from Qiantong to Tonglu"】

Mouse

鳳生鳳，龍生龍，老鼠生的會打洞。 Phoenixes give birth to phoenixes, dragons give birth to dragons, and rats give birth to rats capable of boring holes into walls. 【俗語 Common saying】

滾水潑老鼠 —— 皮爛毛脫。 Like a rat in scalding water. 【歇後語 End-clipper】

老鼠過街，人人喊打。 Everybody yells to kill them when rats cross the street. 【俗語 Common saying】

老鼠看倉 —— 看個精光。When you ask the mice to look after your barn, you will have nothing left behind. 【歇後語 End-clipper】

老鼠拉木鍬 —— 大頭在後頭。A mouse pulls a wooden winnowing spade – the bigger side is following behind. 【歇後語 End-clipper】

老鼠怕見貓。A mouse is afraid of encountering a cat. 【俗語 Common saying】

老鼠尾巴生癤子 —— 出膿也不多。A boil on a rat's tail does not contain much pus. 【歇後語 End-clipper】

老鼠咬烏龜 —— 沒法下手。A rat trying to bite a tortoise does not know where to start. 【歇後語 End-clipper】

哪個老鼠不偷油。What rat won't steal oil? 【俗語 Common saying】

一隻老鼠壞一鍋湯。One mouse spoils a whole pot of soup. 【俗語 Common saying】

Mouth

八哥兒的嘴巴 —— 人云亦云。A myna's tongue – echoing the voices of others. 【歇後語 End-clipper】

八哥兒的嘴巴 —— 專說二話。A myna's tongue – only parroting. 【歇後語 End-clipper】

八哥兒學舌 —— 裝人腔。A myna learning to speak – pretending to sound human. 【歇後語 End-clipper】

八十歲奶奶的嘴 —— 老掉牙了。The mouth of an eighty-year-old granny is toothless. 【歇後語 End-clipper】

白糖嘴巴砒霜心。The mouth is like sugar, and the heart, arsenic. 【俗語 Common saying】

茶壺沒有把兒 —— 光剩嘴兒了。A teapot without a handle – only the spout is left. 【歇後語 End-clipper】

大姑娘說媒 —— 難張口。Find it hard to open one's mouth, like a young girl to act as a match-maker. 【歇後語 End-clipper】

達者三緘口似瓶。A broad-minded person keeps his mouth shut like a corked bottle. 【俗語 Common saying】

戴着斗笠親嘴 —— 差着一帽子。Wearing a straw helmet to kiss and the lips are far apart. 【歇後語 End-clipper】【吳敬梓《儒林外史·第十四回》Wu Jingzi: Chapter 14, *An Unofficial History of the World of Literati*】

防民之口，甚於防川。To guard against rumours from the

people is more difficult than guarding against flooding. 【左丘明《國語・周語》Zuo Qiuming: "The Language of Zhou", *National Languages*】

狗掀門簾 —— 全憑一張嘴。 A dog raising a door screen – all depends on its mouth. 【歇後語 End-clipper】

狗咬刺蝟 —— 下不得嘴。 A dog trying to eat a hedgehog – unable to take a bite. 【歇後語 End-clipper】

急開眼珠慢開口。 Open your eyes quickly but your mouth slowly. 【俗語 Common saying】

口是禍之門。 The mouth is the door to disasters. 【馮道〈舌〉Feng Dao: "Tongue"】

口是傷人斧，言是割人刀。 The mouth is an axe to hurt people and the words are a knife to cut a person. 【俗語 Common saying】

拿得住的是手，掩不住的是口。 You can catch one's hand, but you can't seal one's mouth. 【諺語 Proverb】

人呆得住，嘴呆不住。 People can stop moving, but their mouths can't. 【俗語 Common saying】

三個不開口，神仙難下手。 If a person has decided not to open his mouth, then even fairiescan do nothing about him. 【王濬卿《冷眼觀・第二十九回》Wang Junqing: Chapter 29, *Casting a Cold Eye*】

傷人一語，利如刀割。 Hurting people with a word is as sharp as cutting them with a knife. 【《增廣賢文》Words that Open up One's Mind and Enhance One's Wisdom】

守口如瓶，防意如城。 Keep your mouth shut as you stop a bottle with a cork; guard against selfish desires as you guard a city against the attack by the enemy. 【朱熹《朱子語類・第一百五十卷》Zhu Xi, Chapter 150, *Classified Conversations of Master Zhu*】

壇口好封，人口難捂。 It is easy to seal the mouth of a jar but difficult to cover the mouth of a person. 【陳登科《赤龍與丹鳳・第一部・第二十一章》Chen Dengke: Part 1, Chapter 21, *Red Dragon and Red Phoenix*】

惡利口之覆邦家者。 I dislike those who overthrow kingdoms and families with their sharp tongues. 【孔子《論語・陽貨篇第十七》Confucius: Chapter 17, *The Analects of Confucius*】

笑口常開，青春常在。 Wear a smile often, and feel young all the time. 【俗語 Common saying】

一手難堵眾口。 A single hand cannot muffle the voice of the people. 【俗語 Common saying】

嘴大喉嚨小。 The eye is bigger than the belly. 【俗語 Common saying】

嘴是無底坑。 The mouth is a bottomless pit. 【俗語 Common saying】

Movement

百動不如一靜。 Still is effective.
【西周生《醒世姻緣傳・第三十四回》
Xi Zhousheng: Chapter 34, *Stories of Marriage to Awaken the World*】

動為靜之基，清為濁之源。
Movement is the base of tranquility and purity is the source of turbidity. 【老子《道德經》
Laozi: *Daodejing*】

橄欖屁股 —— 坐不住。 The bottom of a Chinese olive cannot sit firmly – one cannot sit still. 【歇後語 End-clipper】

蛤蟆蹦三蹦，還得歇三歇。 When frogs make three hops, they have to rest three times. 【孔厥，袁靜《新兒女英雄傳・第七回》Kong Jue and Yuan Jing: Chapter 7, *New Biographies of Heroes and Heroines*】

猢猻屁股 —— 坐不住。 A macaque's bottom is hyperactive – one can't sit still. 【歇後語 End-clipper】

老牛拉破車 —— 慢吞吞。 An old ox drags a broken cart, going very slowly. 【歇後語 End-clipper】

靜如處女，動如脫兔。 One who could be still as a coy woman at one moment but agile like an escaping rabbit the next moment. 【孫武《孫子兵法・九地第十一》Sun Wu: Chapter 11, "The Nine Situations", *The Art of War by Sunzi*】

一着不慎，滿盤皆輸。 One careless move and the whole game is lost. 【俗語 Common saying】

一子落錯，滿盤皆輸。 One careless move may lose the whole game. 【俗語 Common saying】

Music

不覺碧山暮，秋雲暗幾重。
Without knowing it, dusk has descended on the green mountain, and the autumn clouds have layers and layers of darkness. 【李白〈聽蜀僧濬彈琴〉
Li Bai: "On Hearing a Monk from Shu Playing His Lute"】

嘈嘈切切錯雜彈，大珠小珠落玉盤。 The thick and fine strings were plucked in a mixed way,

and it sounded like large and small pearls dropping onto a jade tray. 【白居易〈琵琶行，並序〉
Bai Juyi: "Song of a *Pipa* Player, with a Foreword"】

大弦嘈嘈如急雨，小弦切切如私語。 The thick strings rattled like platters of a sudden rain while the fine ones hummed like a hushed whisper. 【白居易

〈琵琶行，並序〉Bai Juyi:"Song of a *Pipa* Player, with a Forward"】

古調雖自愛，今人多不彈。
Though the ancient tune are what I love, most people nowadays don't play them.【劉長卿〈聽彈琴〉Liu Changqing:"Listening to Zither Playing"】

鼓不打不響，鐘不撞不鳴。A drum will not make a sound if it is not struck and a bell will not toll if it is not struck.【名教中人《好逑傳．第十六回》Mingjiao Zhongren: Chapter 16, *A Story of Love*】

故音樂者，所以動蕩血脈，通流精神而和正心也。Music is something that vibrates our pulses, circulates our spirits, and recitifies our mind.【司馬遷《史記．樂書》Sima Qian:"Music", *Records of the Grand Historian*】

好鼓不用重槌敲。A good drum does not need a heavy drumstick.【諺語 Proverb】

將琴代語兮，聊寫衷腸。I use a lute instead of words to express my deep love for her.【司馬相如〈鳳求凰〉Sima Xiangru:"A Phoenix Seeks His Mate"】

驪宮高處入青雲，仙樂飄飄處處聞。The lofty Li Palace enters into the blue clouds, the fairy music floats in the air and can be heard everywhere.【白居易〈長恨歌〉Bai Juyi:"Song of Everlasting Grief"】

目送歸鴻，手揮五弦。My eyes follow the returning swans, and my fingers are plucking the five strings.【嵇康〈贈秀才入軍〉Ji Kang:"Presented to a School on Joining the Army"】

千呼萬喚始出來，猶抱琵琶半遮面。We hailed and urged her many times before she would rise and come, still half-concealing her face with the *pipa* she carried.【白居易〈琵琶行，並序〉Bai Juyi:"Song of a Pipa Player, with a Foreword"】

曲罷不知人在否，餘音嘹亮尚飄空。I wonder if the player stays there when the song ends. The lingering notes of the flute are still floating in the air.【趙嘏〈聞笛〉Zhao Gu:"Hearing a Flute"】

射箭看靶子，彈琴看對象。In shooting, aim one's arrow at the target; in playing a musical instrument, choose a tune for one's audience.【俗語 Common saying】

移風易俗，莫善於樂。There is nothing better than music when it comes to changing the customs and habits of the people.【《孝經．廣要道章第十二》Chapter 12, "Broad and Crucial Doctrine", *Book of Filial Piety*】

一簫一劍平生意，負盡狂名十五年。My love of the flute and the sword has been lifelong. For this, I have been given the name of madman for fifteen years.【龔自珍〈漫感〉Gong Zizhen:"Random Thoughts"】

餘音繞樑儷，三日不絕。The musical notes lingered around the beams of the house and did not die away for three days.【列禦寇《列子‧湯問第五》Lie Yukou: Chapter 5, "Questions of Tang", *Liezi*】

欲將心事付瑤琴。知音少，絃斷有誰聽？I was to confide my feelings to my lute, but admirers are few. Who would listen even when I break my lute strings?【岳飛〈小重山〉Yue Fei: "To the Tune of Manifold Hills"】

欲取鳴琴彈，恨無知音賞。I intend to take my zither and play it. Regrettably, no one would be here to appreciate it.【孟浩然〈夏日南亭懷辛大〉Meng Haoran: "Thinking of Xin the Elder on a Summer Day at the South Pavilion"】

樂者樂也。君子樂得其道，小人樂得其欲。Music is rejoice. A gentleman rejoices in the right principles whereas a petty person rejoices in getting what he desires.【荀況《荀子‧樂論第二十》Xun Kuang: Chapter 20, "On Music", *Xunzi*】

樂者，聖人之所樂也。Music is what is rejoiced by a sage.【荀況《荀子‧樂論第二十》Xun Kuang: Chapter 20, "On Music", *Xunzi*】

樂者，音之所由生也；其本在人心之感於物也。Music is born of sounds and its source is based on people's mind being affected by things.【《禮記‧樂記第十九章》Chapter 19, "Records on the Subject of Music", *The Book of Rites*】

轉軸撥弦三兩聲，未成曲調先有情。She turned the pegs and plucked the the strings a few times, and there was much feeling even before the music was played.【白居易〈琵琶行，並序〉Bai Juyi: "Song of a *Pipa* Player, with a Foreword"】

Name

呼我牛也而謂之牛，呼我馬也而謂之馬。If people call me cow, then my name is cow; if people call me horse, then my name is horse.【莊周《莊子‧外篇‧天道第十三》Zhuang Zhou: Chapter 13, "The Way of Heaven", "Outer Chapters", *Zhuangzi*】

君子疾沒世而名不稱焉。What is of concern to a gentleman is that after his death, his name does not correspond to what it deserves.【孔子《論語‧衛靈公篇第十五》Confucius: Chapter 15, *The Analects of Confucius*】

名不正，則言不順；言不順，則事不成。When names are not proper, what one says will not be smooth; when what is said is not smooth, then things will not be accomplished.【孔子《論語‧子

路篇第十三》Confucius: Chapter 13, *The Analects of Confucius*】

名可名，非常名。The name that can be talked about is not a constant name.【老子《道德經・第一章》Laozi: Chapter 1, *Daodejing*】

名也者，相軋也。To seek a name, people fight against each other.【莊周《莊子・內篇・人間世第四》Zhuang Zhou: Chapter 4, "Human World", "Inner Chapters", *Zhuangzi*】

名者，實之賓也。A name is an object of reality.【莊周《莊子・內篇・逍遙遊第一》Zhuang Zhou: Chapter 1, "Carefree Wandering", "Inner Chapters", *Zhuangzi*】

人有名，樹有影。A person has a name just like a tree has a shadow.【蘭陵笑笑生《金瓶梅・第七十二回》Lanling Xiaoxiaosheng: Chapter 72, *The Plum in the Golden Vase*】

人有人名，地有地名。A person has a name just like a place has a name.【俗語 Common saying】

無名天地之始，有名萬物之母。The unnamed is the beginning of heaven and earth and the named is the mother of myriad things.【老子《道德經・第一章》Laozi: Chapter 1, *Daodejing*】

行不更名，坐不改姓。One never changes one's name whether one travels or stays at home.【施耐庵《水滸傳・第二十七回》Shi Nai'an: Chapter 27, *Outlaws of the Marshes*】

Nature

不恬不愉，非德也。If people do not have desires nor pleasures, this is inconsient with human nature.【莊周《莊子・外篇・在宥第十一》Zhuang Zhou: Chapter 11, "Preserving and Accepting", "Miscellaneous Chapters", *Zhuangzi*】

打得肉爛，本性依然。Even if one is beaten till his flesh is smashed, one's nature remains unchanged.【俗語 Common saying】

哪個貓兒不吃腥。There is no cat that does not eat fish.【施耐庵《水滸傳・第二十一回》Shi Nai'an: Chapter 21, *Outlaws of the Marshes*】

人性本惡，其善者偽。Human nature is originally evil and the goodness of human nature is pretended.【荀況《荀子・性惡第二十三》Xun Kuang: Chapter 23, "Human Nature Is Evil", *Xunzi*】

人性之無分於善與不善也，猶水之無分於東西也。Human nature is indifferent to good and evil, just likethe water is indifferent to the east or west.【孟軻《孟子・告子章句上》Meng Ke: Chapter 6, Part 1, *Mencius*】

人之初，性本惡。Human nature is evil at birth.【荀況《荀子・性

惡第二十三》Xun Kuang: Chapter 23, "Human Nature Is Bad", *Xunzi*】

人之初，性本善。 Human nature is good at birth. 【王應麟《三字經》 Wang Yinglin: *Three-character Classic*】

人之性善惡混。 Human nature is a mixture of good and evil. 【俗語 Common saying】

少無適俗韻，性本愛丘山。 Since youth, I have been out of tune with the vulgar world. By nature, I love hills and mountains. 【陶淵明〈歸田園居〉 Tao Yuanming: "Returning to My Rural Home"】

石可破也，而不可奪堅；丹可磨也，而不可奪赤。 Stone can be smashed, but its hardness cannot be taken away; cinnabar can be ground, but its redness cannot be taken away. 【呂不韋《呂氏春秋‧誠廉》Lu Buwei:"Sincerity and Honesty", *Master Lu's Spring and Autumn Annals*】

食、色，性也。 The desire for food and sex is human nature. 【孟軻《孟子‧告子章句上》Meng Ke: Chapter 6, Part 1, *Mencius*】

偷食貓兒性不改。 A cat that steals food will not change its habit. 【馮夢龍《醒世恆言‧第十七卷》Feng Menglong: Chapter 17, *Stories to Awaken the World*】

偷書不為賊。 One who steals books is not guilty. 【俗語 Common saying】

性不能改，命不能換。 Human nature is unchangeable, so is fate. 【俗語 Common saying】

Neighbour

和得鄰里好，猶如拾片寶。 If you are on good terms with your neighbours, it is like picking up a piece of treasure from the ground. 《增廣賢文》*Words that Open up One's Mind and Enhance One's Wisdom*】

老鷹不吃窩下食。 Even an eagle does not eat what is close around its nest. 【諺語 Proverb】

鄰居好，勝金寶。 Good neighbours are better than treasures. 【諺語 Proverb】

鄰居做官，大家喜歡。 When one's neighbour becomes an official, everyone is happy. 【俗語 Common saying】

寧惱遠親，不惱近鄰。 Rather offend distant relatives than close neighbours. 【諺語 Proverb】

千金賣鄰，八百賣舍。 One would spend a thousand pieces of gold to get good neighbours. 【諺語 Proverb】

兔子不吃窩邊草，老鷹不打窩下食。 A rabbit does not eat

the grass near its own hole and an old eagle doesn't rob its neighbour's henroost.【諺語 Proverb】

毋卜其居，而卜其鄰舍。 Do not choose your house, but choose your neighbours.【晏嬰《晏子春秋‧內篇雜下》Yan Ying: "Micellanous Inner Chapters, Part 2", *Master Yan's Spring and Autumn Annals*】

行要好伴，住要好鄰。 On the road, you need good companions; at home, you need good neighbours.【俗語 Common saying】

遠親不如近鄰。 Distant relatives are not as good as neighbours.【俗語 Common saying】

News

報喜不報憂。 Report only the good news and not the bad.【俗語 Common saying】

財神爺叫門——天大的好事。 The God of Wealth knocking at the door–a heavenly boon.【歇後語 End-clipper】

惡事行千里。 Ill news runs apace.【釋道原《景德傳燈錄‧紹宗禪師》Shi Daoyuan: "Chan Master Shaozong", *Records of the Transmission of the Lamp in the Jingde Period*】

好事不出門，壞事傳千里。 Good news does not go beyond the door, but bad news spreads to a thousand miles.【《增廣賢文》*Words that Open up One's Mind and Enhance One's Wisdom*】

泥牛入海無消息。 A clay ox goes into the sea will no longer be heard of again.【釋普濟《五燈會元‧元日禪師》Shi Puji: "Chan Master Yuanri", *A Compendium of the Five Lamps*】

Nobility

寒門出貴子，白屋出公卿。 A poor family brings forth honourable men, dukes, and ministers.【汪應銓〈題讀書樓〉Wang Yingquan: "Inscription on My Book-reading Tower"】

侯門深似海。 The mansions of the nobility are deep like the

sea.【崔郊〈贈婢詩〉Cui Jiao: "A Poem Presented to a Maid"】

人生何謂貴？閉戶讀我書。 What is nobility in life? Nobility is closing the doors to read my books.【汪應銓〈題讀書樓〉Wang Yingquan: "Inscription on Book-reading Tower"】

時勢為天子，未必貴也；窮為匹夫，未必賤也。貴賤之分，在於行之美惡。 When it is the situation that you become king, it does not mean that you are noble. When you are poor as a commoner, it does not mean that you are low. The distinction between nobility and lowness lies with whether one's behaviour is good or bad.【莊周《莊子‧雜篇‧盜跖第二十九》：Zhuang Zhou: Chapter 29, "Robber Footpad", "Miscellaneous Chapters", *Zhuangzi*】

No turning-back

潑水難收，人逝不返。 Spilt water cannot be gathe Red up again and the dead cannot come back to life.【吳承恩《西遊記‧第十一回》Wu Cheng'en: Chapter 11, *Journey to the West*】

急水沒有回頭浪。 A rapid stream has no adverse currents.【俗語 Common saying】

開弓沒有回頭箭。 Once the arrow is out, it cannot fly back.【俗語 Common saying】

棋盤裏的卒子 —— 只能進，不能退。 Like a pawn on a chessboard, it can only move ahead, and there is no turning back.【歇後語 End-clipper】

肉包子打狗 —— 有去沒回。 Pelting a dog with a meat dumpling, once gone it never returns.【歇後語 End-clipper】

一去不復返。 Once gone, never to return.【司馬遷《史記‧刺客列傳》Sima Qian: "Biographies of Assassins", *Records of the Grand Historian*】

Official

邦有道穀，邦無道穀，恥也。 To think only of one's stipend when the country is in order is a disgrace; to think only of one's stipend when the country is not in order is also a disgrace.【孔子《論語‧憲問篇第十四》Confucius: Chapter 14, *The Analects of Confucius*】

不在其位，不謀其政。 One who is not in office will no longer concern himself with office administration.【孔子《論語‧泰伯篇第八》Confucius: Chapter 8, *The Analects of Confucius*】

朝裏無人別做官。 If one has no connections in the court, one should not serve as an official.【諺語 Proverb】

朝中有人好做官。 If one has connections in the court, it

would be easy for one to serve as an official. 【文康《兒女英雄傳·第三十三回》Wen Kang: Chapter 33, *Biographies of Young Heroes and Heroines*】

廚房有人好做飯，朝裏有人好做官。 If one has connections in the kitchen, it is easy for one to prepare a meal. If one has connections in the court, it is easy for one to serve as an official. 【俗語 Common saying】

當官的動動嘴，當兵的跑折腿。 An official only gives order where his subordinates have to do all the work. 【諺語 Proverb】

當官容易作事難。 It is easy to be an official but difficult to act in his capacity. 【俗語 Common saying】

官愛民，民才敬官。 Only when the officials love the people will the people love them. 【俗語 Common saying】

官不打順民。 Officials will not subject obedient people to torture. 【俗語 Common saying】

官不威，爪牙威。 The official is not awesome, but his runners and lackeys are. 【凌濛初《初刻拍案驚奇·第二十二卷》Ling Mengchu: Chapter 22, *Amazing Tales, Volume One*】

官場如戲場。 Official circles are like theatres. 【諺語 Proverb】

官出於民，民出於土。 Officials depend on people, and people, land. 【諺語 Proverb】

官大一品壓死人。 An official of a higher rank bullies an official of a lower rank. 【諺語 Proverb】

官大有險，權大生謗。 High-ranking officials are faced with dangers and a powerful person is apt to cause slanders. 【俗語 Common saying】【郭小亭《濟公全傳·第二十四回》Guo Xiaoting: Chapter 24, *Biography of Jigong*】

官達者未必當其位，譽美者未必副其名。 A high-ranking official may not be qualified to hold his position; a person who has a good reputation may not match the name he enjoys. 【葛洪《抱朴子·外篇·博喻第三十八》Ge Hong: Chapter 38, "Extensive Analogies", "Outer Chapters", *The Master Who Embraces Simplicity*】

官多則亂，將多則敗。 When there are too many officials, there will be chaos; when there are too many generals, there will be defeats. 【顧炎武《日知錄·醫師》Gu Yanwu: "Doctors", *Records of Daily Knowledge*】

官非其任不處也，祿非其功不受也。 An office that one is not suitable for will not be taken up; a payment that is not due to one's service will not be accepted. 【司馬遷《史記·日者列傳》Sima Qian: "Biographies of Soothsayers", *Records of the Grand Historian*】

官高奴也大。 Servants of high-ranking officials are also highly respected. 【俗語 Common saying】

官官相護，公事相顧。 Officials protect each other and this applies to the handling of official matters.【馮夢龍《醒世恆言・第二十卷》Feng Menglong: Chapter 20, *Stories to Awaken the World*】

官家爭權，百姓遭殃。 When officials scramble for power, people will suffer.【諺語 Proverb】

官禁私不禁。 The government bans something in public but not in private.【羅貫中《平妖傳・第十七回》Luo Guanzhong: Chapter 17, *Taming Devils*】

官滿如花謝。 When the time of holding office is over, an official is like a flower that is withe Red.【佚名《名賢集》Anonymous: *Collected Sayings of Famous Sages*】

官娘死了滿街白，官兒死了沒人抬。 When the wife of an official dies, the entire street will be in white, but when the official himself dies, no one comes to carry his coffin.【俗語 Common saying】

官清民自安，法正天心順。 When the officials are honest, people will be peaceful. When laws are enforced strictly, people will be obedient.【關漢卿〈哭存孝・第二折〉Guan Hanqing: Scene 2, "Tears and Filial Piety"】

官清司吏瘦，神靈廟祝肥。 When officials are honest, their clerks are thin. When the gods reveal accurate predictions, the temple-keepers are fat.【《增廣賢文》*Words that Open up One's Mind and Enhance One's Wisdom*】

官去衙門在。 Officials go but their offices remain there.【俗語 Common saying】

官身不自由。 Officials, bound by their capacity, are not free.【俗語 Common saying】

官無常貴，民無終賤。 The officials cannot be noble forever, and people cannot be humble forever.【墨翟《墨子・尚賢卷八至十》Mo Di: Chapters 8-10, "Exalting the Worthies", *Mozi*】

好官易做，好人難做。 It is easy to be a good official but difficult to be a good person.【李之彥《東谷所見》Li Zhiyan: *What Is Seen by Me*】

賀下不賀上。 Congratulate one who leaves office but not one who takes office.【蘇軾〈東坡志林・卷二〉Su Shi: Chapter 2, *A Forest of Records of Su Dongpo*】

虎惡狼惡沒有奸臣惡。 The most ferocious tigers and wolves are no match for a treacherous court official.【俗語 Common saying】

黃蜂針尾，貪官心狠。 A corrupt official is ruthless and a wasp's sting is poisonous.【俗語 Common saying】

家無讀書子，官從何處來。 If there is not a scholar at home, how can there be an official in the family?【《增廣賢文》*Words that*

Open up One's Mind and Enhance One's Wisdom】

進則兼善天下，退則獨善其身。
When in office, one works to benefit all the people in the world; when retired, he will go in for self-cultivation. 【孟軻《孟子·盡心章句上》Meng Ke: Chapter 7, Part 1, *Mencius*】

其身正，不令而行；其身不正，雖令不從。If an official is upright, his policy will be executed even though he does not give orders. If an official is not upright, his policy will not be executed even though he gives orders.【孔子《論語·子路篇第十三》Confucius: Chapter 13, *The Analects of Confucius*】

千變萬變，官場不變。There might be myriad changes, but the official circles remain unchanged. 【田漢〈琵琶行·第五十八場〉Tian Han: Act 58, "Song of a *Pipa* Player"】

千里為官祇為財。One who goes a thousand miles away to be an official wants nothing but money. 【李伯元《活地獄·第四十三回》Li Boyuan: Chapter 43, *Living Hell*】

千里做官，為了吃穿。One who goes a thousand miles to be an official just wants to have good food and fine clothes. 【郭小亭《濟公全傳·第一百三十三回》Guo Xiaoting: Chapter 133, *Biography of Jigong*】

千里做官祇為口，萬里求財祇為身。One goes a thousand miles to be an official just for the sake of the mouth; one goes ten thousand miles to earn money just for the sake of the body. 【俗語 Common saying】

清官難斷家務事。Even an honest official can't judge domestic cases. 【馮夢龍《喻世明言·第十卷》Feng Menglong: Chapter 10, *Stories to Instruct the World*】

清官萬民愛。A good official is loved by ten thousand people. 【俗語 Common saying】

窮官兒好過富百姓。Even a poor government official is richer than the common people. 【俗語 Common saying】

任官惟賢才。In the appointment of officials, select only talents with morality. 【《尚書·咸有一德》"Common Possession of Pure Virtue", *The Book of History*】

任你官清似水，難逃吏滑如油。No matter how honest and upright officials you are, you cannot avoid being fooled by the cunning and slippery runners. 【馮夢龍《醒世恆言·第二十卷》Feng Menglong: Chapter 20, *Stories to Awaken the World*】

三年清知府，十萬雪花銀。Having serving as an honest prefect for three years, he collected ten thousand taels of snow-white silver. 【吳敬梓《儒林外史·第八回》Wu Jingzi: Chapter 8, *An Unofficial History of the World of Literati*】

仕而優則學，學而優則仕。An official is a good scholar and a good scholar will make an official.【孔子《論語・子張篇第十九》Confucius: Chapter 19, *The Analects of Confucius*】

樹有墩，官有根。A tree must have roots, and an official, backing.【俗語 Common saying】

鐵打的衙門流水的官。The office of an official is as solid as iron, but the officials change as constantly as the flowing water.【俗語 Common saying】

未做官時說千般，做了官時一般。When one has not taken office, he makes a thousand promises, but when he has taken office, he is just the same as other officials.【諺語 Proverb】

文臣不愛錢，武臣不惜死。Civil officials are not greedy for money, and military officials are not afraid of death.【脫脫等《宋史・岳飛傳》Toktoghan, et al: "Biography of Yue Fei", *History of the Song*】

文官把筆安天下，武將持刀定太平。Civil officials make the state stable with their writing brushes and military generals ensure peace for the state with their swords.【朱葵心〈回春記・第十三齣〉Zhu Kuaixin: Scene 13, "The Return of Spring"】

文官動動嘴，武官跑斷腿。Civil officials use their mouths whereas military officials run off their legs.【施世綸《施公案・第三百四十二回》Shi Shilun: Chapter 342, *Cases of Judge Shi*】

文官三隻手，武官四隻腳。The civil officials have three hands and the military officials, four feet.【譚嗣同〈上歐陽中鵠書〉Tan Sitong: "A Letter to Ouyang Zhonggu"】

無官一身輕。One feels carefree when one is no longer an official.【蘇軾〈賀子由生第四孫〉Su Shi: "Congratulating Myself on the Birth of the Fourth Grandson"】

小官抵得富百姓。A petty official is better than an ordinary rich man.【俗語 Common saying】

笑罵由他笑罵，好官我自為之。Let people ridicule or revile as they like, but I happily remain an official.【脫脫等《宋史・鄧綰傳》Toktoghan, *et al*: "Biography of Deng Wan", *History of the Song*】

笑面官，打死人。An official with a smiling face beats people to death.【俗語 Common saying】

新官上任三把火。A new official is vigorous for three days.【羅貫中《三國演義・第四十回》Luo Guanzhong: Chapter 40, *Romance of the Three Kingdoms*】

休官莫問子。Do not ask your son when you are going to resign from office.【吳敬梓《儒林外史・第八回》Wu Jingzi: Chapter 8, *An Unofficial History of the World of Literati*】

衙門八字開，有理無錢莫進來。The gate of a courthouse is

wide open, but those who have justice on their side but are poor should not go in. 【俗語 Common saying】

一代贓官七代娼。 A corrupt official will have seven generations of woman descendants who will become prostitutes. 【諺語 Proverb】

一代做官，七代打磚。 In this general you are an official, but in the coming seven generations your descendants will become bricklayers. 【張恨水《最後關頭・卷上》Zhang Henshui: Part 1, *The Last Moment*】

一封朝奏九重天，夕貶潮陽路八千。 A memorial to the emperor in the morning and I was banished Chaoyang eight thousand miles away in the evening. 【韓愈〈左遷至藍關示侄孫湘〉Han Yu: "To My Nephew Sun Xiang, When I Was Banished to the Blue Gate"】

一肩行李，兩袖清風。 When a good official is relieved of his office, he only has a piece of luggage on his shoulder and a pair of clean hands. 【俗語 Common saying】

一身二任，雖聖莫能。 Even a sage is incapable of holding two posts at the same time. 【俗語 Common saying】

一世為官，七世作磚。 Being an official in his lifetime, he will become a bricklayer for seven generations. 【張恨水《最後關頭・卷上》Zhang Henshui: Part 1, *The Last Moment*】

有才不在官大小。 Talent does not have anything to do with how high one's official rank is. 【俗語 Common saying】

有人辭官歸故里，有人漏夜趕科場。 There are people who resign from their offices to return to their hometowns and there are people who rush to the examination halls to take the civil service examinations. 【諺語 Proverb】【吳敬梓《儒林外史・第四十六回》Wu Jingzi: Chapter 46, *An Unofficial History of the World of Literati*】

於官不貧，賴債不富。 Being an official, one will not be poor; repudiating a debt, one cannot become rich. 【蘭陵笑笑生《金瓶梅・第十九回》Lanling Xiaoxiaosheng: Chapter 19, *The Plum in the Golden Vase*】

只許州官放火，不許百姓點燈。 The magistrates are free to burn down houses, whereas the common people are forbidden to light lamps. 【陸游〈老學庵筆記〉Lu You: *Notebook from the House of a Person Who Studies When He Is Old*】

治則進，亂則退。 Take office in a time of good government and retire on the occurrence of confusion. 【孟軻《孟子・萬章下》Meng Ke: Chapter 10, Part 2, *Mencius*】

做官都是為張嘴。 Officials strive for nothing but their own living. 【俗語 Common saying】

Old age

不知老之將至。 One is not aware that old age is stealing upon oneself.【孔子《論語・述而篇第七》Confucius: Chapter 7, *The Analects of Confucius*】

凡事要好，須問三老。 To do anything well, you must consult the aged.【《增廣賢文》*Words that Open up One's Mind and Enhance One's Wisdom*】

記得當年騎竹馬，看看又是白頭翁。 I still remember the time when we used to ride a bamboo stick as a horse, but in no time we are now white-haired old men.【《增廣賢文》*Words that Open up One's Mind and Enhance One's Wisdom*】

酒債尋常行處有，人生七十古來稀。 At every turn, the bills of wine I owed. From of old, few people lived to be seventy.【杜甫〈曲江二首〉Du Fu:"Twisted River: Two Selections"】

老當益壯，寧移白首之心。 The older we grow, the stronger we become. The heart of a white-haired person would not be wavered.【王勃〈秋日登洪府滕王閣餞別序〉Wang Bo:"Ascending the Tengwang Pavilion of the Hong Family to Bid Farewell on an Autumn Day, with a Preface"】

老而不死是謂賊。 He who does nothing and lives to an old age is a pest.【孔子《論語・憲問篇第十四》Confucius: Chapter 14, *The Analects of Confucius*】

老來日子快。 Old age comes on apace.【俗語 Common saying】

老冉冉其將至兮，恐修名之不立。 As old age draws near, I'm afraid a fair name would not be given to me.【屈原《楚辭・離騷》Qu Yuan:"The Sorrows at Parting", *The Songs of Chu*】

臨老學吹打。 An old dog learns new tricks.【諺語 Proverb】

門神老了不捉鬼。 When the God of the Gate gets old, he does not catch ghosts.【袁靜《淮上人家・第三章》Yuan Jing: Chapter 3, *The People by the Huai River*】

莫笑他人老，終須還到老。 Don't laugh at others who are old for eventually you will also be old.【《增廣賢文》*Words that Open up One's Mind and Enhance One's Wisdom*】

年老知事多。 An old person knows much.【俗語 Common saying】

千金難買老來瘦。 A thousand taels of gold cannot buy slenderness in old age.【俗語 Common saying】

人老心不老。 Old in age but not old at heart.【《增廣賢文》*Words that Open up One's Mind and Enhance One's Wisdom*】

人生七十古稀，我年七十為奇。 A person seldom lives to be seventy years old, I would be surprised if I could live that long. 【唐寅〈七十詞〉Tang Yin:"Written at Seventy"】

人生易老天難老。歲歲重陽，今又重陽。 Human beings grow old easily but it is difficult for Heaven to be old. The Double-nine Festival comes year after after, and now it is another Double-nine Festival. 【毛澤東〈採桑子・重陽〉Mao Zedong:"The Double-nine Festival: To the Tune of Picking Mulberries"】

人已老，事皆非，花前不飲淚沾衣。 I am old and things are not as they were. Among flowers I shun drinking, tears falling on my clothes. 【朱敦儒〈鷓鴣天〉Zhu Dunru."To the Tune of Partridge in the Sky"】

日日人空老，年年春更歸。 Day in and day out, we age to no purpose. Year in and year out, spring comes and goes. 【王維〈送春詞〉Wang Wei:"Farewell to Spring"】

日月催人老。 The days and months hurry people to an old age. 【高明《琵琶記・牛相教女〉Gao Ming:"Niu Xiang Teaching His Daughter", "Tale of the *Pipa*"】

色，老而衰；智，老而多。 Good looks fade with old age, wisdom grows with old age. 【劉向《戰國策・趙策二》Liu Xiang:"Strategies of the State of Zhao, No. 2", *Strategies of the Warring States*】

樹老根多，人老話多。 When old, a tree has a lot of roots, and a man, a lot of words. 【俗語 Common saying】

Old people

家有老，是個寶。 Old people in a family are treasures. 【俗語 Common saying】

家有一老，黃金活寶。 An old member in a family is a living treasure more valuable than gold. 【俗語 Common saying】

劍老無芒，人老無剛。 An old person loses firmness as an old sword its sharpness. 【俗語 Common saying】

老不拘禮，病不拘禮。 The old and the sick need not observe the conventions. 【吳敬梓《儒林外史・第十二回》Wu Jingzi: Chapter 12, *An Unofficial History of the World of Literati*】

老健春寒秋後热。 The healthiest old people last as long as a chilly spring or a hot autumn. 【俗語 Common saying】【曹雪芹《紅樓夢・第五十七回》Cao Xueqin: Chapter 57, *A Dream of the Red Chamber*】

老年人如夕照，少年人如朝陽。 An old person is like the setting sun while a young person, the morning sun. 【俗語 Common saying】

老人不講古，後生會失譜。 If the old folks do not talk about the past, the young will lose their direction. 【諺語 Proverb】

老人如同風前燭。 An old person is like a candle before the wind. 【諺語 Proverb】

老頭吃糖，越扯越長。 Long-winded. 【俗語 Common saying】

老吾老以及人之老。 Take care of one's own aged parents first and then extend the same care to the aged people in general. 【孟軻《孟子‧梁惠王上》Meng Ke: Chapter 1, Part 1, *Mencius*】

老要顛狂少要穩。 The old can be a little frivolous, but the young must be sedate. 【諺語 Proverb】【文康《兒女英雄傳‧第二十二回》Wen Kang: Chapter 22, *Biographies of Young Heroes and Heroines*】

人老奸，馬老猾。 An old person becomes wily and an old horse crafty. 【俗語 Common saying】

人老精，薑老辣。 An old person becomes shrewd and ginger becomes hot when ripe. 【諺語 Proverb】

人老事事通。 An old person sees all things clearly. 【諺語 Proverb】

人老無能，神老無靈。 An old person becomes incapable and an old god cannot work miracles. 【諺語 Proverb】【李漁〈憐香伴‧第三十六齣〉Li Yu: Scene 36, "Cherishing the Fragrant Companion"】

人老心不老。 One may be old in age but young at heart. 【諺語 Proverb】

人老知事多。 An old person knows a lot of things. 【俗語 Common saying】

人老珠黃不值錢。 An old person, like a lusterless pearl, is worthless. 【諺語 Proverb】

晚年惟好靜，萬事不關心。 Late in life, I am only fond of tranquility and have no interest in all other things. 【王維〈酬張少府〉Wang Wei: "A Reply to Vice-prefect Zhang"】

Opportunity

八九不離十。 Most likely. 【諺語 Proverb】

當取不取，坐失良機。 If you do not take what you ought to take, you will miss your opportunity. 【俗語 Common saying】

得時者昌，失時者亡。 Those who grab opportunities thrive, while those who miss opportunities perish. 【列禦寇《列子‧說符第八》Lie Yukou: Chapter 8, "Explaining Conjunctions", *Liezi*】

缸裏捉鱉 —— 十拿九穩。
Catching a turtle in a jar – ninety
percent sure.【歇後語 End-clipper】

過了這個村就沒有那個店。One's
last chance to take advantage of
something.【俗語 Common saying】

機不可失，時不可待。This
opportunity cannot be lost and
time waits for no one.【諺語
Proverb】

機不可失，時不再來。Don't
let such an opportunityslip, it
might never come again.【房玄齡
等《晉書·安重榮傳》Tang Xuanling,
et al:"Biography of An Zhongrong",
History of the Jin】

來而不可失者時也，蹈而不可失
者機也。Do not let slip when
the time comes; do not let pass
when opportunity knocks.【蘇軾
〈代侯公說項羽辭〉Su Shi:"Persauding
Xiang Yu on Behalf of Duke Hou"】

良機難再來。Opportunity knows
but once.【俗語 Common saying】

拿着燒餅當枕頭。Fail to make
the best use of an opportunity.
【俗語 Common saying】

寧叫做過，莫要錯過。Rather try
once than miss the opportunity.
【王濬卿《冷眼觀·第二十五回》Wang
Junqing: Chapter 25, Casting a Cold Eye】

如入寶山空手回。Like going to a
treasure-trove and coming away
empty-handed.【楊顯之〈酷寒亭·
楔子〉Yang Xianzhi: Prologue, "Bitter
Cold Pavilion"】

弱者等待機會，強者創造機
會。Weak men wait for
opportunities; strong men make
them.【諺語 Proverb】

時至不行，反受其殃。When
an opportunity comes and one
does not act accordingly, one
is certain to have disasters.【司
馬遷《史記·越王勾踐世家》Sima
Qian:"House of King Goujian of Yue",
Records of the Grand Historian】

天晴不肯去，祇待雨淋頭。
Refuse to go on clear days but
wait until it rains heavily.【許仲琳
《封神演義·第三十三回》Xu Zhonglin:
Chapter 33, Romance of the Investiture of
the Deities】

瞎貓碰死耗子。Like a blind cat
knocking down a dead rat.【老
舍《四世同堂·第七十七章》Lao She:
Chapter 77, Four Generations under One
Roof】

小車不倒儘管推。Take advantage
of an opportunity to the full
extent.【諺語 Proverb】

Order

將在外，君令有所不受。A
commander far away in a

battlefield can even refuse
to obey the orders from the

emperor.【孫武《孫子兵法·九變第八》Sun Wu: Chapter 8:"Nine Variations in Tactics", *The Art of War by Sunzi*】

君子以申命行事。 A gentleman reiterates his orders in the execution of matters.【《易經·巽·象》"Image", Hexagram *Xun*, *The Book of Changes*】

軍令如山倒。 A military order is like a mountain falling.【俗語 Common saying】

令而不行，令之何益？ If an order cannot be put into force, what is the point of making it?【俗語 Common saying】

令苛則不聽，禁多則不行。 Orders which are too harsh will not be heeded, and prohibitions which are too numerous will not be enforced.【呂不韋《呂氏春秋·適威》Lu Buwei:"Appropriate Authority", *Master Lu's Spring and Autumn Annals*】

拿着雞毛當令箭。 Take a superior's casual remarks as an order to flaunt about.【俗語 Common saying】

其身正，不令而行；其身不正，雖令不行。 If the leader is upright, his subordinates will do well even though he does not give orders; but if he is not upright, they will not listen to the orders he gives.【孔子《論語·子路篇第十三》Confucius: Chapter 13, *The Analects of Confucius*】

王言如天語。 The king's orders are like those of god.【馮夢龍《醒世恆言·第十二卷》Feng Menglong: Chapter 12, *Stories to Awaken the World*】

挾天子以令諸侯。 Have the emperor in one's power and order the feudal lords about in his name.【劉向《戰國策·秦策一》Liu Xiang:"Strategies of the State of Qin, Part 1", *Strategies of the Warring States*】

有令不行，有禁不止。 Orders are not put into force and prohibitions are defied.【俗語 Common saying】

Ox

牛不喝水，按不低牛頭。 You can take a horse to the water, but you cannot make him drink.【俗語 Common saying】【曹雪芹《紅樓夢·第四十六回》Cao Xueqin: Chapter 46, *A Dream of the Red Chamber*】

牛不喝水強按頭。 If an ox does not want to drink water, you can press its head to make it drink.

【曹雪芹《紅樓夢·第四十六回》Cao Xueqin: Chapter 46, *A Dream of the Red Chamber*】

牛耕田，馬吃穀。 The ox ploughs but the horse eats grain.【俚語 slang】

牛口裏扯不出草來。 You cannot pull out grass in an ox's mouth. 【俗語 Common saying】

牛皮燈籠肚裏亮。 A lantern made of ox hide is bright inside. 【孔厥，袁靜《新兒女英雄傳·第七回》 Kong Jue and Yuan Jing: Chapter 7, *New Biographies of Heroes and Heroines*】

牛套馬，累死倆。 When an ox and a horse are pulling the same cart, both will die from exhaustion. 【諺語 Proverb】

牽生要牽牛鼻子。 An ox must be led by the halter. 【俗語 Common saying】

Painting

畫虎不成反類犬。 Try to paint a tiger but end up with one that looks like a dog. 【范曄《後漢書·馬援傳》Fan Ye:"Biography of Ma Huan", *History of the Later Han*】

立錐莫笑無餘地，萬里江山筆下生。 Don't laugh at my cottage which is so small, here, miles and miles of mountains and streams come out from my brush. 【唐寅〈風雨浹旬廚煙不繼滌硯吮筆蕭條若僧因題絕句八首奉寄孫思和〉Tang Yin:"Writing Eight Poems in Quatrain to Sun Sihe When the Wind and Rain Was Falling, the Smoke from the Kitchens Was Rising, and I Was Cleansing the Inkslab and Sucking My Brush for Inspiration"】

世間無限丹青手，一片傷心畫不成。 There are endless painters in this world, yet none of them could paint my sadness. 【高蟾〈金陵晚望〉Gao Chan:"A Reply to Vice-prefect Zhang"】

四十年來畫竹枝，日間揮寫夜間思。 For forty years, I have been painting bamboo. I paint it in the daytime and think about it at night. 【鄭板橋〈畫竹詩〉Zheng Banqiao:"A Poem on Painting Bamboo"】

書畫之妙，當以神會，難以形器求也。 Excellence in painting and calligraphy should be sought through spiritual communion and not in the formal elements. 【沈括《夢溪筆談·卷十七》Shen Kua: Chapter 17, *Notes from Mengxi Studio*】

意態由來畫不成。 Graceful air cannot be painted at any event. 【王安石〈明妃曲〉Wang Anshi:"Song of the Ming Imperial Concubine"】

意在筆先者，定則也；趣在法外者，化機也。 Conceptualize before starting to paint is a guiding principle; the joy of going beyond the principle lies with adjusting to changing conditions. 【鄭板橋〈板橋題畫「竹」〉Zheng Banqiao:"Inscriptions on a Painting of 'Bamboo'"】

Parents

哀哀父母，生我劬勞。 Pitiful are my parents, whom you gave me birth with such toil.【《詩經・小雅・蓼莪》》"Liao E", "Minor Odes of the Kingdom", *The Book of Odes*】

不養兒不知父母恩。 One does not know the love of one's parents only when one raises one's child.【諺語 Proverb】

當家才知鹽米貴，養子方知父母恩。 You only know how expensive salt and rice are when you manage a family and you only realize the love of your parents when you raise your children.【《增廣賢文》*Words that Open up One's Mind and Enhance One's Wisdom*】

父母難保子孫賢。 Parents cannot guarantee that their children and grandchildren will be virtuous.【諺語 Proverb】

父母在，不遠遊。 When one's parents are alive, one does not wander far away.【孔子《論語・里仁篇第四》Confucius: Chapter 4, *The Analects of Confucius*】

虎毒不食子。 Even a vicious tigress will not eat its cubs.【諺語 Proverb】

親不過父母，近不過夫妻。 The most affectionate relation is that between children and parents and the most intimate relation is that between husband and wife.【諺語 Proverb】【袁永思〈母子情〉Yuan Yong'en:"Motherly Love Towards Her Son"】

親情截不斷。 Parental love cannot be servered.【俗語 Common saying】

親情深似海。 Parental love is as deep as the ocean.【俗語 Common saying】

天地有寒燠，母心隨時深。 In heaven and earth, there is coldness and heat, but the heart of a mother is always warm.【王厘成〈秋浦晚歸〉Wang Licheng:"Returning Home Late at Night at the Riverside in Autumn"】

天下無不是的父母。 No parents in the world are in the wrong.【俗語 Common saying】

嚴家無悍勇，慈母有敗子。 A strict father fosters sons who do not have bravery and courage and a kind mother brings up a prodigal son.【韓非《韓非子・顯學第五十》Han Fei: Chapter 50, "Eminence in Learning", *Hanfeizi*】

在家靠父母，出外靠朋友。 At home, one relies on their parents; outside, on their friends.【諺語 Proverb】

Part and whole

大河有水小河滿，大河無水小河乾。When there is water in the main stream, the small streams will be full; when there is no water in the main stream, the small streams will be dry.【俗語 Common saying】

大中見小，小中見大。Show the small in the big, and the big in the small.【蘇轍《洞山文長老語錄》Su Che: *Sayings of the Buddhist Elder Tong Shanwen*】

獨木不能成林。A single tree does not make a forest.【崔駰〈達旨〉Cui Yin:"Expressing My Purpose"】

管中窺豹，可見一斑。Look at a leopard through a bamboo tube and you can visualize the whole animal.【劉義慶《世說新語·方正第五》Liu Yiqing: Chapter 5, "The Square and the Proper", *A New Account of the Tales of the World*】

見木不見林。See the wood for the trees.【俗語 Common saying】

一節見而百節知。Seeing one part of something you can tell the rest of it.【劉向《説苑·卷八尊賢》Liu Xiang: Chapter 8, "Honouring the Worthies", *Garden of Persuasion*】

一粒老鼠屎，壞了一鍋湯。One bit of rat's dung in the soup spoils the whole pot.【俗語 Common saying】

由一斑而知全豹。From one spot one can learn the whole leopard.【劉義慶《世説新語·方正第五》Liu Yiqing. Chapter 5, "The Square and the Proper", *A New Account of the Tales of the World*】

由一知二，脈脈相通。From one learn two and infer all.【俗語 Common saying】

祗見樹木，不見森林。Do not see the forest for the trees.【俗語 Common saying】

Parting

白髮三千丈，離愁似個長。My white hair is three thousand yards long, and my parting sorrows are just as long.【李白〈秋浦歌〉Li Bai:"Song of Qiupu"】

悲莫悲兮生別離，樂莫樂兮新相知。Nothing is sadder than having to part forever; nothing is happier than making new friends.【屈原《離騷·九歌·少司令》Qu Yuan:"The Little Lords of Life", "The Nine Songs", *The Sorrows at Parting*】

別時容易見時難，流水落花春去也，天上人間。Parting is easy but reunion is hard. It is just like the flowing water, the fallen petals, and the passing of spring; once separated, it's like heaven and earth apart. 【李煜〈浪淘沙〉Li Yu: "To the Tune of Waves Washing over Sand"】

道一聲珍重，道一聲珍重，那一聲珍重裏有蜜甜的憂愁 —— 沙揚娜拉。 "Take care of yourself", "take care of yourself", and there is such a sweetness of sorrow in "taking care of yourself" – sayonara. 【徐志摩〈沙揚娜拉一首 —— 贈日本女郎〉Xu Zhimo: "Sayonara: To a Japanese girl"】

多情卻似總無情，唯覺樽前笑不成。 Passionate love always seems to be lacking in love. I only feel that I can't manage to laugh even before a jar of wine. 【杜牧〈贈別〉Du Mu: "Presented at Parting"】

多情自古傷離別，更哪堪，冷落清秋節。 From of old, those who are passionate feel sad when parting with their dear ones, what is more unbearable is to part on a cold, lonely, and clear day in autumn. 【柳永〈雨霖鈴〉Liu Yong: "To the Tune of Bells Ringing in the Rain"】

分手脫相贈，平生一片心。 On parting, I took off my sword and gave it to you as a gift, to express my affection for you all my life. 【孟浩然〈送朱大入秦〉Meng Haoran: "Seeing Zhu Da off to Qin"】

浮雲一別後，流水十年間。 Since we parted like drifting clouds, ten years has passed like flowing water. 【韋應物〈淮上喜會梁州故人〉Wei Yingwu: "A Happy Meeting on the Huai with an Old Friend from Liangzhou"】

好合不如好散。 Better friendly parting than a friendly meeting. 【俗語 Common saying】

恨君不似江樓月，南北東西，南北東西，只有相隨無別離。 Why can't you be like the moon over the riverside tower? South and north, east and west, south and north, east and west, it simply follows me without parting. 【呂本中〈采桑子〉Lu Benzhong: "To the Tune of Picking Mulberry Leaves"】

剪不斷，理還亂，是離愁，別是一番滋味在心頭。 Cut it, it severs not. Comb it, it remains a knot. Such is the sorrow of parting, yet another kind of flavour in my heart. 【李煜〈相見歡〉Li Yu: "To the Tune of the Joy of Meeting"】

將軍不下馬 —— 各自奔前程。 The generals do not dismount from horseback; each goes his own way. 【歇後語 End-clipper】【曹雪芹《紅樓夢‧第六十六回》Cao Xueqin: Chapter 66, A Dream of the Red Chamber】

今日送君須盡醉，明朝相憶路漫漫。 Today I see you off and we should drink to the full, for tomorrow we will miss each other and your journey will be long. 【賈至〈送李侍郎赴常州〉Jia Zhi: "Seeing off Minister Li on His Departure to Changzhou"】

聚散苦匆匆，此恨無窮。 Our meeting and parting are too soon, and my sadness will never go. 【歐陽修〈浪淘沙〉Ouyang Xiu:"To the Tune of Ripples Sifting Sand"】

蠟燭有心還惜別，替人垂淚到天明。 The candle had a heart (wick) and it felt sorry for our parting, shedding tears for us until daybreak. 【杜牧〈贈別〉Du Mu:"Presented at Parting"】

離恨恰如春草，更行更遠還生。 The grief of parting is just like grass in spring: the farther you go, the more it seems to grow. 【李煜〈清平樂〉Li Yu:"To the Tune of Purity and Peace"】

劉郎已恨蓬山遠，更隔蓬山一萬重。 A former Daoist Liu resented that the Penglai Mountain was too far away, yet our separation is a thousandfold more. 【李商隱〈無題〉Li Shangyin:"Untitled Poem"】

千里相送，終有一別。 One might see somebody off for a thousand miles, we have to part in the end. 【無名氏：〈馬陵道〉Anonymous:"Malingdao"】

悄悄的我走了，正如我悄悄的來；我揮一揮衣袖，不帶走一片雲彩。 Quietly I left, as quietly I came. I shook my sleeves, not taking away a patch of the colourful clouds. 【徐志摩〈再別康橋〉Xu Zhimo:"Farewell once Again to Cambridge"】

輕輕的我走了，正如我輕輕的來；我輕輕的招手，作別西天的雲彩。 Quietly I left, as quietly I came. Quietly I waved goodbye to the colourful clouds in the sky of the West. 【徐志摩〈再別康橋〉Xu Zhimo:"Farewell once Again to Cambridge"】

請君試問東流水，別意與之誰短長。 Could you try to ask the east-flowing waters: which is longer, my parting grief or waters? 【李白〈金陵酒肆留別〉Li Bai:"Parting at a Tavern in Jinling"】

去年花裏逢君別，今日花開又一年。 It was in the midst of flowers that we parted a year ago, and now the flowers are in blossom again, marking the passage of another year. 【韋應物〈寄李儋元錫〉Wei Yingwu:"Sent to Li Dan, Styled Yuanxi"】

去時終須去，再三留不住。 If one has to go, he will eventually go, no matter how you repeatedly try to stop him from leaving. 【《增廣賢文》Words that Open up One's Mind and Enhance One's Wisdom】

人去不中留。 If one wants to go, there is no way of holding him back. 【曹雪芹《紅樓夢‧第四十六回》Cao Xueqin: Chapter 46, A Dream of the Red Chamber】

人生聚散無常。 Life is about inconstant unions and separations. 【俗語 Common saying】

人生唯有離別苦。In one's life, the sorrows of parting are hardest to bear. 【俗語 Common saying】

山迴路轉不見君，雪山空留馬行處。The mountains wind, the road turns, and I no longer see you, leaving only the marks on the snow to show where your horse has passed before. 【岑參〈白雪歌送武判官歸〉Cen Shen:"Song of White Snow to Bid Farewell to Secretary Wu on His Return to the Capital"】

山中相送罷，日暮掩柴扉。春草明年綠，王孫歸不歸？Having seen you off down the mountain, I closed my wooden gate as the sun was setting. When the spring grass turns green next year, will you, my friend, come back again? 【王維〈送別〉Wang Wei:"Farewell"】

生離甚於死別。Separated in life is worse than parting in death. 【諺語 Proverb】

十步九回頭。Walk ten steps and look back nine times. 【高明《琵琶記‧伯喈夫妻分別》Gao Ming:"The Separation of the Husband and Wife of Bokai", "Tale of the *Pipa*"】

十年離亂後，長大一相別。After ten years of separation in a world of upheaval, your have grown up and we meet again and then part again. 【李益〈喜見外弟又言別〉Li Yi:"Parting with My Cousin After a Joyful Meeting"】

世情已逐浮雲散，離恨空隨江水長。Things in this world have gradually dispersed like floating clouds, yet the parting sorrow stays as long as the water in the river that flows on and on. 【賈至〈巴陵夜別王八員外〉Jia Zhi:"Parting with Ministry Councillor Wang in the Evening at Baling"】

世上無不散的筵席。No banquet in the world would last forever. 【俗語 Common saying】

送君千里，終須一別。One might escort one's guest a thousand miles to see him off, yet there's bound to be parting in the end. 【《增廣賢文》Words that Open up One's Mind and Enhance One's Wisdom】

桃花潭水深千尺，不及汪倫送我情。The Peach Blossom Lake is one thousand feet deep, but it is not as deep as the parting sorrow that Wang Lun expressed to me. 【李白〈贈汪倫〉Li Bai:"To Wang Lun"】

我寄愁心與明月，隨君直到夜郎西。I entrust to the bright moon the sadness in my heart to accompany you to the west of Yelang. 【李白〈聞王昌齡左遷龍標遙有此寄〉Li Bai:"To Wang Changling on Hearing about His Banishment to Longbiao"】

行行重行行，與君生別離。We walked on and on, and would be parted from you by a life-parting. 【佚名《古詩十九首》Anonymous: *Nineteen Ancient Poems*】

一曲驪歌兩行淚，不知何地再逢君。 A parting song moves us to tears and I don't know when we will meet again. 【韋莊〈江上別李秀才〉Wei Zhuang: "Bidding Farewell to Scholar Li on a River"】

一看一斷腸，好去莫回頭。 Looking at each other causes sadness, just go and don't turn back. 【白居易〈南浦別〉Bai Juyi: "Parting at Nanpu"】

Past and present

春花風秋月何時了，往事知多少？ When will spring flowers and autumn moon cease to come and go? And how much do they know of the past? 【李煜〈虞美人〉Li Yu: "To the Tune of the Beauty of Yu"】

發思古之幽情。 Muse over things of the remote past. 【班固〈西都賦〉Ban Gu: "Rhapsody on West Capitals"】

古今人不相若。 People in ancient times are not the same as people today. 【黃鈞宰《金壺七墨‧醉墨卷一》Huang Junzai: Chapter 1, "Drunken Ink", *Seven Essays from the Golden Pot*】

古為今用，洋為中用。 Make the past serve the present, and foreign things, serve China. 【俗語 Common saying】

觀今宜鑒古，無古不成今。 To understand the present, one should know the past, for without the past, there is no present. 【《增廣賢文》*Words that Open up One's Mind and Enhance One's Wisdom*】

後之視今，猶今之視昔。 When people of later generations look back on today, it is just like people of today looking back on the past. 【王羲之〈蘭亭集序〉Wang Xizhi: "Preface to the Collected Poems of the Orchid Pavilion"】

過去事明如鏡，未來事暗如漆。 Past events are clear as a mirror, but what is to come in the future is pitch dark. 【諺語 Proverb】

看其過去，知其現在。 By looking at one's past, we know his present. 【諺語 Proverb】

來世不可待，往世不可追也。 Life in the future cannot be waited for, and life in the past cannot be sought again. 【莊周《莊子‧內篇‧人間世第四》Zhuang Zhou: Chapter 4, "Human World", "Inner Chapters", *Zhuangzi*】

前不見古人，後不見來者。念天地之悠悠，獨愴然而涕下。 I don't see the men of the past before me and I don't see the people who will come in the future after me. When I think of the endlessness of heaven and earth, I shed tears, alone and forlornly. 【陳子昂〈登幽州臺歌〉Chen Zi'ang: "On Ascending the Youzhou Terrace"】

人不通古今，馬牛而襟裾。 If a person does not know well the past and present, he is like a horse or cow clad in clothes. 【《增廣賢文》 Words that Open up One's Mind and Enhance One's Wisdom】

上無古人，下無來者。 There are no precedents in the past nor successors in the future. 【陳子昂〈登幽州臺歌〉 Chen Zi'ang: "On Ascending the Youzhou Terrace"】

往事已成空，還如一夢中。 Things past are now dead, as though they were in a dream. 【李煜〈子夜歌〉 Li Yu: "Midnight Song"】

往事只堪哀，對景難排。 The thought of the past brings me only grief, which will not be banished before my present vision. 【李煜〈浪淘沙〉 Li Yu: "To the Tune of Waves Washing over Sand"】

往者不可諫，來者猶可追。 What is past cannot be redeemed, but what is yet to come may still be provided against. 【孔子《論語・微子篇第十八》 Confucius: Chapter 18, The Analects of Confucius】

往者不可追。 What is gone is beyond recovery. 【孔子《論語・微子篇第十八》 Confucius: Chapter 18, The Analects of Confucius】

無古不成今。 Without the past, we would never have had the present. 【《增廣賢文》 Words that Open up One's Mind and Enhance One's Wisdom】

悟已往之不諫，知來者之可追。 I realize the past cannot be undone, but I know we can regain things in the future. 【陶淵明〈歸田園居〉 Tao Yuanming: "Returning to My Rurual Home"】

Patriotism

苟利國家，不求富貴。 If what I do benefit the country, I'll not seek wealth and honours for myself. 【《禮記・樂記第十九章》 Chapter 19, "Records on the Subject of Music", The Book of Rites】

苟利國家生死以，豈因禍福避趨之。 I'll do whatever it takes to serve my country even at the cost of my own life, regardless of fortune or misfortune to myself. 【林則徐〈赴戍登程口占示家人〉 Lin Zexu: "For My Family on My Journey to Yili"】

明於識，練於事，忠於國。 Clarity of knowledge, proficiency in affairs, and loyalty to the nation. 【梁啟超：〈嘉慶黃先生墓誌銘〉 Liang Qichao: "Epitaph of Mr Huang Zunxian of Jiaqing"】

死去原知萬事空，但悲不見九州同。 When I die, I know, by my instinct, that everything is but emptiness, but I still feel sad

that I cannot see a unified land.
【陸游〈示兒〉Lu You: "To My Son"】

王師北定中原日，家祭無忘告乃翁。 When the day of the emperor's troops sweeping the North comes, you must not forget to tell me when you offer sacrifices to me before my tombstone. 【陸游〈示兒〉Lu You: "To My Son"】

為國而死，死而光榮。 Dying for one's country is a glorious death. 【俗語 Common saying】

閒居非吾志，甘心赴國憂。 To stay idle is not my wish, and I am ready to engage in tackling matters troubling the country. 【曹植〈雜詩〉Cao Zhi: "Miscellaneous Poems"】

以國家之務為己任。 Take affairs of the country as one's responsibility. 【韓愈〈送許郢州序〉Han Yu: "Preface to Seeing off Xu of Chengzhou"】

People

安民則惠，黎民懷之。 Pacify the people with benefits and they will cherish you in their hearts. 【《尚書‧皋陶謨》"Counsels of Gao Yao", *The Book of History*】

安民之術，在於豐財。 The way to pacify people relies on enhancing their wealth. 【陳壽《三國志‧魏書‧杜畿傳》Chen Shou: "Biography of Du Ji" from "History of the Wei", *Records of the Three Kingdoms*】

百無一用是書生。 Scholars are totally useless. 【黃景仁〈雜感〉Huang Jingren: "Miscellaneous Thoughts"】

百姓昭明，協和萬邦。 We should have amity among people and friendly exchanges among nations. 【《尚書‧舜典》"The Canon of Yao", *The Book of History*】

白樣米養白樣人。 A hundred varieties of rice feed a hundred varieties of people. 【俗語 Common saying】

得民心者興，失民心者亡。 One who wins the hearts of the people will prosper. One who loses the hearts of the people will fall. 【孟軻《孟子‧離婁上》Meng Ke: Chapter 4, Part 1, *Mencius*】

得人心者得天下，失人心者失天下。 One who wins the hearts of the people wins the whole world. One who loses the hearts of the people loses the whole world. 【諺語 Proverb】

得人者昌，失人者亡。 He who wins people prospers and he who loses people, perishes. 【李觀〈項籍故里碑銘序〉Li Guan: "Preface to the Tablet of the Old Lane of Xiang Ji"】

地有高低，人有貴賤。 There are high and low land on earth and there are mean and noble people. 【沈鯨〈雙珠記‧第八齣〉 Shen Jing: Scene 8, "Double Pearls"】

蓋世必有非常之人，然後有非常之事；有非常之事，然後有非常之功。 In the world, there must be extraordinary people, then there will be extraordinary understakings; when there are extraordinary understakings, then there will be extraordinary achievements. 【班固《漢書‧司馬相如傳下》Ban Gu: "Biography of Sima Xiangru, Part 2", *History of the Han*】

嗑瓜子出個臭蟲 —— 甚麼人（仁）都有。 Cracking a melon seed to find a bedbug inside it–you find kernels of all kinds. 【歇後語 End-clipper】

官逼民反，民不得不反。 If the officials oppress the people, people have to revolt against them. 【李寶嘉《官場現形記‧第二十八回》Li Baojia: Chapter 28, *Officialdom Unmasked*】

好人必有好報。 A good person is sure to be repaid by good. 【俗語 Common saying】

好人不當道。 Good people are not in power. 【俗語 Common saying】

好人多落難。 Disasters often befall good people. 【俗語 Common saying】

好人多磨難。 Good people have more suffering. 【俗語 Common saying】

好人有好報。 Good people are sure to be rewarded good. 【俗語 Common saying】

黃金有價人無價。 Gold has a price, but human beings don't. 【俗語 Common saying】

間於天地之間，莫貴於人。 In heaven and earth, nothing is more valuable than human beings. 【孫臏《孫臏兵法》Sun Bin: *Sun Bin's Art of War*】

敬賢如大賓，愛民如赤子。 Respect the virtuous like distinguished guests and love the people like newborns. 【路溫舒〈尚德緩刑書〉Lu Wenshu: "Memorial to the Emperor to Honour Virtue and Relax Punishment"】

絕仁棄義，民復孝慈。 Discard benevolence and abandon righteousness, people will again become filial and kind. 【老子《道德經‧第十九章》Laozi: Chapter 19, *Daodejing*】

絕聖棄智，民利百倍。 Discard sagehood and abandon wisdom, people will be benefitted a hundred times more. 【老子《道德經‧第十九章》Laozi: Chapter 19, *Daodejing*】

郎多好種田。 With many young men, it is easy to till the land. 【諺語 Proverb】

樂民之樂者，民亦樂其樂。 When rulers rejoice at the joys of the people, people will also rejoice at their joys. 【孟軻《孟子‧梁惠王下》Meng Ke: Chapter 1, Part 2, *Mencius*】

裏七層，外八層。 Be crowded with people. 【俗語 Common saying】

裏三層，外三層。 Be crowded with people. 【俗語 Common saying】

民安則國興，民富則國強。 When people are at peace, the country prospers; when people are rich, the country becomes strong. 【俗語 Common saying】

民不可與慮始，而可與樂成。 People cannot be involved when thoughts on plans begin, but they can share the joy when plans are realized. 【商鞅《商君書‧更法》Shang Yang:"Reforming Laws", *The Works of Shang Yang*】

民不畏死，奈何以死懼之。 When people are not afraid of death, why threaten them with death? 【老子《道德經‧第七十四章》Laozi: Chapter 74, *Daodejing*】

民可近，不可下。 People can be approached, but not looked down on. 【《尚書‧夏書‧五子之歌》"Song of Five Masters", "Book of the Xia", *The Book of History*】

民可使由之，不可使知之。 The people should be told to do things without telling them why. 【孔子《論語‧泰伯篇第八》Confucius: Chapter 8, *The Analects of Confucius*】

民生在勤，勤則不匱。 Livelihood hinges on diligence. People will not be poor when they are diligent. 【左丘明《左傳‧宣公十二年》Zuo Qiuming:"The Twelfth Year of the Reign of Duke Xuan", *Zuo's Commentary on the Spring and Autumn Annals*】

民為邦本，本固邦寧。 People are the base of a country; when this base is stable, the country enjoys peace. 【《尚書‧夏書‧五子之歌》"Song of Five Masters", "Book of the Xia", *The Book of History*】

民為貴，社稷次之，君為輕。 People are most valuable, next are the national altars of the soil and grain, and the ruler is insignificant. 【孟軻《孟子‧盡心章句下》Meng Ke: Chapter 7, Part 2, *Mencius*】

民心即天心。 The will of the people is the will of Heaven. 【孟軻《孟子‧梁惠王下》Meng Ke: Chapter 1, Part 2, *Mencius*】

民之所好好之，民之所惡惡之。 Love what the people love and hate what the people hate. 【《禮記‧大學第四十二》Chapter 42, "The Great Learning", *The Book of Rites*】

民之所欲，天必從之。 What is desired by the people will be followed by heaven. 【《尚書‧泰誓上》"The Great Speech, Part 1", *The Book of History*】

破帽之下多好人。 There is many a good man to be found under a shabby hat. 【俗語 Common saying】

人上一百，形形色色。 When there are over one hundred people, they are of every hue. 【俗語 Common saying】【姚雪垠《李自成·第二卷第三十五章》Yao Xueyin: Chapter 35, Volume 2, *Li Zicheng*】

人是鐵，飯是鋼。 Man is iron but food is steel. 【俗語 Common saying】

人有三六九等。 There are all kinds of people. 【俗語 Common saying】

人有十不同，花有十樣紅。 People are different in ten ways as flowers are different in ten colours. 【俗語 Common saying】

人者，其天地之德，陰陽之交，鬼神之會，五行之秀氣也。 A human being is one that has the virtue of heaven and earth, the combination of the male and the female, the unity of body and soul, and the excellence of the five elements of water, fire, metal, wood, and earth. 《禮記·禮運第九》Chapter 9, "Conveyance of Rites", *The Book of Rites*】

人者，天地之心也，五行之端也。 A human being is the mind of heaven and earth and an aspect of the five elements. 【《禮記·禮運第九》Chapter 9, "Conveyance of Rites", *The Book of Rites*】

山山有老虎，處處有強人。 Every mountain has tigers and everywhere has able people. 【張南莊《何典·第一卷》Zhang Nanzhuang: Chapter 1, *From Which Classic*】

山中有直樹，世上無直人。 There are straight trees in the mountains but no straightforward people in the world. 【《增廣賢文》*Words that Open up One's Mind and Enhance One's Wisdom*】

上應天意，下順民心。 Follow the will of heaven and comply with the popular feelings. 【俗語 Common saying】

深人不做淺事。 A circumspect person will not do anything superficial. 【俗語 Common saying】

深人無淺語。 A circumspect person will not say superficial words. 【趙翼《甌北詩話·杜少陵詩》Zhao Yi: "The Poetry of Du Fu", *Poetry Talks by Zhao Yi*】

識時務者為俊傑，通機變者為英豪。 One who understands the times is a great person, one who changes with opportunities is a hero. 【晏嬰《晏子春秋·霸業因時而生》Yan Ying: "Hegemony is Born out of the Times", *Master Yan's Spring and Autumn Annals*】

樹大有枯枝。 There are good and bad people in every group. 【俗語 Common saying】

王者以民為天。 A king regards the people as important as Heaven. 【司馬遷《史記·酈生陸賈列傳》Sima Qian: "Biographies of Li Yiji and Lu Gu", *Records of the Grand Historian*】

為人不自在，自在不為人。 To live as a person, one is not free. If one wants to be free, one should not be a person. 【歇後語 End-clipper】

為人容易做人難。 To live as a person is easy but how to deal with people is difficult. 【俗語 Common saying】

興滅國，繼絕世，舉逸民，天下之民歸心焉。 Revive the extinguished states, restore families without posterity, call to office the retired people, then the hearts of all the people in the world will turn towards you. 【孔子《論語‧堯曰篇第二十》Confucius: Chapter 20, *The Analects of Confucius*】

一根藤上的瓜。 People who share weal and woe. 【諺語 Proverb】

一娘生九種，種種不同。 There are all kinds of people in the world. 【諺語 Proverb】

一人為單，二人為雙，三人成眾。 One person is single, two persons are double and three persons are public. 【俗語 Common saying】

一種米養百種人。 It takes all sorts to make a world. 【俗語 Common saying】

以得為在民，以失為在己；以正為在民，以枉為在己。 Give credit to the people and failure to oneself. Give what is right to the people and what is wrong to oneself. 【莊周《莊子‧雜篇‧則陽第二十五》Zhuang Zhou: Chapter 25, "Sunny", "Miscellaneous Chapters", *Zhuangzi*】

憂民之憂者，民亦憂其憂。 When rulers are concerned about the woes of the people, people will also be concerned about the woes of their rulers. 【孟軻《孟子‧梁惠王下》Meng Ke: Chapter 1, Part 2, *Mencius*】

仗義半從屠狗輩，負心都是讀書人。 Those who are just and upright are mostly people of the dog-slaughterer type and those who are unfaithful to their lovers are all of the educated class. 【陸游〈示兒〉Lu You: "To My Son"】

眾人是面鏡。 The masses serve as a mirror. 【俗語 Common saying】

眾惡之，必察焉；眾好之，必察焉。 When all the people dislike something, it must be investigated; when all the people like something, it must be investigated. 【孔子《論語‧衛靈公篇第十五》Confucius: Chapter 15, *The Analects of Confucius*】

Perfection

甘瓜苦蒂，物無全美。 Melon is sweet, but its base is bitter. Nothing in this world is perfect. 【墨翟《墨子‧兼愛卷十四至十六》Mo

Di: Chapters 14-16, "Universal Love", *Mozi*】

美矣，又盡善也。 It is perfectly beautiful and perfectly good. 【孔子《論語‧八佾篇第三》Confucius: Chapter 3, *The Analects of Confucius*】

寧做有瑕玉，不做無瑕石。 A piece of jade with a flaw is worth more than a stone without imperfections. 【焦竑《玉堂叢語‧卷五》Jiao Hong: Chapter 5, *Collected Accounts from the Jade Hall*】

求士莫求全。 When you look for a scholar do not look for perfection. 【程允升《幼學瓊林‧卷一武職類》Cheng Yunsheng: Chapter 1, "Category of Military Posts", *Treasury of Knowledge for Young Students*】

人不能全，車不能圓。 A person cannot be perfect as a wheel cannot be totally round. 【俗語 Common saying】

人非堯舜，誰能盡善。 As people are not Yao or Shun, how can they be perfect? 【李白〈與韓荊州書〉Li Bai:"A Letter to Han Yu"】

人無完人，金無足赤。 People cannot be perfect as gold cannot be fully pure. 【戴復古〈寄興〉Dai Fugu:"Placing My Feelings"】

十個指頭也有長短。 Even the ten fingers cannot be of the same length. 【俗語 Common saying】

事若求全何所樂。 You cannot enjoy yourself if you expect everything to be perfect. 【曹雪芹《紅樓夢‧第七十六回》Cao Xueqin: Chapter 76, *A Dream of the Red Chamber*】

天地無全功，聖人無全能，萬物無全用。 Heaven and earth do not have all-round functions, sages do not have all-round capacities, and all the things do not have all-round uses. 【列禦寇《列子‧天瑞第一》Lie Yukou: Chapter 1, "Heaven's Gifts", *Liezi*】

天下事總難十全十美。 It is always difficult to make affairs of the world perfect. 【曹雪芹《紅樓夢‧第七十六回》Cao Xueqin: Chapter 76, *A Dream of the Red Chamber*】

天字第一號。 The best in the world. 【俗語 Common saying】

Perseverance

駑馬千里，功在不捨。 An inferior horse relies on perseverance to travel a thousand miles. 【荀況《荀子‧勸學第一》Xun Kuang: Chapter 1, "Exhortation to Learning", *Xunzi*】

鍥而不捨，金石可鏤。 Gold and stone can be carved by working consistently. 【荀況《荀子‧勸學第一》Xun Kuang: Chapter 1, "Exhortation to Learning", *Xunzi*】

人而無恆，不可以作巫醫。 A person without perseverance cannot be a wizard or a doctor. 【孔子《論語‧子路篇第十三》

Confucius: Chapter 13, *The Analects of Confucius*】

人靠有恆，樹靠有根。 A person's success depends on perseverance and a tree depends on its roots. 【諺語 Proverb】

人心堅，石山穿。 When one is perseverant, one can drill through a stony mountan. 【諺語 Proverb】

三天打魚，兩天曬網。 Work by fits and starts. 【曹雪芹《紅樓夢·第九回》Cao Xueqin: Chapter 9, *A Dream of the Red Chamber*】

惜人得人用，惜衣得衣穿。 Treasure manpower and you will have people to use; use clothes sparingly and you will have clothes to wear. 【諺語 Proverb】

祇要人有恆，萬事都可成。 Persevere in what you do, and you are sure to attain your goals. 【諺語 Proverb】

Petty person

才勝德，謂之小人。 He whose talent is better than his virtue is known as a petty person. 【司馬光《資治通鑒·周紀》Sima Guang:"Annals of the Zhou Dynasty", *Comprehensive Mirror to Aid in Government*】

亂生乎小人。 Disorder springs from petty persons. 【荀況《荀子·王制第九》Xun Kuang: Chapter 9, "Sovereign's Regulations", *Xunzi*】

先小人，後君子。 Be a petty person first and then gentleman. 【西周生《醒世姻緣傳·第四十九回》Xi Zhousheng: Chapter 49, *Stories of Marriage to Awaken the World*】

小人不可大受。 A petty person cannot be trusted with great responsibilities. 【孔子《論語·衛靈公篇第十五》Confucius: Chapter 15, *The Analects of Confucius*】

小人長戚戚。 A petty person is always dejected. 【孔子《論語·述而篇第七》Confucius: Chapter 7, *The Analects of Confucius*】

小人道長，君子道消。 When petty persons are in power, good people are unpopular. 【《易經·上經·泰》Book 1, Hexagram *Tai*, *The Book of Changes*】

小人窮斯濫。 A petty person, when reduced to poverty, will do everything to gain his ends. 【孔子《論語·衛靈公篇第十五》Confucius: Chapter 15, *The Analects of Confucius*】

小人無大志。 A petty person has no great aspirations. 【諺語 Proverb】

小人閒居為不善。 A petty person at leisure will do anything evil.

【《禮記・大學第四十二》Chapter 42, "The Great Learning", *The Book of Rites*】

小人乍富，難免有禍。 When a petty person becomes rich suddenly, he will suffer disaster. 【諺語 Proverb】

小人最難防。 What is most difficult to guard against is a petty person. 【俗語 Common saying】

Phoenix

拔了毛的鳳凰不如雞。 A phoenix with its feathers plucked off is not as good as a hen. 【諺語 Proverb】

鳳不離巢，龍不離窩。 Phoenixes do not leave their nests and dragons, their palaces. 【俗語 Common saying】

鳳凰不落無寶之地。 A phoenix does not perch on a ground without treasure. 【俗語 Common saying】

鳳凰不入烏鴉巢。 A phoenix does not enter a crow's nest. 【諺語 Proverb】

鳳凰飛上梧桐樹 —— 自有旁人道短長。 When a phoenix perches on a parasol tree, there are always people who will make comments. 【歇後語 End-clipper】

鳳凰落寶地。 A phoenix perches only on a ground with treasure. 【俗語 Common saying】

鳳凰落架不如雞。 A phoenix off its perch is no match for a chicken. 【諺語 Proverb】

鳳凰台上鳳凰遊，鳳去台空江自流。 Once phoenixes used to perch on the Phoenix Terrace, but now the phoenixes are gone, the terrace is deserted, and the river flows on by itself. 【李白〈登金陵鳳凰台〉Li Bai: "Ascending the Phoenix Tower in Jinling"】

鳳有鳳巢，雞有雞窩。 Phoenixes have nests and chickens, coops. 【俗語 Common saying】

老鵠窩裏出鳳凰。 A phoenix from a crow's nest. 【諺語 Proverb】

Place

大江之南風景殊，杭州西湖天下先。 The scenery south of the Changjiang River is different, and Hangzhou and the West Lake have the best sceneries in the world. 【劉基〈題王潤和尚西湖圖〉Liu Ji: "Inscribing a Painting of West Lake by Monk Wang Run"】

桂林山水甲天下，陽朔山水甲桂林。 The landscape of Guilin is the finest under heaven and that of Yangshuo is the finest in Guilin. 【李曾伯〈重修湘南樓記〉Li Zengbo:"An Account of Renovating the Xiangnan Tower"】

江作青羅帶，山如碧玉簪。 The rivers are like a blue waist belt, and the mountains, a blue jade hairpin. 【韓愈〈送桂州嚴大夫同用南字〉Han Yu:"Presented to Master Yan in Guizhou"】

前不巴村，後不着店。 There is no village ahead and no inn behind. 【施耐庵《水滸傳・第三十七回》Shi Nai'an: Chapter 37, *Outlaws of the Marshes*】

人人盡說江南好，游人祇合江南老。 Everybody says Jiangnan is a nice place, and wanderers after being there hold that it is the place for them to enjoy old age. 【韋莊〈菩薩蠻〉Wei Zhuang:"To the Tune of Buddhist Dancers"】

人生地不熟。 A stranger in a strange place. 【張恨水《夜深沉・第三十三回》Zhang Henshui: Chapter 33, *The Night is Deep*】

人生祇合揚州老，禪智山光好墓田。 Yangzhou is a place for people to die as the beautiful landscape is a good burial place. 【張祜〈游淮南〉Zhang Gu:"Travelling in Huinan"】

日出江花紅勝火，春來江水綠如藍。 When the sun rises at the river, the flowers are redder than fire. When spring comes to the river, the green waters are like blue waters. 【白居易〈憶江南〉Bai Juyi:"Remembering Jiangnan"】

若把西湖比西子，淡妝濃抹總相宜。 If we compare the West Lake to the beautiful lady Xi Shi, we can say that they both are beautiful whether their make-up is light or heavy. 【蘇軾〈飲湖上初晴後雨〉Su Shi:"Drinking Wine on the West Lake When the Sky Begins to Clear up After the Rain"】

上有天堂，下有蘇杭。 There is Paradise above and Suzhou and Hangzhou below. 【范成大《吳郡志》Fan Chengda: *Gazetteer for Wu Commandery*】

食在廣州，着在蘇州。 Eat in Guangzhou and dress in Suzhou. 【諺語 Proverb】

四面荷花三面柳，一城山色半城湖。 The lake has lotus flowers on its four sides and willows on three sides. The entire town has the tints of the mountain and half of the town is occupied by the lake. 【劉鶚《老殘遊記》Liu E: *Travels of Lao Can*】

蘇杭不到枉為人。 One has wasted one's life if one has never been to Suzhou and Hangzhou. 【諺語 Proverb】

一番水土養一方人。 Each place has its own way of supporting its own inhabitants. 【俗語 Common saying】

一在明處，一在暗處。 One is in the open, the other, under cover. 【俗語 Common saying】

有水的風景才美。 Scenic spots with water are really beautiful. 【俗語 Common saying】

Planning

放長線，釣大魚。 Throw a long line to catch a big fish. 【石成金《傳家寶第三集》Shi Chengjin: Volume 3, *Family Heirloom*】

各打各的算盤。 Each has their own plan. 【王少堂《武松・第六回》Wang Shaotang: Chapter 6, *Wu Song*】

計勝怒則強，怒勝計則亡。 One whose planning overcomes anger flourishes; one whose anger overcomes planning perishes. 【荀況《荀子・哀公第三十一》Xun Kuang: Chapter 31, "Duke Ai", *Xunzi*】

君子計成而後行。 A gentleman completes his plan before acting. 【左丘明《國語・魯語下》Zuo Qiuming: "The Language of Lu, Part 2", *National Languages*】

沒得算計一世窮。 Without planning, one will be poor all one's life. 【諺語 Proverb】

謀無主則困，事無備則廢。 You will be in difficulty if you plan without a main theme, and things will be ruined if you have no preparation. 【管仲《管子・霸言第二十三》Guan Zhong: Chapter 23, "Conversations of the Lord Protector", *Guanzi*】

謀先事則昌，事先謀則亡。 If you plan before acting, you will succeed; if you act before planning, you will fail. 【劉向《説苑・卷十六談叢》Liu Xiang: Chapter 16, "The Thicket of Discussion", *Garden of Persuasions*】

窮有窮算盤。 Even a poor person has their own way of calculation. 【俗語 Common saying】【李准〈兩匹瘦馬〉Li Zhun: "Two Thin Horses"】

人上一百，必有奇謀。 When there are over one hundred people gathering together, there will certainly be excellent plans. 【田漢〈西廂記・第五場〉Tian Han: Act 5, "Romance of the Western Bower"】

人無千日計，老來一場空。 A person without a plan for a thousand days will find that he has achieved nothing when he is old. 【徐復祚〈投梭記・第二十四齣〉Xu Fuzuo: Scene 24, "Picking Shuttles"】

細吃細算，油鹽不斷。 Make a careful and detailed calculation and you will not lack oil and salt. 【俗語 Common saying】

細水長流，吃穿不愁。 A long-term plan ensures plenty of food and clothing. 【俗語 Common saying】

細水長流，遇災不愁。 A long-term plan ensures that there will be no worry when a disaster occurs.【諺語 Proverb】

一年之計，莫如樹穀；十年之計，莫如樹木；終身之計，莫如樹人。 The plan for one year is nothing better than growing grains, the plan for ten years is nothing better than planting trees, and the plan for the entire life is nothing better than educating people.【管仲《管子・權修第三》Guan Zhong: Chapter 3, "Cultivation of Political Power", Guanzi】

一年之計在於春，一天之計在於晨。 The plan for one year depends on a good start in spring and the plan for a day depends on a good start in the morning.【蕭繹《纂要・梁元帝》Xiao Yi:"Emperor Yuandi of Liang", Essentials】

走一步，看一步。 Proceed without a plan.【俗語 Common saying】

Poetry

二句三年得，一吟雙淚流。 I spent three years to have these two lines of poem and two rows of tears stream down every time I recite them.【賈島〈題詩後〉Jia Dao:"After Inscribing a Poem"】

李杜詩篇萬口傳，至今已覺不新鮮。 The poems of Li Bai and Du Fu have passed from mouth to mouth for more than ten thousand people, and now they are no longer considered as novel.【趙翼〈論詩絕句〉Zhao Yi:"On Poetry, a Quatrain"】

六十年來妄學詩，功夫深處獨心知。 I have ventured into poetry for more than sixty years, I alone know what I am good at in the writing of poems.【陸游〈夜吟〉Lu You:"A Poem Written at Night"】

詩畫本一律，天工與清新。 Poetry and painting are originally of the same standards: superb skills and freshly clean.【蘇軾〈書鄢陵王主簿所畫折枝二首其一〉Su Shi:"The First Poem of the Two Poems to Inscribe on the Flower Painting by Wang Zhubu of Yanling"】

詩家總愛西崑好，獨恨無人作鄭箋。 Poets generally love the fine quality of Li Shangyin's poetry, it is regrettable that we don't have Zheng Xuan to explicate it.【元好問〈論詩〉Yuan Haowen:"On Poetry"】

詩酒且圖今日樂，功名休問幾時成。 Today, we will enjoy reciting poetry and drinking wine and don't ask when I will accomplish scholarship and official rank.【吳承恩《西遊記・第

五回》Wu Cheng'en: Chapter 5, *Journey to the West*】

詩，可以興，可以觀，可以羣，可以怨。 Poetry can arouse sentiments, stimulate observations, enhance sociability, and express discontent. 【孔子《論語‧陽貨篇第十七》Confucius: Chapter 17, *The Analects of Confucius*】

詩窮而後工。 In poetry one gains depth after suffering. 【歐陽修〈梅聖俞詩集序〉Ouyang Xiu:"Preface to the *Collected Poems of Mei Shengyu*"】

《詩》三百，一言以蔽之，曰：「思無邪」。 The three hundred poems in *The Book of Poetry* can be summarized in one expression, that is:"have no depraved thoughts". 【孔子《論語‧為政篇第二》Confucius: Chapter 2, *The Analects of Confucius*】

詩言志，歌詠言，聲依詠，律和聲。 Poetry expresses one's thoughts, singing speaks one's voice, the voice goes with the expression, and the rhythm accompanies the voice. 【《尚書‧舜典》"The Canon of Shun", *The Book of History*】

詩中有畫，畫中有詩。 There is painting in poetry and poetry in painting. 【蘇軾〈東坡題跋‧書摩詰〈藍田煙雨圖〉〉Su Shi:"Postscript on Wang Wei's Painting 'Mist and Rain over the Blue Fields' "】

熟讀唐詩三百首，不會吟詩也會吟。 If one learns three hundred poems of the Tang Dynasty by heart, one is sure to be able to write poetry. 【孫洙〈唐詩三百首序〉Sun Zhu:"Preface to *Three Hundred Tang poems*"】

天公支與窮詩客，共買清愁不買田。 What the Lord of Heaven pays to impoverished poets is something with which they can only buy pure sorrow, not any fields. 【楊萬里〈戲筆〉Yang Wanli:"Writing a Poem for Fun"】

萬卷山積，一篇吟成。 It is only after reading ten thousand volumes of books piled up like a mountain that I can complete the writing of a poem. 【袁枚《續詩品‧博習》Yuan Mei:"Extensive Study", *A Sequel to Poetry Talks*】

一詩千改始心安，頭未梳成不許看。 I make a thousand emendations to a poem to put my mind to rest, just like a lady would not let anyone to look at her before she combs her hair. 【袁枚〈遣興〉Yuan Mei:"Writing a Poem for Fun"】

一語天然萬古新，豪華落盡見真淳。 Words that are natural remain fresh forever, and sincerity can be seen in poems free of flowery diction. 【元遺山〈論詩三十首〉Yuan Yishan:"Thirty Poems on Poetry"】

Possession

爹有娘有不如己有。 What one's father has and what one's mother has are not as good as what one has. 【諺語 Proverb】

二者不可兼得。 One cannot have both at the same time. 【孟軻《孟子・告子章句上》Meng Ke: Chapter 6, Part 1, *Mencius*】

甘蔗沒有兩頭甜。 A sugarcane is never sweet at both ends. 【諺語 Proverb】

可望不可即。 Within sight but beyond reach. 【劉基〈登臥龍山寫懷二十八韻〉Liu Ji: "My Feelings on Climbing up Mount E'long"】

寧可無了有，不可有了無。 Better go from nothing to something than from something to nothing. 【諺語 Proverb】【凌濛初《初刻拍案驚奇・第二十二卷》Ling Mengchu: Chapter 22, *Amazing Tales, Volume One*】

千賒不如八百現。 A bird in the hand is worth two in the bush. 【諺語 Proverb】

人難再得始為佳。 What is precious is that it is not possible to have a person again. 【龔自珍〈己亥雜詩〉Gong Zizhen: "Miscellaneous Poems of the Year Jihai"】

十賒不如一現。 A bird in hand is worth two in the bush. 【諺語 Proverb】

天地之間，物各有主。 Between the space of heaven and earth, things have their owners. 【蘇軾〈前赤壁賦〉Su Shi: "First Ode to the Red Cliff"】

天上仙鶴，不如手中麻雀。 A bird in hand is better than two in the bush. 【諺語 Proverb】

丫鬟抱小孩 —— 別人的。 A baby held by a servant girl – sb else's. 【歇後語 End-clipper】

閻羅王嫁女 —— 鬼要。 Nobody wants it. 【歇後語 End-clipper】

藥裏的甘草 —— 總有份兒。 Possess oneself of the same as others do. 【俗語 Common saying】

Possibility

方可方不可，方不可方可。 Things are now possible and now impossible, and now impossible and now possible. 【莊周《莊子・內篇・齊物論第二》Zhuang Zhou: Chapter 2, "On the Equality of Things", "Inner Chapters", *Zhuangzi*】

狗頭上生角。 A dog's head growing horns – it's not possible. 【諺語 Proverb】【施耐庵《水滸傳・

第五十一回》Shi Nai'an: Chapter 51, *Outlaws of Them Marshes*】

雞毛飛上天。A chicken feather flies up to heaven. 【諺語 Proverb】

雞窩裏飛出金鳳凰 —— 異想天開。A phoenix soaring out of a chicken coop. 【歇後語 End-clipper】

老虎摘月亮 —— 夢想。A tiger wanting to pluck down the moon – a pipe dream. 【歇後語 End-clipper】

老牛鑽窗眼 —— 騙人。Like trying to drive an ox through the hole in the window. 【歇後語 End-clipper】

年三十晚出月光 —— 不可能。To have moonlight on the night of the Chinese New Year Eve – it's impossible. 【歇後語 End-clipper】

強盜發善心 —— 不可能。A robber showing mercy – it's impossible. 【歇後語 End-clipper】

上天摘月亮 —— 痴心妄想。Cry for the moon. 【歇後語 End-clipper】

西天出太陽 —— 不可能。The sun rises in the West. 【歇後語 End-clipper】

一不離二，二不離三。Things happen in succession. 【俗語 Common saying】

Poverty

安得廣廈千萬間，大庇天下寒士俱歡顏。If only there were thousands of spacious houses, to shelter all the people in the world, much to the joy of the poor. 【杜甫〈茅屋為秋風所破歌〉Du Fu: "Song of My Thatch House Torn down by Autumn Wind"】

家貧不是貧，路貧貧殺人。Poverty at home is not poverty but poverty on the road is killing. 【吳敬梓《儒林外史・第二十四回》Wu Jingzi: Chapter 24, *An Unofficial History of the World of Literati*】

兩個肩膀扛張嘴 —— 淨等吃。With two shoulders carrying one head. 【歇後語 End-clipper】【文康《兒女英雄傳・第二十六回》Wen

Kang: Chapter 26, *Biographies of Young Heroes and Heroines*】

馬行無力皆因瘦，人不貧花衹為貧。A horse runs slowly just because it is too weak and a man does not spend much just because he is too poor. 【《增廣賢文》*Words that Open up One's Mind and Enhance One's Wisdom*】

男做女工，一世命窮。A man who does the work of a woman will be poor all his life. 【俗語 Common saying】

男做女工，越做越窮。The more a man does the work of a woman the poor he becomes. 【俗語 Common saying】【俗語 Common saying】

寧吃少年苦，不受老來窮。
Rather suffer when young than
be poor when old. 【諺語 Proverb】

寧可貧後富，不可富後貧。
Rather get rich after a poor life
than get poor after a rich life. 【俗
語 Common saying】【石君寶〈曲江池・
第二折〉Shi Junbao: Scene 2, "Qujiang
Pool"】

貧而無怨難，富而無驕易。To
be poor and not resentful is far
harder than to be rich and not
arrogant.【孔子《論語・憲問篇
第十四》Confucius: Chapter 14, *The
Analects of Confucius*】

貧窮自在富貴憂。The poor are
happy, while the rich have many
worries.【《增廣賢文》*Words that
Open up One's Mind and Enhance One's
Wisdom*】

貧與賤是人之所惡也，不以其道
得之，不去也。Poverty and low
social status are what people
abhor. If they are not shaken off
in a proper way, they are not to
be evaded.【孔子《論語・里仁篇第
四》Confucius: Chapter 4, *The Analects
of Confucius*】

貧在鬧市無人問，富在深山有
遠親。A poor person in a
bustling place is never greeted,
while a rich person in the deep
mountains has relatives coming
from afar.【《增廣賢文》*Words that
Open up One's Mind and Enhance One's
Wisdom*】

窮命薄如紙。The life of a poor
person is as cheap as a thin

piece of paper.【關漢卿〈裴度還帶・
第一折〉Guan Hanqing: Scene 1, "Pei
Du Returned the Belt He Found"】

窮難惹，饑難擋。The poor
are hard to be dealt with and
hunger is difficult to bear.【諺語
Proverb】

窮怕親戚富怕賊。The poor are
afraid of relatives but the rich,
thieves.【諺語 Proverb】

窮譜兒難打。It is difficult for a
poor person to make his family
budget.【俗語 Common saying】

窮人的飯拿命換。The poor earn
their living with their lives.【諺語
Proverb】

窮人的氣多。Poor people lose
their temper easily.【俗語 Common
saying】

窮人沒災便是福。A poor person
without any disaster is a
blessing in itself.【俗語 Common
saying】

窮人乍富，如同受罪。When
the poor become rich all of a
sudden, it is like torture to them.
【俗語 Common saying】【張恨水《丹
鳳街・第十五章》Zhang Henshui:
Chapter 15, *Crimson Phoenix Street*】

人見人貧親也疏，狗見人貧死
也守。When people see that
their relatives become poor,
they stay away from them, but
when a dog sees that his master
becomes poor, it still defends
him regardless of its life.【《增廣

賢文》Words that Open up One's Mind and Enhance One's Wisdom】

人貧當街賣藝，虎瘦攔路傷人。 A poor person performs in the street to earn a living as a hungry tiger blocks the road to hurt people. 【郭小亭《濟公全傳・第一百六十六回》Guo Xiaoting: Chapter 166, *Biography of Jigong*】

人貧賤，親子離。 A person in poverty becomes lowly and even his own sons will leave him. 【俗語 Common saying】

人窮變形，狗瘦毛長。 A poor person changes in figure and a thin dog has long hair. 【俗語 Common saying】

人窮親戚斷。 A poor person has no relatives. 【俗語 Common saying】 【王璋《吳諺詩鈔》Wang Zhang: *Collected Poems and Proverbs of the Wu Dialect*】

人窮犬也欺。 When a person is poor, he will be bullied even by dogs. 【諺語 Proverb】

人窮心不窮。 One who is poor may not be poor at heart. 【俗語 Common saying】

人窮志不窮。 One who is poor may not be limited in his ambition. 《增廣賢文》Words that Open up One's Mind and Enhance One's Wisdom】

人無三代窮。 No family will be in poverty for more than three generations. 【諺語 Proverb】

人心無剛一世窮。 A person without a strong will suffer poverty all his life. 【諺語 Proverb】 【劉江《太行風雲・第三十三回》Liu Jiang: Chapter 33, *Changes in Taixing*】

日無雞米，夜無鼠糧。 There are no grains to feed the chicken at daytime and no grains for the rats to eat in the evening. 【諺語 Proverb】

若要窮，困到日頭紅。 If one wants to become poor, the best way is to sleep till the sun is bright red. 【諺語 Proverb】

上無片瓦，下無插針之地。 Be in abject poverty. 【釋道原《景德傳燈錄・卷二十》Shi Daoyuan: Chapter 20, *Records of the Transmission of the Lamp in the Jingde Period*.】

手長衫袖短，人窮顏色低。 When the arm is long the sleeve seems short; if a person is poor, he cannot hold up his head. 【俗語 Common saying】

貪產貧，惜產窮。 One who keeps purchasing property but is reluctant to sell it is poor. 【俗語 Common saying】

天無一日雨，人無一世窮。 It seldom rains for a whole day and a person seldom remains poor all his life. 【俗語 Common saying】

田怕秋乾，人怕老窮。 Crops are afraid of drought in autumn and people are afraid of poverty when old. 【諺語 Proverb】

貼人不富自家窮。Financial support to others cannot make them rich but makes yourself poor.【馮夢龍《喻世明言‧第三十九卷》Feng Menglong: Chapter 39, *Stories to Instruct the World*】

外財不富命窮人。A person who is destined to be poor cannot get rich with money that does not belong to him.【諺語 Proverb】

無名草木年年發，不信男兒一世窮。Unnamed grass comes forth every year so do not believe that a man will be poor all his life.【佚名《名賢集》Anonymous: *Collected Sayings of Famous Sages*】

夜不關門 —— 窮壯膽。A poor man does not shut his door at night because he fears no loss of property.【歇後語 End-clipper】

有廉而貧者，貧者未必廉。There are people who become poor because they don't corrupt, but some poor people may not be incorruptible.【劉安《淮南子‧說林訓第十六》Liu An: Chapter 16, "Discourse on Mountains", *Huainanzi*】

Power

豺狼當道，不問狐狸。When jackals and wolves are in power, foxes should not be held responsible.【范曄《後漢書‧張綱傳》Fan Ye: "Biography of Zhang Gang", *History of the Later Han*】

寸權必奪，寸利必得。Wrest every ounce of power and every ounce of gain.【諺語 Proverb】

大權獨攬，小權分散。Have great power in one's hands alone and devolve power on minor issues on others.【俗語 Common saying】

狗是百步王，只在門前狠。Every dog is a lion at home.【諺語 Proverb】

虎死不落架。A tiger is dead, but its skeleton does not fall down.【諺語 Proverb】【王少堂《武松‧第一回》Wang Shaotang: Chapter 1, *Wu Song*】

化阻力為助力。Turn a stumbling block into a stepping stone.【諺語 Proverb】

皇帝輪流做，明年到我家。People become emperors in turn, and next year, it will be my turn.【諺語 Proverb】【吳承恩《西遊記‧第七回》Wu Cheng'en: Chapter 7, *Journey to the West*】

力拔山兮氣蓋世。I have the power to pull up a mountain and my will is unparalleled in the world.【項羽〈垓下歌〉Xiang Yu: "Finale"】

牛有千斤之力，人有倒牛之力。An ox can carry a burden of a thousand catties, but a person has a way to control the ox.【羅

懋登《三寶太監西洋記・第三十一回》Luo Maodeng: Chapter 31, *The Western Voyage of the Eunuch of Three Treasures*】

蚍蜉撼大樹，可笑不自量。 A tiny insect that tries to shake a mighty tree is ludicrously ignorant of its own weakness. 【韓愈〈調張籍〉Han Yu:"Teasing Zhang Ji"】

槍桿子裏面出政權。 Political power comes from the barrel of a gun. 【毛澤東〈八七會議〉Mao Zedong:"Speech at the Meeting on 7 August 1927"】

強權就是公理。 Might is right. 【俗語 Common saying】

人多力量大。 More people, more power. 【諺語 Proverb】

人多勢眾，孤掌難鳴。 When you have more people, you have more power, and when you are all by yourself, it is difficult for you to make your voice heard. 【曹雪芹《紅樓夢・第十回》Cao Xueqin: Chapter 10, *A Dream of the Red Chamber*】

人在勢在，人亡勢亡。 The power of a person exists when he is alive and disappears when he is dead. 【蔡東藩《清史通俗演義・第十八回》Cai Dongfan: Chapter 18, *Popular Romance of the Qing Dynasty*】

勝人者有力，自勝者強。 He who overcomes others is powerful; he who overcomes himself is strong. 【老子《道德經・第三十三章》Laozi: Chapter 33, *Daodejing*】

手大捂不住天。 A big hand cannot cover up the sky. 【諺語 Proverb】

樹倒猢猻散。 When a tree falls, the monkeys on it will run away. 【龐元英《談藪》Pang Yuanying: *Grassland Conversations*】

四兩能夠撥千斤。 Four taels can move a thousand catties. 【俗語 Common saying】

太歲頭上動土。 Provoke somebody in power. 【俗語 Common saying】

藤蘿繞樹生，樹倒藤蘿死。 Wistaria grows on a tree and dies when the tree falls down. 【佚名《名賢集》Anonymous: *Collected Sayings of Famous Sages*】

天上雷公，地上舅公。 Thunder god is most powerful in heaven, mother's uncle is most powerful on earth. 【俗語 Common saying】

問蒼茫大地，誰主沉浮。 I ask the boundless land, who is in command of the rise and fall of this country? 【毛澤東〈沁園春・長沙〉Mao Zedong:"Changsha: To the Tune of Spring in the Garden of Qin"】

無用之用，方為大用。 The use of the useless is the greatest use of usefulness. 【莊周《莊子・內篇・逍遙遊第一》Zhuang Zhou: Chapter 1, "Carefree Wandering", "Inner Chapters", *Zhuangzi*】

要風得風，要雨得雨。 One is able to get what one wants. 【俗語 Common saying】

一分權勢，一分造孽。 More power means more evils. 【俗語 Common saying】

一夫當關，萬夫莫開。 One man blocks the pass, ten thousand others are unable to get through. 【李白〈蜀道難〉Li Bai: "Hard is the Way to Shu"】

一人氣力擔一擔，眾人力量搬倒山。 One person's strength can carry one burden while the strength of the masses can remove mountains. 【諺語 Proverb】【劉江《太行風雲·第三十三回》Liu Jiang: Chapter 33, *Changes in Taixing*】

一人之下，萬人之上。 He has only one over him and thousands under him. 【呂望《六韜》Lu Wang: *Six Secret Teachings*】

一朝權在手，誰敢不低頭。 Once one has power in hand, everybody has to bow before him. 【俗語 Common saying】

以權利合者，權盡而交疏。 Those who come together for power will distance from each other when power goes. 【司馬遷《史記·管晏列傳》Sima Qian: "Biographies of Guan (Zhong) and Yan (Ying)", *Records of the Grand Historian*】

有財便有勢。 Those who are wealthy have power. 【俗語 Common saying】

有勢不可使盡，有福不可享盡。 Do not use your power to the extreme and do not enjoy fortune to the extreme. 【俗語 Common saying】

有勢不使不如無。 One who has the power but does not use it had better give it up. 【俗語 Common saying】

祇有招架之功，沒有還手之力。 Can only ward off blows but lack the ability to hit back. 【俗語 Common saying】

Practice

工多出巧藝。 If you practise often, you become highly skilled. 【諺語 Proverb】

拳不離手，曲不離口。 Practice makes perfect. 【諺語 Proverb】

三日不彈，手生荊棘。 Without playing a musical instrument for three days, you feel as if thorns have grown on one's hands. 【曹雪芹《紅樓夢·第八十六回》Cao Xueqin: Chapter 86, *A Dream of the Red Chamber*】

三天不唱口生，三天不演腰硬。 Without singing for three days, you will become tongue-tied; without performing for three days, you will find your waist stiff. 【諺語 Proverb】

三天不唸口生，三天不做手生。 If you stop practising reading aloud for three days, you will become tongue-tied; if you stop practising a skill for three days, you hand will become clumsy. 【諺語 Proverb】

鐵不磨生锈，水不流發臭。 Iron grows rusty without whetting and water becomes stale without running. 【諺語 Proverb】

一遍功夫一遍巧。 The more practice one does, the cleverer one becomes. 【諺語 Proverb】

Praise

老鼠跌落天平 —— 自己秤自己。 Sing one's own praise. 【歇後語 End-clipper】

Predicament

吊桶落在井裏。 Like a bucket going to the well, one cannot extricate oneself from a predicament. 【施耐庵《水滸傳·第二十一回》Shi Nai'an: Chapter 21, *Outlaws of the Marshes*】

叫天天不應，入地地無門。 One calls to heaven without getting its response. One wants to enter the earth, and there is no door to do so. 【諺語 Proverb】

籠裏的鳥兒 —— 有翅難逃。 A bird in the cage, although it has wings, cannot escape. 【歇後語 End-clipper】

甕中之鱉，釜中之魚。 A turtle in a jar and a fish in a cauldron. 【馮夢龍《喻世明言·第十八卷》Feng Menglong: Chapter 18, *Stories to Instruct the World*】

Preference

愛吃蘿蔔不吃梨 —— 各有所好。 Like eating turnips, but not pears – individuals have their own preferences. 【歇後語 End-clipper】

狗嘴裏拋骨頭 —— 投其所好。 Throwing bones into a dog's mouth – catering to somebody's likes. 【歇後語 End-clipper】

Preparation

安而不忘危，存而不忘亡，治而不忘亂。 When safe, don't forget danger; when alive, don't forget death; when in peace, don't forget chaos.【《易經‧繫辭下》"Appended Remarks, Part 2", *The Book of Changes*】

備而不防，防而不備。 If you are prepared, there is no need to protect yourself. If you are protected, there is no need for preparation.【諺語 Proverb】

常將有日思無日，莫待無時想有時。 If you think of want in time of plenty, you'll have no need to yearn for plenty in time of want.【《增廣賢文》*Words that Open up One's Mind and Enhance One's Wisdom*】

凡事豫則立，不豫則廢。 Preparation ensures success and unpreparedness spells failure.【《禮記‧中庸第三十一章》Chapter 31, "Doctrine of the Mean", *The Book of Rites*】

非針不引線，無水不渡船。 Without a needle there is no way to thread a line. Without water, there is no way to sail a boat.【諺語 Proverb】

豐年要當欠年過，免得欠年挨饑餓。 When there is a bumper harvest, we should practise economy. When there is a crop failure, we have food to fill our bellies.【諺語 Proverb】

積穀防饑，養兒防老。 Store up grain against starvation and give birth to boys to prepare for one's old age.【諺語 Proverb】

居安思危，思則有備，有備無患。 When living in peace, we have to think of danger. If we think, then we will be prepared. If we are prepared, then we will have no worries.【左丘明《左傳‧襄公十一年》Zuo Qiuming: "The Eleventh Year of the Reign of Duke Xiang", *Zuo's Commentary on the Spring and Autumn Annals*】

貓要捕鼠，必先伏下身子。 A cat stoops before it catches a mouse.【俗語 Common saying】

沒事常思有事。 In time of peace, we should prepare ourselves for time of trouble.【諺語 Proverb】【曹雪芹《紅樓夢‧第三十四回》Cao Xueqin: Chapter 34, *A Dream of the Red Chamber*】

磨刀不誤砍柴工。 Sharpening the knife will not delay the work of cutting firewood.【諺語 Proverb】

寧可千日不戰，不可一日不備。 Better have no war for a thousand days than slacken one's vigilance for one day.【諺語 Proverb】

平時不燒香，臨急抱佛腳。 One does not burn incense at ordinary times, but clasp Buddha's feet to seek help when in trouble.【諺語 Proverb】

晴带雨傘，飽带饑糧。 When it is fine, carry an umbrella; when you are full, carry provisions. 【諺語 Proverb】

晴带雨傘飽带糧，洪水未來就先防。 Carry an umbrella when the sun shines and take food when you are still full. Make precautions before a flood arrives. 【諺語 Proverb】

晴天防着下雨。 Be prepared against rain when it is still sunny. 【諺語 Proverb】

萬事俱備，祗欠東風。 Everything is ready, and all that we need is an east wind. 【羅貫中《三國演義·第四十九回》Luo Guanzhong: Chapter 49, *Romance of the Three Kingdoms*】

閒時做下忙時用。 When you have time, prepare something for use at busy times. 【諺語 Proverb】

以備不時之需。 Against a rainy day. 【俗語 Common saying】

宜未雨而綢繆，毋臨渴而掘井。 You had better save against a rainy day rather than digging a well when feeling thirsty. 【朱用純《朱子家訓》Zhu Yongchun: *Percepts of the Zhu Family*】

Presence

承蒙光臨，不勝榮幸。 Your presence is an honour to us. 【俗語 Common saying】

當面鑼，對面鼓。 In one's presence. 【蘭陵笑笑生《金瓶梅·第五十一回》Lanling Xiaoxiaosheng: Chapter 51, *The Plum in the Golden Vase*】

既來之，則安之。 Since we are already here, we may as well stay and enjoy it. 【孔子《論語·季氏篇第十六》Confucius: Chapter 16, *The Analects of Confucius*】

神龍見首不見尾。 Appearing at one moment and disappear the next like a dragon. 【趙執信《談龍錄》Zhao Zhixin: *Records of the Discussions of the Dragon*】

說曹操，曹操就到。 Speak of the devil, and he is sure to appear. 【羅貫中《三國演義·第十四回》Luo Guanzhong: Chapter 14, *Romance of the Three Kingdoms*】

遠在天邊，近在眼前。 Seemingly far away but actually close at hand. 【吳趼人《二十年目睹之怪現狀·第七十九回》Wu Jianren: Chapter 79, *Bizarre Happenings Eyewitnessed over Two Decades*】

Pretention

挨揍打呼嚕 —— 裝糊塗。
Pretending to snore while
being beaten – one is feigning
ignorance. 【歇後語 End-clipper】

背着米討飯 —— 裝窮。Begging
while carrying rice on one's
back – pretending to be poor. 【歇
後語 End-clipper】

打腫臉充胖子。Slap one's face
swollen to make oneself look
imposing. 【俗語 Common saying】

鱷魚淚 —— 假惺惺。A crocodile
shedding tears – hypocritical.
【歇後語 End-clipper】

分明是強盜，卻要裝聖賢。He is
clearly a robber yet he pretends
to be a sage. 【俗語 Common saying】

猴子穿衣 —— 假充人。A monkey
wears clothes to pretend to be a
human being. 【歇後語 End-clipper】

猴子看書 —— 假斯文。A monkey
reading a book is pretending to
be refined in manner. 【歇後語
End-clipper】

老虎唸經 —— 假裝正經。A
tiger chanting scriptures is
pretending to be respectable. 【歇
後語 End-clipper】

貓不吃魚 —— 假斯文。A cat not
eating fish – pretending to be
refined in manner. 【歇後語 End-
clipper】

貓哭老鼠 —— 假慈悲。A cat that
weeps over a dead mouse is
pretending to be merciful. 【歇後
語 End-clipper】

披着羊皮吃羊。Eat sheep on a
sheep's clothing. 【諺語 Proverb】

是馬充不了麒麟。A horse cannot
pose as a Chinese unicorn. 【諺語
Proverb】

烏鴉吃死羊，先要哭一場。Before
a crow eats a dead goat, it will
bewail first. 【諺語 Proverb】

繡花枕頭，虛有其表。Many a
fine dish has nothing on it. 【諺語
Proverb】

Prevention

不吠的狗須提防，平靜的水
要小心。One should take
precaution of a silent dog and
be careful of still waters. 【俗語
Common saying】

吃飯防噎，行路防跌。Beware
of choking when you eat and

stumbling when you walk. 【施
耐庵《水滸傳・第十回》Shi Nai'an:
Chapter 10, *Outlaws of the Marshes*】

防患於未然。Prevention is better
than cure. 【《易經・既濟》Hexagram
jiji, The Book of Changes】

防微杜漸而禁於未然。 Evils should be prevented before they are fully developed. 【宋濂等《元史‧張楨傳》Song Lian, et al.:"Biography of Zhang Zhen", *The History of the Yuan Dynasty*】

Price

價高招遠客。 As long as you are willing to buy at a high price, merchants from afar will come to you. 【羅懋登《三寶太監西洋記‧第七十七回》Luo Maodeng: Chapter 77, *The Western Voyage of the Eunuch of Three Treasures*】

價一不擇主。 When the price is fixed, everybody can buy the goods. 【俗語 Common saying】

蘿蔔花了肉價錢 —— 不合算。 Have paid too dear for the whistle. 【李六如《六十年的變遷‧第一章》Li Liuru: Chapter 1, *The Changes in the Last Sixty Years*】

漫天要價，就地還錢。 The seller demands an exorbitant price, but the buyer gives a down-to-earth offer. 【李汝珍《鏡花緣‧第十一回》Li Ruzhen: Chapter 11, *Flowers in the Mirror*】

便宜無好貨，好貨不便宜。 What is cheap is not good, what is good is not cheap. 【俗語 Common saying】

獅子開大口。 Ask for an exorbitant price. 【俗語 Common saying】

時移俗易，物同價異。 With the passage of time and change of custom, the same thing has different prices. 【葛洪《抱朴子‧外篇‧擢才第十八》Ge Hong: Chapter 18, "Promotion of Talents", "Outer Chapters", *The Master Who Embraces Simplicity*】

羊毛出在羊身上。 The benefit comes from the price which a person has paid. 【俗語 Common saying】

一分錢一分貨。 One gets what one pays for. 【俗語 Common saying】

Pride

傲不可長，慾不可縱。 Pride cannot be allowed to grow and desires, be free of rein. 【《禮記‧曲禮上第一》Chapter 1, "Summary of the Rules of Propriety, Part A", *The Book of Rites*】

驕傲來自淺薄，狂妄出於無知。 Conceit comes from shallowness and arrogance, ignorance. 【諺語 Proverb】

滿招損，謙受益。 Pride incurs losses, while modesty brings

benefits.【《尚書・大禹謨》"Counsels of Yu the Great", *The Book of History*】

Profession

幹一行，愛一行。One likes whatever profession one engages in.【俗語 Common saying】

幹一行，怨一行。One dislikes whatever profession one engages in.【俗語 Common saying】

隔行如隔山。The difference between one profession and another is as wide as the separation of mountains.【諺語 Proverb】

做一行，怨一行。When in the profession, one complains about it.【俗語 Common saying】

Profit

見小利則大事不成。With one's eyes fixed on petty profits, one can hardly succeed in great endeavours.【孔子《論語・子路篇第十三》Confucius: Chapter 13, *The Analects of Confucius*】

刻薄不賺錢，忠厚不析本。Being mean, one does not make profit; being honest, one does not lose money.【馮夢龍《醒世恆言・第三卷》Feng Menglong: Chapter 3, *Stories to Awaken the World*】

貪圖小利，大事難成。One who covets small benefits cannot achieve anything great.【孔子《論語・子路篇第十三》Confucius: Chapter 13, *The Analects of Confucius*】

天下熙熙，皆為利來；天下攘攘，皆為利往。People come here in droves, all for profits; people go there in a bustle, all for profits.【司馬遷《史記・貨殖列傳》Sima Qian:"Biographies of Usurers", *Records of the Grand Historian*】

Progress

長江後浪推前浪，世上新人換舊人。In the Changjiang River, the waves behind push those in front. In the world, the emerging generation replaces the previous one.【《增廣賢文》*Words that Open up One's Mind and Enhance One's Wisdom*】

由近及遠，由淺入深。Proceed from the close to the distant

and from the elementary to the profound. 【諺語 Proverb】

芝麻開花節節高。 A sesame stalk puts forth blossoms notch by notch, higher and higher. 【俗語 Common saying】

牀底下放風箏 —— 不見起。 Flying kites underneath a bed, one is unable to make much progress. 【歇後語 End-clipper】

Promise

百金孰云重，一諾良非輕。 Don't say that a hundred taels of gold is heavy, for a single promise is far from light. 【盧照鄰〈詠史四首‧其一〉Lu Zhaolin: "Four Poems on History, First Poem"】

大丈夫言出如山。 A true gentleman never goes back on his words. 【李雨堂《萬花樓‧第三十回》Li Yutang: Chapter 30, Ten-thousand-flower Tower】

光許願，不供獻。 Make promises but never keep them. 【諺語 Proverb】

好漢一言，快馬一鞭。 A word spoken by a true gentleman is past recalling, just like a whip on a swift horse. 【諺語 Proverb】【釋道原《景德傳燈錄‧袁州南源道明禪師》Shi Daoyuan: "Chan Master Dao Ming of Nanyuan, Yuanzhou", Records of the Transmission of the Lamp in the Jingde Period】

結交一言重，相期千里至。 Good friends highly value their words. They travel a thousand miles to keep their promise for a gathering. 【虞世南〈雜曲歌辭〉Yu Shinan: "A Lyric for a Zaju"】

君子一言，快馬一鞭。 A word spoken by a gentleman is past recalling, just like a whip on a swift horse. 【釋道原《景德傳燈錄‧卷六》Shi Daoyuan: Chapter 6, Records of the Transmission of the Lamp in the Jingde Period.】

空口說白話。 Make empty promises. 【劉昫《舊唐書‧憲宗本紀》Liu Xu: "Annals of Emperor Xianzong", History of the Early Tang】

口惠而實不至，怨災及其身。 If one simply pays, blames and disasters will fall on him. 【《禮記‧表記第三十二》Chapter 32, "Records of Examples", The Book of Rites】

寧許人，莫許神。 Rather make a vow to a man than to a god. 【張南莊《何典‧第一卷》Zhang Nanzhuang: Chapter 1, From Which Classic】

輕諾必寡信，多易必多難。 Those who make promises lightly seldom keep their words and those who take things lightly will definitely end up in great difficulty. 【老子《道德經·第六十三章》Laozi: Chapter 63, *Daodejing*】

人而無信，不知其可也。If a person does not keep his words, I don't know what he gets on in society? 【孔子《論語·為政篇第二》Confucius: Chapter 2, *The Analects of Confucius*】

說的比唱的好聽。Make empty promises. 【俗語 Common saying】

說得出，做得到。What is said is what is done. 【俗語 Common saying】

說得到，做得到。What is said is what is done. 【俗語 Common saying】

說一是一，說二是二。One means everything one says. 【張春帆《宦海·第四回》Zhang Chunfan: Chapter 4, *The Official Circles*】

許人一物，千金不移。If you promise others one thing, you should not break your promise even if you are given a thousand pieces of gold. 【《增廣賢文》*Words that Open up One's Mind and Enhance One's Wisdom*】

言必信，行必果。Promises must be kept and action must be resolute. 【孔子《論語·子路篇第十三》Confucius: Chapter 13, *The Analects of Confucius*】

一言既出，駟馬難追。Even four horses cannot take back what one has said. 【孔子《論語·顏淵篇第十二》Confucius: Chapter 12, *The Analects of Confucius*】

一語為重百金輕。A promise is weightier than one hundred taels of gold. 【王安石〈商鞅〉Wang Anshi:"Shang Yang"】

與朋友交，言而有信。One should honour commitments made to friends. 【孔子《論語·學而篇第一》Confucius: Chapter 1, *The Analects of Confucius*】

Prosperity

得人者昌，失人者亡。One who is well received by the people prospers. One who is not, perishes. 【李觀〈項籍故里碑銘序〉Li Guan:"Preface to the Tablet of the Old Lane of Xiang Ji"】

花無百日好，石頭也有翻轉時。No flower ever blossoms for a hundred days and the day will come when even the rocks will turn over. 【俗語 Common saying】

花無千日紅。Flowers will not blossom for a thousand days. 【施耐庵《水滸傳·第二十二回》Shi Nai'an: Chapter 22, *Outlaws of the Marshes*】

人無千日好，花無百日紅。A person cannot have a smooth running for a thousand days and flowers cannot bloom for a hundred days. 【施耐庵《水滸傳·第二十二回》Shi Nai'an: Chapter 22, *Outlaws of the Marshes*】

三月裏的桃花 —— 紅不了多久。 Peach blossoms in the third month of the lunar year do not last long. 【歇後語 End-clipper】

少年休笑白頭翁，花兒能有幾時紅。 The young should not laugh at the old folks with grey hair; how long can the flowers bloom? 【諺語 Proverb】

生氣勃勃，蒸蒸日上。 Be full of vitality and thriving with each passing day. 【俗語 Common saying】

Prostitute

前門進老子，後門進兒子。 The father enters from the front door and the son from the rear door. 【俗語 Common saying】【蘭陵笑笑生《金瓶梅·第八十回》Lanling Xiaoxiaosheng: Chapter 80, *The Plum in the Golden Vase*】

小娘愛俏，老鴇愛鈔。 A prostitute loves a handsome man, while the procuress loves money. 【俗語 Common saying】【馮夢龍《喻世明言·第十二卷》Feng Menglong: Chapter 12, *Stories to Instruct the World*】

笑娼不笑貧。 People laugh at a prostitute but not a poor woman. 【俗語 Common saying】

笑淫不笑貧。 People laugh at a prostitute but not a poor woman. 【俗語 Common saying】

又想當婊子，又想立牌坊。 Lead a life of prostitution and expect a monument to her chastity. 【俗語 Common saying】

Protection

一棵大樹好遮陽。 A large tree provides shelter from the sun. 【諺語 Proverb】

Punishment

白狗吃肉，黑狗當災。 The white dog eats the meat and the black dog bears the blame. 【俗語 Common saying】

打了不罰，罰了不打。 If one is punished physically, one should not be fined. If one is fined, one should not be punished physically. 【俗語 Common saying】

罰不擇骨肉，賞不避仇讎。 When meting out punishments, one does not choose blood relatives. When giving rewards, one does not avoid enemies. 【諺語 Proverb】

各打五十大板。 Both sides are punished by having fifty strikes. 【諺語 Proverb】

黃犬偷食，白犬當罪。 A yellow dog steals the meat, but a white one is punished. 【何求《閩都別記》 He Qiu: *An Account of the Min Capital*】

家奴犯罪，罪坐家主。 If a servant commits a crime, his master should bear the responsibility. 【施世綸《施公案・第一百三十八回》 Shi Shilun: Chapter 138, *Cases of Judge Shi*】

君子以明慎用刑而不留獄。 A gentleman clearly understands a case and is cautious in meting out punishment, and does not allow litigation to be stalled. 【《易經・旅・象》 "Image", Hexagram *Lu*, *The Book of Changes*】

勸君莫做虧心事，古往今來放過誰。 I advise you not to do anything that is against conscience for from of old no one has gone unpunished for doing things against conscience. 【佚名《名賢集》 Anonymous: *Collected Sayings of Famous Sages*】

賞罰不信，則禁令不行。 When the rewards and punishments are not trusted, then prohibitions cannot be executed. 【韓非《韓非子・外儲說左上第三十二》 Han Fei: Chapter 32, "Outer Congeries of Sayings, Part 1", *Hanfeizi*】

坦白從寬，抗拒從嚴。 Lenient punishment for those who confess, but harsh punishment for those who don't. 【毛澤東〈關於「三反」「五反」的鬥爭〉 Mao Zedong: "On the Struggle Against the 'Three-antis' and 'Five-antis'"】

王者犯法，庶民同罪。 A king who violates the law will be punished like an ordinary person. 【夏敬渠《野叟曝言・第六十七回》 Xia Jingqu: Chapter 67, *Imprudent Discourse of a Wild Old Man*】

違法不究，姑息縱容。 Not punishing law-breakers and tolerate or connive at their crimes. 【俗語 Common saying】

烏狗吃食，白狗當災。 The black dog stole the food but the white dog was punished. 【凌濛初《二刻拍案驚奇・第三十八卷》 Ling Mengchu: Chapter 38, *Amazing Tales, Volume Two*】

誣告加三等。 One who trumps up a charge against another will be punished three times more severely. 【吳承恩《西遊記・第八十三回》 Wu Cheng'en: Chapter 83, *Journey to the West*】

刑不上大夫，禮不下庶人。 Punishments are not for nobles and rites, the common people. 【《禮記・曲禮上第一》Chapter 1, "Summary of the Rules of Propriety, Part 1", *The Book of Rites*】

一佛出世，二佛涅槃。 One beats a person till he is half dead. 【凌濛初《初刻拍案驚奇・第二十三卷》Ling Mengchu: Chapter 23, *Amazing Tales, Volume One*】

一命抵一命。 Demand a life for a life. 【俗語 Common saying】

有事不避難，有罪不避刑。 When something happens, one does not escape from difficulties; when crime is commited, one does not evade punishment. 【左丘明《國語・晉語》Zuo Qiuming:"The Language of Jin", *National Languages*】

治國刑多而賞少，亂國賞多而刑少。 In a well-governed country, punishments are numerous and rewards are few. In a disorderly country, rewards are numerous and punishments are few. 【商鞅《商君書・開塞》Shang Yang:"Opening and Plugging", *The Works of Shang Yang*】

Putting on airs

八仙吹喇叭 —— 神氣十足。 The Eight Taoist Immortals blowing trumpets are full of godlike airs – they put on grand airs. 【歇後語 End-clipper】

Quantity

大能掩小，海納百川。 The big can cover the small and the sea takes in waters from hundreds of rivers. 【李直夫〈虎頭牌・第三折〉Li Zhifu: Scene 3, "Tiger-head Plaque"】

單絲不成線，獨木不成林。 A single strand of silk does not make a thread nor a single tree a forest. 【錢彩《說岳全傳・第四十八回》Qian Cai: Chapter 48, *A Story of Yue Fei*】

貴精不貴多。 It's quality rather than quantity that matters. 【俗語 Common saying】

韓信將兵，多多益善。 The more the better is the way Han Xin recommended for the troops under his control. 【司馬遷《史記・淮陰侯列傳》Sima Qian:"Biography of the Marquis of Huaiyin", *Records of the Grand Historian*】

黃鼠狼拖雞 —— 越拖越稀。 The weasel drags the chickens – the more he drags, the fewer they become. 【歇後語 End-clipper】

積土成山，積水成川。 Heap-up earth becomes a mountain,

accumulated water becomes a river. 【戴德《大戴禮記・勸學》Dai De:"Zengzi Establishes Things", *Records of Rites by Dai the Elder*】

八九不離十 —— 差不多。 Nine times out of ten –pretty close. 【歇後語 End-clipper】

聚沙成塔，集腋成裘。 Many a pickle makes a mickle. 【墨翟《墨子・親士卷一》Mo Di: Chapter 1, "Staying Close to Scholars", *Mozi*】

砍不倒大樹 —— 弄不多柴禾。 If one does not chop down the big trees, one cannot get much firewood. 【歇後語 End-clipper】

牛身上拔了一根毛。 A hair from the hide of an ox. 【李伯元《活地獄・第二十九回》Li Boyuan: Chapter 29, *Living Hell*】

日計不足，歲計有餘。 It is insignificant if counted on a daily basis but it is a surplus if counted on a yearly basis. 【劉安《淮南子・俶真訓第二》Liu An: Chapter 2, "Beginning of Reality", *Huainanzi*】

一朵鮮花做不成花環。 One flower does not make a garland. 【俗語 Common saying】

蟻多可以抬象，蝗多可以蔽天。 Many ants can carry an elephant away and many locusts can cover up the sky. 【俗語 Common saying】

Quarrel

不為左右袒。 Not to take sides in a quarrel. 【司馬遷《史記・孝文本紀》Sima Qian:"Annals of the Xiaowen Emperor", *Records of the Grand Historian*】

公說公有理，婆說婆有理。 Both quarrelling parties claim to be in the right. 【諺語 Proverb】

狗咬狗，兩嘴毛。 When a dog bites another dog, each gets a mouthful of fur. 【諺語 Proverb】

善者不辯，辯者不善。 One who is good does not quarrel and one who quarrels is not good. 【老子《道德經・第八十一章》Laozi: Chapter 81, *Daodejing*】

室無空虛，則婦姑勃豀。 In a house where there is not much space, a woman and her mother-in-law will fall to quarrelling. 【莊周《莊子・雜篇・外物第二十六》Zhuang Zhou: Chapter 26, "External Things", "Miscellaneous Chapters", *Zhuangzi*】

一個巴掌拍不響。 It takes two to make a quarrel. 【俗語 Common saying】

一隻手拍不響。 It takes two to make a quarrel. 【俗語 Common saying】

一隻碗不響，兩隻碗叮噹。 It takes two to make a quarrel.

【施耐庵《水滸傳・第二十二回》Shi Nai'an: Chapter 22, *Outlaws of the Marshes*】

Question and answer

問花花不答。I asked the flowers and they did not answer me.【俗語 Common saying】

問遍千家成行家。A person becomes an expert after asking a thousand professionals.【俗語 Common saying】

一清二楚，無須多問。As everything is crystal clear, there is no need for further questions.【俗語 Common saying】

Rabbit

不見兔子不撒鷹。Don't loose the falcon until you see the hare.【俗語 Common saying】

狡兔有三窟。A clever rabbit has three burrows.【劉向《戰國策・齊策四》Liu Xiang: "Strategies of the State of Qi, No. 4", *Strategies of the Warring States*】

兔子不急不咬人。A rabbit will not bite until it is irritated.【俗語 Common saying】

兔子駕不了轅。A rabbit is never to be harnessed.【諺語 Proverb】

兔子尾巴 —— 長不了。The tail of a rabbit cannot be long.【歇後語 End-clipper】

Rain

悲歡離合總無情，一任階前，點滴到天明。I have become unfeeling to woe, joy, parting, and union, just let the rain before the steps, drip and drip until daybreak.【蔣捷〈虞美人・聽雨〉Jiang Jie: "Listening to the Rain: To the Tune of the Beauty of Yu"】

不雨則已，一雨傾盆。It never rains but pours.【諺語 Proverb】

春雨貴如油。Vernal rain is as precious as oil.【諺語 Proverb】

而今聽雨僧廬下，鬢已星星也。Now I listen to raining under a monk's roof, with hair on my temples already turns white.【蔣捷〈虞美人・聽雨〉Jiang Jie: "Listening to the Rain: To the Tune of the Beauty of Yu"】

近山多得雨。 If you live closer to the mountains, you get more rain. 【俗語 Common saying】

久旱逢甘霖。 Have a sweet shower after a long drought. 【洪邁《容齋隨筆》Hong Mai: *Notes from Rong Studio*】

騎秋一場雨，遍地出黃金。 If it rains in early autumn, there will be a gold-like bumper harvest. 【諺語 Proverb】【潘榮陛《帝京歲時紀勝》Pan Rongbi: *Descriptions of Scenic Spots During Different Seasons in the Imperial Capital*】

山中一夜雨，樹杪百重泉。 A night of rain in the mountain brings a hundred springs on the tree branches. 【王維〈送梓州李使君〉Wang Wei:"Seeing off Prefect Li of Zizhou"】

隨風潛入夜，潤物細無聲。 The spring wind follows the wind and creeps in at night, moisturing things in a small way without a sound. 【杜甫〈春夜喜雨〉Du Fu:"Rain of Joy in a Spring Night"】

天街小雨潤如酥，草色遙看近卻無。 The light rain that fell on the streets in the capital are soft as butter, and the grass that looks green from afar are not there when you go near them. 【韓愈〈初春小雨〉Han Yu:"Light Rain in Early Spring"】

小樓一夜聽春雨，深巷明朝賣杏花。 In a small tower I listened to the vernal rain all night, tomorrow in the deep alley, apricot blooms will be sold. 【陸游〈臨安春雨初霽〉Lu You:"At Lin An After a Vernal Rain"】

煙不出門，大雨將臨。 When smoke lingers in your house, a heavy rain will soon be falling. 【諺語 Proverb】

一場秋雨一場寒。 After each autumn rain, it becomes colder than before. 【諺語 Proverb】

一川煙草，滿城風絮，梅子黃時雨。 My feelings are like a river of smoke and grass, a town filled with flying catkins, and drizzles in a time when plums turn yellow. 【賀鑄〈青玉案〉He Zhu:"To the Tune of Green Jade Table"】

一雨足暝色，孤篷撐暮煙。 After raining, it was getting dark, and a solitary boat sailed amidst mist in the evening. 【俞樾〈夜泊常州〉Yu Yue:"Mooring at Night at Changzhou"】

一陣秋雨一陣涼。 A shower of rain in autumn brings a spell of coolness. 【諺語 Proverb】

雨中黃葉樹，燈下白頭人。 In the rain, there was a yellow-leaved tree. Under the lamplight, there was a white-haired person. 【司空曙〈喜外弟盧綸見宿〉Sikong Shu:"Pleased at My Cousin Lu Lun Passing a Night with Me"】

壯年聽雨客舟中，江闊雲低，斷雁叫西風。 In the middle age, I listened to raining in a passenger boat; the river was wide, the clouds hung low, and there was a stray wild goose crying in the west wind. 【蔣捷〈虞美人·聽雨〉Jiang Jie: "Listening to the Rain: To the Tune of the Beauty of Yu"】

Reading

讀書不求甚解。 In reading a book, it is not necessary to seek a thorough understanding. 【陶淵明〈五柳先生傳〉Tao Yuanming: "Biography of Mister Wu Liu"】

讀書不知意，等於嚼樹皮。 Reading a book without comprehending it is tantamount to chewing the barks of a tree. 【諺語 Proverb】

讀書破萬卷，下筆如有神。 When you have read more than ten thousand books, you can write like being helped by a god. 【杜甫〈奉贈韋左丞丈二十二韻〉Du Fu: "A Twenty-two-Line Poem Presented to Minister Wei Ji"】

讀書雖可喜，何如躬踐履。 Though reading is a delightful thing, it is incomparable to personal practice. 【劉岩〈雜詩〉Liu Yan: "Miscellaneous Poems"】

讀書須用意，一字值千金。 When you study, you have to concentrate, for each character you understand is worth a thousand pieces of gold. 【《增廣賢文》Words that Open up One's Mind and Enhance One's Wisdom】

讀萬卷書不如行萬里路。 It is better to travel ten thousand miles than to read ten thousand books. 【俗語 Common saying】

讀萬卷書，行萬里路。 Read ten thousand books and travel ten thousand miles. 【董其昌〈畫旨〉Dong Qichang: "The Meaning of Painting"】

好鳥枝頭亦朋友，落花水面皆文章。 Fine birds perching on the branches are also our friends, and petals falling on the surface of the water are all literature. 【翁森〈四時讀書樂〉Weng Sen: "The Joy of Reading in the Four Seasons"】

好讀書，不求甚解。 He takes delight in reading but does not seek to understand the details. 【陶淵明〈五柳先生傳〉Tao Yuanming: "Biography of the Scholar Wuliu"】

兩耳不聞窗外事，一心只讀聖賢書。 One's ears are shut to what goes on outside the window and one's mind focuses entirely on the reading of books by sages. 【《增廣賢文》Words that Open up One's Mind and Enhance One's Wisdom】

莫言知識少，還欠讀書多。 Don't say that your knowledge is inadequate, for what is wanting is to read more books. 【諺語 Proverb】

三代不讀書會變牛。 If members of a family do not read books for three generations, they will change into oxen. 【俗語 Common saying】

一章三遍讀，一句十回吟。 One should read a poem three times and recite each line of the poem ten times. 【白居易〈初與元九別後忽夢見之及寤而書適至兼寄桐花詩悵然感懷因以此寄〉Bai Juyi: "I Dreamt of Yuan Zhen after Parting with Him. I Received a Letter from Him with a Poem on Tung Flowers When I Was about to Sleep, with Sad Feelings, I Wrote a Response and Sent It to Him"】

有田不耕倉廩虛，有書不讀子孫愚。 When there is farmland and you do not plough it, your granary will be empty. When there are books and your children and grandchildren do not read them, then they will be stupid. 【《增廣賢文》Words that Open up One's Mind and Enhance One's Wisdom】

Reason

和尚生子 —— 豈有此理。 A monk having a son is outrageous. 【歇後語 End-clipper】

禮拜堂關門 —— 不講道理。 A church closing down means no preaching – it's unreasonable. 【歇後語 End-clipper】

人無理說橫話，牛無力拉橫耙。 An unreasonable person talks senselessly and a weak ox ploughs sidewise. 【諺語 Proverb】

天下逃不過一個理字去。 Everyone has to listen to reason. 【曹雪芹《紅樓夢・第六十五回》Cao Xueqin: Chapter 65, A Dream of the Red Chamber】

天下唯理可服人。 In this world, reason alone can convince people. 【諺語 Proverb】

秀才遇着兵 —— 有理說不清。 One is unable to persuade another person with reason. 【歇後語 End-clipper】

欲加之罪，何患無辭。 If one wants to make charges against another person, there is no lack of pretexts. 【左丘明《左傳・僖公十年》Zuo Qiuming: "The Tenth Year of the Reign of Duke Xi", Zuo's Commentary on the Spring and Autumn Annals】

知其然，不知其以然。 Know the hows but not the whys. 【左丘明《左傳・僖公三十年》Zuo Qiuming: "The Thirtieth Year of the Reign of Duke Xi", Zuo's Commentary on the Spring and Autumn Annals】

Relation

彼亦一是非，此亦一是非。
A "that" is also an affirmation and a denial. A "this" is also an affirmation and a denial.【莊周《莊子‧內篇‧齊物論第二》Zhuang Zhou: Chapter 2, "On the Equality of Things", "Inner Chapters", *Zhuangzi*】

耳鬢廝磨，形影不離。Rub shoulders together and cling to each other like an object and its shadow.【俗語 Common saying】

瓜連蔓兒，蔓兒扯瓜。Melons are linked to vines, and vines intermingle with melons.【俗語 Common saying】

侯門一入深如海，從此蕭郎是路人。The official mansion that you enter is deep as the sea, your master from now on is a stranger to you.【崔郊〈贈詩〉Cui Jiao: "A Dedication"】

古之君子，交絕不出惡聲。The gentlemen in ancient times would not curse each other when breaking up a relationship.【劉向《戰國策‧燕策二》Liu Xiang: "Strategies of the State of Yan, No. 2", *Strategies of the Warring States*】

面和心不和。Remain friendly in appearance but estranged at heart.【黃石公《素書》Huang Shigong: *Book of Plain Truths*】

寧與千人好，不與一人仇。Be good to all and have malice to none.【諺語 Proverb】

情知不是伴，事急切相隨。Though they know clearly that they are not companions, they still follow each other in severe circumstances.【馮夢龍《醒世恆言‧賣油郎獨佔花魁》Feng Menglong: "The Oil Vendor and His Pretty Bride", *Stories to Awaken the World*】

人情莫道春光好，祇怕秋來有冷時。Don't say that human relationships are as good as vernal scenes, for I'm afraid when autumn comes, there are times when the days are cold.【《增廣賢文》*Words that Open up One's Mind and Enhance One's Wisdom*】

日遠日疏，日近日親。Separated far apart, day by day, we are estranged. Closer to each other, day by day, we get closer.【諺語 Proverb】

是亦彼也，彼亦是也。A this is also a that, and a that is also a this.【莊周《莊子‧內篇‧齊物論第二》Zhuang Zhou: Chapter 2, "On the Equality of Things", "Inner Chapters", *Zhuangzi*】

無求到處人緣好，不飲從他酒價高。If you do not ask for help, your relation with others is good. If you do not drink, the price of wine is of no concern to you.【《增廣賢文》*Words that Open up One's Mind and Enhance One's Wisdom*】

眾叛親離，難以濟矣。When the multitude is rebellious and

Relative

快刀割不斷好親戚。 The sharpest knife cannot separate relatives. 【蘭陵笑笑生《金瓶梅・第十五回》 Lanling Xiaoxiaosheng: Chapter 15, *The Plum in the Golden Vase*】

切肉不離皮。 One can't sever meat from skin. 【俗語 Common saying】

親幫親，鄰幫鄰。 Kinsmen help their kinsmen and neighbours, neighbours. 【俗語 Common saying】 【周立波《山鄉巨變・下卷第二十二章》Zhou Libo: Chapter 22, Volume 2, *Great Changes in the Mountain Villages*】

親不間疏，先不僭後。 Distant relatives cannot come between close ones and new friends cannot take the place of the old ones. 【曹雪芹《紅樓夢・第二十回》 Cao Xueqin: Chapter 20, *A Dream of the Red Chamber*】

親家交禮不交財。 Relatives respect each other but do not lend each other money. 【李昉、李穆、徐鉉等《太平御覽・禮儀部二十・媒》Li Fang, Li Mu, and Xu Xuan, et al:, Chapter 20, "Match-making", Rites and Manners Section, *Imperial Reader of the Era of Great Peace*】

親眷莫交財，交財則惡開。 Relatives should not borrow money from each other, otherwise they will be estranged from each other. 【諺語 Proverb】 【胡祖德《滬諺・卷上》Hu Zhude: Part 1, *Shanghainese Proverbs*】

親戚遠來香，隔房打高牆。 Relatives from afar are well-liked and well-treated, while relatives living next door build walls in between their houses. 【李光庭《鄉言解頤・卷四》Li Guangting: Chapter 4, *Country Sayings to Smile at*】

親戚有遠近，朋友有厚薄。 Some relatives are near and some distant, and some friends are close and some ordinary. 【俗語 Common saying】【佚名《薛仁貴征東・第四十七回》Anonymous: Chapter 47, *Xue Rengui's Campaign to the East*】

親是親，財是財。 Relatives are relatives and money is money. 【俗語 Common saying】

人不知親窮知窮，人不知近苦知近。 People do not know who are their close relatives only when they are in poverty and people do not know who are their close friends only when they are in difficulty.【諺語 Proverb】

三年不上門，當親也不親。 Three years without paying a visit and relatives are no longer relatives.【諺語 Proverb】【吳承恩《西遊記‧第四十回》Wu Cheng'en: Chapter 40, *Journey to the West*】

是親人惱不多時。 Relatives do not hate each other long.【俗語 Common saying】

是親三分向。 Blood is thicker than water.【俗語 Common saying】

天子門下有貧親。 Even the Son of Heaven has poor relatives.【諺語 Proverb】【羅懋登《三寶太監西洋記‧第八十七回》Luo Maodeng: Chapter 87, *The Western Voyage of the Eunuch of Three Treasures*】

投親不如訪友。 To ask a relative to help is not as good as to ask a friend.【諺語 Proverb】

有事親人急。 It is your relatives who feel worried when you are in trouble.【俗語 Common saying】

遇急思親戚，臨危托故人。 When in need, one thinks of his relatives, and when in danger, one entrusts his old friends with important things.【諺語 Proverb】【紀君祥〈趙氏孤兒‧第一折〉Ji Junxiang: Act 1, "The Orphan of the Zhao family"】

Reliance

傍生不如傍熟。 To rely on strangers is not as good as to rely on those you know well.【馮夢龍《醒世恆言‧第三十七卷》Feng Menglong: Chapter 37, *Stories to Awaken the World*】

燈草欄杆 —— 不能靠。 A rail made of rotten rushes is a broken reed – it is unreliable.【歇後語 End-clipper】

輔車相依，唇亡齒寒。 The cheekbone and the jaws are mutually dependent. When the lips are gone, the teeth will be cold.【左丘明《左傳‧僖公五年》Zuo Qiuming: "The Fifth Year of the Reign of Duke Xi", *Zuo's Commentary on the Spring and Autumn Annals*】

寄人籬下，有苦難言。 Living under another's roof, one cannot bring himself to mention his misery.【俗語 Common saying】

靠牆牆倒，靠屋屋塌。 When you lean on the wall, it falls down. When you lean on the house, it collapses.【俗語 Common saying】【劉江《太行風雲‧第十五回》Liu Jiang: Chapter 15, *Changes in Taixing*】

靠山吃山，靠水吃水。 When you live near a hill, you get your living from the hill. When you live near water, you get your living from the water. 【馮夢龍《醒世恆言・第三卷》Feng Menglong: Chapter 3, *Stories to Awaken the World*】

皮之不存，毛將焉附。 With the skin gone, to what can the hair attach itself. 【左丘明《左傳・僖公十四年》Zuo Qiuming:"The Fourteenth Year of the Reign of Duke Xi", *Zuo's Commentary on the Spring and Autumn Annals*】

恃人不如自恃也；人之為己者，不如己之自為也。 To rely on others is not as good as relying on yourself; to ask others to do something for you is not as good as doing it by yourself. 【韓非《韓非子・外儲說右下第三十五》Han Fei: Chapter 35, "Outer Congeries of Sayings, Part 2", *Hanfeizi*】

天上下雨地下滑，各自跌倒各自爬。 When it rains and the ground is slippery, one has to get up on one's own feet if one falls. 【諺語 Proverb】【丁玲《太陽照在桑乾河上・第三十四章》Ding Ling: Chapter 34, *The Sun Shines on the Sanggan River*】

與其求人，不如求己。 Better rely on yourself than looking to others for help. 【孔子《論語・衛靈公篇第十五》Confucius: Chapter 15, *The Analects of Confucius*】

指親不富，看嘴不飽。 One who depends on help from one's relatives cannot become rich and one who watches others eating cannot get full. 【諺語 Proverb】【張孟良《兒女風塵記・第一部第一章》Zhang Mengliang: Chapter 1, Volume 1, *Sons and Daughters in Hardship*】

自己跌倒自己爬。 Rise to one's feet after falling all by oneself. 【俗語 Common saying】

嘴上沒毛，辦事不牢。 One is too young to be relied on. 【俗語 Common saying】【李寶嘉《官場現形記・第十五回》Li Baojia: Chapter 15, *Officialdom Unmasked*】

Remedy

船到江心補漏遲。 It is too late to plug the leak when the boat is in midstream. 【關漢卿〈救風塵・第一折〉Guan Hanqing: Scene 1, "Rescued by a Courtesan"】

亡羊而補牢，未為遲也。 It is not too late to mend the fold even after some sheep have been lost. 【劉向《戰國策・楚策四》Liu Xiang:"Strategies of the State of Chu, No. 4", *Strategies of the Warring States*】

往者不可諫。 The past is beyond reproof. 【孔子《論語・微子篇第十八》Confucius: Chapter 18, *The Analects of Confucius*】

小洞不補，大洞受苦。 A small hole unmended will make one

suffer when it becomes a big hole. 【諺語 Proverb】

一針不補，十針難縫。 Ten stitches sewn cannot make up for one stitch missed. 【諺語 Proverb】

Repentance

幡然悔悟，改弦更張。 Repent and mend one's way. 【諺語 Proverb】

苦海無邊，回頭是岸。 The sea of bitterness has no boundary. Repentance is one's shore. 【劉君錫〈來生債‧第一摺〉Liu Junxi: Act 1, "Debt of the Next Life"】

魯莽一時，悔之一世。 A rash action on the spur of the moment makes one repent the rest of one's life. 【諺語 Proverb】

人生不滿百，恆抱千古恨。 The life of a person is less than a hundred years, but the regrets he has last a thousand years. 【諺語 Proverb】

Repetition

一而再，再而三。 Again and again. 【《尚書‧多方》"Multiple States", The Book of History】

Reputation

不飛則已，一飛沖天；不鳴則已，一鳴驚人。 This is a bird that either does not fly at all or once it flies, it soars into the sky; it either does not cry or once it cries, it startles everyone. 【司馬遷《史記‧滑稽列傳》Sima Qian: "Biographies of Jesters", Records of the Grand Historian】

不為名，不為利。 Seek neither fame nor fortune. 【俗語 Common saying】

但看古來盛名下，終日坎壈纏其身。 Just look at those who from of old had great fame, they all suffered from a life of difficulties. 【杜甫〈丹青引贈曹將軍霸〉Du Fu: "Ode on a Painting: To General Cao Ba"】

盜名不如盜貨。 One who steals reputation is worse than one who steals goods. 【荀況《荀子‧不苟第三》Xun Kuang: Chapter 3, "Nothing Indecorous", Xunzi】

爾曹身與名俱滅，不廢江河萬古流。 Both the being and names of the mediocre perish with time, yet the famous and outstanding will stay on like the water of the lakes and rivers flowing continuously forever. 【杜甫〈戲為六絕句〉Du Fu:"Six-line Poems for Fun"】

粉骨碎身全不怕，要留青白在人間。 I'm not afraid of having my bones ground to powder and shredding my entire body, for I want to retain my loyalty and purity in this world. 【于謙〈石灰吟〉Yu Qian:"Song of Limestone"】

功蓋三分國，名成八陣圖。 The achievements of Zhuge Liang are the most distinguished during the period of the Three Kingdoms and his reputation comes from the success of his eight-front strategy. 【杜甫〈八陣圖〉Du Fu:"Eight-front Strategy"】

功名本是無憑事，不及寒江日兩潮。 Fame and honour are originally illusive, they are not as concrete as the ebb and flow of the tides in the Han River. 【陸游〈舟中感懷三絕句呈大傳相公兼簡岳大用郎中〉Lu You:"Feelings When Sailing in a Boat, a Quatrain"】

功名富貴若長在，漢水亦應西北流。 If fame and honour can be there forever, then the water in the Han River should flow north-west. 【李白〈江上吟〉Li Bai:"River Song"】

功名畫地餅，歲月下江船。 Fame and honour are like a cake drawn on the ground and months and years are like a boat sailing down the river. 【周孚〈元日懷陳道人並憶焦山舊遊〉Zhou Fu:"Recalling Chen the Daoist on the New Year's Day and Our Visit to Mount Jiao in the Past"】

古來青史誰不見，今見功名勝古人。 Who does not see all the good deeds since the ancient times recorded in history, but your achievements I see today are superior to what the ancient people did. 【岑參〈輪台歌奉送封大夫出師西征〉Cen Shen:"Song of the Wheel Terrace to Bid Farewell to General Feng Setting Out on an Expedition to the West"】

進不求名，退不辭罪。 We advance not for the sake of fame. We retreat without any fear of punishment. 【孫武《孫子兵法・地形第十》Sun Wu: Chapter 10, "Terrain", *The Art of War by Sunzi*】

久聞大名，如雷貫耳。 I have learned about your reputation long time ago and it sounded like thunder in my ears. 【羅貫中《三國演義・第三十八回》Luo Guanzhong: Chapter 38, *Romance of the Three Kingdoms*】

舉世譽之而不加勸，舉世非之而不加沮。 Though the entire world praises him, he would not for that make great efforts and though the entire world condemns him, he would not be feel more dejected. 【莊周《莊子・

內篇・逍遙遊第一》Zhuang Zhou: Chapter 1, "Carefree Wandering", "Inner Chapters", *Zhuangzi*】

君子所求者，沒世之名；今人所求者，當世之名。What a gentleman seeks is a name after his death; what people today seek is a name in their lifetime. 【顧炎武〈答李紫瀾書〉Gu Yanwu: "A Letter in Reply to Li Zilan"】

留得聲名萬古香。They have left behind a good reputation that will last for ten thousand generations. 【文天祥〈沁園春〉Wen Tianxiang: "To the Tune of Spring in the Garden of Qin"】

美名勝過美貌。A good fame is better than a good face. 【諺語 Proverb】

名世難，失之易。To become famous in the world is difficult, but to lose one's reputation is easy. 【俗語 Common saying】

名豈文章著，官應老病休。One's fame is not gained by one's writings and an official should retire if he is aged or ill. 【杜甫〈旅夜書懷〉Du Fu: "Venting My Feeling While Travelling at Night"】

名者，難立而易廢也。Reputation is hard to build up but easy to be ruined. 【劉安《淮南子・人間訓第十八》Liu An: Chapter 18, "In the World of Man", *Huainanzi*】

莫愁前路無知己，天下誰人不識君。Don't worry about having no bosom friends on your journey ahead, as you are, without exception, known to everyone in this world. 【高適〈別董大〉Gao Shi: "Farewell to a Lutarist"】

寧可曇花一現，不能默默無聞。Rather to be a has-been than a never-was. 【俗語 Common saying】

豹死留皮，人死留名。A leopard leaves its skin behind when it dies and a person leaves a name behind when he dies. 【歐陽修〈新五代史・王彥章傳〉Ouyang Xiu, "Biography of Wang Yanzhang", *A New History of the Five Dynasties*】

憑君莫話封侯事，一將功成萬骨枯。Don't let me hear you talk about titles and promotions, For the success of a general is built on ten thousand corpses. 【曹松〈己亥歲感事〉Cao Song: "Feelings of the War Years of Jihai"】

千秋萬歲後，誰知榮與辱。After tens and thousands of years, who will still know my glory or disgrace? 【陶淵明〈擬挽歌辭之一〉Cao Song: "Elegy I Drafted for Myself, No.1"】

千秋萬歲名，寂寞身後事。One's name might last for tens and thousands of years, but one's fame is little comfort after one's death. 【杜甫〈夢李白二首〉Du Fu: "Dreaming of Li Bai: Two Poems"】

且樂生前一杯酒，何須身後千載名。It is better to enjoy a cup of wine while you're still alive, for what is the use of gaining a thousand years of glory when you're dead? 【李白〈行路難〉Li

Bai: "Moving forward on the road is difficult"】

人被名利牽着走。 People are led by fame and gain. 【俗語 Common saying】

人怕出名豬怕壯。 The reputation of a person portends trouble as the fattening of a pig invites danger. 【俗語 Common saying】

人怕丟臉，樹怕剝皮。 A person is afraid of losing face as a tree is afraid of losing its bark. 【俗語 Common saying】

人生芳穢有千載，世上榮枯無百年。 The good or bad fame in one's life lasts a thousand years, but the rise and fall in this world last not more than a hundred years. 【謝枋得〈和曹東谷韻〉Xie Fangde: "A Poem in Response to the One by Cao Donggu, in the Same Rhyme"】

人為利名牽。 People are pinned down by personal interests and fame. 【俗語 Common saying】

人香千里香。 A person with a good reputation will be known far and wide. 【俗語 Common saying】

人有名，樹有影。 A person has a name as a tree has its shadow. 【蘭陵笑笑生《金瓶梅·第八十六回》Lanling Xiaoxiaosheng: Chapter 86, *The Plum in the Golden Vase*】

人有聲望，其言自重。 The words of a reputable person carry much weight. 【俗語 Common saying】

人之暮名，如水趨下。 People's pursuit of reputation is like water flowing downward. 【司馬光《資治通鑒·上元元年》Sima Guang: "The First Year of the Reign of Shangyuan", *Comprehensive Mirror to Aid in Government*】

三十功名塵與土，八千里路雲和月。 My deeds and fame in the last thirty years are merely dust and dirt, and I have marched eight thousand miles under the clouds and moon. 【岳飛〈滿江紅〉Yue Fei: "To the Tune of the River Is All Red"】

上士忘名，中士立名，下士竊名。 A superior scholar is indifferent to fame; a mediocre scholar establishes fame, and a low scholar steals fame. 【顏之推《顏氏家訓·名實》Yan Zhitui: "Name and Reality", *Family Instructions of Master Yan*】

身敗名裂，遺臭萬年。 One brings ruin and everlasting infamy upon oneself. 【俗語 Common saying】

盛名之下，其實難符。 A reputation that is too high is difficult to live up to. 【范曄《後漢書·黃瓊傳》Fan Ye: "Biography of Huang Qiong", *History of the Later Han*】

生無一日之歡，死有萬世之名。 When alive, one does not have a day of joy; when dead, one enjoys a reputation that lasts ten thousand generations.【列禦寇《列子・楊朱第七》Lie Yukou: Chapter 7, "Yang Zhu", *Liezi*】

十年窗下無人問，一舉成名天下知。 No one asked about me while I was studying for ten years under this window, but once I passed the examination in a single attempt, the entire world knows me.【高明〈琵琶記〉Gao Ming:"Tale of the *Pipa*"】

十年一覺揚州夢，贏得青樓薄倖名。 The ten years I spent in Yangzhou is like a dream, and I was known for being a heartless playboy in the brothels.【杜牧〈遣懷〉Du Mu:"Venting My Feelings"】

樹大招風，名大招忌。 A large tree catches the wind and a great reputation evokes jealousy. 【諺語 Proverb】

未見功名已白頭。 My hair has turned grey before achieving honour and fame.【杜牧〈冬日題智門寺北樓〉Du Mu:"Inscribing on the North Tower of the Zhi'en Temple on a Winter Day"】

無名不知，有名便曉。 When obscure, one is known by nobody, but when one becomes famous, one is known by everybody.【諺語 Proverb】【古立高《隆冬・第九章》Gu Ligao: Chapter 9, *In the Depths of Winter*】

細推物理須行樂，何用浮名絆此身。 The law of nature tells us to make life a happy game, why should I be bound by the vanity

of fame?【杜甫〈曲江二首〉Du Fu:"Twisted River: Two Selections"】

雁過留聲，人去留名。 A wild goose leaves a scream when flying past and a person leaves a name behind when he dies.【文康《兒女英雄傳・第三十二回》Wen Kang: Chapter 32, *Biographies of Young Heroes and Heroines*】

一登龍門，身價十倍。 Once one enters into a house of power, one's fame is ten times greater. 【李白〈與韓荊州書〉Li Bai:"Letter to Han Jingzhou"】

一舉成名天下知。 Once you achieve success at one go, your name will be known far and wide.【高明〈琵琶記〉Gao Ming:"Tale of the Pipa"】

有不虞之譽，有求全之毀。 One might have unexpected praises and defamation out of overall interests.【孟軻《孟子・離婁上》Meng Ke: Chapter 4, Part 1, *Mencius*】

有麝自然香，何必大風揚。 Where there is musk, there is fragrance and it does not need to be wafted everywhere by the wind.【《增廣賢文》*Words that Open up One's Mind and Enhance One's Wisdom*】

爭名者於朝，爭利者於市。 He who is after fame gets it from the court; he who is after profits gets them from the market.【劉向《戰國策・秦策》Liu Xiang:"Strategies of the State of Qin", *Strategies of the Warring States*】

至人無己，神人無功，聖人無名。The perfect man is free of the self, a godly man is free of merits, and a sage is free of fame.【莊周《莊子・內篇・逍遙遊第一》Zhuang Zhou: Chapter 1, "Carefree Wandering", "Inner Chapters", *Zhuangzi*】

Rescue

救人救到底，送人送到家。Save people until they are completely saved. See people off until they are home.【諺語 Proverb】

救人如救火。To save a person is as urgent as to fight a fire.【佚名〈薛仁貴征遼事略〉Anonymous: "Xue Rengui's Expedition to Liao"】

救人一命，勝造七級浮屠。Saving a life is better than building a seven-storied pagoda.【《增廣賢文》 *Words that Open up One's Mind and Enhance One's Wisdom*】

救生不救死。Save those who are still alive, but not dead.【諺語 Proverb】【李寶嘉《官場現形記・第二十三回》Li Baojia: Chapter 23, *Officialdom Unmasked*】

天將救之，以慈衛之。When heaven is about to rescue somebody, it will save him with kindness.【老子《道德經・第六十七章》Laozi: Chapter 67, *Daodejing*】

Resources

挨着大樹有柴燒。If one lives close to big trees, there will be firewood to burn.【諺語 Proverb】

河邊賣水——取之不盡。Selling water by the side of a river – the source is inexhaustible.【歇後語 End-clipper】

靠山的不怕沒柴燒，靠水的不怕沒魚吃。One who lives near a mountain has no fear of the shortage of firewood. One who lives by the side of a river has no fear of having no fish to eat.【李滿天《水向東流・第四十章》Li Mantian: Chapter 40, *Water Flows to the East*】

留得青山在，那怕沒柴燒。As long as the green mountains are there, there is no worry of having no firewood.【俗語 Common saying】【曹雪芹《紅樓夢・第八十二回》Cao Xueqin: Chapter 82, *A Dream of the Red Chamber*】

沒土打不成牆。Without earth, you cannot make a wall.【俗語 Common saying】

內無糧草，外無救兵。Within, there is no food, and without,

there is no reinforcement. 【羅貫中《三國演義‧第七十六回》Luo Guanzhong: Chapter 76, *Romance of the Three Kingdoms*】

巧婦難為無米之炊。 Even a clever housewife cannot cook a meal without rice. 【諺語 Proverb】

取之不盡，用之不竭。 Resources are inexhaustible and they are always available for use. 【蘇軾〈前赤壁賦〉Su Shi:"First Ode to the Red Cliff"】

三日無糧不聚兵。 Without provisions for three days, soldiers will scatter away. 【劉璋《斬鬼傳‧第九回》Liu Zhang: Chapter 9, *Account of Ghost-beheading*】

山裏的人不愁沒柴燒。 People living in the mountain have no worry about a shortage of firewood. 【諺語 Proverb】

無糧不聚兵，無肥不長穗。 With rations and forage, you cannot gather soldiers to fight, as ears of grain cannot grow without fertilizer. 【諺語 Proverb】

Respect

不怕人不敬，祇怕己不正。 We are not afraid of not being respected, but not behaving in a proper way. 【諺語 Proverb】

大不正而小不敬。 If the old do not behave well, they will not be respected by the young. 【諺語 Proverb】

佛燒一炷香，人爭一口氣。 The Buddha needs a burning incense, and a person needs to be respected with dignity. 【蘭陵笑笑生《金瓶梅‧第七十六回》Lanling Xiaoxiaosheng: Chapter 76, *The Plum in the Golden Vase*】

高山仰止，景行行止。 A lofty mountain is to be looked up and a broad road is to be followed. 【《詩經‧小雅‧車舝》"Coach Axle-pin", "Minor Odes of the Kingdom", *The Book of Odes*】

恭不招侮，謙不招忌。 To be respectful invites no insult; modest, no jealousy. 【諺語 Proverb】

恭敬不如從命。 Respect is not as good as obedience. 【趙琦美《古今雜劇‧元‧秦簡夫‧東堂老‧楔子》Zhao Qimei: Qin Jianfu (of the Yuan Dynasty):"Prologue to 'The Elder of the Eastern Hall'", *Dramas of Ancient and Recent Times*】

敬老得老，敬禾得寶。 Respect the old and you will be respected when you are old and honour farm work and you will get treasure. 【諺語 Proverb】

敬人者人恆敬之。 One who respects others will always be respected. 【孟軻《孟子‧離婁下》Meng Ke: Chapter 4, Part 2, *Mencius*】

慢人者，人亦慢之。 Those who treat others disrespectfully will be treated disrespectfully. 【余邵魚《東周列國志・第五十二回》Yu Shaoyu: Chapter 52, *Chronicles of the Eastern Zhou Kingdoms*】

你敬我一尺，我還你一丈。 When you show me some respect, I'll show you ten times more. 【諺語 Proverb】

讓禮一寸，得禮一尺。 If you respect others a little, others will respect you ten times more. 【諺語 Proverb】

人必自敬，爾後人敬之。 Only when you respect yourself will people respect you. 【諺語 Proverb】

人不尊己，則危辱及之。 If others don't respect you, danger and disgrace will befall you. 【列禦寇《列子・説符第八》Lie Yukou: Chapter 8, "Explaining Conjunctions", *Liezi*】

人待我一尺，我待人一丈。 When people respect me one foot, I respect him ten feet. 【諺語 Proverb】

說到做到，威信必高。 Do what you say and you will surely win a high respect. 【諺語 Proverb】

桃李不言，下自成蹊。 Though peach and plum trees do not speak, yet a path has been formed under them. 【司馬遷《史記・李將軍列傳》Sima Qian: "Biography of General Li Guang", *Records of the Grand Historian*】

賢人君子，國家之基也，不可以不敬。 The worthy people and noble men, who are the basis of a country, ought to be respected. 【房玄齡等《晉書・慕容廆載記》Fang Xuanling, *et al*: "Biography of Murong Hui", *History of the Jin*】

仰之彌高，鑽之彌堅。 I look up to him, he towers very high; I study him, he becomes very profound. 【孔子《論語・子罕篇第九》Confucius: Chapter 9, *The Analects of Confucius*】

祇敬衣衫不敬人。 The clothes, not the person, are respected. 【俗語 Common saying】

Responsibility

愛挑的擔子不嫌重。 One does not feel it a burden for a responsibility one likes to take up. 【俗語 Common saying】

得縮頭時且縮頭。 Draw back whenever you can. 【釋惟白《續傳燈錄・第八卷》Shi Weibai: Chapter 8, *A Sequel to the Records of the Transmission of the Lamp*】

父不父，子不子。 Fathers neglect their duties as fathers, while sons neglect their duties as sons. 【孔子《論語・先進篇第十一》Confucius: Chapter 11, *The Analects of Confucius*】

故天將降大任於斯人也，必先苦其心誌，勞其筋骨，餓其體膚，空乏其身，行拂亂其所為，所以動心忍性，曾益其所不能。 Thus, when Heaven is going to give a great responsibility to someone, it first makes his mind endure suffering, his sinews and bones experience toil, and his body to suffer hunger. It inflicts him with poverty and disrupts everything he tries to build. In this way Heaven stimulates his mind, stabilizes his temper and enhances his weak abilities. 【孟軻《孟子‧告子章句下》Meng Ke: Chapter 6, Part 2, *Mencius*】

好漢做事好漢當。 A true man has the courage to accept the consequences of his own actions. 【俗語 Common saying】

居官者當事不避難。 Those who are in official positions should be courageous to shoulder responsibilities and should not avoid difficulties. 【左丘明《國語‧魯語上》Zuo Qiuming: "The Language of Lu, Part 1", *National Languages*】

老鼠抬轎子 —— 擔當不起。 A mouse trying to lift a sedan chair can't beat it; cannot bear the responsibility. 【歇後語 End-clipper】

兩人養馬瘦，兩家養船漏。 When two persons raise the same horse, it will be thin. When two families possess the same boat, it will leak. 【俗語 Common saying】

龍多不治水，雞多不下蛋。 Too many dragons would not attend to rain; too many hens would not lay eggs. 【諺語 Proverb】

貓捉老鼠狗看門 —— 本份事。 A cat catching mice and a dog watching over the house – each has its own duty. 【歇後語 End-clipper】

能管不如能推。 It is better to shift responsibility onto others than take it up yourself. 【俗語 Common saying】【范立本《明心寶鑒》Fan Liben: *The Precious Mirror that Enlightens the Heart*】

人人負責便是沒人負責。 Everybody's business is nobody's business. 【俗語 Common saying】

人人為我，我為人人。 All for one and one for all. 【俗語 Common saying】

士不可以不弘毅，任重而道遠。 A gentleman must be strong and resolute as his burden is heavy and the road is long. 【孔子《論語‧泰伯篇第八》Confucius: Chapter 8, *The Analects of Confucius*】

榮辱之責，在乎己而不在乎人。 The responsibility of glory or disgrace lies with the self, not with others. 【魏徵《羣書治要‧韓子大體》Wei Zheng: "Gist of Han Feizi", *Compilation of Books and Writings on the Important Governing Principles*】

事不關己，高高掛起。 Things that are not of concern to one will be shelved. 【諺語 Proverb】

鐵肩擔道義。 Take up righteousness and justice on one's iron shoulders. 【楊繼盛《楊忠湣公集》Yang Jisheng: *Collected Works of Yang Jisheng*】

一推六二五。 Evade all responsibilities. 【俗語 Common saying】【浩然《艷陽天‧第一百二十七章》Hao Ran: Chapter 127, *Sunny Day*】

以天下為己任。 Take up the management of state affairs as one's own task. 【李延壽《南史‧孔休源傳》Li Yanshou: "Biography of Kong Xiuyuan", *History of the Southern Dynasties*】

Retirement

晨興理荒穢，戴月荷鋤歸。 In the morning I rise and plough the wasted land, under moonlight I carry the hoe on my shoulder and return home. 【陶淵明〈歸田園居〉Tao Yuanming: "Returning to My Rural Home"】

達人樂在退休，傑士急於進取。 A broad-minded person is happy to retire, but a talented person is eager to make progress. 【王澹翁〈櫻桃園‧第四折〉Wang Danweng: Scene 4, "Cherry Garden"】

功成不受爵，長揖歸田廬。 I have rendered my service and would not accept any official position. I make a long bow to you to bid farewell and return to my home in the countryside. 【左思〈詠史〉Zuo Si: "Ode on History"】

幾時歸去，作個閒人。對一張琴，一壺酒，一溪雲。 I wonder when I can retire and live like a recluse, facing a zither, a bottle of wine, and a valley of clouds. 【蘇軾〈行香子〉Su Shi: "To the Tune of Holding the Incense"】

山中無曆日，寒盡不知年。 As there is no calendar in the mountain, so when the cold spell has ended, I still don't know what date it is. 【太上隱者〈答人〉Taishang Yinzhe: "My Answer to Somebody"】

退出歷史舞台。 Retire from the stage of history. 【俗語 Common saying】

賢者辟世，其次辟地，其次辟色，其次辟言。 Some worthy people retire from the world, others, from land, still others, from disrespectful looks, yet others, from contradictory language. 【孔子《論語‧憲問篇第十四》Confucius: Chapter 14, *The Analects of Confucius*】

相逢盡道休官好，林下何曾見一人。 When officials meet they all say that it is better to retire from political life and live in seclusion, but not even one of them is found in the wooded mountain where hermits live. 【靈澈〈東林寺酬韋丹刺史〉Ling

Che: "A Poem to Respond to Premier Wei Dan of the East Forest Temple" 】

Retribution

見色而起淫心，報在妻女。 If you see a beautiful woman and start to have licentious thoughts, retribution will fall on your wife and daughter. 【朱用純《朱子家訓》Zhu Yongchun: *Percepts of the Zhu Family*】

可憐剃頭者，人亦剃其頭。 It is pitiable that those who shave heads will have their heads shaved by others. 【雪庵〈剃頭詩〉Xue An: "Head Shaving"】

善惡到頭終有報，祇爭來早與來遲。 Good and evil will in the end will be retributed, it is only a matter of coming early or late. 【《增廣賢文》*Words that Open up One's Mind and Enhance One's Wisdom*】

善有善報，惡有惡報，不是不報，日子未到。 Do well and have good consequences, and do evil and have evil consequences. If the retribution has not yet been rewarded, it is because the time has not arrived yet. 【《增廣賢文》*Words that Open up One's Mind and Enhance One's Wisdom*】

一人一遭，天公地道。 Turn about is fair play. 【諺語 Proverb】

Revenge

大丈夫報仇，十年不晚。 It is never too late for a true gentleman to take revenge in ten years' time. 【諺語 Proverb】

君子報仇十年未晚。 It is not late for a gentleman to revenge himself in ten years' time. 【司馬遷《史記·范雎蔡澤列傳》Sima Qian: "Biographies of Fan Sui and Cai Ze", *Records of the Grand Historian*】

君子不念舊惡。 A gentleman does not remember the past grudges. 【諺語 Proverb】

往日無冤，近日無仇。 There is no enmity with each other all along. 【俗語 Common saying】

以血還血，以牙還牙。 Blood must be paid for with blood, and a tooth for a tooth. 【俗語 Common saying】

以眼還眼，以牙還牙。 An eye for an eye and a tooth for a tooth. 【俗語 Common saying】

心去意難留，留下結冤愁。 You can't stop someone who has made up his mind to leave; if

you force him to stay, it will
incur enmity. 【張國賓〈合汗衫・第
二折〉Zhang Guobin: Scene 2, "Sweat
Shirts Combined"】

有仇不報非君子。 One who
does not take revenge is not a
gentleman. 【諺語 Proverb】

有冤報冤，有仇報仇。 Requite
hate with hate and like for like.
【施耐庵《水滸傳・第二十六回》Shi
Nai'an: Chapter 26, *Outlaws of the
Marshes*】

Reward

賞不論冤仇，罰不論骨肉。 Be fair
in meting out rewards even to
your personal enemies; be strict
in meting out punishments
even to your kin. 【諺語 Proverb】

賞罰之道，實國之利器。 The
way of reward and punishment
is truly a sharp weapon of a
country. 【韓非《韓非子・內儲說上
第三十》Han Fei: Chapter 30, "Inner
Congeries of Sayings, Part 1", *Hanfeizi*】

好心有好報。 One's kindness
will be rewarded. 【俗語 Common
saying】

投之以桃，報之以李。 Give a
plum in return for a peach. 【《詩
經・大雅・抑》"Pressing", "Greater
Odes of the Kingdom", *The Book of
Odes*】

投以木桃，報以瓊瑤。 Give fine
jade in return for a quince. 【《詩
經・衛風・木瓜》"Quince", "Odes of
Wei", *The Book of Odes*】

有功必賞，有罪必罰。 Merits
must be rewarded and offences
punished. 【韓非《韓非子・外儲說
右上第三十四》Han Fei: Chapter 34,

"Outer Congeries of Sayings, Part 1",
Hanfeizi】

有功不賞，有勞不錄。 Merit goes
unrewarded and distinguished
service unrecorded. 【諺語
Proverb】

有陰德者，必有陽報。 One
who has done good without
being known by others will be
rewarded in this world. 【劉安《淮
南子・人間訓第十八》Liu An: Chapter
18, "In the World of Man", *Huainanzi*】

重賞之下，必有勇夫。 By offering
an ample reward, some brave
people are sure to come out. 【諺
語 Proverb】【王實甫〈西廂記・第二
本第一折〉Wang Shifu: Act 2, Scene 1,
"Romance of the Western Bower"】

Rich and poor

廚中有剩飯，路上有飢人。There are leftovers in the kitchen but starving people on the road. 【佚名《名賢集》Anonymous: *Collected Sayings of Famous Sages*】

富貴不傲物，貧賤不易行。When one is rich and noble, one does not look down on others; when one is poor and low, one does not change one's behaviour. 【晏嬰《晏子春秋・內篇問下》Yan Ying:"Inner Chapters: Questions, Part 2", *Master Yan's Spring and Autumn Annals*】

富人思來年，窮人思眼前。The rich think about things in the coming year and the poor think about things at the moment. 【《增廣賢文》*Words that Open up One's Mind and Enhance One's Wisdom*】

貧而樂，富而好禮。Poor but happy, rich but love rites. 【孔子《論語・學而篇第一》Confucius: Chapter 1, *The Analects of Confucius*】

貧而無怨難，富而無驕易。Poor without grumbling is difficult whereas rich without being arrogant is easy. 【孔子《論語・憲問篇第十四》Confucius: Chapter 14, *The Analects of Confucius*】

貧寒休要怨，富貴不須驕。Don't complain if you are poor and suffering from coldness and don't be arrogant if you rich and high-ranked. 【《增廣賢文》*Words that Open up One's Mind and Enhance One's Wisdom*】

清貧常樂，濁富常憂。Untarnished poverty is always happy and ill-gotten wealth has many worries. 【范立本《明心寶鑒》Fan Liben: *The Precious Mirror that Enlightens the Heart*】

窮不跟富鬥，富不跟官鬥。The poor will not fight the rich, and the rich will not fight officials. 【褚人獲《隋唐演義・第五回》Zhu Renhuo: Chapter 5, *Heroes in Sui and Tang Dynasties*】

窮村有富戶，富村有窮人。There are certainly rich families in a poor village and poor families in a rich village. 【俗語 Common saying】

窮上山，富下川。The poor go up to the mountains while the rich go to the flatlands. 【俗語 Common saying】【張行《武陵山下・第十九章》Zhang Xing: Chapter 19, *Under the Wuling Mountain*】

窮死莫做官，餓死莫做賊。Don't be an official even when one is poor to death and don't be a thief even when one starves to death. 【諺語 Proverb】

窮找窮親，富找富鄰。The poor seek help from their relatives and the rich choose to live with rich neighbours. 【俗語 Common saying】

人愛富的，狗咬窮的。People love the rich and dogs bite the poor. 【俗語 Common saying】

人敬富的，狗咬破的。People respect the rich and dogs bite those in rags.【諺語 Proverb】

人敬有錢的，狗咬提籃的。People respect the rich and dogs bite the poor.【諺語 Proverb】

人親有的，狗咬醜的。People respect the rich and dogs bark at the poor.【諺語 Proverb】

人窮埋短，有錢氣粗。The poor are always on the wrong side, while the rich are always bold and assured.【諺語 Proverb】

人有前後眼，富貴一千年。A person with a hindsight and a foresight will have riches and nobilities for a thousand years.【諺語 Proverb】【克非《春潮急‧第四十章》Ke Fei: Chapter 40, *Spring Tides Come Rapidly*】

若要富，走險路。To get rich, one must take risks.【諺語 Proverb】

十個胖子九個富。Nine out of ten fat men are rich.【俗語 Common saying】

為富不仁，為仁不富矣。The rich are not benevolent and the benevolent are not rich.【孟軻《孟子‧滕文公上》Meng Ke: Chapter 5, Part 1, *Mencius*】

勿貪意外之財。Do not covet unlawful riches.【朱用純《朱子家訓》Zhu Yongchun: *Percepts of the Zhu Family*】

要得富，走險路。To get rich, try the way with risks.【諺語 Proverb】

一闊臉就變。Once one gets rich, one turns one's back on one's old acquaintances.【魯迅〈贈鄔其山〉Lu Xun:"Presented to Wu Qishan"】

有的不知無的苦。The rich do not know how the poor suffer.【俗語 Common saying】

朱門酒肉臭，路有凍死骨。Behind the vermillion gates meat and wine rot while out at the roadside are bones of those frozen to death.【杜甫〈自京赴奉先詠懷五百字〉Du Fu:"Venting My Feelings When Going from the Capital to Fengxian County, in Five Hundred Words"】

濁富不如清貧。Wealth gained by crooked means is not as good as poor with clean hands.【俗語 Common saying】

Right and wrong

彼亦一是非，此亦一是非。That is about a right and a wrong, and this is also about a right and a wrong.【莊周《莊子‧內篇‧齊物論第二》Zhuang Zhou: Chapter 2, "On the Equality of Things", "Inner Chapters", *Zhuangzi*】

不分青紅皂白。One is unable to distinguish right and wrong.

【《詩經‧大雅‧抑》"Tender Mulberry", "Greater Odes of the Kingdom", *The Book of Odes*】

不問是非曲直。 One does not question whether it's right or wrong, or true or false. 【俗語 Common saying】

得理讓三分。 Make some concessions even when you're on the right side. 【諺語 Proverb】

對就是對，錯就是錯。 What is right is right and what is wrong is wrong. 【俗語 Common saying】

公說公有理，婆說婆有理。 Each side claims that they are in the right. 【諺語 Proverb】

兩個啞巴吵嘴 —— 不知誰是誰非。 Two mutes quarrelling – no idea of who is right and who is wrong. 【歇後語 End-clipper】

沒做虧心事，不怕鬼叫門。 Do nothing wrong and no ghost will knock at your door. 【諺語 Proverb】

實迷途其未遠，覺今是而昨非。 Actually I have not gone astray very far, and I feel that I make a right decision now as I made a wrong one in the past. 【陶淵明〈歸去來兮辭〉Tao Yuanming:"Returning Home"】

十目所視，十手所指。 One is being watched by ten eyes and pointed by ten fingers. 【《禮記‧大學第四十二》Chapter 42:"The Great Learning", *The Book of Rites*】

是非曲直自有公論。 The public is the best judge of what's right or wrong and what's true or false.【劉義慶《世說新語‧品藻第九》Liu Yiqing: Chapter 9, "Classification According to Excellence", *A New Account of the Tales of the World*】

是非自有公論。 The public is the best judge of what's right or wrong.【劉義慶《世說新語‧品藻第九》Liu Yiqing: Chapter 9, "Classification According to Excellence", *A New Account of the Tales of the World*】

是非之處，不可以貴賤尊卑論也。 The matter of right or wrong cannot be discussed in terms of whether one is noble, based, respectable or lowly.【宋鈃《文子‧上仁第十》Song Jin: Chapter 10, "The Benevolence of the Ruler", *Wenzi*】

是是、非非謂之知，非是、是非謂之愚。 To say right when it is right and wrong when it is wrong, this is knowledge; to say wrong when it is right and right when it is wrong, this is absurdity.【荀況《荀子‧修身第二》Xun Kuang: Chapter 2, "Cultivating the Person", *Xunzi*】

是謂是，非謂非，曰直。 To say right when it is right and wrong when it is wrong, this is known as being straightforward.【荀況《荀子‧修身第二》Xun Kuang: Chapter 2, "Cultivating the Person", *Xunzi*】

絲瓜纏到豆蔓裏。 Get things all wrong. 【俗語 Common saying】

天老爺睜開眼。 God has opened His eyes. 【俗語 Common saying】

天下理無常是，事無常非。 In this world, principles are not always right and matters are not always wrong. 【列禦寇《列子‧說符第八》Lie Yukou: Chapter 8, "Explaining Conjunctions", *Liezi*】

向理不向人。 Stand by what is right, not by a particular person. 【俗語 Common saying】

Righteousness

國無義，雖大必亡。 A country without righteousness will surely perish even though the country might be large. 【劉安《淮南子‧主術訓第九》Liu An: Chapter 9, "Craft of the Ruler", *Huainanzi*】

以義死難，視死如歸。 Die for righteouness under adverse circumstances and look upon death as home coming. 【司馬遷《史記‧范睢蔡澤列傳》Sima Qian: "Biographies of Fan Sui and Cai Ze", *Records of the Grand Historian*】

義動君子，利動貪人。 Righteousness moves a gentleman; profits attract a greedy person. 【班固《漢書‧匈奴傳》Ban Gu: "Traditions of the Xiongnu", *History of the Han*】

義，人之正路也。 Righteousness is a right path of a person. 【孟軻《孟子‧盡心章句下》Meng Ke: Chapter 7, Part 2, *Mencius*】

義者，宜也；尊賢為大。 Righteousness is about doing what is appropriate, the most important of which is to honour the worthy. 【《禮記‧中庸第三十一章》Chapter 31, "Doctrine of the Mean", *The Book of Rites*】

義之所在，身雖死，無憾悔。 Where there is righteousness, though I might be dead, I have no regrets. 【《易經‧繫辭下》"Appended Remarks, Part 2", *The Book of Changes*】

Rise and fall

按下葫蘆浮起瓢 —— 此落彼起。 As one falls, another rises. 【歇後語 End-clipper】

得人者興，失人者崩。 He who wins the support of the people thrives; he who loses the support of the people perishes. 【司馬遷《史記‧商君列傳》Sima Qian: "Biography of Lord Shang", *Records of the Grand Historian*】

登高必跌重。 The higher one climbs, the greater the fall. 【諺語

Proverb】【曹雪芹《紅樓夢・第十三回》Cao Xueqin: Chapter 13, *A Dream of the Red Chamber*】

跌得倒，爬得起。Be able to rise after a fall. 【俗語 Common saying】

國雖大，好戰必亡；天下雖平，忘戰必危。A country may be large, if it is warlike, it will surely perish. A country may be in peace, if it neglects the threat of war, it will surely be in danger. 【司馬遷《史記・平津侯主父列傳》Sima Qian: "Biographies of the Marquis of Pingjin and Zhufu", *Records of the Grand Historian*】

爬得越高，跌得越重。The higher one climbs, the harder one falls. 【俗語 Common saying】

其興也勃，其亡也忽。Its rise is quick and its fall is sudden. 【左丘明《左傳・莊公十一年》Zuo Qiuming: "The Twenty-ninth Year of the Reign of Duke Zhuang", *Zuo's Commentary on the Spring and Autumn Annals*】

千古興亡多少事，悠悠，不盡長江滾滾流。Rises and falls and many events since the ancient times thousands of years ago are now gone, just like the ever-flowing water of the Changjiang river. 【辛棄疾〈南鄉子・登京口北固亭有懷〉Xin Qiji: "Reflections on Ascending the Beigu Tower at Jingkuo: To the Tune of the Song of the South"】

牆倒眾人推。When a wall is about to collapse, everybody gives it a push. 【俚語 Slang】

情勝欲者昌，欲勝情者亡。He who overcomes desires by reason flourishes; he who overcomes reason by desires perishes. 【劉安《淮南子・繆稱訓第十》Liu An: Chapter 10, "On Erroneous Designations", *Huainanzi*】

擎得高，跌得重。The higher one is raised, the heavier the fall. 【俗語 Common saying】

抬得高，跌得重。The higher one is raised, the heavier one falls. 【俗語 Common saying】

興必慮衰，安必思危。When a country is prosperous, it must think of the possibility of decline; when a country is stable, it must think of the possibility of turbulence. 【司馬遷《史記・司馬相如列傳》Sima Qian: "Biographies of Sima Xiangru", *Records of the Grand Historian*】

禹湯罪己，其興也悖焉；桀紂罪人，其亡也忽焉。Kings Yu and Tang put the blame on themselves when they did something wrong, this accounts for their rapid rise. Kings Jie and Zhou put the blame on others when they did something wrong, this accounts for their sudden fall. 【左丘明《左傳・莊公十一年》Zuo Qiuming: "The Eleventh Year of the Reign of Duke Zhuang", *Zuo's Commentary on the Spring and Autumn Annals*】

Risk

不怕一萬，就怕萬一。 One
cannot afford a single mishap.
【俗語 Common saying】

刀尖上舔糖。 Lick sugar from
a sword's point. 【俗語 Common
saying】

雞蛋碰不過石頭。 Whether the
pot strikes the stone, or the
stone the pot, it will be ill for the
pot. 【俗語 Common saying】

雞蛋碰石頭。 Like an egg dashing
itself against a rock – courting
destruction. 【俗語 Common saying】

老虎頭卜捕蒼蠅。 Catch flies on
a tiger's head. 【吳敬梓《儒林外
史・第六回》Wu Jingzi: Chapter 6, An
Unofficial History of the World of Literati】

老虎頭上搔癢。 Scratch a tiger's
head. 【蔡東藩《後漢通俗演義・第
三十三回》Cai Dongfan: Chapter 33,
Popular Romance of the Later Han】

老虎頭上捉虱子。 Catch the lice
on a tiger's head. 【曹雪芹《紅樓夢・
第四十六回》Cao Xueqin: Chapter 46, A
Dream of the Red Chamber】

老虎嘴裏拔牙 —— 自找死路。
Pull teeth out of a tiger's mouth.
【歇後語 End-clipper】

老虎嘴裏送食。 Stick one's head
into the tiger's mouth. 【諺語
Proverb】

老虎嘴裏討肉吃。 Try to take a
piece of meat out of a tiger's
mouth; 【諺語 Proverb】

摸老虎屁股。 Touch the backsides
of a tiger. 【俗語 Common saying】

寧走十步遠，不走一步險。
Rather go ten paces extra than
take one risky step. 【石玉昆《三
俠五義・第一百一十回》Shi Yukun:
Chapter 110, The Three Heroes and Five
Gallants】

騎馬坐船三分險。 You have to
take certain risks even when
you ride on a horse-back or take
a boat. 【諺語 Proverb】【姚雪垠《李
自成・第一卷第八章》Yao Xueyin:
Chapter 8, Volume 1, Li Zicheng】

千年古樹莫存身。 Do not stay
under a tree that is a thousand
years old. 【孔子《論語・為政篇第
二》Confucius: Chapter 2, The Analects
of Confucius】

上得山多終遇虎。 The fish that
nibbles at every bait will be
caught. 【俗語 Common saying】

往虎口裏探頭。 Put one's head in
a tiger's mouth. 【曹雪芹《紅樓夢・
第六十二回》Cao Xueqin: Chapter 62, A
Dream of the Red Chamber】

Rite / courtesy

安上治民，莫善於禮。 In securing the repose of the ruler and governance of the people, nothing is better than rites. 【《孝經・廣要道章第十二》Chapter 12, "Broad and Crucial Doctrine", *Book of Filial Piety*】

不學禮，無以立。 If you don't learn the rites, there is no way to cultivate your character. 【孔子《論語・季氏篇第十六》Confucius: Chapter 16, *The Analects of Confucius*】

夫禮者，忠信之薄，而亂之首也。 Rites are the wearing thin of loyalty and good faith and the beginning of disorder. 【老子《道德經・第三十八章》Laozi: Chapter 38, *Daodejing*】

壞國、喪家、亡人，必先去其禮。 The ruin of the country, the destruction of the family, and the perishing of individuals are always preceded by the abandonment of rites. 【《禮記・禮運第九》Chapter 9, "Conveyance of Rites", *The Book of Rites*】

來而不往非禮也。 It's impolite not to reciprocate. 【《禮記・曲禮上第一》Chapter 1, "Summary of the Rules of Propriety, Part 1", *The Book of Rites*】

禮不下庶人。 Rites are not extended to the common people. 【《禮記・曲禮上第一》Chapter 1, "Summary of the Rules of Propriety, Part 1", *The Book of Rites*】

禮多人不怪。 No one blames you for being too polite. 【李寶嘉《官場現形記・第三十一回》Li Baojia: Chapter 31, *Officialdom Unmasked*】

禮尚往來。往而不來，非禮也。 Courtesy is reciprocal. A polite action given without a return does not conform to courtesy. 【《禮記・曲禮上第一》Chapter 1, "Summary of the Rules of Propriety, Part 1", *The Book of Rites*】

禮失而求諸野。 When the rite is lost, one seeks it from the countryside. 【班固《漢書・藝文志》Ban Gu: "Bibliographical Treatise", *History of the Han*】

禮下於人，必有所求。 When a person humbles himself before you, he must have a favour to ask you. 【左丘明《左傳・昭公二十九年》Zuo Qiuming: "The Twenty-ninth Year of the Reign of Duke Zhao", *Zuo's Commentary on the Spring and Autumn Annals*】

禮也者，義之實也。 Rites are the substance of righteousness. 【《禮記・禮運第九》Chapter 9, "Conveyance of Rites", *The Book of Rites*】

禮義廉恥，國之四維。 Courtesy, righteousness, integrity, and the sense of shame are the four pillars of the country. 【歐陽修〈新五代史・馮道傳〉Ouyang Xiu, "Biography of Feng Dao", *A New History of the Five Dynasties*】

禮義生於富足。Courtesy and righteousness emerge from wealth and abundance. 【《增廣賢文》 *Words that Open up One's Mind and Enhance One's Wisdom*】

禮，治人之大法；廉恥，立人之大節。Rites and righteousness are the fundamental principles in ruling people; honesty and sense of shame are fundamental requirements for educating people. 【歐陽修〈馮道傳〉Ouyang Xiu: "Biography of Feng Dao"】

禮有輕重，事有緩急。Courtesy should be different in ordinary and special times and work should be done in order of urgency. 【俗語 Common saying】

禮者，君之大柄也。Rites are great utensils of a ruler. 【《禮記‧禮運第九》Chapter 9, "Conveyance of Rites", *The Book of Rites*】

禮之用，和為貴。In the use of rites, harmony is prized. 【孔子《論語‧學而篇第一》Confucius: Chapter 1, *The Analects of Confucius*】

情越疏，禮越多。The more estranged, the more courteous. 【諺語 Proverb】【許廑父《民國演義‧第一百二十六回》Xu Qinfu: Chapter 126, *Romance of the Republic*】

人將禮義為先。People put courtesy and righteousness first. 【石玉崑《小五義‧第六十六回》Shi Yukun: Chapter 66, *The Five Younger Gallants*】

人無禮則不立，事無禮則不成，國無禮則不寧。A person without rites will not establish himself, things without rites will not be accomplished, and a state without rites will not be peaceful. 【荀況《荀子‧修身第二》Xun Kuang: Chapter 2, "Cultivating the Person", *Xunzi*】

人有禮則安，無禮則危。People with rites are safe; people without rites are dangerous. 【《禮記‧曲禮上第一》Chapter 1, "Summary of the Rules of Propriety, Part 1", *The Book of Rites*】

有禮走遍天下，無禮寸步難行。With politeness, one can travel all over the world, but without politeness, one can hardly move an inch. 【俗語 Common saying】

River

春江潮水連海平，海上明月共潮生。The tidal water in the river in spring levels with the sea and the bright moon on the sea rises with the tides. 【張若虛〈春江花月夜〉Zhang Ruoxu: "A Night of Flowers and Moon on a River in Spring"】

當時若不登高望，誰信東流海樣深。If one had not ascended on high to gaze into the distance, who would have known that the

Changjiang River flows east into the unfathomable sea. 【《增廣賢文》 *Words that Open up One's Mind and Enhance One's Wisdom*】

二指深淺的水裏難行船。 It is difficult to sail on a stream which is just two-finger deep. 【俗語 Common saying】

孤帆遠影碧空盡，惟見長江天際流。 The lonely boat and its shadows in the distance have gone to the end of the blue sky and all I could see was the water of the Changjiang River flowing to the edge of heaven. 【李白〈黃鶴樓送孟浩然之廣陵〉Li Bai: "Seeing off Meng Haoran to Guangling at the Yellow Crane Tower"】

黃河遠上白雲間，一片孤城萬仞山。 The Yellow River goes up far into the white clouds, and there is an isolated town at the foot of a mountain of ten thousand feet high. 【王之渙〈涼州詞〉Wang Zhihuan: "Lyric of Liangzhou"】

急水也有回頭浪。 A rapid stream has also adverse currents. 【諺語 Proverb】

江河不曲水不流。 All rivers are winding, otherwise there would be no flowing water. 【俗語 Common saying】

江河不拒細浪，泰山不擇土石。 Rivers do not reject small streams and Mount Tai does not reject earth or stones. 【諺語 Proverb】

江流天地外，山色有無中。 The river flows beyond heaven and earth, and the tints of the mountain are now visible and now invisible. 【王維〈漢江臨眺〉Wang Wei: "Gazing out over the Han River"】

江上柳如煙，雁飛殘月天。 Along the river, willows are like mist and wild geese fly in the sky with a waning moon. 【溫庭筠〈菩薩蠻〉Wen Tingyun: "To the Tune of Buddhist Dancers"】

君不見，黃河之水天上來，奔流到海不復回。 Can't you see the water of the Yellow River comes from heaven, which flows to the sea and never returns? 【李白〈將進酒〉Li Bai: "About to Drink Wine"】

沒有過不去的河。 There is no river that can't be crossed. 【俗語 Common saying】

千流匯江河。 A thousand streams converge into great rivers. 【俗語 Common saying】

水流千遭歸大海。 A river twists and turns a thousand times, it eventually flows into the sea. 【諺語 Proverb】

萬川歸海而不盈。 Ten thousand rivers flow into the sea, but the sea is never full. 【莊周《莊子・外篇・秋水第十七》：Zhuang Zhou: Chapter 17, "Autumn Floods", "Outer Chapters", *Zhuangzi*】

溪淺聲喧，靜水流深。 Shallow rivers make most din; still waters run deep. 【諺語 Proverb】

細流匯江河。Small streams converge into rivers and seas. 【諺語 Proverb】

瞎子過河 —— 不摸水深淺。A blind person crossing a river – he does not know how deep it is. 【歇後語 End-clipper】

一番江水一番魚。Different rivers have different fish. 【諺語 Proverb】

一溪綠水皆春雨，兩岸青山半夕陽。A river of blue water owes to the vernal rain and a half of the setting sun is on the green mountain on its banks. 【端木國瑚〈沙灣放船〉Duanmu Guohu:"Setting a Boat at the Sandy Bay"】

一水護田將綠繞，雨山排達送青來。A river that protects the fields has turned the surrounding green, and the two hills facing the gate brings about the greenness. 【王安石〈茅檐〉Wang Anshi:"Thatched House"】

Road

車走車道，馬走馬路。The cart travels on the cart way while the horse travels its own road. 【諺語 Proverb】

胡同裏扛木頭 —— 直來直去。Walking in a lane with a plank on one's shoulder – taking an arrow-straight course. 【歇後語 End-clipper】

路必有彎，夜長夢多。A road has without exception twists and turns and a long night is fraught with dreams. 【諺語 Proverb】

路不行不到，事不做不成。Without travelling on a road one cannot get to one's destination; without action one can achieve nothing. 【《增廣賢文》Words that Open up One's Mind and Enhance One's Wisdom】

路是人走出來的。Roads are trodden out by people. 【諺語 Proverb】

迷而知反，失道不遠。If you lose your way but know how to find your way back, you are not too far astray. 【陳壽《三國志・魏書・王郎傳》Chen Shou:"Biography of Wang Lang", "History of the Wei", Records of the Three Kingdoms】

前人開路後人走。People in the past opened the roads for the later generations to travel. 【諺語 Proverb】

無路開路，遇水搭橋。Open up a road where there is no road and build a bridge where there is a river. 【諺語 Proverb】

一天星點明歸路，十里荷香送出城。Stars that fill up the sky light up my way home, and ten miles of the fragrance of the

lotus escort me out of the city.
【楊萬里〈六月將晦出夜凝歸門〉Yang Wanli: "Returning Home at Night at the End of the Sixth Month"】

有人有路，無人無路。 Where there are people, there are roads; where there are no people, there are no roads. 【俗語 Common saying】

Root

花在樹上開，莫忘地下根。
Flowers that bloom on top of a tree should not forget the roots on earth. 【諺語 Proverb】

牆上蘆葦，頭重腳輕根底淺。
The reed that grows on the wall has a heavy head, a thin stem, and shallow roots. 【俗語 Common sayings】

人不可以忘本。 People should not forget their origin. 【諺語 Proverb】

樹高千丈，落葉歸根。 A tree may grow a thousand feet high, but its leaves fall back to the roots. 【諺語 Proverb】【錢彩《說岳全傳·第四十六回》Qian Cai: Chapter 46, A Story of Yue Fei】

樹有根，水有源。 A tree has roots and water, a source. 【諺語 Proverb】

Ruler

敗者為賊，成者為王。 He who fails is a rebel, and he who succeeds, a king. 【魯迅《華蓋集續編·談皇帝》Lu Xun: "On Emperors", Sequel to Inauspicious Stars】

村中無犬狗為王。 If there is no mastiff in the village, any cur will rule. 【俗語 Common saying】

大國為臣不如小國為君。 Would rather be a king in a small country than a minister in a big kingdom. 【俗語 Common saying】

君不正，臣投外國。 If the king behaves improperly, his

ministers will go to other states. 【許仲琳《封神演義·第三十一回》Xu Zhonglin: Chapter 31, Romance of the Investiture of the Deities】

君父之仇，不共戴天。 The hatred of killing one's king or father is so deep that one refuses to live with the killer under the same sky. 【《禮記·檀弓上第三》Chapter 3, "Tangong, Part 1", The Book of Rites】

君叫臣死，臣不敢不死。 If the king orders his minister to die, the minister dare not live. 【許仲琳《封神演義·第二十二回》Xu

Zhonglin: Chapter 22, *Romance of the Investiture of the Deities*】

君君，臣臣，父父，子子。 Let the ruler be a ruler, the minister a minister, the father a father and the son a son. 【孔子《論語‧顏淵篇第十二》Confucius: Chapter 12, *The Analects of Confucius*】

君使臣以禮，臣事君以忠。 The king should treat his ministers with rites and the ministers should serve the king with loyalty. 【孔子《論語‧八佾篇第三》Confucius: Chapter 3, *The Analects of Confucius*】

君有諍臣，父有諍子。 The king have ministers who remonstrate with him and the father has sons who oppose his words. 【余邵魚《東周列國志‧第八十九回》Yu Shaoyu: Chapter 89, *Chronicles of the Eastern Zhou Kingdoms*】

君之視臣如犬馬，則臣視君如國人。 When the ruler regards his ministers as his dogs and horses, then they will treat him as an ordinary man of the state. 【孟軻《孟子‧離婁下》Meng Ke: Chapter 4, Part 2, *Mencius*】

君之視臣如手足，則臣視君如腹心。 When the ruler regards his ministers as his hands and feet, then they will treat him as their belly and heart. 【孟軻《孟子‧離婁下》Meng Ke: Chapter 4, Part 2, *Mencius*】

君之視臣如土芥，則臣視君如寇讎。 When the ruler regards his ministers as mud or grass, then they will treat him as a robber or an enemy. 【孟軻《孟子‧離婁下》Meng Ke: Chapter 4, Part 2, *Mencius*】

沒皇帝，不造反。 If there is no king, there would not be rebels. 【俗語 Common saying】

溥天之下，莫非王土。率土之濱，莫非王臣。 All the land under the sky is no exception the king's domain. All the people under the royal reign are the king's subjects. 【《詩經‧小雅‧北山》"The Northern Hills", "Minor Odes of the Kingdom", *The Book of Odes*】

人主使其民信如日月，此無敵矣。 If a ruler makes people believe him like they believe the sun and moon, then he will be invincible. 【商鞅《商君書‧弱民》Shang Yang: "Weakening the People", *The Works of Shang Yang*】

聖王修義之柄，禮之序，以治人情。 A sage king cultivates the handle of righteousness, orders the rites, and regulates the feelings of the people. 【《禮記‧禮運第九》Chapter 9, "Conveyance of Rites", *The Book of Rites*】

誰當皇上，給誰納糧。 We pay taxes to whoever is the emperor. 【周立波《暴風驟雨‧第二部第一章》Zhou Libo: Volume 2, Chapter 1, *Violent Storms and Heavy Showers*】

天子不能以天下與人。 The emperor cannot give the empire to other people. 【《易經‧繫辭上》

"Appended Remarks, Part 1", *The Book of Changes*】

天子以德為車，以樂為御。 The Son of Heaven takes virtue as his chariot and music as his driver. 【《禮記・禮運第九》Chapter 9, "Conveyance of Rites", *The Book of Rites*】

王者以民為天。 A king's life depends on the people. 【司馬遷《史記・酈生陸賈列傳》Sima Qian:"Biographies of Li Yiji and Lu Gu", *Records of the Grand Historian*】

為君難，為臣不易。 It is difficult to be a king or a minister. 【孔子《論語・子路篇第十三》Confucius: Chapter 13, *The Analects of Confucius*】

唯有德者能以寬服民。 Only a ruler with virtue could make people obedient to him with liberty. 【左丘明《左傳・昭公二十年》Zuo Qiuming:"The Twentieth Year of the Reign of Duke Zhao", *Zuo's Commentary on the Spring and Autumn Annals*】

瞎子國裏，獨眼稱王。 Among the blind the one-eyed person is king. 【俗語 Common saying】

先到為君，後到為臣。 He who arrives first is king while he who follows is minister. 【《增廣賢文》*Words that Open up One's Mind and Enhance One's Wisdom*】

賢君必恭儉禮下，取於民有制。 A wise and virtuous ruler must be complaisant, frugal, treat his inferiors with politeness, and take from the people with regulated limits. 【孟軻《孟子・滕文公上》Meng Ke: Chapter 5, Part 1, *Mencius*】

一國不容二主。 There cannot be two sovereigns in the one and the same nation. 【羅貫中《三國演義・第六十回》Luo Guanzhong: Chapter 60, *Romance of the Three Kingdoms*】

有是君，必有是臣。 Like king, like minister. 【羅貫中《三國演義・第六十回》Luo Guanzhong: Chapter 60, *Romance of the Three Kingdoms*】

朝夕勤志，恤民之羸。 A ruler is diligent in pursuing his ideal day and night and cares for the weak among the people. 【左丘明《國語・楚語下》Zuo Qiuming:"The Language of Chu, Part 2", *National Languages*】

政者，口言之，身必行之。 When a ruler says something, he must put it into action. 【墨翟《墨子・公孟卷四十八》Mo Di: Chapter 48, "The Confucianist Gongming Yi", *Mozi*】

主貴臣榮，主憂臣辱。 When the king is respected, his ministers feel honoured; when the king is worried, his ministers feel ashamed. 【羅貫中《三國演義・第三十三回》Luo Guanzhong: Chapter 33, *Romance of the Three Kingdoms*】

Rumour

傳來之言不可信。 Rumour should not be believed.【俗語 Common saying】

荒年傳亂話。 In turmoil and chaos, rumours are rampant.【俗語 Common saying】

流言止於智者。 A wise person does not believe in rumours.【荀況《荀子·大略第二十七》Xun Kuang: Chapter 27, "Great Compendium", *Xunzi*】

聽風就是雨。 Speak or act on hearsay.【李寶嘉《官場現形記·第二十五回》Li Baojia: Chapter 25, *Officialdom Unmasked*】

無風三尺浪。 There are billows three feet high even when there is no wind.【俗語 Common saying】

一傳十，十傳百。 Rumours spread to ten people and ten people spread to one hundred.【陶穀《清異錄·喪葬義疾》Tao Gou: "Funerals, Burials, and Tuberculosis", *Records of the Unworldly and the Strange*】

一人傳虛，百人傳實。 A person spreads something that is false and it becomes true after being repeated by a hundred people.【《增廣賢文》*Words that Open up One's Mind and Enhance One's Wisdom*】

Safety

安在得人，危在失事。 Safety hinges on having the right people in the government and danger, failure on handling things properly.【黃石公《素書·安禮》Huang Shigong: "Securing Rites", *Book of Plain Truths*】

逢橋須下馬，有路莫行船。 Dismount from one's horse when one comes to a bridge and one does not take a boat when there is a road.【錢大昕《恆言錄·卷六》Qian Daxin: Chapter 6, *Record of Common Sayings*】

家累千金，坐不垂堂。 With a thousand pieces of gold at home, one would not sit under the eaves for fear that tiles might fall on and hurt him.【司馬遷《史記·司馬相如列傳》Sima Qian: "Biographies of Sima Xiangru", *Records of the Grand Historian*】

平安就是福。 Safety is a blessing in itself.【俗語 Common saying】

任憑風浪起，穩坐釣魚船。 Despite the rising wind and waves, one sits tight in a fishing boat.【俗語 Common saying】

瓦罐不離井上破。 The pitcher goes so often to the well that the pot is broken at last.【施耐庵《水滸傳·第一百一十回》Shi Nai'an: Chapter 110, *Outlaws of the Marshes*】

Sage

才德全盡，謂之聖人。 He who is perfect in talent and virtue is known as a sage. 【司馬光《資治通鑒‧周紀》Sima Guang: "Annals of the Zhou Dynasty", *Comprehensive Mirror to Aid in Government*】

樂取於人以為善，聖人也；無稽之言勿聽，亦聖人也。 He who is willing to learn from others to do good deed is a sage; he who turns a deaf ear to unfounded talks is also a sage. 【袁枚《隨園詩話》Yuan Mei: *Talks on Poetry from the Sui Garden*】

聖人，百世之師也。 A sage is a teacher of a hundred generations. 【孟軻《孟子‧盡心章句下》Meng Ke: Chapter 7, Part 2, *Mencius*】

聖人不凝滯於物，而能與世推移。 A sage does not get stuck with things but can progress with the times. 【屈原《楚辭‧漁父》Qu Yuan: "The Old Fisherman", *The Songs of Chu*】

聖人不期修古，不法常可，論世之事，因為之備。 A sage does not envy the ancients or follow the standards for all times, but examines the affairs of his age and prepares to deal with them. 【韓非《韓非子‧五蠹第四十九》Han Fei: Chapter 49, "Five Vermins", *Hanfeizi*】

聖人常善救人，故無棄人；常善救物，故無棄物。 A sage is always good at saving people, so there is no deserted person; he is always good at saving things, so there is no deserted thing. 【老子《道德經‧第二十七章》Laozi: Chapter 27, *Daodejing*】

聖人處無為之事，行不言之教。 A sage deals with things without action, practise teaching without words. 【老子《道德經‧第二章》Laozi: Chapter 2, *Daodejing*】

聖人非不好利也，利在於利萬人；非不好富也，富在於富天下。 It is not that a sage does not like benefits, but the benefits should benefit a large number of people; it is not that a sage does not like wealth, but the wealth should enrich all the people under heaven. 【白居易〈策林‧不奪人利〉"Not Taking away the Benefits of the People", *Tactics*】

聖人耐以天下為一家。 A sage can take all under heaven as one family. 【《禮記‧禮運第九》Chapter 9, "Conveyance of Rites", *The Book of Rites*】

聖人去甚，去奢，去泰。 A sage does away with extremity, extravagance, and excess. 【老子《道德經‧第二十九章》Laozi: Chapter 29, *Daodejing*】

聖人無常師。 A sage does not have a regular teacher. 【韓愈《昌黎先生集‧師說》Han Yu: "On Teaching", *Collected Works of Han Yu*】

聖人無常心，以百姓之心為心。 The sage does not have a constant heart, for his heart is for the hearts of the people. 【老子《道德經・第四十九章》Laozi: Chapter 49, *Daodejing*】

聖人一視而同仁，篤近而舉遠。 A sage treats all people in the same way, benefitting people close to them and recommending people far away. 【韓愈《昌黎先生集・原人》Han Yu: "On the Origin of Mankind", *Collected Works of Han Yu*】

聖人以身體力行。 A sage practises what he preaches. 【劉安《淮南子・氾論訓第十三》Liu An: Chapter 13, "Compendious Essay", *Huainanzi*】

聖人與眾人同欲。 A sage has the same desires of the people. 【左丘明《左傳・成公六年》Zuo Qiuming: "The Sixth Year of the Reign of Duke Cheng", *Zuo's Commentary on the Spring and Autumn Annals*】

聖人之道，仁義中正而已矣。 The way of a sage is no more than benevolence, righteousness, moderation, and justice. 【周敦頤《通書・道》Zhou Dunyi: "The Way", *Comprehending The Book of Changes*】

聖人之道，為而不爭。 The Way of the sage is to act for others and does not compete with them. 【老子《道德經・第八十一章》Laozi: Chapter 81, *Daodejing*】

聖人終不為大，故能成其大。 It is because the sage never strives to be great that he manages to achieve great things. 【老子《道德經・第六十三章》Laozi: Chapter 63, *Daodejing*】

聖人自知不自見，自愛不自貴。 The sage knows himself and does not parade his knowledge and he loves himself but does not exalt himself. 【老子《道德經・第七十二章》Laozi: Chapter 72, *Daodejing*】

聖人作而萬物睹。 A sage rises and this is seen by all creatures. 【《易經・坤・文言》"The Record of Wen Yan", Hexagram *Kun*, *The Book of Changes*】

聞而知之，聖也；見而知之，智也。 One who hears something and knows it is a sage; one who sees something and knows it is an intelligent person. 【宋鈃《文子・道德第四》Song Jin: Chapter 4, "The Virtue of the Way", *Wenzi*】

以德分人謂之聖人，以財分人謂之賢人。 He who shares his virtue with others is called a sage; he who shares his wealth with others is called a worthy person. 【列禦寇《列子・力命第六》Lie Yukou: Chapter 6, "Endeavour and Destiny", *Liezi*】

Sailing

潮平兩岸闊，風正一帆懸。The tides are surgeless and the banks are wide. The wind is fair and a sail is hoisted.【王灣〈次北固山下〉Wang Wan: "Mooring at the Foot of Mount Beigu"】

見風就扯篷。Whenever there is wind, one puts up the sail.【俗語 Common saying】

逆水行舟，不進則退。A boat sailing against the water must forge ahead or it will be driven back.【《增廣賢文》*Words that Open up One's Mind and Enhance One's Wisdom*】

Sameness

千部一腔，千人一面。All works are of the same tone and all people have the same faces.【曹雪芹《紅樓夢·第一回》Cao Xueqin: Chapter 1, *A Dream of the Red Chamber*】

Scheming

狐狸尾巴藏不住。A fox cannot hide its tail.【俗語 Common saying】

眉頭一皺，計上心頭。Knit the brows and a stratagem comes to mind.【紀君祥〈趙氏孤兒·第二折〉Ji Junxiang: Scene 2, "The Orphan of the Zhao Family"】

明裏一套，暗裏一套。Act one way in the open and another way in secret.【俗語 Common saying】

明槍易躲，暗箭難防。It is easy to dodge a spear in the open, but difficult to guard against an arrow shot in the dark.【佚名〈劉千病打獨角牛〉Anonymous: "Liu Qianbing Fighting with a Unicorn Ox"】

明是一盆火，暗是一把刀。Make a show of great warmth while stabbing somebody in the back.【曹雪芹《紅樓夢·第六十五回》Cao Xueqin: Chapter 65, *A Dream of the Red Chamber*】

明修棧道，暗度陳倉。Pretend action in one place and make the real move in another.【趙琦美《古今雜劇·韓元帥·暗度陳倉》Zhao Qimei: Han Yuanshuai: "Making the Real Move in Another Place", *Dramas of Ancient and Recent Times*】

人算不如天算巧。Heaven calculates better than man.【周楫《西湖二集·第二十四卷》Zhou Ji: Chapter 24, *The West Lake, Second Volume*】

入山不怕傷人虎，衹怕人情兩面刀。 When people enter a mountain, they are not afraid of tigers that hurt them but of people who play double games. 【俗語 Common saying】

司馬昭之心路人皆知。 What one is up to is only too evident. 【陳壽《三國志・魏書・高貴鄉公傳》 Chen Shou:"Biography of the Township Duke of Gaogui", "History of the Wei", *Records of the Three Kingdoms*】

Scholar

士別三日，即更刮目相待。 A scholar who has been away for three days must be looked at with a new pair of eyes. 【陳壽《三國志・吳書・呂蒙傳》 Chen Shou:"Biography of Lu Meng", "History of the Wu", *Records of the Three Kingdoms*】

士不以利移，不為患改。 A scholar does not change for the sake of profits nor waver in the face of perils. 【劉向《説苑・卷十六談叢》 Liu Xiang: Chapter 16, "The Thicket of Discussion", *Garden of Persuasion*】

士而懷居，不足以為士矣。 A person who indulges in comfort is not fit to be a scholar. 【孔子《論語・憲問篇第十四》 Confucius: Chapter 14, *The Analects of Confucius*】

士窮不失義，達不離道。 A scholar does not lose his righteousness when he is poor nor deviate from the right path when he is prosperous. 【孟軻《孟子・盡心章句上》 Meng Ke: Chapter 7, Part 1, *Mencius*】

士窮乃見節義。 The integrity and righteousness of a scholar is revealed when he is in adversity. 【韓愈〈柳子厚墓誌銘〉 Han Yu:"An Epitaph for Liu Zihou"】

士之為人，當理不避其難，臨患忘利，遺生行義，視死如歸。 The behaviour of a scholar as a person is not to escape difficulty in face of truth, forget about one's interests in front of a disaster, sacrifice one's life to practise rigthteousness, and look upon death as home coming. 【呂不韋《呂氏春秋・士節》 Lu Buwei:"The Integrity of a Scholar", *Master Lu's Spring and Autumn Annals*】

士者國之寶，儒為席上珍。 A scholar is a treasure of his country and a Confucian scholar is like a delicacy in a feast. 【《增廣賢文》 *Words that Open up One's Mind and Enhance One's Wisdom*】

文人相輕，自古而然。 From of old, scholars have scorned each other. 【曹丕《典論・論文》 Cao Pei:"On Writing", *On Classics*】

學者於貧賤富貴不動其心，死生禍福不變其守。 A scholar will not be moved by poverty, low position, wealth, and nobility or change his conduct because of death, life, fortune and misfortune. 【王廷相〈慎言〉Wang Tingxiang: "Prudence in Speech"】

有道之士，貴以近知遠，以今知古，以所見知所不見。 A scholar with the Way is valued for knowing the distant by the near, the ancient by the present, and what he cannot see by what he sees. 【呂不韋《呂氏春秋‧察今》Lu Buwei: "Perceive the Present", *Master Lu's Spring and Autumn Annals*】

Scolding

挨罵的不低，罵人的不高。 The abused is not low, and the abuser is not high. 【俗語 Common saying】

不挨罵長不大。 If one is not scolded from time to time, one cannot grow up. 【俗語 Common saying】

對客不得嗔狗。 Don't scold your dog before a guest. 【俗語 Common saying】【佚名〈村樂堂‧第一折〉Anonymous: Scene 1, "Village Happiness Hall"】

罵人無好口，打人無好手。 To curse, one will not use fine language; to beat, one will not use a light hand. 【諺語 Proverb】

莫罵酉時妻，一夜受孤淒。 Don't scold your wife in the evening, otherwise you have to endure a night of lonliness and misery. 【《增廣賢文》*Words that Open up One's Mind and Enhance One's Wisdom*】

人隨大眾不挨罵，羊隨大眾不挨打。 A person who follows the majority will not be scolded and a sheep that follows the herds will not be beaten. 【諺語 Proverb】【李滿天《水向東流‧第二十三章》Li Mantian: Chapter 23, *Water Flow to the East*】

萬人唾罵，遺臭萬年。 One who is cursed by ten thousand people and defamed for ten thousand years. 【房玄齡等《晉書‧桓溫傳》Fang Xuanling, *et al*: "Biography of Heng Wen", *History of the Jin*】

指冬瓜，罵葫蘆。 One points at the wax gourd to abuse the calabash. 【諺語 Proverb】

指雞罵狗，指桑罵槐。 One points at the chicken to abuse the dog and at the mulberry to abuse the locust. 【周立波《暴風驟雨‧第一部第十章》Zhou Libo: Chapter 10, Volume 1, *Violent Storms and Heavy Showers*】

指桑樹，罵槐樹。 One points at the mulberry to abuse the locust. 【蘭陵笑笑生《金瓶梅‧第六十二回》Lanling Xiaoxiaosheng: Chapter 62, *The Plum in the Golden Vase*】

指着和尚罵禿子。 Point at a monk and abuse the bald-headed. 【羅

Sea

不積小流，無以成江海。 Without accumulating the water of small streams, there is no way to form rivers and oceans.【荀況《荀子‧勸學第一》Xun Kuang: Chapter 1, "Exhortation to Learning", *Xunzi*】

大海呵，哪一顆星沒有光？哪一朵花沒有香？哪一次我的思潮裏，沒有你波濤的清響？ Oh, the vast sea, has there ever been a star without light? Has there ever been a flower without fragrance? Has there ever been a time when I did not have the clear sound of your waves in my thoughts?【冰心〈繁星〉Bing Xin: "Stars"】

海闊從魚躍，天高任鳥飛。 The sea is so wide that it allows the fish to leap about and the sky is so high that it allows birds to fly freely.【阮閱《詩話總龜前集》Ruan Yue: *Remarks on Poetry, First Volume*】

洋闊有邊，海深有底。 An ocean, however vast, has an edge; a sea, however deep, has a bottom.【俗語 Common saying】

Search

打着燈籠沒處找。 Something is so rare that it cannot be found if even one searches for it with a lantern.【文康《兒女英雄傳‧第九回》Wen Kang: Chapter 9, *Biographies of Young Heroes and Heroines*】

可遇而不可求。 One may come by something with luck but not by searching for it.【班固《漢書‧郊祀志下》Ban Gu: "Suburban Sacrifices, Part 2", *History of the Han*】

路漫漫其修遠兮，吾將上下而求索。 The road is endless and my journey is long, yet I go uphill and down dale to search for my destination.【屈原〈離騷〉Qu Yuan: *The Sorrows at Parting*】

騎着驢找驢。 Look for a donkey while one is riding it.【釋道原《景德傳燈錄‧卷二十八》Shi Daoyuan: Chapter 28, *Records of the Transmission of the Lamp in the Jingde Period*】

曲終人不見，江上數峯青。 When the music ended, the player was nowhere to be seen, and what was left were a few green mountains near the river.【錢起〈湘靈鼓瑟〉Qian Qi: "Xiang Goddess's Harp"】

上窮碧落下黃泉，兩處茫茫皆不見。 He seeks in the paradise up in the sky and down in hell, and yet her ghost is not there in either place. 【白居易〈長恨歌〉Bai Juyi:"Song of Everlasting Grief"】

踏破鐵鞋無覓處，得來全不費工夫。 Find something by accident after tracking miles in vain for it. 【夏元鼎〈絕句〉Xia Yuanding: :"A Quatrain"】

天上難找，地下難尋。 Something cannot be found in heaven nor on earth. 【俗語 Common saying】

祇在此山中，雲深不知處。 I only know that the recluse is right here in this mountain, but he is deep in the cloud and nobody knows where he is. 【賈島〈尋隱者不遇〉Jia Dao:"Failing to Meet the Recluse I looked for"】

眾裏尋他千百度，驀然回首，那人卻在，燈火闌珊處。 For a thousand and a hundred times, I looked for her in the crowd. Then suddenly, as I turned my head, there she was, in a place where the lanterns were burning low. 【辛棄疾〈元夕‧青玉案〉Xin Qiji:"The Lantern Festival Night: To the Tune of Green Jade Cup"】

Secret

臣不密則失身。 If a minister does not keep secrets, he will lose his life. 【《易經‧繫辭上》"Appended Remarks, Part 1", *The Book of Changes*】

機事不密則害成。 If confidential matters are not kept secret, it will harm their accomplishment. 【《易經‧繫辭上》"Appended Remarks, Part 1", *The Book of Changes*】

君不密則失臣。 If a ruler does not keep secrets, he will lose his ministers. 【《易經‧繫辭上》"Appended Remarks, Part 1", *The Book of Changes*】

謀泄者事無功，計不決者名不成。 He who does not keep things secretive will achieve nothing and he who fails to decide on his plans will not gain reputation. 【劉向《戰國策‧齊策三》Liu Xiang:"Strategies of the State of Qi, No.3, *Strategies of the Warring States*】

神不知，鬼不覺。 Unknown even to gods and ghosts. 【馮夢龍《警世通言‧第三十一卷》Feng Menglong: Chapter 31, *Stories to Caution the World*】

沒有不透風的牆。 There is no wall which does not allow the wind to go through. 【郭泳戈，海草《劉公案‧第七十一回》Guo Yongge and Hai Cao: Chapter 71, *Cases of Judge Liu*】

事以密成，語以泄敗。 Things succeed through secrecy; promises fail through divulgence. 【韓非《韓非子‧說難第

十二》Han Fei: Chapter 12, "Difficulties in Persuasion", *Hanfeizi*】

天機不可泄漏。 Heaven's secrets must not be divulged.【曹雪芹《紅樓夢・第十三回》Cao Xueqin: Chapter 13, *A Dream of the Red Chamber*】

天有眼，牆有耳。 Heaven has eyes and walls ears.【周立波《山鄉巨變・下卷第九章》Zhou Libo: Chapter 9, Volume 2, *Great Changes in the Mountain Villages*】

一語道破天機。 Divulge Heaven's secrets with a single word.【諺語 Proverb】

Self

不能靠己，焉能靠人。 If you can't rely on yourself, how can you rely on others?【俗語 Common saying】

姜太公封神 —— 忘了自己。 Jiang Tai Gong making others deities – forgetting himself【歇後語 End-clipper】

老西兒拉胡琴 —— 自顧自。 Chaozhou music – everyone for themselves.【歇後語 End-clipper】

人不為己，天誅地滅。 Anyone who does not look after his own interests will be destroyed by heaven and earth.【諺語 Proverb】

人在江湖，身不由己。 One's life is bound by rules of the underworld.【俗語 Common saying】

上無老，下無小。 One has no old folk and no children – all by oneself.【俗語 Common saying】

手電筒 —— 對人不對己。 A flash light – one who is always strict with others but never with oneself.【歇後語 End-clipper】

犧牲自己，保全他人。 Sacrifice oneself to safeguard others.【俗語 Common saying】

責己嚴，待人寬。 Be strict with oneself and lenient towards others.【俗語 Common saying】

丈八燈台 —— 照見人家，照不見自己。 Like a six-foot lampstand that lights up others but stays dark itself.【歇後語 End-clipper】

知己莫若己。 The person who knows you best is your ownself.【俗語 Common saying】

Selfishness

各人自掃門前雪，莫管他人瓦上霜。 Each clears away the snow in front of his door and would not care about the frost on the tiles of another person's roof. 【陳元靚《事林廣記·卷九》Chen Yuanliang: Chapter 9, *Comprehensive Records of Affairs*】

黃牛過河 —— 各顧各。 When oxen cross a river, each of them looks after itself. 【歇後語 End-clipper】

叫化子照火 —— 祇往自己懷裏扒。 Beggars trying to get warm by a fire – everyone wants to get nearer to it. 【歇後語 End-clipper】

哪個腹中無算盤。 Who does not calculate for himself? 【李汝珍《鏡花緣·第十一回》Li Ruzhen: Chapter 11, *Flowers in the Mirror*】

千可貴，萬可貴，無私最可貴。 A thousand is valuable, ten thousand is valuable, most valuable, nevertheless, is selflessness. 【俗語 Common saying】

人無三分為己，天也不容。 A person who does not somehow looks after his interests is not tolerated even by heaven. 【俗語 Common saying】

心底無私天地寬。 The world is boundless for a selfless person. 【俗語 Common saying】

以其無私，故能成其私。 It is without the self that makes it possible to realize the self. 【老子《道德經·第七章》Laozi: Chapter 7, *Daodejing*】

祇知有己，不知有人。 One is self-centred without considering others. 【諺語 Proverb】

Self-praise

打擊別人，抬高自己。 Attack others to promote oneself. 【俗語 Common saying】

夫子廟前賣文章。 Sell one's essay before the temple of Confucius. 【俗語 Common saying】

關公面前耍大刀 —— 獻醜。 Display one's limited skill before an expert. 【歇後語 End-clipper】

耗子爬稱鈎 —— 自己稱自己。 Self-praise. 【歇後語 End-clipper】

誇嘴大夫 —— 無好藥。 A doctor who boasts has no good medicine. 【歇後語 End-clipper】

老王賣瓜 —— 自賣自誇。 Every cook praises his own broth. 【歇後語 End-clipper】

賣瓜的說瓜甜，賣醋的說醋酸。 One who sells melons says that

his melons are the sweetest. One who sells vinegar says that his vinegar is sour. 【俗語 Common saying】【克非《春潮急·第四十二章》Ke Fei: Chapter 42, *Spring Tides Come Rapidly*】

天不言自高，地不言自厚。 Good wine needs no push. 【諺語 Proverb】

王婆賣瓜 —— 自吹自誇。 Ring one's own bell. 【歇後語 End-clipper】

自伐者無功，功成者墮，名成者虧。 He who brags about himself would not succeed. Even if he succeeds, he will fail, and his reputation will wane. 【莊周《莊子·外篇·山木第二十》Zhuang Zhou: Chapter 20, "The Mountain Tree", "Outer Chapters", *Zhuangzi*】

Separation

悲莫悲兮生別離，樂莫樂兮新相知。 Nothing is sadder than the separation of the living and the dead; nothing is happier than making new bosom friends. 【屈原《離騷·九歌·少司令》Qu Yuan: "The Little Lords of Life", "The Nine Songs", *The Sorrows at Parting*】

明日巴陵道，秋山又幾重。 Tomorrow we shall again part on the Baling way and be separated again by mountains in autumn. 【李益〈喜見外弟又言別〉Li Yi: "Delighted to Meet My Cousin, Only to Part Again"】

年年今夜，月華如練，長是人千里。 Every year this night, in bright moonlight, we are always a thousand miles apart. 【范仲淹〈御街行〉Fan Zhongyan: "Imperial Street"】

同心而離居，憂傷以終老。 We are of the same heart but have to live apart, ending our old age with grief and sadness. 【佚名《古詩十九首》Anonymous: *Nineteen Ancient Poems*】

一懷愁緒，幾年離索。 I have a heartful of sorrowful feelings as we have been separated for a few years. 【陸游〈釵頭鳳〉Lu You: "To the Tune of Phoenix Hairpin"】

Serenity

大漠孤煙直，長河落日圓。 In the vast desert, there is a pillar of smoke; in the long river, the setting sun is round. 【王維〈使至塞上〉Wang Wei: "On the Frontier as an Envoy"】

大漠沙如雪，燕山月似鈎。In the vast desert, the sands are white as snow; over the Mount Yan, the moon is like a hook. 【李賀〈馬詩〉Li He: "A Poem on Horses"】

非淡泊無以明志，非寧靜無以致遠。Without indifference to fame and fortune, one cannot express one's ambition; without tranquility, one cannot achieve something lasting. 【諸葛亮〈誡子篇〉Zhuge Liang: "Admonition to My Son"】

枯藤老樹昏鴉，小橋流水人家，古道西風瘦馬。Withe Red vines, old trees, and crows at dusk. A small bridge, flowing water, and cottages. An ancient road, the west wind, and a skinny horse. 【馬致遠〈天淨沙·秋思〉Ma Zhiyuan: "Autumn Yearnings: To the Tune of Sky-cleaned Sand"】

結廬在人境，而無車馬喧。I built my hut in the world of men, away from the hubbub of horses and carriages. 【陶淵明〈飲酒〉Tao Yuanming: "Drinking Wine"】

靜以修身，儉以養德。Serenity is for the cultivation of the person and frugality, the nourishment of virtue. 【諸葛亮〈誡子篇〉Zhuge Liang: "Admonition to My Son"】

犬吠一山秋意靜，敲門時有夜歸僧。The barking of a dog breaks the serenity of the mountain in autumn, and from time to time, there are knocks on the door by monks who return late to the temple. 【趙渢〈晚宿山寺〉Zhao Feng: "Stay at Night at a Mountain Temple"】

清靜為天下正。Through inaction and serenity, you become a leader of the world. 【老子《道德經·第四十五章》Laozi: Chapter 45, Daodejing】

清時有味是無能，閒愛孤雲靜愛僧。It's a pity that I am unable to enjoy peaceful days. At leisure I love lonely clouds and in serenity, I like the monastic way of life. 【杜牧〈將赴吳興登樂遊原〉Du Mu: "Ascending the Leyou Plateau Before Leaving for Wuxing"】

人閒桂花落，夜靜春山空。People at rest and cassia flowers fall. The night is still and mountains in spring are deserted. 【王維〈鳥鳴澗〉Wang Wei: "Birds Singing in the Ravine"】

山光悅鳥性，潭影空人心。The light of the mountain suits the nature of birds and reflections in the pool cleanse people's heart. 【常建〈題破山寺後禪院〉Chang Jian: "Inscribing on the Meditation Court behind a Ruined Temple"】

山靜似太古，日長如小年。Mountains are so quiet, it is like ancient times; the day is long and I feel like that this moment is forever. 【唐庚〈醉睡〉Tang Geng: "Sleeping in Drunkenness"】

深林人不知，明月來相照。In the deep forest, nobody knows me, only the moon comes to pour its light on me. 【王維〈竹里館〉Wang Wei: "Zhuli Lodge"】

水清石出魚可數，林深無人鳥相呼。 The water was clear enough to expose rocks and count the fish. The grove was deep and without people, and birds could call out to one another. 【蘇軾〈臘日游孤山訪惠勤惠思二僧〉Su Shi: "Travelling Mount Gu on the Last Day of the Year to Visit Monk Hui Qin and Monk Huien"】

松風吹解帶，山月照彈琴。 The wind blowing through the pines loosens my girdle, the moon shining on the mountain illuminates the lute I play. 【王維〈酬張少府〉Wang Wei: "A Reply to Vice-prefect Zhang"】

野曠天低樹，江清月近人。 The wild plain is vast and the sky is beneath the trees. The river is clear and the moon is so near. 【孟浩然〈宿建德江〉Meng Haoran: "Passing the Night on the Jiande River"】

一鳥不鳴山更幽。 The mountain will be more quiet when not a single bird is chirping. 【王安石〈鍾山即事〉Wang Anshi: "Written on Mount Zhong"】

Service

吃自己的飯，管別人的事。 Run errands for other people. 【俗語 Common saying】

敬其事而後其食。 Perform one's service dutifully and then get the payment. 【孔子《論語・衛靈公篇第十五》Confucius: Chapter 15, *The Analects of Confucius*】

鞠躬盡瘁，死而後已。 I have devoted my life to serving the people and will always do my best in the service until death. 【諸葛亮〈後出師表〉 Zhuge Liang: "Second Memorial on Dispatching the Troops"】

一人不能事二主。 A person cannot serve two masters. 【褚人獲《隋唐演義・第四十九回》Zhu Renhuo: Chapter 49, *Heroes in Sui and Tang Dynasties*】

一人為大家，大家為一人。 The individual should serve the public and the public should serve the individual. 【俗語 Common saying】

Sex

飽暖思淫慾，饑寒起盜心。 When one is well-fed and well-clad, one's sexual desire will come up. When one is hungry and cold, one has the temptation to steal.【沈采〈千金記・第二齣〉Shen Cai: Scene 2, "A Story of One Thousand Pices of Gold"】

多沐浴，少情慾。 More baths, less lust.【俗語 Common saying】

甘作一生拼，盡君今日歡。 I am willing to spend all that I have in this life to enjoy to the full the pleasure of today.【牛嶠〈菩薩蠻〉Niu Qiao: "To the Tune of Buddhist Dancers"】

清官不愛色。 An honest official is not indulged in lust.【諺語 Proverb】

三姑六婆，實淫盜之媒。 Women in disreputable occupations are really intermediaries for illicit sexual relations and thefts.【朱用純《朱子家訓》Zhu Yongchun: Percepts of the Zhu Family】

色膽大如天。 One who seeks sexual relations must be very bold.【施耐庵《水滸傳・第四十五回》Shi Nai'an: Chapter 45, Outlaws of the Marshes】

色是殺人刀。 Sexual pleasures are like knives that kill.【俞達《青樓夢・第五十四回》Yu Da: Chapter 54, Dream of the Green Chamber】

色字頭上一把刀。 Womanizing is dangerous.【俗語 Common saying】

貪色乃人之天性。 Indulging in sex is human nature.【俗語 Common saying】

萬惡淫為首。 Of all vices, lust comes first.【《增廣賢文》Words that Open up One's Mind and Enhance One's Wisdom】

有奇淫者，必有大禍。 One who indulges in lust excessively will have great disasters.【余邵魚《東周列國志・第十五回》Yu Shaoyu: Chapter 15, Chronicles of the Eastern Zhou Kingdoms】

Shame

不識人間有羞恥事。 There are people who don't know that there are shameful things in this world.【歐陽修〈與高司諫書〉Ouyang Xiu: "Letter to Gao Sijian"】

寡婦養子 —— 醜事。 A widow giving birth to a baby–a shameful act.【歇後語 End-clipper】

苦好受，羞難遮。 Hardships are easy to bear, but shame is hard to cover up.【俗語 Common saying】

寧可無錢，不可無恥。 Rather be penniless than shameless.【諺語 Proverb】

人不可以無恥，無恥之恥，無恥矣。 People cannot be without shame. The shame of without shame is shameless.【孟軻《孟子・

盡心章句上》Meng Ke: Chapter 7, Part 1, *Mencius*】

人無羞恥，百事可為。 If a person is dead to shame, they can do all sorts of evil things. 【俗語 Common saying】

無面見江東父老。 One feels too ashamed to see again one's elders of one's home place. 【司馬遷《史記・項羽本紀》Sima Qian:"Annals of Xiang Yu", *Records of the Grand Historian*】

仰不愧天，俯不愧人，內不愧心。 When looking up, one has no occasion for shame before heaven; when looking down, he has no occasion to blush before people; when looking inside, he has no occasion for guilt before his heart. 【韓愈〈與孟尚書書〉Han Yu:"Letter to Minister Meng"】

知恥近乎勇。 Knowing shame is close to courage. 【《禮記・中庸第三十一章》Chapter 31, "Doctrine of the Mean", *The Book of Rites*】

Sincerity

不實心，不成事。 One who is not sincere cannot achieve anything. 【石成金《傳家寶第三集》Shi Chengjin: Volume 3, *Family Heirloom*】

精誠所至，金石為開。 Where there is utmost sincerity, even gold and stones will fall apart. 【范曄《後漢書・廣陵思王荊傳》 Fan Ye:"Biography of Si Wangjing of Guangling", *History of the Later Han*】

所謂誠其意者，毋自欺也。 What is known as"making one's mind sincere" means that one should not deceive oneself. 【《禮記・大學第四十二》Chapter 42, "The Great Learning", *The Book of Rites*】

至誠金石開。 Utmost sincerity breaks up even gold and stones. 【范曄《後漢書・廣陵思王荊傳》 Fan Ye:"Biography of Si Wangjing of Guangling", *History of the Later Han*】

Singing

不惜歌者苦，但傷知音稀。 I do not pity the suffering of the singer, but is hurt that those who understand her singing are scare. 【佚名《古詩十九首・五》Anonymous: Poem No. 5, *Nineteen Ancient Poems*】

得意高歌，夜靜聲偏朗；無人賞，自家拍掌，唱得千山響。 In high spirits, I sing loudly, which is particularly clear in the quiet night. No one praises me. I clap my hands in applause, and my song is echoed by a thousand mountains. 【僧正岩〈點絳脣〉Seng

今日聽君歌一曲，暫憑杯酒長精神。 Today I listened to a song you sang, at the moment I relied on a cup of wine to make the wish that we stay in high spirits forever. 【劉禹錫〈酬樂天揚州初逢席上見贈〉Liu Yuxi:"Responding to Bai Juyi's Poem on Our First Meeting at Yangzhou"】

千人唱，萬人和。 One thousand people sing and ten thousand people echo. 【劉勰《文心雕龍‧事類》Liu Xie:"Classifying Things", *The Literary Mind and the Carving of Dragons*】

善歌者使人繼其聲。 A good singer makes the audience ask for more of his singing. 【《禮記‧學記第十八》Chapter 18, "Records on the Subject of Education", *The Book of Rites*】

楊柳青青江水平，聞郎江上唱歌聲。 The willows are green and the waters in the river flow smoothly. I heard the singing of my lover on the river. 【劉禹錫〈竹枝詞〉Liu Yixi:"To the Tune of Bamboo Branches"】

一曲高歌一樽酒，移舟穩臥荻蘆邊。 With a bottle of wine, I sing loudly, move my boat besides the giant reed, and sleep tightly. 【吳樹本〈漁家〉Wu Shuben:"Fisherman"】

字字清脆，聲聲婉轉。 Every word is distinct and every note is melodic. 【劉鶚《老殘遊記‧第二回》Liu E: Chapter 2, *The Travels of Lao Can*】

Situation

八寶飯摻漿糊 —— 糊塗到一塊兒了。 Eight-treasure steamed rice pudding mixed with paste – all muddled up together. 【歇後語 End-clipper】

彼一時，此一時。 That was the situation then and this is the situation now. 【孟軻《孟子‧公孫丑下》Meng Ke: Chapter 2, Part 2, *Mencius*】

處順境須謹慎，處逆境須忍耐。 When things are in one's way, one has to be cautious. When things are not in one's way, one has to be patient. 【諺語 Proverb】

打他廊下過，誰敢不低頭。 As one passes by the low eaves of another one's house, one does not dare to hold one's head high. 【施耐庵《水滸傳‧第二十八回》Shi Nai'an: Chapter 28, *Outlaws of the Marshes*】

狗長角 —— 出洋（羊）相。 A dog with horns – making a spectacle of oneself. 【歇後語 End-clipper】

顧大局，識大體。 Bear the overall situation in mind and put the

general interest above all. 【李寶嘉《官場現形記・第十四回》Li Baojia: Chapter 14, *Officialdom Unmasked*】

好景難常，名花易落。 Favourable situations do not last long and beautiful flowers wither easily. 【程趾祥《此中人語・卷五》Cheng Zhixiang: Chapter 5, *Sayings of an Insider*】

虎落平陽被犬欺。 If the tiger went down to the level and, it would be insulted by dogs. 【《增廣賢文》*Words that Open up One's Mind and Enhance One's Wisdom*】

井水不犯河水。 The water in the well does not intrude into the water in the river. 【曹雪芹《紅樓夢・第六十九回》Cao Xueqin: Chapter 69, *A Dream of the Red Chamber*】

可以速而速，可以久而久，可以處而處，可以仕而仕。 If you can leave, then leave; if you can stay longer, then stay longer; if you can retire, then retire; and if you can take office, then take office. 【孟軻《孟子・萬章下》Meng Ke: Chapter 10, Part 2, *Mencius*】

爐中添炭，火上加油。 The situation is like adding charcoal in the furnace and pouring oil on the fire. 【施耐庵《水滸傳・第六十三回》Shi Nai'an: Chapter 63, *Outlaws of the Marshes*】

兩人恰恰好，人多一團糟。 Two persons are just right and too many people cause chaos. 【俗語 Common saying】

騎上虎背 —— 欲罷不能。 As one is riding on a tiger's back, one can't get off from it. 【歇後語 End-clipper】

前頭虎，後頭狼 —— 進退兩難。 Be faced with tigers ahead and wolves behind – one is in a dilemma. 【歇後語 End-clipper】

前有高山，後有深谷。 There are high mountains in front and deep valleys behind. 【孫臏《孫臏兵法・雄牝城》Sun Bin: "Xiongpin town", *Sun Bin's art of war*】

前有狼，後有虎 —— 進退維谷。 Be faced with a wolf ahead and a tiger behind – one is in a dilemma. 【歇後語 End-clipper】

窮則獨善其身，達則兼濟天下。 In adversity, you cultivate your own virtue; in prosperity, you extend what you have to benefit the whole world. 【孟軻《孟子・盡心章句上》Meng Ke: Chapter 7, Part 1, *Mencius*】

如入無人之境。 Like entering a piece of land without any people. 【佚名〈薛仁貴征遼事略〉Anonymous: "Xue Rengui's Expedition to Liao"】

上天無路，入地無門。 One is in desperate straits. 【施耐庵《水滸傳・第三十四回》Shi Nai'an: Chapter 34, *Outlaws of the Marshes*】

十個甕缸九個蓋。 Fail to make both ends meet. 【俗語 Common saying】

獸窮則齧，鳥窮則啄，人窮則詐。
Animals in a dead end will bite, birds in a dead end will strike with the beak, and people in a dead end will cheat.【韓嬰《韓詩外傳‧卷二》Han Ying: Chapter 2, *Supplementary Commentary on the Book of Songs by Master Han*】

順得哥情失嫂意。 One is between the devil and the deep blue sea. 【俗語 Common saying】

投之亡地然後存，陷於死地然後生。 One will survive when put in a desperate situation, and stay alive when threathened by death.【孫武《孫子兵法‧九地第十一》Sun Wu: Chapter 11, "The Nine Situations", *The Art of War by Sunzi*】

王小二過年 —— 一年不如一年。 One's case is getting more run-down year after year. 【歇後語 End-clipper】

陷之死地而後生，置之死地而後存。 When one has fallen into a desperate situation, one will come off alive; when one is placed in a desperate situation, one will survive. 【司馬遷《史記‧淮陰侯列傳》Sima Qian:"Biography of the Marquis of Huaiyin", *Records of the Grand Historian*】

一面砌牆兩面光。 Both sides benefit.【諺語 Proverb】

雨天挑稻草 —— 越挑越重。 One's burden becomes greater.【歇後語 End-clipper】

正氣高，邪氣消。 When a healthy atmosphere prevails, the evil influence vanishes.【俗語 Common saying】

Skill

積財千萬，不如薄技在身。 To accumulate thousands and thousands of dollars is not as good as learning a simple skill.【顏之推《顏氏家訓‧勉學》Yan Zhitui:"Exhortation to Learning", *Family Instructions of Master Yan*】

將錢學藝，學藝賺錢。 Spend money on skills and make money with skills.【俗語 Common saying】

教會徒弟，餓死師父。 When a master taught his apprentice his skills, he could starve to death. 【俗語 Common saying】

久練為熟，熟能生巧。 Skill is acquired through repeated practice and practice makes perfect.【諺語 Proverb】

慢工出巧匠。 Slow work makes a skilled person.【諺語 Proverb】

慢工出細貨。 Slow work produces skilled work.【俗語 Common saying】

能書不擇筆。One who is good at calligraphy does not choose the writing brush.【王肯堂《鬱岡齋筆麈》Wang Kentang: *Notes from the Yugang Studio*】

人丁上百，武藝皆全。When there are more than a hundred people, you have people with different skills.【諺語 Proverb】

人多一技有益，物多一備有用。It is beneficial to a person with one more skill and useful when there is one more thing to spare.【馮德英《山菊花‧第十三章》Feng Deying: Chapter 13, *Wild Chrysanthemum*】

色色都會，件件不精。He who has the skills of everything is usually slack in their execution.【諺語 Proverb】

授人以魚，三餐之需。授人以漁，終生之用。If you give a fish to a person, it meets his needs for three meals, but if you teach a person to fish, he learns a skill that he can use for life.【劉安《淮南子‧說林訓第十六》Liu An: Chapter 16, "Discourse on Mountains", *Huainanzi*】

熟讀唐詩三百首，不會作詩也會吟。Skill comes from constant practice.【諺語 Proverb】

戲法人人會變，各有巧妙不同。Each juggler has his own tricks.【俗語 Common saying】

學到知羞處，方知藝不高。When one feels ashamed of one's learning, one begins to understand that one's skills need improving.【諺語 Proverb】

學會百藝不壓人。Grasp a hundred skills and you will not be weighed down by life.【諺語 Proverb】

學藝終身福，是藝不虧人。The acquisition of skills is a life-long blessing and no skill will ever let you down.【諺語 Proverb】

腰纏萬貫，不若一技在身。It is better to learn a certain trade than to possess a large fortune.【諺語 Proverb】

要學驚人藝，須下苦功夫。To learn great skills, you must make great efforts.【諺語 Proverb】

一技在身，吃着不盡。With a useful skill, one can eat one's fill and wear good clothes.【諺語 Proverb】

一藝不精，誤了終身。Without good skill, your whole life is ruined.【諺語 Proverb】

一招鮮，吃遍天。When one has the skill, one can eat one's fill.【諺語 Proverb】

一招鮮，走遍天。When one has the skill, one will be respected wherever one goes.【諺語 Proverb】

藝多思，藝不精，專攻一藝可成名。If one learns too many skills, he cannot be proficient at any; if one specializes in one skill, he will become famous.【諺語 Proverb】

藝高功夫深。 Perfect skills result from hard work. 【諺語 Proverb】

藝高人膽大。 A person with superb skills is bold. 【石玉昆《三俠五義・第六十六回》Shi Yukun: Chapter 66, *The Three Heroes and Five Gallants*】

有腳不愁沒路走，學會百藝不壓身。 With healthy feet one does not worry about having no road to walk on; learning a hundred skills, one does not worry about having no job to do. 【俗語 Common saying】

Sky

上不着天，下不着地。 Touch neither the sky nor the ground. 【韓非《韓非子・解老第二十》Han Fei: Chapter 20, "Commentaries on Laozi's Teachings", *Hanfeizi*】

上有青冥之高天，下有淥水之波瀾。 High above is the blue and lofty sky, and down below are the waves of the clear water. 【李白〈長相思〉Li Bai: "Everlasting Longing"】

天不會塌下來。 The sky will not fall down. 【俗語 Common saying】

天不可一日無日，國不可一日無君。 The sky cannot be without the sun for a day just as a country cannot be without the king for a day. 【諺語 Proverb】【羅懋登《三寶太監西洋記・第二十一回》Luo Maodeng: Chapter 21, *Sanbao Eunuch's Voyage to the Western Ocean*】

天不言自高，地不言自厚。 The sky does not boast, but it is high; the earth does not boast, but it is thick. 【俗語 Common saying】

天蒼蒼，野茫茫，風吹草低見牛羊。 The sky is boundless; the grassland is endless. When the wind blows and grass bends low, sheep and cattle will emerge before your eyes. 【佚名〈敕勒歌〉Anonymous: "Song of Chi'le"】

天憑日月，人憑志氣。 The sky relies on the sun and moon, and people, high aspirations. 【俗語 Common saying】

我仰望星空，它是那樣寥廓而深邃；那無窮的真理，讓我苦苦地求索、追隨。 I look up at the starry sky, which is so vast and profound; the infinite truth attracts my persistent search and pursuit. 【溫家寶〈仰望星空〉Wen Jiabao: "Looking up at the Starry Sky"】

一手遮不了天。 A hand cannot cover the key. 【諺語 Proverb】

一在天上，一在地下。 One is high up in the sky, while the other is down on earth. 【俗語 Common saying】

Slander

大雪壓不矮高山。 Heavy snow cannot press the mountain low. 【俗語 Common saying】

惡語傷人六月寒。 Vicious slander makes one feel cold even in the hottest sixth month of the year. 【《增廣賢文》 Words that Open up One's Mind and Enhance One's Wisdom】

腳正不怕鞋歪。 With well-shaped feet, one is not afraid of ill-shaped shoes. 【俗語 Common saying】

利刀傷人瘡猶合，惡語傷人恨不清。 The cut by a sharp knife can be healed, but the hatred caused by vicious slanders cannot be dispelled. 【《增廣賢文》 Words that Open up One's Mind and Enhance One's Wisdom】

名之所在，謗之所歸。 Where there is fame, there will be a gathering of slanders. 【諺語 Proverb】

止謗莫如修身。 The best way to avoid slanders is to cultivate the person. 【徐幹《中論·貴言》Xu Gan: "Valuing Speech", Balanced Discourses】

Sleep

春眠不覺曉，處處聞啼鳥。 In spring, I sleep and when I wake up, I do not know it's dawn. Everywhere the chirping of the birds can be heard. 【孟浩然〈春曉〉Meng Haoran: "Daybreak in Spring"】

牛背牧兒酣午夢，不知風雨過前山。 The shepherd boy on the back of an ox is deep in his afternoon nap, without knowing that the wind and rain have passed through the mountain in front. 【劉宰〈雲邊阻雨〉Liu Zai: "Holding back by the Rain by the Side of Clouds"】

其寢不夢，其覺無憂。 He who sleeps with no dreams will wake up without worries. 【莊周《莊子·內篇·大宗師第六》：Zhuang Zhou: Chapter 6, "The Great Ancestral Teacher", "Inner Chapters", Zhuangzi】

如今但欲關門睡，一任梅花作雪飛。 Now I only want to shut myself indoors and sleep, paying no attention to the plum blossoms flying about like snow. 【朱敦儒〈鷓鴣天〉Zhu Dunru: "To the Tune of Partridge in the Sky"】

睡多了夢長。 Long sleep has long dreams. 【王令〈客次寄王正叔〉Wang Ling: "Letter to Uncle Wang Zheng While Travelling"】

睡眠是賊偷半生。 Sleep is a thief who steals half of one's life. 【俗語 Common saying】

夜中不能寐，起坐彈鳴琴。I could not sleep in the middle of the night, so I rose and sat to play my zither.【阮籍〈詠懷〉Ruan Ji:"My feelings"】

一夜不眠，十日不安。One sleepless night will make you feel uneasy for ten days.【俗語 Common saying】

早起早睡身體好。Early to bed, early to rise makes one healthy.【俗語 Common saying】

Smell

頂風也臭四十里。Stink for miles around.【張笑天《太平天國‧第三十三章》Zhang Xiaotian: Chapter 33, The Taiping Heavenly Kingdom】

狗肉滾一滾，神仙站不穩。The smell of boiling dog meat makes gods unable to stand still.【諺語 Proverb】

老太太的裹腳布 —— 又臭又長。An old woman's foot binds are stinking and long.【歇後語 End-clipper】

老鷹放屁 —— 臭氣熏天。When an eagle passes wind, it stinks to high heaven.【歇後語 End-clipper】

茅廁裏打哈欠 —— 滿嘴臭氣。When yawning in a latrine, the whole mouth is full of stench–one is using foul language.【歇後語 End-clipper】

茅廁裏的石頭，又臭又硬。Like the stone in a privy, it's hard and stinking.【歇後語 End-clipper】

入鮑魚之肆，久而不聞其臭。It's like staying long in a fish market and getting used to the stinking smell.【王肅《孔子家語‧六本》Wang Su: Volume 6, *The School Sayings of Confucius*】

Snake

打蛇不死，給蛇咬死。If one beats but fails to kill a snake, it will surely bite one to death.【俗語 Common saying】

打蛇打七寸。If you beat a snake, beat it seven inches from the head.【王有光《吳下諺聯‧第四卷》Wang Youguang: Chapter 4, *Proverb Couplets of the Wu Dialect*】

打蛇打頭，殺雞割喉。To kill a snake, beat its head. To kill a chicken, cut its throat.【俗語 Common saying】

打蛇隨竿上。 If one beats a snake with a stick, it crawls up the stick. 【俗語 Common saying】

惡蛇不咬善人。 Even ferocious snakes will not bite a good person. 【俗語 Common saying】

蛇死要擺尾，虎死跳三跳。 When a snake is dying, it wags its tail and when a tiger is dying, it jumps three times. 【諺語 Proverb】

蛇咬一口，見了黃鱔都怕。 Once bitten by a snake, one dreads the sight of an eel. 【俗語 Common saying】

蛇鑽的窟窿蛇知道。 A snake knows the hole that it has drilled. 【俗語 Common saying】

小蛇出大蟒。 A small snake can grow into a large boa. 【劉江《太行風雲》 Liu Jiang: *Changes in Taixing*】

一蛇九尾，首動尾隨；一蛇二首，不能寸進。 If a snake had nine tails, when the head moved, the tails followed. But if the snake had two heads, it cannot move even an inch. 【宋濂《元史‧姚天福傳》 Song Lian: "Biography of Yao Tianfu", *History of the Yuan*】

一淵不能兩蛇。 A deep pool cannot accommodate two snakes. 【俗語 Common saying】

一朝被蛇咬，十年怕井繩。 Once bitten by a snake, one shies at a coiled rope for the next ten years. 【俗語 Common saying】

Snow

北國風光，千里冰封，萬里雪飄。 The landscape of the northern part of the country is a thousand miles of frozen earth and ten thousand miles of whirling snow. 【毛澤東〈沁園春‧雪〉 Mao Zedong: "Snow: To the Tune of Spring in the Garden of Qin"】

冬雪勝如寶。 Winter snow is as precious as treasures. 【俗語 Common saying】

瑞雪兆豐年。 A timely snow promises a good harvest. 【曲波《橋隆飆‧第十九章》 Qu Bo: Chapter 19, *Qiao Longbiao*】

三九無雪休種麥。 If there is no snow in mid-winter, there is no way to grow wheat. 【諺語 Proverb】【李光庭《鄉言解頤‧卷一》 Li Guangting: Chapter 1, *Country Sayings to Smile at*】

山南山北雪晴，千里萬里月明。 To the south of the mountain and the north of the mountain, snow is clear. For a thousand miles and ten thousand miles, the moon is bright. 【戴叔倫〈轉應曲‧邊草〉 Dai Shulun: "Border Grass: To the Tune of Transpositions"】

下雪不冷化雪寒。 It is not cold when it snows, but when the

snow melts, it is extremely cold. 【諺語 Proverb】

一片兩片三四片，五六七八九十片，千片萬片無數片，飛入梅花總不見。 One flake, two flakes, three, and four flakes; five flakes, six flakes, seven flakes, eight flakes, nine flakes, and ten flakes; a thousand flakes, ten thousand flakes and countless flakes. When the flakes float into the plum blossoms, they can no longer be seen. 【鄭板橋〈詠雪〉 Zheng Banqiao: "Snow Flakes"】

有梅無雪不精神，有雪無詩俗了人。 When there are plum blossoms without snow, there is a lack of spirit and when there is snow without a poem, it makes people vulgar. 【盧梅坡〈雪梅〉Lu Meipo: "Snow and Plum Blossoms"】

Solution

車到山前必有路。 The cart will find its way round the hill when it gets there. 【諺語 Proverb】

船到橋頭自然直。 The boat naturally goes straight when it reaches a bridge. 【諺語 Proverb】

船頭上跑馬 —— 走投無路。 Riding a horse on the bow of a ship, one has nowhere to go. 【歇後語 End-clipper】

此路不通那路通。 If this way does not work, the other way will. 【俗語 Common saying】

大事化小，小事化了。 Turn big issues into smaller ones, and smaller ones into nothing. 【曹雪芹《紅樓夢·第六十二回》Cao Xueqin: Chapter 62, A Dream of the Red Chamber】

東河裏沒水西河裏走。 If there is no water in the east river, sail in the west river. 【諺語 Proverb】

逢山開路，遇水搭橋。 Cut paths through mountains and build bridges across river. 【紀君祥〈趙氏孤兒·楔子〉Ji Junxiang: Prologue, "The Orphan of the Zhao Family"】

蜂蠆入懷，解衣去趕。 If a wasp gets in one's bosom, remove one's coat to shake it off. 【諺語 Proverb】

耗子鑽水溝 —— 各有各的路。 Rats passing through a sewer have their own ways. 【歇後語 End-clipper】

解鈴還須繫鈴人。 It is the person who tied to bell that should untie it. 【曹雪芹《紅樓夢》Cao Xueqin: A Dream of the Red Chamber】

沒有翻不過的山，沒有渡不過的河。 There is no mountain in the world that cannot be travelled over and no river that cannot be crossed. 【諺語 Proverb】

山不轉路轉，河不彎水彎。 The mountain does not make way, but the road finds its way; the river course does not bend, the water makes it bent. 【諺語 Proverb】

頭痛醫頭，腳痛醫腳。 Treat the head when it aches, treat the foot when it hurts. 【諺語 Proverb】

揚湯止沸，不如釜底抽薪。 To stop water from boiling by scooping it up and pouring it back is not as effective as taking out the burning firewood under the pot. 【班固《漢書・董仲舒傳》 Ban Gu: "Biography of Dong Zhongshu", *History of the Han*】

一把鑰匙開一把鎖。 Use a key to open a lock. 【諺語 Proverb】

以簡制煩惑，以易御險難。 Solve the troublesome and doubtful problems with simple means and handle the dangerous and difficult situations in easy ways. 【尹文《尹文子・大道上》Yin Wen: "The Great Way, Part 1", *Yinwenzi*】

Son

愛子，教之以義方，弗納於邪。 When you love a son, you should teach him righteous ways so that he would not go into depravity. 【左丘明《左傳・隱公三年》Zuo Qiuming: "The Third Year of the Reign of Duke Yin", *Zuo's Commentary on the Spring and Autumn Annals*】

曹操的兒子 —— 奸種。 Cao Cao's son – a self-seeking sort. 【歇後語 End-clipper】

獨柴難燒，獨子難教。 A single log is hard to burn and the only son is difficult to teach. 【諺語 Proverb】

獨子成龍，獨女成鳳。 The only son becomes a dragon, the only daughter, a phoenix. 【諺語 Proverb】

兒不嫌母醜，狗不嫌主貧。 A son does not cold-shoulder an ugly mother and a dog, a poor master. 【徐啞〈殺狗記・第十六折〉Xu Ya: Scene 16, "An Account of Dog-killing"】

兒大不由爹，女大不由娘。 When a son grows up, he does not follow the instructions of his father. When a daughter grows up, she will not listen to her mother about her marriage. 【諺語 Proverb】

兒女最長情。 Sons and daughters cherish the deepest love for their parents. 【諺語 Proverb】

兒行千里母擔憂。 When the son has to travel a thousand miles, his mother is worried about him. 【諺語 Proverb】【褚人獲《隋唐演義・第二十四回》Zhu Renhuo:

兒要親生，財要自振。 A son has to be born by oneself and money should be earned by oneself. 【諺語 Proverb】

兒要自養，穀要自種。 One's own son should be brought up by oneself and grains should be grown by oneself. 【諺語 Proverb】

兒子不如女兒親。 Sons are not as close to their parents than daughters. 【俗語 Common saying】

兒子自己的好，娘子別人的好。 One's own son is good, but another one's wife is good. 【俗語 Common saying】

兒子做官歸，不如丈夫討飯歸。 A son return home in glory as an official is not as good as a husband returning home as a beggar. 【諺語 Proverb】

兒做的兒當，爹做的爹當。 What is done by the son should be borne by the son, what is done by the father, by the father. 【諺語 Proverb】

富家兒子傲，貴家女兒嬌。 The sons of a rich family are conceited and the daughters of a noble family are pampered. 【諺語 Proverb】

醬油煮雞蛋 —— 混蛋。 Eggs boiled in soy sauce are muddy eggs – son of a bitch. 【歇後語 End-clipper】

癩痢頭兒子自己的好。 The best boy in the world is one's own son, though he may be affected with favus on the head. 【俗語 Common saying】

浪子回頭金不換。 Even gold cannot exchange a prodigal son who has mended his way. 【俗語 Common saying】【張恨水《八十一夢・第三十二夢》Zhang Henshui: "The Thirty-second Dream", *Eighty-one Dreams*】

寧養頑子，莫養呆子。 Rather have a naughty son than a stupid one. 【俗語 Common saying】【周楫《西湖二集・第四卷》Zhou Ji: Chapter 4, *The West Lake, Second Volume*】

天下老，祇向小。 All parents under heaven favour their youngest child. 【俗語 Common saying】

心好家門生貴子。 If one's heart is good, a noble son will be born in the family. 【佚名《名賢集》Anonymous: *Collected Sayings of Famous Sages*】

養兒不讀書，不如養口豬。 A son who does not go to school is not as good as a pig raised at home. 【諺語 Proverb】

養兒防老，積穀防饑。 Raise children to provide against one's old age and store grain to provide against famine. 【諺語 Proverb】

一娘養九子，九子九個心。 A mother gives birth to nine sons

and all of them have their own thinking. 【俗語 Common saying】

有兒靠兒，無兒靠婿。 Having a son, one depends on his son for a living; having no son, one depends on his son-in-law. 【諺語 Proverb】【蘭陵笑笑生《金瓶梅·第二十回》Lanling Xiaoxiaosheng: Chapter 20, *The Plum in the Golden Vase*】

有兒窮不久，無子富不長。 Having a son, one cannot remain poor for long; having no son, one cannot remain rich for long. 【《增廣賢文》*Words that Open up One's Mind and Enhance One's Wisdom*】

有錢難買新生子，無錢可討有錢妻。 With money, you cannot buy a son, but without money, you canmarry a rich woman. 【俗語 Common saying】

有錢無子未為貴。 One who has money but no sons is not valued. 【俗語 Common saying】

有子莫嫌愚。 As long as you have a son, do not dislike him for his foolishness. 【施世綸《施公案·第九十回》Shi Shilun: Chapter 90, *Cases of Judge Shi*】

有子萬事足。 Having a son, one is satisfied with everything. 【蘇軾〈賀子由生第四孫〉Su Shi:"Congratulating Myself on the Birth of the Fourth Grandson"】

Song

此曲祇應天上有，人間能得幾回聞。 This piece of music should only exist in heaven above, how rare can it be heard in the world of men? 【杜甫〈贈花卿〉Du Fu:"To the Goddess of Flowers"】

其曲彌高，其和彌寡。 The more high-brow the songs are, the fewer echoes you get. 【宋玉〈對楚王問〉Song Yu:"Responding to the Question of the King of Chu"】

Sorrow

悲歡離合一台戲。 Sorrow and joy, parting and union are merely a show on the stage of life. 【俗語 Common saying】

長痛不如短痛。 A pain of a short time is better than a pain of a long time. 【俗語 Common saying】

抽刀斷水水更流，舉杯消愁愁更愁。 I draw my sword to cut the water, yet the water still flows on. I raise my cup of wine to drown my sorrow, yet it makes me more sorrowful. 【李白〈宣州謝朓樓餞別校書叔雲〉Li Bai:"Farewell

而今識盡愁滋味，欲說還休，欲說還休，卻道天涼好個秋。 Now that I have known all the taste of sorrow, I hold back when I want to speak, I hold back when I want to speak, except to say, "What a cool autumn day!"【辛棄疾〈醜奴兒〉Xin Qiji:"To the Tune of an Ugly Maid"】

舊愁未去新愁來。 While the old sorrows are still around new sorrows have come.【俗語 Common saying】

暝色入高樓，有人樓上愁。 The dusk enters the high tower, and somebody in the tower is sad.【李白〈菩薩蠻〉Li Bai:"To the Tune of Buddhist Dancers"】

莫將愁緒比飛花，花有數，愁無數。 Don't compare sorrow to falling flowers: flowers can be counted, sorrow cannot.【朱敦儒〈一落索〉Zhu Dunru:"To the Tune of One Falling Rope"】

牽牛過獨木橋 —— 難過。 Leading an ox to cross over a single-plank bridge is difficult to get across –feeling sad.【歇後語 End-clipper】

傷心橋下春波綠，曾是驚鴻照影來。 To see the green waves beneath the bridge would break my heart, for they have once reflected your shadows.【陸游〈沈園〉Lu You:"Garden of Shen"】

少年不識愁滋味，愛上層樓，愛上層樓，為賦新詞強說愁。 When I was young, I did not know the taste of sorrow: I loved to climb storied towers, I loved to climb storied towers. To write new poems, I forced myself to speak of grief.【辛棄疾〈醜奴兒〉Xin Qiji:"To the Tune of an Ugly Maid"】

天長地久有時盡，此恨綿綿無盡期。 Heaven and earth will eventually end, but this sorrow will be everlasting.【白居易〈長恨歌〉Bai Juyi:"Song of Everlasting Grief"】

天無涯兮地無邊，我心愁兮亦復然。 Heaven is endless and earth is boundless, and this is also the case with the sorrows on my mind.【蔡琰〈胡笳十八拍〉Kui Tan:"Eighteen Stanzas for a Barbarian Reed Leaf Pipe"】

問君能有幾多愁？恰似一江春水向東流。 You ask me, "How much sorrow can you bear?""As much as the waters of a whole river in spring flood flowing towards the sea."【李煜〈虞美人〉Li Yu:"To the Tune of the Beauty of Yu"】

祇恐雙溪舴艋舟，載不動，許多愁。 I only fear that the small boat of the Double Stream, could not bear so much sorrow that I have.【李清照〈武陵春〉Li Qingzhao:"To the Tune of Spring at Wuling"】

Sound

鞭炮齊鳴，鑼鼓喧天。 The air was filled with the sound of bursting firecrackers and the din of clashing gongs and drums. 【俗語 Common saying】

伐木丁丁，鳥鳴嚶嚶。 The sound of cutting trees is *dingding*, the chirping of the birds is *yingying*. 【《詩經‧小雅‧伐木》“Cutting Trees”, "Minor Odes of the Kingdom", *The Book of Odes*】

破鐘無好音。 A cracked bell does not sound well. 【俗語 Common saying】

唧唧復唧唧，木蘭當戶織。不聞機杼聲，唯聞女歎息。 Click clack and again click clack, Mulan is weaving near the door. Then the sounds of weaving stop, and what is heard is only her sighs. 【佚名〈木蘭詞〉Anonymous: "Poem of Mulan"】

聲無細而不聞，行無隱而不形。 No sound is too slight to be heard and no action is too imperceptible to be revealed. 【慎到《慎子‧外篇》Shen Dao: "Outer Chapters", *Shenzi*】

一個碗不響，兩個碗叮噹。 One bowl is quiet while two bowls give out ding-dong sounds. 【諺語 Proverb】

Source

凡木有本，是水有源。 Every tree has its roots and all water has its source. 【諺語 Proverb】

水從源流樹從根。 A river flows from its source and a tree grows from its roots. 【石玉昆《三俠五義‧第六十六回》Shi Yukun: Chapter 66, *The Three Heroes and Five Gallants*】

水有源，樹有根。 A river has its source and a tree, its roots. 【諺語 Proverb】

無本之水，涸可立待。 When a stream has no source, it will soon dry. 【孟軻《孟子‧離婁下》Meng Ke: Chapter 4, Part 2, *Mencius*】

無源之水，無本之木。 A river without a source is like a tree without roots. 【左丘明《左傳昭公九年》Zuo Qiuming: "The Ninth Year of the Reign of Duke Zhao", *Zuo's Commentary on the Spring and Autumn Annals*】

Space

處小而不逼，處大而不窕。The place is small, but it is not crowded; the place is large, but it is not spacious. 【劉安《淮南子‧原道訓第一》Liu An: Chapter 1, "Searching out the Way", *Huainanzi*】

量無窮，時無止。Space is limitless and time, eternal. 【莊周《莊子‧外篇‧秋水第十七》: Zhuang Zhou: Chapter 17, "Autumn Floods", "Outer Chapters", *Zhuangzi*】

室雅何須大，花香不在多。A room that is elegant does not need to be large, and the fragrance of flowers does not rely on their number. 【鄭板橋《板橋全集》: Zheng Banqiao: *Complete Works of Zheng Banqiao*】

Spirit

乘興而往，興盡而返。Go off in high spirits but return with a low mood. 【房玄齡等《晉書‧列傳第五十》Fang Xuanling, *et al*: Chapter 50, "Biograpies", *History of the Jin*】

獨與天地精神往來。I only communicate with the spirit of heaven and earth. 【莊周《莊子‧雜篇‧天下第三十三》Zhuang Zhou: Chapter 33, "All under Heaven", "Miscellaneous Chapters", *Zhuangzi*】

氣可鼓而不可泄。Morale should be boosted, not dampened. 【崔巍《剿蜂記》Cui Wei: *Killing Bees*】

人逢喜事精神爽，悶上心來瞌睡多。People will be in high spirits when having a happy event and when things are bored, they fall asleep mostly. 【吳承恩《西遊記》Wu Cheng'en: *Journey to the West*】

三軍可奪氣，將軍可奪心。For the entire army, you can rob of its morale; for a general, you can make him disheartened. 【孫武《孫子兵法‧軍爭第七》Sun Wu: Chapter 7, "Military Fighting", *The Art of War by Sunzi*】

身如枯木，心如死灰。One's body is like a withe Red tree, and one's spirits, dying embers. 【莊周《莊子‧內篇‧齊物論第二》Zhuang Zhou: Chapter 2, "On the Equality of Things", "Inner Chapters", *Zhuangzi*】

吾善養浩然之氣。I am good at nourishing my vast spirit. 【孟軻《孟子‧公孫丑上》Meng Ke: Chapter 2, Part 1, *Mencius*】

一鼓作氣，再而衰，三而竭。The fighting spirit aroused by the first beat of the drum is diminished by the second and extinguished by the third. 【左丘明《左傳‧莊公十年》Zuo Qiuming: "The Tenth Year of the Reign of Duke Zhuang", *Zuo's Commentary on the Spring and Autumn Annals*】

長他人志氣，滅自己威風。Boost the morale of other people and dampen one's own spirit.【吳承恩《西遊記‧第三十二回》Wu Cheng'en: Chapter 32, *Journey to the West*】

壯士氣如虹。The spirit of a brave person is like a rainbow.【諺語 Proverb】

Spring

春二三月一片青。Spring is an expanse of greenness in the second and third months of the year.【諺語 Proverb】

春風、春暖、春日、春長，春山蒼蒼，春水漾漾。The wind in spring, the warmth of spring, the days in spring, and the long period of spring. Mountains in spring are green, and waters in spring are wavy.【鄭板橋〈春詞〉Zheng Banqiao: "Song on Spring"】

春風又綠江南岸，明月何時照我還。The breeze in spring has again made the banks of the Changjiang River green, when will the bright moon guide me home with its light?【王安石〈泊船瓜州〉Wang Anshi: "Mooring My Boat at Guazhou"】

春露秋霜，夏雨冬雪。We have dew in spring, frost in autumn, rain in summer, and snow in winter.【俗語 Common saying】

春秋多佳日。There are many fine days in spring and autumn.【陶淵明〈移居二首‧其二〉Tao Yuanming: "Two Poems on Moving House, Second Poem"】

春色滿園關不住，一枝紅杏出牆來。A courtful of spring beauty cannot be contained, and a branch of red apricot stretches over the fence.【葉紹翁〈遊園不值〉Ye Shaoweng: "Visiting a Garden When the Host Was Absent"】

春宵一刻值千金，花有清香月有陰。A moment of joy on a spring night values a thousand taels of gold. Flowers have fragrance and the moon wanes.【蘇軾〈春宵〉Su Shi: "To the Tune of Water Dragon Chant"】

等閒識得東風面，萬紫千紅總是春。I feel the touch of the east wind here and there; after all spring blossoms with a blaze of colours.【朱熹〈春日〉Zhu Xi: "A Spring Day"】

簾外雨潺潺，春意闌珊。Outside the bamboo curtains, the rain was splashing, and the spring in the air began to fade.【李煜〈浪淘沙〉Li Yu: "To the Tune of Waves Washing over Sand"】

莫道今年春將盡，明年春色倍還人。Don't say that this year's spring is about to end, as the scenery of spring will be twice as enchanting next year.【杜審言〈春日京中有壞〉Tu Shenyan:"My Feelings on a Spring Day in the Capital"】

若到江南趕上春，千萬和春住。 If you catch up spring in the South, make sure not to let it slip away.【王觀〈卜算子・送鮑浩然之浙江〉Wang Guan:"Seeing off Bao Haoran Who Leaves for Zhejiang: To the Tune of Divination"】

若有人知春去處，喚取歸來同住。 If you know where spring is today, please call her back to stay.【黃庭堅〈清平樂〉Huang Tingjian:"To the Tune of Purity and Peace"】

三春不趕一秋忙。 Three springs are not as busy as one autumn.【周立波《暴風驟雨・第一部第二十一章》Zhou Libo: Chapter 21, Volume 1, *Violent Storms and Heavy Showers*】

三分春色二分愁，更一分風雨。 Two-thirds of spring are sorrows, and the remaining one-third, wind and rain.【葉清臣〈賀聖朝〉Ye Qingcheng:"Congratulations to the Holy Court"】

山色滿園春雨後，一簾風絮捲春歸。 The tints of the mountain wrapped the entire garden after a rain in spring and a curtain of catkins rolls up the spring that is on its way out.【史彌寧〈春暮同社會飯張圓小樓分韻得飛字〉Shi Nining:"Dining at a Small Tower"】

生意忽滿眼，不知春淺深。 Suddenly a scene of vitality

fills my eyes, and I don't know how long spring has been with us.【方孝孺〈上己約友登南樓〉Fang Xiaoru:"Climbing up the South Tower with My Friend"】

樹木吐葩春臨近。 When flowers on the trees start to blossom, spring is approaching.【俗語 Common saying】

送春春去幾時回。 Spring is now going away, when will it come back again?【張先〈天仙子〉Zhang Xian:"To the Tune of Angels in the Sky"】

一花獨放不是春，百花齊放春滿園。 The blooming of a single flower does not make a spring; when one hundred flowers blossom, spring is in the garden.【諺語 Proverb】

一片花飛減卻春，風飄萬點正愁人。 A flurry of flying flowers signals the passing of the spring and thousands of petals floating in the wind brings sorrows to me.【杜甫〈曲江二首〉Du Fu:"Twisted River: Two Selections"】

鶯花猶怕春光老，豈可教人枉度春。 Even orioles and flowers are worried about the fading away of the spring scenery, how can one teach people to idle away their youth?【《增廣賢文》Words that Open up One's Mind and Enhance One's Wisdom】

祇消幾日懵騰醉，看得春風到牡丹。 It only takes a few days for us to stay dead drunk, then we can see the spring breeze blowing the peony. 【張昱〈春日〉 Zhang Yu: "Spring Day"】

最是一年春好處，絕勝煙柳滿皇都。 This is by far the best place in spring in the entire year, far better than the time when mists and willows embrace the imperial capital. 【韓愈〈初春小雨〉 Han Yu: "Drizzle in Early Spring"】

Star

七八個星天外，兩三點雨山前。 Beyond the sky, seven or eight stars; in front of the mountain, two or three drops of rain. 【辛棄疾〈西江月〉 Xin Qiji: "To the Tune of Moon in the West River"】

星垂平野闊，月涌大江流。 Stars hang over the vast flat plain and the moon surges in the water of the Changjiang River. 【杜甫〈旅夜書懷〉 Du Fu: "Venting My Feeling While Travelling at Night"】

Stealing

嫦娥應悔偷靈藥，碧海青天夜夜心。 Chang E should regret stealing the elixir of life, for night after night, her heart is with the green sea and blue sky. 【李商隱〈嫦娥〉 Li Shangyin: "Chang E, Lady of the Moon"】

虎餓要吃人，人窮起盜心。 When a tiger is hungry, it will eat people and when a man is poor, he is apt to steal. 【諺語 Proverb】

饑寒起盜心。 When one is hungry and cold, one is tempted to steal. 【《增廣賢文》 Words that Open up One's Mind and Enhance One's Wisdom】

今日偷針，明日偷金。 When one steals needles today, one will steal money in the future. 【諺語 Proverb】

年年防旱，夜夜防盜。 Guard against famine year after year. Guard against thieves night after night. 【《增廣賢文》 Words that Open up One's Mind and Enhance One's Wisdom】

寧可餓死，不可行竊。 One would rather die of hunger than resort to stealing. 【俗語 Common saying】

強盜碰着賊爺爺 —— 黑吃黑。 A robber being robbed by a thief – one bad person taking advantage of another. 【歇後語 End-clipper】

強盜照相 —— 賊頭賊腦。 A robber taking his own photo looks stealthy. 【歇後語 End-clipper】

竊鈎者誅，竊國者王。 Those who steal a hook would be executed

while those who steal the throne would become kings. 【莊周《莊子·內篇·逍遙遊第一》Zhuang Zhou: Chapter 1, "Carefree Wandering", "Inner Chapters", *Zhuangzi*】

情願獨偷一隻狗，不願合偷一隻牛。 Rather steal a dog by oneself than steal an ox with a partner. 【諺語 Proverb】

人贓現獲，百喙難辭。 When the thief and his booty are caught at the same time, there is no way to defend himself even he has a hundred mouths. 【李伯元《活地獄·第四十一回》Li Boyuan: Chapter 41, *Living Hell*】

三討不如一偷。 To beg three times is not as good as to steal once. 【吳敬梓《儒林外史·第二十一回》Wu Jingzi: Chapter 21, *An Unofficial History of the World of Literati*】

門戶不關緊，聖賢起盜心。 An open door may tempt a sage. 【諺語 Proverb】

手腳不乾淨。 Be light-fingered. 【俗語 Common saying】

疏忽招賊盜。 Negligence invites thieves. 【俗語 Common saying】

偷不着雞丟把米。 Go for wool and come back shorn. 【俗語 Common saying】

偷吃不肥，做賊不富。 Sneaking food does not make one grow fat and stealing does not make one rich. 【諺語 Proverb】

偷的鑼兒敲不得。 One cannot beat a stolen gong. 【曹雪芹《紅樓夢·第六十五回》Cao Xueqin: Chapter 65, *A Dream of the Red Chamber*】

偷風不偷月，偷雨不偷雪。 A thief steals on windy but not moonlit nights, on rainy but not snowy nights. 【諺語 Proverb】【周楫《西湖二集·第十三卷》Zhou Ji: Chapter 13, *The West Lake, Second Volume*】

小時偷針，大時偷金。 When one steals needles in boyhood, one will steal money when grown up. 【諺語 Proverb】

野賊好捉，家賊難防。 A thief from outside can be caught easily but a thief from within is hard to guard against. 【釋普濟《五燈會元·卷三十七》Shi Puji: Chapter 37, *A Compendium of the Five Lamps*】

一不偷，二不搶。 We don't steal things nor rob people. 【俗語 Common saying】

一次做賊，下次手癢。 Once you start to steal, you will do it again. 【俗語 Common saying】

賊偷一更，防賊一夜。 A thief steals at a certain watch of the night but our efforts to prevent the thief from stealing take up the entire evening. 【俗語 Common saying】

Strategy

逮雀兒也捨一把米。 To catch birds, one needs to spread a handful of rice as bait. 【諺語 Proverb】【崔復生《太行志・第十九章》Cui Fusheng: Chapter 19, *Records of Taixing*】

道高一尺，魔高一丈。 When virtue rises one foot, vice rises ten. 【吳承恩《西遊記・第五十回》Wu Cheng'en: Chapter 50, *Journey to the West*】

敵強用智，敵弱用勢。 Conquer a strong enemy by strategy and subdue a weak enemy by force. 【崔鴻《十六國春秋・第一卷》Cui Hong: Chapter 1, *The Spring and Autumn of the Sixteen States*】

多用兵不如巧用計。 A clever use of strategies is better than the deployment of more soldiers. 【劉江《太行風雲・第四回》Liu Jiang: Chapter 4, *Changes in Taixing*】

逢強智取，逢弱活擒。 Use a strategy when facing a strong enemy and capture it alive when the enemy is weak. 【石玉崑《小五義・第一百一十回》Shi Yukun: Chapter 110, *The Five Younger Gallants*】

趕人不可趕上。 Don't drive a person into a corner. 【錢彩《說岳全傳・第七十九回》Qian Cai: Chapter 79, *A Story of Yue Fei*】

攻城為下，攻心為上。 Capturing a town is secondary, while winning the heart of the people is primary. 【陳壽《三國志・蜀書・馬謖傳》Chen Shou:"Biography of Ma Su", "History of the State of Shu", *Records of the Three Kingdoms*】

攻其無備，出其不意。 Strike when the enemy is unprepared and do what the enemy does not expect. 【孫武《孫子兵法・始計第一》Sun Wu: Chapter 1, "Initial Estimations", *The Art of War by Sunzi*】

將欲敗之，必姑輔之。 If you want to defeat your enemy, you must first yield a little. 【劉向《戰國策・魏策一》Liu Xiang:"Strategies of the State of Wei, No.1", *Strategies of the Warring States*】

將欲奪之，必固與之。 If you want to take, you must first give. 【老子《道德經・第三十六章》Laozi: Chapter 36, *Daodejing*】

將欲廢之，必固興之。 If you want to get rid of something, you must promote it first. 【老子《道德經・第三十六章》Laozi: Chapter 36, *Daodejing*】

將欲取之，必姑與之。 If you want to take, you must first give. 【劉向《戰國策・魏策一》Liu Xiang:"Strategies of the State of Wei, No.1", *Strategies of the Warring States*】

將欲弱之，必固強之。 If you want to weaken a thing, you must strengthen it first. 【老子《道德經・第三十六章》Laozi: Chapter 36, *Daodejing*】

將欲歙之，必固張之。 If you want something to shrink, you must first stretch it. 【老子《道德經·第三十六章》Laozi: Chapter 36, *Daodejing*】

將者，國之輔也。 Generals are the guardians of the country. 【孫武《孫子兵法·謀攻第三》Sun Wu: Chapter 3, "Attack by Stratagem", *The Art of War by Sunzi*】

將者，智、信、仁、勇、嚴也。 A general is one who has wisdom, faith, benevolence, courage, and rigour. 【孫武《孫子兵法·始計第一》Sun Wu: Chapter 1, "Initial Estimations", *The Art of War by Sunzi*】

力貴疾，智貴卒。 To resort to force, one should be vigorous; to take by strategy, one should be quick. 【呂不韋《呂氏春秋·貴卒》Lu Buwei: "Valuing the Soldiers", *Master Lu's Spring and Autumn Annals*】

眉頭一皺，計上心頭。 When one knits one's brows, a stratagem comes to one's mind. 【馬致遠〈漢宮秋·第一折〉Ma Zhiyuan: Scene 1, "Autumn in the Han Palace"】

你有關門計，我有跳牆法。 You have your strategy, I have mine. 【俗語 Common saying】

三十六着，走為上着。 Of all the thirty-six stratagems, running away is the best. 【蕭子顯《南齊書·王敬則傳》Xiao Zixian: "Biography of Wang Jingze", *History of the Southern Qi*】

善出奇者，無窮如天地，不竭如江河。 Those who are good at surprise tactics have strategies which are inexhaustible as heaven and earth and unending as rivers and lakes. 【孫武《孫子兵法，兵勢第五》Sun Wu: Chapter 5: "Strategic Military Power", *The Art of War by Sunzi*】

上有政策，下有對策。 The higher authorities have policies, the localities have their counter-measures. 【俗語 Common saying】

射人先射馬，擒賊先擒王。 In shooting a rider, shoot his horse first; in capturing the robbers, capture their chief first. 【杜甫〈前出塞〉Du Fu: "First Series on Going out of the Border"】

先下手為強，後下手遭殃。 He who acts first prevails; he who acts late suffers. 【吳承恩《西遊記·第八十一回》Wu Cheng'en: Chapter 81, *Journey to the West*】

一計不成，又生二計。 When one tactic fails, one comes up with another. 【俗語 Common saying】

一人計短，二人計長。 Two heads are better than one. 【黃谷柳《蝦球傳·第二部第十四章》Huang Guliu: Chapter 14, Volume 2, *Biography of Prawns*】

一手硬一手軟。 Promote one thing and neglect another thing at the same time. 【俗語 Common saying】

以近待遠，以佚待勞。 Wait at a close distance for the faraway. Wait at one's ease for the fatigued.Close to the field of battle, the army awaits an enemy coming from afar; at rest, the army awaits a fatigued enemy.【劉向《戰國策・秦策》Liu Xiang:"Strategies of the State of Qin", *Strategies of the Warring States*】

以子之矛，攻子之盾。 Use one's own spear to attack one's own shield.【韓非《韓非子・難一第三十六》Han Fei: Chapter 36, "Criticisms of the Ancients", *Hanfeizi*】

用兵之法，十則圍之，五則攻之，倍則分之。 In deploying troops, when the enemy are outnumbered by ten to one, surround them; by five to one, attack them; by two to one, divide them.【孫武《孫子兵法・謀攻第二》Sun Wu. Chapter 3:"Attack by Stratagem", *The Art of War by Sunzi*】

有大略者不可責以捷巧，有小智者不可任以大功。 He who has overall strategies should not be entrusted with things requiring simple skills and he who has mediocre intelligence should not be entrusted with significant services.【劉安《淮南子・主術訓第九》Liu An: Chapter 9, "Craft of the Ruler", *Huainanzi*】

運籌帷幄之中，決勝千里之外。 Sit in a commander tent and devise strategies that will assure victory in a thousand miles away.【司馬遷《史記・高祖本紀》Sima Qian:"Annals of Gaozu", *Records of the Grand Historian*】

運用之妙，存乎一心。 Ingenuity in applying strategies depends on hard thinking.【脫脫等《宋史・岳飛傳》Toktoghan, et al:"Biography of Yue Fei", *History of the Song*】

爭取多數，孤立少數。 Win over the majority and isolate the minority.【俗語 Common saying】

指東打西，指南打北。 Point east but attack west and point south but attack north.【文康《兒女英雄傳・第六回》Wen Kang: Chapter 6, *Biographies of Young Heroes and Heroines*】

祇能智取，不可力敵。 We could only win by strategy, not by force.【施耐庵《水滸傳・第四十二回》Shi Nai'an: Chapter 42, *Outlaws of the Marshes*】

Strengths and weaknesses

表壯不如裏壯。 Inner power counts more than outward strength.【施耐庵《水滸傳・第二十二回》Shi Nai'an: Chapter 22, *Outlaws of the Marshes*】

尺有所短，寸有所長。 A foot has its shortness and an inch, its longness.【屈原《楚辭・卜居》Qu Yuan:"Living", *The Songs of Chu*】

打鐵先得本身硬。 To strike iron, the striker must be strong.【諺語 Proverb】

刀越磨越亮，人越煉越強。 A sword becomes sharper with more whetting and a person become stronger with more tempering.【諺語 Proverb】

刀在石上磨，鋼在火中煉。 A knife is sharpened on the grindstone and steel is tempered in fire.【諺語 Proverb】

獨拳難打虎。 A single fist is difficult to subdue a tiger.【諺語 Proverb】

方木頭不滾，圓木頭不穩。 A square log does not roll and a round log is not steady.【諺語 Proverb】

見人之失，知己之失。 Seeing the shortcomings of others, one sees one's own.【諺語 Proverb】

強者必怒於言，懦者必怒於色。 People with a strong character will express their anger in words and people with a weak character, in facial expression.【韓愈〈原毀〉Han Yu: "Inquiry into the Origin of Slander"】

取人之長，補己之短。 Learn from others' strengths to overcome one's weaknesses.【孟軻《孟子‧滕文公上》Meng Ke: Chapter 5, Part 1, Mencius】

人多力量大，柴多火焰高。 The more the number of people, the more is the strength. The more the firewood, the higher is the flame.【諺語 Proverb】

人有所短，乃見所長。 One's weaknesses reveal one's strengths.【司馬光《資治通鑒‧卷一百九十五》Sima Guang: Chapter 195, Comprehensive Mirror to Aid in Government】

柔能克剛，弱能制強。 The soft can conquer the hard and the weak can control the strong.【范曄《後漢書‧臧宮傳》Fan Ye: "Biography of Zang Gong", History of the Later Han】

弱不可以敵強，寡不可以敵眾。 The weak cannot resist against the strong, nor a few against many.【孟軻《孟子‧梁惠王上》Meng Ke: Chapter 1, Part 1, Mencius】

樹怕剝皮，人怕揭短。 A tree is afraid of peeling and a person, of muckraking.【諺語 Proverb】

勿道人之短。 Don't speak of others' shortcomings.【崔瑗《座右銘》Cui Yuan: My Mottos】

以己之長比人之短。 / 以己之長攻人之短。 Compare one's strong points with others' weak points./ Use one's strong points to attack others' weak points.【諺語 Proverb】

由小到大，由弱到強。 From small to large, from weak to strong.【俗語 Common saying】

Student

弟子不必不如師，師不必賢於弟子。A student may not be inferior to his teacher and the teacher may not be more virtuous than his student. 【韓愈《昌黎先生集 · 師說》Han Yu: "On Teachers", *Collected Works of Han Yu*】

弟子三千，賢人七十二。Of the three thousand students of Confucius, seventy-two were sages. 【佚名《名醫集》Anonymous: *Collected Sayings of Famous Sages*】

青出於藍而勝於藍。Blue is extracted from the indigo plant but is bluer than the plant it comes from. 【荀況《荀子 · 勸學第一》Xun Kuang: Chapter 1, "Exhortation to Learning", *Xunzi*】

桃李滿天下。One has students all over the world. 【司馬光《資治通鑒 · 唐紀 · 武后久視元年》Sima Guang: "The First Year of the Reign of Jiushi of Empress Wu", "Annals of the Tang Dynasty", *Comprehensive Mirror to Aid in Government*】

Study

讀書患不多，思義患不明。In studying, one suffers from not reading many books; in thinking, one suffers from not clear about meanings. 【韓愈〈贈別元十八協律六首〉Han Yu: "Presented to Yuan the Eighteenth, Six Poems"】

讀書有三到：謂心到，眼到，口到。In studying, there are three approaches: they are called the approach of the heart, the approach of the eyes, and the approach of the mouth. 【朱熹〈訓學齋規〉Zhu Xi: "Rules for Exhortation to Study"】

凡學之不勤，必其志之未篤也。All those who are not diligent in their study are surely due to their lack of determination. 【列禦寇《列子 · 說符第八》Lie Yukou: Chapter 8, "Explaining Conjunctions", *Liezi*】

黑髮不知勤學早，轉眼便是白頭翁。One who does not realize that one has to work hard at an early age will become a white-haired old man in the twinkling of an eye. 【《增廣賢文》*Words that Open up One's Mind and Enhance One's Wisdom*】

勤學如春起之苗，不見其增，日有所長。Studying hard is like growing seedlings in spring; you can't see their growth, yet they are growing day by day. 【陶淵明〈歸去來兮辭〉Tao Yuanming: "Returning Home"】

勤學雖苦，其果卻甜。Though intensive study is hard, its fruit is sweet. 【諺語 Proverb】

三更燈火五更雞。 Stay up reading till midnight under a lit lamp and rise early at dawn when cocks first crow. 【顏真卿〈勸學〉Yan Zhenqing: "Exhortation to Study"】

少年不知勤學早，白頭方悔讀書遲。 He who does not study diligently in his youth will, when old, repent that he puts it off till it is too late. 【顏真卿〈勸學〉Yan Zhenqing: "Exhortation to Study"】

少小須勤學，文章可立身。 One must study hard at an early age. One's writings can help one live well in the world. 【汪洙〈神童詩〉Wang Zhu: "Poem of a Talented Boy"】

書生不離學房。 A scholar does not leave his study. 【文康《兒女英雄傳‧第三十一回》Wen Kang: Chapter 31, *Biographies of Young Heroes and Heroines*】

鐵硯磨窮，寒氈坐破。 One studies so hard that an ink-slab made of iron is worn through and a felt blanket is worn out for sitting on it for a long time. 【方汝浩《東度記‧第三十四回》Fang Ruhao: Chapter 34, *Passage to the East*】

萬般皆下品，惟有讀書高。 All pursuits are base, book-learning is exalted. 【汪洙〈神童詩〉Wang Zhu: "Poem of a Talented Boy"】

為學當先立志，修身當先知恥。 In studying, one must first makes one's determination; in the cultivation of the person, one must first know what shame

is. 【傅山《霜紅龕集》Fu Shan: *Collected Works from the Frosty Red House*】

為學讀書，須是耐煩。 In studying and reading books, one has to be patient. 【張洪〈朱子讀書法‧一‧熟讀精思〉Zhang Hong: "Zhu Xi's Method of Reading Books, No.1, Read It Through and Think Deeply"】

為學之道，莫先於窮理；窮理之要，必先於讀書。 The way of studying must begin with a full exploration of the principles and the essence of a full exploration of the principles must begin with reading books. 【朱熹〈甲寅行宮便殿奏劄二〉Zhu Xi: "Second Memorial to the Emperor in His Temporary Dwelling Palace in the Year of Jiayin"】

學其上，僅得其中；學其中，斯為下矣。 When you set a high standard in your study, you only get to a medium level; when you set a medium standard in your study, you only get to a low level. 【嚴羽《滄浪詩話‧詩辯》Yan Yu: Chapter 19, "Poetic Analysis", *Canglang Poetry Talks*】

學問勤中得，螢窗萬卷書。 Learning is acquired through diligence, reading ten thousand volumes of books under the window lit by glowworms. 【汪洙〈神童詩〉Wang Zhu: "Poem of a Talented Boy"】

循序而漸進，熟讀而精思。 Follow an orderly way in learning to move ahead gradually; read thoroughly and think meticulously.【朱熹〈讀書之要〉Zhu Xi: "The Essence of Studying"】

業精於勤荒於嬉，行成於思毀於隨。 One's study advances with diligence but it is retarded by indolence; one's deed is accomplished by thinking but it is destroyed by thoughtlessness.【韓愈〈進學解〉Han Yu: "Explanation of Progress in One's Study"】

幼而學者，如日出之光；老而學者，如秉燭夜行。 One who studies young is like the light of the sun at dawn; one who studies in old age is like the light of a candle when walking at night.【顏之推《顏氏家訓・勉學》Yan Zhitui: "Exhortation to Learning", *Family Instructions of Master Yan*】

知人無務，不若愚而好學。 An intelligent person who does not study hard is not as good as a slow-witted person who studies hard.【劉安《淮南子・修務訓第十九》Liu An: Chapter 19, "Necessity of Training", *Huainanzi*】

輟學如磨刀之石，不見其損，日有所虧。 Stop studying is like a grinding stone for knives; you can't see its erosion, yet it is losing day after day.【陶淵明〈歸去來兮辭〉Tao Yuanming: "Returning Home"】

Success

百年成之不足，一日敗之有餘。 A hundred years is not enough to achieve something, but a day is more than enough to destroy it.【《增廣賢文》*Words that Open up One's Mind and Enhance One's Wisdom*】

不成功，便成仁。 To win or to die.【諺語 Proverb】

不榮通，不醜窮。 Don't be arrogant when you are successful and don't feel repulsive when you are poor.【莊周《莊子・外篇天地第十二》Zhuang Zhou: Chapter 12, "Heaven and Earth", "Outer Chapters", *Zhuangzi*】

長風破浪會有時，直掛雲帆濟滄海。 When the time for the long wind cleaving the waves comes, I will hoist the sails as high as the clouds to sail across the dark blue sea.【李白〈行路難〉Li Bai: "Hard is the Way of the World"】

成功不驕傲，失敗不氣餒。 When one succeeds, one should not be arrogant. When one fails, one should not get upset.【商鞅《商君書・戰法》Shang Yang: "Military Strategy", *The Works of Shang Yang*】

成功屬於勤者。 Success belongs to the diligent.【諺語 Proverb】

成也蕭何，敗也蕭何。 The success owes to Xiao He and the failure also owes to Xiao He.【馬

致遠〈蟾宮曲〉Ma Zhiyuan:"To the Tune of the Toad Palace"】

成則運也，敗則命也。I succeed by luck; I fail by destiny. 【俗語 Common saying】

達則兼善天下。When one has succeeded in getting what one wants, one strives to benefit others in the world. 【孟軻《孟子・盡心章句上》Meng Ke: Chapter 7, Part 1, *Mencius*】

凡事無捷徑。There is no shortcut to success. 【諺語 Proverb】

功成而弗居。One does not claim credit for success. 【老子《道德經・第八章》Laozi: Chapter 8, *Daodejing*】

好的開始是成功的一半。Well begun is half done. 【俗語 Common saying】

良好的開端，成功的一半。A good beginning is half the battle. 【俗語 Common saying】

民之從事，常於幾成而敗之。People often fail on the verge of success. 【老子《道德經・第六十四章》Laozi: Chapter 8, *Daodejing*】

明君賢將，能以上智為間者，必成大功。Wise rulers, good generals, and the highly-intelligent who can serve as spies, is a sure guarantee of great success. 【孫武《孫子兵法・用間第十三》Sun Wu: Chapter 13, "The Deployment of Spies", *The Art of War by Sunzi*】

貧賤憂戚，庸玉汝於成也。Poverty, low position, worries, and depression all help a person to achieve success. 【張載《西銘》Zhang Zai: *The Western Inscriptions*】

勤勉為成功之本。Industry is the parent of success. 【諺語 Proverb】

人有得意日，狗有稱心時。A person has his hour, a dog, his day. 【諺語 Proverb】

若要好，大作小。If you want to be successful, you must be humble and modest even if you are in a high position. 【諺語 Proverb】【吳承恩《西遊記・第八十七回》Wu Cheng'en: Chapter 87, *Journey to the West*】

世事有成必有敗，為人有興必有衰。In mundane affairs, there are successes as well as failures. In human life, there are rises and falls. 【施耐庵《水滸傳・第一百一十四回》Shi Nai'an: Chapter 114, *Outlaws of the Marshes*】

是非成敗轉頭空，青山依舊在，幾度夕陽紅。Right or wrong, success or failure become nothing in an instant; the green hills are still there to witness time and again the red sunsets. 【楊慎〈臨江仙・說秦漢〉Yang Shen:"Chatting about Qin and Han Dynasties: To the Tune of an Immortal by the River"】

事敗垂成多矣。In many cases one falls short of success at the very last step. 【諺語 Proverb】

太上無敗，其次敗而有以成。The best is to have no defeat, and the second best is to have defeat but there is still something achieved.【墨翟《墨子・親士卷一》Mo Di: Chapter 1: "Staying Close to Scholars", *Mozi*】

為者如牛毛，獲者如麟角。Doers are numerous like hairs on an ox, but those who succeed are as rare as unicorn's horns.【葛洪《抱朴子・內篇・極言第十三》Ge Hong: Chapter 13, "The Ultimate Words about Immortality", "Inner Chapters", *The Master Who Embraces Simplicity*】

小挫之後，反有大獲。A small setback could lead to a great success.【俗語 Common saying】【曾樸《續孽海花・第四十三回》Zeng Pu: Chapter 43, *Sequel to Flower on an Ocean of Sin*】

一事成，事事成。Nothing succeeds like success.【俗語 Common saying】

祇許成功，不許失敗。One has to succeed without fail.【俗語 Common saying】

自信是成功的第一秘訣。Self-trust is the first secret of success.【俗語 Common saying】

Suffering

白骨露於野，千里無雞鳴。
生民百遺一，念之斷人腸。
White bones are exposed in the wilderness and there is no cock crowing for a thousand miles. Only one in a hundred people survives. When I think of this, it breaks my heart.【曹操〈蒿里行〉Cao Cao: "Overgrown with Bambles"】

城門失火，殃及池魚。A fire on the city gate brings disaster to the fish in the moat.【杜弼〈檄梁文〉Du Bi: "War Proclamation against Liang"】

吃二遍苦，受二茬罪。Suffer once again.【俗語 Common saying】

吃過苦頭，方知甜頭。One who has suffered knows best what is sweetness.【俗語 Common saying】

吃苦在先，享樂在後。First suffer the hardship, then enjoy comfort.【俗語 Common saying】

覆巢之下無完卵。When the nest is overturned, no eggs will remain intact.【劉義慶《世說新語・言語第二》Liu Yiqing: Chapter 2, "Speech and Conversation", *A New Account of the Tales of the World*】

好了瘡疤忘了疼。Forget the pain once the wound is healed.【俗語 Common saying】

後生苦，風吹過；老來苦，真難過。Suffering in one's youth passes easily like winds, but suffering in one's old age is really hard to bear.【俗語 Common saying】

壞人當道，好人受苦。When evildoers are in power, good people suffer.【俗語 Common saying】

開水淋臭蟲 —— 不死也夠受。A bedbug under a shower of boiling water – unbearably painful.【歇後語 End-clipper】

人生在世，痛苦難免。Living in this world, people unavoidably would have to suffer pain.【俗語 Common saying】

如吞苦丸，有苦難言。It is like swallowing bitter pills – it is hard to tell the pain.【俗語 Common saying】

啞巴吃黃蓮 —— 有苦說不出。A dumb person, when eating japonica, is unable to tell others his suffering.【歇後語 End-clipper】

啞子吃黃蓮 —— 有苦自己知。A dumb person, when eating japonica, only he himself knows his own suffering.【歇後語 End-clipper】

一時之苦，終身受惠。A moment of suffering benefits one a lifetime.【俗語 Common saying】

一時之樂，終身之苦。A moment of happiness causes a lifetime of suffering.【俗語 Common saying】

summer

暑退九霄淨，秋澄萬景清。The retreat of summer makes the sky clean and the shiny autumn moon makes everything clear.【劉禹錫〈八月十五夜玩月〉Liu Yuxi:"Watching the Moon on the Evening of the Fifteenth Day of the Eighth Month of the Lunar Year"】

孤燕不成夏。One swallow does not make a summer.【俗語 Common saying】

四時皆是夏，一雨便成秋。All the year round it is like summer, but one rainfall makes it as cool as autumn.【諺語 Proverb】

一燕不成夏。One swallow does not make a summer.【俗語 Common saying】

Sun

白日依山盡，黃河入海流。The sun goes down behind the mountains, and the Yellow River flows into the sea.【王之渙〈登黃鶴樓〉Wang Zhihuan:"Climbing up the Yellow Crane Tower"】

大漠孤煙直，長河落日圓。In the boundless desert, the lonely smoke rises straight and in the long river, the setting sun sinks round.【王維〈使至塞上〉Wang Wei:"On Mission to the Frontier"】

秋陽如老虎。The sun in autumn is like a tiger.【諺語 Proverb】

山映斜陽天接水，芳草無情，更在斜陽外。Mountains reflect the setting sun and water merges with heavens.Fragrant grass, being void of passion, lies further beyond the setting sun.【范仲淹〈蘇幕遮‧懷舊幕〉Fan Zhongyan:"Missing My Old Colleagues: To the Tune of Painted Hat"】

太陽從西邊出來。When the sun rises in the west.【俗語 Common saying】

太陽雖暖不當衣，牆上畫馬不能騎。The sun, though warm, cannot be worn as a piece of clothing; a painted horse is not meant for riding.【諺語 Proverb】

無日無光，萬物不長。Without sun, there is no light and the myriad things cannot grow.【俗語 Common saying】

夕陽方在半，忽墮亂流中。The setting sun is hanging in the middle of the sky, but all of a sudden it falls into the fast-flowing water of the river.【郭麟〈登吳山望江〉Guo Lin:"Climbing Mount Wu to Look at the River"】

夕陽勸客登樓去，山色將秋繞郭來。The setting sun attracted visitors to climb the tower to watch and the tints of the mountain brings autumn here through the city walls.【黃景仁〈都門秋思〉HuangJingren:"Autumn Thoughts at Doumen"】

夕陽無限好，祇是近黃昏。The setting sun is infinitely beautiful, only that dusk is drawing near.【李商隱〈登樂游原〉Li Shangyin:"Ascending the Leyou Plain"】

夕陽西下，斷腸人在天涯。The setting sun goes down in the west, and the heart-broken person is at the end of the world.【馬致遠〈天淨沙‧秋思〉Ma Zhiyuan:"Autumn Yearnings: To the Tune of Sky-cleaned Sand"】

夕陽西下幾時回。When will the sun, which is setting in the west, come back again?【晏殊〈浣溪沙〉Yan Shu:"To the Tune of Sand of Silk-washing Stream"】

一輪紅日，萬道霞光。A red sun with myriad shimmering rays.【俗語 Common saying】

一輪紅日倚青山，祇見湖光數里間。The setting sun rests at the green mountains, and the light of the lake can be seen several miles.【宋伯仁〈西湖晚歸〉Song Boren:"Returning Home Late at the West Lake"】

Superior and subordinate

上不緊則下慢。 If the superior does not grasp firmly, the subordinates will act slowly. 【施耐庵《水滸傳・第十七回》Shi Nai'an: Chapter 17, *Outlaws of the Marshes*】

上不正，下參差。 When the superiors behave unworthily, the inferiors will do worse. 【楊泉《物理論》Yang Quan: *On Metaphysics*】

上明不知下暗。 Even a wise superior does not know the dark sides of his subordinates. 【張國賓〈薛仁貴・第一折〉Zhang Guobin: Scene 1, "Xue Rengui"】

上人不好，下人不要。 If the superior does not express his fondness of something, the subordinates will not do it. 【俗語 Common saying】

上有所好，下必甚焉。 What is loved by those above will be loved all the more by those below. 【孟軻《孟子・滕文公上》Meng Ke: Chapter 5, Part 1, *Mencius*】

Support

百柱載梁，千歲不僵。 When there are one hundred pillars supporting the beam, the beam will not collapse in one thousand years. 【焦延壽《焦氏易林・歸象之四》Jiao Yanshou:"Returning to the Images, No.4", *Thoughts on The Book of Changes by Master Jiao*】

背靠大樹有柴燒。 With big trees around, there will certainly be firewood. 【俚語 Slang】

大樹底下好乘涼。 There is good shade under a big tree. 【佚名〈劉弘嫁婢・第一折〉Anonymous: Scene 1, "Liu Hong Marrying His Maid"】

大樹之下，草不沾霜。 Under a big tree, grass will not be frosted. 【諺語 Proverb】

得道多助，失道寡助。 One who has the Way will have many to support him, while one who does not will have few to support him. 【孟軻《孟子・公孫丑下》Meng Ke: Chapter 2, Part 2, *Mencius*】

扶起不扶倒。 Help those who can stand on their own feet but not those who can't. 【羅懋登《三寶太監西洋記・第十二回》Luo Maodeng: Chapter 12, *The Western Voyage of the Eunuch of Three Treasures*】

荷花雖好，也要綠葉扶。 Though lotus flowers are lovely, they still need the support of green leaves to set off their beauty. 【俗語 Common saying】

紅花雖好，綠葉扶持。 With all its beauty the red flower needs the

green of its leaves to set it off. 【俗
語 Common saying】

花兒好還得綠葉扶。 Though
flowers are lovely, they still need
the support of green leaves to
set off their beauty. 【諺語 Proverb】

吉凶相救，患難相扶。 The
fortuneate help the unfortunate
and those in trouble support
each other. 【羅貫中《三國演義·第
六十回》Luo Guanzhong: Chapter 60,
Romance of the Three Kingdoms】

接人要一世，怪人祇一次。 When
you aid a person, you aid him
all your life. When you blame
a person, you blame him just
once. 【馮夢龍《警世通言·第二十五
卷》Feng Menglong: Chapter 25, *Stories
to Caution the World*】

牡丹雖好，仍要綠葉扶持。
Though the peony is lovely, it
still needs the support of green
leaves to set off its beauty. 【文康
《兒女英雄傳·第十九回》Wen Kang:
Chapter 19, *Biographies of Young Heroes
and Heroines*】

同甘共苦，患難相扶。 Share joys
and sorrows with one's friends
and support one another in
adversity. 【諺語 Proverb】

土幫土成牆，窮幫窮成王。 Earth
sticks to earth to form a wall and
the poor sticks to the poor to
make a kingdom. 【諺語 Proverb】

相濡以沫，不如相忘於江湖。
Instead of sticking together and
suffering in a drying brooklet,
it would be better to forget
each other and swim freely in
the rivers and lakes. 【莊周《莊
子·內篇·大宗師第六》；Zhuang
Zhou: Chapter 6, "The Great Ancestral
Teacher", "Inner Chapters", *Zhuangzi*】

朽木不可以為柱。 Rotten wood
cannot be used as pillars. 【班固
《漢書·劉輔傳》Ban Gu: "Biography of
Liu Fu", *History of the Han*】

一個籬笆三個樁，一個好漢三人
幫。 A fence needs the support
of three stakes and an able
fellow needs the help of three
other people. 【諺語 Proverb】

一木焉能支大廈。 How can a
single log support a mansion?
【諺語 Proverb】

Surface

表面是人，暗中是鬼。 A human
being in appearance but a
demon at heart. 【諺語 Proverb】

貌似天仙，心如魔鬼。 She looks
like an angel but has the heart
of a devil. 【俗語 Common saying】

貌似鮮花，心如蛇蠍。 She looks
as beautiful as a flower but has
the heart of a serpent. 【俗語
Common saying】

外表道貌岸然，心裏男盜女娼。
On surface one is a person

of high morals, at heart one is as shameful as thieves and prostitutes. 【俗語 Common saying】

外表老實，骨子奸詐。 An honest appearance but inwardly full of machinations and deceit. 【俗語 Common saying】

外表溫順，內藏心計。 Gentle and obedient on surface, but inwardly full of machinations. 【俗語 Common saying】

外貌雖變，骨子依舊。 One's appearance has changed but inwardly one remains the same as before. 【俗語 Common saying】

外作賢良，內藏奸滑。 One feigns to be worthy and kind, but one is actually cunning and deceitful. 【曹雪芹《紅樓夢·第六十九回》Cao Xueqin: Chapter 69, *A Dream of the Red Chamber*】

外作忠良，內藏叵測。 One feigns to be loyal and kind, but one is actually full of evil intentions. 【俗語 Common saying】

祗重表面，不重實質。 More sail than ballast. 【俗語 Common saying】

Suspicion

非我族類，其心必異。 Those who are not of our own race must have different intentions. 【左丘明《左傳·成公四年》Zuo Qiuming: "The Fourth Year of the Reign of Duke Cheng", *Zuo's Commentary on the Spring and Autumn Annals*】

瓜田不納履，李下不正冠。 Don't put on your shoes in a melon patch or adjust your cap under a plum tree. 【佚名《樂府·君子行》Anonymous: "The Gentleman", *Folk-song-style Poems*】

寡門不入宿，臨甑不取塵。 Don't stay overnight in a widow's house or dust near a cooking pot. 【馬總《意林·鄒子》Ma Zong: "Master Zou", *Forest of Opinions*】

人之病祗知他人之說可疑，而不知己說之可疑。 A mistake of the people is that they only suspect what is said by others and do not suspect what is said by themselves. 【朱熹《朱子語類》Zhu Xi, *Classified Conversations of Master Zhu*】

聽見風就是雨。 Whenever one hears the wind, he thinks that it is raining. 【李寶嘉《官場現形記·第二十五回》Li Baojia: Chapter 25, *Officialdom Unmasked*】

一疑無不疑。 Once a person is suspected, he will be suspected for everything. 【陸人龍《三刻拍案驚奇·第二十九回》Lu Renlong: Chapter 29, *Amazing Tales, Volume Three*】

疑心生暗鬼。 Suspicion creates ghosts out of one's imagination.

【呂本中《師友雜誌》Lu Benzhong: *Remarks on Teachers and Friends*】

在可疑而不疑者，不曾學，學則須疑。 If you have no doubts when there should be doubts, you have not learned. In learning, you should have doubts. 【張載《經學理窟》Zhang Zai: *The Profundities of the Classics*】

Sword

寶劍也有鈍時。 The sharpest sword sometimes becomes blunt. 【俗語 Common saying】

大雪滿弓刀。 The bows and swords are covered with heavy snow. 【盧綸〈塞下曲〉Lu Lun: "Frontier Song"】

得十良劍，不若得歐冶。 Having ten good swords is not as good as having a sword expert Ou Ye. 【呂不韋《呂氏春秋‧贊能》Lu Buwei: "Praising the Capable", *Master Lu's Spring and Autumn Annals*】

十年磨一劍，霜刃未曾試。 It has taken me ten years to whet my sword, and its frosty edge has yet to be tested. 【賈島〈劍客〉Jia Dao: "Swordsman"】

已到窮途猶結客，風塵相贈值千金。 I have come to the end of the tethers and I still make friends, and in this mundane world, I give my sword, which is worth a thousand taels of gold, to my friend as a gift. 【石達開〈寶劍〉Shi Dakai: "Sword"】

勇劍敵一人，智劍敵萬人。 The sword of courage can resist but one person while the sword of wisdom can resist ten thousand. 【俗語 Common saying Talent】

不傲才以驕人，不以寵而作威。 Don't be arrogant to others because of your talents; don't flaunt your power because of your favouritism. 【諸葛亮〈將誡〉Zhuge Liang: "Admonition to Generals"】

不才明主棄，多病故人疏。 Lack of talent, I am deserted by a wise master and due to my chronic illness, my old friends alienated me. 【孟浩然〈歲暮歸南山〉Meng Haoran: "Returning to the South Mountain at Year End"】

才高八斗，學富五車。 One's talent is high as eight bushels and one's learning, much as five cartloads. 【羅貫中《平妖傳》Luo Guanzhong: *Taming Devils*】

才高必狂，藝高必傲。 One who is greatly talented is sure to be presumptuous. One who is greatly skilled is sure to be haughty. 【俗語 Common saying】【石玉昆《三俠五義‧第三十一回》Shi Yukun: Chapter 31, *The Three Heroes and Five Gallants*】

才苟適治，不問世冑。If one has the talent suitable to govern a state, nobody will ask the question if one comes from a noble family or not.【劉晝《劉子‧薦賢第十九》Liu Zhou: Chapter 19, "Recommending the Virtuous", *Works of Master Liu Zhou*】

才可必傳能有幾。How many people have the talent that has to be transmitted?【趙翼〈西湖晤竹月才喜贈〉Zhao Yi: "To Yuan Mei, Whom I Met at the West Lake"】

才也養不才。Those who are talented train those who are not.【孟軻《孟子‧離婁下》Meng Ke: Chapter 4, Part 2, *Mencius*】

才以用而日生，思以引而不竭。Talent grows daily by use and thinking is resourceful through quotation.【王夫之《周易外傳》Wang Fuzhi: *Supplementary Commentary on The Book of Changes*】

才子佳人，一雙兩好。A talented man and a beautiful lady make a perfect couple.【佚名〈梧桐葉‧第三摺〉Anonymous: Scene 3, "Leaves of the Wutong Trees"】

大方無隅，大器晚成。A large square does not have corners and a great talent matures late.【老子《道德經》Laozi: *Daodejing*】

江山代有才人出，各領風騷數百年。There were generations and generations of talents coming out from this country, with each generation dominating for several hundred years.【趙翼〈論詩絕句〉Zhao Yi: "On Poetry, a Quatrain"】

空心大樹──不成材。A huge tree with a hollow trunk is not good building material – a person of little talent.【歇後語 End-clipper】

人才雖高，不務學問，不能致聖。Though a person may be highly talented, if he does not learn and consult, he cannot reach sagehood.【劉向《說苑‧卷三建本》Liu Xiang: Chapter 3, "Building the Foundation", *Garden of Persuasion*】

山高出俊鳥。In high mountains beautiful birds are bred.【諺語 Proverb】

十步之內，必有芳草。There is certainly fragrant grass within ten paces.【劉向《說苑‧卷十六談叢》Liu Xiang: Chapter 16, "The Thicket of Discussion", *Garden of Persuasion*】

天才是百分之一的靈感，百分之九十九的汗水。Talent is one percent inspiration and ninety-nine percent perspiration.【俗語 Common saying】

天才天生，無可使成。Talents are born, they cannot be made.【俗語 Common saying】

天才在於勤奮，知識在於積累。Talents come from diligence and knowledge is gained by accumulation.【諺語 Proverb】

我勸天公重抖擻，不拘一格降人才。I urge the Lord of Heaven to bestir himself again, sending down all kinds of talents to our country. 【龔自珍〈己亥雜詩〉Gong Zizhen:"Poems Written in the Year of Jihai"】

一個西湖一才子。 A beautiful West Lake, a talented person. 【趙翼〈西湖晤子才喜贈〉Zhao Yi:"To Yuan Mei, Whom I Met at the West Lake"】

有大才必有大用。 Great talent is sure to find great occupation. 【蘭陵笑笑生《金瓶梅‧第七十八回》 Lanling Xiaoxiaosheng: Chapter 78, *The Plum in the Golden Vase*】

有能則舉之，無能則下之。 Those who have talent are promoted and those who have no talent are dismissed. 【墨翟《墨子‧尚賢卷八至十》Mo Di: Chapters 8-10, "Exalting the Worthies", *Mozi*】

Talking

八十歲學吹笙 —— 老調。 An eighty-year-old person learning to play a pipe – it's the same old stuff. 【歇後語 End-clipper】

把話說在前頭。 Give somebody a forewarning. 【俗語 Common saying】

不敢說半個不字。 Dare not mutter dissent. 【俗語 Common saying】

不以言舉人，不以言廢人。 Don't recommend a person by his words or reject a person by his words. 【孔子《論語‧衛靈公篇第十五》Confucius: Chapter 15, *The Analects of Confucius*】

長話不可短說。 A long story cannot be told short. 【俗語 Common saying】

車軲轆話來回轉。 Sing the song of burden. 【俗語 Common saying】

吃蜂蜜，說好話 —— 甜言蜜語。 Speaking fine words while eating honey – sweet words and honeyed phrases. 【歇後語 End-clipper】

持之有故，言之成理。 Support one's opinions with sufficient grounds and what is presented is reasonable. 【荀況《荀子‧非十二子第六》Xun Kuang: Chapter 6, "Against the Twelve Masters", *Xunzi*】

處世戒多言，言多必失。 In conducting yourself in society, do not talk more than is necessary, otherwise there will be slips in what you say. 【朱用純《朱子家訓》Zhu Yongchun: *Percepts of the Zhu Family*】

從頭至尾，一五一十。 Tell the whole story blow-by-blow and from beginning to end. 【曹雪芹《紅樓夢‧第十回》Cao Xueqin: Chapter 10, *A Dream of the Red Chamber*】

粗話無害，甘言無益。Hard words are harmless and fine words are of no benefit.【諺語 Proverb】

打開話匣子。Start a conversation.【俗語 Common saying】

打開天窗說亮話。Not to mince one's words.【俗語 Common saying】

大言炎炎，小言詹詹。Great speech is bland while petty speech, mere blathering.【莊周《莊子‧內篇‧齊物論第二》Zhuang Zhou: Chapter 2, "On the Equality of Things", "Inner Chapters", *Zhuangzi*】

道上人說話，草窩有人聽。People talking on the road may be overheard by people hiding in the haystack.【諺語 Proverb】

得其言，不若得其所以然。Understanding what is said is not as good as understanding why it is being said.【劉安《淮南子‧氾論訓第十三》Liu An: Chapter 13, "Compendious Essay", *Huainanzi*】

燈不點不亮，話不說不明。A lantern is not bright if it is not lit. What is said is not clear if it is not explained.【俗語 Common saying】

東扯葫蘆西扯瓢。Talk aimlessly.【柯藍《瀏河十八彎》Ke Lan: *Eighteen Turns of the Liu River*】

東一句，西一句。Drag in irrelevant matters.【俗語 Common saying】

對啥人說啥話。Say the right thing to the right person.【俗語 Common saying】

多虛不如少實。A lot of empty talk is not as good as a little practical work.【諺語 Proverb】

多言獲利，不如默而無言。To gain by talking a lot is not as good as to gain by silence.【羅貫中《三國演義‧第四十三回》Luo Guanzhong: Chapter 43, *Romance of the Three Kingdoms*】

多言數窮，不如守中。Talking much is exhaustive, and it would be better to keep things to oneself.【老子《道德經》Laozi: *Daodejing*】

多嘴討人厭。Loquacity is disgusting.【俗語 Common saying】

飯可以亂吃，話不能亂講。Watch what you say.【俗語 Common saying】

飛機上拉二胡 —— 唱高調。Playing *erhu* on board an airplane – mouthing high-sounding words.【歇後語 End-clipper】

飛機上聊天 —— 空談。Chatting on board an airplane is talking in the air – empty talk.【歇後語 End-clipper】

逢人但說三分話，莫把真心一鍋端。When you talk to people, you tell them a small part of what you want to say, and don't tell them all what is really on your mind.【諺語 Proverb】【《增廣賢

文》Words that Open up One's Mind and Enhance One's Wisdom】

逢人且說三分話，未可全拋一片心。 When you talk to people, you tell them a small part of what you want to say, don't tell them all what is really on your mind. 【諺語 Proverb】【《增廣賢文》Words that Open up One's Mind and Enhance One's Wisdom】

骨鯁在喉 —— 不吐不快。 If one does not speak out, one feels suffocated. 【歇後語 End-clipper】

過耳之言，不可聽信。 Words overheard are not to be trusted. 【諺語 Proverb】【吳承恩《西遊記·第九回》Wu Cheng'en: Chapter 9, *Journey to the West*】

好話不瞞人，瞞人非好話。 Fine words are not hidden from others, but those words hidden from others are not fine words. 【施世綸《施公案·第二百九十七回》Shi Shilun: Chapter 297, *Cases of Judge Shi*】

好言難得，惡語易施。 Good words are hard to get and vicious comments can be easily used. 【《增廣賢文》Words that Open up One's Mind and Enhance One's Wisdom】

好一句，歹一句。 Use all means of persuasion. 【諺語 Proverb】【曹雪芹《紅樓夢·第一百回》Cao Xueqin: Chapter 100, *A Dream of the Red Chamber*】

狐狸吵架 —— 一派胡言。 Foxes quarrelling in the fox language– it's sheer nonsense. 【歇後語 End-clipper】

話到口中留半句，理從是處讓三分。 Say just half of what you want to say when you're about to say it and leave others a way out even when you're on the right side. 【碩果山人《訓蒙增廣改本》Shuoguo Shanren: *Revised Edition of the Words that Open up One's Mind and Enhance One's Wisdom for Enlightening Children*】

話多了不甜。 Too much talk is unpleasant. 【諺語 Proverb】

話裏有文章。 There is something else deeper and more complicated in the words. 【曹雪芹《紅樓夢·第十九回》Cao Xueqini Chapter 19, *A Dream of the Red Chamber*】

話沒腿，跑千里。 Words have no legs, but they go a thousand miles. 【俗語 Common saying】

話是開心的鑰匙。 Words are the keys to the heart. 【諺語 Proverb】

話說給知人，飯送給饑人。 Words are said to people who understand you and rice is given to the hungry people. 【諺語 Proverb】

話說為空，落筆為實。 Talk is empty but writing is binding. 【諺語 Proverb】

雞一嘴，鴨一嘴。 The chicken chips in and the duck chips in. 【俗語 Common saying】

家有十五口 —— 七嘴八舌。
There are fifteen people in the family–all talking at once. 【歇後語 End-clipper】

見啥人說啥話。 Talk differently to different people. 【俗語 Common saying】

酒後吐真言。 Truth is exposed in wine. 【俗語 Common saying】

君子必貴其言。 A gentleman surely cares about what he says. 【徐幹《中論·貴言》Xu Gan:"Caring about One's Language", *Balanced Discourses*】

開口不如緘口穩。 It is safer to keep silent than to speak. 【俗語 Common saying】

可與言而不與之言，失人；不可與之言而與之言，失言。 If you don't talk to somebody whom you can talk to, you lose the person; if you talk to somebody whom you cannot talk to, you waste your words. 【孔子《論語·衞靈公篇第十五》Confucius: Chapter 15, *The Analects of Confucius*】

空口說白話。 Pay lip service. 【俗語 Common saying】

口惠而實不至。 Make a promise but not keep it. 【《禮記·表記第三十二》Chapter 32:"Records of Examples", *The Book of Rites*】

口裏擺菜碟兒。 Pay lip service. 【吳承恩《西遊記·第五十四回》Wu Cheng'en: Chapter 54, *Journey to the West*】

口若懸河，成事無多。 Great boast, small roast. 【俗語 Common saying】

枯樹不長葉，空話不頂用。 Withe Red trees do not have leaves, and empty words are useless. 【俗語 Common saying】

枯樹無果實，空話無價值。 As withe Red trees bear no fruit, so empty words have no value. 【諺語 Proverb】

癩蛤蟆打哈欠 —— 好大的口氣。 A toad yawning has a big breath–one talks big. 【歇後語 End-clipper】

兩喜必多溢美之言，兩怒必多溢惡之言。 When both sides are on good terms, there are many good words to say about each other; when both sides are on hostile terms, there are many bad words to say against each other. 【莊周《莊子·內篇·人間世第四》Zhuang Zhou: Chapter 4, "Human World", "Inner Chapters", *Zhuangzi*】

路上說話，草裏有人。 When talking on the road, you might be overheard by somebody hiding in the grass. 【吳承恩《西遊記·第九回》Wu Cheng'en: Chapter 9, *Journey to the West*】

滿口仁義道德，滿肚子男盜女娼。 One who talks a lot about virtue and morality but is a scoundrel at heart. 【宋喬《侍衛官雜記·卷上》Song Qiao: Volume 1, *Notes of a Guard Officer*】

盲人吹喇叭 —— 瞎吹。A blind person blowing a trumpet is blowing it blindly – one is talking rubbish.【歇後語 End-clipper】

美言可以市尊，美行可以加人。Fine words can be in respect and good deeds can add grace to people.【老子《道德經‧第六十二章》Laozi: Chapter 62, *Daodejing*】

木耳朵 —— 說不通。Wooden ears can't be persuaded.【歇後語 End-clipper】

你一言，我一語。Every tongue wags at once.【俗語 Common saying】

琵琶斷了弦 —— 談（彈）不下去了。A Chinese lute with broken strings can't be plucked any more – something can't be discussed any more.【歇後語 End-clipper】

七月七日長生殿，夜半無人私語時。On the seventh day of the seventh month in the Long-living Palace, they whispered together at midnight, all by themselves.【白居易〈長恨歌〉Bai Juyi: "Song of Everlasting Grief"】

千年紙墨會說話。Contracts and deeds of a thousand years old can still talk.【劉江《太行風雲‧第五回》Liu Jiang: Chapter 5, *Changes in Taixing*】

前言不搭後語。Utter words that do not hang together.【俗語 Common saying】

巧言不如直道，明人不必細說。A flowery speech is not as good as a straightforward talk; to a clever man, a detailed explanation is not necessary.【諺語 Proverb】

巧言不如直說。A straightforward talk is better than flowery speech.【諺語 Proverb】

巧言令色鮮矣仁。Fine words and an insinuating appearance are seldom associated with true virtue.【孔子《論語‧學而篇第一》Confucius: Chapter 1, *The Analects of Confucius*】

禽有禽言，獸有獸語。Birds have the bird language and animals have the animal talk.【吳承恩《西遊記‧第七十二回》Wu Cheng'en: Chapter 72, *Journey to the West*】

羣居終日，言不及義。Gather together the whole day without talking about things righteous.【孔子《論語‧衞靈公篇第十五》Confucius: Chapter 15, *The Analects of Confucius*】

人有人言，獸有獸語。Human beings have their language and animals, theirs.【郭小亭《濟公全傳‧第一百三十五回》Guo Xiaoting: Chapter 135, *Biography of Jigong*】

人嘴兩張皮 —— 各說各有理。The mouth of a human being consists of but two lips.【郭小亭《濟公全傳‧第一百二十一回》Guo Xiaoting: Chapter 121, *Biography of Jigong*】

仁者，其言也訒。A benevolent person is cautious and slow in

his speech. 【孔子《論語·顏淵篇第十二》Confucius: Chapter 12, *The Analects of Confucius*】

少說空話，多做實事。 Less empty talk, more practical work. 【俗語 Common saying】

矢出難追，言出不回。 An arrow which has been shot is hard to be caught and words that have been spoken cannot be taken back. 【俗語 Common saying】

守口莫談人過短，自短何曾說與人。 If one shuts one's mouth and does not talk about the mistakes and shortcomings of others, then how can his shortcomings be talked about by others. 【諺語 Proverb】

說出去的話，潑出去的水。 Words spoken are like water split. 【俗語 Common saying】

說的比唱的還好聽。 What one says is more agreeable than songs. 【俗語 Common saying】

說得好不如做得好。 Well-said is not as good as well-done. 【俗語 Common saying】

說話不明，猶如昏鏡。 Unclear remarks are like unclear mirrors. 【文康《兒女英雄傳·第二十三回》Wen Kang: Chapter 23, *Biographies of Young Heroes and Heroines*】

說話不蝕本，舌頭打個滾。 Talking does not cost you anything; you just wag your tongue. 【諺語 Proverb】

說來容易做來難。 Easier said than done. 【諺語 Proverb】

說是說，笑是笑。 Joking is joking. 【俗語 Common saying】

說是一回事，做是一回事。 To say is one thing, to practise is another. 【俗語 Common saying】

說者無心，聽者有意。 The speaker has no particular intention in saying something, but the listener reads his own meaning into it. 【俗語 Common saying】

隨口之言，有口無心。 Say whatever comes to one's mind. 【蘭陵笑笑生《金瓶梅·第三十九回》Lanling Xiaoxiaosheng: Chapter 39, *The Plum in the Golden Vase*】

談笑有鴻儒，往來無白丁。 I chat and laugh with great scholars and none of the people with whom I communicate is uneducated. 【劉禹錫〈陋室銘〉Liu Yuxi: "Eulogy on my Humble Abode"】

天不怕，地不怕，就怕廣東人講普通話。 Fear neither heaven nor earth, but what is most fearful is the Cantonese people speaking Putonghua. 【俗語 Common saying】

天子不輕言。 The Son of Heaven does not speak lightly. 【俗語 Common saying】

天子無戲言。 The Son of Heaven does not speak in jest. 【呂不韋《呂氏春秋·重言》Lu Buwei: "Emphasis on Words", *Master Lu's Spring and Autumn Annals*】

聽君一席話，勝讀十年書。What I get from listening to you in a conversation is more rewarding than what I can get from reading books for ten years. 【《增廣賢文》Words that Open up One's Mind and Enhance One's Wisdom】

聞其言而知其人。A person is judged by the things he says. 【諺語 Proverb】

無心人說話，祇怕有心人來聽。One may speak unintentionally, but the listener may think that it is deliberate. 【諺語 Proverb】【文康《兒女英雄傳・第十七回》Wen Kang: Chapter 17, *Biographies of Young Heroes and Heroines*】

喜時之言多失信，怒時之言多失體。One often breaks one's promise which is made when happy, and one often speaks in inappropriate terms when angry. 【陳繼儒〈安得長者言〉Chen Jiru:"How to Get Advice from the Elders"】

戲謔之中寓真理。Profound truths rest in jokes. 【俗語 Common saying】

下巴掛鈴鐺 —— 想（響）到哪說到哪兒。A bell hanging on the chin–speaking whatever occurs to one. 【歇後語 End-clipper】

夏蟲不可以語冰。One cannot talk to summer insects about ice. 【莊周《莊子・外篇・秋水第十七》：Zhuang Zhou: Chapter 17, "Autumn Floods", "Outer Chapters", *Zhuangzi*】

先說斷，後不亂。Have an agreement first and you will not have disputes later. 【蘭陵笑笑生《金瓶梅・第七回》Lanling Xiaoxiaosheng: Chapter 7, *The Plum in the Golden Vase*】

小辯害大智，巧言使信廢，小惠妨大義。Trivial disputes harm great intelligence, elusive words ruin trust, and small favours block great righteousness. 【劉向《說苑・卷十六談叢》Liu Xiang: Chapter 16, "The Thicket of Discussion", *Garden of Persuasion*】

雄辯是銀，沉默是金。Speech is silver, and silence is gold. 【諺語 Proverb】

言不及義，好行小惠。Never talk about fundamentals but take pleasure only in giving small favours. 【孔子《論語・衛靈公篇第十五》Confucius: Chapter 15, *The Analects of Confucius*】

言不亂發，筆不妄動。Do not speak carelessly nor write recklessly. 【諺語 Proverb】

言而當，知也；默而當，亦知也。Speak when it is proper to speak, this is wisdom; be silent when it is proper to remain silent, this is also wisdom. 【荀況《荀子・非十二子第六》Xun Kuang: Chapter 6, "Against the Twelve Masters", *Xunzi*】

言顧行，行顧言。Be consistent in speech and action. 【《禮記・中庸第三十一章》Chapter 31:"Doctrine of the Mean", *The Book of Rites*】

言乃心之聲。 Words are the voice of the mind. 【諺語 Proverb】

言有物，行有格。 Speak with substance and act by rules. 【《禮記‧緇衣第三十三》Chapter 33:"The Black Robes", *The Book of Rites*】

言者無心，聽者有意。 An unintentional remark could mean something to a listener. 【俗語 Common saying】

言者諄諄，聽者藐藐。 The speaker is earnest, but the listener pays little attention to what he says. 【《詩經‧大雅‧抑》"Pressing", "Greater odes of the kingdom", *The Book of Odes*】

一言既出，駟馬難追。 What has been said cannot be unsaid. 【《增廣賢文》*Words that Open up One's Mind and Enhance One's Wisdom*】

以人言善我，必以人言罪我。 If you treat me well when you hear something good about me, you will certainly penalize me when you hear something bad about me. 【韓非《韓非子‧說林上第二十二》Han Fei: Chapter 22, "On Forests, Part 1", *Hanfeizi*】

有話說在明處。 If you have anything to say, say it openly. 【俗語 Common saying】

有話則長，無話則短。 If there is much to be said, the story will be long. If there is not much to be said, the story will be short. 【施耐庵《水滸傳‧第二十四回》Shi Nai'an: Chapter 24, *Outlaws of the Marshes*】

有甚麼說甚麼。 Say what is on one's mind. 【俗語 Common saying】

有一句，說一句。 Say everything that one knows. 【蘭陵笑笑生《金瓶梅‧第九十一回》Lanling Xiaoxiaosheng: Chapter 91, *The Plum in the Golden Vase*】

有一說一，有二說二。 Call a spade a spade. 【俗語 Common saying】

與君一夕話，勝讀十年書。 To talk with you for an evening is more beneficial than reading books for ten years. 【劉鶚《老殘遊記‧第九回》Liu E: Chapter 9, *The Travels of Lao Can*】

灶王爺上天 ── 有啥說啥。 Say whatever one likes. 【歇後語 End-clipper】

知無不言，言無不盡。 Say all that one knows and say it without reserve. 【蘇洵《衡論‧遠慮》Su Xun:"Farsightedness", *Criteria for Evaluation*】

祇聽樓梯響，不見人下來。 All talk and no cider. 【俗語 Common saying】

祇聞雷聲，不見雨點 Full of sound and fury but without action. 【俗語 Common saying】

醉是醒時言。 What is said when drunken is what intends to be said when sober. 【施耐庵《水滸傳‧第四十五回》Shi Nai'an: Chapter 45, *Outlaws of the Marshes*】

Taste

百人吃百味。A hundred people have a hundred tastes. 【諺語 Proverb】

不登大雅之堂。Of a taste that is unfit for the higher circles. 【沈德潛《說詩晬語》Shen Deqian: *Remarks on Poetry*】

吃過黃蓮苦，更知蜜糖甜。If one has tasted the bitterness of gall, one knows better the sweetness of honey. 【諺語 Proverb】

蜂蜜拌紅糖 —— 甜到底。Honey mixed with brown sugar – thoroughly sweet. 【歇後語 End-clipper】

蜂蜜加香油 —— 又香又甜。Honey plus sesame oil – both savoury and sweet. 【歇後語 End-clipper】

囫圇吞棗不覺味。If one swallows dates whole, one cannot know how they taste. 【諺語 Proverb】

緊行無好步，慢嚼得滋味。In a rush, you cannot walk steadily. In slow chewing, you can know the real taste. 【諺語 Proverb】

涼水沏茶 —— 沒味兒。Making tea with cold water is tasteless. 【歇後語 End-clipper】

蘿蔔青菜，各有所愛。Everyone to his taste. 【俗語 Common saying】

未諳姑食性，先遣小姑嚐。I had no idea about my mother-in-law's taste in food, I asked my sister-in-law to try it first. 【王建〈新嫁娘詞〉Wang Jian: "Words of the Newly wed Woman"】

武大郎玩夜貓子 —— 甚麼人玩甚麼鳥。Wu the Elder finding sport with the night owl–there is a bird to suit every kind of person. 【歇後語 End-clipper】

羊羔雖美，眾口難調。Though lamb soup is delicious, it cannot suit everyone's taste. 【佚名《名賢集》Anonymous: *Collected Sayings of Famous Sages*】

一菜難合百人味。A single dish cannot satisfy the taste of a hundred people. 【諺語 Proverb】

豬八戒吃人參果 —— 不知啥滋味。Pigsy eating the ginseng fruit does not know its taste. 【歇後語 End-clipper】

Tea

茶為花博士，酒是色媒人。Tea is a go-between for flowers, wine, for man and woman. 【俗語 Common saying】【凌濛初《初刻拍案驚奇‧第七卷》Ling Mengchu: Chapter 7, *Amazing Tales, Volume One*】

茶香寧靜卻可以致遠，茶人淡泊卻可以明志。The fragrance of tea is tranquil but it reaches far; a connoisseur of tea is indifferent to fame and fortune, but it expresses one's aspirations. 【陸羽《茶經》Lu Yu: *The Classic of Tea*】

茶者，南方之嘉禾也。Tea is a golden grain of the South. 【陸羽《茶經》Lu Yu: *The Classic of Tea*】

啜苦咽甘，茶也。Tea is something that tastes bitter but sweet when drunk. 【陸羽《茶經》Lu Yu: *The Classic of Tea*】

好茶不怕品。Tea of good quality can stand any critical sipping. 【諺語 Proverb】

早茶晚酒飯後煙。Morning tea, evening wine and after-meal cigarettes. 【俗語 Common saying】

Teaching

但開風氣不為師。I blaze a trail but do not teach. 【龔自珍〈己亥雜詩〉Gong Zizhen: "Poems Written in the Year of Jihai"】

當仁不讓於師。If something is benevolent, you don't have to be too modest with your teacher. 【孔子《論語·衛靈公篇第十五》Confucius: Chapter 15, *The Analects of Confucius*】

道吾好者是吾賊，道吾惡者是吾師。He who says that I'm good is my enemy and he who says that I'm bad is my teacher. 【《增廣賢文》*Words that Open up One's Mind and Enhance One's Wisdom*】

凡學之道，嚴師為難。Of all the ways relating to learning, respecting the teacher is difficult. 【《禮記·學記第十八》Chapter 18, "Records on the Subject of Education", *The Book of Rites*】

各師父各傳授，各把戲各變手。Each teacher has his own method and every trade its own trick. 【劉鶚《老殘遊記·第十三回》Liu E: Chapter 13, *The Travels of Lao Can*】

攻吾之短者是吾師。He who criticizes my weaknesses is my teacher. 【王陽明《傳習錄·答周道通書》Wang Yangming: "A Letter in Reply to Zhou Daotong", *Records of Teaching and Practising*】

記問之學，不足以為人師。One whose learning is by memory and consultation is not qualified to be a teacher. 【《禮記·學記第十八》Chapter 18, "Records on the Subject of Education", *The Book of Rites*】

教不倦，仁也。Teaching without feeling tired is benevolence. 【孟軻《孟子·公孫丑上》Meng Ke: Chapter 2, Part 1, *Mencius*】

教不嚴，師之惰。To educate without severity is a teacher's indolence. 【王應麟《三字經》Wang Yinglin: *Three-character Classic*】

教婦初來，教兒嬰孩。Instruct a daughter-in-law when she is just married and teach a child in his infancy. 【顏之推《顏氏家訓・教子》Yan Zhitui: "Teaching the Children", *Family Instructions of Master Yan*】

教然後知困。In teaching, one knows one's limitations. 【《禮記・學記第十八》Chapter 18, "Records on the Subject of Education", *The Book of Rites*】

教人者，成人之長，去人之短也。In teaching people, one should accentuate one's strong points and remove one's shortcomings. 【魏源《魏源集・默觚》Wei Yuan: "Mogu", *Works of Wei Yuan*】

教是為了不教。Teaching is in order not to teach. 【葉聖陶《葉聖陶教育文集》Ye Shengtao: *A Collection of Ye Shengtao's Writings on Education*】

教學不離書，窮人不離賭。Teaching relies on books and poverty comes from gambling. 【俗語 Common saying】

經師易得，人師難求。It is easy to have a teacher of the classics but difficult to get a teacher of the person. 【《禮記・學記第十八》Chapter 18, "Records on the Subject of Education", *The Book of Rites*】

名師出高徒。A great teacher will have great pupils. 【諺語 Proverb】

千個師傅千個法。A thousand masters, a thousand methods. 【諺語 Proverb】

千教萬教，教人求真。Whatever we teach is all about the pursuit of truths. 【陶行知〈小學教師與民主運動〉Tao Xingzhi: "Primary School Teachers and Democratic Movement"】

人之患，在好為人師。A common trouble with people is that they are too eager to assume the role of a teacher to others. 【孟軻《孟子・離婁上》Meng Ke: Chapter 4, Part 1, *Mencius*】

三人行，必有我師。In a group of three people, there will always be one person I can learn from. 【孔子《論語・述而篇第七》Confucius: Chapter 7, *The Analects of Confucius*】

善待問者如撞鐘，叩之以小則小鳴，叩之以大則大鳴。A teacher who is good at answering questions is like the striking of a bell: a light strike is responded with a light ring and a big strike, a loud ring. 【《禮記・學記第十八》Chapter 18, "Records on the Subject of Education", *The Book of Rites*】

善教者使人繼其志。A good teacher makes his students carry on his ideals. 【《禮記・學記第十八》Chapter 18, "Records on the Subject of Education", *The Book of Rites*】

善者固吾師，不善者亦吾師。People who are good are my teachers, and those who are not good are also my teachers. 【王陽明《傳習錄》Wang Yangming: *Records of Teaching and Practising*】

身教勝於言教。 Example is better than precept. 【諺語 Proverb】

師父領進門，修行在個人。 The master teaches the trade, but the apprentice's skills are self-acquired. 【諺語 Proverb】

師徒如父子。 The relation between a master and his apprentices are like that of a father and his sons. 【諺語 Proverb】

師者，所以傳道受業解惑也。 A teacher is one who propagates the cardinal principles, imparts knowledge, and resolves doubts. 【韓愈《昌黎先生集・師說》Han Yu:"On Teachers", *Collected Works of Han Yu*】

十年教書不富，一年不教就窮。 Teaching for ten years does not make one rich but if one stops teaching for just one year, one becomes poor. 【俗語 Common saying】

堂前教子，枕邊教妻。 Lecture your son in public, but your wife in bed. 【碩果山人《訓蒙增廣改本》Suoguoshanren: *Revised Edition of the Words that Open up One's Mind and Enhance One's Wisdom for Enlightening Children*】

桃李不言，下自成蹊。 Peaches and plums do not speak, yet a path is trampled out beneath them. 【司馬遷《史記・李將軍列傳》Sima Qian:"Biography of General Li Guang", *Records of the Grand Historian*】

天下的事非教不行。 Things under heaven must be taught. 【俗語 Common saying】

同門不同道。 Under the tutelage of the same teacher but go different ways in their learning. 【俗語 Common saying】

為師不嚴，誤人子弟。 A teacher who is not strict with his students is misguiding the children. 【俗語 Common saying】

溫故而知新，可以為師矣。 When you review what has been learned and learn something, you are worthy of being a teacher. 【孔子《論語・為政篇第二》Confucius: Chapter 2, *The Analects of Confucius*】

先做學生，後做先生。 Be a pupil before you are a teacher. 【諺語 Proverb】

學莫便乎近其人。 The best way to learn is to stay close to the person you learn from. 【荀況《荀子・勸學第一》Xun Kuang: Chapter 1, "Exhortation to Learning", *Xunzi*】

學為人師，行為世範。 Learn, so as to teach others; act, so as to serve as an example to all. 【劉昫《舊唐書》Liu Xu: *History of the Early Tang*】

言教不如身教。 To teach others by one's own example is better than to teach with words. 【諺語 Proverb】

嚴師出高徒。A strict master produces outstanding apprentices.【諺語 Proverb】

要做先生，必須先做學生。If one wants to be a teacher, one has to be a student first.【諺語 Proverb】

一日為師，終身是友。He who teaches me for one day is my friend for life.【俗語 Common saying】

一日為師，終身為父。He who teaches me for one day is my father for a lifetime.【關漢卿〈玉鏡台〉Guan Hanqing: "Jade Dressing Table"】

一日為師，終生為師。He who teaches me for one day is my teacher for life.【俗語 Common saying】

以言教者訟，以身教者從。Those who teach in words will be criticized and those who teach in deeds will have their followers.【范曄《後漢書·第五倫傳》Fan Ye: "Biography of Diwu Lun", History of the Later Han】

有其師必有其徒。Like master, like apprentice.【俗語 Common saying】

智如泉源，行可以為表儀者，人師也。When a person has wisdom like the source of a spring and his conduct is a good model to be followed, such a person is qualified to be a teacher.【韓嬰《韓詩外傳·卷五》Han Ying: Chapter 5, Supplementary Commentary on the Book of Songs by Master Han】

Tear

不見棺材不落淚。One will only shed tears when one sees the coffin.【蘭陵笑笑生《金瓶梅·第九十八回》Lanling Xiaoxiaosheng: Chapter 98, The Plum in the Golden Vase】

滿紙荒唐言，一把辛酸淚。Pages full of idle words, brushed with bitter tears.【曹雪芹《紅樓夢》Cao Xueqin: A Dream of the Red Chamber】

男兒有淚不輕彈，祇因未到傷心時。A man does not shed tears easily. He shed tears only when his heart is broken.【李開先〈林沖寶劍記·第三十七齣〉Li Kaixian: Scene 37, "The Story of Lin Chong's Sword"】

人不傷心不落淚。People shed tears only when sad.【薛旭升《龍泉村奇聞》Xue Xusheng: Strange Tales of the Longquan Village】

人生有情淚霑臆。In human life, tears would come out of sentiment.【杜甫〈哀江頭〉Du Fu: "In Sadness beside the River"】

眼淚往肚裏流。One has to swallow his tears.【葉紹翁《四朝見聞錄》Ye Shaoweng: Record of Things Seen and Heard in the Last Four Dynasties】

一聲何滿子，雙淚落君前。 As soon as she hears the palace song "Youngest Daughter He", her tears stream down in the presence of her lord. 【張祜〈宮詞〉Zhang Gu: "Palace Song"】

玉容寂寞淚欄杆，梨花一枝春帶雨。 Her jade-white face, looking lonely, is covered with tears like balustrades, resembling a twig of pear blossom with raindrops in spring. 【白居易〈長恨歌〉Bai Juyi: "Song of Everlasting Grief"】

丈夫非無淚，不灑離別間。 It is not that man does not shed tears, it is just that they don't shed them in partings. 【陸龜蒙〈別離〉Lu Guimeng: "Parting"】

Temper

急性子，慢手腳。 One's temper is quick but one's action is slow. 【俗語 Common saying】

敬之而不喜，侮之而不怒。 One is not overjoyed when esteemed, nor infuriated when humiliated. 【莊周《莊子·雜篇·庚桑楚第二十三》Zhuang Zhou: Chapter 23, "Gengsang Chu", "Miscellaneous Chapters", Zhuangzi】

皮球性子——一拍就跳。 A rubber ball temper – you pat it and it will jump. 【歇後語 End-clipper】

千人千脾氣，萬人萬模樣。 A thousand people have a thousand temperaments and ten thousand people have ten thousand appearances. 【俗語 Common saying】【王厚選《古城青史·第二十回》Wang Houxuan: Chapter 20, History of an Old Town】

隨錢添脾氣。 The richer one is the more ill-tempered one becomes. 【俗語 Common saying】

心急等不得人，性緊釣不得魚。 A short-tempered person cannot wait for people and an impatient person cannot go fishing. 【諺語 Proverb】

Temple

姑蘇城外寒山寺，夜半鐘聲到客船。 Outside the Gu Su City lies the Hanshan Temple. At midnight, the chimes of the bell reached the traveller's boat. 【張繼〈楓橋夜泊〉Zhang Ji: "Mooring at Night by the Maple Bridge"】

南朝四百八十寺，多少樓台煙雨中。 Of the four hundred and eighty temples built in the Southern Dynasties, how many of them are still there in the misty rain?【杜牧〈江南春〉Du Mu:"Spring in Jiangnan"】

人不祈禱不上廟。 A person who has no prayer to make will not go to a temple. 【俗語 Common saying】

Thief

絕巧棄利，盜賊無有。 Discard machinations and abandon profits, there will not be robbers and thieves. 【老子《道德經·第十九章》Laozi: Chapter 19, *Daodejing*】

拿不盡的跳蚤，殺不盡的賊。 All fleas cannot be caught and all thieves cannot be eliminated. 【俗語 Common saying】

賊不打貧人家。 A thief does not rob a poor family. 【俗語 Common saying】【釋普濟《五燈會元·卷三草堂和尚》Shi Puji: Chapter 3, "Monk Caotang", *A Compendium of the Five Lamps*】

賊不怕銅牆壁，獨怕健人兇狗。 A thief is not afraid of solid walls but of strong people and fierce dogs. 【俗語 Common saying】

賊沒種祇怕哄。 There are no born thieves, they are lured to be thieves. 【諺語 Proverb】【周楫《西湖二集·第一卷》Zhou Ji: Chapter 1, *The West Lake, Second Volume*】

賊是小人，智過君子。 A thief is a petty person yet he might be more intelligent than a gentleman. 【《增廣賢文》*Words that Open up One's Mind and Enhance One's Wisdom*】

祇有千日做賊，哪有千日防賊。 Thieves steal everyday, but people cannot guard against theft everyday. 【李寶嘉《中國現在記·第七回》Li Baojia: Chapter 7, *Present-day China*】

捉到強盜連夜解。 As soon as thieves are caught, take them to jail the same day or night. 【張恨水《金粉世家·第六十一回》Zhang Henshui: Chapter 61, *A Golden Family*】

做賊三年，不打自招。 Being a thief for three years, one confesses without duress. 【俗語 Common saying】

做賊偷蔥起。 People become thieves by first stealing onions. 【諺語 Proverb】

Things

背人沒好事，好事不背人。 Things done behind others are not good things, whereas good things will not be done in secret. 【俗語 Common saying】

不關己事不張口。 Do not say things that do not concern one. 【曹雪芹《紅樓夢・第五十五回》Cao Xueqin: Chapter 55, *A Dream of the Red Chamber*】

不關己事隨他便。 Let things be if they are of no concern to one. 【俗語 Common saying】

不管閒事終無事。 Mind your own business and trouble will not trouble you. 【俗語 Common saying】

不如意事十八九，可與人言無二三。 Eight out of ten things one does may go against one's wishes and no more than two or three things can be told to others. 【馮夢龍《醒世恆言》Feng Menglong: *Stories to Awaken the World*】

不以物喜，不以己悲。 Don't be happy because of material things; don't feel sad because of your situation. 【范仲淹〈岳陽樓記〉Fan Zhongyan: "Song of the Yueyang Tower"】

成事不足，敗事有餘。 Be unable to achieve but more than capable of ruining things. 【俗語 Common saying】

池子裏捕魚，太湖裏放生。 Be fussy about trifles but careless about big things. 【諺語 Proverb】

打破沙鍋問到底。 Get to the bottom of the matter. 【黃庭堅〈拙軒頌〉Huang Tingjian: "Ode to My Humble Studio"】

多一事不如少一事。 To have one thing less is better than to have one too many. 【劉鶚《老殘遊記・第十二回》Liu E: Chapter 12, *The Travels of Lao Can*】

狗拿耗子 —— 多管閒事。 A dog trying to catch mice is meddling into other people's business. 【歇後語 End-clipper】

好事不瞞人，瞞人沒好事。 One does not hide good things from others, those one hides are not good things. 【諺語 Proverb】

好戲在後頭。 The best show is yet to follow. 【俗語 Common saying】

好物不賤，賤物不好。 Good things are not cheap and cheap things, not good. 【諺語 Proverb】【西周生《醒世姻緣傳・第八十五回》Xi Zhousheng: Chapter 85, *Stories of Marriage to Awaken the World*】

好物不在多。 It is the quality of a thing that counts, not the quantity. 【馮夢龍《古今譚概・卷六》Feng Menglong: Chapter 6, *Stories Old and New*】

見怪不怪，其怪自敗。 If you see strange things and do not regard them as strange, then strangeness will destroy itself. 【曹雪芹《紅樓夢・第九十四回》Cao Xueqin: Chapter 94, *A Dream of the Red Chamber*】

見物不見人。 Notice only material but not human factors. 【諺語 Proverb】

君子役物，小人役於物。 A gentleman uses things and a petty man is used by things. 【荀

況《荀子‧修身第二》Xun Kuang: Chapter 2, "Cultivating the Person", *Xunzi*】

事者，難成而易敗也。 **Things are difficult to succeed but easy to fail.**【劉安《淮南子‧人間訓第十八》Liu An: Chapter 18, "In the World of Man", *Huainanzi*】

世事短如春夢，人情薄似秋雲。 **Things in the world are as short as a spring dream and human relationship is as thin as autumn clouds.**【朱敦儒〈西江月〉Zhu Dunru: "To the Tune of the Moon over the West River"】

天下難事，必作於易；天下大事，必作於細。 **Difficult things in the world must begin with the easier ones and great things in the world must begin with the small things.**【老子《道德經》Laozi: *Daodejing*】

天下萬物生於有，有生於無。 **All things in the world are born of something and something is born of nothing.**【老子《道德經》Laozi: *Daodejing*】

天下之事，常成於困約，而敗於奢靡。 **Things in the world are usually accomplished through toil and hardship and ruined by extravagance and luxury.**【陸游〈放翁家訓〉Lu You: *Family Instructions of Lu You*】

物必先腐也，而後蟲生之。 **Things must have first been rotten before worms grow.**【蘇軾〈范增論〉Su Shi: "On Fan Zeng"】

物固莫不有長，莫不有短。 **Things have, without exception, their own strengths and weaknesses.**【呂不韋《呂氏春秋‧用眾》Lu Buwei: "Fulfill the Number" in *Master Lu's Spring and Autumn Annals*】

物離鄉貴，人離鄉賤。 **Articles leaving home become precious, but people, demeaned.**【諺語 Proverb】

物物而不物於物。 **Treat things as things and do not let things treat you as a thing.**【莊周《莊子‧外篇‧山木第二十》Zhuang Zhou: Chapter 20, "The Mountain Tree", "Outer Chapters", *Zhuangzi*】

物以罕為貴。 **When a thing is rare, it becomes precious.**【諺語 Proverb】

物以類聚，人以羣分。 **Things of one kind come together; people alike form a community.**【劉向《戰國策‧齊策三》Liu Xiang: "Strategies of the State of Qi, No.3, *Strategies of the Warring States*】

物以稀為貴。 **When a thing is scarce, it is precious.**【俗語 Common saying】

物有本末，事有始終。 **Everything has its proper sequence of foundation and end results.**【《禮記‧大學第四十二》Chapter 42, "The Great Learning", *The Book of Rites*】

物有必至，事有固然。 **Things have their inevitable outcomes and matters have their own courses to follow.**【司馬遷《史記‧孟嘗君列傳》Sima Qian: "Biography of

Lord Mengchang", *Records of the Grand Historian*】

小有所繫，大必所忘也。 When you concentrate on small things, the big things are bound to be neglected. 【劉晝《劉子・觀量第四十四》Liu Zhou: Chapter 44, "Observing the Volume", *Works of Liuzi*】

一物降一物。 One thing is always subdued by another. 【吳承恩《西遊記・第五十一回》Wu Cheng'en: Chapter 51, *Journey to the West*】

一物自有一主。 Everything has its owner. 【許仲琳《封神演義・第四十七回》Xu Zhonglin: Chapter 47, *Romance of the Investiture of the Deities*】

Thinking

百思不得其解。 Be unable to get an answer even after much thinking. 【紀昀《閱微草堂筆記・卷十三》Ji Yun: Chapter 13, *Jottings from the Thatched Hut for Reading the Subtleties*】

打如意算盤。 Indulge in wishful thinking. 【李寶嘉《官場現形記・第四十四回》Li Baojia: Chapter 44, *Officialdom Unmasked*】

居不隱者，思不遠也。 If one does not live in seclusion, one's thinking cannot be far-reaching. 【劉晝《劉子・激通第五十二》Liu Zhou: Chapter 52, "Strike to Penetrate", *Works of Master Liu Zhou*】

敏而好學，不恥下問。 Be quick in thinking, fond of learning, and feel no shame to learn from the inferiors. 【孔子《論語・公冶長篇第五》Confucius: Chapter 5, *The Analects of Confucius*】

明主慮之，良將修之。 A wise ruler does the thinking and a good general does the execution. 【孫武《孫子兵法・火攻第十二》Sun

Wu: Chapter 12, "Attack by Fire", *The Art of War by Sunzi*】

人多道道多。 The more people, the more ideas. 【俗語 Common saying】

人多智謀高。 More people mean more ideas. 【俗語 Common saying】

人之進學在於思，思則能知是與非。 The progress of a person's study lies in thinking; when one thinks, one can distinguish the right from wrong. 【朱熹〈九思〉Zhu Xi: "Nine Thoughts"】

日有所思，夜有所夢。 What one thinks about in the day, one will dream of it at night. 【諺語 Proverb】

三思而後行。 Think thrice before you act. 【孔子《論語・公冶長篇第五》Confucius: Chapter 5, *The Analects of Confucius*】

三思而行，再思可矣。 Think thrice before you act, and you can still think it over again. 【《增

廣賢文》Words that Open up One's Mind and Enhance One's Wisdom】

事不三思，終有後悔。 Without thinking thrice before doing anything, you will regret. 【馮夢龍《喻世明言・第二卷》Feng Menglong: Chapter 2, *Stories to Instruct the World*】

思而不學則殆。 Thought without learning is perilous. 【孔子《論語・為政篇第二》Confucius: Chapter 2, *The Analects of Confucius*】

思所以危則安，思所以亂則治，思所以亡則存。 Only when we think about where danger looms can we ensure our security. Only when we think about why chaos occurs can we ensure our peace. And only when we think about why a country falls can we ensure our survival. 【歐陽修，宋祁，范鎮，呂夏卿《新唐書・魏徵傳》Ouyang Xiu, Song Qi, Fan Zhen, Lu Xiaqing: "A Biography of Wei Zhen", *A New History of the Tang*】

心之官則思。思則得之，不思則不得也。 The function of the mind is thinking. It is through thinking that we acquire knowledge, and we cannot acquire knowledge if we don't think. 【孟軻《孟子・告子章句上》Meng Ke: Chapter 6, Part 1, *Mencius*】

玄之又玄，眾妙之門。 The more you study the Way, the more profound it gets, and this is the door to all wonders. 【老子《道德經・第一章》Laozi: Chapter 1, *Daodejing*】

要知心中事，且聽口中言。 If you want to know what is on one's mind, you must listen to what one says. 【諺語 Proverb】

一念之差，終身之悔。 A slight error in thought may constitute a lifelong regret. 【諺語 Proverb】

愚者千慮，必有一得。 Even a fool after thinking a thousand times occasionally hits on a good idea. 【司馬遷《史記・淮陰侯列傳》Sima Qian: "Biography of the Marquis of Huaiyin", *Records of the Grand Historian*】

Thunder

乾打雷，不下雨。 There is just thunder, but no rain. 【諺語 Proverb】

雷打眼前報。 When a person is struck by thunder, it is a case of overt retribution. 【俗語 Common saying】

雷公先唱歌，有雨也不多。 If it thunders before the rain falls, the rain won't last long for sure. 【諺語 Proverb】

雷聲大，雨點小。 Loud thunder but small raindrops. 【釋道原《景德傳燈錄・卷二十八》Shi Daoyuan: Chapter 28, *Records of the Transmission of the Lamp in the Jingde Period.*】

雷聲繞圈轉，有雨不久遠。 When the thundering echoes round and round, the rain will soon come.【俗語 Common saying】

平地一聲雷。 A sudden clap of thunder.【趙崇祚《花間集·韋莊·喜遷鶯》Zhao Chongzuo: Wei Zhuang:"To the Tune of a Happy Oriole Moving Nest", *Anthology of Poems Written among the Flowers*】

迅雷不及掩耳。 A swift clap of thunder leaves no time for one to cover one's ears.【佚名《六韜·龍韜·軍勢》Anonymous: *Six Arts, the Dragon Way, and the Military Situation*】

夜雷三日雨。 If it thunders at night, there will be rain for three days in succession.【諺語 Proverb】

一個霹靂天下響。 A thunderclap is heard all over the world.【俗語 Common saying】【陸人龍《三刻拍案驚奇·第二十七回》Lu Renlong: Chapter 27, *Amazing Tales, Volume Three*】

一夜起雷三夜雨。 When it thunders in the night, it'll rain for three nights on end.【徐光啟《農政全書·農事·占候》Xu Guangqi:"Agricultural Tasks", "Divination", *Complete Treatise on Agriculture*】

早雷不過午，夜雷十日雨。 Thunder in the morning, rain gone before noon; thunder at night, a ten-day shower.【諺語 Proverb】

Tiger

打虎不着，反被虎傷。 If one cannot catch a tiger, one might be wounded by it.【俗語 Common saying】【錢彩《說岳全傳·第十三回》Qian Cai: Chapter 13, *A Story of Yue Fei*】

縛虎容易縱虎難。 It is easier to tie a tiger up than to let it go.【錢彩《說岳全傳·第六十一回》Qian Cai: Chapter 61, *A Story of Yue Fei*】

虎負隅，莫之敢攖。 No one is dare to challenge a tiger at bay.【孟軻《孟子·盡心章句下》Meng Ke: Chapter 7, Part 2, *Mencius*】

虎死不倒威。 The tiger dies without loss of dignity.【田漢〈獲虎之夜〉Tian Han:"The Night a Tiger Was Captured"】

畫虎不成反類犬。 Try to paint a tiger but end up having a tiger that looks like a dog.【范曄《後漢書·馬援傳》Fan Ye:"Biography of Ma Huan", *History of the Later Han*】

老虎入山洞 —— 顧前不顧後。 When a tiger enters a mountain cave, it sees things just in front of but not behind it.【歇後語 End-clipper】

猛虎不吃回頭食。 A tiger will not go back to look for prey.【諺語 Proverb】【施世綸《施公案·第

一百一十三回》Shi Shilun: Chapter 113, *Cases of Judge Shi*】

人防虎，虎防人。 People guard against tigers and tigers against people.【諺語 Proverb】

人有三分怕虎，虎有七分怕人。 People are afraid of tigers in a small way, but tigers are afraid of people in a big way.【諺語 Proverb】【謝覺哉《不惑集‧說「怕」》Xie Juezai:"On Fear", *Collected Works of Without Doubt*】

搔虎頭，弄虎鬚。 Offend the mighty and the powerful.【施耐庵《水滸傳‧第五回》Shi Nai'an: Chapter 5, *Outlaws of the Marshes*】

養虎遺患，姑息養奸。 To rear a tiger is to court calamity; to tolerate evil is to abet it.【《禮記‧檀弓上第三》Chapter 3:"Tangong, Part 1", *The Book of Rites*】

一個山頭一隻虎。 There is a tiger in each mountain.【褚人獲《隋唐演義‧第十二回》Zhu Renhuo: Chapter 12, *Heroes in Sui and Tang Dynasties*】

一虎可抵千羊。 One tiger can fight against one thousand sheep.【俗語 Common saying】

一虎十羊，勢無全羊。 One tiger fights against ten sheep, and no sheep can survive.【陳子壯《昭代經濟言‧卷八》Chen Zizhuang: Chapter 8, *On the Economy of the Dynasty*】

捉虎容易放虎難。 It is easy to catch a tiger and difficult to set it free.【施世綸《施公案‧第一百一十二回》Shi Shilun: Chapter 112, *Cases of Judge Shi*】

縱虎歸山 —— 必有後患。 If you let a tiger escape back to the mountain, you'll cause trouble in the future.【歇後語 End-clipper】

Time

不貴尺之璧，而貴寸之陰。 Don't treasure jade of a foot long, but treasure every inch of time.【劉安《淮南子‧原道訓第一》Liu An: Chapter 1, "Searching out the Way", *Huainanzi*】

尺璧非寶，寸陰是競。 A piece of one-foot jade is not precious, but an inch of time is.【劉安《淮南子‧原道訓第一》Liu An: Chapter 1:"Searching out the Way", *Huainanzi*】

春爭日，夏爭時。 In spring, every day counts in sowing seedlings; in summer, every moment, in reaping harvest.【諺語 Proverb】

隔年的黃曆 —— 過時了。 Last year's almanac – out of date.【歇後語 End-clipper】

瓜熟蒂落，水到渠成。 When a melon is ripe, it falls off its stem and when water flows, a channel is formed.【諺語 Proverb】

光陰似箭，日月如梭。Time passes like an arrow and the days and months move as fast as a shuttle.【增廣賢文】*Words that Open up One's Mind and Enhance One's Wisdom*】

光陰似駿馬加鞭，浮世似落花流水。The years gallop by like swift horses and worldly affairs pass like fallen flowers or the waters of a flowing stream.【關漢卿〈單刀會‧第四折〉Guan Hanqing: Scene 4, "Single-sword Meeting"】

光陰似流水，一去不回頭。Time passes like flowing waters, it goes without returning.【俗語 Common saying】

光陰勿虛度，青春不再來。Don't waste your precious time for youth, once spent, will never come again.【諺語 Proverb】

光陰一去不復返。All time is no time when it is past.【諺語 Proverb】

光陰者，百代之過客。Time is a passer-by of a hundred generations.【李白〈春夜宴桃李園序〉Li Bai: "Preface to a Banquet on a Night in Spring in the Peach and Plum Garden"】

花開花謝自有時。Time for flowers to bloom or wither is fixed.【諺語 Proverb】

花有重開日，人無再少年。Flowers may blossom again, but a person can never be young again.【關漢卿〈竇娥冤〉Guan Hanqing: "The Injustice to Dou E"】

歡娛嫌夜短，寂寞恨更長。In pleasure and happiness, one thinks that the night is too short. In loneliness, one feels that the night is too long.【羅貫中〈風雲會‧第三折〉Luo Guanzhong: Scene 3, "The Meeting of Wind and Clouds"】

及時當勉勵，歲月不待人。Strive hard while you have time, as years and months wait for no one.【陶淵明〈雜詩〉Tao Yuanming: "Miscellaneous Poems"】

賤百璧而重寸陰。Value each minute of time more than a foot-long jade.【曹丕《典論‧論文》Cao Pi: "Essay on Literature", *Discourse on Canon*】

節令不等人。Time and tide wait for no man.【俗語 Common saying】

今年歡笑復明年，秋月春風等閒度。The joy and laughters of this year will be repeated next year, I have idled away so many years.【白居易〈琵琶行，並序〉Bai Juyi: "Song of a *Pipa* Player, with a Foreword"】

苦時難熬，歡時易過。Time goes by slowly in hard times but fast in happy times.【諺語 Proverb】【馮夢龍《喻世明言‧第一卷》Feng Menglong: Chapter 1, *Stories to Instruct the World*】

年光似鳥翩翩過，世事如棋局局新。Time, like birds, flies quickly away, and affairs in the world, like chess playing, change anew from game to game.【僧

志文〈西閣〉Seng Zhiwen: "Western Pavillion"】

破題兒第一遭。 For the first time.【俗語 Common saying】

日月如流水。 Time passes like flowing water.【俗語 Common saying】

韶華不為少年留，恨悠悠，幾時休？ Time would not wait for us and let us stay young. It is a long long regret that we can never forget.【秦觀〈江城子〉Qin Guan: "To the Tune of a Riverside Town"】

時乎時，不再來。 Time never comes back.【司馬遷《史記·淮陰侯列傳》Sima Qian: "Biography of the Marquis of Huaiyin", *Records of the Grand Historian*】

時間沖淡一切。 Time will weaken everything.【俗語 Common saying】

時間就是金錢。 Time is money.【諺語 Proverb】

時間就是生命。 Time is life.【諺語 Proverb】

說時遲，那時快。 In a twinkling.【施耐庵《水滸傳·第二十三回》Shi

Nai'an: Chapter 23, *Outlaws of the Marshes*】

歲月不待人。 Time and tide wait for no one.【陶淵明〈雜詩〉Tao Yuanming: "Miscellaneous Poems"】

歲月既往，不可復追。 Lost time cannot be found again.【曾國藩〈賢人論惜陰〉Zeng Guofan: "The Sages on Saving Time"】

仙家日月長。 In the fairyland, time goes slower than on earth.【馬戴〈送于道士〉Ma Dai: "Seeing off Wang the Daoist"】

閒覺日偏長。 When idle you feel the day is long.【諺語 Proverb】

一寸光陰一寸金，寸金難買寸光陰。 An inch of time is an inch of gold, but it is difficult to buy an inch of time with an inch of gold.【《增廣賢文》*Words that Open up One's Mind and Enhance One's Wisdom*】

早起三朝當一工。 Getting up early for three mornings is equal to a day in time.【諺語 Proverb】【樓鑰〈午睡戲作〉Lou Yue: "When Taking a Nap in the Afternoon"】

Toil

採得百花成蜜後，為誰辛苦為誰忙。 After making honey with hundreds of flowers, the bees do not know for whom they toil.【羅隱〈蜂〉Luo Yin: "Bees"】

君子勞心，小人勞力。 A gentleman works with his mind and the ordinary people toil with labour.【左丘明《左傳·襄公九年》Zuo Qiuming: "The Ninth Year of the Reign of Duke Xiang", *Zuo's*

Commentary on the Spring and Autumn Annals】

馬上不知馬下苦。 The one on horseback does not know the toil of the one on foot. 【陳登科《風雷‧第一部第二十二章》Chen Dengke: Chapter 22, Volume 1, *Wind and Thunder*】

沒有功勞，也有苦勞。 Even if one has not achieved much, one has at least toiled. 【俗語 Common saying】

騎驢的不知趕腳苦。 A person who rides on a donkey's back does not understand the toil of a porter. 【俗語 Common saying】【李英儒《野火春風鬥古城‧第十六章》Li Yingru: Chapter 16, *The Wildfire and Spring Breeze Fighting against the Ancient City*】

人言田家樂，爾苦誰得知。 Everybody talks about the joy of farming, who knows the toil farmers suffer. 【陳師道〈田家〉Chen Shidao: "Farming Family"】

生勞不如死逸。 Live in toil is not as good as die in peace. 【蒲松齡〈聊齋誌異‧黃九郎‧卷三〉Pu Songling: Chapter 3, "Huang Jiulang", *Strange Stories from a Chinese Studio*】

誰知盤中餐，粒粒皆辛苦。 One should know that every grain on the plate is the fruit of hard toil. 【李紳〈憫農〉Li Shen: "Sympathy for the Peasants"】

心中為念農桑苦，耳裏如聞飢凍聲。 My mind is on the hardship and suffering of the farmers, and my ears seem to hear the sighs of the people in hunger and cold. 【白居易〈新製綾襖成感而有詠〉Bai Juyi: "A Poem Written upon Making a New Cotton Jacket"】

Tolerance

必有忍，其乃有濟。 You must exercise tolerance, which helps you to succeed. 【《尚書‧君陳》"Lord Chen", *The Book of History*】

不忍一時有禍，三思百歲無妨。 A moment of impatience brings a disaster and thinking thrice before doing anything saves one from trouble for a hundred years. 【錢德蒼《解人頤》Qian Decang: *Jokes to Relieve People*】

得忍且忍，得耐且耐，不忍不耐，小事成大。 Endure if you could endure and tolerate if you could tolerate. If you don't endure or tolerate, a small trouble will become a big problem. 【《增廣賢文》 *Words that Open up One's Mind and Enhance One's Wisdom*】

忍得十日破，忍不得一日餓。 One can endure ten days in rags but cannot endure one day in hunger. 【俗語 Common saying】

忍得一時忿，終身無煩悶。
Endurance of a temporary indignation will save you from worries all your life. 【曹雪芹《紅樓夢・第九回》Cao Xueqin: Chapter 9, *A Dream of the Red Chamber*】

忍得一時之氣，免得百日之憂。
To repress a moment's anger may save you from worries of a hundred days. 【《增廣賢文》*Words that Open up One's Mind and Enhance One's Wisdom*】

忍氣饒人禍自消。 Endure indignation and forgive others and you will be free of disasters. 【馮夢龍《警世通言・第十一卷》Feng Menglong: Chapter 11, *Stories to Caution the World*】

忍所不能忍，容所不能容，惟識量過人者能之。 To tolerate what cannot be tolerated and accept what cannot be acceptable can only be practised by those who have exceptional knowledge and magnanimity. 【薛瑄《理學粹言》Xue Xuan: Chapter 3, *Quotes from the Idealist Confucian Philosophy*】

忍天下之小忿者，始可以成大功；忍大辱者，始可以雪天下之大恥。 Only those who tolerate small insults can achieve great success; only those who tolerate great insults can remove the greatest humiliation under heaven. 【王源《居業堂文集》Wang Yuan: *Collected Works from the Hall of Occupation*】

忍一句，息一怒。 If you bear with an angry man by not saying a sentence, you may suppress his anger. 【《增廣賢文》*Words that Open up One's Mind and Enhance One's Wisdom*】

忍字家中寶，不忍惹煩惱。
Forbearance should be the motto in every family as want of forbearance produces discord. 【俗語 Common saying】

忍字心頭一把刀。 Tolerance when stretched to the limit can become a knife. 【俗語 Common saying】

容忍便是福。 Tolerance is a blessing in itself. 【俗語 Common saying】

是可忍也，孰不可忍也。 If this can be tolerated, what else cannot? 【孔子《論語・八佾篇第三》Confucius: Chapter 3, *The Analects of Confucius*】

小不忍則亂大謀。 A little impatience spoils great plans. 【孔子《論語・衛靈公篇第十五》Confucius: Chapter 15, *The Analects of Confucius*】

Tongue

儒生三寸舌，將軍一紙書。 The tongue of a scholar is better than a general's order. 【湯顯祖

〈牡丹亭・第四十六齣〉Tang Xianzu: Scene 46, "Peony Pavillion"】

三寸不爛之舌。 An eloquent tongue.【司馬遷《史記・平原君虞卿列傳》Sima Qian: "Biographies of Lord Pingyuan and Yu Qing", *Records of the Grand Historian*】

三寸舌害了六尺身。 It is your three-inch tongue that harms your six-foot body.【諺語 Proverb】

舌尖殺人不用刀。 The tongue can kill people without using a knife.【釋普濟《五燈會元・卷十七》Shi Puji: Chapter 17, *A Compendium of the Five Lamps*】

舌頭是扁的，說話是圓的。 The tongue is flat, but words can be round.【俗語 Common saying】

舌頭無骨，任意圓扁四方。 The tongue has no bone, so it can be shaped in different way – round, flat or square.【俗語 Common saying】

泰山壓不死人，舌頭能壓煞人。 Mount Tai cannot press a person to death, but a tongue can.【俗語 Common saying】

拙婦巧舌頭。 A woman with clumsy hands often has a glib tongue.【諺語 Proverb】

Tool

割雞焉用牛刀。 There is no need to kill a chicken with a knife that is used for killing an ox.【孔子《論語・陽貨篇第十七》Confucius: Chapter 17, *The Analects of Confucius*】

工欲善其事，必先利其器。 A workman who wants to do his job well must sharpen the tools he uses first.【孔子《論語・衛靈公篇第十五》Confucius: Chapter 15, *The Analects of Confucius*】

國之利器，不可以示人。 The powerful weapons of a country should not be shown to others.【老子《道德經・第三十六章》Laozi: Chapter 36, *Daodejing*】

劣工尤其器。 An ill workman quarrels with his tools.【俗語 Common saying】

沒有大網，打不着大魚。 Without big nets, one cannot catch big fish.【諺語 Proverb】

器具質而潔，瓦臼勝金玉。 Utensils should be simple and clean, then earthen ware is better than gold or jade ware.【諺語 Proverb】

人笨怨刀鈍。 A clumsy person complains that the knife he uses is blunt.【諺語 Proverb】

善御者不忘其馬，善射者不忘其弩。 One who is good at driving carriages does not ignore one's horses; one who is good at shooting does not ignore one's bows.【劉安《淮南子・謬稱訓第十》Liu An: Chapter 10, "On Erroneous Designations", *Huainanzi*】

Trade

吃一行，怨一行。 One who earns a living in a trade complains about it. 【俗語 Common saying】

打鐵賣糖，各幹一行。 Each person to their trade, regardless of being a blacksmith or a candy seller. 【諺語 Proverb】

打魚的不離船邊，打柴的不離山邊。 A fisherman does not leave his boat and a woodman does not leave the mountain. 【諺語 Proverb】

隔行不隔理。 Professions may be different, but the principles are the same. 【諺語 Proverb】

隔行如隔山。 Difference in profession is like worlds apart. 【諺語 Proverb】

敲鑼賣糖 —— 各幹一行。 Beat gongs or selling sweets – each has his own line of business. 【歇後語 End-clipper】

行家看門道，外行看熱鬧。 An expert observes the way to do something, while a layman watches something for fun. 【諺語 Proverb】

男怕入錯行。 A man is afraid of choosing a wrong profession. 【俗語 Common saying】

千行萬行，莊稼是頭一行。 Among all trades farming is the most important. 【俗語 Common saying】【李綠園《歧路燈‧第八十五回》Li Luyuan: Chapter 85, *Lamp on a Forked Road*】

入行三日無劣把。 Three days after you enter a trade, you are no longer a layman. 【諺語 Proverb】【文康《兒女英雄傳‧第三十三回》Wen Kang: Chapter 33, *Biographies of Young Heroes and Heroines*】

三百六十行，行行吃飯着衣裳。 There are three hundred and sixty trades and each of them can provide you with food and clothes. 【諺語 Proverb】【張南莊《何典‧第六卷》Zhang Nanzhuang: Chapter 6, *From Which Classic*】

三百六十行，行行出狀元。 There are three hundred and sixty trades and every trade has its master. 【馮惟敏〈玉抱肚‧贈趙今燕〉Feng Weimin: "Presented to Zhao Jinyan: To the Tune of Jade Embracing the Stomach"】

三百六十行，行行有規矩。 There are three hundred and sixty trades and every trade has its rules and regulations. 【俗語 Common saying】

三句不離本行。 Talk shop all the time. 【李寶嘉《官場現形記‧第三十四回》Li Baojia: Chapter 34, *Officialdom Unmasked*】

同行如敵國。 Bitter rivalries and hatreds exist among people in the same profession. 【俗語 Common saying】

同行是冤家。 People of the same trade are rivals. 【俗語 Common saying】

與子千金不如教子一藝。 It is better to teach one's son a trade than to leave him a lot of money. 【諺語 Proverb】

在一行，怨一行。 One who is in a trade complains about it.【俗語 Common saying】

治百業者必無一精。 Jack of all trades and master of none. 【俗語 Common saying】

Training

好鐵不經三爐火。 Good iron does not need to be melted in the furnace three times. 【俗語 Common saying】

人鈍人上磨，刀鈍石上磨。 A slow person should be tempered by working with people and a blunt knife should be sharpened on a stone. 【俗語 Common saying】

人在世上練，刀在石上磨。 A person is tempered in life and a knife is sharpened on a stone. 【諺語 Proverb】

Trap

蠶子牽絲 —— 自網自。 A silkworm spinning silk is entrapping itself. 【歇後語 End-clipper】

飛蛾攆蜘蛛 —— 自投羅網。 A moth trying to drive out a spider is casting itself into the net. 【歇後語 End-clipper】

老狐狸難上圈套。 It is difficult to snare an old fox. 【俗語 Common saying】

圈套易入難出。 It is easy to fall into a trap but difficult to get out from it. 【俗語 Common saying】

Travel

浮雲遊子意，落日故人情。 A floating cloud is like the will of a traveller and the setting sun is like the fond feelings of an old friend. 【李白〈送友人〉Li Bai: "Seeing off a Friend"】

父母在，不遠遊，遊必有方。 When your parents are alive,

you should not travel too far away. If you do travel, let them know your whereabouts. 【孔子《論語・里仁篇第四》Confucius: Chapter 4, *The Analects of Confucius*】

蜀道之難難於上青天。 The difficulty of travelling to Shu is harder than ascending the blue sky. 【李白〈蜀道難〉Li Bai: "Hard is the Way to Shu"】

五嶽尋仙不辭遠，一身好入名山遊。 I search for the celestial beings in the Five Peaks without minding the distance as I have always been fond of visiting famous mountains. 【李白〈廬山謠寄盧侍御盧舟〉Li Bai: "Song of Mount Lu to Censor Li Xuzhou"】

行百里者半九十。 If a journey is one hundred miles long, travelling ninety is half of it. 【劉向《戰國策・秦策五》Liu Xiang: "Strategies of the State of Qin, No.5", *Strategies of the Warring States*】

早霞不出門，晚霞行千里。 A rainbow in the morning is a warning not to travel, while a rainbow at night is an omen to travel a thousand miles. 【俗語 Common saying】

朝辭白帝彩雲間，千里江陵一日還。 At dawn, I left the White Emperor Town amidst rosy clouds, and arrived at Jiangling a thousand miles away in a day. 【李白〈早發白帝城〉Li Bai: "Leaving the White Emperor Town at Dawn"】

Tree

柳樹上開花 —— 沒結果。 A willow tree blossoms but does not bear fruit. 【歇後語 End-clipper】【孔厥，袁靜《新兒女英雄傳・第六回》Kong Jue and Yuan Jing: Chapter 6, *New Biographies of Heroes and Heroines*】

沒有梧桐樹，引不到鳳凰來。 Without Chinese parasol trees, phoenixes will not come. 【諺語 Proverb】

千年老幹屈如鐵，一夜東風都作花。 The old branches of a thousand-year-old tree is strong as iron, but with a night of east wind they turn into blossoms. 【張庸〈梅〉Zhang Yong: "Plum"】

樹不修不成材，兒不育不成人。 Trees without pruning will not be grown into useful timber; a son without strict discipline cannot grow up to be useful. 【俗語 Common saying】

樹大分杈，人大分家。 When a tree grows big, it branches out; when people grow up, they divide their family property. 【諺語 Proverb】【周立波《山鄉巨變・上卷第十三章》Zhou Libo: Chapter 13, Volume 1, *Great Changes in the Mountain Villages*】

樹大有枯枝。 When a tree grows big, there are certainly withe Red branches. 【諺語 Proverb】

樹倒猢猻散。 Once a tree falls, the monkeys scatter. 【龐元英《談藪‧曹詠妻》Pang Yuanying: "Wife of Cao Yong", *Concourse on Conversation*】

水明知月上，木落見梅尊。 When the surface of the water is bright, we know that the moon has risen, and when we see the trees are withe Red, we see the uniqueness of the plum tree. 【仇遠〈冷坐〉Chou Yuan: "Sitting in the Cold"】

松柏參天傲霜雪。 The towering pine and cypress tress defy frost and snow. 【諺語 Proverb】

歲寒三友 —— 松竹梅。 Three friends in water – the pine, bamboo, and plum. 【諺語 Proverb】

停車坐愛楓林晚，霜葉紅於二月花。 I stopped my carriage and sat there to enjoy the maple trees at dusk. Their frosted leaves were redder than flowers in the second month of the year. 【杜牧〈山行〉Du Mu: "Travelling in the Mountain"】

無邊落木蕭蕭下，不盡長江滾滾來。 The boundless forests shed their yellow leaves with rustles, the everflowing Changjiang River rolls on and on. 【杜甫〈登高〉Du Fu: "Climbing the Height"】

一樹春風千萬枝，嫩於金色軟於絲。 The willow tree, in spring breeze, has tens of thousands branches; they are more tender than the gold colour and softer than silk. 【白居易〈永豐坊園中垂柳〉Bai Juyi: "The Drooping Willow in the Garden in Yongfeng Lane"】

早晨栽下樹，晚來要趁涼。 One plants a tree in the morning and wants to enjoy the cool in its shade in the afternoon. 【馬致遠〈岳陽樓‧第一折〉Ma Zhiyuan: Scene 1, "Yueyang Tower"】

直尺難量彎木。 A straight ruler cannot measure a bending tree. 【諺語 Proverb】

Trend

大勢所趨，人心所向。 The general trend and the desire of the people. 【俗語 Common saying】

天下大勢，分久必合，合久必分。 The general trend under heaven is that there will be unity after prolonged division and division after prolonged unity. 【羅貫中《三國演義》Luo Guanzhong: *Romance of the Three Kingdoms*】

Trouble

飽暖生閒事。 Those who are well-fed and warmly-clad are apt to create trouble. 【諺語 Proverb】【蘭陵笑笑生《金瓶梅‧第三回》Lanling Xiaoxiaosheng: Chapter 3, *The Plum in the Golden Vase*】

不栽桃李種薔薇。 One does not plant peach and pear trees but grow roses. 【賈島〈題興化寺園亭〉Jia Dao:"Inscribing the Garden Pavilion of the Xinghua Temple"】

踩一頭，翹一頭。 As soon as one trouble is settled another crops up. 【俗語 Common saying】

打蛇不死——後患無窮。 Beating a snake without killing it leaves no end of trouble in the future. 【歇後語 End-clipper】

但能依本份，終須無煩惱。 If you can conduct yourself according to your position, there would be no troubles for you all your life. 【《增廣賢文》Words that Open up One's Mind and Enhance One's Wisdom】

多一位菩薩多一爐香。 With one more Buddha, one has to have one more incense burner. 【諺語 Proverb】

惡虎難鬥肚裏蛇。 A fierce tiger is incapable of fighting against a snake hidden inside one's belly. 【諺語 Proverb】【李六如《六十年的變遷‧第四章》Li Liuru: Chapter 4, *The Changes in the Last Sixty Years*】

煩惱不尋人，人自尋煩惱。 Trouble does not trouble a person, it is the person who brings about trouble himself. 【諺語 Proverb】

煩惱皆因強出頭。 One is troubled because one strives to take the lead. 【《增廣賢文》*Words that Open up One's Mind and Enhance One's Wisdom*】

飯飽生逸事。 A well-fed person creates trouble. 【俗語 Common saying】

風不刮樹不搖，心裏沒事不煩惱。 When there is no wind, a tree does not shake. When there is nothing on one's mind, one does not have worries. 【諺語 Proverb】

逢人不說人間事，便是人間無事人。 When one does not talk about affairs of the world when meeting people, then one is somebody who is free from troubles of the world. 【杜荀鶴〈贈質上人〉Du Xunhe:"Presented to Monk Zhi"】

耗子逗貓——沒事找事 A mouse teasing a cat is asking for trouble. 【歇後語 End-clipper】

呼蛇容易遣蛇難。 It is easy to summon a snake but difficult to send it away. 【諺語 Proverb】【馮夢龍《警世通言‧第十六卷》Feng Menglong: Chapter 16, *Stories to Caution the World*】

虎頭抓蒼蠅。 Catching flies on the tiger's head is asking for trouble. 【諺語 Proverb】

花錢買了個氣布袋。 Spend money just to buy oneself a bag of trouble. 【俗語 Common saying】

君子以思患而豫防之。 A gentleman thinks of troubles that may come and guard against them in advance. 【《易經‧既濟‧象》"Image", Hexagram *jiji*, *The Book of Changes*】

開水淋臭蟲 —— 不死也夠受。 One gets out of distress but into trouble. 【歇後語 End-clipper】

母雞叫鳴，家宅不安。 If hens crow, the family will have trouble. 【俗語 Common saying】

拿草棍兒戳老虎鼻子。 Tickle the tiger's nose with a straw – to stir up trouble. 【俗語 Common saying】 【曹雪芹《紅樓夢‧第四十六回》Cao Xueqin: Chapter 46, *A Dream of the Red Chamber*】

平地起風波。 Stir up trouble out of nothing. 【關漢卿〈魯齋郎‧第二折〉Guan Hanqing: Scene 2, "Luzailang"】

破船偏遇打頭風。 One trouble coming on top of another. 【馮夢龍《醒世恆言‧第一卷》Feng Menglong: Chapter 1, *Stories to Awaken the World*】

窮有窮愁，富有富愁。 The poor have their troubles and the rich, their problems. 【俗語 Common saying】【柳青《創業史‧第一卷第二十一章》Liu Qing: Chpater 21, Volume 1, *History of Creating Business*】

去了咳嗽添了喘 —— 禍不單行。 Leap out of the frying pan into the fire. 【歇後語 End-clipper】

扇陰風，點鬼火。 Stir up trouble. 【俗語 Common saying】

少管閒事少麻煩。 If you don't mind other people's business, you seldom get into trouble. 【俗語 Common saying】

天下本無事，庸人自擾之。 There is nothing happening in the world and yet those unenlightened make a fuss of it by themselves. 【歐陽修，宋祁，范鎮，呂夏卿等《新唐書‧陸象先傳》Ouyang Xiu, Song Qi, Fan Zhen, Lu Xiaqing, et al:"Biography of Lu Xiangxian", *A New History of the Tang*】

無事不登三寶殿。 Call on somebody only when one is in trouble. 【張南莊《何典‧第四卷》Zhang Nanzhuang: Chapter 4, *From Which Classic*】

無與禍臨，禍乃不存。 Do not get involved in troubles and you will have no trouble. 【馬總《意林‧卷一》Ma Zong: Chapter 1, *Forest of Opinions*】

野草不種年年有，煩惱無根日日生。 Without planting, there is wild grass every year; without reason, there is trouble coming up every day. 【柯丹丘〈荊釵記〉Ke Danqiu:"The Wooden Hairpin"】

一波方平，一波又起。 One trouble has just settled when another rises. 【俗語 Common saying】

一波未平，一波又起。 One trouble follows another. 【俗語 Common saying】

自己有苦自己知。 One knows where the trouble is with oneself. 【俗語 Common saying】

Trust

人非信不立。 A person who is not trustworthy cannot establish himself in the society. 【劉畫《劉子‧履信第八》Liu Zhou: Chapter 8, "Practise Trust", *Works of Master Liu Zhou*】

小信成則大信立，故明主積於信。 When trust in small things is accomplished, trust in big things will be established. An intelligent ruler therefore is serious about building up trust. 【韓非《韓非子‧外儲説左上第三十二》Han Fei: Chapter 32, "Outer Congeries of Sayings, Part 1", *Hanfeizi*】

信，國之寶也，民之所庇也。 Trust is a treasure of a country, with which people are protected. 【左丘明《左傳‧僖公二十七年》Zuo Qiuming: "The Twenty-seventh Year of the Reign of Duke Xi", *Zuo's Commentary on the Spring and Autumn Annals*】

信近於義，言可復也。 Trust is close to righteousness for what is spoken can be made good. 【孟軻《孟子‧告子章句上》Meng Ke: Chapter 6, Part 1, *Mencius*】

至信之人可以感物也。 A most trustworthy person can move inanimate things. 【列禦寇《列子‧黃帝第二》Lie Yukou: Chapter 2, "The Yellow Emperor", *Liezi*】

Truth and falsehood

醜媳婦也得見公婆。 Truth will come to light one day. 【俗語 Common saying】

此地無銀三百兩。 Never try to prove what nobody doubts. 【俗語 Common saying】

道路越走越寬，真理越辯越明。 A road becomes wider with more people walking on it. Truth becomes clearer through more debates. 【俗語 Common saying】

燈不撥不亮，理不辯不明。 An oil lamp becomes brighter after trimming, a truth becomes clearer after being discussed. 【諺語 Proverb】

耳聞是虛，眼見是實。 What one hears is vague, but what one sees is real. 【諺語 Proverb】

弓是彎的，理是直的。 A bow is bent, but truth is straight. 【諺語 Proverb】

假作真時真亦假，無為有處有還無。 When false is taken for true, true becomes false; if non-being turns into being, being becomes non-being. 【曹雪芹《紅樓夢》Cao Xueqin: *A Dream of the Red Chamber*】

經目之事，猶恐未真，背後之言，豈能全信？ When things that are seen by your own eyes are still not truly real, how can you fully believe in what is said behind your back? 【蘭陵笑笑生《金瓶梅》Lanling Xiaoxiaosheng: *The Plum in the Golden Vase*】

鏡中花，水中月。 It is as illusive as flowers in a mirror or the moon in the water. 【曹雪芹《紅樓夢·第五回》Cao Xueqin: Chapter 5, *A Dream of the Red Chamber*】

路有千條，理祇有一條。 There are thousands of roads but only one truth. 【諺語 Proverb】

牆上畫餅 —— 中看不中吃。 To draw a cake on the wall is nice to look at, but it cannot be eaten. 【歇後語 End-clipper】

去粗取精，去偽存真。 Discard the dross and select the essential; eliminate the false and retain the true. 【俗語 Common saying】

人多講出理來，稻多打出米來。 With many people, truth can be found and with a lot of paddies, rice is produced. 【黎汝清《萬山紅遍·第四十七章》Li Ruqing: Chapter 47, *Redness All over Ten Thousand Mountains*】

實的虛不得。 What is true cannot be covered with anything untrue. 【馮夢龍《喻世明言·第二十六卷》Feng Menglong: Chapter 26, *Stories to Instruct the World*】

實即是虛，虛即是實。 What is real is empty and what is empty, real. 【諺語 Proverb】

實中有虛，虛中有實。 There is emptiness in reality, and there is reality in emptiness. 【諺語 Proverb】

是真難假，是假難真。 What is real cannot be unreal and what is unreal cannot be real. 【諺語 Proverb】

是真難滅，是假易除。 What is true is difficult to destroy and what is false is easy to get rid of. 【諺語 Proverb】【施耐庵《水滸傳·第六十二回》Shi Nai'an: Chapter 62, *Outlaws of the Marshes*】

雖是笑話，卻含真理。 Though it is just a joke, it has some truth in it. 【諺語 Proverb】

談笑之中存至理。 There is truth in joking and jesting. 【諺語 Proverb】

小兒口裏出真言。 Children tell the truth. 【俗語 Common saying】

虛則實之，實則虛之。 The unreal is to be regarded as real and the real as unreal. 【孫武《孫子兵法‧虛實第六》Sun Wu: Chapter 6, "The Void and Substance", *The Art of War by Sunzi*】

一人傳虛，萬人傳實。 When one person circulates a false story, ten thousand people would circulate it as a fact. 【王符《潛夫論‧賢難》Wang Fu: "Difficulties of Worthies", *Remarks by a Recluse*】

一人為私，六眼為公。 What a person says may be false but what three persons say may be true. 【諺語 Proverb】

朝聞道，夕死可矣。 Truth is so valuable that one is willing to die in the evening after learning it in the morning. 【孔子《論語‧里仁篇第四》Confucius: Chapter 4, *The Analects of Confucius*】

真的假不了，假的真不了。 What is true cannot become false and what is false cannot become true. 【黎汝清《萬山紅遍‧第三十一章》Li Ruqing: Chapter 31, *Redness All over Ten Thousand Mountains*】

真理越辯越明。 The more truth is debated, the clearer it becomes. 【諺語 Proverb】

紙包不住火。 Paper cannot wrap fire. 【古華《芙蓉鎮‧第二章》Gu Hua: Chapter 2, *Hibiscus Town*】

醉漢口裏說真話。 A drunk man tells the truth. 【諺語 Proverb】

Two-facedness

棒槌打人手撫摸。 Give one a hard time while pretending to be warm-hearted. 【俗語 Common saying】

表面是人，暗中是鬼。 They are human beings in appearance but ghosts at heart. 【諺語 Proverb】

當面不說，背後亂說。 Say nothing in one's face, but gossip a lot behind one's back. 【俗語 Common saying】

當面叫哥哥，背後摸傢伙。 Honey on one's lips and murder in one's heart. 【俗語 Common saying】

當面捧場，背後罵娘。 Praise one to one's face and abuse one behind one's back. 【諺語 Proverb】

當面是人，背後是鬼。 Act one way in public and another in private. 【俗語 Common saying】

當面說得好聽，背後又在搞鬼。 Say nice things to one's face but

use dirty tricks behind one's back. 【俗語 Common saying】

當面說好，背後捅刀。 Say nice things to one's face, but stab one in the back. 【俗語 Common saying】

當面頌揚，背後罵娘。 Praise one to one's face, but curse one behind one's back. 【俗語 Common saying】

當面一套，背後一套。 Act one way in one's face but another behind one's back. 【李行道〈灰闌記・第二折〉Li Xingdao: Scene 2, "The Chalk Circle"】

翻臉不認人。 Change one's countenance and does not recognize one's acquaintance. 【老舍《駱駝祥子・第十四章》Lao She: Chapter 14, *Rickshaw Boy*】

芙蓉其面，蛇蝎其心。 A woman with a beautiful face, but her heart is as vicious as a snake. 【諺語 Proverb】

好面譽人者，亦好背而毀之。 One who is fond of praising you in your presence is also one who is fond of defaming you behind your back. 【莊周《莊子・盜跖・雜篇第二十九》Zhuang Zhou: "Robber Zhi", Chapter 29, "Miscellaneous Chapters", *Zhuangzi*】

話好聽如鈴，心彎曲如鈎。 One's words are as agreeable as a bell but one's heart is as crooked as a hook. 【諺語 Proverb】

見人說人話，見鬼說鬼話。 A double-faced person who says one thing before one, and another thing before another. 【李寶嘉《官場現形記・第三十八回》Li Baojia: Chapter 38, *Officialdom Unmasked*】

講的是一套，做的又是一套。 Say one thing but do another. 【俗語 Common saying】

口善心不善。 Say fine words but be cruel at heart. 【袁於令〈西樓記・一三齣〉Yuan Yuling: Scene 13, "The West Tower"】

口似蓮花心似刀。 One has a glib tongue but a cruel heart. 【馮夢龍《喻世明言・第三十五卷》Feng Menglong: Chapter 35, *Stories to Instruct the World*】

口談道德，而志在穿窬。 Talk about virtue but think of vice. 【李贄《焚書・又與焦弱侯》Li Zhi: "Another Letter to Jiao Hong", *A Book to Burn*】

口有蜜，腹有劍。 Honey-mouthed but dagger-hearted. 【司馬光《資治通鑒・唐紀・唐玄宗天寶元年》Sima Guang: "The First Year of the Reign of Tianbao of Emperor Xuanzong", "Annals of the Tang Dynasty", *Comprehensive Mirror to Aid in Government*】

臉上帶笑，袖裏藏刀。 With smiles on the face but a knife in the sleeve. 【諺語 Proverb】

面帶忠厚，內藏奸詐。 One has an honest appearance but is actually cunning and deceitful. 【俗語 Common saying】

面若桃花，心存蛇蝎。A woman having a beautiful face but a foul heart.【俗語 Common saying】

面上笑呵呵，心裏壽蛇窩。Have a face wreathed in smiles and a heart filled with gall.【諺語 Proverb】

明是一盆火，暗是一把刀。A pot of fire on surface but a knife in secret.【曹雪芹《紅樓夢‧第六十五回》Cao Xueqin: Chapter 65, A Dream of the Red Chamber】

明一套，暗一套。Act one way in the open and another in secret.【諺語 Proverb】

入山不怕傷人虎，祇怕人情兩面刀。When entering a mountain, we are not afraid of tigers who might injure people. We only fear people who resort to double dealings in their human relationships with others.【《增廣賢文》Words that Open up One's Mind and Enhance One's Wisdom】

上頭笑着，底下就使絆子。All the time one is smiling when one tries to trip somebody up.

【曹雪芹《紅樓夢‧第六十五回》Cao Xueqin: Chapter 65, A Dream of the Red Chamber】

說一套，做一套。Say one thing but do another.【諺語 Proverb】

台上握手，台下踢腳。Shaking hands on stage, but kicking each other off stage.【姜樹茂《漁港之春‧第五章》Jiang Shumao: Chapter 5, The Spring of a Fishing Port】

陽一套，陰一套。Act in one way in public and another in private.【諺語 Proverb】

陰一套，陽一套。Act one way in private and another in public.【諺語 Proverb】

又唱紅臉又唱白臉。Play the role of a gentleman and a villian.【諺語 Proverb】

嘴裏說東，心裏想西。To say one thing, while there's another thing on one's mind.【諺語 Proverb】

一隻手捏香，一隻手捏槍。With joss sticks in one hand but a gun in the other.【俗語 Common saying】

Ugliness

老鴉笑黑豬，自醜不覺得。A crow calls a pig black, but does not know its own ugliness.【諺語 Proverb】

人醜愛戴花。The uglier a woman is, the more flowers she wants

to wear in her hair.【周立波《暴風驟雨‧第一部第七章》Zhou Libo: Chapter 7, Volume 1, Violent Storms and Heavy Showers】

一白遮百醜。White skin relieves ugliness.【俗語 Common saying】

Uniqueness

古今中外，前所未有。It is unprecedented in the past or present, China or abroad. 【俗語 Common saying】

天上少有，人間無雙。One is rare in heaven and unparalleled on earth. 【俗語 Common saying】

Unity

不怕浪頭高，祇怕槳不齊。We are not afraid of towering billows, but fear that our oars cannot be pulled in unison. 【諺語 Proverb】

大家一條心，鋒利可斷金。When we are united, our strength is so great that it can even snap a block of gold. 【俗語 Common saying】

單者易折，眾者難摧。A single person is easy to be frustrated. Many people gathering together is difficult to be defeated. 【李延壽《北史・吐谷渾傳》Li Yanshou: "Annals of Tuyuhun", *History of the Northern Dynasties*】

高山也要低頭，河水也要讓路。Mountains bow their heads and rivers give way. 【俗語 Common saying】

合則存，分則亡。United, we survive; divided, we perish. 【諺語 Proverb】

三人一條心，黃土變成金。When three persons are of the same mind, yellow earth becomes gold. 【諺語 Proverb】

萬眾一條心，力量大無邊。When all the people are of the same mind, the power is boundless. 【諺語 Proverb】

我中有你，你中有我。You are among us and we are among you. 【管道昇〈我儂詞〉Guan Daosheng: "A Poem of You and I"】

團結就是力量。Unity is strength. 【諺語 Proverb】

一虎不敵眾犬。A single tiger is no match to a peck of dogs. 【諺語 Proverb】

眾人一條心，黃土變成金。When all the people are of the same mind, the yellow earth can be turned into gold. 【諺語 Proverb】

Urgency

不分輕重緩急。 Work without regard to the relative importance or urgency.【諺語 Proverb】

貓不急不上樹，兔不急不咬人。 A cat does not climb up a tree unless it is irritated; a hare does not bite unless it is nettled.【劉江《太行風雲‧第四回》Liu Jiang: Chapter 4, *Changes in Taixing* 】

人急智生，狗急跳牆。 When in urgency, a person will come up with a way to get out of the predicament and a dog will jump over a wall.【曹雪芹《紅樓夢‧第二十七回》Cao Xueqin: Chapter 27, *A Dream of the Red Chamber*】

事急無法律，路急無君子。 Necessity knows no law.【諺語 Proverb】

Use

大炮打麻雀 —— 大材小用。 Using a cannon to shoot a sparrow is to employ a large tool for petty use.【歇後語 End-clipper】

放諸四海而皆準。 Applicable everywhere.【《禮記‧祭義第二十四章》Chapter 24, "The Meaning of Sacrifices", *The Book of Rites*】

古為今用，洋為中用。 To use the ancient for the present and the West for China.【俗語 Common saying】

好鋼用在刀刃上。 Use the best material where it is needed most.【俗語 Common saying】

沒藥性的砲仗 —— 中看不中用。 A fire-cracker without powder is good only for show – it's useless.【歇後語 End-clipper】

桐油罐子無二用。 A tung oil canister is merely for holding the tung oil.【俗語 Common saying】

物有所歸，各盡其用。 There is a place for everything and everything in its place.【俗語 Common saying】

Victory and defeat

敗莫敗於不自知。 The major cause of defeat lies with not knowing what one is incapable of.【呂不韋《呂氏春秋‧自知》Lu Buwei: "Self-knowledge", *Master Lu's Spring and Autumn Annals* 】

被打敗的公雞 —— 垂頭喪氣。A defeated cock – dejected. 【歇後語 End-clipper】

不獲全勝，決不收兵。Not to withdraw troops until complete victory is won. 【俗語 Common saying】

不可勝在己，可勝在敵。Not being able to win has to do with oneself, but being able to win has to do with the opponent. 【孫武《孫子兵法・軍形第四》Sun Wu: Chapter 4, "Tactical Dispositions", *The Art of War by Sunzi*】

不戰則已，戰則必勝。One goes into a battle sure of victory. 【孟軻《孟子・公孫丑下》Meng Ke: Chapter 2, Part 2, *Mencius*】

不爭一日之長短。One does not strive for temporary superiority. 【俗語 Common saying】

不知鹿死誰手。Don't know in whose hands will the deer die. 【房玄齡等《晉書・石勒載記下》Fang Xuanling, *et al*: "Records of Shi Le, Part 2", *History of the Jin Dynasty*】

操必勝之券。Hold the trump card in one's hands. 【管仲《管子・明法第四十六》Guan Zhong: Chapter 46, "Making the Law Clear", *Guanzi*】

成則為王，敗則為寇。The victors become kings and the defeated are branded thieves. 【孫中山《國民黨第一次代表大會之演講》Sun Yat-sen: "Address at the First National Congress of Kuomintang"】

得勝的貓兒歡似虎。A victorious cat is happy as a tiger. 【吳承恩《西遊記・第六十一回》Wu Cheng'en: Chapter 61, *Journey to the West*】

風無常順，兵無常勝。The wind is not always favourable and an army is not always victorious. 【馮夢龍《醒世恆言・第三十四卷》Feng Menglong: Chapter 34, *Stories to Awaken the World*】

假不能以勝真，邪不能以壓正。The false cannot defeat the true and the evil cannot triumph over the virtuous. 【羅懋登《三寶太監西洋記・第二十一回》Luo Maodeng: Chapter 21, *Sanbao Eunuch's Voyage to the Western Ocean*】

凱歌陣陣，喜報頻傳。Songs of triumph are sung and reports of victory keep pouring in. 【俗語 Common saying】

柔弱勝剛強。The soft and weak overcome the rigid and strong. 【老子《道德經・第三十六章》Laozi: Chapter 36, *Daodejing*】

弱之勝強，柔之勝剛，天下莫不知，莫能行。All people in the world know that the soft overcomes the hard, and the weak the strong, but they are unable to put it into practice. 【老子《道德經・第七十八章》Laozi: Chapter 78, *Daodejing*】

勝敗乃兵家常事。Victories and defeats are common things for soldiers. 【劉昫《舊唐書・裴度傳》Liu Xu: "Biography of Pei Du", *History of the Early Tang*】

勝不驕，敗不餒。 Don't be proud when you win or upset when you lose. 【商鞅《商君書‧戰法》Shang Yang:"Military Strategy", *The Works of Shang Yang*】

勝可知而不可為。 Victory can be known but cannot be created. 【孫武《孫子兵法‧軍形第四》Sun Wu: Chapter 4, "Tactical Dispositions", *The Art of War by Sunzi*】

勝利沖昏了頭腦。 One becomes dizzy when one wins. 【俗語 Common saying】

勝人者有力，自勝者強。 One who is victorious over others is powerful; one who is victorious over oneself is strong. 【老子《道德經‧第三十三章》Laozi: Chapter 33, *Daodejing*】

天下之至柔，馳騁天下之至堅。 The softest in the world manipulates the hardest in the world. 【老子《道德經‧第四十三章》Laozi: Chapter 43, *Daodejing*】

先為不可勝，以待敵之可勝。 Place yourself in an invulnerable position and wait for an opportunity to defeat the enemy. 【孫武《孫子兵法‧軍形第四》Sun Wu: Chapter 4:"Tactical Dispositions", *The Art of War by Sunzi*】

以少勝多，以弱勝強。 The few defeating the many, the weak defeating the strong. 【諺語 Proverb】

知彼知己，勝乃不殆；知天知地，勝乃不窮。 Knowing the enemy and the self, victory is safe; knowing heaven and earth, victory is endless. 【管仲《管子‧牧民第一》Guan Zhong: Chapter 1, "Shepherding the People", *Guanzi*】

知己知彼，百戰百勝。 One who knows one's own strength and that of the enemy is sure to win every battle. 【孫武《孫子兵法‧謀攻第三》Sun Wu: Chapter 3, "Attack by Stratagem", *The Art of War by Sunzi*】

View

卑之無甚高論。 What is said is far from lofty. 【司馬遷《史記‧張釋之馮唐列傳》Sima Qian:"Biographies of Zhang Shizhi and Feng Tang", *Records of the Grand Historian*】

不隨俗而雷同，不逐聲而寄論。 Don't drift along with the crowd and follow what they do; don't follow their views and engage in empty talk. 【王符《潛夫論‧交際》Wang Fu:"On Social Relationships", *Remarks by a Recluse*】

不以人廢言。 Not to reject a view because of the person expressing it. 【孔子《論語‧衛靈公篇第十五》Confucius: Chapter 15, *The Analects of Confucius*】

成見不可有，定見不可無。 One should not have biases, but one

should have one's own views. 【諺語 Proverb】

你說長，他說短。 You say that it is long, but he says that it is short. 【俗語 Common saying】

仁者見之謂之仁，智者見之謂之智。 A benevolent person may look at something and call it benevolence and a wise person may look at the same thing and call it wisdom. 【《易經・繫辭上》 "Appended Remarks, Part 1", *The Book of Changes*】

人各有心，心各有見。 Everyone has one's own mind and each mind has its own view. 【《增廣賢文》Words that Open up One's Mind and Enhance One's Wisdom】

同聲相應，同氣相求。 Similar voices echo each other, and similar odours merge together. 【《易經・乾・文言》 "The Record of Wen Yan", Hexagram *Qian*, *The Book of Changes*】

同乎己者未必可用，異於我者未必可忽也。 Those who have the same views with me may not be appointable for office; those who have different views with me may not be neglected. 【葛洪《抱朴子・外篇・清鑒第二十一》Ge Hong: Chapter 21, "The Pure Mirror", "Outer Chapters", *The Master Who Embraces Simplicity*】

Virtue

不矜細行，終累大德。 Not cautious to small actions will eventually have a negative effect on one's great virtue. 【《尚書・旅獒》"Hounds of Lu", *The Book of History*】

不以一眚掩大德。 Don't devalue one's great contributions by a small fault one makes. 【左丘明《左傳・僖公三十三年》Zuo Qiuming: "The Thirty-third Year of the Reign of Duke Xi", *Zuo's Commentary on the Spring and Autumn Annals*】

大德之人必得其壽。 A person of great virtue is sure to have a long life. 【《禮記・中庸第十七章》 Chapter 17, "Doctrine of the Mean", *The Book of Rites*】

大上有立德，其次有立功，其次有立言。 The best is to establish virtue, the second best, have achievements, and the third best, have one's philosophy. 【左丘明《左傳・襄公二十四年》Zuo Qiuming: "The Twenty-fourth Year of the Reign of Duke Xiang", *Zuo's Commentary on the Spring and Autumn Annals*】

德不孤，必有鄰。 Virtue is not alone for it is bound to have neighbours. 【孔子《論語・里仁篇第四》Confucius: Chapter 4, *The Analects of Confucius*】

德如寒泉，假有沙塵，弗能污也。Virtue is like a clear fountain, even though there might be sand and dirt, it cannot be soiled.【劉晝《劉子·通塞第二十三》Liu Zhou: Chapter 23, "Penetration and Blockade", *Works of Master Liu Zhou*】

德者本也，財者末也。Virtue is primary, wealth, secondary.【《禮記·大學第四十二》Chapter 42, "The Great Learning", *The Book of Rites*】

度德而處之，量力而行之。Managing affairs according to the magnitude of one's virtue and taking actions according to the estimation of one's strength.【左丘明《左傳·隱公十一年》Zuo Qiuming: "The Eleventh Year of the Reign of Duke Yin", *Zuo's Commentary on the Spring and Autumn Annals*】

功無大乎進賢。No service is greater than recommending the virtuous people.【呂不韋《呂氏春秋·贊能》Lu Buwei: "Praising the Capable", *Master Lu's Spring and Autumn Annals*】

賤貨而貴德。Despise wealth and esteem virtue.【《禮記·中庸第二十章》Chapter 20, "Doctrine of the Mean", *The Book of Rites*】

君子強梁以德，小人強梁以力。A gentleman's strength lies with virtue while that of a petty peron, force.【揚雄《太玄·強》Yang Xiong: "Strength", *Great Mystery*】

君子以德，小人以力。A gentleman's strength lies with virtue while that of a petty peron, force.【荀況《荀子·富國第十》Xun Kuang: Chapter 10, "Enriching the State", *Xunzi*】

君子在德不在衣。The essence of a gentleman lies on his virtue, not on the clothes he wears.【諺語 Proverb】

君子以多識前言往行，以畜其德。A gentleman relies on knowing much of what has been said and done previously to cultivate his own virtue.【《易經·大畜》"Hexagram Da Chu", *The Book of Changes*】

立天下之大本。Establish the great fundamental virtues of the world.【《禮記·中庸第三十二章》Chapter 32, "Doctrine of the Mean", *The Book of Rites*】

男子有德便是才，女子無才便是德。A man with virtue is intelligent and a woman without intelligence is virtuous.【張岱〈公祭祁夫人文〉Zhang Dai: "Essay for the Public Memorial Service for Mrs. Qi"】

棄德崇奸，禍之大者也。To abandon virtue and favour evils is the greatest disaster.【左丘明《左傳·僖公二十年》Zuo Qiuming: "The Twentieth Year of the Reign of Duke Xi", *Zuo's Commentary on the Spring and Autumn Annals*】

上德不德，是以有德。A person of superior virtue does not claim to have virtue and this is true virtue.【老子《道德經·第三十八章》Laozi: Chapter 38, *Daodejing*】

上德若谷，大白若辱，廣德若不足。 Superior virtue is like a valley, pure whiteness is like having been stained, and one who has many virtues is like being inadequate in virtue. 【老子《道德經‧第四十一章》Laozi: Chapter 41, *Daodejing*】

恃德者昌，恃力者亡。 He who relies on virtue will thrive and he who relies on force will perish. 【司馬遷《史記‧商君列傳》Sima Qian: "Biography of Lord Shang", *Records of the Grand Historian*】

樹德務滋，除惡務本。 To establish virtue, one should spread it; to remove evil, one must do it from the roots. 【《尚書‧泰誓》"The Great Speech", *The Book of History*】

樹高不能撐着天。 Even the tallest tree cannot reach the heaven. 【諺語 Proverb】

吾未見好德如好色者也。 I have yet to meet a man who is fond of virtue as he is of beauty. 【孔子《論語‧子罕篇第九》Confucius: Chapter 9, *The Analects of Confucius*】

賢能不待次而舉，不肖不待須而廢。 The virtuous and talented must be recommended without delay and the incapable must be dismissed from office immediately. 【韓嬰《韓詩外傳‧卷五》Han Ying: Chapter 5: *Supplementary Commentary on the Book of Songs by Master Han*】

賢為國之寶。 The able and virtuous are treasures of the country. 【《增廣賢文》Words that Open up One's Mind and Enhance One's Wisdom】

賢者容不辱。 A person of virtue forgives and never insults others. 【桓寬《鹽鐵論‧申韓》Huan Kuan: "On Preparedness against the Steppe Peoples", *Discussions on Salt and Iron*】

以德防患，憂禍不存。 To prevent troubles from happening with virtue, worries and disasters will not occur. 【焦延壽《焦氏易林‧泰之‧乾》Jiao Yanshou: "Taizhi, Hexagram *Qian*", *Thoughts on The Book of Changes by Mr Jiao*】

以德服人，使人心服。 Win popularity with your virtue and you will win people's heart. 【孟軻《孟子‧公孫丑上》Meng Ke: Chapter 2, Part 1, *Mencius*】

以直報怨，以德報德。 Return enmity with justice and return kindness with kindness. 【劉向《戰國策‧秦策三》Liu Xiang: "Strategies of the State of Qin, Part 3", *Strategies of the Warring States*】

有德不可敵。 Those with virtue are invincible. 【左丘明《左傳‧僖公二十八年》Zuo Qiuming: "The Twenty-eighth Year of the Reign of Duke Xi", *Zuo's Commentary on the Spring and Autumn Annals*】

知者莫大於知賢，政者莫大於官賢。 The most important thing for a wise person is to discover a worthy person; the most important thing for a government administer is to offer appointments to the virtuous people. 【戴德《大戴禮記‧主言》Dai De: "Royal Speeches", *Records of Rites by Dai the Elder*】

智仁勇三者，天下之達德也。 Wisdom, benevolence, and courage are the three virtues that are universally acknowledged. 【《禮記‧中庸第三十一章》Chapter 31, "Doctrine of the Mean", *The Book of Rites*】

忠，德之正也；信，德之固也；卑讓，德之基也。 Loyalty is the centre of virtue; trust is the consolidation of virtue, and modesty is the foundation of virtue. 【左丘明《左傳‧文公元年》Zuo Qiuming: "The First Year of the Reign of Duke Wen", *Zuo's Commentary on the Spring and Autumn Annals*】

重積德則無不克。 If one stresses the accumulation of virtue, there is nothing that cannot be overcome. 【老子《道德經‧第五十九章》Laozi: Chapter 59, *Daodejing*】

尊德樂義，則可以囂囂矣。 Honour virtue and delight in righteousness, then you can always be satisfied. 【孟軻《孟子‧盡心章句上》Meng Ke: Chapter 7, Part 1, *Mencius*】

作德，心逸日休；作偽，心勞日拙。 If you act virtuously, your mind is at ease, and you feel comfortable every day. If you act pretentiously, your mind is toiled and you feel tired every day. 【《尚書‧周官》"Zhou Ministers", *The Book of History*】

Vision

筆筒子裏觀天。 Have a very narrow vision. 【周立波《山鄉巨變‧上卷第六章》Zhou Libo: Chapter 6, Volume 1, *Great Changes in the Mountain Villages*】

不登高山，不知天之高也。不臨深谷，不知地之厚也。 One who has not climbed up to the top of a high mountain does not know the height of the sky. One who has not been to a deep valley does not know the depth of the earth. 【荀況《荀子‧勸學第一》Xun Kuang: Chapter 1, "Exhortation to Learning", *Xunzi*】

戴着有色眼鏡。 Look at something or somebody through coloured spectacles. 【俗語 Common saying】

顧大局，識大體。 Have the overall situation in mind and put the general interest above all. 【李寶嘉《官場現形記‧第十四回》Li Baojia: Chapter 14, *Officialdom Unmasked*】

見小不見大。 Strain at a gnat and swallow a camel. 【俗語 Common saying】

老太太打哈欠 —— 一望無涯（牙）。 When you look at an old woman yawning, she has no teeth – as far as the eye can see. 【歇後語 End-clipper】

明察秋毫，不見輿薪。 See the minute details but miss the major issue. 【孟軻《孟子・梁惠王上》Meng Ke: Chapter 1, Part 1, *Mencius*】

識遠者貴本，見近者務末。 One who is far-sighted values the roots; one who is short-sighted focuses on the trivialities. 【葛洪《抱朴子・外篇・博喻第三十八》Ge Hong: Chapter 38, "Extensive Analogies", "Outer Chapters", *The Master Who Embraces Simplicity*】

天下事當於大處着眼，小處下手。 In dealing with things in the world, we must set our sight on the whole situation, and start in a small way. 【曾國藩《曾文正公全集》Zeng Guofan: *Complete Works of Zeng Guofan*】

一眼平疇三十里，際天白水立青秧。 At a glance, the flat fields run into thirty miles, and the green seedlings in the white water are boundless. 【楊萬里〈晚登多稼亭〉Yang Wanli: "Climbing up the Duojia Tower in the Evening"】

愚者昧於成事，智者見於未萌。 An unintelligent person remains ignorant even when something has happened while an intelligent person senses it before something happens. 【劉向《戰國策・趙策二》Liu Xiang: "Strategies of the State of Zhao, No. 2", *Strategies of the Warring States*】

欲窮千里目，更上一層樓。 If you want to stretch your sight to a thousand miles, you have to climb up one more storey of the tower. 【王之渙〈登鸛雀樓〉Wang Zhihuan: "Ascending the Stock Tower"】

站得高，看得遠。 Stand high and see far ahead. 【王充《論衡・別通第三十八卷》Wang Chong: Chapter 38, "On Intelligence", *Critical Essays*】

只見其一，不見其二。 See just one side of the matter and overlook the other. 【俗語 Common saying】

Waiting

半夜裏屙屎 —— 等不得。 Having to defecate in the middle of the night – can't wait. 【歇後語 End-clipper】

放長線釣大魚。 Wait patiently for a long time in order to get something big. 【俗語 Common saying】

守得雲開見月明。Wait till the clouds roll by. 【俗語 Common saying】

Walking

常在河邊走，哪能不濕鞋。If you frequently walk along a river, how could it be possible that your shoes do not get wet? 【俗語 Common saying】

穿大街，走小巷。Walk through a maze of main roads and narrow lanes. 【俗語 Common saying】

穿新鞋，走老路。Wear new shoes but take the old road. 【俗語 Common saying】

飯後百步走，活到九十九。Walk a hundred steps after dinner, you will live up to ninety-nine years old. 【俗語 Common saying】

急行無好步。In a rush, one cannot walk very steadily. 【俗語 Common saying】

心慌行路慢。When one is anxious, one walks with a slow pace. 【俗語 Common saying】

行不愧影，寢不愧衾。One does not let his shadow down when walking and does not let his quilt down when sleeping. 【脫脫等《宋史・蔡元定傳》Toktoghan, et al: "Biography of Cai Yuanding", History of the Song】

行路難，行路難。多歧路，今安在。Moving forward on the road is difficult, and it is so difficult. There have been many crossroads, but where are they now? 【李白〈行路難〉Li Bai: "Moving Forward on the Road is Difficult"】

一步三回頭。With every step one looks back three times. 【俗語 Common saying】

一腳高，一腳低。Walking in an awkward way. 【關漢卿〈詐妮子調風月・第二折〉Guan Hanqing: Scene 2, "A Deceitful Hussy Toys with Romance"】

有道難行不如醉，有口難言不如睡。When the way is difficult to travel, it is better to get drunk, and when things are difficult to be said, it is better to sleep. 【蘇軾〈醉睡者〉Su Shi: "Drunken Sleeper"】

War

兵貴乎勇，不在乎多。Soldiers are highly valued for their courage, not for their numbers. 【陳壽《三國志・魏書・郭嘉傳》Chen

Shou:"Biography of Guo Jia", "History of the State of Wei", *Records of the Three Kingdoms*】

兵貴勝，不貴久。 In war, what is valued is victory, not prolonged war. 【孫武《孫子兵法・作戰第二》 Sun Wu: Chapter 2, "Waging War", *The Art of War by Sunzi* 】

兵無常勢，水無常形。 Wars do not have fixed scenerios; water has no constant shape. 【孫武《孫子兵法・虛實第六》 Sun Wu: Chapter 6, "The Void and Substance", *The Art of War by Sunzi* 】

兵者，不祥之器。 Arms are tools of ill omen. 【老子《道德經・第三十一章》 Laozi: Chapter 31, *Daodejing*】

刀槍入庫，馬放南山。 The swords and guns are put back in the arsenal and war horses are grazed in the hillside. 【錢彩《說岳全傳・第一回》 Qian Cai: Chapter 1, *A Story of Yue Fei*】

弓上弦，刀出鞘。 The arrow is on the bowstring and the sword is unsheathed. 【施耐庵《水滸傳・第九十五回》 Shi Nai'an: Chapter 95, *Outlaws of the Marshes*】

故善用兵者，避其銳氣，擊其惰歸。 One who is skilled in military strategy avoids an enemy when the enemy's spirits are high but one attacks the enemy who has become sluggish and inclined to return. 【孫武《孫子兵法・軍爭第七》 Sun Wu:

Chapter 7, "Military Fighting", *The Art of War by Sunzi*】

國雖大，好戰必亡。 Though a country may be large, if it likes to go to war, it will inevitably fall. 【司馬穰苴《司馬法・仁本》 Sima Rangju:"Benevolence as a Basis", *The Art of War by Sima Rangju*】

化干戈為玉帛。 Bury the hatches and work for peace. 【劉安《淮南子・原道訓第一》 Liu An: Chapter 1, "Searching out the Way", *Huainanzi*】

禍莫大於輕敵。 There is no calamity greater than underestimating the strength of your enemy. 【老子《道德經・第六十九章》 Laozi: Chapter 69, *Daodejing*】

軍中無戲言。 There is no jesting in war. 【羅貫中《三國演義・第四十六回》 Luo Guanzhong: Chapter 46, *Romance of the Three Kingdoms*】

兩國相爭，不斬來者。 Envoys should not be beheaded when two states are at war against each other. 【羅貫中《三國演義・第四十五回》 Luo Guanzhong: Chapter 45, *Romance of the Three Kingdoms*】

寧作太平犬，莫為離亂人。 Rather be a dog in times of peace than a person in the midst of wars. 【馮夢龍《醒世恆言・第三卷》 Feng Menglong: Chapter 3, *Stories to Awaken the World*】

妻離子散，家破人亡。 War causes the breakup of countless families by death or separation.

【孟軻《孟子·梁惠王上》Meng Ke: Chapter 1, Part 1, *Mencius*】

輕傷不下火線。 Not to leave the front line due to slight wounds. 【俗語 Common saying】

善戰者，立於不敗之地，而不失敵之敗也。 He who is good at warfare places himself in an invincible position and does not miss any opportunity to defeat the enemy. 【孫武《孫子兵法·軍形第四》Sun Wu: Chapter 4, "Tactical Dispositions", *The Art of War by Sunzi*】

善戰者，其勢險，其節短。 He who is good at warfare has an advantageous position and attacks within a short time. 【孫武《孫子兵法·兵勢第五》Sun Wu: Chapter 5, "Strategic Military Power", *The Art of War by Sunzi*】

善戰者，求之於勢，不責於人。 He who is good at warfare seeks victory from the situation and does not rely on others. 【孫武《孫子兵法·兵勢第五》Sun Wu: Chapter 5, "Strategic Military Power", *The Art of War by Sunzi*】

十五從軍征，八十始得歸。 I joined the army and fought in a war at the age of fifteen, but could only return home until I am eighty years old. 【佚名《古詩十九首》Anonymous: *Nineteen Ancient Poems*】

天下雖安，忘戰必危。 Though the world is at peace, it will certainly be dangerous if war is forgotten. 【房玄齡等《晉書·杜預傳》Fang Xuanling, *et al*: "Biography of Du Yu", *History of the Jin*】

犧牲車馬，保存將帥。 Sacrifice the pawns to save the generals. 【俗語 Common saying】

一面東風百萬軍，當年此處定三分。 It was the east wind and an army of a million soldiers that the three kingdoms were formed here at that time. 【袁枚〈赤壁〉Yuan Mei: "Red Cliff"】

一年動刀兵，十年不太平。 A war in one year will bring about ten years of turbulence. 【俗語 Common saying】

一日動干戈，十年不太平。 Once a war breaks out, there will be no peace for ten years. 【俗語 Common saying】

以不教民戰，是謂棄也。 To involve people who have not received military training in war can be described as sacrificing them. 【孔子《論語·子路篇第十三》Confucius: Chapter 13, *The Analects of Confucius*】

陣而後戰，兵法之常。運用之妙，存乎一心。 When a formation is set up, the army goes to war. This is commonplace in military strategy. The knack of its application relies on the mind. 【脫脫等《宋史·岳飛傳》Toktoghan, et al: "Biography of Yue Fei", *History of the Song*】

醉臥沙場君莫笑，古來征戰幾人回。 Don't laugh at me when I lay drunk on the battlefield, for from of old, how many soldiers return safe and sound from wars?【王翰〈涼州詞〉Wang Han:"Lyric of Liangzhou"】

Waste

好花插在牛糞上 —— 白糟蹋了。Sticking a good flower in cow dung – wasted.【歇後語 End-clipper】

剪牡丹餵牛。Feed oxen with peony.【李壽卿〈度柳翠·第二折〉Li Shouqing: Scene 2, "Redeeming Willow Green"】

瞎子點燈 —— 白費蠟。To light a lamp for a blind person is a sheer waste.【歇後語 End-clipper】

瞎子看戲 —— 白搭功。A blind person sees a play – a waste of time.【歇後語 End-clipper】

學書者紙費，學醫者人費。One who learns calligraphy wastes paper and one who learns medicine wears out the body.【蘇軾〈墨寶堂記〉Su Shi:"Account of Ink-treasure Hall"】

Water

冰，生於水，而寒於水。Ice, which is produced from water, is colder than water.【荀況《荀子·勸學第一》Xun Kuang: Chapter 1, "Exhortation to Learning", *Xunzi*】

滄浪之水清兮，可心濯吾纓；滄浪之水濁兮，可心濯吾足。When the waters of Canglang are clear, I can wash my hat-strings in them; when the waters of Canglang are muddy, I can wash my feet in them.【屈原《楚辭·漁父》Qu Yuan:"The Old Fisherman", *The Songs of Chu*】

飛流直下三千尺，疑是銀河落九天。The waterfall pours three thousand feet straight down, looking like the Milky Way tumbling from high heaven.【李白〈望廬山瀑布〉Li Bai:"Watching the Waterfall at Mount Lu"】

渴時一滴如甘露，醉後添杯不如無。When you are thirsty, a drop of water is like sweet dew. After you are drunk, adding wine to your cup is not as good as not adding anything.【《增廣賢文》Words that Open up One's Mind and Enhance One's Wisdom】

喉嚨裏冒煙。One's throat burns like fire – very thirsty.【俗語 Common saying】

後浪推前浪。The waves behind drive on those before.【文珦〈過

苕溪〉Wen Xiang:"Crossing the Tiao Brook"】

井乾方知水可貴。One realizes the value of water only when the well is dry.【諺語 Proverb】

流靜水深，人靜心深。Still waters run deep and reticent people are adept at scheming.【俗語 Common saying】

流水不腐，戶樞不蠹。Running water is never stale and a door-hinge never gets worm-eaten. 【呂不韋《呂氏春秋・盡數》Lu Buwei:"Fulfill the Number", *Master Lu's Spring and Autumn Annals*】

沒水不煞火。Without water, fire cannot be put out.【西周生《醒世姻緣傳・第六十四回》Xi Zhousheng: Chapter 64, *Stories of Marriage to Awaken the World*】

美不美，鄉中水。Sweet or not, it's water from one's hometown. 【俗語 Common saying】【蘭陵笑笑生《金瓶梅・第九十二回》Lanling Xiaoxiaosheng: Chapter 92, *The Plum in the Golden Vase*】

逝者如斯夫，不捨晝夜。What passes is just like water. It flows day and night and never lets up. 【孔子《論語・子罕篇第九》Confucius: Chapter 9, *The Analects of Confucius*】

水火不留情。Water and fire have no mercy.【俗語 Common saying】 【羅懋登《三寶太監西洋記・第四十二回》Luo Maodeng: Chapter 42, *The Western Voyage of the Eunuch of Three Treasures*】

水火不相容。Water and fire are not compatible.【王符《潛夫論・慎微》Wang Fu:"On Scrupulous Attention to Details", *Remarks by a Recluse*】

水流千轉歸大海。A river winding through a thousand curves will eventually flow into the sea.【俗語 Common saying】

水流下，不爭疾，故去而不遲。Water flows downward without vying for speed, it goes not too slowly.【宋鈃《文子・符言第四》Song Jin: Chapter 4, "Words from Registers", *Wenzi*】

水能載舟，亦能覆舟。While water can carry a boat, it can also overturn it.【荀況《荀子・王制第九》Xun Kuang: Chapter 9, "Sovereign's Regulations", *Xunzi*】

天下莫柔弱於水，而攻堅強者莫之能勝。Nothing in the world is weaker and softer than water, but when it comes to overpowering the hard and strong, water is second to none. 【老子《道德經・第七十八章》Laozi: Chapter 78, *Daodejing*】

問渠那得清如許，為有源頭活水來。I asked him how the pond can be so clear. It's because fresh water comes from its source.【朱熹〈觀書有感〉Zhu Xi:"Thoughts on Reading Books"】

一水接天，風帆隱隱。The water joins the sky at the horizon and sailing boats can be dimly seen. 【沈復《浮生六記・卷四》Shen Fu: Chapter 4, *Six Chapters of a Floating Life*】

在山泉水清，出山泉水濁。The spring water is pure in the mountain, but once it leaves the mountain, the water gets muddied. 【杜甫〈佳人〉Du Fu:"A Beautiful Lady"】

祇要有水，何患無魚。As long as there is water, there is no worry about having no fish. 【俗語 Common saying】

Way, the

大道不稱，大辯不言。The great Way cannot be enunciated and great eloquence does not resort to words. 【莊周《莊子・內篇・齊物論第二》Zhuang Zhou: Chapter 2, "On the Equality of Things", "Inner Chapters", *Zhuangzi*】

大道之行也，天下為公。When the great Way prevails, the whole world is one community. 【《禮記・禮運第九》Chapter 9, "Conveyance of Rites", *The Book of Rites*】

道不可言，言而非也。The Way cannot be expressed in words for what can be expressed in words is not the Way. 【老子《道德經・第二十二章》Laozi: Chapter 22, *Daodejing*】

道常無為而無不為。The Way always does nothing and so there is nothing which it does not do. 【老子《道德經・第三十七章》Laozi: Chapter 37, *Daodejing*】

道大，天大，地大，人大。The Way is great, heaven is great, earth is great, and man is great. 【老子《道德經・第二十五章》Laozi: Chapter 25, *Daodejing*】

道高龍虎伏，德重鬼神欽。One has the ability to subdue dragons and tigers and the virtue to overcome devils and gods. 【吳承恩《西遊記・第二十九回》Wu Cheng'en: Chapter 29, *Journey to the West*】

道高益安，勢高益危。The higher your Way, the safer you are; the higher your position, the more dangerous you are. 【司馬遷《史記・日者列傳》Sima Qian: "Biographies of Soothsayers", *Records of the Grand Historian*】

道可道，非常道。The Way that can be spoken of is not the constant way. 【老子《道德經・第一章》Laozi: Chapter 1, *Daodejing*】

道生一，一生二，二生三，三生萬物。The Way begets one, one begets two, two begets three, and three begets the myriad things. 【老子《道德經・第四十二章》Laozi: Chapter 42, *Daodejing*】

道者，萬物之奧，善人之寶。The Way is the innermost secret of the myriad things and a treasure of the good people. 【老子《道德

經・第六十二章》Laozi: Chapter 62, *Daodejing*】

道者，萬物之始，是非之紀也。 The Way is the beginning of all beings and the measure of right and wrong.【韓非《韓非子・主道第十五》Han Fei: Chapter 15, "The Way of the Ruler", *Hanfeizi*】

君子憂道不憂貧。 A gentleman is concerned about the Way, not poverty.【孔子《論語・衛靈公篇第十五》Confucius: Chapter 15, *The Analects of Confucius*】

人能弘道，非道弘人。 People can propagate the Way, not the Way propagating the people.【孔子《論語・衛靈公篇第十五》Confucius: Chapter 15, *The Analects of Confucius*】

天下有道，小德役大德，小賢役大賢。 When the Way prevails in the world, the less virtuous are submissive to the much virtuous, and the less worthy are submissive to the much worthy. 【孟軻《孟子・離婁上》Meng Ke: Chapter 4, Part 1, *Mencius*】

天下有道，以道殉身；天下無道，以身殉道。 When the Way prevails in the world, one should devote oneself to the Way. When the Way does not prevail in the world, one should sacrifice one's life to save the Way.【孟軻《孟子・盡心章句上》Meng Ke: Chapter 7, Part 1, *Mencius*】

天下有道則見，無道則隱。 When the Way prevails in the world, one shows oneself. When the Way does not prevail in the world, one conceals oneself.【孔子《論語・泰伯篇第八》Confucius: Chapter 8, *The Analects of Confucius*】

天下有道，則政不在大夫。天下有道，則庶人不議。 When the Way prevails in the world, governance will not be in the hands of the senior officials. When the Way prevails in the world, the common people will have no gossips.【孔子《論語・季氏篇第十六》Confucius: Chapter 16, *The Analects of Confucius*】

天下之道，可一言而盡也：其為物不貳，則其生物不測。 The way of heaven and earth can be concluded in one sentence: as it is unique, its creation of things is therefore unpredictable.【《禮記・中庸第二十六章》Chapter 26, "Doctrine of the Mean", *The Book of Rites*】

形而上者謂之道，形而下者謂之器。 That which is above a form is called the Way, and that which is below a form is called the utensil.【《易經・繫辭上》"Appended Remarks, Part 1", *The Book of Changes*】

一陰一陽之謂道。 A female and a male is called the Way.【《易經・繫辭上》"Appended Remarks, Part 1", *The Book of Changes*】

以道佐人主者，不以兵強天下。 He who assists the ruler with the Way does not conquer the world by military strength. 【老

子《道德經·第三十章》Laozi: Chapter 30, *Daodejing*】

朝聞道，夕死可矣。If I could learn the Way in the morning, I am willing to die in the evening.【孔子《論語·里仁篇第四》Confucius: Chapter 4, *The Analects of Confucius*】

Wealth

百萬豪家一焰窮。A millionaire can become very poor after a fire.【羅貫中《平妖傳·第十八回》Luo Guanzhong: Chapter 18, *Taming Devils*】

暴富欺貧，暴寒欺人。An upstart bullies the poor and a cold winter, the people.【諺語 Proverb】

不以富貴驕人。Do not throw one's weight with one's wealth and rank to boast before others.【李延壽《南史·魯悉達傳》Li Yanshou:"Biography of Lu Shida", *History of the Southern Dynasties*】

財大莫折人，勢大莫欺人。Do not torment others with one's great wealth and bully others with one's great power.【諺語 Proverb】

財多惹禍，樹大招風。Great wealth invites disasters and large trees catch wind.【諺語 Proverb】

常將有日思無日，莫把無時當有時。Always think of the days of have-nots when you're in the days of haves and don't treat the days when you don't have anything as days when you have everything.【《增廣賢文》*Words that Open up One's Mind and Enhance One's Wisdom*】

誠知此恨人人有，貧賤夫妻百事哀。I know indeed that this kind of regret may occur to anyone. For a couple in poverty, everything is sad.【元稹〈遣悲懷〉Yuan Zhen:"Giving Vent to Sorrow"】

從來為富難為仁，自古盡忠難盡孝。It has been the case that one who pursues wealth cannot be benevolent and from of old, one who has been loyal to one's country cannot perform their filial duties.【諺語 Proverb】

大富由命，小富由勤。Great wealth rests with the will of Heaven while a well-off living comes from diligence.【俗語 Common saying】

丹青不知老將至，富貴於我如浮雲。Absorbed in painting, I do not notice the coming of old age. To me, wealth and nobility are like floating clouds.【杜甫〈丹青引贈曹霸將軍〉Du Fu:"Introduction to a Painting: Presented to General Cao Ba"】

富不學奢而奢，貧不學儉而儉。The rich are luxurious

without having to learn how to be luxurious and the poor are frugal without having to learn how to be frugal. 【馬總《意林‧任子十卷》Ma Zong: "Ten Chapters on Renzi", *Forest of Opinions*】

富而不吝，寵而不驕。 One is rich but not mean and favoured but not arrogant. 【曹植〈黃初六年令〉Cao Zhi: "An Edict of the Sixth Year of Huangchu"】

富而無驕，貧而無諂。 One is rich but not haughty. One is poor but not flattering. 【孔子《論語‧學而篇第一》Confucius: Chapter 1, *The Analects of Confucius*】

富貴本無根，盡從勤裏得。 Riches and honours have no roots, they all come from diligence. 【馮夢龍《醒世恆言‧第三十五卷》Feng Menglong: Chapter 35, *Stories to Awaken the World*】

富貴不能淫，貧賤不能移。 One cannot be corrupted by riches and honours nor sway from one's principle as a result of poverty or low position. 【孟軻《孟子‧滕文公下》Meng Ke: Chapter 5, Part 2, *Mencius*】

富貴草頭露。 Riches and honours are like dew on grass. 【杜甫〈送孔巢父謝病歸遊江東兼呈李白〉Du Fu: "Presented to Kong Juefu Who Returned to Tour Jiangdong After Recovery from Illness, Also Presented to Li Bai"】

富貴生驕奢。 Riches and honours give rise to pride and extravagance. 【俗語 Common saying】

富貴有前因。 Riches and honours have their antecedents. 【俗語 Common saying】

富靠窮，窮靠力。 The rich rely on the poor, and the poor, their strength. 【俗語 Common saying】

富人思來年，窮人思眼前。 A rich person thinks ahead to the coming year, while a poor person thinks about the present. 【俗語 Common saying】

富人乍窮，寸步難行。 When a rich person suddenly becomes poor, he finds it hard to move even a single step. 【徐明華〈韓玉無意揮窗紗〉Xu Minghua: "Han Yu has No Intention to Dust the Window Gauze"】

富潤屋，德潤身。 Wealth enriches one house, virtue, one's person. 【《禮記‧大學第四十二》Chapter 42, "The Great Learning", *The Book of Rites*】

富日子當窮日子過。 Though one could live quite well, one lives frugally. 【俗語 Common saying】

富無三代享。 The wealth of a family will not last for three generations. 【俗語 Common saying】【黃世仲《廿載繁華夢‧第一回》Huang Shizhong: Chapter 1, *A Rich Dream that Lasted Two Decades*】

富嫌千口少，貧恨一身多。 When one is rich, a thousand people are not enough. When one is poor, one person is more than enough. 【釋普濟《五燈會元‧卷十九》Shi Puji: Chapter 19, *A Compendium of the Five Lamps*】

富與貴，是人之所欲也，不以其道得之，不處也。 Wealth and high social status are what people desire. If they are not obtained in a proper way, they are not to be accepted. 【孔子《論語‧里仁篇第四》Confucius: Chapter 4, *The Analects of Confucius*】

富則盛，貧則病。 When rich, one is energetic. When poor, one is dispirited. 【諺語 Proverb】

富者未必多福。 The rich may not be always fortunate. 【諺語 Proverb】

富者愈富，貧者愈貧。 The rich become richer, and the poor poorer. 【俗語 Common saying】

狠心做財主。 A cruel-hearted person becomes a rich person. 【范寅《越諺‧卷上》Fan Yin: Part 1, *Proverbs of the State of Yue*】

橫財不富命窮人。 A person of poor fate will not get rich even with ill-gotten gains. 【俗語 Common saying】

黃牛雖瘦三籮骨。 Though a cow is thin, it still has three baskets of bones. 【俗語 Common saying】

金也空，銀也空，死後何曾在手中。 Gold is empty, silver is empty, for no one can hold them in their hands when he dies. 【悟空〈萬空歌〉Wu Kong: "Song of Ten-thousand Emptiness"】

金銀不露白。 Don't show your gold and silver. 【俗語 Common saying】

刻薄成家，理無久享。 If you make your fortune by avarice, there is no reason for you to enjoy your fortune for a long time. 【朱用純《朱子家訓》Zhu Yongchun: *Percepts of the Zhu Family*】

良賈深藏若虛。 A good merchant never shows off his riches. 【戴德《大戴禮記‧曾子制言上》Dai De: "Zengzi about Behaviour, Part 1", *Records of Rites by Dai the Elder*】

錢財如糞土，仁義值千金。 Money and wealth are like dung and soil and benevolence and righteousness are worth a thousand taels of gold. 【《增廣賢文》*Words that Open up One's Mind and Enhance One's Wisdom*】

錢財是倘來之物。 Riches are only something gained by chance. 【趙琦美《古今雜劇‧元‧秦簡夫‧東堂老‧第三折》Zhao Qimei: Qin Jianfu: Scene 3, "The Elder of the Eastern Hall", *Dramas of Ancient and Recent Times*】

人生富貴由天命。 Whether there is wealth and nobility in the life of a person is decided by heaven. 【孔子《論語‧顏淵篇第十二》Confucius: Chapter 12, *The Analects of Confucius*】

人生何謂富？山水繞吾廬。 What is abundance in life?

Abundance is having mountains and rivers surrounding my house. 【汪應銓〈題讀書樓〉Wang Yingquan:"Inscription on My Book-reading Tower"】

人無橫財不富，馬無夜草不肥。 Without ill-gotten wealth, a person cannot get rich; without being fed at night, a horse cannot put on weight. 【張國賓〈合汗衫・第三折〉Zhang Guobin: Scene 3, "Sweat Shirts Combined"】

人有盜而富者，富者未必盜。 There are people who get rich by stealing, but some rich people may not steal. 【劉安《淮南子・說林訓第十六》Liu An: Chapter 16, "Discourse on Mountains", Huainanzi】

三更窮，五更富。 One is poor at the third watch of the night, but by the fifth watch of the night, one is rich. 【俗語 Common saying】

善人富，謂之賞；淫人富，謂之殃。 When a good person gets rich, we call it reward; when a bad person gets rich, we call it disaster. 【左丘明《左傳・襄公二十八年》Zuo Qiuming:"The Twenty-eighth Year of the Reign of Duke Xiang", Zuo's Commentary on the Spring and Autumn Annals】

生前富貴草頭露，死後風流陌上花。 Wealth before you die is dew on grass and the reputation after you die is flowers on the paddy field path. 【蘇軾〈陌上花〉Su Shi:"Flowers on the Paddy Field Path"】

生死由命，富貴由天。 Life and death are determined by fate, and wealth, heaven. 【孔子《論語・顏淵篇第十二》Confucius: Chapter 12, The Analects of Confucius】

生之者眾，食之者寡，為之者疾，用之者舒。 The way to accumulate wealth is to have many producers but few consumers, and to have activity in the production and economy in the expenditure. 【《禮記・大學第四十二》Chapter 42, "The Great Learning", The Book of Rites】

世人都曉神仙好，惟有功名忘不了。 Everyone knows that it is nice to be an immortal, but the search for fame and fortune is always on their mind. 【曹雪芹《紅樓夢・第一回》Cao Xueqin: Chapter 1, A Dream of the Red Chamber】

世人結交須黃金，黃金不多交不深。 In this world, friendship is based on gold. If you do not have much gold, friendship would not be close. 【張謂〈題長安主人壁〉Zhang Wei:"Inscribing on the Wall of the Master in Chang'an"】

試金以石，試人以財。 Gold is tested by a touchstone and a person, by wealth. 【俗語 Common saying】

視榮華富貴如浮雲。 Regard rank and wealth as floating clouds. 【孔子《論語・述而篇第七》Confucius: Chapter 7, The Analects of Confucius】

鐵公雞 —— 一毛不拔。 An iron cock from which never a single

feather can be plucked – a miser.
【歇後語 End-clipper】

一番富貴，一番精神。The more
wealth one possesses, the higher
spirit one has. 【俗語 Common
saying】

一富遮三醜。Wealth can cover
up scandals. 【俗語 Common saying】

祇愁富貴不愁貧。What makes
one worry is not poverty but
wealth. 【凌濛初《初刻拍案驚奇・第
二十卷》Ling Mengchu: Chapter 20,
Amazing Tales, Volume One】

Weather

不知十月江寒重，陡覺三更布
被輕。I did not know that the
riverside in the tenth month
was so cold and I suddenly felt
in the third watch that the cloth
quilt was light. 【查慎行〈寒夜〉Cha
Shenxing: "Cold Night"】

出門看天色，進門看臉色。When
one goes out from one's place,
watch the weather. When one
gets into a person's place, watch
the looks on his face. 【諺語
Proverb】

春天後母面。Spring weather is as
changeable as a step-mother's
face. 【俗語 Common saying】

東虹日頭西虹雨。When there is
a rainbow in the east, it is sunny,
when the rainbow is in the west,
it is rainy. 【諺語 Proverb】

東邊日出西邊雨，道是無晴還有
晴。On the east, the sun rises
and on the west, there's rain.
You can say that it is not fine,
yet it is still fine. 【劉禹錫〈竹枝
詞〉Liu Yuxi: "To the Tune of Bamboo
Branches"】

冷得早，回暖早。If the cold
season begins early, it will turn
warm early. 【諺語 Proverb】

冷得足，晴得足。If it is extremely
cold, the sky is extremely clear.
【諺語 Proverb】

露水重，天氣晴。When there is
heavy dew, it will be sunny. 【諺語
Proverb】

麻雀屯食，將會下雪。When the
sparrows are storing food, it will
be snowing soon. 【諺語 Proverb】

螞蟻搬家要下雨。When the ants
are moving home, it will soon
be raining. 【諺語 Proverb】

螞蟻壘窩要下雨。When the ants
are reinforcing their ant-hill,
it will soon be raining. 【諺語
Proverb】

青蛙集中有大雨。When the frogs
are gathering, a heavy rain will
soon be falling. 【諺語 Proverb】

蜻蜓低飛將有大雨。When the
dragonflies are flying low, it is a

sure sign of a downpour. 【諺語 Proverb】

秋早寒則冬必暖矣，春多雨則夏必旱矣。When it is cold in early autumn, winter will be warm; when it is rainy in spring, there will be drought in summer. 【呂不韋《呂氏春秋‧情慾》 Lu Buwei: "Feelings and Desires", *Master Lu's Spring and Autumn Annals*】

羣雁南飛天將冷，羣雁北飛天轉暖。When flocks of wild geese are flying south, it will soon turn cold; when flocks of wild geese are flying north, it will soon turn warm. 【諺語 Proverb】

人變一日，天變一時。It takes a day for a man to change, but just a moment for the weather to change. 【諺語 Proverb】

日暈而雨，月暈而風。When there is solar halo, it will rain; when there is a lunar halo, it will be windy. 【諺語 Proverb】

霜重見晴天。Heavy frost heralds a fine day. 【諺語 Proverb】

天公不作美。The heaven does not give us a fine weather. 【俗語 Common saying】

天上鈎鈎雲，地下雨淋淋。Hook-shaped clouds in the sky foretells a heavy rain. 【諺語 Proverb】

天上有了掃帚雲，不出三天大雨淋。If a broom-shaped cloud appears in the sky, there will be a heavy rain within three days. 【諺語 Proverb】

天無三日晴，地無三尺平。There were never three sunny days in a row, or three square feet of level land. 【諺語 Proverb】

天有不測風雲。There are unexpected winds or clouds in the sky. 【諺語 Proverb】【臧懋循《元曲選‧佚名‧合同文字‧第四折》 Anonymous: Scene 4, "The Story of a Bond", Zang Maoxun: *Anthology of Yuan Plays*】

晚晌火燒雲，明早曬殺人。Rosy clouds in the evening predicts a scorching day tomorrow. 【俗語 Common saying】

晚霞晴千里，早霞別出門。If there is an evening glow, it will be sunny tomorrow; if there is a morning glow, you had better stay at home. 【諺語 Proverb】

烏雲攔東，不雨也風。When black clouds are gathering in the eastern sky, rain will arrive or wind will rise. 【諺語 Proverb】

五月南風漲大水，六月南風井底乾。When the south wind blows in the fifth month of the year, the river will rise; when the south wind blows in the sixth month of the year, the well will run dry. 【諺語 Proverb】

霧露不收即是雨。If the mist does not disperse when the sun rises, there will be rain. 【諺語 Proverb】

西北雲開天鎖，明天晴朗氣爽。If the northwestern part of the sky is clear, tomorrow the weather will be agreeable and fair. 【諺語 Proverb】

下雪不冷化雪寒。It is not cold when it snows, but it is freezing when the snow melts. 【諺語 Proverb】

一日春雷十日雨。When for a whole day the spring thunders roar, there will be a ten-day downpour. 【諺語 Proverb】

已涼天氣未寒時。It's getting chilly, but is not cold yet. 【韓偓〈已涼〉Han Wo:"Cooler Weather"】

魚鱗天，不雨也風顛。When there are fish-scale-shaped clouds in the sky, it will rain or have a strong wind. 【諺語 Proverb】

月暈而風，礎潤而雨。A halo round the moon indicates the rising of wind, and dampness on a plinth is a sign of approaching rain. 【蘇洵〈辨奸論〉Su Xun:"Criticism of Corrupt Officials"】

雲紋雲，雨淋淋。When the clouds are twisting, it will soon be raining. 【諺語 Proverb】

早晨山頂有霧罩，午後必有大雨到。If the mountain top is enshrouded in mist in the morning, it will certainly rain heavily in the afternoon. 【諺語 Proverb】

早蚯出太陽，晚蚯衣迎雨場。When the earthworm appears in the morning, the sun will shine brightly; when the earthworm appears in the evening, it will rain heavily. 【諺語 Proverb】

早上出現虹，出門帶笠篷。When a rainbow appears in the morning, take a raincoat with you when you go out. 【諺語 Proverb】

早霞雨，晚霞晴。Rosy morning clouds indicate rain and a rosy sunset means fine weather. 【諺語 Proverb】

豬銜草墊窩，將有寒潮過。When pigs are fetching straw to mat their pens, a wave of coldness is drawing near. 【諺語 Proverb】

Wedding

春宵一刻值千金。Every moment of the wedding night is worth a thousand taels of gold. 【蘇軾〈春宵〉Su Shi:"Spring Night"】

三日入廚下，洗手作羹湯。Three days after my wedding, I went to the kitchen, washed my hands to prepare soup. 【王建〈新嫁娘詞〉Wang Jian:"Words of the Newly-wed Woman"】

新婚不如久別。 Reunion after a long separation is better than a wedding night. 【諺語 Proverb】

新人上了床，媒人丟過牆。 When the newly-wedded go to bed, the match-maker is forgotten and thrown over the wall. 【吳趼人《糊塗世界‧第三回》Wu Jianren: Chapter 3, *Confused World*】

一女不二聘。 A girl should not be betrothed to two men. 【諺語 Proverb】

Wife

不賢妻，不孝子，沒法可治。 An unvirtuous wife and an unfilial son are beyond correction. 【俗語 Common saying】【黃世仲《廿載繁華夢‧第九回》Huang Shizhong: Chapter 9, *A Rich Dream that Lasted Two Decades*】

糟糠之妻不下堂。 Do not desert your wife who shared your hard lot. 【范曄《後漢書‧宋弘傳》Fan Ye:"Biography of Song Hong", *History of the Later Han*】

醜是家中寶，可喜惹煩惱。 An ugly wife is a treasure at home, while a beautiful wife often brings trouble. 【俗語 Common saying】【蘭陵笑笑生《金瓶梅‧第九十一回》Lanling Xiaoxiaosheng: Chapter 91, *The Plum in the Golden Vase*】

當面教子，背後教妻。 One may teach one's children in the presence of other people, but admonish one's wife in privacy. 【俗語 Common saying】

蕩子行不歸，空牀難獨守。 My roaming husband travels and does not return home, it is difficult for me to be in the empty bed all by myself. 【佚名《古詩十九首》Anonymous: *Nineteen Ancient Poems*】

好妻難為夫。 It is difficult to be the husband of a good woman. 【俗語 Common saying】

家花不及野花香，轉做家花也不香。 One's wife may not be as charming as the harlot, but when the harlot becomes a wife, she is no longer charming. 【胡祖德《滬諺‧卷上》Hu Zhude: Part 1, *Shanghainese Proverbs*】

家花不及野花香，野花沒有家花長。 One's wife may not be as charming as the harlot, but the latter does not last as long as the former. 【俗語 Common saying】

家花不如野花香。 The harlot is more charming than one's own wife. 【俗語 Common saying】

家貧思賢妻。 With a poor family, one cherishes the hope of having a virtuous wife to manage it. 【司馬遷《史記‧魏世家》Sima Qian:"House of Wei", *Records of the Grand Historian*】

家有賢妻，夫不吃淡飯。 With a virtuous wife at home, the husband will not eat tasteless food.【安遇時《包公案・卷三》An Yushi: Chapter 3, *Cases of Judge Bao*】

家有賢妻，丈夫不遭橫事。 With a virtuous wife at home, the husband can avert disasters.【佚名〈盆兒鬼・第一折〉Anonymous: Scene 1, "The Ghost of the Pot"】

老婆是人家的好，孩子是自己的好。 The wife of another person is better and one's own children are better.【俗語 Common saying】【吳越《括蒼山恩仇記・第十四回》Wu Yue: Chapter 14, *Revenge at Mount Kuocang*】

兩姑之間難為婦。 A wife finds it difficult to handle the relationship between two mothers-in-law.【蔡東藩《南北史通俗演義・第七十六回》Cai Dongfan: Chapter 76, *Popular Romance of the Southern and Northern Dynasties*】

莫圖顏色好，醜婦家中寶。 Don't choose your wife by her beauty, for an ugly wife is a treasure at home.【羅貫中《平妖傳・第三十五回》Luo Guanzhong: Chapter 35, *Taming Devils*】

朋友妻，不可欺。 Do not bully your friend's wife.【俗語 Common saying】

朋友妻，不可戲。 Do not take liberties with your friend's wife.【俗語 Common saying】

妻不如妾，妾不如偷。 The wife is not as good as a concubine, and a concubine, a mistress.【曹雪芹《紅樓夢・第四十四回》Cao Xueqin: Chapter 44, *A Dream of the Red Chamber*】

妻妾切忌艷裝。 The wife or concubine should avoid dressing themselves with beautiful clothes.【朱用純《朱子家訓》Zhu Yongchun: *Percepts of the Zhu Family*】

妻是枕邊人，十事商量九事成。 Your wife is beside you by your pillow and you will succeed in settling things nine out of ten times.【俗語 Common saying】【佚名〈殺狗記・第六齣〉Anonymous: Scene 6, "An Account of Dog-killing"】

妻賢夫禍少。 A good wife makes the husband safe.【《增廣賢文》 *Words that Open up One's Mind and Enhance One's Wisdom*】

妻賢夫省事，子孝父心寬。 A virtuous wife saves the husband a lot of trouble and a filial son makes his father feel relieved.【《增廣賢文》*Words that Open up One's Mind and Enhance One's Wisdom*】

妻有大小，子無嫡庶。 One may have a wife and a concubine, but the sons by both are the same.【佚名《郭公案第四編》Anonymous: Chapter 4, *Cases of Judge Guo*】

妻子是別人的好，文章是自己的好。 Another's wife is always better and one's own articles are always better.【俗語 Common saying】

巧妻常伴拙夫眠。 A beautiful wife often has a stupid husband.

【武漢臣〈生金閣・第一折〉Wu Hancheng: Scene 1, "Gold-creating Studio"】

請壞長工一年窮，討壞老婆一世窮。 A bad farm-hand spoils a year but a bad wife spoils your whole life.【俗語 Common saying】

窮媳婦知米貴。 The wife of a poor man knows that rice is expensive.【馮德英《迎春花・第六章》Feng Deying: Chapter 6, *Winter Jasmine*】

娶老婆是接財神。 To get a wife is to take home the God of Wealth.【俗語 Common saying】【劉江《太行風雲・第六十二回》Liu Jiang: Chapter 62, *Changes in Taixing*】

娶妻娶德，娶妾娶色。 You take a wife for her virtue and a concubine for her beauty.【俗語 Common saying】

娶妻要小，嫁漢要老。 One should take a wife much younger than one and a girl should marry a man much older than she.【李滿天《水向東流・第四十五章》Li Mantian: Chapter 45, *Water Flows to the East*】

娶媳求淑女，毋計厚奩。 When you take a wife, you look for a kind and gentle woman, and don't consider getting a generous dowry.【朱用純《朱子家訓》Zhu Yongchun: *Percepts of the Zhu Family*】

捨不得嬌妻，做不得好漢。 It is not possible for a man to be a great person if he cannot leave his dear wife.【俗語 Common saying】

他妻莫愛，他馬莫騎。 Do not fall in love with another's wife and do not ride another's horse.【諺語 Proverb】【馮夢龍《醒世恆言・第三十三卷》Feng Menglong: Chapter 33, *Stories to Awaken the World*】

討了老婆，丟了父母。 When a man gets a wife, he leaves his parents.【俗語 Common saying】

頭妻嫌，二妻愛。 A man dislikes his first wife but loves his second wife.【諺語 Proverb】

頑妻劣子，無藥可醫。 A stupid wife or an unfilial son cannot be cured by any medicine.【俗語 Common saying】【馮夢龍《醒世恆言・第二十七卷》Feng Menglong: Chapter 27, *Stories to Awaken the World*】

無婦不成家。 Without the wife, a home is not a home.【俗語 Common saying】【馮夢龍《醒世恆言・第十卷》Feng Menglong: Chapter 10, *Stories to Awaken the World*】

賢婦令夫貴，惡婦令夫敗。 A virtuous woman makes her husband honourable and a wicked woman can bring failure to her husband.【《增廣賢文》*Words that Open up One's Mind and Enhance One's Wisdom*】

新來媳婦三日勤。 A newlywed wife keeps herself busy for three days.【諺語 Proverb】【西周生《醒世姻緣傳・第八十四回》Xi Zhousheng: Chapter 84, *Stories of Marriage to Awaken the World*】

眼選妻不如耳選妻。To choose a wife by your eyes is not as good as by your ears. 【俗語 Common saying】

一代娶矮妻，三代沒高人。One short wife will have short off-springs for three generations. 【諺語 Proverb】

糟糠之妻不下堂。A wife who shared poverty may not be divorced in times of comfort. 【范曄《後漢書・宋弘傳》Fan Ye: "Biography of Song Hong", *History of the Later Han*】

Wind

不是東風壓倒西風，就是西風壓倒東風。If it isn't the east wind that prevails over the west, then it's the west wind prevailing over the east. 【曹雪芹《紅樓夢・第八十二回》Cao Xueqin: Chapter 82, *A Dream of the Red Chamber*】

春風桃花，十里飄香。The fragrance of peach blossoms in the spring breeze wafts to ten miles away. 【俗語 Common saying】

大風起兮雲飛揚，威加海內兮歸故鄉。A strong wind rises and clouds fly. I have exerted my power within the four seas and so I return to my hometown. 【劉邦〈大風歌〉Liu Bang: "Song of Strong Wind"】

東風夜放花千樹，更吹落，星如雨。The east wind in a night adorns a thousand trees with flowers, and blows down stars in showers. 【辛棄疾〈青玉案〉Xin Qiji: "To the Tune of Green Jade Table"】

長風幾萬里，吹度玉門關。The wind, travelling over thousands of miles, blows across the Yumen Pass. 【李白〈關山月〉Li Bai: "Moon over the Mountain Pass"】

風不定，人初靜，明日落紅應滿徑。The wind blows unsteadily, the noise of human beings has just become dim. Tomorrow, the fallen petals should have covered up all the pathways. 【張先〈天仙子〉Zhang Xian: "To the Tune of Angels in the Sky"】

風裏來，雨裏去。Go through wind and rain. 【俗語 Common saying】

風是雨的頭。Wind heralds rain. 【諺語 Proverb】【柳青《種穀記・第十六章》Liu Qing: Chapter 16, *Growing Rice*】

風無定止，雲無定形。The wind does not fix a destination and the cloud, a pattern. 【諺語 Proverb】

風雨無晦，雞鳴不已。The wind and rain make the sky very dark, but the cocks keep crowing. 【《詩經・國風・鄭風・風雨》"Wind and

Rain", "Odes of the State of Zheng", "Odes of the States", *The Book of Odes*】

風乍起，吹縐一池春水。The breeze suddenly begins to blow, ruffling a pool of waters in spring. 【馮延巳〈謁金門〉Feng Yansi:"Homage at the Golden Gate"】

和風吹柳綠，細雨點花紅。The gentle breeze blows the willows green and the drizzle turns the flowers red. 【吳承恩《西遊記‧第九回》Wu Cheng'en: Chapter 9, *Journey to the West*】

和風煦日，碧波粼粼。The breeze is gentle, the sunshine is warm, and the blue water shimmers. 【諺語 Proverb】

簾捲西風，人比黃花瘦。The west wind blows up the curtain, and I find myself thinner than yellow flowers. 【李清照〈醉花陰〉Li Qingzhao:"To the Tune of Intoxicated in the Flower Shade"】

南風不過午，過午連夜吼。The south wind usually blows before noon; if it lasts until afternoon, it'll blow fiercely the whole night. 【諺語 Proverb】

南風吹暖北風寒，東風多濕西風乾。The south wind brings warmth and the north wind brings coldness. The east wind brings dampness and the west wind brings dryness. 【諺語 Proverb】

飄風不終朝，驟雨不終日。A strong wind does not last all morning and a violent storm, all day. 【老子《道德經》Laozi: *Daodejing*】

秋風起兮白雲飛，草木黃落兮雁南歸。The autumn wind rises and white clouds fly. Grass and trees turn yellow, leaves fall, and wild geese go south again. 【劉徹〈秋風辭〉Liu Che:"Song of the Autumn Wind"】

秋風掃落葉。The autumn wind sweeps away the fallen leaves. 【陳壽《三國志‧魏書‧辛毗傳》Chen Shou:"Biography of Xin Pi", "History of the Wei", *Records of the Three Kingdoms*】

秋後北風緊，夜靜有白霜。In late autumn the north wind blows hard and when the night is quiet, there is white frost. 【諺語 Proverb】

山雨欲來風滿樓。The wind sweeping through the tower heralds the falling of rain in the mountain. 【許渾〈咸陽城東樓〉Xu Hun:"The East Tower at Xianyang City"】

無風不刮雨，有雨便有風。Where there is no wind there is no rain. Where there is rain, there is wind. 【諺語 Proverb】

行得春風有夏雨。Only after the spring breeze blows does summer rain come. 【諺語 Proverb】

一場春風，對一場秋雨。A breeze in spring is a forecast of a rain in autumn. 【諺語 Proverb】

一夜東風吹雨過，滿江新水長魚蝦。A night of east wind blew

the rain away, the rivers were full of fresh waters that raised fish and shrimps. 【祁珊洲：A Line of Poem by a Qing Poet Qi Shanzhou】

願乘長風破萬里浪。I wish to follow the strong wind to sail ten thousand miles of waves. 【沈約《宋書‧宗愨傳》Shen Yue:"Biography of Zong Que", *History of the Song*】

願為西南風，長逝入君懷。I would rather be the southwesterly wind, blowing all the way to your chest. 【曹植〈七哀詩〉Cao Zhi:"Poem on Seven Sorrows"】

晝風久，夜風止。When the wind blows a long time during the day, it will stop at night. 【孫武《孫子兵法‧火攻第十二》Sun Wu: Chapter 12, "Attack by Fire", *The Art of War by Sunzi*】

Wine

背鄉出好酒。Good wine is found in a remote village. 【俗語 Common saying】【老舍《四世同堂‧偷生第四十章》Lao She: Chapter 40, "Dragging out an Ignoble Existence", *Four Generations under One Roof*】

不是春來偏愛酒，應須得酒遣春愁。It is not that I take a special liking in wine when spring comes, for it should be that we must take wine to drive away the sorrows of spring. 【徐凝〈春飲〉Xu Ning:"Drinking in Spring"】

陳酒味醇，老友情深。The taste of old wine is mellow and the feelings among old friends are deep. 【諺語 Proverb】

吃酒不言公務事。When drinking wine together, we do not talk about business. 【俗語 Common saying】【錢彩《說岳全傳‧第四十八回》Qian Cai: Chapter 48, *A Story of Yue Fei*】

東籬把酒黃昏後，有暗香盈袖。I drink wine at the east fence after dusk, and my sleeves are filled with faint fragrance. 【李清照〈醉花陰〉Li Qingzhao:"To the Tune of Intoxicated in the Flower Shade"】

斷送一生唯有酒。The only thing that ruins one's life is wine. 【韓愈〈遣興〉Han Yu:"Expressing One's Feelings"】

古來聖賢皆寂寞，惟有飲者留其名。Sages have since the ancient times been little known, only the drinkers are still known to us. 【李白〈將進酒〉Li Bai:"About to Drink Wine"】

好酒不用幌。Good wine needs no wavering. 【諺語 Proverb】

好酒除百病。Good wine kills a hundred diseases. 【諺語 Proverb】

好酒說不酸，酸酒說不甜。Do not call good wine not sour nor

sour wine sweet. 【俗語 Common saying】

呼兒將出換美酒，與爾同銷萬古愁。 I call my son to take the things I mentioned to exchange for wine, so that together, we could banish the sorrow that is everlasting. 【李白〈將進酒〉Li Bai: "About to Drink Wine"】

幾時杯重把，昨夜月同行。 When shall we hold the wine cups again? Last night the moon was with us when we walked. 【杜甫〈奉濟驛重送嚴公四韻〉Du Fu: "Seeing off Lord Yan Wu Again at Fengji Post-station"】

借問酒家何處有，牧童遙指杏花村。 May I ask where can I find a tavern? The shepherd boy points to a distant village with apricots in full bloom. 【杜牧〈清明〉Du Mu: "The Qingming Festival"】

今朝有酒今朝醉，明日愁來明日愁。 This morning we have wine and we will get drunk this morning, and we will worry about troubles of tomorrow when tomorrow comes around. 【羅隱〈自遣〉Luo Yin: "Self-consolation"】

敬酒不吃吃罰酒。 One is forced to drink wine which is offered at first as a toast. 【諺語 Proverb】

酒病酒藥醫。 Disease caused by wine can be cured with wine. 【諺語 Proverb】【蘭陵笑笑生《金瓶梅·第五十四回》Lanling Xiaoxiaosheng: Chapter 54, The Plum in the Golden Vase】

酒不解真愁。 Wine can never dispel real sorrow. 【《增廣賢文》Words that Open up One's Mind and Enhance One's Wisdom】

酒不醉人人自醉，色不迷人人自迷。 It is not wine that intoxicates people but people intoxicating themselves and it is not women who beguile men but men beguiling themselves. 【施耐庵《水滸傳·第四回》Shi Nai'an: Chapter 4, Outlaws of the Marshes】

酒逢知己千杯少，話不投機半句多。 With bosom friends it is not much to drink a thousand cups of wine. With incompatible people, even uttering half a sentence is too much. 【歐陽修〈遙思故人〉Ouyang Xiu, "Thinking of My Old Friends Far away"】

酒逢知己飲，詩向會人吟。 Wine is to be drunk with bosom friends and poems are recited to people who write poems. 【《增廣賢文》Words that Open up One's Mind and Enhance One's Wisdom】

酒好客自來。 Good wine needs no push. 【俗語 Common saying】

酒後多失言。 There is many a slip between the cup and lip. 【施耐庵《水滸傳·第四十六回》Shi Nai'an: Chapter 46, Outlaws of the Marshes】

酒後見真情。 True feelings are revealed in wine. 【俗語 Common saying】

酒後吐真言。 In wine there is truth. 【俗語 Common saying】

酒極則亂，樂極則悲。Excess of wine results in disorder and excess of happiness, sorrow. 【司馬遷《史記‧滑稽列傳》Sima Qian:"Biographies of Jesters", *Records of the Grand Historian*】

酒老味醇，人老識深。Vintage wine tastes mellow, and old people have profound knowledge. 【俗語 Common saying】

酒亂性，色迷人。Wine makes one lose his reason and beauty ensnares him. 【施耐庵《水滸傳‧第四十五回》Shi Nai'an: Chapter 45, *Outlaws of the Marshes*】

酒能成事，也能敗事。Wine can accomplish things, but it can also ruin things. 【諺語 Proverb】【施耐庵《水滸傳‧第四回》Shi Nai'an: Chapter 4, *Outlaws of the Marshes*】

酒能祛百慮，菊為制頹齡。Wine can relieve me of many worries and chrysanthemums are for restraining the declining years. 【陶淵明〈九日閒居詩〉Tao Yuanming:"Spending the Ninth Day in Solitude"】

酒入愁腸，化作相思淚。Wine in sad bowels would turn into nostalgic tears. 【范仲淹〈蘇幕遮〉Fan Zhongyan:"To the Tune of Screened by Southern Curtain"】

酒色禍之媒。Wine and beautiful women are vehicles of disasters. 【沈鯨〈雙珠還‧第十四齣〉Shen Jing: Scene 14, "Returning the Two Pearls"】

酒香不愁巷子深。Good wine attracts people from afar. 【諺語 Proverb】

酒要少吃，事要多知。Drink less wine and gain more knowledge. 【佚名《名賢集》Anonymous: *Collected Sayings of Famous Sages*】

酒已盡，意未消。Wine has been drunk up and yet our emotions have not yet spent. 【俗語 Common saying】

酒在口頭，事在心頭。One who often drinks wine must have something weighing on his mind. 【顧起元《客座贅語‧卷一》Gu Qiyuan: Chapter 1, *Superfluous Words from My Salon*】

酒中不語真君子。One who does not speak carelessly after drinking wine is a true gentleman. 【《增廣賢文》*Words that Open up One's Mind and Enhance One's Wisdom*】

酒中含毒，色上藏刀。There is poison in wine and a knife in beauty. 【蔡東藩《元史通俗演義‧第四十八回》Cai Dongfan: Chapter 48, *Popular Romance of the Yuan Dynasty*】

酒醉吐真言。Drunkenness reveals what soberness conceals. 【俗語 Common saying】

舊瓶裝新酒。Put new wine in old bottles. 【俗語 Common saying】

莫思身外無窮事，且盡生前有限杯。Don't think about the endless matters unrelated to you, simply drink up the limited cups of wine that you can drink before your life ends. 【杜甫〈絕句漫興〉Du Fu: "A Quatrain Written in Joke"】

莫飲卯時酒，昏昏醉到酉。Don't drink wine early in the morning, otherwise you will be drunk till evening. 【《增廣賢文》 *Words that Open up One's Mind and Enhance One's Wisdom*】

千家吃酒，一家還錢。A thousand people drink wine, but only one pays for it. 【湯顯祖〈紫釵記‧第五十三齣〉Tang Xianzu: Scene 53, "Purple Hairpin"】

人逢喜事千杯少。When people have happy things, a thousand cups of wine is nothing. 【俗語 Common saying】

人生有酒須當醉，一滴何曾到九泉。You should get drunk when you have wine in your life, not a single drop could reach you when you are in your grave. 【高翥〈清明日對酒〉Gao Zhu: "Facing the Wine on the Qingming Festival Day"】

若要不喝酒，醒眼看醉人。If you want to abstain from drinking, look at a drunken person when you are sober. 【俗語 Common saying】【黎汝清《雨雪霏霏‧第八章》Li Ruqing: Chapter 8, *In the Midst of the Rain and Snow*】

三杯和萬事，一醉解千愁。After drinking three cups of wine, all differences will be gone and when one is drunk, all cares will be dissipated. 【武漢臣〈生金閣‧第三折〉Wu Hanchen: Scene 3, "Gold-creating Studio"】

三杯通大道，一斗合自然。When you drink three cups of wine, you are united with the Way, and when you drink a bushel, you are one with nature. 【李白〈月下獨酌〉Li Bai: "Drinking Alone under the Moon"】

三杯下肚話鋒來。After having three cups of wine, one begins to talk without cease. 【俗語 Common saying】

三杯下肚，情不自禁。After having three cups of wine, one cannot control one's feelings. 【俗語 Common saying】

山僧過嶺看茶老，村女當爐煮酒香。A monk in the mountain climbs over to another one to visit his old friend who makes tea, and the village woman warmed the wine in a stove, wafting the fragrance of the wine. 【祝允明〈首夏山中行吟〉Zhu Yunming: "Poem Written When Walking in the Mountain in Early Summer"】

十觴亦不醉，感子故意長。Ten cupfuls of wine does not make us drunk. I am grateful to you for your long friendship. 【杜甫〈贈衛八處士〉Du Fu: "Presented to Scholar-recluse Wei the Eighth"】

數甕猶未開，來朝能飲否？We have a couple of jugs of wine not yet opened. Shall we drink them tomorrow morning? 【儲光羲〈田

家雜興〉Chu Guangxi:"A Rencontre of a Peasant House"】

天有酒星，地有酒泉，人有酒緣。 There is the Wine Star in heaven, a wine spring on earth, and wine appeals to people. 【劉璋《斬鬼傳·第九回》Liu Zhang: Chapter 9, *Account of Ghost-beheading*】

天子避醉漢。 Even the Son of Heaven avoids a drunkard. 【施耐庵《水滸傳·第四回》Shi Nai'an: Chapter 4, *Outlaws of the Marshes*】

天子呼來不上船，自稱臣是酒中仙。 When the emperor summoned Li Bai to a boat, he refused to go aboard and proclaimed that he, a subject of the emperor, is an immortal in wine. 【杜甫〈飲中八仙詩〉Du Fu:"Eight Immortals of the Wine"】

晚來天欲雪，能飲一杯無。 At dusk, it is like going to snow. How about having a cup of wine? 【白居易〈問劉十九〉Bai Juyi: "A Question to Liu the Nineteenth"】

晚酌一杯，亦不為惡。 It is not amiss to drink a glass of wine at supper. 【俗語 Common saying】

萬事不如杯在手。 There is nothing better than a cup of wine in the hand. 【何良俊《四友齋叢說》He Liangjun: *Collection of Tales from the Four-Friends Studio*】

我有旨酒，與汝樂之。 I have mellow wine and I would like to share with you the pleasure of drinking it. 【陶淵明〈答龐參軍·其三〉Tao Yuanming:"Poems in Reply to Military Counsellor Pang, No.3"】

相歡有尊酒，不用惜花飛。 With a jar of wine, we can have a happy gathering. Why should we grieve over the falling blossoms? 【王維〈送春詞〉Wang Wei:"Farewell to Spring"】

言多語失皆因酒，義斷情疏祇為錢。 If you drink wine, you will talk too much and offend people; relatives and friends are estranged from you just because of money. 【佚名《名賢集》Anonymous: *Collected Sayings of Famous Sages*】

眼看人盡醉，何忍獨為醒？ I see with my own eyes that everybody is drunk, can I alone remain sober? 【王績〈過酒家〉Wang Ji:"Passing a Tavern"】

眼前一杯酒，誰論身後名。 A cup of wine before my eyes, who cares to talk about fame after one's death. 【庾信〈擬詠懷〉Yu Xin:"Imitating the Yonghuai"】

一杯在手，萬事全丟。 Forget everything when a cup of wine is in one's hand. 【俗語 Common saying】

一壺酒，一竿身，世上如儂有幾人。 With a bottle of wine and a fish rod, you go fishing, how many in the world can be like you? 【李煜〈漁父〉Li Yu:"Fisherman"】

一壺濁酒喜相逢，古今多少事，都付笑談中。 With a pot of turbid

wine, we meet in happiness, laughing away many things in the past and present. 【楊慎〈臨江仙·説秦漢〉Yang Shen: "Chatting about Qin and Han Dynasties: To the Tune of an Immortal by the River"】

一人不食酒，兩人不賭錢。 You don't drink when you're all by yourself and you don't gamble when there are just the two of you. 【俗語 Common saying】

一盞能消萬古愁。 A cup of wine can dispel one's thousand-year-old worries. 【翁綬〈詠酒〉Weng Shou: "Poem on Wine"】

倚酒三分醉。 Behave wildly as if one were dead drunk. 【曹雪芹《紅樓夢·第四十四回》Cao Xueqin: Chapter 44, A Dream of the Red Chamber】

遇酒且呵呵，人生能幾何？ Drink while wine comes your way, for how long can your life be? 【韋莊〈菩薩蠻〉Wei Zhuang: "To the Tune of Buddhist Dancers"】

遇飲酒時須飲酒，得高歌處且高歌。 When there is wine to drink, you should drink it. When you can sing loudly, do so. 【《增廣賢文》Words that Open up One's Mind and Enhance One's Wisdom】

糟鼻子不吃酒 —— 枉擔虛名。 A red nose without drinking wine is to have a reputation one does not deserve. 【歇後語 End-clipper】

醉翁之意不在酒，在乎山水之間也。 The old tippler is really not interested in wine, but in the mountains and rivers. 【歐陽修〈醉翁亭記〉Ouyang Xiu: "The Story of the Old Drunkard Pavillion"】

Winter

冬季乾冷春季寒。 Winter season is dry and cold and spring season, chilly. 【諺語 Proverb】

冬日可愛，夏日可畏。 The sun in winter is lovable while the sun in summer, oppressive. 【左丘明《左傳·文公七年》Zuo Qiuming: "The

Seventh Year of the Reign of Duke Wen", Zuo's Commentary on the Spring and Autumn Annals】

冬至長，夏至短。 Daytime is long after the Winter Solstice and short after the Summer Solstice. 【諺語 Proverb】

Wisdom

聰明乃是苦功夫。 Wisdom comes from hard work. 【諺語 Proverb】

大智若愚，大巧若拙。 A person of great wisdom behaves like a fool and a person of great skill behaves like a clumsy one. 【老子《道德經‧第四十五章》Laozi: Chapter 45, *Daodejing*】

鬥智不鬥力。Competing with wisdom but not with force. 【司馬遷《史記‧項羽本紀》Sima Qian: "Annals of Xiang Yu", *Records of the Grand Historian*】

人多智多生諸葛。More people, more wisdom. 【俗語 Common saying】

事後諸葛亮。One is wise after an event. 【俗語 Common saying】

雖有智慧，不如乘勢。You might have wisdom, but it is not as good as taking advantage of the right opportunity. 【孟軻《孟子‧公孫丑上》Meng Ke: Chapter 2, Part 1, *Mencius*】

唯上智與下愚不移。Only those who are extremely intelligent and those who are extremely stupid cannot be changed. 【孔子《論語‧陽貨篇第十七》Confucius: Chapter 17, *The Analects of Confucius*】

下下人有上上智。There are people of great wisdom among the inferiors. 【慧能《六祖壇經‧行由品第一》Hui Neng: "Section One: The Sources of My Practice", *The Sixth Patriarch's Platform Sutra*】

仙機人不識，妙算鬼難猜。Extraordinary wisdom cannot be understood by ordinary people and wonderful foresight cannot be detected even by ghosts. 【羅貫中《粉妝樓‧第二十七回》Luo Guanzhong: Chapter 27, *Cosmetical Building*】

星多天空亮，人多智慧廣。The more the stars, the brighter the sky; the more the people, the greater the wisdom. 【諺語 Proverb】

詢問者，智之本；思慮者，智之道也。Consultation is the basis of wisdom; thinking is the way to wisdom. 【劉向《說苑‧卷三建本》Liu Xiang: Chapter 3, "Building the Foundation", *Garden of Persuasions*】

一人不如二人智。Two heads are better than one. 【西周生《醒世姻緣傳‧第八十四回》Xi Zhousheng: Chapter 84, *Stories of Marriage to Awaken the World*】

有大智就有大勇。Great wisdom is sure to bring about great courage. 【俗語 Common saying】

有智不在年高。Wisdom has nothing to do with age. 【俗語 Common saying】

有智贏，無智輸。The wise win, and the foolish lose. 【俗語 Common saying】

知人則哲，能官人。He who understands people is wise and can make official appointments. 【《尚書‧皋陶謨》"Counsels of Gao Tao", *The Book of History*】

知者不惑，仁者不憂，勇者不懼。A wise person is not baffled, a benevolent person is not worried, and a brave person is fearless. 【孔子《論語‧子罕篇第九》

Confucius: Chapter 9, *The Analects of Confucius*】

知者不言，言者不知。A wise person does not speak up, and he who speaks up is not wise. 【老子《道德經·第五十六章》Laozi: Chapter 56, *Daodejing*】

智者不上兩回當。A wise person will not be fooled twice. 【諺語 Proverb】

智者不妄為，勇者不妄殺。A wise person does not act recklessly; a courageous person does not kill casually. 【劉向《説苑·卷十六談叢》Liu Xiang: Chapter 16, "The Thicket of Discussion", *Garden of Persuasion*】

智者不襲常。A wise person does not stick to the established practice. 【顧炎武《天下郡國利病書·卷二八》Gu Yanwu: Chapter 28, *The Strengths and Weaknesses of the Prefectures and Provinces of the Empire*】

智者不再計，勇士不怯死。A wise person is not indecisive and a brave person is not afraid of death. 【司馬遷《史記·魯仲連鄒陽列傳》Sima Qian: "Biographies of Lu Zhonglian and Zou Yang", *Records of the Grand Historian*】

智者動，仁者靜。The wise are active, the benevolent, inactive. 【孔子《論語·雍也篇第六》Confucius: Chapter 6, *The Analects of Confucius*】

智者貴於趁時。A wise person takes the occasion when it serves him. 【羅貫中《三國演義·第六十七回》Luo Guanzhong: Chapter 67, *Romance of the Three Kingdoms*】

智者樂，仁者壽。The wise are joyful, and the benevolent are long-lived. 【孔子《論語·雍也篇第六》Confucius: Chapter 6, *The Analects of Confucius*】

智者樂水，仁者樂山。The wise delight in water and the benevolent, in mountains. 【孔子《論語·雍也篇第六》Confucius: Chapter 6, *The Analects of Confucius*】

智者棄其所短，而採其所長，以致其功。A wise person abandons other people's weaknesses and stress their strengths so that they can make achievements. 【王符《潛夫論·實貢》Wang Fu: "On Recommendations of Substance", *Remarks by a Recluse*】

智者千慮，必有一失。Even the wise are not always free from errors. 【司馬遷《史記·淮陰侯列傳》Sima Qian: "Biography of the Marquis of Huaiyin", *Records of the Grand Historian*】

智者無不知也，當務之為急。A wise man knows everything, but he considers urgently only matters of top priority. 【孟軻《孟子·盡心章句上》Meng Ke: Chapter 7, Part 1, *Mencius*】

Wolf

狼改不了吃人。A wolf cannot change its man-eating nature. 【諺語 Proverb】

狼披羊皮還是狼。A wolf remains a wolf even though it is dressed in sheep's skin. 【諺語 Proverb】

狼易其衣，不改其性。The wolf changes his coat, but not his disposition. 【諺語 Proverb】

狼走千里吃人，狗走千里吃屎。A wolf walks a thousand miles to eat man and a dog, dung. 【俗語 Common saying】

披着羊皮的狼。A wolf in sheep's clothing. 【諺語 Proverb】

外披羊皮，內藏狼心。Outside he is clad in sheep's skin, but inside his heart is a wolf's. 【諺語 Proverb】

野狼養不成家狗。A wild wolf cannot be tamed into a domestic dog. 【諺語 Proverb】【胡正《汾水長流‧第二十四章》Hu Zheng: Chapter 24, *The Fen River Flows on and on*】

越是怕，狼來嚇。When you are scared, the wolf is sure to come. 【俗語 Common saying】

Woman

薄命女子負心漢。An infatuated girl deserted by a heartless man. 【俗語 Common saying】

婦女能頂半邊天。Women can hold up half the sky. 【毛澤東：一九六八年語 Mao Zedong: His Saying in 1968】

婦人長舌為厲之階。A woman with a malicious tongue is a peddler of trouble. 【《詩經‧大雅‧瞻卬》"Looking up", "Greater Odes of the Kingdom", *The Book of Odes*】

婦人水性無常。Woman's nature, like water, is not constant. 【馮夢龍《警世通言‧第三十二卷》Feng Menglong: Chapter 32, *Stories to Caution the World*】

婦人無德有三，曰獨妒毒。A woman lacks virtue in three ways: selfishness, jealousy, and viciousness. 【俗語 Common saying】

姑娘的心 —— 難捉摸。A lady's heart is hard to understand. 【歇後語 End-clipper】

黃毛丫頭十八變。A girl changes all the time before reaching womanhood. 【諺語 Proverb】

苦中出好女。A good lady grows up from hardships. 【俗語 Common saying】

毛頭姑娘十八變。A girl changes all the time before reaching womanhood. 【諺語 Proverb】

女大不由娘。A girl, when grown up, will not listen to her mother's advice on marriage. 【俗語 Common saying】

女大不中留。A girl, when grown up, cannot be kept unmarried for long. 【董解元《西廂記諸宮調·卷六》Dong Jieyuan: Chapter 6, *The Romance of the Western Bower in All Keys and Modes*】

女大十八變。A girl changes eighteen times in appearance before reaching womanhood. 【釋道原《景德傳燈錄·幽州譚空和尚》Shi Daoyuan: "Monk Tan Kong of Youzhou", *Records of the Transmission of the Lamp in the Jingde Period*】

人生莫作婦人身，百年苦樂由他人。One would not like to be a woman, for her happiness or suffering is all decided by others. 【白居易〈太行路〉Bai Juyi: "The Grand Pass"】

三個閨女一台戲。When three girls come together, it will be as noisy as a play on a stage. 【俗語 Common saying】

三個女人一個墟。When women get together they make a lot of noise chattering. 【俗語 Common saying】

三女一鵝成市。Three women and a goose make a market. 【俗語 Common saying】

侍夫如侍君。A woman serves her husband in the same way she serves the lord. 【俗語 Common saying】

唯女人與小人為難養也，近之則不遜，遠之則怨。Women and petty men are hard to deal with. If you get close to them, they become insolent. If you keep a distance from them, they harbour resentment. 【孔子《論語·陽貨篇第十七》Confucius: Chapter 17, *The Analects of Confucius*】

鄉裏姑子鄉裏樣。Girls in the rustic areas have rustic manners. 【俗語 Common saying】

邪花不宜人宅。Evil flowers should not be taken into the house. 【俗語 Common saying】【黃世仲《廿載繁華夢·第二十四回》Huang Shizhong: Chapter 24, *A Rich Dream that Lasted Two Decades*】

秀而不媚，清而不寒。A lady who is charming but not coquettish, delicate but not mean. 【劉鶚《老殘遊記·第二回》Liu E: Chapter 2, *The Travels of Lao Can*】

妍皮不裹痴骨 One is beautiful in appearance and clever in mind. 【房玄齡等《晉書·慕容超載記》Fang Xuanling, *et al*: "Biography of Murong Chao", *History of the Jin*】

一代紅妝照汗青。This woman of her generation Chen Yuanyuan will shine in history. 【吳偉業〈圓圓曲〉Wu Weiye: "Song of the Beautiful Lady Chen Yuanyuan"】

一女不事二夫。A woman should not serve two husbands. 【左丘明《左傳·莊公十四年》Zuo Qiuming: "The Fourteenth Year of the Reign of Duke Zhuang", *Zuo's*

Commentary on the Spring and Autumn Annals】

有志女人勝男人。 A woman with aspirations is better than a man without them.【俗語 Common saying】

幼從父兄，嫁從夫，夫死從子。 A woman is obedient to her father and elder brother when young, to her husband after marriage, and to her son when her husband passes away.【《禮記‧郊特牲第十一》Chapter 11: "Special Livestock for Suburban Sacrifice", *The Book of Rites*】

Word

不着一字，盡得風流。 Without using a single word, the literary elegance is revealed completely.【司空圖《二十四詩品》Sikong Tu: *Twenty-four Modes of Poetry*】

附耳之語，流聞千里。 A whisper at one's ear could travel a thousand miles away.【宋鈃《文子‧微明第七》Song Jin: Chapter 7, "The Illumation of the Minuscule", *Wenzi*】

君子贈人以軒，不若以言。 A gentleman giving a carriage as a gift to somebody is not as good as giving him advice.【晏嬰《晏子春秋‧內篇雜上第五》Yan Ying: Chapter 5, "Miscellanous Inner Chapters", *Master Yan's Spring and Autumn Annals*】

君子重正言之惠，賢於軒璧之贈。 A gentleman values more the benefit of honest advice than receiving the gifts of carriages or jade.【劉晝《劉子‧貴言第三十一》Liu Zhou: Chapter 31, "Valuing advice", *Works of Master Liu Zhou*】

良玉不雕，美言不文。 Beautiful jade does not need carving and well-meant words do not need refinement.【揚雄《法言‧寡見》Yang Xiong: "My Views", *Exemplary Sayings*】

貌言華也，至言實也，苦言藥也，甘言疾也。 Polite words are flowers, honest words are fruit, harsh words are medicine, and sweet words are sickness.【司馬遷《史記‧商君列傳》Sima Qian: "Biography of Lord Shang", *Records of the Grand Historian*】

美言可以市尊，美行可以加人。 Beautiful words can bring honour and fine deeds can gain respect from others.【老子《道德經‧第六十二章》Laozi: Chapter 62, *Daodejing*】

舌劍利於刀劍。 Words cut more than swords.【諺語 Proverb】

書不盡言，言不盡意。 Words cannot express in full what I want to say, and speech cannot express in full what I have in mind.【《易經‧繫辭上》"Appended Remarks, Part 1", *The Book of Changes*】

同心之言，其臭如蘭。 Words of agreement are as fragrant as orchids.【《易經‧繫辭上》"Appended Remarks, Part 1", *The Book of Changes*】

心之孔嘉，其言藹如。 The kindness in one's heart makes one's words gentle and affable.【袁枚《續詩品‧齊心》Yuan Mei: "Unity of Hearts", *A Sequel to Poetry Talks*】

信言不美，美言不信。 Faithful words are not beautiful and beautiful words are not faithful.【老子《道德經‧第八十一章》Laozi: Chapter 81, *Daodejing*】

信者，言之瑞也，善之主也。 Trust is the treasure of speech and the centre of good conduct.【左丘明《左傳‧襄公九年》Zuo Qiuming: "The Ninth Year of the Reign of Duke Xiang", *Zuo's Commentary on the Spring and Autumn Annals*】

言不顧行，行不顧言。 One's words do not agree with one's deeds and the reverse is true.

【孟軻《孟子‧盡心章句下》Meng Ke: Chapter 7, Part 2, *Mencius*】

言無實不祥。 Words which are not true are inauspicious.【孟軻《孟子‧離婁下》Meng Ke: Chapter 4, Part 2, *Mencius*】

言有盡而意無窮。 Words have an end, messages do not.【嚴羽《滄浪詩話‧詩辯》Yan Yu: Chapter 19, "Poetic Analysis", *Canglang Poetry Talks*】

一言僨事，一人定國。 A single remark ruins things and a single person stabilizes a country.【《禮記‧大學第四十二》Chapter 42: "The Great Learning", *The Book of Rites*】

一語驚醒夢中人。 A person suddenly becomes clear-minded upon listening to a word of wisdom.【俗語 Common saying】

與人善言，暖於布帛；傷人以言，深於矛戟。 Give people friendly words, this is warm as clothes. Hurt people with words, this is pain deeper than that of spears.【荀況《荀子‧榮辱第四》Xun Kuang: Chapter 4 "Honour and Disgrace", *Xunzi*】

Work

得人錢財，替人消災。 One must be committed to complete the task for which one has been paid.【俗語 Common saying】

多勞多得，少勞少得，不勞不得。 He who works more gets more,

he who works less gets less, and he who does not work gets nothing.【俗語 Common saying】

工作在先，享樂在後。 Work first, enjoy yourself later.【俗語 Common saying】

慢工出細活。Slow work yields fine products. 【俗語 Common saying】

木匠多了蓋歪房。Too many carpenters make the house shapeless. 【諺語 Proverb】

起五更，睡半夜。Rise very early and go to bed very late. 【俗語 Common saying】【西周生《醒世姻緣傳‧第五十六回》Xi Zhousheng: Chapter 56, *Stories of Marriage to Awaken the World*】

巧者多勞拙者閒。A clever and able person is often busy while a clumsy and stupid person is often at leisure. 【諺語 Proverb】【莊周《莊子‧雜篇‧列御寇第三十二》Zhuang Zhou: Chapter 32, "Lie Yukou", "Miscellaneous Chapters", *Zhuangzi*】

人多手腳亂。Too many people make things chaotic. 【俗語 Common saying】

日出而作，日入而息。Start work at daybreak and retire at sunset. 【《古逸：擊壤歌》Ancient Poems: "Song of the Peasants in the Time of Yao"】

三天打魚，兩天曬網。Go fishing for three days and then dry the nets for two days. 【俗語 Common saying】

三早抵一工。Three mornings makes a day. 【俗語 Common saying】

少說空話，多做實事。Less empty talk and more hard work. 【諺語 Proverb】

生命不止，工作不息。As long as one is alive, one's work never ends. 【俗語 Common saying】

食其祿者忠其事。Earning salary from one, you should fulfill your tasks assigned by one. 【諺語 Proverb】

五更起牀，百事興旺。If you rise at the fifth watch of the day, everything would thrive. 【諺語 Proverb】

一步一個腳印。Every step leaves its print. 【諺語 Proverb】

一個蘿蔔一個坑。Each has one's own task and no one can be spared for any other work. 【俗語 Common saying】

一人難唱一台戲。One person cannot perform a play. 【諺語 Proverb】

一日不作，一日不食。Without working for a day, you will have nothing to eat for the day. 【俗語 Common saying】

一日不作，百日不食。Without working for a day, you will have nothing to eat for a hundred days. 【司馬遷《史記‧趙世家》Sima Qian: "House of Zhao", *Records of the Grand Historian*】

欲得亨通，日日作工。To get prosperous, you must work hard everyday. 【俗語 Common saying】

坐在坑頭數芝麻 —— 用上細工了。Sitting on a pit to count sesame seeds – it requires meticulous work. 【歇後語 End-clipper】

World

百事大吉，天下太平。Everything is fine and the world is in peace. 【周密《癸辛雜識續集下・桃符獲罪》Zhou Mi: "Convicted by Peach-wood Charms", Part 2, *Sequel to the Miscellaneous Notes from the Guixin Quarter*】

不食人間煙火。Be otherworldly. 【諺語 Proverb】

大千世界，無奇不有。In this boundless world, there are things of every description. 【俗語 Common saying】

世事紛紛一局棋。The changes in the affairs of this world are like those of a game of chess. 【馮夢龍《醒世恆言・第九卷》Feng Menglong: Chapter 9, *Stories to Awaken the World*】

世事深如海，要得細思量。Affairs in the world are as deep as the sea, which need careful pondering. 【諺語 Proverb】

世事要多知，香酒要少吃。One needs to know more about the world but drinks less wine. 【俗語 Common saying】

世治用文，世亂用武。In times of peace and prosperity, civil officials are important; in times of turbulence, generals are important. 【俗語 Common saying】

世治則禮詳，世亂則禮簡。In times of peace and prosperity, rites can be detailed; in times of turbulence, rites should be simple. 【陳壽《三國志・魏書・袁渙傳》Chen Shou: "Biography of Yuan Huan", "History of the Wei", *Records of the Three Kingdoms*】

天下非一人之天下，乃天下人之天下也。The world is not a world of a single person; it is a world of all the people. 【呂不韋《呂氏春秋・貴公》Lu Buwei: "Esteeming Impartiality", *Master Lu's Spring and Autumn Annals*】

天下之本在國，國之本在家，家之本在身。The base of the world is the state, the base of the state is the family, and the base of the family is self-cultivation. 【孟軻《孟子・離婁上》Meng Ke: Chapter 4, Part 1, *Mencius*】

唯恐天下不亂。Be anxious to see the world plunged into chaos. 【洪應明《菜根譚》Hong Yingming: *The Roots of Wisdom*】

Worry

吃了定心丸。 Be free of worries.
【俗語 Common saying】

吃肉不長肉，衹為多憂愁。 If one
eats meat and does not put on
weight, it is because one has too
many things to worry about.【俗
語 Common saying】

幹活不死人，愁要愁死人。 Work
won't kill a person, worry will.
【俗語 Common saying】

工作不傷身，愁要愁死人。 Work
does not cause any harm to
a person's health, but worry
does kill a person.【俗語 Common
saying】

借酒消愁愁上愁。 To turn to
wine to dispel your worries will
only increase your worries.【李
開先〈後岡陳提學傳〉Li Kaixian:
Scene 37, "Biography of Chen Tixue of
Hougang"】

卻看妻子愁何在，漫卷詩書喜欲
狂。 I notice that all of my wife's
worries are now gone, I am wild
with glee among my books and
poems.【杜甫〈聞官軍收河南河北〉
Du Fu: "Recapture of the Regions North
and South of the Yellow River"】

窮有窮愁，富有富憂。 The poor
have the poor's troubles and the
rich, the rich's worries.【曹雪芹
《紅樓夢·第八十一回》Cao Xueqin:
Chapter 81, A Dream of the Red Chamber】

人愁不要喜悅。 When people
have worries, they are not in the
mood of seeking pleasure.【佚

名《古詩十九首》Anonymous: Nineteen
Ancient Poems】

人生識字憂患始。 When a person
learns the characters, it is the
beginning of his worries.【蘇軾
〈石蒼舒醉墨堂〉Su Shi: "Shi Cangshu's
Hall of Inebriant Ink"】

人無遠慮，必有近憂。 A person
who does not think about the
distant future will sure to have
worries at hand.【孔子《論語·衛
靈公篇第十五》Confucius: Chapter 15,
The Analects of Confucius】

身無半畝，心憂天下；讀破萬卷，
神交古人。 I don't have half an
acre of land to myself, but I care
about my people across the land.
I read over ten thousand books
and I am spiritually attracted to
the ancient people.【左宗棠〈對聯〉
Zuo Zongtang: "Couplet"】

生年不滿百，常懷千歲憂。 A
person does not live a hundred
years, yet what he worries is
longer than a thousand years.
【佚名《古詩十九首》Anonymous:
Nineteen Ancient Poems】

無事一身輕。 Without worry,
without care.【俗語 Common
saying】

伍子胥過昭關，一夜頭髮白。 It
is like Wu Zixu passing through
the Zhao Gate, one's hair
turning grey overnight owing to
excessive anxiety.【俗語 Common
saying】

先天下之憂而憂，後天下之樂而樂。 To worry before the whole world worries, and to rejoice after the whole world rejoices. 【范仲淹〈岳陽樓記〉Fan Zhongyan: "Song of the Yueyang Tower"】

心裏有事渾身重，心上無事一身輕。 Having something to worry about, one feels heavy all over; without anything to worry about, one feels light on one's feet. 【俗語 Common saying】

心事更壓人。 Worry weighs on one's mind most heavily. 【俗語 Common saying】

心有千載憂，身無一日閒。 My heart is filled with concerns that last one thousand years and my body does not idle for a single day. 【白居易〈秋山〉Bai Juyi: "Mountains in Autumn"】

憂民之憂者，民亦憂其憂。 When a ruler grieves at the sorrow of his people, they also grieve at his sorrow. 【孟軻《孟子‧梁惠王下》Meng Ke: Chapter 1, Part 2, Mencius】

知我者，謂我心憂。不知我者，謂我何求。 Those who know me say that I am sad at heart while those who don't know me ask me what I am after. 【《詩經‧王風‧黍離》"The Millets Separated", "Odes around the Capital", The Book of Odes】

Writing

白紙寫上黑字 —— 賴不掉。 When it is in black and white, it cannot be denied. 【歇後語 End-clipper】

筆鋒如利刃。 The tip of one's pen is as keen and powerful as a sword. 【俗語 Common saying】

筆落驚風雨，詩成泣鬼神。 When Li Bai puts pen to paper, he stuns the wind and the rain; when he finishes a poem, he moves ghosts and gods to tears. 【杜甫〈寄李太白二十韻〉Du Fu: "To Li Bai"】

不薄今人愛古人，清詞麗句必為鄰。 I would not belittle the moderns or love the ancients. Clear phrases, lovely lines shall surely be my company. 【杜甫〈戲為六絕句〉Du Fu: "Six Quatrains Composed for Fun"】

不露文章世已驚。 Zhuge Liang did not write articles and yet his talents have stunned the world. 【杜甫〈古柏行〉Du Fu: "Ode to an Old Cypress"】

不願文章高天下，祇願文章中考官。 One does not wish that one's article is the best of the world, but that the article is to the liking of the examiner. 【諺語 Proverb】【文康《兒女英雄傳‧第

三十四回》Wen Kang: Chapter 34, *Biographies of Young Heroes and Heroines*】

藏之名山，傳之其人。I will hide my writings in a famous mountain and pass them on to the like-minded people.【司馬遷〈報任少卿書〉Sima Qian: "A Letter in Reply to Ren An"】

春秋多佳日，登高賦新詩。There are so many fine days in spring and autumn for one to go up the hills and write new poems.【陶淵明〈移居〉Tao Yuanming: "Moving Residence"】

凡作人貴直而作詩文貴曲。In all cases, what is valued in conducting oneself is straightforwardness and what is valued in writing poems and essays is insinuation.【袁枚《隨園詩話》Yuan Mei: *Talks on Poetry from the Sui Garden*】

蓋文章，經國之大業，不朽之盛事。Literature is a significant matter in the governing of a state and a grand undertaking that is everlasting.【曹丕《典論・論文》Cao Pei: "On Writing", *On Classics*】

借問因何太瘦生，祇為從來作詩苦。Could I ask you why you have grown so slim since we parted? It was all because you find it difficult to write poems.【李白〈戲子美〉Li Bai: "Teasing Du Fu"】

孔子放屁 —— 文氣衝天。Confucius being flatulent –

literary airs fill the heavens.【歇後語 End-clipper】

李杜文章在，光焰萬丈長。The writings of Li Bai and Du Fu will remain, shedding their splendour far and wide.【韓愈〈調張籍〉Han Yu: "Teasing Zhang Ji"】

奇文共欣賞，疑義相與析。Together we share the pleasure of reading a rare piece of writing and discuss its subtleties.【陶淵明〈移居〉Tao Yuanming: "Moving Residence"】

人以文傳，文以人傳。A person is propagated by his writings, and his writings will be propagated among people.【魯迅〈阿Q正傳〉Lu Xun: "The Story of Ah Q"】

人之於文學也，猶玉之於琢磨也。Classics to people is like craving and polishing to jade.【荀況《荀子・大略第二十七》Xun Kuang: Chapter 27, "Great Compendium", *Xunzi*】

述而不作，信而好古。I talk but do not write; I believe and I am fond of the ancient.【孔子《論語・述而篇第七》Confucius: Chapter 7, *The Analects of Confucius*】

天恐文章中道絕，再生賈島在人間。Heaven worried about the termination of good writings after the death of Meng Jiao, so it gives birth to Jia Dao to this world.【韓愈〈贈賈島〉Han Yu: "To Jia Dao"】

為文不能關教事，雖工無益也。An article that is not instructive

does not have any benefit no matter how articulated it is. 【葉適〈贈薛子長〉Ye Shi: "To Xue Zichang"】

文籍雖滿腹，不如一囊錢。 The articles and books that fill your belly are not as good as a bag of money. 【趙壹〈疾邪詩〉Zhao Yi: "Poem to Cure Evil"】

文若春華，思若湧泉。 His writings are like flowers in spring and his thoughts, like gushing springs. 【曹植〈王仲宣誄〉Cao Zhi: "Elegy for Wang Can"】

文所以載道也。 Literature is a vehicle of the Way. 【周敦頤《通書·文辭》Zhou Dunyi: "Literature and Words", *Comprehending The Book of Changes*】

文以行立，行以文傳。 One's writing is established by what one practises; what one practises is shown through one's writing. 【劉勰《文心雕龍·宗經》Liu Xie: "Honouring the Classics", *The Literary Mind and the Carving of Dragons*】

文章本天成，妙手偶得之。 The words are already there, you get them by chance through clever skills. 【陸游〈文章〉Lu You: "Words"】

文章可立身。 Writing good articles can establish oneself in this world. 【汪洙〈神童詩〉Wang Zhu: "Poem of a Talented Boy"】

文章千古事，得失寸心知。 Writing is a deed of eternity and its failure and success are known only to the author. 【杜甫〈偶題〉Du Fu: "Occasional Poem"】

文章體制本天生，模宋規唐徒自苦。 The format of an article is originally natural, you're being harsh to yourself if you pattern after the Song scholars or follow the norms of the Tang literary people. 【張問陶〈論文〉Zhang Wentao: "On Literature"】

文章已滿行人耳，一席思卿一愴然。 Your writings have been fully heard by all people and as soon as I think of you, I feel sad. 【唐宣宗〈懷白居易〉Emperor Xuanzong of Tang: "In Memory of Bai Juyi"】

文章易作，通峭難為。 Essays are easy to write, but to create a flavour in it is difficult. 【袁枚《隨園詩話》Yuan Mei: *Talks on Poetry from the Sui Garden*】

文章自古無憑據。 From of old, there has never been a fixed standard for writings. 【呂祖謙《詩律武庫·卷四》Lu Zuqian: Chapter 4, *Arsenal of Poetic Rules*】

文字緣同骨肉深。 Our fate with characters is as deep as meat to bones. 【龔自珍〈己亥雜詩〉Gong Zizhen: "Poems Written in the Year of Jihai"】

我手寫我口。 My hand writes what my mouth says. 【黃遵憲〈雜感〉Huang Zunxian: "Random Thoughts"】

無感不成詩。 Without feelings, you cannot produce poems. 【俗語 Common saying】

下筆千言，離題萬丈。 A thousand words from the writing brush and yet what is written is ten thousand feet away from the theme. 【朱自清〈論廢話〉Zhu Ziqing: "On Nonsense"】

寫神則生，寫貌則死。 If you describe the spirit of something, your writing will be vivid; if you describe the appearance of something, your writing will be rigid. 【許槤《六朝文絜》Xu Lian: *Anthology of the Six Dynasties*】

言以足志，文以足言。 Words are to supplement a will and writings are to supplement speech. 【左丘明《左傳·襄公二十五年》Zuo Qiuming: "The Twenty-fifth Year of the Reign of Duke Xiang", *Zuo's Commentary on the Spring and Autumn Annals*】

言愈多，於道未必明，故言以簡為貴。 With too many words, the Way may not be understood, this is why economy of words is valued. 【程顥，程頤《河南程氏粹言·論學篇》Cheng Hao and Cheng Yi: "On Learning", *Sayings of Masters Cheng of Henan*】

言之無文，行之不遠。 Without literary elegance, words go a short way. 【左丘明《左傳·襄公二十五年》Zuo Qiuming: "The Twenty-fifth Year of the Reign of Duke Xiang", *Zuo's Commentary on the Spring and Autumn Annals*】

一字害一句。 One word, when misused, spoils the whole sentence. 【孟軻《孟子·萬章上》Meng Ke: Chapter 10, Part 1, *Mencius*】

一字值千金。 A single word is worth a thousand taels of gold. 【司馬遷《史記·呂不韋列傳》Sima Qian: "Biography of Lu Buwei", *Records of the Grand Historian*】

因字而生句，積句而成章，積章而成篇。 Words generate sentences, sentences form sections, and sections form texts. 【劉勰《文心雕龍·章句》Liu Xie: "Texts and Sentences", *The Literary Mind and the Carving of Dragons*】

有佳意必有佳語。 When there are good ideas, there are surely good expressions. 【孫聯奎《詩品臆說》Sun Liankui: *Conjectures on Talks on Poetry*】

語不驚人死不休。 If my lines do not startle others, I will be restless until death. 【杜甫〈江上值水如海勢聊短述〉Du Fu: "Having a Short Chat When the Water in the River is Running into the Sea"】

玉皇若問人間事，亂世文章不值錢。 If the Jade Emperor asked you about things in the world of sentient beings, tell Him that literary writings in a chaotic world are worthless. 【呂蒙正〈祭灶詩〉Lu Mengzheng: "Offering Sacrifices to Zao Jun"】

字字看來皆是血，十年辛苦不尋常。 Every character that you read is laboured by my blood.

Ten years of hardship is not all that simple. 【曹雪芹《紅樓夢》Cao Xueqin: *A Dream of the Red Chamber*】

Yearning

滴不盡相思血淚拋紅豆，開不完春柳春花滿畫樓。 Dripping endlessly are blood and tears of longing, as I throw the forget-me-not red beans; blooming ceaselessly are willows and flowers in spring that fill the entire painted tower. 【曹雪芹《紅樓夢‧紅豆詞》Cao Xueqin:"Song of Red Beans", *A Dream of the Red Chamber*】

羈鳥戀舊林，池魚思故淵。 A bird in a cage yearns for the old forest; a fish in a pond thinks of its former river. 【陶淵明〈歸田園居〉Tao Yuanming:"Returning to My Rural Home"】

癩蛤蟆想吃天鵝肉。 A toad thinks of eating the swan's meat. 【曹雪芹《紅樓夢‧第十一回》Cao Xueqin: Chapter 11, *A Dream of the Red Chamber*】

相思一夜情多少，地角天涯未是長。 How much love there is for yearning in a whole night; the ends of the world are not as long, 【張仲素〈燕子樓〉Zhang Zhongsu:"The Swallow Tower"】

休別有魚處，莫戀淺灘頭。 Don't leave a place where there is fish to catch and don't long for a shallow beach where there is no fish to catch. 【《增廣賢文》*Words that Open up One's Mind and Enhance One's Wisdom*】

有了千田想萬田，做得皇帝想成仙。 When you have a thousand fields, you want ten thousand; when you become a king, you want to be a fairy. 【諺語 Proverb】

Yielding

處世讓一步為高。 In life, it is better to yield a step. 【洪應明《菜根譚》Hong Yingming: *The Roots of Wisdom*】

大丈夫能屈能伸。 A true man knows when to yield and when not. 【俗語 Common saying】【李伯元《文明小史‧第三十六回》Li Boyuan: Chapter 36, *A Short History of Civilization*】

富貴不能淫，貧賤不能移，威武不能屈。 One who cannot be corrupted by riches or honours, swayed by poverty or low positions, or subdued by power or force. 【孟軻《孟子‧滕文公下》Meng Ke: Chapter 5, Part 2, *Mencius*】

花好開，果難結。 It is easy to get a tree to bloom but difficult to get it to yield fruit. 【俗語 Common saying】

爭之不足，讓之有餘。 By quarrelling you can never get enough, by yielding you will get more than you want. 【俗語 Common saying】【劉安《淮南子・齊俗訓第十一》 Liu An: Chapter 11: "Placing Customs on a Par", *Huainanzi*】

Youth

白日莫閒過，青春不再來。 Don't idle away one's days, as one's youth will never come back. 【俗語 Common saying】

不經事少年。 A young man without experience. 【房玄齡等《晉書・桓沖傳》 Fang Xuanling, *et al*: "Biography of Huan Chong", *History of the Jin*】

不羨神仙羨少年。 I do not envy the celestial beings, but I do envy the young. 【袁枚〈湖上雜詩〉 Yuan Mei: "Miscellaneous Poems Written at the Lake"】

後生可畏，焉知來者之不如今也？ The young is awesome. How do we know that the future generations will not be as good as that of the present? 【孔子《論語・子罕篇第九》 Confucius: Chapter 9, *The Analects of Confucius*】

枯木逢春猶再發，人無兩度再少年。 A withe Red tree can still blossom flowers when spring comes, but a person cannot be young twice. 【《增廣賢文》 *Words that Open up One's Mind and Enhance One's Wisdom*】

莫等閒白了少年頭，空悲切。 Don't dawdle, the young head is soon white. What is the use of feeling sad then? 【岳飛〈滿江紅〉 Yue Fei: "To the Tune of the River Is All Red"】

勸君莫惜金縷衣，勸君惜取少年時。 I urge you not to hanker for dresses threaded with gold; I urge you to treasure the time when you are young. 【杜秋娘〈金縷衣〉 Du Qiuniang: "The Gold-threaded Dress"】

少年安得長少年，海波尚變為桑田。 How can the young stay young forever, for even oceans can become cropland. 【李賀〈嘲少年〉 Li He: "Teasing the Young"】

少年樂新知，哀暮思故友。 When young, people are happy to make new friends; when weak and aged, people think of old friends. 【韓愈〈除官赴闕至江州寄鄂嶽李大夫〉 Han Yu: "Presented to Master Li of E E When I Was Demoted to Jiangzhou"】

少年十五二十時，步行奪得胡馬騎。 When I was young, may be

around fifteen or twenty, I could on foot snatch a horse from the Tartar and ride on it. 【王維〈老將行〉Wang Wei:"Ode to an Old General"】

少年聽雨歌樓上，紅燭昏羅帳。 When young, I listened to raining in the singing parlour and the red candles dimmed in the silk canopy. 【蔣捷〈虞美人·聽雨〉Jiang Jie:"Listening to the Rain: To the Tune of the Beauty of Yu"】

少年心事當拿雲。 The aspirations of a youth should be to catch clouds. 【李賀〈致酒行〉Li He:"Ode to Wine"】

少年辛苦真食蓼，老景清閒如啖蔗。 It is truly like chewing knotweed when toiling in youth and it is like chewing sugarcane when leading a leisurely life in old age. 【蘇軾〈定惠院寓居月夜偶出次韻〉Su Shi:"Going out in a Moonlit Night When Staying at the Dinghui Court, with Matching Rhymes"】

少壯能幾時，鬢髮各已蒼。 How long can we stay young and strong? The sideburns and hair of each of us have turned white. 【杜甫〈贈衛八處士〉Du Fu:"Presented to Scholar-recluse Wei the Eighth"】

四時可愛唯春日，一事能狂便少年。 Of the four seasons, spring time is most enjoyable and the only thing that excites me is the liberty of youth. 【王國維〈曉步〉Wang Guowei:"Walking in the Morning"】

小時了了，大未必佳。 He who is clever and understanding when young doesn't necessarily mean he will be successful in his adulthood. 【劉義慶《世説新語·言語第二》Liu Yiqing: Chapter 2, "Speech and Conversation", *A New Account of the Tales of the World*】

宣父猶能畏後生，丈夫未可輕年少。 Even Confucius could still respect the young, the aged should not look down on the young. 【李白〈上李邕〉Li Bai:"To Li Yong"】

幼吾幼以及人之幼。 Take care of one's own young ones first and then extend the same care to the young people in general. 【孟軻《孟子·梁惠王上》Meng Ke: Chapter 1, Part 1, *Mencius*】

Authors and works quoted in the dictionary
引文之作者及其著作

[A]

安遇時 An Yushi, author of《包公案》*Cases of Judge Bao*

[B]

白居易 Bai Juyi, author of《策林》*A Forest of Strategies*
班固 Ban Gu, author of《漢書》*History of the Han*
鮑昌 Bao Chang, author of《庚子風雲》*The War in 1900-1901*

鮑令暉 Bao Linghui
邊貢 Bian Gong
冰心 Bing Xin
《般若波羅蜜多心經》*Prajna Paramita Heart Sutra*

[C]

蔡東藩 Cai Dongfan, author of《民國史通俗演義》*Popular Romance of the Republican Period*,《後漢通俗演義》*Popular Romance of the Later Han*,《元史通俗演義》*Popular Romance of the Yuan Dynasty*,《南北史通俗演義》*Popular Romance of the Southern and Northern Dynasties*,《清史通俗演義》*Popular Romance of the Qing Dynasty*, and《明史通俗演義》*Popular Romance of the Ming Dynasty*
曹操 Cao Cao
曹靖華 Cao Jinghua, author of《歎往昔，獨木橋頭徘徊無終期》*A Sigh on the Past: Hovering at the End of a Single-log Bridge without End*
曹丕 Cao Pei, author of《典論》*On Classics*
曹松 Cao Song
曹雪芹 Cao Xueqin, author of《紅樓夢》*A Dream of the Red Chamber*
曹禺 Cao Yu
曹玉林 Cao Yulin, author of《甦醒的原野》*The Awakened Plain*
曹植 Cao Zhi
岑參 Cen Shen
查慎行 Cha Shenxing
囅然子 Chan Ranzi, author of《拊掌錄》*Clapping-hand Stories*
常建 Chang Jian
陳忱 Chen Chen, author of《水滸後傳》*A Sequel to the Outlaws of the Marshes*
陳淳 Chen Chun, author of《北溪字義》*Meanings of Characters at Northern River*
陳登科 Chen Dengke, author of《赤龍與丹鳳》*Red Dragon and Red Phoenix* and《風雷》*Wind and Thunder*

陳繼儒 Chen Jiru
陳亮 Chen Liang, author of《漢論》*On Han Dynasty*
陳琳 Chen Lin
陳汝衡 Chen Ruheng, author of《説唐演義全傳》*Romance of the Tang Dynasty*
陳師道 Chen Shidao
陳壽 Chen Shou, author of《三國志》*Records of the Three Kingdoms*
陳叔寶 Chen Shubao
陳陶 Chen Tao
陳希夷 Chen Xiyi, author of《心相篇》*Essay on Mind and Appearance*
陳于王 Chen Yuwang
陳玉蘭 Chen Yulan
陳元覯 Chen Yuanliang, author of《事林廣記》*Comprehensive Records of Affairs*
陳造 Chen Zao
陳子昂 Chen Zi'ang
陳子壯 Chen Zizhuang, author of《昭代經濟言》*On the Economy of the Dynasty*
程顥 Cheng Hao, co-author of《二程全書》*Complete Works of Cheng Hao and Cheng Yi*,《河南程氏粹言》*Sayings of Cheng Hao and Cheng Yi of Henan*
程頤 Cheng Yi, co-author of《二程全書》*Complete Works of Cheng Hao and Cheng Yi*,《河南程氏粹言》*Sayings of Cheng Hao and Cheng Yi of Henan*
程允升 Cheng Yunsheng, author of《幼學瓊林》*Treasury of Knowledge for Young Students*
程趾祥 Cheng Zhixiang, author of《此中人語》*Sayings of an Insider*
仇遠 Chou Yuan

儲光羲 Chu Guangxi

崔復生 Cui Fusheng, author of《太行志》
Records of Taixing

崔顥 Cui Hao

崔鴻 Cui Hong, author of《十六國春秋》*The Spring and Autumn of the Sixteen States*

崔護 Cui Hu

崔郊 Cui Jiao

崔巍 Cui Wei, author of《剿蜂記》*Killing Bees*

崔駰 Cui Yin

崔瑗 Cui Yuan, author of《座右銘》*My Mottos*

[D]

《大般涅槃經》*Mahāparinirvāṇa Sūtra*

戴德 Dai De, author of《大戴禮記》*Records of Rites by Dai the Elder*

戴復古 Dai Fugu

戴叔倫 Dai Shulun

鄧小平 Deng Xiaoping, author of《鄧小平文選》*Selected Works of Deng Xiaoping*

翟灝 Di Hao, author of《通俗編》*Common Things*

丁玲 Ding Ling, author of《太陽照在桑乾河上》*The Sun Shines on the Sanggan River*

董解元 Dong Jieyuan, author of《西廂記諸宮調》*The Romance of the Western Bower in All Keys and Modes*

董其昌 Dong Qichang

董説 Dong Shuo, author of《西遊補》*Supplement to Journey to the West*

董仲舒 Dong Zhongshu

董卓 Dong Zhuo

杜弼 Du Bi

杜甫 Du Fu

杜來 Du Lai

杜牧 Du Mu

杜秋娘 Du Qiuniang

杜荀鶴 Du Xunhe

端木國瑚 Duanmu Guohu

端木蕻良 Duanmu Hongliang, author of《曹雪芹》*Cao Xueqin*

[E]

《鶡冠子》Eguanzi *Eguanzi*

[F]

范成大 Fan Chengda, author of《吳郡志》*Gazetteer for Wu Commandery*

范立本 Fan Liben, author of《明心寶鑑》*The Precious Mirror that Enlightens the Heart*

范受益 Fan Shouyi

范曄 Fan Ye, author of《後漢書》*History of the Later Han*

范寅 Fan Yin, author of《越諺》*Proverbs of the State of Yue*

范仲淹 Fan Zhongyan

方東樹 Fang Dongshu, author of《昭昧詹言》*Casual Words by Zhaomei*

方回 Fang Hui

方汝浩 Fang Ruhao, author of《東度記》*Passage to the East*

方孝孺 Fang Xiaoru

房玄齡 Fang Xuanling, one of the editors of《晉書》*History of the Jin*

封特卿 Feng Teqing

馮道 Feng Dao

馮德英 Feng Deying, author of《山菊花》*Wild Chrysanthemum*

馮夢龍 Feng Menglong, author of《警世通言》*Stories to Caution the World*,《醒世恆言》*Stories to Awaken the World*, and《喻世明言》*Stories to Instruct the World*,《古今譚概》*Stories Old and New*

馮惟敏 Feng Weimin

馮延巳 Feng Yansi

馮志 Feng Zhi, author of《敵後武工隊‧第四章》*Armed Working Team Behind Enemy Lines*

霍諝 Fo Xu

傅山 Fu Shan, author of《霜紅龕集》*Collected Works from the Frosty Red House*

傅玄 Fu Xuan

[G]

高蟾 Gao Chan

高明 Gao Ming

高適 Gao Shi

高士談 Gao Shitan

高文秀 Gao Wenxiu

高陽 Gao Yang, author of《胡雪巖全傳》*A Biography of Hu Xueyan*

高雲覽 Gao Yunlan, author of《小城春秋》*Spring and Autumn of a Small Town*

高則誠 Gao Zecheng

[J]

紀君祥 Ji Junxiang
紀昀 Ji Yun, author of《閱微草堂筆記》 *Jottings from the Thatched Hut for Reading the Subtleties*
集成 Ji Cheng, author of《宏智禪師廣錄》 *Extended Records of Chan Master Hong Zhi*
嵇康 Ji Kang
霽園主人 Jiyuan Zhuren, author of《夜譚隨錄》 *Random Notes of Evening Chats*
賈島 Jia Dao
賈思勰 Jia Sixie, author of《齊民要術》 *Important Ways to Unite the People*
賈誼 Jia Yi, author of《新書》 *New Writings*
賈至 Jia Zhi
賈仲名 Jia Zhongming

姜夔 Jiang Kui
姜樹茂 Jiang Shumao, author of《漁港之春》 *Spring in a Fishing Port*
蔣濟 Jiang Ji
蔣捷 Jiang Jie
焦竑 Jiao Hong, author of《玉堂叢語》 *Collected Accounts from the Jade Hall*
焦延壽 Jiao Yanshou, author of《焦氏易林》 *Thoughts on The Book of Changes by Master Jiao*
鶡冠子 Jie Guanzi, author of《鶡冠子》 *Jieguanzi*
金誠 Jin Cheng
金纓 Jin Ying, author of《格言聯璧》 *Couplets of Maxims*

[K]

康海 Kang Hai
柯丹丘 Ke Danqiu
柯藍 Ke Lan, author of《瀏河十八彎》 *Eighteen Turns of the Liu River*
克非 Ke Fei, author of《春潮急》 *Spring Tide Comes Rapidly*

孔厥，袁靜 Kong Jue and Yuan Jing, authors of《新兒女英雄傳》 *New Biographies of Heroes and Heroines*
孔融 Kong Rong
孔子 Kongzi (Confucius),《論語》 *The Analects of Confucius*
況周頤 Kuang Zhouyi
葵埭 Kui Tan

[L]

蘭陵笑笑生 Lanling Xiaoxiaosheng, author of《金瓶梅》 *The Plum in the Golden Vase*
郎瑛 Lang Ying, author of《七修類稿》 *Draft Arranged in Seven Categories*
老舍 Lao She, author of《正紅旗下》 *Under the Red Banner*,《鼓書藝人》 *The Drum Singers*,《駱駝祥子》 *Rickshaw Boy*,《四世同堂》 *Four Generations under One Roof*
老子 Laozi, author of《道德經》 *Daodejing*
黎汝清 Li Ruqing, author of《萬山紅遍》 *Redness All over Ten Thousand Mountains* and《雨雪霏霏》 *in the Midst of the Rain and Snow*
李白 Li Bai
李百藥 Li Baiyao, author of《北齊書》 *History of the Northern Qi*
李寶嘉 Li Baojia, author of《官場現形記》 *Officialdom Unmasked* and《中國現在記》 *Present-day China*
李伯元 Li Boyuan, author of《文明小史》 *A Short History of Civilization* and《活地獄》 *Living Hell*
李昉，李穆，徐鉉 Li Fang, Li Mu, and Xu Xuan, co-editors of《太平御覽》 *Imperial Reader of the Era of Great Peace*

李復言 Li Fuyan, author of《續玄怪錄》 *Sequel to the Records of the Mysterious and Strange*
李覯 Li Gou
李觀 Li Guan
李光庭 Li Guangting, author of《鄉諺解頤》 *Country Sayings to Smile at*
李涵秋 Li Hanqiu, author of《近十年目睹之怪現狀》 *Bizarre Happenings Eyewitnessed over the Last Ten Years*
李賀 Li He
李節 Li Jie
李開先 Li Kaixian
李康 Li Kang
李六如 Li Liuru, author of《六十年的變遷》 *The Changes in the Last Sixty Years*
李綠園 Li Luyuan, author of《歧路燈》 *Lamp on a Forked Road*
李滿天 Li Mantian, author of《水向東流》 *Water Flows to the East*
李匡乂 Li Qiangyi, author of《資暇集》 *Collection of Leisure Time Notes*
李清照 Li Qingzhao
李汝珍 Li Ruzhen, author of《鏡花緣》 *Flowers in the Mirror*

盧照鄰 Lu Zhaolin

魯迅 Lu Xun, author of《而已集》And that's that,《彷徨》Wandering, and《隨感錄》Records of My Random Thoughts,《花邊文學》Fringed Literature,《兩地書》Letters between Two Places, and《華蓋集續編》Sequel to Inauspicious Stars

陸佃 Lu Dian, author of《埤雅》Enlarged Erya

陸龜蒙 Lu Guimeng

陸九淵 Lu Jiuyuan, author of《語錄》Records of My Sayings

陸人龍 Lu Renlong, author of《三刻拍案驚奇》Amazing Tales, Volume Three

陸游 Lu You, author of《天彭牡丹譜》Treatise on Tianpeng Peonies,《老學庵筆記》: Notebook from the House of a Person Who Studies When He Is Old,《放翁家訓》Family Instructions of Lu You

陸羽 Lu Yu, author of《茶經》The Classic of Tea

呂本中 Lu Benzhong, author of《師友雜誌》Remarks on Teachers and Friends

呂不韋 Lu Buwei, author of《呂氏春秋》Master Lu's Spring and Autumn Annals

呂德勝 Lu Desheng, author of《小兒語》Words for Young Boys

呂坤 Lu Kun, author of《呻吟語》Groaning Words

呂蒙正 Lu Mengzheng

呂南公 Lu Nangong

呂望 Lu Wang, author of《六韜》Six Secret Teachings

呂岩 Lu Yan

呂夷簡 Lu Yijian

呂祖謙 Lu Zuqian, author of《詩律武庫》Arsenal of Poetic Rules

[N]

納蘭性德 Nalan Xingde

聶海 Nie Hai, author of《靠山堡》Near-mountain Fort

牛嶠 Niu Qiao

牛希濟 Niu Xiji

鈕驃 Niu Biao

[O]

歐陽山 Ouyang Shan, author of《三家巷》Three-family Lane

歐陽修 Ouyang Xiu, author of《五代史》History of the Five Dynasties

歐陽修、宋祁,范鎮,呂夏卿 Ouyang Xiu, Song Qi, Fan Zhen, Lu Xiaqing, compilers of《新唐書》A New History of the Tang

羅大經 Luo Dajing《鶴林玉露》Jade Dew of the Crane Forest

羅貫中 Luo Guanzhong, author of《三國演義》Romance of the Three Kingdoms,《平妖傳》Taming Devils,《粉妝樓》Cosmetical Building

羅懋登 Luo Maodeng, author of《三寶太監西洋記》Sanbao Eunuch's Voyage to the Western Ocean

羅隱 Luo Yin

羅願 Luo Yuan, author of《爾雅翼》Wings to the Erya

駱賓王 Luo Binwang

[M]

馬戴 Ma Dai

馬烽 Ma Feng, author of《呂梁英雄傳》Heroes of the Lu Liang Mountain

馬銀春 Ma Yinchun, author of《沒有最好只有更好》The Best Has Gotten Better

馬致遠 Ma Zhiyuan

馬總 Ma Zong, author of《意林》Forest of Opinions

毛澤東 Mao Zedong

茅盾 Mao Dun, author of《霜葉紅似二月花》The Frosty Leaves Are Red As Flowers in the Second Month of the Year

枚乘 Mei Cheng

梅貽琦 Mei Yiqi

孟德耀 Meng Deyao

孟浩然 Meng Haoran

孟郊 Meng Jiao

孟軻 Meng Ke, author of《孟子》Mencius

《名賢集》Collected Sayings of Famous Sages

明思宗 Emperor Sizong of Ming

墨翟 Mo Di, author of《墨子》Mozi

歐陽元源 Ouyang Yuanyuan, author of《負曝閒談》Chats When Basking in the Winter Sun

[P]

潘榮陛 Pan Rongbi, author of《帝京歲時紀勝》Descriptions of Scenic Spots During Different Seasons in the Imperial Capital

潘嶽 Pan Yue

龐元英 Pang Yuanying, author of《談藪》Grassland Conversations

裴休 Pei Xiu

彭定求 Peng Dingqiu, co-editor of《全唐詩》Complete Tang Poems

彭汝礪 Peng Ruli

彭養鷗 Peng Yang'ou, author of《黑籍冤魂》*The Curse of Opium*

蒲松齡 Pu Songling, author of《聊齋誌異》*Strange Stories from a Chinese Studio*

[Q]

錢彩 Qian Cai, author of《說岳全傳》*A Story of Yue Fei*

錢大昕 Qian Daxin, author of《恆言錄》*Record of Common Sayings*

錢德蒼 Qian Decang, author of《解人頤》*Jokes to Relieve People*

錢鶴灘 Qian Hetan

錢起 Qian Qi (?-766)

錢希言 Qian Xiyan, author of《戲瑕》*Jokes about Flaws*

喬孟符 Qiao Mengfu

秦觀 Qin Guan

秦嘉 Qin Jia

秦韜玉 Qin Taoyu

邱心如 Qiu Xinru, author of《筆生花》*The Flowering Writing Brush*

秋瑾 Qiu Jin

曲波 Qu Bo, author of《林海雪原》*Tracks in the Snowy Forest* and《橋隆飆》*Qiao Longbiao*

屈大鈞 Qu Dajun

屈復 Qu Fu

屈原 Qu Yuan

瞿時行 Qu Shixing

權德輿 Quan Deyu

[R]

任昉 Ren Fang, author of《述異記》*Accounts of Strange Things*

戎昱 Rong Yu

阮籍 Ruan Ji

阮閱 Ruan Yue, author of《詩話總龜前集》: *Remarks on Poetry, First Volume*

[S]

僧正岩 Seng Zhengyan

僧志文 Seng Zhiwen

《山海經》*Shanhaijing, Classic of Mountains and Seas*

商鞅 Shang Yang, author of《商君書》*The Works of Shang Yang*

《尚書》*The Book of History*

邵雍 Shao Yong

申涵光 Shen Hanguang, author of《荊園小語》*Remarks from the Jing Garden*

申居鄖 Shen Juyun, author of《西岩贅語》*Remarks by Shen Juyun*

沈德潛 Shen Deqian, author of《說詩晬語》*Remarks on Poetry*

沈復 Shen Fu, author of《浮生六記》*Six Chapters of a Floating Life*

沈璟 Shen Jing

沈鯨 Shen Jing

沈受先 Shen Shouxian

沈泰 Shen Tai, author of《盛明雜劇》*Variety Plays from the High Ming*

沈約 Shen Yue, author of《宋書》*History of the Song*

沈倬 Shen Zhuo

沈自晉 Shen Zijin

慎到 Shen Dao, author of《慎子》*Shenzi*

《詩經》*The Book of Songs*

施惠 Shi Hui, author of《幽閨記》*Stories from the Secluded Chamber*

施耐庵 Shi Nai'an, author of《水滸傳》*Outlaws of the Marshes*

施世綸 Shi Shilun, author of《施公案》*Cases of Judge Shi*

史彌寧 Shi Nining

史清溪 Shi Qingxi

石成金 Shi Chengjin, author of《傳家寶》*Family Heirloom*

石達開 Shi Dakai

石君寶 Shi Junbao

石印紅 Shi Yinhong, co-author of《護國皇娘傳》*A Biography of the Protect-the-country Imperial Concubine*

石玉昆 Shi Yukun, author of《三俠五義》*The Three Heroes and Five Gallants* and《小五義》*The Five Younger Gallants*, and《續小五義》*A Second Sequel to The Five Younger Gallants*

釋道原 Shi Daoyuan, author of《景德傳燈錄》*Records of the Transmission of the Lamp in the Jingde Period*

釋普濟 Shi Puji, author of《五燈會元》*A Compendium of the Five Lamps*

釋惟白 Shi Weibai, author of《續傳燈錄》*A Sequel to the Records of the Transmission of the Lamp*

釋悟明 Shi Wuming, author of《聯燈會要》*Essential Materials from the Chan School's Successive Lamp Records*

《說呼全傳》*Shuofu Quanzhuan, A History of the Shuo family*

碩果山人 Shuoguo Shanren, author of《訓蒙增廣改本》*Revised Edition of the Words*

that Open up One's Mind and Enhance One's
Wisdom for Enlightening Children
尸佼 Shi Jiao, author of《尸子》Shizi
司空曙 Sikong Shu
司空圖 Sikong Tu, author of《二十四詩品》
Twenty-four Modes of Poetry
司馬光 Sima Guang, author of《資治通鑒》
Comprehensive Mirror to Aid in Government
and《司馬文正公集》Collected Works of
Sima Guang
司馬遷 Sima Qian, author of《史記》Records
of the Grand Historian
司馬穰苴 Sima Rangju, author of《司馬法》
The Art of War by Sima Rangju
司馬文森 Sima Wensen, author of《風雨桐
江》The Tong River in Wind and Rain
司馬相如 Sima Xiangru
宋伯仁 Song Boren
宋鈃 Song Jin, author of《文子》Wenzi
宋濂 Song Lian, co-compiler of《元史》The
History of the Yuan Dynasty
宋凌雲 Song Lingyun
宋喬 Song Qiao, author of《侍衛官雜記》
Notes of a Guard Officer
宋禧 Song Xı

宋繡 Song Xun, author of《古今藥石》
Medical Herbs Past and Present
宋玉 Song Yu
宋之問 Song Zhiwen
蘇伯玉妻 Wife of Su Boyu
蘇轍 Su Che, author of《洞山文長老語錄》
Sayings of the Buddhist Elder Dong Shanwen
蘇復之 Su Fuzhi
蘇麟 Su Lin
蘇軾 Su Shi
蘇武 Su Wu
蘇洵 Su Xun, author of《權書》Book of Power
Strategy and《衡論》Criteria for Evaluation
孫臏 Sun Bin, author of《孫臏兵法》Sun
Bin's Art of War
孫錦標 Sun Jinbiao, author of《通俗常言
疏證》Mistakes and Corrections in Nantong
Dialects and Proverbs
孫聯奎 Sun Liankui, author of《詩品臆説》
Conjectures on Talks on Poetry
孫武 Sun Wu, author of《孫子兵法》The Art
of War by Sunzi
孫星衍 Sun Xingyan
孫中山 Sun Yat-sen
孫洙 Sun Zhu

[T]

太上隱者 Taishang Yinzhe
譚嗣同 Tan Sitong, author of《仁學》An
Exposition of Benevolence
湯顯祖 Tang Xianzu
唐庚 Tang Geng, author of《唐子西語錄》
Sayings of Tang Geng
唐裴休 Tang Peixiu, author of《黃蘗山斷際
禪師傳心法要》Essentials in the Method of
the Transmission of Mind by the Chan Master
Duanji of the Huang Nie Mountain
唐太宗 Emperor Taizong of the Tang, author
of《帝範》Rules for an Emperor
唐宣宗 Emperor Xuanzong of Tang
唐寅 Tang Yin

唐芸洲 Tang Yunzhou, author of《七劍十三
俠》Seven Swords and Thirteen Swordsmen
陶榖 Tao Gou, author of《清異錄》Records of
the Unworldly and the Strange
陶谷 Tao Gu
陶弘景 Tao Hongjing
陶行知 Tao Xingzhi
陶淵明 Tao Yuanming
天然癡叟 Tianran Chisou, author of《石點
頭》Stone Nodding
田漢 Tian Han
脫脫 Toktoghan, compiler of《金史》History
of the Jin and《宋史》History of the Song

[W]

《丸經》Wanjing, The Classic of Herbal Pills
汪灝，張逸少 Wang Hao, Zhang Yishao,
editors of《廣羣芳譜》Extended Notes of the
Peiwen Study on All Various Herbs
汪時元 Wang Shiyuan
汪廷訥 Wang Tingna
汪琬 Wang Wan
汪應銓 Wang Yingquan
王安石 Wang Anshi
王勃 Wang Bo
王昌齡 Wang Changling

王充 Wang Chong, author of《論衡》Critical
Essays
王澹翁 Wang Danweng
王定保 Wang Dingbao, author of《唐摭言》
Garnered Words from Tang Dynasty
王夫之 Wang Fuzhi, author of《張子正蒙
注》Annotations on Correct Discipline for
Beginners by Zhang Zai and《周易外傳》
Supplementary Commentary on The Book of
Changes

王符 Wang Fu, author of《潛夫論》 *Remarks by a Recluse*

王觀 Wang Guan

王翰 Wang Han

王厚遷 Wang Houxuan, author of《古城青史》 *History of an Old Town*

王績 Wang Ji

王驥德 Wang Jide

王建 Wang Jian

王濬卿 Wang Junqing, author of《冷眼觀》 *Casting a Cold Eye*

王肯堂 Wang Kentang, author of《鬱岡齋筆麈》 *Notes from the Yugang Studio*

王厘成 Wang Licheng

王令 Wang Ling

王冕 Wang Mian

王圻 Wang Qi, author of《續文獻通考》 *Sequel to the Comprehensive Study of Literary and Documentary Sources*

王少堂 Wang Shaotang, author of《武松》 *Wu Song*

王士禎 Wang Shizhen

王世貞 Wang Shizhen, author of《鳴鳳記》 *Records of a Phoenix's Cry*

王實甫 Wang Shifu, compiler of《孤本元明雜劇》 *Unique Copies of Zaju in Yuan and Ming*

王肅 Wang Su, author of《孔子家語》 *The School Sayings of Confucius*

王廷相 Wang Tingxiang

王庭筠 Wang Tingyun

王通 Wang Tong, author of《中說》 *Analects of Wenzhongzi*

王灣 Wang Wan

王維 Wang Wei

王文祿 Wang Wenlu

王羲之 Wang Xizhi

王詡 Wang Xu, author of《鬼谷子》 *Master of the Ghost Valley*

王陽明 Wang Yangming, author of《傳習錄》 *Records of Teaching and Practising*

王應麟 Wang Yinglin, author of《三字經》 *Three-character Classic*

王有光 Wang Youguang, author of《吳下諺聯》 *Proverb Couplets of the Wu Dialect*

王有齡 Wang Youling

王禹偁 Wang Yucheng

王源 Wang Yuan, author of《居業堂文集》 *Collected Works from the Hall of Occupation*

王璋 Wang Zhang, author of《吳諺詩鈔》 *Collected Poems and Proverbs of the Wu Dialect*

王之渙 Wang Zhihuan

王重民、王慶菽、向達、周一良、啟功、曾毅公 Wang Zhongmin, Wang Qingshu, Xiang Da, Zhou Yiliang, Qi Gong, Zeng Yigong, editors of《敦煌變文集》 *A Collection of Proses at Dunhuang*

王晫 Wang Zhuo, author of《今世說》 *Modern Tales of the World*

惟白 Wei Bai, author of《建中靖國續燈錄》 *Continuation of the Record of the Transmission of the Lamp from the Jianzhong to Jingguo Years*

韋應物 Wei Yingwu

韋莊 Wei Zhuang

魏際瑞 Wei Jirui

魏泰 Wei Tai, author of《東軒筆錄》 *Remarks Recorded at the East Studio*

魏源 Wei Yuan, author of《魏源集》 *Works of Wei Yuan*

魏徵 Wei Zheng, author of《隋書》 *History of the Sui* and《羣書治要》 *Compilation of Books and Writings on the Important Governing Principles*

魏子安 Wei Zi'an

溫家寶 Wen Jiabao

溫庭筠 Wen Tingyun

文康 Wen Kang, author of《兒女英雄傳》 *Biographies of Young Heroes and Heroines*

文天祥 Wen Tianxiang

文珣 Wen Xiang

翁森 Weng Sen

翁綬 Weng Shou

無垢道人 Wugou Daoren, author of《八仙全傳》 *Biographies of the Eight Immortals*

吳承恩 Wu Cheng'en, author of《西遊記》 *Journey to the West*

吳德旋 Wu Dexuan, author of《初月樓聞見錄》 *A Sequel to What I Hear and See from the Crescent Moon Tower*

吳晗 Wu Han

吳趼人 Wu Jianren, author of《二十年目睹之怪現狀》 *Bizarre Happenings Eyewitnessed over Two Decades* and《糊塗世界》 *Confused World*

吳敬梓 Wu Jingzi, author of《儒林外史》 *An Unofficial History of the World of Literati*

吳浚 Wu Jun, author of《飛龍全傳》 *A Complete History of the Flying Dragon*

吳南生 Wu Nansheng, author of《革命母親李梨英》 *My Revolutionary Mother Li Liying*

吳樹本 Wu Shuben

吳偉業 Wu Weiye

吳文英 Wu Wenying

吳越 Wu Yue, author of《括蒼山恩仇記》 *Revenge at Mount Kuocang*

吳中情奴 Wuzhong Qingnu

武漢臣 Wu Hancheng

悟空 Wu Kong

余邵魚 Yu Shaoyu, author of《東周列國志》 *Chronicles of the Eastern Zhou Kingdoms*
虞世南 Yu Shinan
俞達 Yu Da, author of《青樓夢》 *Dream of the Green Chamber*
俞萬春 Yu Wanchun, author of《蕩寇志》 *A Record of the Eradication of Bandits*
俞文豹 Yu Wenbao, author of《清夜錄》 *Records of a Clear Night*
俞樾 Yu Yue
魚玄機 Yu Xuanji
《玉泉子》 *Master Jade Sources*
郁達夫 Yu Dafu
元好問 Yuan Haowen
元遺山 Yuan Yishan

元稹 Yuan Zhen
袁采 Yuan Cai, author of《袁氏世範》 *Models for the World by Master Yuan*
袁靜 Yuan Jing, author of《淮上人家》 *The People by the Huai River*
袁凱 Yuan Kai
袁了凡 Yuan Liaofan
袁枚 Yuan Mei, author of《隨園詩話》 *Talks on Poetry from the Sui Garden* and《續詩品》 *A Sequel to Poetry Talks*
袁永恩 Yuan Yong'en
袁於令 Yuan Yuling
岳飛 Yue Fei
《越謠歌》 *Folksongs of Yue*

[Z]

臧懋循 Zang Maoxun, compiler of《元曲選》 *Anthology of Yuan Plays*
曾鞏 Zeng Gong
曾國藩 Zeng Guofan, author of《曾國藩日記》 *The Diary of Zeng Guofan* and《冰鑒》 *Ice Judge*
曾樸 Zeng Pu, author of《續孽海花》 *Sequel to Flower on an Ocean of Sin*
《增廣賢文》 *Words that Open up One's Mind and Enhance One's Wisdom*
曾廷枚 Zeng Tingmei, author of《古諺閒譚》 *Chats on Ancient Proverbs*
章炳麟 Zhang Binglin
章程 Zhang Cheng, co-author of《護國皇娘傳》 *A Biography of the Protect-the-country Imperial Concubine*
張伯行 Zhang Boxing, author of《困學錄集粹》 *Collections of Difficult Subjects of Study*
張春帆 Zhang Chunfan, author of《宦海》 *The Official Circles*
張岱 Zhang Dai
張端義 Zhang Duanyi, author of《貴耳集》 *Collection of Things Heard*
張祜 Zhang Gu
張國賓 Zhang Guobin
張恨水 Zhang Henshui, author of《夜深沉》 *The Night is Deep*,《啼笑姻緣》 *Cry and Laugh Marriage*,《丹鳳街》 *Crimson Phoenix Street*,《最後關頭》 *The Last Moment*, and《八十一夢》 *Eighty-one Dreams*
張洪 Zhang Hong
張華 Zhang Hua
張籍 Zhang Ji
張繼 Zhang Ji
張九齡 Zhang Jiuling
張居正 Zhang Juzheng, author of《張太岳文集》 *Collected Works of Zhang Juzheng*

張履祥 Zhang Luxiang, author of《初學備忘》 *Memorandum for Beginners of Learning*
張孟良 Zhang Mengliang, author of《兒女風塵記》 *Sons and Daughters in Hardship*
張泌 Zhang Mi
張南莊 Zhang Nanzhuang, author of《何典》 *From Which Classic*
張若虛 Zhang Ruoxu
張謂 Zhang Wei
張問陶 Zhang Wentao
張先 Zhang Xian
張笑天 Zhang Xiaotian, author of《太平天國》 *The Taiping Heavenly Kingdom*
張孝祥 Zhang Xiaoxiang
張行 Zhang Xing, author of《武陵山下》 *Under Mount Wuling*
張庸 Zhang Yong
張昱 Zhang Yu
張載 Zhang Zai, author of《張子語錄》 *The Sayings of Zhang Zai*,《經學理窟》 *The Profundities of the Classics*, and《西銘》 *The Western Inscriptions*
張仲超 Zhang Zhongchao, author of《錢氏家訓》 *Family Instructions of Master Qian*
張仲素 Zhang Zhongsu
張作為 Zhang Zuowei, author of《原林深處》 *Deep in the Forest*
趙秉文 Zhao Bingwen
趙崇祚 Zhao Chongzuo, author of《花間集》 *Anthology of Poems Written among the Flowers*
趙爾巽 Zhao Erxun, author of《清史稿》 *Draft History of the Qing Dynasty*
趙渢 Zhao Feng
趙嘏 Zhao Gu
趙恆 Zhao Heng

References 參考書目

Birch, Cyril (ed.) (1965) *Anthology of Chinese Literature: From Early Times to the Fourteenth Century*, New York: Grove Press.

Bynner, Witter (tr.) (1929) *The Jade Mountain, a Chinese Anthology: Being Three Hundred Poems of the T'ang Dynasty*, New York: Knopf.

Chang, H. C. (1977) *Chinese Literature 2: Nature Poetry*, New York: Columbia University Press.

Chan, Hong-mo (2011) *The Birth of China Seen through Poetry*, Singapore: World Scientific.

Chan, Sin-wai (2018) "Translating Chinese Famous Quotes into English", in Chan Sin-wai (ed.), *An Encyclopedia of Practical Translation and Interpreting*, Hong Kong: The Chinese University Press, 201-70.

Chang, Kang-i Sun (1980) *The Evolution of Chinese Tz'u Poetry: From Late T'ang to Northern Sung*, Princeton: Princeton University Press.

Chaves, Jonathan (ed.) (1986). *The Columbia Book of Later Chinese Poetry: Yüan, Ming, and Ch'ing Dynasties (1279–1911)*, New York: Columbia University Press.

Davis, Albert Richard, (ed.) (1970) *The Penguin Book of Chinese Verse*, Baltimore: Penguin Books.

Dolby, William (tr.) (2006) *Three Hundred Tang Dynasty Poems*, Edinburgh: Carreg Publishers.

Fletcher, W.J.B. (tr.) (1919) *Gems of Chinese Verse, Translated into English Verse*, Shanghai: The Commercial Press.

Giles, Herbert (ed. and tr.) (1884) *Chinese Poetry in English Verse*, Shanghai: Kelly and Walsh.

Hinton, David (ed.) (2008) *Classical Chinese Poetry: An Anthology*, New York: Farrar, Straus, and Giroux.

Jenyns, Soame (tr.) (1944) *A Further Selection from the Three Hundred Poems of the T'ang Dynasty*, London: John Murray.

Jiao, Liwei (2014) *500 Common Chinese Proverbs and Colloquial Expressions: An Annotated Frequency Dictionary*, London and New York: Routledge.

Landau, Julie (1994) *Beyond Spring Tz'u Poems of the Sung Dynasty: Translations from the Asian Classics*, New York: Columbia University Press.

Lévy, André (2000) *Chinese Literature, Ancient and Classical*, translatd into English by William H. Nienhauser, Bloomington: Indiana University Press.

Liu, James J.Y. (1962) *The Art of Chinese Poetry*, Chicago: University of Chicago Press.

Liu, Kezhang (2006) *An Appreciation and English Translation of One Hundred Chines (i.e. Chinese) cis During the Tang and Song Dynasties*, Pittsburgh, Penn: RoseDog Books.

Liu, Shicong 劉士聰 and Gu Qinan 谷啟楠 (trs.) (2014) 《漢英對照中國經典名句》(*Famous Quotes of Chinese Wisdom*), Hong Kong: The Commercial Press.

Liu, Shih Shun (1979) *Chinese Classical Prose: The Eight Masters of the Tang-Sung Period*, Hong Kong: The Chinese University Press.

MacKintosh, Duncan and Alan Ayling (1967) *A Collection of Chinese Lyrics*, Nashville: Vanderbilt University Press.

Mair, Victor H., Nancy Shatzman Steinhardt, and Paul Rakita Goldin (eds.) (2005) *Hawai'i Reader in Traditional Chinese Culture*, Honolulu: University of Hawai'i Press.

Mair, Victor H. (2001) *The Columbia History of Chinese Literature*, New York: Columbia University Press.

Mair, Victor H. (1994) *The Columbia Anthology of Traditional Chinese Literature*, New York: Columbia University Press.

Major, John S., Queen, Sarah, Meyer, Andrew; Roth, Harold (2010) *The Huainanzi: A Guide to the Theory and Practice of Government in Early Han China, by Liu An, King of Huainan*, New York: Columbia University Press.

Mao, Xian (2013) *Children's Version of 60 Classical Chinese Poems*, eBook: Kindle Direct Publishing.

Nienhauser, William H (ed.) (1986) *The Indiana Companion to Traditional Chinese Literature*, Bloomington: Indiana University Press.

Owen, Stephen (2006) *The Late Tang: Chinese Poetry of the Mid-Ninth Century (827-860)*, Cambridge, MA: Harvard University Press.

Owen, Stephen (ed.) (1996) *An Anthology of Chinese Literature: Beginnings to 1911*, New York and London: W.W. Norton.

Owen, Stephen (1981) *The Great Age of Chinese Poetry: The High T'ang*, New Haven: Yale University Press.

Payne, Robert (ed.) (1947) *The White Pony: An Anthology of Chinese Poetry*, New York: John Day Company.

Qian, Housheng 錢厚生 (2010) 《漢英對照中國古代名言辭典》 (*Dictionary of Classic Chinese Quotations with English Translation*), Nanjing: 南京大學出版社 Nanjing University Press.

Stimson, Hugh M. (1976) *Fifty-five T'ang Poems*, New Haven: Far Eastern Publications: Yale University.

Sze, Arthur (2001) *The Silk Dragon: Translations from the Chinese*, Port Townsend, Washington: Copper Canyon Press.

Turner, John A. (1989) *A Golden Treasury of Chinese Poetry*, Hong Kong : Research Centre for Translation, The Chinese University of Hong Kong.

Wagner, Marsha L. (1984) *The Lotus Boat: The Origins of Chinese Tz'u Poetry in T'ang Popular Culture*, New York: Columbia University Press.

Watson, Burton (1984) *The Columbia Book of Chinese Poetry, from Early Times to the Thirteenth Century*, New York: Columbia University Press.

Watson, Burton (1971) *Chinese Lyricism: Shih Poetry from the Second to the Twelfth Century*, New York: Columbia University Press.

Weinberger, Eliot (2004) *The New Directions Anthology of Classical Chinese Poetry*, New York: New Directions.

Wu, John C. H. (1972) *The Four Seasons of Tang Poetry*, Rutland, Vermont: Tuttle Publishing.

Xu Yuan-zhong (tr.) (1986) *1, 000 Tang and Song Ci poems*, Hong Kong: The Commercial Press.

Yin Bangyan 尹邦彥 and Yin Haibo 尹海波 (eds.) (2007) 《中國歷代名人名言》 (*A Collection of Chinese Maxims*), Beijing: Yiling Publishing House 譯林出版社.

Yip Wai-lim (1997) *Chinese Poetry: An Anthology of Major Modes and Genres*, Durham: Duke University Press.

Zhou, Yanxian (2017) *Two Thousand Zhuang Proverbs from China with Annotations and Chinese and English Translation*, Bern: Peter Lang.

Reference translations
參考譯著

Bai Juyi 白居易
Howard S. Levy (tr.) (1971) *Translations from Po Chü-I's Collected Works*, New York: Paragon Book Preprint Corporation.

Ban Gu 班固
Hanshu《漢書》
Dubs, Homer H. (tr.) (1938-1955) *The History of the Former Han Dynasty*, 3 volumes, Baltimore: Waverly.

Borepoluomiduoxinjing《般若波羅蜜多心經》
Gyatso, Geshe Kelsang (2012) *The New Heart of Wisdom: An Explanation of the Heart Sutra*, Cumbria: Tharpa Publications.

Pine, Red (2004) *The Heart Sutra: The Womb of Buddhist Thought*, Berkeley, California: Counterpoint Press.

Cao Xueqin 曹雪芹
Hongloumeng《紅樓夢》
Hawkes, David and John Minford (trs.) (1979-1987) *The Story of the Stone*, 5 volumes, Harmondsworth: Penguin Classics; Bloomington: Indiana University Press.

McHugh, Florence and Isabel McHugh (trs.) (1958) *A Dream of the Red Chamber*, London: Routledge and Kegan Paul.

Yang, Xianyi and Gladys Yang (trs.) (1999) *A Dream of Red Mansions*, Beijing: Foreign Languages Press and Hunan People's Publishing House.

Chen Shou 陳壽
Sanguozhi《三國志》
Cutter, Robert Joe and William Gordon Crowell (trs.) (1999) *Empresses and Consorts: Selections from Chen Shou's Records of the Three States With Pei Songzhi's Commentary*, Honolulu: University of Hawaii Press.

Du Fu 杜甫
Cooper, Arthur (tr.) (1986) *Li Po and Tu Fu: Poems*, Viking Press.

Cooper, Arthur (tr.) (1973) *Li Po and Tu Fu: Poems Selected and Translated with an Introduction and Notes*, London: Penguin Classics.

Hawkes, David (1967) *A Litter Primer of Du Fu*, Oxford: Clarendon Press.

Hung, William (1952) *Tu Fu: China's Greatest Poet*, Cambridge, MA: Harvard University Press.

Owen, Stephen (2016) (tr.) *The Poetry of Du Fu*, 6 volumes, Berlin: De Gruyter.

Seth, Vikram (tr.) (1992) *Three Chinese Poets: Translations of Poems by Wang Wei, Li Bai, and Du Fu*, London: Faber and Faber.

Watson, Burton (tr.) (2002) *The Selected Poems of Du Fu*, New York: Columbia University Press.

Young, David (tr.) (2008) *Du Fu: A Life in Poetry*, New York: Random House

Fan Chengda 范成大
James M. Hargett (tr.) (2008) *Riding the River Home: A Complete and Annotated Translation of Fan Chengda's (1126–1193) Travel Diary Record of a Boat Trip to Wu (Wuchuan lu)*, Hong Kong: The Chinese University Press.

Schmidt, J.D. (1992) *Stone Lake: The Poetry of Fan Chengda 1126-1193*, Cambridge: Cambridge University Press.

Feng Menglong 馮夢龍
Gujin Tanqai《古今譚概》
Yang, Shuhui and Yang Yunqin (trs.) (2000) *Stories Old and New: A Ming Dynasty Collection, Vol.1*, Washington: Washington University Press.

Jingshi Tongyan《警世通言》(馮夢龍)
Yang, Shuhui and Yang Yunqin (trs.) (2007) *Stories to Caution the World, A Ming Dynasty Collection, Vol. II*, Washington: University of Washington Press.

Xingshi Hengyan《醒世恆言》(馮夢龍)
Yang, Shuhui and Yang Yunqin (trs.) (2009) *Stories to Awaken the World: A Ming Dynasty Collection, Vol. III*, Washington: University of Washington Press

Gao Yang 高陽
Chan, Sin-wai (tr.) (1989) *Stories by Gao Yang: "Rekindled Love" and "Purple Jade Hairpin"*, Hong Kong: The Chinese University Press.

Ge Hong 葛洪

Shenxianzhuan《神仙傳》
Robert Ford Campany (tr.) (2002) *To Live As Long As Heaven and Earth: A Translation and Study of Ge Hong's Traditions of Divine Transcendents*, California: University of California Press.

Gushi Shijiushou《古詩十九首》
Ho, Kenneth P. H. (tr.) (1977) *The Nineteen Ancient Poems*, Hong Kong: Kelly and Walsh.

Gu Yanwu 顧炎武
Johnston, Ian (tr.) (2015) "Gu Yanwu: Translations of Letters, Poems and Essays", *Cordite Poetry Review*

Guan Hanqing 關漢卿
Yang Xianyi and Gladys Yang (trs.) (1919) *Selected Plays of Guan Hanqing*, Beijing : Foreign Languages Press.

Guan Zhong 管仲
Guanzi《管子》
Rickett, Allyn W. (1985) *Guanzi: Political, Economic, and Philosophical Essays from Early China: A Study and Translation*, Princeton: Princeton University Press.

Guo Xiaoting 郭小亭
Jigong Quanchuan《濟公全傳》
John Robert Shaw (tr.) (2014) *Adventures of the Mad Monk Ji Gong: The Drunken Wisdom of China's Famous Chan Buddhist Monk*, North Clarendon, Verment: Tuttle Publishing.

Han Fei 韓非
Hanfeizi《韓非子》
Liao, W. K. (1939) *The Complete Works of Han Fei Tzu*, London: Arthur Probsthain.

Liao, W. K. (1959) *The Complete Works of Han Fei Tzu*, Volume II, London: Arthur Probsthain.

Watson, Burton (1964) *Han Fei Tzu: Basic Writings*, New York: Columbia University Press.

Han Ying 韓嬰
Hanshi Waizhuan《韓詩外傳》
Hightower, James R. (tr.) (1952) Han Shih Wai Chuan: *Han Ying's Illustrations of the Didactic Application of the "Classic of Songs"*, Cambridge, MA: Harvard University Press.

Huan Kuang 桓寬
Yantie Lun《鹽鐵論》
Gale, Esson M. (tr.) (1931) *Discourses on Salt and Iron: A Debate on State Control of Commerce and Industry in Ancient China*, Leyden: E. J. Brill.

Jia Dao 賈島
O'Connor, Mike (tr.) (2000) *When I Find You Again, It Will Be in Mountains: Selected Poems of Chia Tao*, Somerville, MA: Wisdom Publications.

Kongzi 孔子
Lunyu《論語》
Ames, Roger T. and Henry Rosemont, Jr. (tr.) (1998) *The Analects of Confucius: A Philosophical Translation*. Ballantine.

Brooks, E. Bruce and Taeko Brooks (trs.) (2001) *The Original Analects: Sayings of Confucius and His Followers*, New York: Columbia University Press.

Huang, Chi-chung (tr.) (1997) *The Analects of Confucius*, Oxford: Oxford University Press.

Lau, D. C. (tr.) (2000) *The Analects*, Hong Kong: Chinese University Press.

Watson, Burton (tr.) (2007) *The Analects of Confucius*, New York: Columbia University Press.

Lanling Xiaoxiaosheng 蘭陵笑笑生
Jinpingmei《金瓶梅》
Egerton, Clement (tr.) (1939) *The Golden Lotus*, 4 volumes, London and New York: Routledge.

Miall, Bernard (tr.) (1942) *Chin P'ing Mei: The Adventurous History of Hsi Men and His Six Wives*, London: John Lane.

Roy, David Tod (tr.) (1993-2013) *The Plum in the Golden Vase*, 5 volumes, Princeton, N.J.: Princeton University Press.

Lao She 老舍
Hu, Jieqing (1985) *Lao She: Crescent Moon and Other Stories*, Beijing: Panda Books.

Chaguan〈茶館〉
Howard-Gibbon, John (tr.) (1980) *Teahouse: A Play in Three Acts*, Beijing: Foreign Languages Press; reprinted Hong Kong: The Chinese University Press.

Gushu Yiren《鼓書藝人》
Kuo, Helena (tr.) (1952) *The Drum Singers*, New York: Harcourt, Brace.

Luotuo Xiangzi《駱駝祥子》
Goldblatt, Howard (tr.) (2010) *Rickshaw Boy: A Novel*, New York: Harper Perennial Modern

Chinese Classics.

James, Jean (tr.) (1979) *Rickshaw*, Honolulu: University Press of Hawaii.

King, Evan (tr.) (1945) *Rickshaw Boy*, New York: Reynal and Hitchcock.

Shi, Xiaoqing (tr.) (1981) *Camel Xiangzi*, Beijing: Foreign Languages Press; (2005) Hong Kong: Chinese University Press.

Sishi Tongtang《四世同堂》
Pruitt, Ida (tr.) (1951) *The Yellow Storm*, New York: Harcourt, Brace.

Laozi 老子

Daodejing《道德經》
Ames, Roger T. and David Hall (2003) *Daodejing: A Philosophical Translation*, New York: Ballantine Books.

Lau, D. C. (tr.) (2001) *Tao Te Ching*, Hong Kong: Chinese University Press.

Li Bai 李白
Cooper, Arthur (tr.) (1986) *Li Po and Tu Fu: Poems*, Viking Press.

Cooper, Arthur (tr.) (1973) *Li Po and Tu Fu: Poems Selected and Translated with an Introduction and Notes*, London: Penguin Classics.

Hinton, David (1998) *The Selected Poems of Li Po*, Anvil Press Poetry.

Holyoak, Keith (tr.) (2007) *Facing the Moon: Poems of Li Bai and Du Fu*, Durham, NH: Oyster River Press.

Obata, Shigeyoshi (1922) *The Works of Li Po, the Chinese Poet*, New York: Dutton; reprinted (1965) New York: Paragon

Seth, Vikram (tr.) (1992) *Three Chinese Poets: Translations of Poems by Wang Wei, Li Bai, and Du Fu*, London: Faber and Faber.

Sun, Yu 孫瑜 (1982) *Li Po – A New Translation*, Hong Kong: The Commercial Press.

Li Baojia 李寶嘉

Guanchang Xianxingji《官場現形記》
Yang, T.L. (tr.) (2001) *Officialdom Unmasked*, Hong Kong: Hong Kong University Press.

Li He 李賀
J. D. Frodsham (tr.) (2016) *The Collected Poems of Li He*, Hong Kong: The Chinese University Press.

Li Qingzhao 李清照

Mayhew, Lenoreand William McNaughton (1977) *As Though Dreaming: The Tz'u of Pure Jade by Li Ch'ing-chao*. Berkeley: Serendipity Books; Tokyo: Mushinsha.

Rexroth, Kenneth and Chung Ling (trs.) (1979) *Li Ching-chao: Complete Poems*, New York: New Directions.

Wang, Jiaosheng (tr.) (1989) *The Complete Ci-poems of Li Qingzhao: A New English Translation*, Philadelphia: Department of Oriental Studies, University of Pennsylvania.

Kwock, C.H. and Vincent McHugh (1962) *The Lady and the Hermit: 30 Chinese Poems* (by Li Qingzhao and Wang Fanchih), San Francisco: Tao Press, 1962.

Hamill, Sam (tr.) (1985) *The Lotus Lovers: Poems and Songs* (by Tzu Yeh and Li Ch'ing-chao), Saint Paul: Coffee House Press.

Li Shangyin 李商隱
Chan, Kwan-Hung (tr.) (2012) *The Purple Phoenix : Poems of Li Shangyin*, West Conshohocken, PA : Infinity Publishing.

Li Yu 李漁
Mao, Nathan K. (tr.) (1979) *Twelve Towers: Short Stories*, Hong Kong: The Chinese University Press.

Li Yu 李煜
Bryant, Daniel (1982) *Lyric Poets of the Southern T'ang: Feng Yen-ssu, 903–960, and Li Yü, 937–978*, Vancouver: University of British Columbia Press.

Koh, Malcolm Ho Ping; Nair, Chandran (1975). *A Translation: The Poems & Lyrics of Last Lord Lee*. Singapore: Woodrose Publications.

Liu, Yih-ling and Shahid Suhrawardy (1948) *Poems of Lee Hou-chu*, Calcutta: Orient Longmans.

Pannam, Clifford L. (2000) *The Poetry of Li Yu*, Ormond, Victoria: Hybrid Publishers.

Liji《禮記》
Nylan, Michael (2001), *The Five "Confucian" Classics*, New Haven: Yale University Press.

Ling Mengchu 凌濛初

Chuke Pai'an Jingqi《初刻拍案驚奇》
Wen, Jingen (tr.), *Amazing Tales, Volume One*, Beijing: Panda Books.

Erke Pai'an Jingqi《二刻拍案驚奇》
Ma, Perry W. (tr.), *Amazing Tales, Volume Two*, Beijing: Panda Books.

Lie Yugou 列禦寇

Liezi《列子》

Giles, Lionel (tr.) (1912) *Taoist Teachings from The Book of Lieh-Tzŭ*, London: Wisdom of the East.

Graham, A.C. (tr.) (1960, revised 1990), *The Book of Lieh-tzŭ: A Classic of Tao*, New York: Columbia University Press.

Liang, Xiaopeng (tr.) (2005) *Liezi*, Beijing: Zhonghua Book Company.

Wong, Eva (tr.) (2001) *Lieh-Tzu: A Taoist Guide to Practical Living*, Boston: Shambhala.

Liu An 劉安

Huainanzi《淮南子》

Ames, Roger T. (1983) *The Art of Rulership: A Study in Ancient Chinese Political Thought*, Honolulu: University of Hawaii Press.

Major, John S. Sarah A. Queen, Andrew Seth Meyer, and Harold D. Roth (eds. and trs.) (2010), *The Huainanzi*, New York: Columbia University Press.

Liu Xiang 劉向

Zhanguoce《戰國策》

Crump, James I. Jr. (tr.) (1970) *Chan-kuo ts'e*, Oxford: Clarendon Press.

Liu Xie 劉勰

Wenxin Diaolong《文心雕龍》

Shih, Vincent Yu-chung (tr.) (1983) *The Literary Mind and the Carving of Dragons*, Hong Kong: The Chinese University Press.

Yang, Guobin (2003) *Dragon-carving and the Literary Mind*, Beijing: Foreign Language Teaching and Research Press.

Liu Yiqing 劉義慶

Shishuo Xinyu《世說新語》

Liu, Jun and Richard B. Mather (trs.) (2002) *A New Account of Tales of the World*, Ann Arbor: Centre for Chinese Studies, University of Michigan.

Liu Zongyuan 柳宗元

Jan, W. and Lloyd Neighbors (1973) *Liu Tsung-yüan*, New York: Twayne Publishers Inc.

Lu Xun 魯迅

Lovell, Julia (tr.) (2007) *The Real Story of Ah-Q and Other Tales of China: The Complete Fiction of Lu Xun*, Penguin.

Yang Hsien-yi and Gladys Yang (trs.) (1960) *Selected Stories of Lu Hsun*, 4 volumes, Beijing: Foreign Languages Press; republished in 2007.

Lu You 陸游

Burton Watson (tr.) (1994), *The Old Man Who Does As He Pleases*, New York: Columbia University Press.

Lu Buwei 呂不韋

Lushi Chunqiu《呂氏春秋》

Di, Jiang Yuejin 翟江月今 (tr.) (2005)《呂氏春秋》(漢英對譯) (*The Spring and Autumn of Lu Buwei*), Guangxi: Guangxi Normal University Press 廣西師範大學出版社.

Knoblock, John and Jeffrey Riegel (trs.) (2000) *The Annals of Lü Buwei: A Complete Translation and Study*, Stanford: Stanford University Press.

Luo Guanzhong 羅貫中

Sanguo Yanyi《三國演義》

Brewitt-Taylor, Charles Henry (tr.) (1925) *Romance of the Three Kingdoms*, Shanghai: Kelly and Walsh.

Roberts, Moss (tr.) (1991) *Three Kingdoms: A Historical Novel*, California: University of California Press.

Mao Zedong 毛澤東

Nancy T. Lin (tr.) *Reverberations: A New Translation of Complete Poems of Mao Tsetung*, Hong Kong: Joint Publishing (Hong Kong) Ltd.

Meng Ke 孟軻

Mengzi《孟子》

Bloom, Irene (2009) *Mencius*, New York: Columbia University Press.

Dobson, W.A.C.H. (tr.) (2003) *Mencius*, New Bilingual Edition, Hong Kong: The Chinese University Press.

Dobson, W.A.C.H. (tr.) (1963) *Mencius, A New Translation Arranged and Annotated for the General Reader*, London: Oxford University Press.

Lau, D. C. (tr.) (2003) *Mencius*, Hong Kong: The Chinese University Press.

Lau, D. C. (1970) *Mencius*, London: Penguin Books.

Van Norden, Bryan (2008) *Mencius: With Selections from Traditional Commentaries*, Indianapolis: Hackett Publishing Company.

Ware, James R. (tr.) (1960) *The Sayings of Mencius*, New York: Mentor Books.

Mo Di 墨翟

Mozi《墨子》
Johnston, Ian (tr) (2010) *The Mozi: A Complete Translation*, Hong Kong: The Chinese University Press.

Ouyang Xiu
Colin Hawes (1997) *Competing with Creative Transformation: The Poetry of Ouyang Xiu (1007-1072)*, PhD thesis, Vancouver: The University of British Columbia

Pu Songling 蒲松齡
Denis, C. and Victor H. Mair (trs.) (1989) *Strange Tales from Make-do Studio*, Beijing: Foreign Languages Press.

Giles, Herbert A. (tr.) (1880) *Strange Stories from a Chinese Studio*, London: T. De La Rue.

Lu Yunzhong, Chen Tifang, Yang Liyi, and Yang Zhihong (trs.) (1982) *Strange Tales of Liaozhai*, Hong Kong: The Commercial Press.

Minford, John (tr.) (2006) *Strange Tales from a Chinese Studio*, London: Penguin.

Sondergard, Sidney L. (tr.) (2008) *Strange Tales from Liaozhai*, Jain Pub Co.

Soulie, George (tr.) (1913) *Strange Stories from the Lodge of Leisure*, London: Constable.

Zhang, Qingnian, Zhang Ciyun, and Yang Yi (trs.) (1997) *Strange Tales from the Liaozhai Studio*, Beijing: People's China Publishing.

Qian Cai 錢彩
Shuo Yue Quanzhuan《説岳全傳》
Yang, T.L. (tr.) (1995) *General Yue Fei*, Hong Kong: Joint Publishing (H.K.) Co., Ltd.

Qu Yuan 屈原
Hawkes, David (1959) *Ch'u Tz'u: The Songs of the South, an Ancient Chinese Anthology*, Oxford: Clarendon Press.

Shi Jiao 尸佼
Shizi《尸子》
Fischer, Paul (2012) *Shizi: China's First Syncretist*, New York: Columbia University Press.

Shangshu《尚書》
Legge, James (tr.) (1865) *The Chinese Classics, Volume III: the Shoo King or the Book of Historical Documents*, London: Trubner.

Waltham, Clae (tr.) (1971) *Shu Ching: Book of History. A Modernized Edition of the Translation of James Legge*, Chicago: Henry Regnery.

Shen Fu 沈復

Fousheng Liuji《浮生六記》
Sanders, Graham (tr.) (2011) *Six Records of A Life Adrift*, Indianapolis: Hackett Publishing Co.

Shen Dao 慎到
Shenzi《慎子》
Harris, Eirik Lang (tr.) (2016) *The Shenzi Fragments: A Philosophical Analysis and Translation*, New York: Columbia University Press.

Shijing《詩經》
Karlgren, Bernhard (tr.) (1950) *The Book of Odes*, Stockholm: Museum of Far Eastern Antiquities.

Legge, James, (tr.) (1871) *Classic of Songs. The Chinese Classics 4*, Rpt. (1960) Hong Kong: Hong Kong University Press.

Pound, Ezra (tr.) (1954) *The Confucian Odes: The Classic Anthology Defined by Confucius*, New York: New Directions.

Waley, Arthur (tr.) (1937) The Book of Songs, New York: Grove Press.

Xu, Yuanzhong 許淵沖 (tr.) (1993) *The Book of Poetry*, : the Hunan Publishing House 湖南出版社.

Shi Yukun 石玉昆
Sanxia Wuyi《三俠五義》
Blader, Susan (tr.) (1998) *Tales of Magistrate Bao and His Valiant Lieutenants: Selections from Sanxia Wuyi*, Hong Kong: The Chinese University Press.

Sima Guang 司馬光
Zizhi Tongjian《資治通鑑》
Yap, Joseph P. (tr.) (2009) *Wars with The Xiongnu, A Translation from Zizhi Tongjian*, Bloomington, Indiana: Author House.

Yap, Joseph P. (tr.) (2016) *Zizhi Tongjian: Warring States and Qin by Sima Guang Volume 1 to VIII*, North Charleston, S. C.: CreateSpace.

Sima Qian 司馬遷
Shiji《史記》
Nienhauser, William H. Jr. (ed.) (1994–) *The Grand Scribe's Records*, 9 vols, Bloomington: Indiana University Press.

Watson, Burton (tr.) (1961). *Records of the Grand Historian of China*, New York: Columbia University Press.

Yang, Hsien-yi and Gladys Yang (trs.) (1974)

Records of the Historians, Hong Kong: The Commercial Press.

Song Jin 宋鈃

Wenzi《文子》

Cleary, Thomas, (tr.) (1991) *Wen-tzu: Understanding the Mysteries, Further Teachings of Lao-tzu*, Boston-Shaftsbury: Shambhala.

Su Shi 蘇軾

Drummond, Cyril and Le Gros Clark (1974) *Selections from the Works of Su Tung-po (A.D. 1036-1101)*, New York: AMS Press.

Lin Yu-tang (tr.) (1994) *Selected Poems and Prose of Su Tungpo*, Taipei: Zhengzhong Shuju 正中書局.

Osing, Gordon (1999) *Blooming Alone in Winter: Poems of Su Dong-po*, Zhengzhou: Henan People's Publishing House.

Watson, Burton (tr.) (1994) *Selected Poems of Su Tung-po*, Port Townsend, WA: Copper Canyon Press, 1994.

Watson, Burton (tr.) (1965) *Su Tung-p'o: Selections from a Sung Dynasty Poet*, New York: Columbia University Press, 1965.

Xu Yuan-zhong (tr.) (1982) *Su Dong-po: A New Translation*, Hong Kong: The Commercial Press 商務印書館.

Yang, Vincent (1989) *Nature and Self: A Study of the Poetry of Su Dongpo, with Comparisons to the Poetry of William Wordsworth*, Bern: Peter Lang.

Sun Wu 孫武

Sunzi Bingfa《孫子兵法》

Ames, Roger T. (tr.) (1993) *Sun-tzu: The Art of War*, New York: Ballantine Books.

Cleary, Thomas (tr.) (1987) *Sun Tzu, The Art of War*, Boston-Shaftsbury: Shambhala.

Giles, Lionel (tr.) (1910) *Sun Tzu on The Art of War*, London: Luzac and Company.

Griffith, Samuel B. (tr.) (1963) *The Art of War*, Oxford: Oxford University Press.

Huang, J.H. (tr.) (1993) *The Art of War: The New Translation*, New York: Quill William Morrow.

Huynh, Thomas (tr.) (2008) *The Art of War: Spirituality for Conflict*, Nashville: Skylight Paths Publishing.

Kaufman, Stephen F. (tr.) (1996) *The Art of War: The Definitive Interpretation of Sun Tzu's Classic Book of Strategy*, North Clarendon, Verment: Tuttle Publishing.

Lin, Wusun (tr.) (2001) *Sunzi: The Art of War*, Beijing: Foreign Language Press.

Mair, Victor H. (tr.) (2007) *The Art of War: Sunzi's Military Methods*, New York: Columbia University Press.

Minford, John (tr.) (2002) *The Art of War*, New York: Viking.

Sawyer, Ralph D. (tr.) (1994) *The Art of War*, Boulder: Westview Press.

Wing, R.L. (tr.) (1988) *The Art of Strategy*, Seattle, Washington: Main Street Books.

Zhang, Huimin (tr.) (1995) *Sunzi: The Art of War with Commentaries*, Beijing: Panda Books.

Tan Sitong 譚嗣同

Renxue《仁學》

Chan, Sin-wai (1984) *An Exposition of Benevolence: The Jen-hsueh of Tan Ssu-t'ung*, Hong Kong: The Chinese University of Hong Kong.

Tao Yuanming 陶淵明

Acker, William (tr.) (1952) *T'ao the Hermit: Sixty Poems by T'ao Ch'ien, 365-427*, London and New York: Thames and Hudson.

Davis, Albert R. (1983) *T'ao Yuan-ming: His works and Their Meaning*, 2 Volumes, Cambridge: Cambridge University Press.

Hinton, David (tr.) (1993) *The Selected Poems of T'ao Ch'ien*, Copper Canyon Press.

Wang Chong 王充

Lunheng《論衡》

Forke, Alfred (tr.) (1907, 2015) *Lun-hêng, Philosophical Essays of Wang Ch'ung*, Wiesbaden: Harrassowitz Verlag.

Wang Fu 王符

Qianfulun《潛夫論》

Kinney, Anne Behnke (1992) *The Art of the Han Essay: Wang Fu's Ch'ien fu lun*, Tempe: Centre for Asian Studies, Arizona State University.

Pearson, Margaret J. (tr.) (1989) *Wang Fu and the Comments of a Recluse*, Tempe: Centre for Asian Studies.

Wang Wei 王維

Seth, Vikram (tr.) (1992) *Three Chinese Poets: Translations of Poems by Wang Wei, Li Bai, and Du Fu*, London: Faber and Faber.

Weinberger, Eliot, and Octavio Paz (1987) *Nineteen Ways of Looking at Wang Wei: How a Chinese Poem Is Translated*. Wakefield, R.I.:

Moyer Bell.

Yip, Wai-lim (tr.) (1972) *Hiding the Universe: Poems by Wang Wei*, New York: Grossman.

Yu, Pauline (tr.) (1980) *The Poetry of Wang Wei: New Translations and Commentary*, Bloomington: Indiana University Press.

Wen Jiabao 溫家寶

Chan, Sin-wai (tr.) (2009) *Famous Chinese Sayings Quoted by Wen Jiabao*, Hong Kong: Chung Hwa Book Co., (H.K.) Ltd. 中華書局(香港)有限公司.

Wu Chng'en 吳承恩

Xiyouji《西遊記》

Waley, Arthur (1942) *Monkey: A Folk-tale of China*, London: George Allen & Unwin Ltd.

Yang, Xianyi and Gladys Yang (trs.) *Journey to the West*, 4 volumes, Beijing: Panda Publications.

Yu, Anthony C. (tr.) (1977-1983) *Journey to the West*, 4 volumes, Chicago: University of Chicago Press.

Wu Jianren 吳趼人

Ershinian Mudu Zhi Guaixianzhuang《二十年目睹之怪現狀》

Shih Shun Liu (tr.) (1976) *Vignettes from the Late Ch'ing: Bizarre Happenings Eyewitnessed over Two Decades*, Hong Kong: The Chinese University Press.

Wu Jingzi 吳敬梓

Rulin Waishi《儒林外史》

Yang, Xianyi and Gladys Yang (trs.) (2004) *The Scholars*, Beijing: Foreign Language Press.

Xi Zhoushng 西周生

Xingshi Yinyuanzhuan《醒世姻緣傳》

Nyren, Eve Alison (tr.) (1995) *The Bonds of Matrimony (Hsing-shih Yin-yuan Chuan), Volume I: A Seventeenth-century Chinese Novel*, Lewiston, New York: Edwin Mellen.

Xu Zhimo 徐志摩

Fung, Mary M. Y. and David Lunde (trs.) (2017) *Xu Zhimo: Selected Poems*, Hong Kong: Research Centre for Translation, The Chinese University of Hong Kong.

Xun Yue 荀悅

Xunzi《荀子》

Knoblock, John (tr.) (1994) *Xunzi: A Translation and Study of the Complete Works*, Stanford: Stanford University Press.

Yan Ying 晏嬰

Yanzi Chunqiu《晏子春秋》

Milburn, Olivia (tr.) (2016) *The Spring and Autumn Annals of Master Yan*, London: Brill.

Yijing《易經》

Ritsema, Rudolf and Stephen Karcher (trs.) (1995) *I Ching: The Classic Chinese Oracle of Change: The First Complete Translation with Concordance*, Michigan: Element Books Ltd.

Zheng Banqiao 鄭板橋

Cheung, Anthony and Paul Gurofsky (eds. and trs.) (1987) *Cheng Pan-ch'iao: Selected Poems, Calligraphy, Paintings and Seal Engravings*, Hong Kong: Joint Publishing Co. (HK) 三聯書店(有限)公司.

Zhuang Zhou 莊周

Zhuangzi《莊子》

Giles, Herbert (tr.) (1889) *Chuang Tzŭ: Mystic, Moralist and Social Reformer*, London: Bernard Quaritch; 2nd edition, revised (1926), Shanghai: Kelly and Walsh; reprinted (1961), London: George Allen and Unwin.

Graham, A. C. (tr.) (1981) *Chuang-tzu, The Seven Inner Chapters and Other Writings from The Book Chuang-tzu*, London: George Allen and Unwin.

Legge, James (tr.) (1891) *The Texts of Taoism*, in *Sacred Books of the East*, Vols. XXXIX and XL, Oxford: Oxford University Press.

Mair, Victor H. (tr.) (1994) *Wandering on the Way: Early Taoist Tales and Parables of Chuang Tzu*, New York: Bantam Books; republished (1997), Honolulu: University of Hawaii Press.

Watson, Burton (tr.) (1968) *The Complete Works of Chuang Tzu*, New York: Columbia University Press.

Watson, Burton (tr.) (1964, 1996, 1997) *Chuang Tzu: Basic Writings*, New York: Columbia University Press.

Ziporyn, Brook (tr.) (2009) *Zhuangzi: The Essential Writings with Selections from Traditional Commentaries*, Indianapolis: Hackett Publishing.

Zuo Qiuming 左丘明

Zuozhuan《左傳》

Hu, Zhihui 胡志揮 and Chen Kejiong 陳克炯 (trs.) (1996) *Zuo Zhuan: Zuo's Commentary*, Changsha: Hunan People's Publishing House 湖南人民出版社.

主題索引
Topic index